Lockhart Road

GORDON JOHN THOMSON

Copyright © 2020 Gordon John Thomson

All rights reserved.

ISBN:
ISBN-13:9798600128248

DEDICATION

For my brother Alan Thomson, and his wife Theresa.

Lockhart Road

Hong Kong...in the sweltering month of August 1937...

Lockhart Road is a street in the waterfront district of Wanchai on Hong Kong Island...a microcosm of the seamy side of Hong Kong life...a place of sexual temptations, of greed and lust, intrigue and murder...

In the summer of 1937 Hong Kong is a city in turmoil, where war clouds are looming as thousands of refugees flee the war in China. The Japanese have invaded deep into China territory and this new war is threatening to spill over into Hong Kong. The privileged British expatriate community tries to stay aloof from this turmoil around them, yet it soon threatens to engulf their complacent lives too...

Inspector Paul Jericho of the Hong Kong Police leads the hunt in the seamen's area of Wanchai for the killer of two young women, bar hostesses, who worked on the Wanchai waterfront. At first he suspects that the killer must be a violent Western seaman, but his investigation soon leads him to suspect a connection with the rich and privileged expatriate community of the Mid-levels...

Paul Jericho has another more personal case to solve too: the death of his wife Susan in a hit-and-run incident six months before...

In Government House, a young code-breaker with the Secret Intelligence Service, Edith Starling, has found a way to read the coded signals between Japanese High Command in Tokyo and their rampaging army in China. Edith is leading a dangerous life, for she is sleeping with a Chinese lawyer, Michael Yip, who might also be a spy of some sort. But when her own SIS chief, Ralph Ogden, dies in mysterious circumstances, she begins to suspect that there might be a traitor inside Government House itself...

CONTENTS

Prologue   Pg 1

Chapter 1   Pg 14

Chapter 2   Pg 38

Chapter 3   Pg 54

Chapter 4   Pg 70

Chapter 5   Pg 85

Chapter 6   Pg 101

Chapter 7   Pg 112

Chapter 8   Pg 129

Chapter 9   Pg 134

Chapter 10   Pg 141

Chapter 11   Pg 152

Chapter 12   Pg 158

Chapter 13   Pg 171

Chapter 14   Pg 184

Chapter 15   Pg 195

Chapter 16   Pg 206

Chapter 17   Pg 213

Chapter 18   Pg 222

Chapter 19   Pg 231

Chapter 20	Pg 240
Chapter 21	Pg 250
Chapter 22	Pg 267
Chapter 23	Pg 278
Chapter 24	Pg 288
Chapter 25	Pg 296
Chapter 26	Pg 304
Chapter 27	Pg 311
Chapter 28	Pg 321
Chapter 29	Pg 332
Chapter 30	Pg 345
Chapter 31	Pg 353
Chapter 32	Pg 364
Chapter 33	Pg 373
Chapter 34	Pg 380
Chapter 35	Pg 389
Epilogue	Pg 404

PROLOGUE

Monday morning, 9 August 1937

A narrow and fetid alleyway, early on a Monday morning in the British Crown Colony of Hong Kong...

Not a pleasant place for a young woman to die, Paul Jericho thought, as he examined the scene with his professional policeman's eye.

This could have been a mean street in any poor quarter of any East Asian city, he decided, yet something about this festering place said that this back alley was Chinese to its very core, no matter what the Union Jack flag flying on the flagpole of the nearby China Fleet Club might say to the contrary. The alleyway was a short cul-de-sac that separated two crumbling old tenement buildings on the south side of Lockhart Road, one of the main thoroughfares that cut east-west through the eastern waterfront district of Wanchai. A stern-faced young police constable stood guard at the doorways at the back of the alleyway that provided a rear access to those tenements: the occupants had already been told that they had to use only the front entrance to their buildings in Lockhart Road until further notice.

This place was only a mile or so east of the fashionable Central business district of Hong Kong Island yet it was a different world entirely. Jericho had not looked inside the rear doorways to the tenements yet, but he had no doubt what he would find if he did: a concrete staircase strewn with litter and stained with spittle, leading to a warren of narrow cell-like rooms above, divided up into cubicles or bed spaces. The vast influx of migrants and refugees from war-torn China over the last few years had led to a severe housing shortage in Hong Kong, and the class of coolies who lived and worked in Wanchai would be crammed into these tenements, sometimes twenty to a room. Even through the solidity of those concrete block walls, Jericho could hear that the buildings on each side resounded faintly with the sing-song chatter of Chinese voices, even the wail of young children.

Although it was only seven o'clock in the morning, the heat and the humidity were already as oppressive as usual in the month of August, so that the alleyway felt like a hot and particularly steamy corner of Hell. Jericho could feel the sweat trickling down his neck, and took off his dark blue police cap for a moment to run a hand through his damp hair.

Replacing his peaked cap on his head, Jericho stretched his stiff neck and looked up at the thin strip of sky visible above, still savouring the distinctive Chinese essence of this place, which seemed to him to summarize so much of the present painful Chinese struggle for life within its narrow confines. This place did truly seem more like a narrow tunnel than a public street, because, in addition to the encroaching featureless walls of the tenement buildings on each side, the sky was almost blocked out by a virtual ceiling of tattered laundry on the criss-cross of bamboo poles above.

Yet even with all this abundant evidence of Chinese life clearly visible, this mean little alley did however also contain an essence of that Chinese fixation with death and mortality too. For halfway along the alleyway, partly hidden behind a midden heap of foul-smelling and congealing garbage, was the body of the young woman that had brought all these policemen here so early on a Monday morning...

Jericho went over regretfully to the body again, and bent down to examine the woman's features, which were frozen into what he knew must be a sad and distorted caricature of her living face. He realized that this had been a pretty girl – perhaps even a beautiful one – but violent death was no respecter of fragile beauty. The woman was fully dressed at least in a Western cotton summer dress of good quality, and her long nails were painted a shade of pink, therefore she was certainly no labouring woman...

In his fifteen years with the Hong Kong Police, Jericho had seen more dead bodies than he could remember, for death was a common and pervasive presence here in this tiny outpost of the empire. Yet he had still never become completely immune to the sight of death, as so many of his colleagues had, and could never entirely conceal his sympathy for the dead, even for those people judged to be from the lowest ranks of society. His superior, Superintendent Charlie Hebdon, thought this a great weakness on Jericho's part, and dismissed it as an unfortunate tendency for sentimentality that impaired his performance as a policeman. Yet Jericho could not change his ways any more than he could change the coarse wiry texture of his hair or the steel-blue colour of his eyes...

He wondered with annoyance what had happened to the young police surgeon, Dr Formby. Jericho himself had only arrived on the scene ten minutes ago, but he still expected that Eric Formby should have been here by now, since he only lived up the hill from here in the more affluent and salubrious surroundings of Queens Road East. The police had even paid for a telephone to be installed in Formby's apartment so that he could be summoned quickly outside normal working hours. Even Jericho himself hadn't been given a perk like that, but this particular perquisite didn't seem to be working very well, for Formby was still invariably late on the scene...

Nor was there any sign of Jericho's sergeant, George Dorling, which was even more annoying than the doctor's absence, since George should certainly have been here on the job by now and taking statements. Although George Dorling lived over in Ashley Road in Kowloon, and therefore had to use the Wanchai ferry to get to work, he was supposed to have started his shift at six this morning. Yet the duty officer at the station hadn't seen him, or had any message from him to explain his absence.

Jericho wondered if George was perhaps having some renewal of his marital problems with his wife Tess that might justify his being elsewhere. Dorling's wife was rumoured among George's police colleagues to be of a moody and difficult disposition, although Jericho himself had never seen any direct evidence of such behaviour. But then Tess Dorling had lost her first baby due to a miscarriage earlier this year so might well have some reasonable excuse for her moody nature, if such a thing was even true.

Jericho almost hoped that the reason for George's absence *was* something to do with his wife, for the alternative was even worse. Yet he could hardly believe that Dorling would have been stupid enough to go out on another drinking binge last night after Jericho had given him a severe warning about his behaviour only the previous week. Jericho had just been forced by Charlie Hebdon to hand over a major investigation that George had been leading – the murder of a police informer called Ricky Sun – because of an alleged lack of progress. Jericho would normally have fought tooth-and-nail to avoid handing over his cases to Central, but in this case he had gone along with the decision without too much complaint. And Jericho had to admit to himself that George's excessive drinking and aberrant behaviour of late had been a factor in his unusually acquiescent decision...

Jericho heard a footfall behind him and turned to see that Senior Constable Thomas Sung had followed him. Sung had been the first officer on the scene after the body had been reported forty minutes ago, and had already been speaking at length to the crowd of curious local bystanders gathered in Lockhart Road to find out if any of them had seen anything.

'Any luck?' Jericho asked him.

Sung looked apologetic. 'Not yet, Inspector Jericho. The only person who has been of any help so far is the woman who found the body. I let her go back to her own room in Lockhart Road to do something urgent, but she said she would come back in a few minutes to speak to you, sir.'

'I hope you've got this woman's name and that you know where she lives, Thomas?' Jericho growled warningly. The local Chinese were invariably reluctant to get involved with the police in any way, and Chinese witnesses to crimes did have an unfortunate habit of disappearing in this teeming city, never to be found again.

'Of course, sir.' Sung was not intimidated by the tone of Jericho's question. 'Her name is Yiu Pui Wah, or Maggie Yiu, and I made sure to follow her and see where she lived...it's just up the street...' He turned his head suddenly as he heard someone approaching behind him. 'And here she is, sir, returning promptly as she promised.'

Jericho could hear a note of relief in Sung's voice despite his apparent show of confidence. Thomas Sung was the most competent Chinese officer in his station on the Wanchai waterfront, and, truth to tell, Jericho had more trust in his ability, and in his incorruptibility, than was the case with many of his senior expatriate officers. Most police officers were unfortunately only too happy to take "squeeze" money to look the other way when it suited them, but Jericho would have bet his house that Sung had never taken a penny from anyone. Sung should by rights be a Station Sergeant by now after twenty years exemplary service, but it was almost impossible to get such a promotion for a Chinese. Not unless they could demonstrate to Charlie Hebdon that they could walk on water anyway...

And Sung's case wasn't helped by the fact that, at forty years of age, he still looked so alarmingly young and boyish...

Jericho was happy to leave the depressing task of studying the body for the present, so was grateful for the chance to talk with a witness instead. He stood up quickly and went over to meet this Miss Yiu Pui Wah. He had been expecting that the woman who had actually found the body would be either a coolie or a local worker in one of the many small shops and businesses in Lockhart Road. Yet he saw immediately that she was neither of those, but rather a sophisticated-looking young woman of mixed race.

'I'm Chief Inspector Jericho,' he said, offering her his hand. 'Shall we talk in Cantonese, Miss Yiu, or are you all right with English?' After fifteen years of practice, Jericho spoke reasonably fluent Cantonese, although his accent bore little resemblance to the language spoken by the wealthy merchants and compradors of Hong Kong, and had much more in common with the crude lingua franca of the streets.

'I'm afraid that my Cantonese is still not perfect, Inspector,' Miss Yiu said with a faint smile of apology. 'I am from Shanghai, you see, and have only lived here for a year. So English would be best. I went to an English language school in Shanghai.'

'Then I want to thank you firstly for returning so promptly. I know this can't be pleasant for you. Shall we talk here in the alleyway, Miss Yiu?' Jericho glanced uneasily at the body behind him. 'Or would you prefer to talk in the street away from the...err..?'

The woman swallowed hard. 'I have already experienced the shock of finding her, so I believe I can bear the continued pain of seeing her in this state.'

'How did you happen to see the body before anyone else?' Jericho asked. He had no suspicions that this young woman was involved in any way, but he was still puzzled that this woman had noticed the body before any of the residents of the tenements on each side.

'I doubt sincerely that I was the first person to notice the body, Inspector,' Miss Yiu said dryly. 'But I suspect most of the people in these buildings would be very reluctant to go to the police. They will mostly be new arrivals from China, where no one in their right minds would ever go to the police voluntarily. Therefore it was far more sensible for them *not* to notice the body...perhaps I should have been as sensible too...'

Jericho nodded ruefully, knowing the situation in Hong Kong concerning public distrust of the police was little different. 'Yes, but how did you happen to see the body at all, when it is concealed from the main street by that waste heap?'

'Not entirely concealed...' Miss Yiu shivered slightly, despite the intense heat in the alleyway. 'The truth is that I found a rat in my room this morning, feasting on my little store of rice. I tried to catch it, but it was too quick for me. And I couldn't bear the thought of coming home late tonight, and hearing that monstrous rat scurrying about in the dark as I tried to sleep. So I went out at quarter past six this morning – first light almost - to buy some rat poison to leave in my room. There is a shop in Fenwick Street that sells rat poison, and I was on my way back from there, walking along Lockhart Road, when I happened to glance into this alleyway and saw a shoe sticking out from behind that rubbish heap...'

Jericho didn't contradict her, but decided that he would check for himself that the dead woman's shoe was actually visible from the street, when he had a spare moment.

Miss Yiu saw the clear look of doubt on Jericho's face. 'That's why I asked your constable if I could return home for a few minutes,' she went on hurriedly. 'I had already bought the rat poison, so I wanted to set some traps with it around my room before going to work.'

Jericho glanced at Constable Sung to see whether he had noticed if Miss Yiu had really been carrying a pack of rat poison when he had talked to her earlier. From the wry shake of his head, it seemed not...

Miss Yiu hesitated fractionally, before finally nodding in the direction of the dead woman. 'I believe her name is Kam Mei-ling, and that she comes from Shanghai too. She used the name Dora Kam here in Hong Kong, though...'

'Ah, you *knew* her?' Jericho said in surprise. He glanced again at Constable Sung and wondered why his officer had not mentioned this earlier.

Sung shook his head again in slight puzzlement.

Miss Yiu caught that pointed exchange of looks between the two policemen and quickly explained. 'I didn't mention it earlier to this constable, Inspector. Frankly I was tempted not to tell the police that I knew this girl because it might inevitably arouse your suspicions. It does seem like a significant coincidence, even to me, that Dora's body should be found by someone who knew her.'

Jericho studied the woman's face with interest. 'What made you change your mind?'

'I suspect you would have got to the truth eventually, since I am a very poor liar, and then my behaviour would have seemed even more suspicious. So better to get this suspicious coincidence over with now.' Miss Yiu looked at the bulging eyes and distorted features of the dead woman with a suggestion of a tear in her own almond-shaped eyes. 'She was quite beautiful when she was alive, you know...'

Jericho had guessed that much already about the dead woman, although, speaking personally, he thought that Miss Yiu herself was probably even more beautiful than her old acquaintance had been.

Miss Yiu composed herself with difficulty. 'But beauty is always a fleeting thing and is soon eclipsed by death, is it not, Inspector...' She sighed heavily. '...*Like as the waves make towards the pebbled shore, so do our minutes hasten to their end...*' She looked discomforted for a moment by her own sudden loquaciousness. 'I'm sorry. My father was a Russian émigré in Shanghai but he rather enjoyed the works of your national poet, so passed his tastes onto me,' she explained, half-embarrassed. 'And I am a teacher of English too, so inclined to pedantry like most teachers,' she added with an apologetic smile.

Jericho couldn't help wondering if her father and her mother had actually been married, since she seemed to be using her mother's Chinese family name. 'Oh? Where do you teach?'

'At St Stephen's Girls' College up in Mid-Levels - Lyttelton Road. Unfortunately I cannot afford to live up there so have to make do with a room in Wanchai at present...'

'Yes, I know St Stephen's.' Jericho was tempted to add that his wife Susan had been a teacher there too, but quickly decided not to venture into that painful subject.

Miss Yiu grimaced as she glanced at the body again. 'How did Dora die?'

Jericho wondered if he should keep this knowledge to himself for the moment, since even the police surgeon hadn't seen the body yet to confirm his own findings. But then curiosity overcame his normal adherence to police protocol and he decided to test her reaction. 'I think the evidence is clear enough to me that she was strangled, probably sometime late last night close to midnight...'

'Who would do such an evil thing?' Miss Yiu said with a deep sigh.

Jericho shrugged. 'Who indeed? I don't think she was actually strangled here in the alleyway because there's no evidence of a struggle near the body. She is also fully dressed, and there is no evidence that she was sexually molested in any way. Most likely she was killed in some room or building nearby, although she might have been attacked on Lockhart Road itself, and her body then simply dumped here out of direct sight...' Jericho paused as he reflected that the murderer had still taken a significant risk because a busy street like Lockhart Road would never be completely devoid of potential witnesses, even in the early hours of the morning. 'How is it that you know this woman? Are you old friends from Shanghai? Is that it?'

Miss Yiu shook her head vigorously. 'No, nothing like that. I never said we were friends. I only met Dora perhaps a dozen times in the two months that I knew her. She used to lodge in the same building as me in Lockhart Road; she had the room immediately below mine, so I used to see her on the stairs sometimes. We soon discovered that we were both from Shanghai so we naturally talked a little. But she left my building a month ago, and I hadn't seen her since...'

'Do you know where she moved to? Or what she did for a living?' Jericho had a suspicion, because of Dora Kam's undoubted beauty, and also because of the fact that she had apparently been able to afford a room to herself, that Dora might have worked in one of the hotels or bars in this area: Wanchai was infamous after all as a place where expatriate soldiers and sailors could find willing female company...

Certainly no Englishwoman would ever speak to a common sailor in Hong Kong; Englishwomen were in short supply here, and most were upper crust and well-off anyway so even the plainest of them would not be tempted by any ordinary Jack Tar. Therefore the only options for female company open to ordinary seamen and soldiers were Chinese girls. The China Fleet Club and the Soldiers' and Sailors' Home were both close by in Wanchai, as was the naval dockyard, so it was only natural that Chinese hotels like the Luk Kwok, or bars like Nagasaki Joe's or The Black Dog, would cater to the needs of the lower ranks of the British services by providing access to pretty Chinese women.

The women were not officially employed by these hotels and bars, of course, but simply had a mutually beneficial business arrangement with them. The bars made money from selling booze to the sailors tempted in by the presence of the girls, and the hotels profited from renting out rooms to them for short times with the girls, while the girls themselves kept whatever money they could negotiate directly from their amorous clients.

Yet there was a problem now because this business was no longer legal as it had once been. Brothels had been made officially illegal five years ago after a bunch of liberal do-gooders from the English parliament had visited

Hong Kong and, horrified at what they had found in Wanchai, had forced the Governor to change the law. But trying to stop this age-old practice with mere legislation was like trying to hold back the tide with a bucket and spade. All the do-gooders had achieved in practice was to drive the business underground, to close the women's health clinics, and to make it more difficult to regulate the activities of these often desperate women. As a consequence, the age old diseases of sin were now rife in Wanchai again, and competing for victims with the regular scourges of smallpox and cholera...

Miss Yiu sighed, as if reluctant to betray a confidence. 'Dora did tell me once that she was working in the bar in the Tin Hau Hotel on the waterfront road...'

Jericho's heart missed a beat for a moment at the mention of the Tin Hau Hotel. But he said nothing and allowed Miss Yiu to keep talking.

'...But she said it was only a temporary measure until she could find something better...she had only been in Hong Kong since May. The last time that I saw her, she told me she had left the Tin Hau, but she didn't tell me where she was working now. And she didn't even let me know that she was moving out of my building...she just disappeared one night a month ago. But then, as I said, we weren't really friends, just passing acquaintances...'

Jericho found this general story believable enough: Dora Kam had certainly been tall and white-skinned, and probably elegant-looking too, therefore was a definite cut above most of the young Cantonese women who worked in sailors' dives in Wanchai. And the Tin Hau Hotel was certainly a dive, despite being named after the Chinese Taoist Goddess of the Sea; the bar in the Tin Hau wasn't quite as crude a pickup place as Nagasaki Joe's or the Black Dog, but it was no London Ritz either. Therefore it would not be a surprise that a good-looking woman like Dora Kam would soon discover that there were better places to ply her trade. Yet it was still disturbing to hear that Dora Kam had worked at the Tin Hau at all, because this seemed like the first definite link to another recent murder in Wanchai...*and one that bore a disturbing similarity to this one...*

Jericho wondered if Dora had left the Tin Hau because she had perhaps found herself a more permanent arrangement with one particular client; most of these women preferred having a regular sailor boyfriend to the lottery of picking up different men every night in a seedy hotel bar.

Miss Yiu suddenly looked at her watch and gave a gasp. 'It's after seven-thirty, and I must be in school by eight-fifteen...'

Jericho shook his head. 'I'm afraid I'm going to have to ask you to come to the station and make a formal statement of everything you've told me, Miss Yiu.'

'Right now?' Miss Yiu frowned, and Jericho thought he saw a glimpse of some unexpected steel in those dark magnetic eyes. 'I can't miss school today; the head is away and is relying on me to hold assembly. Can't I come to the station after work, or even tomorrow morning? I have some free periods on a Tuesday, so that would suit me much better.'

Jericho didn't want to put Miss Yiu's back up unnecessarily, particularly as she was such a helpful witness. 'All right. I dare say I can stretch a point this one time. Shall we say seven o'clock tomorrow morning? I presume you know where the station is?'

'I suppose you work in the big new station on the waterfront road? The one that faces directly onto the harbour?'

'That's it; my office is on the fourth floor so I have one of the best views in Hong Kong...or in Wanchai anyway. The address is one hundred and twenty three Gloucester Road, if you come by rickshaw.'

'I never use rickshaws; I feel uncomfortable at having some poor undernourished man pulling me up Hong Kong's steep streets. But I will find the station on foot well enough,' Miss Yiu said primly. 'Seven o'clock tomorrow morning will be fine for me.'

Jericho nodded reassuringly. 'I am always there by that time so it suits me too. And it should only be an hour at most to take a formal statement, so you can still probably get to work by nine.'

'Thank you. That would be a great help.' She nodded formally. 'You're very kind.'

Jericho escorted Miss Yiu out of the alleyway into Lockhart Road proper. 'May I walk back to your building with you?'

She looked at him askance. 'Why? Are you scared that I might abscond?'

'It has been known with witnesses,' Jericho admitted dryly. 'But that's not the reason in this case. I simply want to see the room where Dora Kam used to live.'

'I doubt that she left anything behind. The room has been divided up into bed spaces since she left so that our landlord can cram a dozen people in there. He's also trying to double my rent to fifty dollars a month, which I can hardly afford when I only earn a hundred a month. I am only a junior teacher at St Stephen's, and still on probation until I complete twelve months' service in December.'

Jericho reflected that his wife Susan had been making six times that as a teacher in the same school. But Miss Yiu was no doubt treated as local Chinese staff because of her mixed blood, so clearly didn't qualify for European rates of pay.

Jericho privately agreed that there would almost certainly be nothing left of Dora Kam's possessions in her old room, yet he still insisted on walking with Miss Yiu to her front door.

Miss Yiu could see she wasn't going to win this point, so finally gave in with a graceful sigh and pointed the way east up Lockhart Road.

Jericho saw that the street was already bustling with morning activity. The ground floors of the tenement buildings on each side were all occupied by businesses or shops of one kind or another: tailors, carpenters, metal workers, undertakers, sellers of spices, and food stalls offering breakfasts of fish, barley, kidney or pork congee to passers-by. The busy noise of sewing machines issued from a shirt maker's, where emaciated-looking young men in shirt sleeves worked feverishly under the glare of a single bare electric light bulb. From a workshop came the blinding white flare of a welding arc that caused shadows to dance among the ceiling-high stacks of metal junk. A red painted sign over a lighted doorway seemed like the entrance to a bar, yet a great clatter came from within, like the noise of a factory.

Jericho and Miss Yiu passed a naval tailor's where the fat beaming proprietor did his best to entice Jericho across his threshold. The blackboard in front of the shop said: "*Welcome to all members of...*" and had three numbers chalked below – the numbers of the three American navy ships presently in port. Jericho was glad that he was wearing his summer khaki green police uniform, otherwise his purpose in walking up this street with a beautiful Eurasian girl in tow might have looked highly questionable.

They came finally to Miss Yiu's tenement, which was certainly no smarter than any other on this street, and was topped with the usual rooftop structures of old sacking, rotting wood, and flattened-out tin cans in which some hardy souls were eking out an existence. They entered the main door between the premises of a restaurant and a tailor, and climbed the usual seedy concrete staircase. From deep within the bowels of the building, Jericho could smell the stench of an earth privy; few of these tenements had modern plumbing so coolies would have to come every few days to collect and dispose of the night soil in that age-old Chinese practice. Miss Yiu did not seem at all embarrassed by the degrading poverty of her surroundings, although, to Jericho, she seemed in this dismal place like some angel ascending a road through the chaos of Hell.

The interior of the building seethed with humanity, a gabble of noise and the ubiquitous clatter of mah-jong tiles. A door opened on one landing and a blue close-shaven scalp appeared, with a waft of cooking smells following behind this curious head. The rooms at each level were partitioned into bed spaces with sacking, as Jericho suspected they would be. Greedy landlords, and the notorious practice of sub-letting, meant that some unconscionable people in Hong Kong were making a fortune out of the misery of these wretched people.

They came to the second floor where Miss Yiu indicated a doorway. 'This was Dora's room. But I think there are a dozen labourers sleeping there now, although most will be out at work already.'

Jericho knew he would be wasting his time by going in there, but decided he would have to make some kind of cursory search anyway. He pushed the door open and peered inside briefly. In the first cubicle, just inside the doorway, he glimpsed burning joss sticks stuck like fireworks into an old soup can, some tattered almanacs, a Tibetan rosary.

Miss Yiu frowned. 'May I go up to my own room now? I just need to get my school papers, then I will have to run and catch a tram in Hennessey Road.'

Jericho assented with an attempt at a smile. 'Yes, of course.' But something made him follow her up the last flight of stairs to her own door even though Miss Yiu clearly didn't want him to.

She opened the door of her own room with a slightly petulant show of defiance. 'It seems you want to see my room too, Inspector,' she challenged him.

Jericho peered inside and saw that her room was the only oasis of civilization remaining in this dismal building. The pastel colours of the plaster walls had long since faded, but the dusty windows were shaded by a bright awning of red and gold. The furniture was of bamboo and rattan, although one cabinet was of lacquer work and there was a fine silk painting on the wall. Dust motes danced where a bright beam of sunlight pierced the dimness, and a caged bird, a Java sparrow, seemed to recognize Miss Yiu on her return, and began chirping merrily.

Jericho now put the important question that he had been holding back until now to test her reaction. 'Are you by any chance acquainted with a woman called Wong Yu-lan? Sometimes known as Judy Wong?'

Miss Yiu looked curious at the manner of the question, but Jericho was sure the name meant nothing particular to her. 'No. Why do you ask? *Should* I be acquainted with this woman?' She had a sudden thought, and her face fell. 'Oh, is that the name of the other young woman who was murdered recently in Wanchai?'

'I'm afraid it is,' Jericho admitted uneasily.

Miss Yiu stared at him with open hostility for the first time. 'It seems that you really do suspect *me* of some part in these murders...'

'No, not at all. It was just a thought...I'm looking for any possible connections between the two cases, that's all, and there was just a possibility that you might have known both women.' He tried a look of contrition. 'I assure you that I have no reason to suspect you. On the contrary your willingness to come forward as a witness suggests you are completely innocent. After all, it is very unlikely that any murderer would report the body of the victim themselves when they had no need to...' Jericho smiled apologetically as he finally turned back to begin his search of the room on the floor below. 'Thank you again for all your help. I trust I will see you tomorrow at seven at the station,' he said pointedly, hoping she would understand the seriousness of the situation she'd be in if she didn't turn up as promised. Suddenly he realized with chagrin, though, that he was actually *looking forward* to his formal interview with this striking young woman tomorrow. It made him suddenly realize the sad sterility of his own life now, when an interview with a witness to a murder might turn out to be the social high point of his week...

*

When Jericho got back to the scene of the crime fifteen minutes later, he was glad to see that both George Dorling and the young police surgeon Eric Formby had finally arrived. They were both heavily engrossed in studying the body, though, so did not notice his arrival until he coughed loudly behind them to announce his return.

George Dorling sprang guiltily to his feet. 'Ah, there you are, sir!' His eyes fell for a moment. 'I'm sorry that I was late this morning. Had a small domestic emergency. Tess took a tumble at home in the bathroom and smacked her head against the edge of the bath. So I had to take her to hospital to get a nasty cut over her eye stitched.'

Jericho studied Dorling's weary unshaven face and uncombed ginger hair with slight professional cynicism as he wondered if this excuse was genuine. But it seemed too contrived not to be; if he'd simply wanted an excuse, Dorling could have come up with a much simpler story than that. Jericho did however wonder bleakly if George himself might have struck his wife in a fit of drunken temper; such things were unfortunately a common enough occurrence in policemen's marriages, given the stressful lives that they led.

Jericho still liked George Dorling on the whole and knew this young Yorkshireman to be highly accomplished at his job. He came originally from the port of Hull, from a family of fishermen, and his character had all the characteristics that you would associate with those tough-minded people – hard, resourceful and stubborn. But the last year had seen a distinct falling off in the quality of this young man's work, particularly with the case of the murdered police informer, Ricky Sun, where he had got precisely nowhere despite two months of major investigation. Dorling also seemed a troubled soul these days. Gone were the cheerful manner and the amiable jokes that he had been known for when he'd first come to Hong Kong six years ago, and in its place was a hard-drinking and bitter man seemingly in a downward and destructive spiral. Jericho had seen this before with many young officers, whose youthful enthusiasm soon gave way under the pressure of the job to a cynical and unpleasant venality.

Unlike the incorruptible Thomas Sung, Jericho was fairly sure that Dorling was now supplementing his normal income with a generous amount of squeeze money. Yet the practice was so widespread in the Hong Kong Police that it had to be generally overlooked unless the scale of an officer's corruption got so bad that it was interfering with his normal work. If Jericho had decided to go gunning for all his colleagues taking squeeze, then he would have ended up taking on at least half the force. But Jericho had lately taken Dorling to task over his excessive drinking at least, which simply had to stop if he wanted to stay in the police force...

This morning Dorling seemed even more out of sorts than usual of late, though that might be explained of course by his wife's accident, if it really was genuine. George's usually reddened and freckled face looked white and strained, and his manner seemed almost wild and nervous.

Jericho explained to George where he had been and what he had learned about the victim Dora Kam from the elegant Miss Yiu. Jericho had made a point on his return to the crime scene of checking the visibility of the body from Lockhart Road and had been reassured to see that one of Dora Kam's shoes was indeed clearly visible from the main street, sticking out from behind that rubbish heap in the alleyway just as Miss Yiu had said.

Dorling whistled softly when he heard that Dora Kam had also been working lately in the bar of the Tin Hau Hotel. 'Just like Judy Wong...that can't be a coincidence, can it?'

'I doubt it. So now it seems that *two* women who recently worked in the bar of the Tin Hau Hotel have been strangled to death in very similar fashion. First this woman Judy Wong two weeks ago, now this second victim Dora Kam. Judy Wong was also found fully dressed with her underwear intact, and showed no apparent signs of any sexual assault, just like this woman...'

The youthful Dr Formby now finally spoke up. 'Yes, but there is a notable difference, isn't there? Judy Wong was killed and then left in her own room, wasn't she? While this woman was killed and then dumped in an alley?' Jericho still couldn't hear the slightest trace of Liverpool accent in young Dr Formby's voice, though that was where he was supposed to be from. In truth he sounded like any public school boy brought up in the Home Counties. In fact, Formby's accent was very like Paul Jericho's own, though even Jericho had to concede that Formby was a lot younger and better looking than himself. Formby looked in fact like a rather younger version of the actor Robert Donat, down to his pencil-thin moustache and thick glossy hair.

Jericho grunted sourly. 'Nevertheless, I would stake my life that this was done by the same man.' And not only the same man, but almost certainly a seaman of some sort, and probably a Westerner, he wanted to add. At least that was what his instincts as a policeman told him.

And a more worrying point now occurred to Paul Jericho: had this man now perhaps developed a taste for killing Chinese women? *Was this only the start of his killing spree...?*

CHAPTER 1

Monday, 9th August 1937

Edith Starling was strolling in the gardens of Government House as the sun began to set on another achingly hot Hong Kong day. This was always her favourite time of the day as she enjoyed the tranquillity of the gardens, and listened to the soothing evening calls of the magpie robins and white eyes as they flitted through the Bauhinia trees above her head. Above her, Victoria Peak was still fully lit by the setting sun, rising in green magnificence and shedding the lower social orders as it climbed, until there remained only a sprinkling of white bungalows and luxury apartment buildings on the highest roads, May Road and Conduit Road. Higher still, but invisible from here, were the even more exclusive residences of the Peak itself, the luxurious mansions of Hong Kong's taipans and diplomats, enjoying their splendid isolation from the rest of the colony while fortified by magnificent views of the blue harbour far below.

Edith followed her favourite path as it meandered through the wooded garden, and then emerged from the cover of the trees on the north side of Government Hill where she could see the blue harbour below in all its beauty and bustle. The heat was still intense despite the fading light, a humid blanket of warmth that seemed to envelop the island like a heavy shroud. Immediately below her were the imposing colonial buildings of the Central District, with the new Art Deco headquarters of the Hong Kong and Shanghai Bank now dominating the view like a massive square fist.

The *Praya* – the main road along the waterfront - constituted in effect the principal business street of the city; it was here that the 19th century taipans and compradors of the noble business houses had held court in the line of distinguished colonnaded neo-classical buildings that crowded the waterfront. These days, those terms "taipan" and "comprador" were going out of fashion a little, yet trade and commerce still seemed to be conducted in the business district of Hong Kong much as it had always been. On each side of Central District, the long waterfront stretched for nearly five miles in each direction, from Kennedy Town in the west to Shaukeiwan in the east. Almost all of the Chinese residents of Hong Kong Island were wedged into that thin coastal urban strip, particularly in the Tai Ping Shan area of Western District, and in Wanchai in the Eastern. And they were now packed even more tightly than previously, Edith reflected, for the long-running civil war in China had caused the population of the Crown Colony to swell to a million and a half because of the flood of new refugees and migrants from the mainland, three times what it had been twenty five years ago.

Edith watched as the dusk took hold of the busy streets below, and the street lights came on one by one, forming glowing chains of pearls in the falling darkness. When she had first arrived in Hong Kong two years ago, she had thought this the most beautiful place she had ever seen, with its majestic sweep of granite peak, green hillsides and sunlit water, with its harbour of blue-green water and its ungainly red-sailed junks and sampans, with its picturesque scatter of white colonial buildings climbing the wooded slopes above the dense little metropolis towards the towering green Peak. Even now, she still thought the scenery as beautiful as ever, yet her appreciation of Hong Kong was tempered these days by her unease at the poverty she had seen here, and by the extreme contrast between the lives of pampered expatriates like herself, and those Chinese masses toiling in the shadows below.

Only this lunchtime, having walked down to Royal Square to visit the bank, she had seen something that had disturbed her greatly. Royal Square, with its lawns and statues and its lines of tall Cuban palms, was normally the most sedate and orderly place in Hong Kong. But coming out of the bank, Edith had become aware of a great commotion next to the cupola housing the bronze statue of Victoria, with a crowd of local Chinese milling about in a fever, and an outnumbered group of policemen trying vainly to control the situation. Eventually she had discovered the cause of the uproar: a leper had been found wandering in the square and frightening passersby with his hideous and deformed face.

Two years ago lepers had been a common sight in Hong Kong. But the government, conscious of the fear and loathing that these poor wretches instilled in the healthy, had built an asylum in the New Territories to house them and keep them out of public sight, a measure which had solved the problem in their eyes – out of sight and therefore out of mind. But the war in China had now led to a fresh influx of destitute lepers from the mainland. This particular man had apparently been sleeping at the foot of the statue of the Great White Empress herself, until his presence was noted by panicked locals, who had called the police. As the poor man was herded away to be housed in the dilapidated buildings of the former Tung Wah Smallpox Hospital, Edith had glimpsed the man's terrifying features and had been ashamed of the revulsion and fear it had caused in her...

With a sigh, Edith took one last lingering look at the green hillsides of Mid-levels above, dotted with apartment blocks and hillside temples and the mansion roofs of the wealthy, then returned to the main portico entrance of the building on the south side of Government House. The grounds of Government House were protected from the public by a tall perimeter wall so formed a privileged enclave that was only accessible to a very select group of people. At the driveway entrance to the grounds on Upper Albert Road, Edith could see an armed contingent of the Government House guards standing rigidly to attention at the tall iron entrance gate, which was framed by a pair of elegant gate lodges. With all the civil unrest and rioting in Hong Kong in recent months, the guards looked as if they were taking their task of protecting the Governor a lot more seriously than in former easier times...

Even though Edith spent every working day in the Central Government offices on the north side of this building, she had not yet grown blasé in her appreciation of its architectural perfection. Government House, built in a Colonial Renaissance style, had stood in white splendour here on Government Hill for the last eighty years, and had been the official residence of all the governors of Hong Kong during that time, as well as the main seat of British power. The Governor and his cabinet, or Executive Council, were housed here, while the Legislative Council also used the main ballroom as their meeting chamber. While the Executive Council was composed entirely of British colonial officials, the Legislative Council was a minor nod to local democracy, for it was made up of a selection of the colony's taipans and business elite, as well as some local citizens of note, including some Chinese.

Yet, as Edith knew, these small concessions to democracy were no more than wafer thin for the role of the Legislative Council was purely advisory; in reality, the Governor and his chief cohorts had almost complete autonomy over the running of Hong Kong, and were as powerful here as any Oriental potentate. The only real constraints on their conduct that the Governor and his staff had to worry about were the views of their political masters back in Whitehall; the mandarins of the Foreign Office did not generally like their colonial officials being overly presumptuous and regal in their conduct of Hong Kong affairs, and were always quick to stamp on any governor who they suspected of overreaching himself.

As Edith came into the main entrance hall, the balding avuncular figure of her superior, Ralph Ogden, emerged from the drawing room. 'Oh, hello, Edith. Are you ready for tonight's do? I know this sort of thing is hardly your cup of tea, but it should be interesting enough anyway.' Ogden had probably been a very handsome man in his youth, Edith thought, but time had taken a heavy toll on him and left him with a sagging belly, a flabby double chin and an unhealthy sallow complexion. He led her to the rear of the building where a covered walkway connected the main block to the modern annexe buildings at the back which contained the government offices, including their own communications section.

Edith knew the image that she projected to most of the staff in Government House: the shy, bespectacled and unworldly secretary, the ultimate bluestocking. However Ogden knew her better than anyone here and certainly fully understood what she was capable of as a work colleague. Yet it seemed that even he had no more comprehension of her true character than any of the other men in Government House. It should have annoyed her to be dismissed so easily – a minor female cog in this male-dominated government machine - yet Edith preferred the relative anonymity of her position. In her line of work there were many advantages to being ignored and underestimated. Of course she knew that if she had been a more handsome and amenable woman, then attitudes towards her from her male colleagues would have been entirely different. Yet she was glad to be spared their pestering attentions too, for she truly was as little interested in them as they were in her.

She adopted a neutral expression as she reached the entrance to the suite of rooms that served as the government communications centre. 'Actually I'm looking forward to tonight, Ralph. It's not often that I get to mix socially with the great and good of Hong Kong.' Edith suspected that Ogden thought he had done her a great favour by getting her an invitation to tonight's reception in the ballroom for the business leaders of Hong Kong, so she decided to be politic and to butter him up a little for a change.

Ogden glanced a little uneasily at her plain and dowdy cotton floral-print dress, and at her straight brown hair, which was scraped back from her brow in what even she knew to be a highly unflattering style. 'I do hope that you are not intending to come to the party dressed like that, are you?'

Edith looked down at her slender figure and her sensible shoes. 'Of course…why not?' But then she smiled faintly at Ogden's uneasy expression. 'Don't worry. I brought an evening dress to work with me today, Ralph, so I will change before all these taipans and their regal ladies arrive at seven-thirty. And I will even try to do something with my dreadful hair.'

'Oh, it's not dreadful at all, Edith,' Ogden demurred. 'It has a very fine chestnut colour and texture, and would look wonderful if you ever wore it up or invested in a perm, I'm sure,' he added with gentlemanly tolerance.

Something in his patronising tone made Edith suddenly decide that she would do her level best to surprise her boss this evening. Certainly her evening dress of black velvet was from the Spanish couture house of Balenciaga and was therefore the finest item of clothing she possessed by a mile; it also showed off her best features to fine effect, she knew, her strikingly long neck and her tall and graceful figure.

Ogden hesitated for a moment. 'I hope you will take this reception seriously, Edith. The Governor is determined to put on a good show tonight and demonstrate that it is business as usual in Hong Kong.'

Yet Edith knew that the present situation in Hong Kong was very far from business as usual. '*Acting* Governor, I think you mean,' she corrected him tartly. The Colonial Secretary Norman Lockhart Smith was presently acting as a rather ineffectual governor after the departure of the last governor in April, and until the arrival of his successor, while his own deputy George Carothers was standing in as Colonial Secretary. The new governor was to be Sir Geoffrey Northcote, a man who had served as the Chief Secretary of the Gold Coast until 1934, and then more lately as Governor and Commander-in-Chief of British Guiana. Yet Sir Geoffrey seemed in no hurry to arrive in Hong Kong, and - given the problems that he would face when he did finally arrive - Edith could well understand his reluctance.

The civil war in mainland China between the Nationalists and the Communists had long caused huge problems in the tiny colony of Hong Kong, but a new and potentially disastrous dynamic had entered the political arena in China last month when the Japanese had invaded the country.

An increasingly belligerent and militaristic Japan had long been making territorial incursions into a China weakened by civil war and a lack of any central authority. But this Japanese aggression has entered a new and ominous phase last month when they had invaded China en masse. The justification for this aggression had been a rather minor incident at a railway junction, thirty three days ago on July 7th. Twelve miles west of Peking, at a place called Lukouchaio where the railway line from Tientsin crossed the Peking-Hankow line, the Japanese Kwantung Army had been carrying out night exercises in an area of Chinese territory previously ceded to them, and one of their number had been shot in the dark by some unknown bullet near the ancient Marco Polo Bridge. Japan had used this incident to demand the complete handover of the two northern Chinese provinces of Hopei and Chahar, and had threatened that there would be a major retaliation if their extortionate demands were not met. The Nationalist Chinese leader, Chiang Kia-shek, had previously ignored the many Japanese land grabs on Chinese territory, more concerned with fighting his home-grown Communist enemies. But this time the Generalissimo had not been prepared to accede to this brazen new Japanese ultimatum and had said simply that no more of China would be surrendered. A few days later, ten thousand Japanese troops had crossed the Great Wall and invaded Hopei province without any formal declaration of war, and this undeclared war now seemed likely to sweep down the whole length of China in time, even to the South...

Ogden was clearly thinking similar thoughts to Edith about the situation in China, for he frowned as he suddenly remembered a relevant part of her personal history. 'You grew up in Japan, didn't you, Edith?'

'It was more than that; I was actually *born* in Tokyo,' she admitted. 'And I lived there more or less continuously until I was seventeen years old. My father was in the diplomatic service there initially, and then stayed on when he retired as ambassador because he loved the place and the people so much.'

Ogden grunted cynically. 'I doubt if he would approve of what the Japanese military is getting up to in China these days, though, would he?'

Edith didn't answer that directly. But she knew that her father would have been mystified, and even devastated, by what had happened in Japan over the last ten years – how a civilized and cultured people had been corrupted by their military leaders and seen their natural patriotism and energy misdirected instead to the cause of bigotry, xenophobia and perverted nationalism. Edith herself found it difficult to reconcile her own memories of the Japanese she had grown up with – their gentle and polite charm – with the tales of bloodthirsty atrocities now coming out of China...

Ogden looked suddenly sombre. 'We must try and maintain confidence, Edith, despite the threat from the Japanese. I would hope that the Japs will not dare to push into Southern China, though something tells me that those shots fired near the Marco Polo Bridge might have signalled the start of a new and terrible world war...'

'Now who is being defeatist, Ralph?' Edith remonstrated. She felt like reminding him that it had been *she* who had actually intercepted and decoded the signals from Japanese High Command to the Kwantung Army, ordering them to invade Hopei province, and that the British had therefore known about the timing of this attack probably long before Chiang Kia-shek. But privately she agreed with Ogden's grim assessment that this new Japanese incursion was much more serious than any that had gone on before. Ogden was a very astute man of course behind that deceptively bland Cambridge academic's facade: a fine classics scholar in his own right, an unlikely hero of the Somme twenty years ago as a volunteer army captain, and now, at fifty-three years of age, Britain's chief spymaster in the Far East. Therefore he might well be right: no one really knew where this new conflagration in China would lead, but it might well end up setting fire to the whole world.

War was also threatening to overwhelm Europe too, of course, with a bitter civil war in progress in Spain. Hitler's Germany had predictably taken the side of the Nationalist rebels, while Russia was supporting the left wing Republican government. In April the Luftwaffe had destroyed the Basque town of Guernica, and a new age of cynical warfare had started in earnest, where civilian populations were seen as being just as much fair game for the belligerents as the armies in the field...

And the threat of war spilling over from China wasn't the only problem facing the new Governor of Hong Kong when he did finally arrive to take up his post. Edith had heard that the number of smallpox and cholera cases in the colony was showing a disturbingly fast rise of late, perhaps because of the influx of migrants. There seemed every chance that these new cases might blow up into a major epidemic of one of these dread diseases in the coming months...

'I saw a leper in Royal Square today,' she said reluctantly.

'I'm sorry. That must have been very distressing for you,' Ogden said kindly.

'Not as distressing as it was for that poor man,' Edith commented bitterly. 'I thought that any lepers from China were supposed to be stopped at the border now, or else removed to that quarantine facility at Swatow?'

'That is the supposed plan,' Ogden said. 'But the system isn't foolproof, and the occasional one will still get through,' he admitted. 'By the way, did you hear the sad news? It seems the Americans have finally called off the search for Amelia Earheart...'

Edith was disappointed to hear it, because the American flier Amelia Earheart was a personal hero of hers. Earheart had disappeared with her navigator in the Pacific on July 2nd during a round-the-world flight, yet hopes had persisted that she might have landed in the sea and got into a boat, or else made landfall on some remote Pacific island. Rumours had even emerged that her Lockheed Electra might have been shot down by the Japanese, and she and her navigator imprisoned. Edith would have liked even that wild rumour to be true, yet she was realistic enough to know when it was time to give up forlorn hopes. 'Then that's a great pity,' she said with a sigh as she imagined poor Amelia Earhart in her final watery grave, deep beneath the Pacific Ocean...

*

At seven o'clock, Edith returned to the main block of Government House and entered the sumptuously furnished neo-classical drawing room, where she had been told that there would be a small briefing from the Acting Governor before the VIP guests started arriving for the main reception. She was now dressed in her evening finery and had her hair worn up, and had even applied some rouge and powder to her face.

She was gratified to see that all the four men already assembled in the room in their best dinner jackets looked distinctly startled by her change of appearance, and that the Attorney General, Julian Colby, had not even apparently recognized her at first without her glasses. Ronnie Grantham's jaw had positively dropped when he had noticed the provocative shade of lipstick she was wearing. Edith had not been sure about that final embellishment when she had regarded her scarlet-painted mouth in the mirror earlier. That violent shade of red did make her look disturbingly like a high-priced Mayfair tart, particularly when combined with such a low cut gown. But in the end she had decided to be bold; tonight she felt that she wanted to be noticed for once.

Ian Luff, who was second in command in the financial team to the Colonial Treasurer Bob Harmsworth, was the first to get over his surprise and speak up. Rising quickly from his armchair, he whistled softly in appreciation. 'My, my, you look wonderful, Edith.' His voice rose in slight perplexity. 'Is that a *Balenciaga* gown that you're wearing?'

Edith smiled at his reaction. Ian Luff was one of the nicer and less affected young men who worked at Government House. 'It is. But I should also admit that it is five years old, Ian, and therefore completely out of date with this season's fashion lines in Paris.'

Luff's superior in the Hong Kong Treasury, Bob Harmsworth, had also leapt to his feet and now regarded her with something like wonder. 'Nevertheless it is a revelation, young Edith. I am always astonished at the way that young women can transform themselves at will into such ravishing creatures.'

Edith almost blushed at Harmsworth's roguish smile. Yet she knew that she would soon lose Harmsworth's attention once the main party started, for the business leaders of Hong Kong naturally all had beautiful and glamorous wives to show off, who would soon put Edith's own small attempt at glamorising herself into the shade. So Harmsworth would soon have many other temptingly beautiful women on which to practice his well-known flirtatious skills. Yet, despite his tendency for lascivious behaviour, Harmsworth had always struck Edith as a gentleman at heart, and was probably the nicest of the senior government officials. He was a handsome widower in his fifties with a full head of shining silver hair and the face of a distinguished Shakespearean actor. Rather more improbably, he was also an old friend of Ralph Ogden from their days serving together in France with the 8th Service Battalion of the Norfolk Regiment. Both Ogden and Harmsworth had volunteered with noble self-sacrifice to serve in France when they were already established professional men well into their thirties, and had fought side-by-side on the first day of the Battle of the Somme on 1 July 1916, which ordeal had probably swayed Edith's opinions in both their favours a little.

Julian Colby, a rather unprepossessing man with a bald close-shaven head and piercing blue eyes, had been Attorney General in Hong Kong for several years and was therefore the most senior government official in the room, despite being younger than Harmsworth. He made no comment on Edith's radically different appearance, but did venture a long and thoughtful examination of her figure, starting at her feet and then working his eyes slowly upwards. Edith could see that her cleavage in particular had attracted Colby's unwanted attention in this low cut gown, and that he was making no secret of his interest. The presumption of his calculated inspection irritated her, and for a moment she was tempted to turn her back rudely on him. Colby was certainly the most irritating and patronising of the gentlemen here, as well as the most senior in rank. He also had a truly terrifying wife; Eileen Colby was renowned as the most terrible snob in the whole of the Mid-levels, and widely feared for her bitter and waspish tongue. Certainly Edith had never received an invitation to any of her famous soirees at their luxurious house on Bonham Road.

But then, as far as Eileen Colby was concerned, Edith Starling was of course a social nonentity - no more than a mere secretary in Government House assigned to the communications chief Ralph Ogden. The real truth about her was known only to Ogden: that she was Secret Service too, and that she was an expert in Japanese military codes. The Secret Intelligence Service had recruited her direct from Oxford after she graduated with a doctorate in mathematics from Somerville College where she had done original research into the new field of coding theory. Edith had acquired her love of mathematics from her mother, a wealthy American anglophile from an old Boston family, who had done original mathematical work of her own before finally marrying an eccentric English diplomat. Edith's PhD supervisor at Somerville had been so enthusiastic about her research that he had even declared it to be the beginnings of a whole new branch of mathematics, which he had decided in his wisdom to call "information theory". Edith's particular research had been concerned with finding explicit methods for increasing the efficiency of data communication by data compression and error-correction techniques. This work had led her naturally into a wider interest in cryptographic algorithms, both codes and ciphers.

Edith's late father, Henry Starling, had been a senior British diplomat in Tokyo during the Taishoo period of the 1910s, before eventually becoming British ambassador in the early twenties, therefore Edith also had the unusual distinctions for an Englishwoman of having been born in Japan, and speaking fluent Japanese. So these two talents of hers - the linguistic and the mathematical - had combined to make her a perfect choice for the code-breakers section of the SIS at their headquarters near St James's Park in London. Then, when a vacancy had arisen for an expert in Japanese military codes to work at Government House in Hong Kong, she had been the logical choice, particularly as she would be able to pose as only a simple secretary to the intelligence chief in Hong Kong, Ralph Ogden...

Ronnie Grantham came over to her with a shy smile. 'May I get you a drink before the Governor arrives, Edith? A glass of white wine perhaps?'

Ronnie was a lawyer by training, and deputy to the Attorney General Julian Colby. Edith found him to be genial enough but it seemed his chief Colby deemed him to be rather incompetent and unreliable, or so Edith had heard privately from Ogden. Of course, this might only be Colby's sour and biased assessment; Edith doubted that Colby ever had a good word to say about anyone. At the age of thirty-eight Grantham still had the looks of a Cambridge undergraduate, with shining blond hair and pink cheeks, which was possibly one particular reason why the bald and ugly Colby had not taken to him. Colby was only eight years older than Ronnie, but looked twenty five years older. Ronnie's beautiful wife Faye was famed in the expatriate community for her serene beauty and her vibrant personality, and she and Ronnie made one of the handsomest couples in town. Yet Edith had often wondered how Ronnie had managed to win Faye's hand for, despite his boyish looks, he always seemed a little dull and ill-at-ease when in company with his effervescent and gorgeous wife.

Edith had no opportunity, however, to accept the offer of a drink from Ronnie Grantham, for at that moment the Acting Governor Norman Lockhart Smith bustled into the room with Colonial Secretary George Carothers at his side.

Ralph Ogden also sidled into the drawing room in the wake of the Governor, and did a double take when he noticed how Edith was dressed. He came over discreetly to her side and whispered in her ear. 'I only told you to smarten yourself up, Edith, not turn yourself into Mata Hari...'

Edith didn't take offence for she could see that Ogden was actually quite taken with the way she looked. 'I take it that you like this dress, then, Ralph?'

Ogden smiled. 'Very much. But you could have warned me to be prepared. I'm not sure that shocks like this are good for my health. You do remember that I am still recovering from that recent heart attack, don't you?'

'I doubt the fact that I am wearing lipstick for a change should be enough to cause a relapse of your heart condition, Ralph. And it was only angina that you were suffering from, wasn't it, not a full blown coronary...' Edith then noticed that his face was twisted a little, as if in pain. 'Are you sure that you're all right?' she asked, now with some genuine concern.

Ogden relaxed his face. 'Just a little indigestion, I'm sure...nothing more.' He saw that Lockhart Smith was finally ready to begin his pep talk, so dropped his voice to a whisper. 'Let's have some fun and count how many clichés Norman manages to insert into his five-minute speech of encouragement, shall we...?'

*

An hour later, the party was in full swing in the ballroom, with a spirited babble of conversation and the continuous chink of glasses. Electric fans turned slowly in the fine moulded plaster ceiling, providing some relief to the guests from the oppressive evening humidity. Great blocks of ice had also been laid out around the room, with more fans arranged at ground level to blow some cooling air at the guests. This was the grandest room in Government House, over sixty feet long, and seemed a fitting place for all these assembled taipans and their statuesque and beautiful wives. Edith had decided to persist with not wearing her spectacles this evening even though it meant as a result that she had to squint most indecorously to see any of her companions up close. Yet even without the encumbrance of her glasses, Edith had still begun to feel distinctly dowdy again in the presence of all these gloriously attired Hong Kong wives and daughters. In the spirit of improving relations with the Chinese community, the Acting Governor had also decided that the leaders of the Chinese business community should be invited to this reception too, and some of their exotic-looking wives were dressed in even more fabulous splendour than the expatriate wives.

Edith knew from the Governor's pep talk beforehand that this evening was intended to be a relatively sober occasion rather than a light-hearted and frivolous celebration; that type of party seemed insensitive and inappropriate in the circumstances, given the grim news coming out of China in recent weeks. The main practical consequence of this decision by the Acting Governor was that there would be no dancing on offer tonight, which had rather disappointed Edith. Unknown to most of her colleagues at Government House, she was an accomplished dancer and had been looking forward to tripping the dance floor in a foxtrot or rumba with some of Hong Kong's most eminent gentlemen. But there was nevertheless plenty of good food and drink being dispensed from the well-stocked tables on one side of the room, while a local amateur string quartet played selections from Bach and Mozart with discreet and airy skill. Despite the intention to keep this a low key affair, Edith had noticed that the mood had certainly lightened as more drink had been consumed, so the conversations around the room had become less serious and business-orientated as the evening went on, and perhaps more flirtatious and even scandalous.

Edith saw that the young Taipan of the Noble House, Jardine-Matheson - the Honourable Sir John Keswick - was very much in evidence during the party, circulating among all his competitors and rivals with practised charm. At the age of only thirty-one he was now in charge of the company's operations in Hong Kong, while his (slightly) older brother Tony ran their mainland operations from their Shanghai office. Like most of the large hongs in Hong Kong, Jardine-Matheson had expanded their activities in China hugely in the last thirty years, though they, like many other Hong Kong businesses, had to be looking at the present political instability in China, and at the new hostilities with Japan, with some trepidation, for these disturbing events could potentially wipe out the value of their investments on the mainland overnight.

Despite the unexpectedly light mood of the party, Edith could still sense the underlying tensions in this room, particularly from all these business leaders with so much money invested in China: the heads of Butterfield and Swire, and of Hutchinson Whampoa, for example; or of the Hong Kong and Shanghai Bank, or even the directors of the main department store in Hong Kong, Lane Crawford, who had also heavily invested in new stores in China.

Edith became aware that Faye Grantham had joined her. 'Ah, Edith. May I say how charming you look tonight? That shade of lipstick works wonderfully well with your natural colouring. And without your glasses for once, I see that you have very beautiful eyes.'

'You're very kind, thank you, Faye,' Edith said formally, a little taken aback by such an encomium from someone who was famed in Hong Kong for her own beauty. Edith didn't know Faye's age but suspected that Faye was even younger than her – perhaps only twenty-six or twenty-seven. Yet Faye Grantham carried so much more assurance in her manner than most women of that age. Of course she was very wealthy; she came originally from South Africa where her family owned one of the largest gold mines in the Witwatersrand. So such assurance must come naturally when you were an heiress worth five million pounds or so, Edith thought cynically. As if that wasn't enough, though, she had also been blessed with the face and flaxen hair of a sculpted Renaissance angel and a body that any sensible man would die for. If any woman in this room seemed designed to make Edith feel insecure about her own appearance, then it was undoubtedly Faye Grantham.

'Your husband seems very happy tonight,' Edith said neutrally, glancing at the far side of the room where she could see that Ronnie Grantham was deep in an apparently high-spirited conversation with Eileen Colby. Edith wondered what on earth he could be saying that would entertain that sour old dragon so much.

Faye gave her handsome blonde husband a long thoughtful look. 'Yes, he does, doesn't he?' She returned her attention to Edith with some apparent reluctance. 'We don't see much of you socially, Edith. You need to get out a bit more from your dusty files in Government House, and come to one of our parties.'

This seemed a disingenuous remark to Edith since she was never invited to any of Faye's parties in Robinson Road. 'Well, work does keep me very busy,' she said innocuously.

'In fact I don't think I've seen you socially since that beach party we held last autumn at Repulse Bay,' Faye commented. 'You created quite a stir that day...'

'Did I?' Edith thought that her black flannel bathing costume had been rather modest and plain compared to the gorgeous and daring red two-piece that Faye Grantham herself had been wearing that day.

'Yes, you did.' Faye saw Edith's puzzled look and quickly explained. 'Oh, I meant that wonderful Yank car that you turned up in.'

Edith nodded resignedly. 'Oh, you mean my Studebaker?'

'Yes, it looks a wonderful car. And such a heavenly colour – dark blue. I was simply green with envy and wanted to buy it from you on the spot. I haven't seen another like that in Hong Kong.'

Edith smiled at Faye's unlikely enthusiasm for American cars. 'That's because it's the only one.' American cars – Studebakers and Chryslers - were relatively common among the two thousand motor vehicles registered in Hong Kong, but not the model that Edith had bought from a friend. 'It was a nineteen-thirty Studebaker President passenger tourer, series FE seven...very rare and very nice...'

Faye looked disappointed. 'It sounds as if you no longer have it.'

'I haven't,' Edith admitted. 'I had a slight accident with it in the New Territories during the winter – I went to watch a meeting of the Fan-ling Hunt – and I ran off the road into a ditch...' The New Territories was the area of mainland China leased by the British from the Chinese as a buffer zone to Kowloon, and was still largely a wild and untamed area roamed by occasional tigers, and more often by wild boar and Chinese bandits. Therefore Edith's experience of being stuck in a ditch had been a little more frightening that she was prepared to admit. 'Fortunately a kind Chinese man from the village stopped and arranged to send a truck to pull me out and tow me back to Kowloon. The owner of the garage in Nathan Road in Kowloon which repaired the damage was very taken with the car and offered me a fortune for it. So I sold it to him; it was in truth far too large a car for a single girl like me. So now I drive a little Austin Seven, which is much easier to park in Hong Kong's narrow little streets, though not nearly as much fun as the Studebaker...'

Faye pouted a little. 'That's a pity. I wish you'd thought of selling it to me. What was the name of this fortunate garage owner? Perhaps he might sell the car on to me...'

'His name is Dominic Tien; he's a Eurasian, I think,' Edith said. 'But I wouldn't build your hopes up, Faye. It was eight months ago, after all. And this Mr Tien said he was going to give the Studebaker to his favourite cousin as a birthday present.'

Faye was about to say something more in response when her attention was distracted by a couple of new arrivals at the party, a middle-aged Englishman and a younger Chinese man.

Edith saw that Faye's eyes were directed at the newly arrived Englishman too. Edith didn't recognize the man, but he looked interesting, a dark and brooding Celtic face, thick wavy hair that shone jet black under the ballroom chandeliers, and a lean and athletic build. He was very close to Edith's mental image of what Heathcliff from Emily Bronte's *Wuthering Heights* might look like, if his wild dark curls had been tamed by a smart haircut, and his muscular body concealed within an elegant dinner jacket. 'Who is that man?' she asked Faye casually.

Faye tossed her head a little dismissively. 'Oh, *him*? That's Sebastian Ride, the chairman of Saunders-Woo Holdings.'

'Ah, *that* is the infamous Sebastian Ride?' Edith knew this man by reputation at least, and had some particular intimate knowledge of him too, for she knew that Sebastian Ride had once pursued an affair with a close friend of hers. In fact it seemed he had become quite besotted with her friend Susan and had pestered her repeatedly with his attentions. Eventually it seemed that this pressure had worked, for Edith was almost convinced that her friend had given in to Mr Ride's seductive persuasion in the end. Edith remembered that *Wuthering Heights* had been Susan's favourite book, so perhaps that was the reason why she had been attracted to this modern day Heathcliff.

Poor Susan...she had deserved so much better from life than her sad fate...

Now Edith could finally understand for the first time just why Susan might have betrayed her loving and devoted husband, for Sebastian Ride would be hard for any woman to resist... 'Isn't he married?' Edith persisted. 'He seems to be here on his own.'

Faye shrugged. 'I believe he *is* married...'

Suddenly Edith became conscious of the hungry look on Faye Grantham's face as she watched Sebastian Ride make his way confidently across the room, greeting people with a well-practised smile as he went. Edith almost had to suppress a gasp of astonishment as she understood instinctively just what that look meant – those bright eyes and those suddenly flushed cheeks, and a perceptible rise in her breathing. It seemed as clear to Edith as if Faye Grantham had just run across the room and fallen into Mr Ride's muscular arms...*she was yet another of his female conquests...*

Faye glanced uneasily at Edith at her side, and seemed consciously to try and relax her facial muscles. 'He rarely brings his wife to these affairs. It seems that Gloria Ride drinks rather a lot and has a reputation as a difficult woman.'

Edith had an uncomfortable feeling that she might know just why Gloria Ride drank so much. But she said nothing. *Who was she to judge Faye Grantham anyway?* She had a much deeper and darker secret of her own, after all...

She limited herself instead to a simple question. 'Who was that young Chinese man with Mr Ride?' Edith had noted that this Chinese man was also very handsome – pretty as a girl almost – yet with a petulant and arrogant look about him that suggested a far from amiable character.

Faye was almost her normal self again. 'That gentleman is James Woo, the vice-chairman of Saunders-Woo Holdings. The company was founded back in the nineteenth century when the Scots Taipan James Saunders went into partnership with the wealthy Woo family of Canton. Sebastian Ride started with them only as a junior clerk; but he rose through the ranks of the company over the last twenty years and is now chairman since the last of the Saunders retired. James Woo is the young scion of the Woo clan and is now his deputy, even though he's only thirty-two years old.'

'You seem to know a lot about them,' Edith said guardedly. She thought that Woo barely looked twenty years old, with his smooth olive skin and slender build and his pretty girlish features.

Faye blinked uncertainly as if conscious that she might have given away too much of her personal feelings. 'One tries to keep abreast of Hong Kong affairs.'

Edith noticed that Ride was now speaking in a close huddle with James Woo; the discussion did not look particularly warm, though - in fact a little bad-tempered, she would have said. But she was prevented from making any comment on this disagreement, because Ralph Ogden suddenly appeared at her side.

'Would you like to take a turn in the garden, Edith?' he asked solicitously. Ogden smiled apologetically at Faye Grantham. 'Edith loves stargazing, and it seems it might be possible to see the Southern Cross from the garden tonight...'

*

Once out in the starlit garden, and safely away from any prying eyes beneath the branches of a Flame-of-the-Forest tree, Edith said wryly, 'I hope that Faye Grantham is not an amateur astronomer, otherwise your excuse for wresting me away from her company might look a little suspicious. In fact it's almost impossible to see the Southern Cross from anywhere in Hong Kong, except perhaps from the Peak where it might appear very low down near the Southern horizon in May and June. And then only on an exceptionally clear night with no sea haze. There is certainly no chance of ever seeing the Southern Cross from here in the grounds of Government House, Ralph.' Edith was suddenly struck by an embarrassing thought: that Faye would think instead that Ralph had invited her out into the garden for a much more obvious reason...

Ralph Ogden smiled. 'Doesn't matter, I doubt that Faye would know you can't see the Southern Cross from here. In fact I doubt that Faye Grantham would know the difference between the Southern Cross and the Big Dipper.'

Ogden had suggested that they should walk on even further into a more remote part of the garden. But Edith was in a fretful mood now and would have none of it; her evening shoes were hardly suited for a walk along an uneven and mossy garden path in the dark. She presumed that Ogden must have something important to say to justify dragging her out here into the garden, but she still wasn't prepared to walk any further and see her best pair of shoes ruined. 'On the contrary Faye should know all about the Southern Cross,' she pointed out tartly, '...she's from South Africa, remember, where it must be high in the night sky most of the time.'

Ogden was not to be distracted even by that argument. 'But only if you look up at the night sky, which I am sure the gorgeous Faye would never waste her time on. She would be far too busy ogling all the handsome gentlemen at eye level, just as she was ogling Mr Ride when he arrived just now.'

'So it's true,' Edith muttered in disbelief, though she was quietly pleased to have her guess confirmed. 'She's having an affair with this Mr Ride.'

'Oh, yes. It's been going on for some time,' Ogden said breezily. 'I just hope it comes to a natural conclusion before Ronnie finds out. He's a nice boy; I wouldn't want to see him get hurt.'

'He's not such a boy, is he? I mean he's thirty-eight, isn't he?' Edith protested mildly.

'Still a naive little boy inside, though, when it comes to his marriage, I suspect.' Ogden looked up through the fronds of the Delonix tree at the night sky, where the constellation of Cygnus the Swan, otherwise known as the Northern Cross, was at least clearly discernable above the outline of the Peak, if not the Southern Cross. 'Fortunately my knowledge of the classics is much sounder than my knowledge of the stars. Which is just as well, for I intend to go back to my roots when I retire, and teach the classics again...'

'*Are* you planning to retire, Ralph?' This was a new and worrying development to Edith, for she had formed a close working rapport with Ogden over the last two years. *Was this why he had brought her out here in the garden?* To break this bad news?

'Well, I am fifty-three after all, I have a dicky heart, and this game that we are in is a young man's business,' Ogden said mildly. 'But don't worry; I am not intending to desert the battlefield quite just yet. There are too many important things to do first...'

Edith guessed that the most vital of these was to close down the huge network of Japanese agents that was operating in Hong Kong. Edith doubted that the Japanese would ever be bold enough to attack Hong Kong itself, yet the fact was that they were doing their best to discover all the details of Britain's military defences along the border with China, which was a worry. The SIS knew that Japanese espionage in South China, Malaya and Hong Kong was being orchestrated through a bogus company, the King Chung Company, based in Shameen, Canton province, which was known to be a subsidiary of the South Manchurian Railway, whose salaries and expenses were paid by the Japanese War Ministry. But even knowing this, the SIS had not been able to identify the most important Japanese agents in Hong Kong, even though it was obvious that their activities were being coordinated through the Japanese Consulate in Macdonnell Road, close to where Ogden himself lived. There were many hundreds of Japanese working in Hong Kong as waiters, barmen, hairdressers and masseurs, and a good proportion of them had to be passing on the confidences of their more important expatriate customers to the Japanese Consulate. But it was the leaders of this network that Ogden wanted to catch...*catch them and he could close this network down...*

'Do you know that I haven't been home in ten years?' Ogden said. 'I stopped taking home leave after my wife died.'

Edith had learned enough about her boss's past to know that Ogden had been completely devoted to his late wife, and that her painful death from liver cancer had knocked the stuffing completely out of him. Despite his very English sense of humour, he did wear a permanent air of melancholy, like an enveloping black cloak.

Ogden smiled ruefully. 'We now have a *second* new king since I was last in England, which makes me feel like I've been away a hundred years, rather than ten. I hope this new one does rather better than the last, though I am hardly confident of it with such a stuttering lightweight individual...'

The new King, George VI, had been crowned in May after his brother Edward had renounced the throne the previous December to marry his American mistress, Wallis Simpson. Edith didn't know much about the character of the new king, who had formerly been the Duke of York, but no one seemed to have very high hopes for him...

'It would be a great blessing in our business, Edith, if we could read minds and understand a man's real thoughts, wouldn't it?' Ogden said, suddenly changing the subject, '... particularly those of our closest friends and acquaintances. Though it might shock us to discover the dark soul hidden behind a familiar and friendly face,' he added. Then a fresh thought seemed to strike him. 'Have you ever heard of Ephialtes of Trachis, Edith?'

Edith guessed that this was a rhetorical question since most of Ogden's were, at least when it came to anything to do with his beloved classics. But she decided to surprise him and answer anyway. 'Wasn't he the man who betrayed the Spartans at Thermopylae by showing the Persians a secret path that gave them access behind the Greek lines?'

'Bravo, Edith! You astonish me with your erudition as usual. Yes, you are quite right. The name of Ephialtes is now a byword not only for treason, but for the worst kind of betrayal as well. History might have ended up quite differently if the Greeks had been able to read the mind of this traitor in their midst.'

'And then again, perhaps not... Didn't the Greeks win that war anyway, despite this man's betrayal?' Edith wondered what Ogden could mean with this talk of an Ancient Greek traitor. *Was he trying to tell her in his usual oblique way that he suspected that there might be a traitor embedded somewhere at high level in Hong Kong...perhaps even in Government House itself?*

Ogden soon confirmed Edith's bleak suspicions. 'I have lately received a report brought by a personal courier from our embassy in Tokyo. It seems that our SIS staff in Tokyo have received a tipoff from one of their own local informants - a man in the Japanese War Ministry, the *Hyōbu-sho* - that the contents of several recent coded messages between the Foreign Office in London and Government House in Hong Kong are known to the Japanese. Until now, as you know, we had been confident that the Japanese weren't able to break our own codes. This is mainly thanks to your own sterling work in breaking the main Japanese military codes, Edith, which has enabled us to read *their* High Command messages to their army in China with ease, all of which seemed to show how little the Japanese understood about our own plans and defences in the Far East. But this report from Tokyo three days ago suggests that the Japanese may now be able to read our own secret transmissions at will...'

Edith wondered with irritation why Ralph had not told her this earlier, since he seemed to have known about this security leak for three days or more. And it seemed even more perverse of him to have decided to break this worrying news to her on an evening like this when she would have preferred to forget work entirely for once and simply enjoy the party.

Ogden hesitated. 'Naturally we have changed our codes at once to try and make our messages secure from the Japanese again. However, if they manage to break our new code too, then it will naturally be highly suspicious. Of course it might just be that the Japanese have found themselves some new mathematical genius like yourself who is able to break our codes with some clever mathematical algorithm. I almost hope that that *is* the reason. Yet we must be mindful of the possibility that this knowledge of how to break our codes has been given to them by a traitor in our own midst...' Ogden frowned heavily. 'Our embassy staff in Tokyo certainly suspect that we might have an informer right here in Hong Kong...and perhaps even in Government House itself...'

'Why?' Edith asked, perplexed. 'The leak – if there *is* one - could equally well be someone in the Tokyo embassy, or perhaps in one of our consulates in mainland China. Or even in the Foreign Office in London, come to think of it...'

'That's true, I suppose...except for the fact that the same man from the *Hyōbu-shō* who gave us this information has also told us that he believes the Japanese have an agent embedded here in Government House. Yet I hope to God that this is simply a mistake of some sort...' Ogden took her hands in an usually intimate gesture, and squeezed them gently. 'Please keep this information strictly to yourself for now, Edith.'

'Do ABC know about this?' Edith asked. "ABC" was the slightly flippant way that Ralph always referred to his three top SIS agents here in Hong Kong - Noah Adam, Geoffrey Broadbent and Elliot Casaubon. Adam and Broadbent were comparatively green young men, but Casaubon was a very experienced government agent.

Edith didn't like Casaubon much - though only forty years old, he was balding, bespectacled, and burdened with a personality that was dry to the point of desiccation. He also had the prim superior air of a schoolmaster with a taste for using the birch. Noah Adam was nicer, an earnest young man from Oxford with a subtle sense of humour, while Broadbent was a dour young Scot from Edinburgh who looked like an athlete. Broadbent was certainly the only one of the three who had any of the physical look of Bulldog Drummond about him; Adam and Casaubon looked instead like they would be much more at home in the reading room of the British Museum, studying dusty manuscripts.

Yet all three of these men spoke fluent Mandarin and Cantonese, and knew their way around China, therefore their importance to SIS operations could not be discounted. Casaubon had been out in the East for fifteen years already. Adam's parents had been missionaries in China during the twenties, so he had spent a lot of time there as a child, while Broadbent had taken a first in Oriental languages at Oxford...

Ogden looked sheepish. 'No, I haven't spoken to Casaubon yet. In fact the Governor doesn't even know about this yet. So I am being very improper in telling *you* about this before anyone else. So please respect your privileged position, Edith, and speak of this possibility to nobody for the present, not even privately to your young man, if you have one...'

'Of course I would never do such a thing, Ralph,' Edith remonstrated angrily, astonished that he should make such an insulting suggestion. 'Even if I had a "young man", as you put it, which I do not...'

'Of course you wouldn't do such a thing.' Ogden took hold of her hand again and squeezed it again briefly. 'And I apologize most humbly for even suggesting such a thing. I shouldn't perhaps have told you of these suspicions of our embassy people, yet I felt you had the right to know, when you have personally been so instrumental in breaking these Japanese military codes. And it is best that *someone else* in Government House knows about this possibility of a traitor, apart from just me. At the moment, you are the only person whom I feel I can trust completely...' Ogden suddenly fell silent as he saw a figure approaching them in the starlit garden.

The figure came closer along the path under the trees, and stepped into a faint pool of illumination from an electric lamp suspended from a tree branch. The light revealed him to be a young Chinese man dressed in a dinner jacket and therefore presumably one of the guests at the party.

'Good evening, Miss Starling,' the man said unexpectedly, then seemed to notice Ogden for the first time. 'And you...err...Mr Ogden.'

'Good evening, Mr Yip,' Ogden said smoothly. 'I hope you are enjoying the party.'

The man nodded his head politely. 'Very much so, despite arriving so late. But I needed a little break from the stuffy air inside, as you apparently did too.' Mr Yip bowed again, slightly awkwardly this time, then proceeded on his way back to the main house.

Edith wondered what to say to Ralph as she watched Michael Yip leave. She hadn't noticed him earlier in the ballroom, so thought that he could not have been there long at all.

Ogden looked at her a trifle suspiciously. 'I didn't know that you knew Michael Yip, Edith,' he said with a hint of accusation in his voice.

'I don't really,' she denied. 'I went to a play at the Theatre Royal in the City Hall a couple of months ago – an amateur production of *Private Lives* by the Bowen Players – and I happened to meet him in the bar during the interval.'

'How did you "happen" to meet him? Can you be sure that he didn't pick you out deliberately for his attentions?'

'I'm sure he didn't; we just happened to find ourselves standing next to each other, and it seemed rude not to speak,' Edith said.

'Hmm,' Ogden grunted cynically. 'Yet I wager it was him who spoke up first.'

Edith had to admit that much was true, so she wondered if there might be something in what Ogden had said after all.

'I advise you to steer well clear of that man, Edith. He is not to be trusted,' Ogden said emphatically.

'Why do you say that? I was only chatting with the man; it's not as if I'm planning to sleep with him,' Edith protested icily. 'Anyway he can't be too controversial otherwise he wouldn't be getting invitations to parties at Government House like this one.'

Ogden looked at her warningly. 'Yet even so, he is most certainly a dubious character, and no friend of the British Empire. I imagine he was invited here only as a gesture of tolerance towards the Chinese community, certainly not because the Governor approves of him. Mr Yip is only twenty-seven years old, yet for such a young man he is *very* well connected both here and in mainland China, a fact which no one seems quite able to explain. Despite coming from a very wealthy family of Shanghai merchants, his politics are most decidedly left wing and anti-colonial. As a lawyer working here in Hong Kong, he is always representing left wing troublemakers and union men, and other members of the awkward squad, in their various tangles with the Law...'

Edith wisely decided not to say any more on the subject of Michael Yip, but simply nodded to end this unwelcome discussion. She and Ogden finally began to walk back to the main block of Government House.

Arriving at the main entrance again, Edith saw that Sebastian Ride was leaving early. It was only ten o'clock but it seemed that Mr Ride had had more than enough of his fellow taipans for one evening. He brushed past her without a word, his handsome Celtic face twisted into an impatient frown. He strode across the forecourt and climbed into the front seat of an open two-seater Bugatti Type 55 painted bright blue, then screeched away with a spurt of gravel from his rear wheels.

Ian Luff was standing at the entrance, enjoying a cigarette. He smiled at Edith and Ralph in his usual charming way as his eyes followed the tracks in the gravel left by Sebastian Ride's sports car. 'It seems the evening didn't agree with Mr Ride, at least.'

Edith smiled wanly at him in return. 'No, it seems not...'

*

Sebastian Ride made it back from Government House to his own sprawling three-storey mansion at the end of Conduit Road in less than six minutes. The frantic drive at high speed up the steep incline of Garden Road had improved his mood at least, which had been soured tonight by James Woo's boorish behaviour at the Governor's party. James had made rather an exhibition of himself with his tiresome manners, Ride thought. He had got into an ill-tempered argument with Julian Colby which had threatened to turn into a physical confrontation. Ride had spotted the danger quickly and managed to extricate James from this contretemps, but James had only become even more loud and abusive when Ride had tried to quieten him afterwards. James had certainly done the reputation of Saunders-Woo no good at all with his petulant display of childish ill temper in front of the Acting Governor of Hong Kong.

Ride had done his best not to acknowledge Faye openly tonight for fear of being observed. He had made love to her only last night at the empty company flat in Bowen Road that he used for his regular assignations with her, and he had warned her then to be careful at tonight's party for fear of giving herself away. But his warning, and his own discreet behaviour at the party, had been of little use, for Faye was simply not equipped for deceit and had made her feelings towards him so glaringly obvious that everybody at that party must have some suspicions by now of the affair. Even that nice looking young woman in the black gown who had been talking to Faye had clearly noticed it, Ride thought.

Faye was a wonderful looking woman, and had a surprisingly warm and homely personality behind that cool and sophisticated exterior, yet he still had to wonder if the benefits of continuing this affair were worth the eventual likely aggravation. He had fallen for a married woman once before, and pursued her shamelessly, before it had all ended in a mysterious tragedy that still haunted him. After such a tragic outcome he had told himself that he would never do such a thing again and pursue an affair with a married woman. Yet it seemed he could not learn from his mistakes; within a few weeks of that tragedy he had started this new affair with Faye Grantham, which threatened to be even more dangerous than the last, and would perhaps ruin his reputation in Hong Kong for good if it became public knowledge. Given the parlous state of the company's business affairs in China, he simply couldn't afford to upset his social peers in Hong Kong by being labelled publicly as a predatory seducer of married women. Faye's husband, Ronald Grantham, was of little account himself, and there was little problem with upsetting him personally. Yet Grantham had some very powerful friends, right up to the Acting Governor himself, who could make his life very uncomfortable if they wished, and whose sanctions could even threaten his business empire if they wished. Therefore, for the first time, Sebastian Ride began to consider how he might end his affair with Faye with as little fuss as possible...

Ride let himself in through the front door with his own key. The house was eerily quiet apart from the sounds of the wireless upstairs; the four servants — houseboys, laundry boy and amah - all apparently retired to the basement below for the night. He loosened his bow tie and climbed the stairs, trying not to make any noise on the creaking wooden steps.

But he needn't have worried about disturbing Gloria at least. When he got to the master bedroom, he saw that she was lying stretched out on the double bed, still dressed in the evening gown she'd planned to wear to the party tonight, and dead to the world. The radio by the bed was on, and Hong Kong's only radio station, ZBW, was broadcasting a live relay of the dance orchestra from The Gripps - the ballroom in the Hong Kong Hotel. Ride had been fully intending to take Gloria with him to Government House this evening, but he'd found to his dismay on returning home at six from the office that she had broken her promise and had been drinking all afternoon, therefore was in no fit state to be paraded in front of Hong Kong's elite. In her sudden violent fury at his refusal to take her, she had thrown an empty whisky decanter at him which had only missed him by a whisker...

Worriedly he now looked at a half empty bottle of Gordon's Gin on the bedside table and wondered if she could have really drunk half its contents while he had been out at the party tonight. He didn't know where she had got that bottle from, for he had locked up all the alcohol in the house in the cellar, and only he had the key. The amah and the houseboys had been forbidden to buy her any alcohol on threat of instant dismissal. Yet Gloria was still apparently resourceful enough to find booze when she wanted. With a groan of disappointment he unfastened a few of the buttons at the top of her gown, and straightened her tousled red head to make sure that she could breathe unimpeded.

With even more weary resignation, he turned the radio off, then slumped down on a rattan chair in the corner of the room and regarded his sleeping wife with deep concern. They had been married for nearly ten years in all, though in many ways it seemed to him much longer than that. Sometimes it truly did feel like a self-imposed prison sentence. The first two years had been generally happy, but things had quickly gone downhill after that, though Ride wasn't quite sure why. He had loved this woman once, so his distaste for her now seemed a difficult thing for him to explain or justify to himself.

He remembered when he had first met her back in the autumn of 'twenty-six. Gloria was the daughter of a colonel in the Indian Army, so had spent most of her life either in India or at boarding school in England. She had come out to Hong Kong that autumn ostensibly to stay with some family friends on the Peak, but in reality she had been part of the "fishing fleet" of young Englishwomen looking for a wealthy young husband in the colony. Ride had found her pretty and bubbly, if of no great intellectual depth. Yet she also had many unusual and surprisingly sexy talents: she could imitate the voice of her own Chinese houseboy with absolute perfection and drive the poor man into a fit of embarrassed giggles. And she could also sing lusty jazz songs just like Helen Kane: when she had sung *I Wanna be Loved by You* to him one night in that sexy little American girl voice, Ride had been completely hooked.

Her connections were nothing special, although obviously better than his own, for he was only the son of an engine driver from Manchester. (Yet an engine driver who had clearly had ambitions for his son, for no other Manchester locomotive driver but Jack Ride would ever have given their son an upper crust name like Sebastian.) He had left school at fourteen, and then wandered the world for a few years as a lowly seaman in the British Merchant Navy, before eventually finding his way to Hong Kong and deciding to try his luck ashore. Yet Gloria had been willing to overlook his lack of breeding given his dark brooding looks and his clear ability for getting on. He had after all worked himself up into a senior position in one of the great business houses in Hong Kong from nowhere, simply by his own natural instinct for business and his single-minded dedication to getting on.

In the end it was she who had forced the issue by seducing him on a quiet Shek-O beach. Ride had been surprised by her earthy passion – not what he had expected at all from such a refined-looking woman – therefore he had decided to take the plunge and marry her, despite all his lingering doubts. Their marriage, when it came, was hardly one made in heaven, yet it had worked for a while. Yet after two years of married life, Ride had to admit to himself that he had simply fallen out of love with his wife. It would have been better, and fairer, in the circumstances if she had also fallen out of love with him, but unfortunately she had seemed more besotted with him than ever by then, and in an increasingly clinging and unhealthy way. He tried to make it work, staying faithful to her, but finding it increasingly hard to keep his marriage vows when faced with all the enticements of the many seductive and glamorous women that he came into regular social contact with.

He realized now that it would have been better for everyone if he had left her then and forced a generous divorce settlement on her. In staying with her and keeping up the pretence of being a loyal and affectionate husband, he had only made things worse. Gloria was astute enough not to be fooled by his protestations of continued affection, and that knowledge seemed to drive her into a dark depression that could only be relieved by drink. Things with her had taken even more of a turn for the worse six months ago, for her dark moods and her drinking had intensified since then. Ride had no idea what had triggered this new and deepening crisis, yet the effects on Gloria had been devastating. Now, her condition was so severe that it was too late to talk to her about a possible divorce; he worried that such talk might even drive her to suicide. Gloria's doctor had told him privately just yesterday that she was doing severe damage to her liver with her drinking, and had advised him to put her into a sanatorium where she could be weaned off her alcohol habit. In some odd way, Ride had found that he was now becoming closer to her again in her desperate state, for he felt some undoubted responsibility for what had happened to her. That closeness had more to do with pity now than with love, it was true, yet he found the thought of simply abandoning her callously to her fate to be quite impossible...

Gloria stirred suddenly on the bed, disturbed by some bad dream. Her dress had ridden up her legs and revealed her black silk stockings and her suspenders. Ride went over and rearranged her dress to cover her panties and her exposed legs again, though he hardly knew why when no one but himself would see her in this indecorous pose. It was perhaps the token act of a man wanting to atone for his sins, but not knowing how. At this moment he did have a feeling of unexpected tenderness towards his sadly disturbed wife. He could not help noticing, though, as he rearranged Gloria's dress, that her legs were still as shapely and fine as they had been ten years ago. He was surprised to find that those shapely legs could still produce a flicker of his old desire for her. Yet nothing else about her seemed the same...

With a sigh, Ride went into the connecting second bedroom and began to undress...

CHAPTER 2

Tuesday, 10th August 1937

Paul Jericho had left his flat in Happy Valley before six this morning, then walked to Causeway Bay in the humid pre-dawn twilight where he caught an electric tram west to Wanchai. As usual he took a seat on the open top deck, enjoying the breeze created by the slow and lumbering motion of the elderly tram, and watching the dawn break around him. He kept his own car at his apartment – an old Austin – but rarely used it to go to work since he had a police car and driver at his disposal at Wanchai station when he needed it.

He was still finding it difficult to sleep these days, and often got up well before first light after a mostly sleepless night. Yet the thought of taking pills to help him sleep was anathema to him; he'd been brought up to believe that such things were a sign of weakness and dissipation. Paul Jericho was not a man who could live easily with the evidence of his own natural weaknesses.

The building where he worked, Wanchai Police Station, was an uncompromisingly modern art deco building on the new waterfront road through Wanchai; it comprised four stories of white-painted concrete, and had a striking facade of exposed columns that ran all the way from ground level up to the roof and formed a full-height protective atrium to the interior glazed facade of the building. The station building was only five years old, having been built on land reclaimed under the Praya East Reclamation Scheme of the 1920s, and was therefore one of the newest and most modern police buildings on the island. It was officially known as No. 2 Police Station or Eastern Police Station, which reflected its importance to the force, second only to the main police headquarters building in Central Hong Kong.

At a quarter to seven, Jericho stood in his office on the fourth floor and contemplated the view across the harbour to the line of bare and serrated mountain peaks that separated Kowloon from the New Territories and China beyond. That imposing line of mountains soon fell away however into a less impressive scarred landscape of mean and ugly hills pockmarked by rock quarries and mean little shanty towns that formed the immediate backdrop to urban Kowloon. The flat peninsula of Kowloon was a mass of grey and undistinguished buildings, with nothing of any architectural note apart from the grand new Peninsula Hotel at its very southern tip, and the terminus of the Kowloon-Canton railway, right on the Kowloon waterfront. Yet in the early morning light, with the main harbour channel suffused with fiery shades of red and gold, and under that apricot-coloured morning sky, even urban Kowloon managed to look beautiful and mysterious today to Paul Jericho.

Among the mass of anchored shipping in the main roadsteads of the harbour, east of Stonecutter's Island, three sleek grey destroyers of the US Navy Asiatic Fleet stood out like sinister predatory grey sharks. They rather put the modest Royal Navy ships in port to shame, Jericho thought, including the stately shape of the converted frigate *HMS Tamar*, which was used as the navy's floating headquarters, in its permanent mooring near the dockyard. The three American ships explained the sudden glut of American seamen in the bars of Wanchai for the last two weeks, but this glut would end soon, for the ships were due to leave in the next few days to join up with the rest of the US Asiatic Fleet in the Philippines.

A ferry was just crossing the harbour from the Kowloon terminal, taking a curving diagonal path that threaded its way past the busy Kowloon wharves, then through the mass of anchored junks, sampans and rusting tramp steamers in the open channel. Immediately below Jericho's vantage point, at the Wanchai ferry terminal, a crowd of locals was waiting impatiently at the ferry turnstile for this approaching vessel to arrive. Jericho could see a complete panorama of Hong Kong life in that murmuring crowd of five cent passengers waiting to board the lower deck: women in cotton pyjama suits, coolies in blue tattered trousers, old men in felt slippers and faded old Chinese robes. A line of emaciated-looking rickshaw drivers stood waiting in stoic silence for the next flood of passengers to arrive. A street vendor in a battered old felt hat was selling melon seeds to the waiting crowd, dispensing them into twirled cones of Chinese newspaper for ten cents a time. A girl with a pony tail picked at her cone of melon seeds with care, while a wizened old ancient with a wispy white foot-long ribbon of beard leaned on an ebony stick and discreetly adjusted the folds of his high-necked Chinese gown. Babies with tufts of straight black hair like tussock grass peeped out from slings on the backs of their patient mothers, and intense-looking youths in horn-rimmed glasses studied their Chinese school books with rapt attention.

The ferryboat finally came chugging alongside the jetty, its propellers churning up the water into a coffee-like foam. The slatted bench seats on the covered top deck were almost invisible under the press of people on board. The waiting crowd on the quayside moved forward in readiness as the gangplank was lowered to the newly berthed ferry. The arriving passengers disgorged from the ferry like a colourful wave, then scattered along the Praya and disappeared into the network of alleys and side-streets like water down a plughole. A few of them – the wealthier ones – departed in rickshaws. In a minute more, the waiting passengers had swarmed aboard the vessel to take their places, and the overloaded ferry was ready to leave again. Water churning, engines rumbling, deck plates vibrating, the little ferry pulled wearily away from the jetty again and began her endless journey back to Kowloon...

Jericho's attention was finally distracted from the ferry and its passengers by a sharp knock on his door. George Dorling poked his head around the door and coughed loudly. 'That witness, Miss Yiu, has arrived, sir. I've put her into Interview Room Number Two on the ground floor.'

'All right, George.' Jericho studied Dorling's face with fresh concern, for his sergeant was looking distinctly worse for wear again this morning, with bloodshot eyes and an uneasy manner. 'By the way, have you handed over all your case notes on the Ricky Sun murder to Inspector Ball at Central Station?' Ricky Sun had been a police informer, and a very useful one, since he had been a long-time member of a major triad society in Hong Kong, the Kao Ki-kan. Ricky Sun came from Shanghai originally but had been in Hong Kong for ten years where he had made a name for himself as a dubious businessman and wheeler-dealer on the fringe of the legitimate business community. He was known for his flashy suits and big American cars, and always seemed to be in the money, some of which came from the police for information provided on his triad connections. But his career as an informer had come to a brutal end on June 12th this year when his body had been found that Saturday night in an alleyway off Lockhart Road with two bullets in the back of his head. It seemed obvious that the murder was the work of this triad gang, but it also seemed possible that someone on the force had betrayed Sun to his triad masters...

Dorling looked uneasy; that case was still a sore point since Jericho had taken it off him and passed it over to Headquarters at Charlie Hebdon's instigation. 'I have, sir. I had a long meeting with Inspector Ball yesterday afternoon in Central, and briefed him fully.' Inspector Kevin Ball was Charlie Hebdon's blue-eyed boy, but an object of derision to his Wanchai colleagues for the way that he blatantly toadied to his superiors. At twenty-eight, he was the youngest inspector on the force by a long way, two years younger even than Dorling, so his servile sycophancy had certainly paid off. Yet Jericho had to admit that, despite his shameless boot-licking to his superiors, Ball was a top class investigator who had achieved several major successes in prosecuting cases against the triad gangs.

Dorling didn't look as if he had much enjoyed his long meeting with the pushy Inspector Ball yesterday but Jericho could hardly blame him for that. Dorling bit his lip nervously, before asking: 'Do you want me to sit in on the interview with you and Miss Yiu, or can Thomas or Gary Ho do it?'

'Better you should be there, George, and that you should ask the questions. I've made you the lead officer in this enquiry, after all.' After relieving Dorling of the Ricky Sun investigation, and also lately tearing him off a strip over his excessive drinking, Jericho had sweetened the medicine a little by putting him in charge of this new murder investigation. It was meant to be an expression of confidence in Dorling, and hopefully a means of bringing him back into the fold and encouraging him to return to being the sort of policeman he had once been. Yet Jericho knew he was taking a big risk that might backfire on him if Dorling didn't respond and mend his ways... 'I think it should just be the two of us, George. We don't want to frighten the girl to death with a whole room full of coppers. She already seems half-convinced that I suspect her of being involved...'

'And do you?'

'No, not at all,' he denied lamely.

*

Interview Room Number Two was hardly a place designed to calm a nervous witness, being a bare windowless room, unadorned by any decoration, and lit by a harsh down-light over the central table that made everyone look like a potential criminal. The dusty wooden blades of a ceiling fan turned slowly above their heads; from the alarming wrenching noise that the fan made, it seemed that the main bearing was badly worn and about to go.

But Miss Maggie Yiu seemed to be coping well enough with this intimidating place, Paul Jericho thought; even in that unforgiving light she managed to look quite serenely beautiful. She sat opposite him and George Dorling, and seemed perfectly composed too, with no hint of nervousness at the manner of George's questions. Her beauty was in stark contrast to the plain looks of the two policemen who were interviewing her, Jericho had to admit to himself. Dorling's red face looked blotchy and unhealthy in that unforgiving glaring light, and his carrot-coloured hair was sticking up in unruly fashion and glistening with sweat. And Paul Jericho knew that he himself was certainly no oil painting either, with his own coarse wiry hair and rough skin and plain features.

Dorling's harsh Yorkshire accent was also a harsh dissimilarity with Miss Yiu's polished tones, which were as soothing as a sea breeze by comparison. George was certainly being much harsher in the manner of his questioning than Jericho himself had been with her yesterday, but she hadn't put a foot wrong so far that Jericho could see, and her answers had all been exactly the same as yesterday. In fact her answers had been almost word-for-word repeats of what she had told him yesterday during his own more informal questioning. Some might consider this a possible black mark, for it suggested the possibility that she had memorized those answers. Yet Jericho simply could not believe that she had any complicity in the murder of Dora Kam, for it would have been lunacy itself to then report the body when she had no need to.

At the end of his questioning, Dorling glanced perceptibly at Jericho to see if he had any additional questions of his own to put to Miss Yiu.

So far all the questions had been about the murder of Dora Kam, but Jericho decided that he must ask Miss Yiu again about the other victim, Judy Wong. The initial post-mortem on Dora Kam had confirmed that she had died from strangulation, just like Judy Wong, and that the perpetrator was almost certainly a man since few women possessed that sort of strength in their fingers.

Miss Yiu seemed almost to know what he was thinking. 'Where is Mei-ling's body now, Inspector?'

Jericho hesitated fractionally. 'Oh, you mean Dora?' He had forgotten the victim's Chinese name for the moment. 'Her body is in the police mortuary in Central District.'

'And is the other woman's body there too?'

'You mean Wong Yu-lan? Or I should rather say Judy Wong, as that was how she was known here in Hong Kong...' Jericho was grateful that Miss Yiu herself had brought the subject around to that of the other victim, though he did wonder why she had. 'Yes, it is. Miss Wong's body still hasn't been released for burial. Like Dora, Judy was also a relatively new arrival in Hong Kong; we think she had only been here since March. She was a northerner too, from Hopei Province, so perhaps she left there because of the imminent threat of a Japanese invasion. Apparently she has no relatives in Hong Kong. Or at least no one has come forward to claim her body, so we *presume* she has no family or close friends here...'

'Then that's very sad,' Miss Yiu said. 'From what Dora said to me, I don't believe that she has any relatives in Hong Kong either. As for friends, it seems that *I* might have been the closest thing to a friend that Dora had here in Hong Kong, which is an even sadder thing when I know so little about her...' She saw the look on Jericho's face and her face flushed a little. 'But I cannot take responsibility for her body, Inspector, if that's what you're suggesting. I was only a casual acquaintance, after all, and I certainly can't afford to pay the cost of her funeral.'

Jericho held up a reassuring hand. 'No one is expecting you to do that, Miss Yiu.'

Her face relaxed a little, and Jericho took the opportunity to study her face again with secret pleasure. She did have an extraordinarily serene and beautiful face. She was as white-skinned as any full Northern European, yet with a silky complexion and features that very few Europeans could match: high sculpted cheekbones, almond eyes of a striking shade of brown, a perfectly proportioned mouth and a long elegant neck. She had been wearing her hair tied up at the back yesterday, but today she had let it down to show its full magnificence, a mass of shining raven hair that fell straight to her shoulders. It seemed she was not taken with the Western fashion for perming her hair into artificially sculpted waves and curls, something which Jericho was glad of.

'Are you sure that you never met this other woman, Judy Wong?' Jericho asked her.

'No, I told you already,' Miss Yiu said almost brusquely. 'Why do you keep asking me that? Do you think I'm lying about it?'

Jericho rushed to placate her. 'No, not at all. It's just that we know that Judy Wong also worked for a while in the bar at the Tin Hau Hotel – we think between April and June – therefore must have known Dora Kam, who, according to you, also worked there for a couple of months from about May to July. Therefore, since their periods of employment overlapped a little in June, there is a possibility that Dora and Judy might have been friends, or might have been seeing some of the same men...'

Miss Yiu nodded thoughtfully. 'Ah, I see. You clearly think that the same man killed both these women, and might have met them in the Tin Hau Hotel...'

Jericho noticed that Dorling had turned a rather bilious shade of green at this point as if he was about to be sick; it seemed disappointingly that George might have been drinking again last night after all, despite the warnings he had been given. But Jericho hid his dismay about his colleague as best he could and carried on with his questions to Miss Yiu. 'That is a possibility. In which case the man we are looking for might be a Western sailor or soldier. Both Dora and Judy had not stayed long at the Tin Hau, therefore this might be confirmation that they wanted to escape the attentions of a particular individual...'

Miss Yiu looked concerned. 'Ah...you think they might have left the Tin Hau because they were *afraid* of someone they had met there? Someone violent?'

'Exactly so. But there is another possibility too. Both Dora Kam and Judy Wong were extremely attractive-looking young women of Northern Chinese stock - tall and pale-skinned - and perhaps even elegant by comparison with most of the young Cantonese women of more lowly stock who work in bars in Wanchai. We don't know the details of their life in China, but both girls seem to be of relatively high class; that is, they were certainly not peasants or coolie women. Therefore they might both have left the bar at the Tin Hau Hotel simply to work in a better sort of establishment with richer clients, who would be attracted by their better manners and looks. In which case, they might have met the man who killed them in this *second* establishment that we presently know nothing about...'

'But who's to say that Dora and Judy were still working at all?' Miss Yiu protested mildly.

Jericho shook his head. 'I think we can be relatively sure that Dora and Judy were still plying their trade in some fashion at the time of their deaths. For how else would they be making money to live on? The third possibility is that they had both taken up with a particular client in a longer term relationship – most of these girls prefer a more permanent boyfriend, if they can find one who is generous enough, and who is here in port for more than just a few days.'

Miss Yiu looked resigned. 'Well, I would dearly like to help you catch this evil man, whoever he is. But I don't think I can help further. I have no idea where Dora went to work after leaving my building, or if she had moved in with one particular man somewhere.'

Jericho nodded. 'I understand, and I don't want to put too much pressure on you about this. But please, when you have time, try and think of anything that Dora might have said to you - anything that could give us a clue where she might have gone to work after leaving the Tin Hau, or whom she might have been seeing...'

*

Afterwards, Jericho chose to escort Miss Yiu personally through the security door that separated the private working areas of Wanchai Police Station from the public entrance hall. Then he led her out through the main entrance into the shaded atrium at the front of the building, where they were met by a blast of humid heat and the bustling sounds of the waterfront emanating from across the Praya.

The harbour was as full of shipping as usual; in the choppy blue-green water, the hulls of moored steamers rocked violently in the swell of passing ferries and sampans. Echoing across the water, ships' horns competed with the raucous shouts of Hoklo and Tanka women on the quayside. A line of sinewy coolies on the waterfront continued to unload a cargo of rice from a berthed ship, building up a veritable mountain of hessian bags on top of the jetty wall.

'Does this place remind you of Shanghai at all?' he asked her, not wanting her to leave immediately. It was quite improper of him to be making small talk with a witness, yet he was reluctant to just let this woman leave without saying something. This might be his only remaining chance to talk to her...

She turned her head to look at all the bustle on the quayside. 'Yes, a little. And Shanghai is just as hot and humid as this in August.'

Yet she didn't look like she was bothered by the heat at all; on the contrary she seemed as cool and unruffled as ever. Unlike Jericho himself, who could already feel his khaki police shirt sticking to his back, and a bead of sweat forming on his forehead.

He was encouraged to see that she seemed in no pressing hurry to leave this time. 'You said your father was a Russian émigré? How did he end up in Shanghai?'

She seemed a little surprised by the question. 'Oh, the International Settlement in Shanghai has always attracted every sort of foreigner under the sun. I was very happy, growing up there. But then the Westerners in the Shanghai International Settlement are generally more tolerant of Eurasians like me than they are here; Hong Kong English society is not generally open to Eurasians, as you must know.'

'Perhaps,' Jericho conceded reluctantly. But he knew she was right of course; there was very little social interaction here between the races, and any establishment Englishman who was foolish enough to marry a Chinese or Eurasian girl would be ostracized by his peers, and would almost certainly lose his well paid job at the Bank or in the government. Yet some expatriate men in the lower reaches of society - merchant ship's officers, railway engineers, dockyard supervisors - still did it, and kept Chinese mistresses, although they tended to live over in Kowloon away from the disapproving eyes of the memsahibs on the Peak. It was an old joke in Hong Kong that was asked about expatriate men: *Are you married, or do you live in Kowloon...?* Certainly many junior police officers "lived in Kowloon", as Jericho well knew. And seeing the beauty of this woman in front of him, Jericho could well understand why they did...

'But at least I can work here easily enough,' Miss Yiu was saying. 'My school, St Stephen's Girls' College, has treated me very well, and most of the English teachers there have been very welcoming and supportive. The pupils are now all Chinese of course, no Europeans at all any more, so this makes it easier for me. I'm still struggling a little with teaching in Cantonese. Even though I teach English language and literature, yet I still have to use Cantonese as the main medium of instruction. The girls would be lost if I just spouted nothing but English at them.'

'Is Mrs Adela Marr still involved with the school?' Jericho asked without thinking. 'I know she was the headmistress there for many years. She was born in Hong Kong, I think, and has long been known in the colony as a passionate advocate for the education of Chinese girls.'

'Yes, she is still involved with the school that she founded thirty years ago, and still as indomitable as ever, even though she is now in her seventies. Of course she is retired from full time work now, yet she still comes to the school regularly to give talks and even occasional lessons.' Miss Yiu suddenly exclaimed in surprise. 'How is it that you know Mrs

Marr? Have you been asking her about me?' she added suspiciously.

Jericho could see that he would have to tell her the truth, if he wanted to avoid offending her further. 'No, I haven't. I know Mrs Marr because my wife used to work as a teacher at St Stephen's Girls' College. My wife, though a Westerner, was also born in Hong Kong, you see, and spoke Cantonese like a local.'

Miss Yiu suddenly realized the significance of that. 'Ah...so Mrs Jericho was *your* wife...' She swallowed uncomfortably, completely disconcerted for the first time. 'I should have guessed...Jericho is an unusual name...'

'Did you know my wife at all? Jericho asked quickly, to relieve her embarrassment. 'I suppose you must have if you started work at the school last December.'

'Yes, I did meet her. But she was head of the maths department, while I teach English, so we never saw much of each other. And I had only been there a few weeks when she had that terrible accident...' Miss Yiu hesitated. 'She seemed a very nice lady. You must miss her a lot.'

'Of course I do.' Susan was the last thing that Jericho had intended to talk about with Miss Yiu, but he seemed stuck with it now.

'Where do you come from, yourself, Inspector?' she asked him, as if consciously trying to move away from the painful subject of his dead wife. 'Your accent is hard for me to pin down. Not exactly English, I would say...'

'Well, I was born in Rangoon of all places. My father was a superintendent in the colonial police in Burma, and my mother was a Scots girl from Aberdeen.'

'So that's how you became a policeman. You were following in your father's footsteps.'

'I suppose so, though it certainly wasn't my original plan. My mother died of cholera in Rangoon in the epidemic of nineteen-o-six so I was brought up by a Burmese amah...' Even after all these years Jericho could still remember the warmth and the smiles of his pretty amah; in truth she had been the nearest thing to a mother to him as a small child. It probably explained his enduring sympathy for Orientals in general, and his regard for Oriental women in particular, given that they seemed to have such a tough lot in life yet always made the best of it. 'My widowed father sent me back to boarding school in England – near Guildford in Surrey - when I was ten years old, but I never saw him again. He was killed by bandits a year after I left Burma.'

'So you were left alone in England?' Miss Yiu murmured.

'I suppose so. But I was lucky. I had made good friends with a boy at school called Johnny Grantham, and he and his family more or less adopted me unofficially, so that I spent all my school holidays from then on with them in Guildford. So I suppose Guildford is the nearest thing I have to a real home. When I finished school, I started training as a solicitor in London, but the work bored me. So Johnny's father suggested that I apply for a career with the Hong Kong Police. One of his sons was already out here with the government service and loving it. So I took the plunge and joined the police here when I was twenty-one – that's fifteen years ago...' Jericho knew that he looked older than his thirty-six years, with his wiry hair already going grey at the temples, and his sad middle-aged face, and wondered uneasily if Miss Yiu would think that he was lying about his age.

But Miss Yiu seemed not to notice his unease, and made no comment. Instead she looked at her watch. 'It's eight o'clock, so I'm afraid that I must dash to Hennessy Road for a tram now.'

'I could order my car brought round from the compound and ask my driver to take you up to Lyttelton Road, if you wish?' he offered quickly.

But she wouldn't hear of it. 'No thank you, Inspector. I prefer to take my usual means of transport – the tram, and then what I believe you English call "Shank's pony".' She held out her hand formally. 'Goodbye, Inspector Jericho. I promise I will give your suggestion some thought, and see if I can remember anything else useful that Dora might have said to me. But I truly doubt that I know anything else that will help you catch this man...'

With that she took her leave, and Jericho watched her disappear among the crowds and the rickshaws on the waterfront road with real regret...

*

As Jericho returned to the public entrance hall, he saw his superior, Superintendent Charlie Hebdon, standing at the main inquiry desk, with an amused smile playing on his lips. 'Who was your girlfriend?' he asked ironically. 'I must say you can pick them, Paul. She's a looker...'

Jericho had never got on particularly well with Charlie Hebdon, a blunt Northerner from Rochdale, but they respected each other's abilities as policemen. 'That was the woman who found the second victim.'

Hebdon didn't need to ask *which* second victim, of course. He knew exactly which case Jericho was talking about; both men feared that these two murders might just be the start of a wave of repeat murders on the Wanchai waterfront. This case now certainly took precedence over the murder of the informer Ricky Sun two months ago, which the police knew had almost certainly been carried out on the orders of a triad leader called "Lucky" Lam, although it would be near impossible to prove it in a court of law. Lucky Lam was the de facto leader of the Kao Ki-kan, one of the largest of the Hong Kong triad societies, but this man allegedly had friends in some very high places so was a difficult man for the police to pursue directly...

'And who is this woman who found the second body?' Hebdon asked. 'Did she work with the two dead women? Is she a tart too? She's a good-looking one, if she is...'

Jericho shrugged. 'No, not at all. She's a schoolteacher up at St Stephen's College.'

Hebdon raised his shaggy grey eyebrows; they needed to be shaggy and prominent, though, Jericho thought, to be even noticed in that hard and uncompromising face. 'Isn't that the same school where your wife...err...?'

'Yes, it is.'

'A *schoolmarm*, eh...' Hebdon looked like he was about to say something provocative about Jericho's apparent preference for female schoolteachers but then wisely thought twice about it. Hebdon was normally based at police headquarters in Central, though he tried to get over to Wanchai Station at least two days a week in his schedule. Since the murder of Judy Wong, he had been coming here more often, though, anxious to be updated when he had his own chief, Commissioner of Police Gregory Matlock, pressing him so hard to make an arrest. The fact that this appeared to be a case of a Western man murdering a local Chinese woman made it an embarrassing one for the Acting Governor at a time of great tensions between the colonial government and the mass of their Chinese subjects. And now that there had been a second similar murder, the stakes had suddenly become even higher. Riots and demonstrations by Chinese mobs were already commonplace now given the economic hardships and dire living conditions being faced by the lowest class of Chinese worker, and no one wanted to see the anger of the mob directed blindly against innocent Westerners because of these murders...

'Are you making any progress with the case yet?' Hebdon asked hopefully, after a long silence.

'That depends on what you mean by progress, sir,' Jericho said resignedly.

Hebdon led the way to the stairs. There was a granite edge to his voice as he said: 'We'd better go to your office, then, where you can tell me everything that you *do* know...'

*

At 10 a.m. on this hot and muggy Tuesday morning, Sebastian Ride sat in his office on the top floor of the Saunders Building in Queens Road Central.

His stern-looking private secretary, Frances Leung, immaculate in her formal woman's pinstripe suit, brought him a cup of green tea, though it wasn't her job to do it, of course, since there were three floor boys in the corridor outside with nothing else to do at the moment. Yet she prided herself on her personal attention to him, so Ride allowed her to do these more menial things for him if she wanted. Yet she was much more than a menial of course; in fact Ride didn't know how he would manage this company without her at his beck and call. The unruffled Frances was never at a loss; always there with a report, or a financial statement, or a credit check on a rival, or even with insider knowledge of the finances of all their rival companies. Ride suspected that if he had asked her to go out and commit a murder on his behalf, she would simply have pursed her lips with slight disapproval, then agreed without a qualm. *'Very well, Mr Ride...'*

Ride had the windows open fully to let in some moving air, but with that outside air also came the constant raucous buzz and clatter of noise from the street below. Queens Road Central was Hong Kong's main commercial avenue and looked superficially like many similar busy streets in the centre of Liverpool or Manchester or Birmingham, with its shops and its offices and its big modern cinema. But Queens Road soon narrowed as it ran west, and the gracefully arcaded Victorian buildings of the Central District quickly gave way to a narrow heaving thoroughfare of endless Chinese shop fronts and closely packed tenements and godowns, which had no resemblance to Liverpool or Manchester at all. As Sebastian Ride looked eastwards down Queens Road West, he saw that every building in sight was festooned with a dazzling array of Chinese signs and calligraphy, fading into the hot muggy distance. There were still far more rickshaws filling the street below than cars or motor buses, but he imagined that even the rickshaws would soon have had their day and would disappear from these busy streets, as the sedan chair, once a mainstay of public transport here, already had.

Ride thought that it was demeaning and wasteful that humans should still be used as beasts of burden in this city, and particularly at the fact that rickshaw coolies were so badly paid for their backbreaking work; he knew that the average rickshaw man only made twenty dollars a month. And these tough durable men only got *that* amount if they worked every day from sunrise to sunset. Sebastian Ride was a hard-headed businessman, and no sentimentalist when it came to exploiting people, but nor did he like waste. Ride had a vision that this mass of Chinese labour could be far more productively employed than this, and could with proper training turn the colony from a colonial backwater into a great commercial centre. Yet such visions of a golden economic future for Hong Kong were definitely on hold at present, given this constant flood of near starving refugees crossing from the mainland, which prevented any proper planning for the future, and which had turned the Chinese areas of the city into squalid ghettoes rife with disease...

Ride was sipping his green tea in thoughtful contemplation of these problems when his partner James Woo barged into his room without even knocking at the open door. Frances Leung, a sheaf of papers in her hands, turned her trim figure and looked at James with undisguised hostility but did not say anything.

'I need to talk to you, Sebastian...' - Woo fixed the stubbornly loyal

Frances with a pointed stare - '...*and alone.*'

Ride sighed, knowing he was in for yet another difficult conversation with this man. 'I think you'd better excuse us, Frances,' he apologized.

Frances nodded resignedly and left for her own adjacent office through the connecting door, while Ride mentally prepared himself for what was to come.

'Now, what can I do for you, James?' Ride had always got on extremely well with James's father, Woo Man Lo, and their business had prospered as a result of this warm relationship, and grown ten-fold over the last dozen years. Ride had always been treated by the Woo clan very kindly – even as one of their extended family. But Man Lo was now nearly bed-ridden with heart disease, so it had been only natural that his eldest son would take over the reins of power in his company. In preparation for this, Woo Man Lo had even sent his son to the US to study business management at Yale College in Connecticut. Ride had welcomed James's elevation when it came in April last year, for he had known James since he was a boy, and had always had almost a brotherly affection for him. But that feeling of optimism had soon worn off, for Ride had quickly discovered that the adult James had been completely changed by his years in the US and was nothing like the amiable boy he had once been. Instead Woo had turned into an arrogant and decadent playboy with scant regard for the niceties of business, and even scanter regard for the feelings of the people who worked for him.

James didn't sit down but faced him angrily from a standing position. 'I wanted to tell you, Sebastian, that I didn't appreciate your intervention last night,' he said sourly. 'If you ever insult me again in public like that, I swear to God that I will punch you in the fucking mouth...'

Ride refused to be drawn, and merely sat back in his chair, sipping his tea calmly. 'I didn't insult you, James. I merely broke up that pointless argument you were having with Julian Colby, and led you away from him...' Since his return to Hong Kong, Ride knew that James had also come under the influence of some very unsettling people on the wilder fringes of Hong Kong society, including a group of very wealthy young Chinese – mostly, like himself, the pampered western-educated sons of some of the richest Chinese families - who indulged in wild drinking parties and even wilder sexual adventures. Ride did not know the names of all these people that James consorted with, but he had heard disturbing reports of their activities.

'I won't stand for being treated by you like some menial coolie!' James snapped.

Ride suspected that James himself now openly indulged in taking the fashionable drug cocaine, like his self-indulgent friends. Working late one night, Ride had entered Woo's private office to recover some papers he had left there for Woo's signature, only to find an ominous trace of distinctive white powder on James's desk. There seemed no other explanation for it being there other than James being a regular user. *And if James was prepared to indulge his unsavoury habit in the office, then who knew what he got up to elsewhere...?* 'I did not speak to you like a coolie, James. In fact I was perfectly polite,' Ride explained patiently. 'What was the argument with Colby about, anyway?'

'He is like all you arrogant English. He thinks he is being wonderfully tolerant by even speaking to a Chink. But when he started lecturing me in his boorish way about what is wrong with China and the Chinese, my patience snapped.'

Ride studied James's face. He was still a fine-looking man with a more youthful face than even his thirty two years suggested, and with no signs of dissipation as yet from his wanton lifestyle. But the rot would soon begin to show if he didn't mend his ways, Ride thought... 'I agree that Colby is a tactless oaf. But he is also Attorney General of this colony, and we can't afford to antagonize such people, James.'

'That's all right for you to say, Sebastian; you're one of them! You patronize me just as much as that oaf Colby did. I know that you and your devoted Frances...' – here James couldn't resist a sneering glance through the adjoining doorway - '...have been deliberately conspiring against me and keeping me ignorant of your new business plans. And I have to tell you that this must stop, as of now...' he added threateningly.

Ride wondered what he could say to end this discussion, which was threatening to boil over into open warfare. Working closely with this man was a real problem for him now, and there seemed no easy solution that might get his business relationship with James back on track. In addition to his cocaine habit, Ride suspected that James might also be bisexual. Although James had always shown a clear sexual interest in beautiful women, Ride had noticed something about his manner since his return from America that suggested that he might be open to affairs with men too. And that possibility was ringing real warning bells in Ride's head, for it was anybody's guess whom James might be sleeping with, and with whom he might also possibly be sharing their business secrets. Sebastian Ride was no prude himself when it came to sexual matters, yet even when young he had always prided himself on keeping his wilder pleasures private. James on the other hand seemed determined to broadcast his errant behaviour to the world, and this was causing some undoubted problems for the company, which had to deal with some very straight-laced people among its investors.

'I have not been conspiring against you, James. That's arrant nonsense,' Ride said with as much conviction as possible. It wasn't actually *complete* nonsense, of course, for the fact was that Ride and Frances had managed to minimize the disruptive effects of Woo's behaviour by sidelining him as much as possible, and keeping him away from the most important business decisions that affected the company. Yet this tactic was going to be more difficult now, since James had clearly worked out what was happening.

'You think I'm a fool, don't you?' James said, his anger continuing to simmer.

'No, of course not. I think you're a very clever man. But you still need to learn to play by the rules of business here in Hong Kong; the establishment here will simply not tolerate rash or ungentlemanly behaviour.' Ride had not worked up the nerve yet to take the ultimate step and speak to James's father about this problem, and ask him to rein his son in, for frankly he did not know how Man Lo would take this criticism of his son. Like most devoted Chinese fathers, Man Lo was still mostly blind to the faults of his children, therefore might react very badly. Ride could simply not afford a breakdown in his relationship with the sickly patriarch of the family too, not when so many other things were going wrong for the company at present.

'*Rash behaviour*? What the hell do you mean by that?'

'Just what I say,' Ride said, his own anger rising. 'And you need to start taking my advice, James. I have been at this game for twenty years after all.' At the age of only forty-one, Ride told himself that he still held most of the cards as far as the day-to-day running of the company was concerned, therefore it was perhaps time to put his foot down with this man. After all, he was still undisputed Chairman of Saunders-Woo Holdings' shipping and property empire, with a thirty percent stake that he owned outright. It was true that another thirty percent of the company was owned by the Woo family, but James fortunately still only had direct control of a quarter of those family shares. The other part of the Woo holding was held in the names of other family members, including the patriarch Man Lo and the eldest daughter Grace, who all presently listened to Ride more than they did to James where business matters were concerned.

James leaned over Ride's desk, his face flushed with boiling resentment. 'Then perhaps it's time for an old man like you to move on, Sebastian, and make way for some fresh blood and some fresh ideas.' His face contorted into a semblance of a smile. 'And don't lecture me about morality, Sebastian. Not when I know that you are sleeping with a married woman. That oaf Julian Colby certainly wouldn't like it if he discovered that you were sleeping with his colleague Grantham's beautiful wife...' With that James turned on his heel and stalked out of the room.

Ride heard his boots thumping down the corridor to the main staircase, as Frances poked her head through the adjacent doorway. 'Well, that could have gone better,' he said conversationally.

Frances looked nervous. 'Yes, indeed. Do you think he will make trouble with our investors?' she asked.

'Perhaps.' Ride was pensive for a moment. The other forty percent of the Saunders-Woo company was owned by various private investors and banks, and Ride was always conscious that he needed to keep on the right side of these powerful individuals. Even though they constituted a minority holding, and couldn't therefore out-vote him at shareholders' meetings even if they combined their efforts, Ride was still careful to listen to their concerns. Yet signs of dissent from these shareholders were growing lately with the recent slump in profits, and some of them were becoming distinctly hostile, and possibly even considering ways of taking control of the company and forcing Ride out of his position as Chairman of the Board. That however could only be achieved if one or more of the Woo family sided with the dissenters, which had never happened to date. Yet Ride no longer trusted James Woo in this regard; if James chose to take the side of these hostile parties, then the outcome of such a challenge would be more difficult to predict.

It was a galling thought to Sebastian Ride, but – if he wasn't careful - he might well find himself being forced out of his own company...

CHAPTER 3

Tuesday, 10th August 1937

The bar in the Tin Hau Hotel was busy even early on a Tuesday evening, Paul Jericho saw...

After his meeting with an ill-tempered and argumentative Charlie Hebdon today, Jericho had decided that he would have to visit the Tin Hau himself in civvies this evening to see what he could discover by his own efforts. Hebdon was certainly not satisfied with the limited progress in the case so far, and wanted urgent action to bring the culprit to justice, so Jericho had decided to take some personal intervention even though George Dorling might be annoyed when he found out about it. The last thing that Jericho wanted was for Hebdon to take this case off them as well, and pass it to his blue-eyed boy, Inspector Ball at Central, as he had done with the Ricky Sun case...

Jericho should perhaps have sent Dorling or one of his junior officers on this speculative mission, but he suspected that his younger expatriate officers would all be quite well known in the local bars, whereas he would be relatively anonymous. He had never been in this bar in his life before, even though it was only a hundred yards along the waterfront from Wanchai Police Station. And Jericho had never frequented the bars of Wanchai much at all during his fifteen years in Hong Kong, therefore should be unknown here to both the staff and the bar girls, and certainly unknown to the other customers, most of whom were sailors passing briefly through the port. During his five years of marriage to Susan, Jericho had been far too contented with his domestic life at home in Happy Valley to ever venture at night into Wanchai's seedy alleyways. Tonight, dressed in an old linen jacket and well-worn drill trousers, Jericho thought he could pass easily enough for a ship's captain or first engineer himself.

American sailors were far better represented tonight in the bar than either the Royal Navy or the British Merchant Navy, for the three destroyers of the US Asiatic Fleet were still here and their sailors were clearly still doing their best to cement close personal relations between America and China by consorting so generously with these friendly local girls. The exotic accents of Oklahoma and Idaho and Vermont were therefore mingled tonight with the kittenish broken English of compliant Chinese girls. A grizzled middle-aged British matelot did not seem put out by all this youthful competition from America but sucked on his pipe and snuggled up to the tiny Chinese girl on his lap like a man infinitely comfortable with life. The Chinese manager of the place – a local man of forty with slicked back hair and a prominent gold tooth – circulated among the noisy sailors with the practised manner of his trade. He was wearing a dinner jacket and a wing collar that was twenty-five years out of date and shiny with age, yet those worn clothes suited his oily manner perfectly.

The atmosphere of the bar was smoky, but lit like a cheap night club with a rosy diffused glow from its pink wall lamps. The windows were curtained, and the entrance door from the lobby of the hotel was a swing door like in an American western saloon. The place was just about big enough for twenty tables, but only at a very tight squeeze. The wooden table tops smelled of spilt San Miguel beer and carried the stains of countless unfortunate encounters with drunken seamen. There was a bar counter in the corner of the room stocked with glass shelves of wine and spirits, while there was a fancy coin-operated American gramophone in another corner, next to a tiny circle of polished wood decking that served as a dance floor. The gramophone played the same tunes in endless succession, which seemed to have been picked deliberately to suit the visiting Americans' tastes: Bing Crosby singing *Pennies from Heaven,* Benny Goodman playing *Goody Goody* and *The Glory of Love,* Fats Waller's *It's a Sin to Tell a Lie,* and *The Music Goes Round and Round* by the Tommy Dorsey Orchestra...

Jericho sat by himself at a table and sipped a beer as he studied the girls at the other tables. Since the bar was so busy tonight with good-looking young American sailors, he was not being pestered by any bored girls looking for a customer, and could therefore study them at some leisure. They seemed on the whole far nicer girls than the type of cold and mercenary Englishwomen who sold themselves in the nightclubs of Mayfair or Soho; these local Cantonese girls were driven into this business by poverty and their lack of education. Jericho had no doubt that many of them would be supporting whole families with the money they earned in this questionable trade: mothers, sick fathers, younger brothers and sisters. None of the women he could see at the adjacent tables could be called beautiful, as Dora Kam and Judy Wong had been, but many were pretty and lively with lots of cheery conversation and winning smiles. Few of them dressed the part of a woman for sale therefore it would have been hard to distinguish them on the streets from respectable girls like office typists or shop girls.

There were a couple of exceptions, though: one girl called Minnie had a rather ugly little face, but had overcome her defects by sporting garish scarlet lips and huge false eyelashes. The split in her tight skirt rose almost to her stocking tops, and showed off her shapely figure and legs. She had playfully borrowed her sailor companion's hat and placed it rakishly on her own head of permed black curls. In the middle of some playful banter with the men at her table, she sprang up from her chair, legs planted firmly apart, long red fingernails on her hips, and kissed one of the sailors boldly on the lips.

Another tall girl called Betty was even more obvious in her endeavours, with a black split skirt stretched taut over her undulating hips, black stockings and enormous high heels. She had also clearly modelled her walk on the lately deceased Jean Harlow, who was famous for her waggling behind. Betty tottered about the room on this extraordinary pair of high heels, and her undulating posterior was clearly one of the star attractions of the bar, judging from the whistles, catcalls and lewd comments it drew from the assembled American sailors as she bumped and grinded deliberately by their tables.

Despite his serious purpose in being here tonight, Jericho had nevertheless found his own attention drawn frequently to Betty's wobbling behind, so failed to notice that one of the other girls had finally approached his table. When she cleared her throat to attract his attention, he turned his head to find a tall white-skinned girl standing at his side with a shy smile on her face. 'May I join you, Mister?' she asked modestly in sing-song English.

Jericho saw that he had, for some strange reason, attracted the prettiest girl in the place. Perhaps she had just arrived for work tonight, and he had luckily proved to be the last man without a girl at his table. This young woman was certainly far closer in looks to Dora Kam and Judy Wong than to any of the other dark-skinned Southern girls here tonight, therefore was certainly worth talking to. Jericho was still working on the theory that both Judy and Dora had met the man who had ultimately killed them in this bar, though it still seemed hard to believe that any ordinary British seaman would do such a thing. Yet there had been no US Navy ships in port from May to July, so if Judy and Dora had met their killer here, then the odds were high – *unfortunately* - that the man in question was British...

Jericho responded to her in Cantonese. '*Yes, please sit down. I could use some nice company.*'

But the girl only stared blankly at this, and Jericho realized that she couldn't speak Cantonese at all. He tried a little Mandarin on her, although he only knew a few words. '*Where are you from, Miss? Are you a Northerner?*'

She smiled gratefully; she could understand that at least, and replied in the same language. *'Yes, from the city of Zhangjiakou in Chahar province.'*

Jericho had understood that reply - just about anyway - though he had never heard of the town she had mentioned. But he knew Chahar province was one of the places lately threatened with invasion by the Japanese Kwantung Army.

Jericho bought her a drink of cold tea that cost him five dollars. That was about a week's wage for a labouring man in Hong Kong, which extravagance made him wince mentally, for he doubted that he would be able to claim this money back.

'What is your name?' he asked her ruefully as he paid the waiter for the drink.

'*Kwok Yaw-lim...*' The girl switched suddenly to broken English. 'But here I called Cherry Kwok. Cherry very beautiful flower in North China.'

Jericho smiled back and spoke in English too. 'Yes, it's a perfect name for someone with your clear white skin.' He thought he understood now why she might be the only available girl tonight. This was clearly a newish girl in the bar, and almost a foreigner to the other girls working here, who were all Cantonese. "Cherry" might share a written language with these other girls, but otherwise she was as alien here among these Cantonese women as a Turk or a Bengali.

Jericho didn't want to spook this girl by asking her questions about Judy Wong and Dora Kam immediately. He sensed that she was nervous already, so certainly didn't want to give away the fact that he was a policeman investigating that case.

Cherry sipped at her tea with pretended relish. 'Where you from, Mister?'

'I'm from England...'

'Ah, nice. *London?*'

Jericho nodded. 'Yes, quite near London.'

Cherry regarded him thoughtfully. 'You look like big man, important man.'

Jericho gave her a self-deprecating smile. 'No, not at all.'

Cherry weighed up him through narrowed eyes. 'I think so. You ship's captain or something.'

Jericho answered carefully. 'You're very clever, Cherry. How did you know that?'

'Most men come here, work on ship. You not American. You quite old so I think captain.'

Her logic was sound enough, Jericho had to admit ruefully.

'You marry?' Cherry asked.

He shook his head, conscious that the gold-toothed manager of the bar was lingering suspiciously close to his table as if trying to eavesdrop. Jericho wondered uneasily if he'd been spotted as a policeman in plain clothes. 'No.'

'Why not?'

Jericho smiled again. 'It could be because I've never found anyone like you, Cherry.'

She didn't smile back. 'You have honey tongue, Mister Englishman. What your name anyway?'

'Paul.' Jericho suddenly had the oddest feeling that he was not only talking to this girl Cherry, but that he was also conversing in some way with the two dead girls too. He thought that both Judy and Dora must have been very like this pretty girl when they were alive. It made him suddenly even more determined to catch the sick wretch who had done this terrible thing. The lower ranks of Western seamen inevitably contained some very low class and violent individuals among their number, men who were used to treating women like these bar girls with nastiness and abuse when it suited them. What was troubling Jericho, though, was that this man had repeated such a terrible act of violence against a defenceless young woman within two weeks of the first; it suggested an individual who was far more depraved and evil than any average Jack Tar....*someone who actually enjoyed the process of killing for its own sake...*

The bar manager with the gold tooth and the oily slicked-back hair had finally moved away from them, apparently happy that nothing untoward was going on between Jericho and Cherry. 'Who is that man?' he asked her, nodding in the direction of his retreating back.

Cherry shrugged. 'He's the bar manager, Freddie Ling. He speak good English. Lived in America - San Francisco...' She frowned. 'He not nice man. But we have to be nice to him, otherwise he stop us coming here...'

'How long have you worked in this bar?' Jericho asked her gently.

'I start in May. Just arrive from mainland then,' she admitted. 'I leave last month for a short while. But come back again tonight.'

This seemed so much like the experiences of Judy Wong and Dora Kam that Jericho had to resist a feeling of quiet satisfaction at finding a girl with such a similar history. Except that Judy and Dora had never come back here to work, of course; they'd never had the opportunity given their grisly fate. Jericho wondered where Cherry had been working recently, and why she had decided to leave that second place of employment and come back to the Tin Hau bar. *Could it be that she had even gone to work in the very same bar or nightclub that Judy and Dora had moved to?*

It seemed to Jericho that he had, by exceedingly good fortune, happened on the one girl in this place who might be able to help his inquiry. 'I was in here at the end of May,' he lied glibly, 'but I don't remember seeing you here then.' He took a long breath and decided to take a chance. 'I think I was talking to two other girls that night – one called Judy, I believe, and the other, Dora.'

Cherry barely reacted to that, which was disappointing. 'I not know those names,' she stated flatly. She sipped her tea again, not even pretending to enjoy it now. 'You want to go for short time upstairs?' she demanded pointedly. 'I show you very nice time.'

Cherry clearly wasn't one for small talk with her clients, and preferred to get quickly to the crux of the matter.

Jericho wasn't sure how to respond to this sudden invitation. But in his capacity as an undercover policeman, he certainly couldn't afford to accept her offer, which had come much earlier in the conversation, and more directly, than he had wished. He would have preferred to keep this girl engaged in quiet conversation in the bar where he might have some chance of leading the discussion in the right direction and uncovering what she might know about the two murdered girls. He wasn't entirely convinced that Cherry hadn't known either Judy or Dora; her denial seemed to carry a false note. There were only twenty or thirty women working here in the bar on a regular basis, after all, so Cherry *must* have known Dora and Judy by sight at least. Perhaps she didn't know their English names, but that was also quite odd considering that both the dead girls were Northerners like herself. It was true that Dora was from Shanghai, which wasn't particularly close to Cherry's home province in the far north of China, therefore there might not have been any reason for a special connection to develop between her and Dora. But Judy came from the neighbouring Hopei province therefore must have spoken almost the same Northern dialect as Cherry...

Jericho could feel Cherry's look becoming suspicious as he vacillated over what to say. In the end he made do with: 'I can't go with you tonight, Cherry, much as I'd like to. I have to leave in a few minutes. Can't we just stay here and drink a little more...'

With that, Jericho surreptitiously took out a couple of ten-dollar bills from his wallet and passed them to her discreetly under the table. 'This is for your time,' he said with a note of apology, hoping it would encourage her to stay with him a little longer, for twenty Hong Kong dollars was certainly generous enough to cover the normal cost of a short excursion upstairs.

But this display of generosity didn't encourage her. Instead Cherry simply pocketed the money like a professional, and got to her feet with an exaggerated sweep of her arms. Her eyes had now taken on a hard and avaricious glitter that Jericho didn't much like. 'No, I don't need any more talk. But please come back if you want see me again.' With that she turned her back on him and walked away to the ladies' room.

The grizzled middle-aged British matelot at the next table gave Jericho a rueful grin. 'Looks like you've just been shafted, mate...*and not in the way you were expecting...*' he commented with ribald humour.

*

George Dorling's apartment was on the third floor of a modern block in Ashley Road, Kowloon, near the busy junction with Hankow Road that was occupied by the huge new air-conditioned Star Cinema. It was convenient for Tess having a cinema so close to the apartment, and even Dorling himself, though no movie fan, thought it a pleasant place to watch a film, since the dress circle where the expatriates always sat didn't have individual seats like a normal cinema, but plush couches with white covers on them...

Yet there were disadvantages too in living so close to a cinema, for the late night crowds were always noisy and raucous as they left, while the expatriates among them also filled the street outside the Dorlings' apartment with parked Austins and Rovers. As he walked up Hankow Road at 10:30, Dorling saw that the Star was presently showing *Captains Courageous* with Spencer Tracy, and the giant billboard over the entrance was covered with a garish picture of the actor in the unlikely guise of a Portuguese fisherman. Dorling's return home tonight had coincided unluckily with the end of this main feature and he soon found himself swallowed up in this sudden mass outpouring of theatregoers who appeared on the street. Yet he managed to fight his way through the boisterous crowd in the end, and take the familiar turning into Ashley Road.

He should have felt some pleasure at finally returning home after such a long day. Yet pleasure was a commodity in distinctly short supply in George Dorling's life at present: in fact his life seemed to be falling apart, and dark forces were closing in on him from every direction, threatening to destroy him.

He didn't know how he had got himself into this terrible situation, although greed and stupidity certainly had much to do with it. The last two days had been the worst of all. Dorling didn't know how he had got through the last forty-eight hours: first the discovery of the body of Dora Kam, then that interview this morning with the witness Maggie Yiu. He felt sure that he would give himself away somehow, so that his head had felt about to burst with the pressure building inside, like a steam boiler about to blow. Paul Jericho was a smart man, and could see that something was wrong with him; Dorling was terrified of Jericho discovering the truth, for that would be the end of him...*the end of everything...*

Now, as he entered the lobby of his building and climbed the stairs to his third floor flat, Dorling tried to prepare himself for his homecoming. He knew there would be no domestic comfort to be found here in the arms of his wife, though. His marriage was as much of a disaster as everything else in his life...

He realized now that he made a big mistake in bringing Tess out here, so far away from everything that she knew and was comfortable with. He had met her working as a "Nippy" waitress in a Lyons teahouse on the Scarborough seafront, on his first home leave three years ago, and in a whirlwind courtship had married her within three weeks of that first meeting. And in another week, he and his pretty little Lyons waitress had found themselves on their way to Hong Kong on board the P & O liner, the *SS Rajputana*. Tess had only been twenty-one at the time, a fishmonger's daughter from Scarborough, so that voyage on the *Rajputana* had seemed like a Hollywood movie to her: the glamorous passengers even in Second Class, the bustle and warm amber light of Marseilles, the azure and gold skies of the Mediterranean, the bumboats at Port Said selling all kinds of unimagined goods – Turkish Delight, baskets, Arab hats – then Suez and the slow, hot, star-filled nights steaming through the Red Sea. Hong Kong too had seemed like a dream place to Tess when she first arrived.

Yet reality had soon set in; the reality being a small poky flat on a busy and noisy road in downtown Kowloon. She did have a house boy and an amah to do all the housework for her, but that only made it worse for Tess if anything, and made her feel even more inadequate and helpless. She had not found any close friends here – certainly not among Hong Kong's snooty elite on the Island - nor even among the more ordinary expat residents of Kowloon, where Tess's Northern accent and working class manners still made her stand out. Probably she would have been all right if she could have had a child to shower her affections on; but the loss of that baby in pregnancy three months ago had broken her spirit, for it seemed she might not be able to have any more. She was now consumed by homesickness and just wanted to go home...

Yet Dorling had always known that he would never find another job back in Blighty that could remotely compare with the one he had here. But the pressure that Tess had put on him to leave had pushed George Dorling into taking huge risks which were now coming home to roost. Even three years ago, he had already been taking a small amount of squeeze from local criminals and businesses; everybody in the police did, and no one thought twice about it. But for the last year he had abandoned any restraint in this direction, trying to make as much money as he could in the next year or two so that he and Tess could return home with enough of a nest egg to start a business in Yorkshire. Yet the gamble had failed and left him in this dark chasm that he could presently see no way of escaping from...

He let himself in through the front door with his key, rather than knocking. It was nearly eleven o'clock after all, and Tess often retired early. The servants too usually slept early for they were up before dawn, doing the daily laundry and cooking his breakfast.

But this time Tess was still awake, sitting by a lamp in the living room and darning one of his police socks. The bruising over her eye was getting better, he was glad to see, but the stitches still looked red and raw. No doubt everyone at the station would think that he had blacked her eye for her; ironically the story that he had told Paul Jericho was the gospel truth. She *had* slipped in the bathroom yesterday morning and hit her head on the corner of the enamel bath...

He attempted a smile as he kissed her on the forehead. 'Do you really have to do that? Can't Ah Tong do it for you?' Ah Tong was their elderly amah.

'Of course...and probably much better than me,' Tess declared with a grimace. 'But what else have I got to do?'

Dorling decided to let that remark pass. Whatever he said only seemed to make things worse with her these days, yet sullen reciprocal silence seemed even more soul destroying.

'You've been drinking again,' she said accusingly. 'Don't deny it; I can smell it on your breath.'

'It was just one beer,' he said, truthfully for a change. 'I was working in that roasting hot station until nine, so was desperate for something cold to drink.'

'Are you sure it wasn't something hot you were desperate for, like your Chinese floozy...?' Her voice was bitter.

'I don't have any Chinese floozy,' he denied sullenly.

Tess stood up, her pretty face transformed by an ugly snarl of anger. 'You liar!'

'It's not a lie.' Dorling tried to compose himself. He turned to go into the kitchen to make some tea, but she pulled him back roughly by the shoulders.

'I even know her name, George,' Tess said balefully.

'No, you can't, Tess,' he muttered in exasperation. 'Because there's no such person.'

'Yes, I can, George. Her name is Dora...' Tess was almost triumphant.

Dorling tried to hide his profound shock. *How could she possibly know that name...?*

Tess's little triumph had not lasted long, though, and she was now close to tears. 'You can't deny it. I heard her name from your own bloody lips...*in bed last night*. If you want to keep secrets from me, George, then you'd better learn not to talk in your sleep...'

*

Paul Jericho was also returning home to his flat in Happy Valley as a distant public clock struck eleven. He had not stayed long in the bar of the Tin Hau Hotel after his talk with Cherry Kwok, yet had not felt like going home directly. So he had wandered eastwards on foot along the Wanchai waterfront, which was still busy even at this late hour.

Hong Kong was a strange and contradictory place to him: on the one hand a place of fabulous wealth where the grandest families lived like royalty; yet also a place where the mass of Chinese coolies went barefoot. It was also a city that still depended very much on the ubiquitous rickshaw and its legions of weary coolies to keep it moving, as Jericho could plainly see this evening as he walked along the hot crowded quayside.

Yet just over the harbour at Kai Tak airfield, there was now a regular commercial aircraft flight operating to Penang, linking the colony to London. Until very recently the future of long distance air travel had seemed likely to reside with those great gleaming, futuristic German airships, yet the *Hindenburg* disaster three months ago in the United States had changed all that forever. Jericho had seen the newsreel pictures of the *Hindenburg* crashing to earth in a ball of flame as it attempted to dock with its mooring mast in Lakehurst, New Jersey, and had been as profoundly shocked as everyone else at the terrible scenes. Suddenly it appeared that *aircraft* might now offer a rather safer alternative to these fragile floating palaces in the sky, as proven by the new commercial flights now operating successfully in stages from Hong Kong to London.

It was true that Hong Kong's airfield was still a gimcrack affair at present, since the runway crossed the main road from Kowloon to the Saikung peninsula and the traffic therefore had to be stopped every time a plane took off. But it was nevertheless a clear sign of the changes coming to Hong Kong. Also just inaugurated was the new flying boat service of Imperial Airways, which amazingly took only *ten days* to get to London instead of six weeks by ship. Pan American Airways was also about to initiate a flying clipper service to connect Hong Kong to Manila, and then across the Pacific to San Francisco, which would reduce the crossing of the Pacific to a mere *six days*...

Getting to the west coast of America from Hong Kong in only six days seemed almost like magic to Paul Jericho...

The modern world was now intruding on Hong Kong and its grossly unequal society whether it liked it or not, and Jericho could only hope that the benefits of this modernization would be enjoyed by all the population here in time. Yet with war clouds looming on the horizon, Jericho did wonder how long the peace of this tiny colony could endure when faced with all these huge challenges coming from abroad. Jericho had heard unsettling rumours that the Japanese intended ultimately to take over the whole of China. If that happened, he doubted if the Japanese army would stop their divisions obligingly at the Hong Kong border...

His late night walk eventually took him to Causeway Bay, and then inland towards his home in Happy Valley. For Paul Jericho, this little valley was one of the loveliest places on the island, a place of inspiring beauty nestling in a natural bowl below verdant hillsides and towering granite peaks. The main feature of the valley was of course the racecourse, which had to be one of the most scenically sited racecourses in the world. Jericho had spent many happy days here at race meetings with Susan, for she had been an unlikely aficionado of the Sport of Kings. She had liked nothing better than to stroll among the crowds in the picturesque grandstand, eyeing the diplomats in their plumed helmets, the swaggering young subalterns, the elegantly dressed taipans and their gorgeous ladies revelling in the sheen of their Chinese silk dresses.

Happy Valley had been the place where the first English merchant colonists had built their fine houses nearly a century ago, but the place had been less than happy for them at first. The beautiful hillside cemetery above Happy Valley, with its jungle greenery and giant banyan and strong-wood trees, was also full of the moss-covered headstones of English merchants and their young families cut down in the prime of life by malaria and typhus. But the swamps had been drained and the mosquitoes mostly defeated eventually, and Happy Valley had finally begun to live up to its name for its later, more fortunate, residents. Yet not for Paul Jericho in the end, for his wife Susan was now buried in Happy Valley cemetery too, her white marble headstone now joining all those other English headstones in that melancholy if beautiful place...

Paul Jericho lived in a flat at the top of a small three-storey apartment building in Blue Pool Road, situated on a green hillside above the racecourse. Forest-covered hills rose steeply behind the block and sheltered it from the worst of tropical storms. Susan had loved this apartment, particularly the open balcony at the rear where the only sounds that could be heard were of trickling forest streams and echoing birdsong...

None of Susan's fashionable and well-connected friends had been able to understand just why a beautiful and vibrant young woman like her had married a rather dull and dour policeman like Paul Jericho. Yet when he was with her, the truth was that the stolid Paul Jericho became a quite different person that few others ever saw. And perhaps that was enough for Susan; knowing that she was with a man who was completely bewitched by her...

Jericho entered the small lobby of his building and climbed the familiar staircase to the top floor. He had been tempted to sell this flat after Susan's death in January, for he didn't know how he would be able to cope with living here without her. It still felt more like her apartment than his; it was mostly her money that had paid for it, after all, since she had inherited most of her wealthy parents' money a few years before. Every object, memento, and piece of furniture in the flat held some personal memory for him of Susan, and the recurring sight of those intimate details of her life had left him overwhelmed by grief for a while. Yet in the end he had stayed here and endured the sadness. For he knew that Susan would have hated him ever giving up this wonderful apartment and its magical views, and in a way he felt that he would be betraying her memory by selling up. In the end, it was only those objects in the flat, and the sweet memories of her living in this place, which had kept him going for the last seven months...

He let himself in and was dismayed for a moment afresh by the terrible silence. No one had told him that his biggest problem would be the silence of his empty home; that the soul of this apartment had died with Susan, and would never recover fully, now that her voice and her gentle distinctive laugh had been stilled forever. He should perhaps have hired some live-in servants just to relieve that silence, yet found he couldn't do it. Susan had always preferred that it was just the two of them in the apartment, and Jericho now preferred to be left alone with his memories rather than have to put up with the background chatter of live-in servants.

After lighting the mosquito coils in the living room and the main bedroom, he walked out onto the balcony at the back of the apartment, and was relieved just to hear the sounds of the hot evening wind stirring the forested hillside above. Susan had died seven months before on a very different night from this – a cold and blustery January night - the victim of a hit-and-run accident in the Eastern Mid-levels. The actual spot where Susan had died was in Kennedy Road close to the turning with Bowen Drive, which led even higher up the hillside towards Macdonnell Road, and then finally to the highest road in that part of the Mid-levels, Bowen Road. No one knew what Susan had been doing there at 11pm, apparently walking along Kennedy Road, for she had no friends that Jericho knew of in that part of the Eastern Mid-levels, which lay directly above Queens Road East in Wanchai.

Susan had merely told Jericho that she would be staying late after school that day, and then meeting some girlfriends for an evening get together. Jericho had been on police duty that night, so had not questioned exactly where she would be, though he assumed that she was visiting someone in the *Western* Mid-levels. Susan had lots of teacher friends in that western area of Mid-levels – Robinson Road, Kotewall Road, Caine Road – so Jericho had not thought twice about it until he had received the terrible news close to midnight. But what had taken Susan to Kennedy Road on that unusually cold night remained a mystery, and no friends had ever come forward to say that they had seen Susan that evening. It seemed regretfully that Susan had been keeping some secret from him, though Jericho was still reluctant to believe the worst interpretation of her behaviour.

Even if she had been betraying him with another man as some were suggesting, it hardly mattered now. For his part Paul Jericho preferred to believe in his wife's integrity, and that there was some perfectly reasonable explanation as to why she had been in Kennedy Road that night...

Another policeman had been assigned to investigate the death, of course – actually Charlie Hebdon's obsequious favourite yet again, Inspector Kevin Ball. But even the pushy and aggressive Inspector Ball had drawn a blank this time, for there had been no witnesses to the accident, and little useful evidence of what had gone on. Certainly the vehicle in question had disappeared from the scene and had never been tracked down, although it must have been a sizeable car of some sort to have inflicted such terrible injuries. From the limited residual tyre marks on the road, the driver had not braked at all before the impact, but had apparently stopped briefly after hitting Susan, before then driving on again with callous disregard for the woman he had struck down. An anonymous phone call, later traced to a public phone box in Macdonnell Road, had reported the incident to the police emergency line at exactly 11:15 – most likely this had been the remorseful driver of the car who had phoned in, although that wasn't completely certain. The voice had sounded like a Chinese man speaking broken English, although the police officer who answered the call couldn't be entirely sure of the caller's sex, since the voice had been no more than a hoarse whisper.

Inspector Ball had in his usual thorough way checked with every repair garage in Hong Kong in an effort to find the car and the driver – even on Kowloon side. But no likely car had been found: all those drivers who had had appropriate repairs carried out to the front bodywork of their cars between the day of the accident in January and the end of April could also prove that they had been elsewhere on the night of Tuesday, January 19th. Nor had Ball had any luck in establishing what Susan had been doing in Kennedy Road that evening, though Jericho had soon understood that Ball suspected that Susan had been meeting a man that evening. Yet with no proof of that, Ball had soon abandoned that line of enquiry too, since it seemed unlikely to help with finding the driver of the car.

Strangely, Jericho had shown little interest at the time in investigating the accident himself; his loss had left him so emotionally crippled that he was quite unable to think rationally for many weeks afterwards. Yet now, nearly seven months later, he was beginning to be consumed with the desire to know who had hit his wife with a car that night and then driven off without calling for help at once. It probably would have made no practical difference if the driver had remained at the scene, for Susan's internal injuries had been so severe that she would have died anyway long before ever getting to a hospital. Yet Jericho still wanted to know the identity of this person.

What he would do if he ever did discover the name of this person was somewhat more problematical. For he wanted that person to know just what enormous damage they had done to him by depriving him of his beautiful wife...*and perhaps to make them suffer a little of the same pain too...*

*

Edith Starling was also in reflective mood on this hot muggy Tuesday night as she left the main gate of Government House at 11:15 and turned west along Upper Albert Road. It was one of the principal advantages of her job that her flat in Wyndham Street was only seven minutes' walk away, almost straight down the hill. Given that she worked long hours at Government House six days a week, she hardly made any use of her little car - or of any other form of transport, come to think of it, except her own two feet. In fact she normally left her Austin Seven parked below in Pedder Street near the Hong Kong Hotel all week, since it was impossible to park it in the narrow road outside her apartment, and the only time she ever got to drive it was a Sunday anyway. And quite often – given her relentless work habits – not even then, for she often worked on Sundays too...

Today she had arrived at her desk at seven in the morning, and apart from a twenty-minute walk around the Botanical Gardens at lunchtime, had not stirred outside the building since then. What Ralph Ogden had told her last night at the party had troubled her greatly; it was staggering to think that there might be a traitor at Government House passing secrets to the Japanese.

Yet *someone* was clearly passing secrets to the Japanese...

Edith knew this without a doubt after what she had discovered today. She had been looking at a fresh batch of coded signals between the Japanese War Ministry and their Kwantung Army headquarters in Northern China. At first the signals looked similar to those she had seen many times before, and she'd had no doubt that she would be able to decipher them within a few hours using the techniques she had worked out herself. All Japanese signals were first written in the simplified Romanized form of Japanese, *romanji*, before being encrypted, since this was much more amenable to encoding than the more complicated *hiragana* script or the *Kanji* pictographic characters which the Japanese had taken over wholesale from Chinese. But this simplification also made them easier for a code-breaker to decipher them.

Japanese military codes were unlike the new German codes in that they were still primarily unsophisticated "book" ciphers, while German codes now used mechanical encipherment which was a much more difficult problem to crack. With book ciphers, the plain text of messages was replaced with a group of numbers and letters in accordance with a standard code book. The relative simplicity of the Japanese coding system therefore made it possible to decipher the messages, though it was still a considerable challenge for the code-breaker's skill. Edith's success with breaking these Japanese codes had been mainly to do with the clever mathematical algorithms she had invented to incorporate standard techniques such as frequency analysis: these algorithms provided a logical step-by-step process by which the codes could gradually be obtained, though they still needed to be applied with a certain amount of mathematical ingenuity.

Edith had soon found however that these new signals were completely indecipherable using her trusted algorithms. A horrible suspicion began to grow on her as she realized the truth: that these messages had been encrypted, not once, but *twice*. Somebody had encoded the plain text into code, then had applied a second code to the already coded text, something that was called *super-encipherment*...

This was like picking a difficult lock, only to find, after a titanic struggle to get through it, that there was another lock inside the first, smaller and even more devilish to pick than the last...

That meant there was no way that she could read these messages with her current techniques. The encoding was so complicated and convoluted that it must make it difficult even for the signals officers with the Kwantung Army to decipher the messages even when they had the key. But much worse for Edith than the realization that she was locked out of these particular messages was the obvious conclusion: *somebody had tipped off the Japanese that the British could read their army signals*...

So there was certainly an informer somewhere. And if the information obtained by the British embassy in Tokyo was correct, then this informer was operating in Government House itself. Edith hoped to God that this information from Tokyo was wrong, though; that sort of treachery would be hard to take.

She hadn't even been able to confide in Ralph Ogden about this frightening conclusion for he had been away from Government House today, probably on one of his frequent flying visits to the border with China to assess the military situation there.

Edith turned from Upper Albert Road into Wyndham Street. The road fell away steeply from here down to Central. At the bottom of the street, where it met Queens Road Central, was the place where the women flower-sellers gathered every day beneath the spreading branches of an old banyan tree with their bright baskets of freesia, lilies and geraniums, so that Wyndham Street was known unofficially as "Flower Street". Edith's flat was half way down the street, so on Sundays when she was at home she often enjoyed the powerful scents of the massed flowers as they drifted up the hill and wafted in through her open windows.

She entered her building lobby and climbed the stairs to the second floor. She had just opened the door of her flat and was reaching for the light switch on the inside wall when she was suddenly grabbed roughly from behind.

Her assailant planted his hands on her breasts, then spun her around roughly to face him.

Edith regarded him coldly. 'Take your hands off me, you Chinese dog.'

'You're late,' the man said with annoyance.

'Does it really matter?' she answered him. 'I'm here now, aren't I, Michael...?' Then she pulled him forward to her and kissed him hard on the lips.

CHAPTER 4

Wednesday, 11th August 1937

Edith Starling stirred uneasily in her bed, and saw through the gap in the bedroom curtains that it was getting light outside. Because of the oppressive heat at night in her apartment, she invariably slept entirely naked in summer with only a thin cotton sheet to cover her. She looked at her bedside clock - a Liberty Arts and Crafts clock attributed to the famous designer Archibald Knox. The clock had been given to her as a twenty-first birthday present by her American mother so was her most prized possession. By the enamel-on-silver dial she saw that it was a quarter to six, therefore nearly time to get up and begin a new day.

Michael was still asleep beside her, breathing gently. She could see the clear outline of his slim body beneath the same thin cotton sheet and thought she had never seen anything more beautiful. He aroused her physically in a way that no Western man ever had. Something about her own countrymen had always repelled her – or at least the thought of taking one as a lover anyway. Most of the Englishmen she met in Hong Kong were in any case loud-mouthed obnoxious colonial bores with nothing appealing about them at all; they had all been out here far too long and their minds had ossified into an unpleasant and complacent arrogance. Therefore it was perhaps natural that she would be attracted by someone entirely different from her own kind.

Yet she knew that she was risking potential disaster by meeting this man here brazenly in her own apartment. It was bad enough taking a Chinese lover – that by itself would be enough to make her a social pariah and destroy her life in Hong Kong if it became public knowledge – yet it was even worse because of Michael's high profile in Hong Kong as a gadfly lawyer with left wing sympathies.

Edith remembered her enigmatic conversation with Ralph Ogden in the garden at Government House on Monday night, and wondered if he suspected the truth about her relationship with Michael. That meeting with Michael in the garden had been entirely accidental – Edith hadn't even known that he would be there at the reception that night for he was hardly a man held in high esteem at Government House. But it occurred to her now that perhaps Ogden had thought the starlit encounter in the garden was deliberate. So *had he perhaps been warning her off in his subtle fashion from this unfortunate infatuation...?*

She had told Ogden the truth at least about how she had first met Michael – in the interval of a play at the Theatre Royal in the City Hall a couple of months ago – but she had not admitted of course that she and Michael had become lovers within two weeks of that first meeting. It was complete madness on her part, she knew, since the affair could only end in bitterness and recrimination.

Or perhaps even in complete disaster for her...

Yet she still couldn't stop and change course, even though she knew she was heading pell-mell for a dangerous precipice from which there might be no way back...

Edith wondered again if what Ralph had suggested might be true – that Michael had picked her out deliberately for his attentions. He certainly had spoken to her first that night in the bar in the City Hall, though very diffidently and politely at first. Yet if he had cultivated her acquaintance deliberately in order to get access to government secrets, then he had been singularly subtle and relaxed about it, for he had never quizzed her since about any aspects of her work. She was sure that Michael believed her to be only a junior secretary at Government House, and certainly not a senior code expert with the Secret Intelligence Service. The only people who knew differently, after all, were Ralph Ogden and a handful of her senior colleagues in the communications section at Government House.

But perhaps Michael was still just biding his time, she thought with a fresh rush of doubt, for they had only been lovers for six weeks. Yet Michael had been very open about telling her about his own background and his own political sympathies, which was odd behaviour if he was trying to get secretly into her confidences. He had told her that he came from a very wealthy family of Shanghai merchants, and that he had taken a law degree in London. But he had also confessed freely that his patriotic love for China meant that he could never be a friend of the colonial powers – England, Germany, Russia, and now Japan - who had bled China dry for the last century. Perhaps *because* of his wealthy background - rather than in spite of it - he had become quietly attuned to the problems of China's vast army of the poor. So it had been almost natural, given his sympathies for the plight of the Chinese peasant, that his politics would be left wing and anti-colonial, and that his career as a lawyer would be in accordance with those principles. He had never really explained to her why he had come to Hong Kong in particular to practise, which was a slight mark against him perhaps. Yet the one thing that even Michael's natural political enemies in Government House had to admit was that he was a most accomplished lawyer, for he had an enviable record of defending his clients in court against everything from public order offences to accusations of robbery with violence...

At twenty-seven, he was also a year younger than her, a fact which made her a little uncomfortable too, as she knew that she looked rather older than her real age, while he was the opposite. She studied his sleeping face in repose now - the golden skin, the glossy black hair and the delicate features – and couldn't stop herself from gently stroking his cheek.

His eyes flickered open, then he yawned extravagantly and smiled at her.

'I think you have to go now, Michael, before anybody sees you sneaking out of my apartment,' she said in a whisper.

'When can we meet again?' he asked, leaning over and touching the bridge of his nose affectionately with hers.

'Saturday afternoon, maybe,' she said wistfully. 'We could drive out to Stanley again and find that empty beach at Tai Tam Bay.' They had been there together once before, to a remote beach on the most south-easterly bay of the island where there was little chance that anyone would ever see them together. It had been the most glorious and sensual afternoon of Edith's life.

He nodded, still yawning. 'All right. But only if you find yourself a better bathing suit. That black flannel one you wore last time looked like something a grandmother would wear.'

Edith smiled. 'Ah, I should perhaps have told you before about my three grandchildren – little Ignatius, Reginald and Algernon. You do know that I am fifty-seven years old, Michael, don't you? I think I'm remarkably well preserved for my age, though...'

Michael laughed. 'Fool! Will you pick me up in your little Austin, like before?'

'Yes, of course. But I won't park near your flat in Happy Valley this time; there are too many nosy memsahibs in Broadwood Road. So I'll pick you up near the cemetery...'

'A little morbid...'

'But safe from prying eyes.' Edith ran her finger along the line of his clean sculpted jaw. 'I wish I still had my big Studebaker President now. My little Austin Seven has a real struggle to get over the mountains, whereas my Studebaker used to get up Stubbs Road and soar across the Wong Nei Chung Gap like a bird, with no problems at all...'

'You had a Studebaker?' he asked idly. 'What kind?'

'It was a Studebaker President series FE seven passenger Tourer. A wonderful dark blue. There wasn't another car like it in Hong Kong,' she said proudly.

His genial smile faded. 'Then perhaps the Austin is a better choice for us after all, for it is much less likely to be noticed, even with a Chinese man and a wicked English girl on board...'

'I suppose I am wicked, aren't I?' she said quietly. 'Or perhaps ridiculous.'

He kissed her softly on the lips. 'You are not ridiculous, Edith. You are entrancing...'

She fell silent for a moment. 'Do you ever think about the future, Michael?'

'I try not to, for the immediate future of my country is bleak indeed.' His voice had taken on a bitter note.

'No, I meant *our* future,' Edith said patiently.

'*Our future?*' Michael smiled sadly. 'That's easy, Edith. We have no future together. I'm afraid that you *are* being ridiculous now, to even contemplate such things.' He kissed her again. 'I told you...we must simply live for the present and enjoy this little time that we have together. For we both know that it cannot last...'

For some reason, the bleakness of that remark quelled all her doubts that this man was being deceitful with her. Reluctantly, she pulled back the sheet and got out of bed. 'I must get ready for work; I have to be there by seven.'

He lay back in bed studying with obvious pleasure her naked figure, which was silhouetted against the dawn light filtering through the curtain behind her. Edith felt no shame at being studied so assiduously; it was a compliment if anything. She knew that she had a fine figure, which made up for the many imperfections of her rather ordinary face.

'You're very beautiful, you know,' he said unexpectedly. 'I hope your boss Mr Ogden appreciates you.'

This was the first time that Michael had ever mentioned the fact that he knew Ralph Ogden to be her direct boss. She felt a sudden shiver of apprehension at this surprising admission, for *she* had certainly never told him this. And if Michael knew this much, then he might also know that Ralph Ogden was Britain's chief spymaster in the Far East. It might even mean that Michael also knew much more about *her* real work at Government House than he had ever let on...

*

Dressed in a fine white linen suit of tropical cut, Sebastian Ride sat at his desk on this hot and steamy Wednesday morning in the offices of Saunders-Woo Holdings in Queens Road Central. He had many business worries presently on his mind to distract him, yet his overriding concern on this grey and oppressively hot morning was actually for his stricken wife.

Gloria had been drunk again last night when he had got home, though still conscious this time at least. Although she had put on a pretence of normality for him – or as much slurred normality as she could manage with so much gin inside her – he was now convinced that he would have to find professional nursing help to look after her. It was either that or put her into some sort of institution where she could be gradually weaned off her alcohol dependency...

He looked up from his morbid reflections at his desk as Frances Leung knocked on the connecting door and marched forcefully into the room, immaculately turned out as ever in her formal woman's pinstripe suit. She cleared her throat with pointed effect. 'Is this a good time to give you that summary you were asking for, Mr Ride?'

Ride had asked her last week to prepare a summary report of all their current projects in China, to see how they might be impacted by the Japanese invasion of the Northern provinces. Elsewhere in China, the problems of doing business were almost as bad as in the North for there was still no central controlling authority over the whole country. It was true that Chiang Kia-shek's Nationalists controlled much of the South, after the Communists had retreated to the West and North in their infamous "Long March" two years ago. Yet much of the country still remained in the control of local warlords who were corrupt and violent individuals on the whole, and who could not be trusted when it came to business dealings with foreign companies.

The list of projects made for grim listening as Frances went through them in her usual imperturbable manner. Despite her stern and unsmiling appearance, Frances was a quietly attractive woman. She had worked for him for nearly ten years now, yet Ride still knew surprisingly little about her life away from the office. He did know that she was the daughter of a renowned Chinese doctor – a specialist in tropical diseases - and an adventurous Austrian mother who had travelled with her younger sister to Asia at the end of the last century. Both these Austrian sisters had ended up marrying distinguished Chinese doctors. This parental ancestry explained Frances's unusual looks, and perhaps her unusual personality too. Her mother's Germanic ancestry was evident in the strong sculpted lines of her face and in her tall and erect physique, while her father had given her raven black hair and smooth golden skin. And both her parents had clearly played their part in moulding Frances's forceful and sober character. She also had a cousin whom she was very close to because of his identical Austrian and Chinese heritage; Ride had met him once when he had called at the office one evening to take Frances to dinner. Dominic Tien was a local businessman, who seemed quite well off, and who owned a considerable property portfolio as well as a string of motor dealerships and garages.

Frances finally got to the project that was causing Ride so much particular concern: the construction of a new steel rolling mill in Hopei province, which had only been completed last year. It had seemed like a very good idea four years ago when it was being planned, for China was critically short of its own steel making facilities. Frances still spoke in the same flat voice as she gave him the bad news. 'According to our latest information, the plant has had to halt production because of the Japanese aggression. Although the plant is still notionally in Chinese-held territory, it is less than fifty miles from the Japanese front lines therefore is likely to be overrun within days...'

Ride cursed under his breath. 'Then I commend you for not displaying some satisfaction that your worst predictions have come true, Frances. You warned me not to go ahead with that project because of the political uncertainty in the North. Now it means that we have probably lost our part of the investment for good... four million Hong Kong dollars...'

'Yet even I didn't foresee that the Japanese would have the effrontery to invade Hopei Province so my advice was based on entirely false assumptions,' Frances said mildly. 'But for that unexpected aggression by the Japanese Army, I think the investment would have proved a very profitable one after all. And it might well be so in the future, if the Japanese eventually withdraw from Hopei.'

'Nevertheless, it would have been far better if *you* had been sitting in this chair, and making the decisions rather than me,' Ride said ruefully.

Ride thought he detected a faint flush of pleasure in Frances's amber cheeks at the compliment, as she tried to look on the positive side. 'Yet the news from outside China is good. Our shipping line is making record profits throughout Asia and the Pacific, while our recent investments in rubber plantations in Malaya and in large scale agricultural projects in the Philippines are bearing valuable fruit...'

Ride smiled. 'Literally, in the latter case, for our company farms are now the largest producers of mangoes and pineapples in Asia, are they not?'

Frances gave him one of her rare smiles. 'They are.'

Ride couldn't help noticing for the first time how appealing she looked when she smiled. He could honestly say that he had never been sexually attracted to Frances in the slightest before, perhaps because she was a year or two older than himself, as much as by the fact that she was Eurasian. She was also unfailingly proper in her behaviour in the office too, which had probably also reined in his natural tendencies in this case. This unusual reticence on his part was probably just as well for their working relationship, as the unwelcome distraction of sexual feelings had fortunately never interfered to spoil it. Yet Ride had to admit that she had a nice face and a slender graceful figure for a middle-aged woman, therefore he was not entirely sure why he had never succumbed even slightly to her attractions. For a man who idolized beautiful women, it was an odd lapse, particularly when she had such beautiful long legs that were always displayed so pleasingly in sheer silk stockings.

Frances had clearly picked up on his unusual attention towards her, and particularly the long admiring look he had bestowed on her legs. She flushed again slightly, and patted her hair as if worried something was wrong with her appearance.

Ride became business-like again. 'Is there anything else I should know about? Is one of our ships about to hit an iceberg?'

Frances didn't smile this time, apparently determined not to be distracted again. 'Not at this time of the year, Mr Ride. But there is one thing that has been troubling me about a couple of our vessels...'

Ride looked up in concern. 'And what is that?'

Frances frowned. 'I have been doing checks on the seaworthiness certificates for our fleet, and I happened to notice that two of our vessels have lately been making regular deliveries of goods to unusual destinations...'

"What vessels do you mean?'

Frances consulted her notes. 'The *SS Corazon* and the *SS Maribeth*...'

'I don't know either of those vessels,' Ride said, puzzled.

'That's probably because we bought them only recently from a shipping company in the Philippines. The two vessels in question are sister ships – a pair of old tramp steamers, each of two thousand tons gross displacement.'

'So where have these two old tramp steamers been calling?'

Frances frowned. 'Well, since March, the *SS Corazon* has been making a regular run from Singapore to the port of Dalian in the south of Liaoning Province in Northern China.'

'That's odd. We shouldn't be shipping anything that far north. That's near Port Arthur on the Liaodong Peninsula, isn't it? That's very close to Korea, which must lie just across the Yellow Sea to the east of Dalian.' Ride was worried now for he couldn't see any reason why a Saunders vessel should be delivering cargo there.

Frances nodded. 'Yes, that's right. I believe that Russia took possession of the Liaodong Peninsula from China in the last century since it was one of the few areas in the Pacific region that could provide them with an ice-free port. But the Japanese took over control of the peninsula after defeating the Russians in a war thirty years ago. Just this year, Japan has enlarged both ports on the peninsula: the northern one, Dalian, and the southern one Lüshun, or Port Arthur as you Europeans call it. This was probably done deliberately as part of their plans to invade more Chinese territory.'

'Doesn't matter what they call the damned place!' Ride muttered. 'We shouldn't be delivering to any Jap ports. There is no official trade embargo on Japan yet, I know, but we have been advised by the Governor to terminate all non-essential trade with areas of China controlled by the Japanese. What was on the ship's manifest?'

Frances looked down at her notes again. 'Medical supplies and general provisions.'

And what about the other ship? The *SS Maribeth?* Where has that vessel been visiting?'

Frances looked doubtful. 'It's a similar story. Apparently it has been making a regular run since May from Manila to the port of Tsingtao in the east of Shandong Province, which is also on China's Yellow Sea coast.'

'So not that far south of Dalian?'

'No, not far at all. And Tsingtao must also be in Japanese hands by now,' she pointed out.

Ride knew that Tsingtao was another Chinese port that had been taken over in the nineteenth century by an aggressive European power, in this case Imperial Germany. Although China had regained temporary control of it again after the Great War, this was another area where Japan had lately taken over effective possession after its recent incursions into Chinese territory. 'So, don't tell me,' he said sarcastically, '– the *SS Maribeth* was also no doubt carrying "medical supplies and general provisions".'

Frances shrugged uneasily. 'Yes, it was. At least if you believe the manifest anyway.'

Ride turned and looked out of the window at busy Queens Road for a moment as he tried to think. 'We need to find out what is going on here, Frances and why we seem to be trading with the Japanese when it's completely against company policy. Somebody in the company must have authorized this, but it certainly wasn't me.' Ride had a nasty suspicion that there was something ominous behind this mystery.

Frances seemed about to say something, but then thought better of it.

Ride guessed what it might be. 'You think James might be behind these shipments, don't you, Frances?'

'He normally deals with our shipping business in Singapore and Manila,' she said, wrinkling her brow.

'That's true.' Ride stood up suddenly. 'Then I'd better go and have a word with him about it, despite our angry words yesterday.'

'You won't be able to talk to him immediately. I saw him going out just before I came in here,' Frances explained.

'Oh? Do you know where he's gone?'

Frances nodded. 'Of course. He's gone to that old quarry site east of Shaukeiwan. I overheard him talking to his secretary.'

'Why has he gone there? I thought we were selling that site to some factory owner?'

'That was the agreed decision of the Board. But I think Mr Woo is now of a mind to keep it, though I don't know what he plans to do with it. I assume he must be meeting someone out there to discuss his plans, whatever they are.'

Ride made a sudden decision, and picked up his white Panama hat from the nearby hat stand. 'Then I think I will drive along there and see just what James is getting up to.'

Frances looked thoughtful. 'I think that might be wise, Mr Ride...'

*

Sebastian Ride did not often venture this far east on the island, and was conscious that his bright blue Bugatti Type 55 was causing something of a sensation with Chinese bystanders as he drove it along Queens Road East, and then further east beyond Causeway Bay. His destination, Shaukeiwan, was the easternmost point of that dense ribbon of urban development that ran along almost the entire length of the north shore of Hong Kong Island, so it was also naturally the eastern terminus of the tram line. In his open-topped sports car, he found that the oppressive morning heat was less of a problem than it had been in his office; in fact the steady cooling draft of air blowing over the car windscreen was a welcome relief, though he did have to hold on to his Panama hat from time to time as it was caught by a sudden swirl of hot gusting wind.

After passing Causeway Bay, Ride found that the road ahead became progressively narrower and meaner, and the buildings on each side poorer and more ramshackle. This road that ran east from Causeway Bay to Shaukeiwan, through North Point and Quarry Bay on the way, had originally closely followed the natural shoreline of the north side of Hong Kong Island, but various reclamation projects over the last century had gradually left the old waterfront road stranded several hundred yards inland. The road now had a new name too: two years ago, the section between the east end of Causeway Bay and the East Gate of Taikoo Dockyard had been renamed as King's Road to honour the silver jubilee of King George V, even though a mean and narrow road like this one hardly lived up to the grandeur of that name.

Sebastian Ride was still mulling worriedly over what Frances had told him in the office. She obviously suspected from the discovery of those surprising ship manifests that James Woo might have authorized some illicit trading with the Japanese. It would be bad enough if this was really only medical supplies and general provisions that were being traded, but Ride had a nasty suspicion that James might have been selling something more lucrative to the Japanese, like rubber or chemicals. Saunders-Woo was unusual for a Hong Kong trading company in that many of its investors were wealthy overseas Chinese. So if it was discovered that the company had been assisting the Japanese war effort in any way, then all hell would break loose. These outside investors were nervous enough as it was because of falling profits from their Chinese operations, and if it was found that the company had been profiting directly from trade with the warmongering Japanese, they might start selling their shares and driving the company into a real crisis.

Ride drove on through North Point and Quarry Bay and past the huge Taikyoo Dockyard, before turning a last bend and seeing the township of Shaukeiwan directly ahead. In the early days of British Hong Kong, Shaukeiwan had been a small picturesque harbour that served as a typhoon shelter for local fishermen. But it had also been an infamous refuge for pirates, so the English had been forced to clean up the area in the last century by hanging the pirates and clearing out their slums. Hakka people from Huizhou had begun to move into the cleared area after that to work in the rock quarries, and had built a small town on the shore to add to the floating village of fishermen's boats. Now the settlement was known as a centre for shipbuilding and stone quarrying, as well as fishing, and had a number of temples dedicated to popular fisherman's deities such as Tin Hau and Tam Kung. Even more recently, for the last ten years or so, Shaukeiwan had begun to develop into an industrial area with the arrival of many new light industries.

Saunders-Woo owned a rock quarry on the east side of Shaukeiwan, but the good quality granite was now worked out and the site disused. The company had therefore been in negotiation with a Chinese manufacturer of machine parts to sell the site to them for a new factory. But it seemed that James Woo had other ideas about this now, though he had not had the courtesy to discuss this first with his chairman, Sebastian Ride.

Ride drove on through the high street of Shaukeiwan. As with all of Hong Kong's coastal urban strip, everything here was concentrated into a very compact area, with squalid tenements and dismal workshops and crumbling warehouses all jammed together into a dense grey mass, but with verdant green hillsides rising behind to relieve the gloom. Yet at Shaukeiwan, these hills were less scenic than elsewhere on the island because of all the quarrying that had taken place, which had left great ugly gouges and chasms in the scarred hillside. The hillsides above Shaukeiwan were even less prepossessing these days because many new refugees from mainland China had settled illegally on those steep bluffs above the township and built rusting shantytowns of clapboard and corrugated iron, from where they tapped illegally into the overhead electric lines.

A hundred yards past the outlying buildings of Shaukeiwan, and Ride came finally to the Saunders-Woo Quarry where he parked his Bugatti on a patch of waste ground near the old quarry offices. He had forgotten how large this quarry was, for it had been worked for over fifty years and had created a great rolling expanse of rubble the size of three football fields, backed by near vertical man-made cliffs behind. There was no housing or other buildings between the quarry and the sea, for an overhead iron gantry bridge had been used to transport the excavated stone over the coastal road to an old timber jetty for eventual loading onto ships and barges.

Ride looked around and thought he might have wasted his journey here, for the quarry seemed to be empty, and there was no sign of James's distinctive car, an American gold Cadillac.

But no sooner had he decided reluctantly to give up and return to Central than James Woo appeared suddenly from behind a giant boulder. He was on his own, which surprised Ride a little for he had thought, like Frances, that James must be meeting someone here.

James walked over with a frown etched on his handsome face. He was still dressed in an elegant business suit and broad-brimmed Fedora; his only concession to his dusty surroundings was a pair of thick-soled boots. 'What are you doing here, Sebastian? Have you followed me here?'

Ride was tempted to deny it for a moment, but then realized that he had no other plausible explanation for being here. 'Yes, I did, James. Frances told me where you'd gone, and that you might be reconsidering our plans to sell this site to a factory owner.'

It was eleven o'clock in the morning by now, and the sun was beating down fiercely on the stone rubble in the quarry, throwing up a volcanic wall of heat at their feet. Ride was particularly glad to be wearing his wide-brimmed Panama hat as protection from the sun. James Woo seemed to be coping better than him with the savage heat, although, when he removed his Fedora for a moment to mop his brow, the harsh glare of the sunlight, falling near vertically, revealed some lines and blemishes in his boyish face that Ride had not noticed before.

James was still apparently in as difficult and touchy a mood as he had been yesterday, and seemed ready to take offence again at anything that Ride might say. Therefore Ride decided to be wary about making any fresh accusations until he knew what was going on here.

But then James surprised Ride with a genuine-looking smile, which was a reminder to Ride of the pleasant and amiable boy he had once been. 'I believe I might have found a much more lucrative use for this site, Sebastian.'

Ride responded with a quizzical smile of his own. 'Would you like to tell me what?'

'Simple...we use it for *housing*...' James looked up at the distant hillside to the west and at the ugly shanties that littered its slopes. '*For those people up there...*'

Ride was a little confused, for he doubted if James had ever been motivated by sympathy for the plight of his fellow Chinese, and certainly not for the kind of refugee peasants who had taken over these hillsides. 'And who is going to pay us for this generosity? Not those poor wretches themselves, who probably haven't got five dollars between them.'

James was unperturbed. 'I happen to know that the Acting Governor, Norman Lockhart Smith, and the Colonial Secretary George Carothers, have decided on a massive building program to house the poor in Hong Kong. The government has nearly thirty million dollars in its tax reserves from the recent years of plenty, and Lockhart Smith wants to use a large part of the surplus to cement his legacy with some timely social spending.'

Ride was sceptical. 'Lockhart Smith would never do that; he will surely leave any huge decisions like that until the new governor, Sir Geoffrey Northcote, arrives.'

James smiled smugly. 'On the contrary, my information is that the Acting Governor is determined to make these decisions quickly before the new governor arrives; he doesn't want to give Northcote the chance to rescind his plans.'

'How do you know all this?' Ride demanded.

'I have a very reliable source in Government House who tells me everything.'

Ride wondered who that might be; it certainly didn't sound like one of James's normal circle of intimate friends, who were mostly pampered western-educated young Chinese addicted to wild excess and extravagance. There certainly were not too many people like *that* working in Government House...

James could obviously see what Ride was thinking. 'Don't worry, Sebastian. I know what I'm talking about. The plans for this housing are well advanced. Four potential sites have already been earmarked for up to twenty-five thousand dwellings on each...'

Ride was astonished. *'Twenty-five thousand...?'*

James Woo shrugged casually, clearly pleased at Ride's surprised reaction. 'On *each* site...that's *a hundred thousand* family units in total.' He smiled slyly. 'Of course they won't be luxury apartments. Just simple mass housing without frills.'

'Where are these four sites?' Ride asked.

James glanced around him. 'One of them is right here. The other three designated areas are on Kowloon side: the first is in Sham Shui Po, and the other two are in Yau Ma Tei and Lai Chi Kok.'

'We already own land for development in all those three areas,' Ride said suspiciously. 'We bought those plots in a government land auction earlier this year, on your father's advice.'

James smiled. 'Actually it was on *my* advice, Sebastian, but I thought it better that you believed this recommendation came from my father. And it's no coincidence, of course, that the proposed areas for this mass public housing are all located on the plots of land that we purchased. It's called business planning, Sebastian. Which you would do well to study a bit more after your disastrous investment in that steel rolling mill in Hopei province.

Now, with all the turmoil in China, this is the time to concentrate on safe projects here in Hong Kong that can generate real profit for us.'

Ride was beginning to think that he might have underestimated James Woo. The man was certainly a decadent rake, with a disreputable taste for drugs and dangerous sexual liaisons, yet he did seem to have inherited some of his father's head for business too...

Another thought struck Ride as he studied James Woo's triumphant expression. 'You also made a recent deal with an American construction company for the licensed use of some of their building products and construction methods. If I remember, this company specialises in the design and construction of prefabricated concrete buildings up to ten stories high.'

James laughed. 'So finally you are beginning to understand that there is some method in my madness. With this building system, we will be able to erect mass housing on our own land at a quarter of the cost and the construction time of conventional buildings.'

Ride doubted that this was true, for labour for building conventional housing was dirt cheap in Hong Kong at present, while imported building materials were expensive. But he was more interested to know how definite these plans were, for he had heard nothing of such an ambitious building programme himself. And the Acting Governor, Norman Lockhart Smith, did not seem to him the sort of man to take such a huge responsibility on his own head; he had always struck Sebastian Ride as a man of limited ambition who would never rock the boat by taking excessive risks with public money. 'But this is not certain, is it? Your man in Government House may be able to tell you what is going on but...'

James didn't let him finish. 'He is doing far more than that, Sebastian. He has been working behind the scenes on this for a year or more, using his influence quietly to promote this scheme. It was because of his advice that I bought those plots of land, since they seemed like the most suitable sites for this mass housing...'

'Who is this man, James? I need to know more about this individual before I go along with this plan.'

James smiled wryly. 'I'm afraid that information is confidential for the moment, even to you. I don't want you interfering with this scheme of mine until the thing is done and dusted. You will have to trust me and my inside man for the moment. But don't concern yourself too much with trying to identify this man; just be content to know that he is working hard for us on the inside, and that he is fully capable of manipulating events in our favour and winning over any doubting voices in the Executive Council. He is also using his best endeavours to ensure that this work is directly awarded to our construction subsidiary in the end, and is not put out to general tender.'

Ride snapped the brim of his Panama hat forward to give his face more shade from the fierce sun. 'So there are *some* doubting voices in Government House who could still stop this grand scheme of yours?'

For the first time, James Woo showed a brief sign of doubt. 'Perhaps. But I am working with my man on the inside to ensure that nothing derails this deal. I do know that Lockhart Smith and Carothers rely heavily on the advice and support of four key men in their establishment: Attorney General Julian Colby, his deputy Ronald Grantham, the Colonial Treasurer Robert Harmsworth, and lastly, the colony's intelligence chief, Ralph Ogden. Any of those gentlemen could possibly veto the plan as being too extravagant with the public finances, since it will deplete the government's coffers considerably and leave them little money for dealing with other unforeseen emergencies. And Lockhart Smith might unfortunately be swayed by such arguments. Therefore we have to ensure that we get all these gentlemen on board, and suitably enthused with the plan...'

'It hardly helped, then, that you had a flaming public row with Colby on Monday evening, did it?' Ride said sarcastically.

James clearly did not like being reminded of that episode, and retaliated swiftly. 'Nor would it help our case much, Sebastian, if it came out that you were bulling Ronald Grantham's beautiful wife,' he said icily.

Ride felt his cheeks burn but otherwise he did not rise to James's cheap remark. The fact was that he had already decided to end his relationship with Faye as soon as he decently could, even though she might possibly resent his rejection and turn on him publicly.

James Woo clearly saw that he was not going to get the angry reaction that he had hoped for, so relented a little in his tone. 'Don't worry about Colby and Grantham, or indeed Harmsworth; we can easily manipulate those gentlemen in the right direction. Ogden is the only one who concerns me, for he is a law unto himself. Did you know that he is head of the British Secret Intelligence Service in the Far East? In terms of Whitehall power, he even outranks the Governor. Yet because of that, I doubt that Ogden will use his influence to stop this housing scheme. He must know that Hong Kong is in a dangerously volatile situation with so many refugees flooding in, and great unrest among the coolie population, with food riots and protests about the rising cost of living. This new housing project may help to stabilize things, so Ogden will almost certainly give it his backing...' James glanced at Ride. 'Aren't you going to say anything positive about this, Sebastian? This scheme could rescue our finances after all our problems on the mainland - especially that damned steel rolling mill of yours in Hopei Province...'

Ride decided to be conciliatory. 'Of course I will be very pleased if this plan of yours comes off, James, though I would have preferred to know about this before now. I *am* supposed to be the chairman of this company, after all,' he added sarcastically. 'And I'm just not sure how you can be so confident that you can actually win over Colby, Grantham and Harmsworth to the scheme – at least to the point of simply awarding all this construction work to us. Harmsworth in particular is likely to have something to say on that score since he runs the Hong Kong Treasury. I have met the man several times...he is a hard-nosed devil and will almost certainly want to get competitive tenders for such a massive building scheme...'

'And I've told you that it is all in hand, Sebastian,' James said smoothly. 'Now I must get back to Central and start to put the next steps in motion. My car and driver are over there just behind the quarry foreman's wooden hut...'

James started to walk away, but Ride called him back. 'James, do you know anything about two ships of ours – the *SS Corazon* and the *SS Maribeth?* It seems that the *SS Corazon* has been making a regular run from Singapore to the port of Dalian in Northern China, while the *SS Maribeth* has been delivering goods from Manila to the port of Tsingtao in the east of Shandong Province...'

James frowned. 'What sort of goods?'

'According to their manifests, medical supplies and general provisions.'

'I have never heard of either of these vessels,' James said, still frowning.

Ride studied James Woo's face for signs of deceit, but had to admit that he saw none.

'Is this of some concern to you, Sebastian?' James asked.

'Yes, it's a concern, because both ports are under the control of the Japanese. Therefore it might be that somebody is selling something illicit to the Japanese using our vessels. The Japanese are short of petroleum and rubber and many other products needed for their war effort. It would be easy for the Japanese to tranship such goods on to ports in Japan, which is just across the Yellow Sea from Tsingtao and Dalian.'

'Perhaps that's true,' James admitted. 'Yet I know nothing about it.'

His denial seemed quite convincing to Sebastian Ride. 'Then I will have to find out who has authorized these regular shipments, since it seems it was not you, and it certainly wasn't me.'

James began to walk away finally to his car. 'Then, when you find out, Sebastian, please let me know. It does sound as if something suspicious is going on...'

CHAPTER 5

Thursday, 12th August 1937

At three o'clock in the afternoon, Chief Inspector Paul Jericho of the Hong Kong Police stood at the window of his office on the fourth floor of Wanchai Police Station and contemplated the usual sunny view across the harbour. The temperature of the room was relatively comfortable because of the cooling effect of the ceiling fans that turned slowly above his head, yet through the glass he could feel the wall of volcanic afternoon heat outside, which caused the distant mountains on Kowloon side to shimmer like a mirage, and bathed the crowded Wanchai waterfront below in a fierce burnished light. He turned and sat down in his chair again, facing George Dorling who was sitting a little nervously on the other side of his desk, shuffling a file of case notes. Jericho had asked George to come up to his office and give him an update on the investigation into the deaths of Judy Wong and Dora Kam.

Jericho was glad to see that Dorling seemed to have pulled himself together in the last couple of days, so perhaps his warnings about Dorling's excessive drinking had finally got through to the man. Sitting there in his clean khaki green summer uniform, and with his webbing straps freshly cleaned and his leather pistol holster polished to a high shine, he looked much more like the old George Dorling. He was neatly shaved too and had just had his untidy crop of ginger hair trimmed to a respectable short-back-and-sides. And his face looked much healthier than even two days ago, Jericho thought, his eyes no longer bloodshot and his manner more open and relaxed again.

'How is Tess?' Jericho asked him.

Dorling looked confused for a moment. 'Err...*Tess?*'

'You told me that she'd had a fall in your bathroom on Monday morning and had hit her head on the edge of the bath. You said she'd had to go to hospital to get a nasty cut over her eye stitched,' Jericho prompted him.

Dorling swallowed hard, but looked relieved. 'Oh, you mean that... yes, she's much better. The bruising over her eye is nearly gone, and the cut is healing well. The stitches can probably come out in a few more days.'

'I'm glad to hear it,' Jericho said. 'And how is her general condition? Women can get themselves into a very depressed state after they lose a baby. It's only natural that it must hit them hard. And it was only three months ago, wasn't it?'

Dorling looked glum for a moment. 'Yes, it's only three months.' He hesitated. 'I wouldn't say that she's back to normal yet, sir, but she's bearing up. She's still very homesick, of course. Even after three years out here, she hasn't got used to this place, and certainly not enough to like it. She wants me to quit Hong Kong and go back home with her, but I've told her it's out of the question for the moment. I would probably end up on the dole if I moved back to Yorkshire, the way things are in England now,' he added ruefully.

'I see.' Jericho was beginning to understand why George had been under such strain of late, and why this had perhaps led to him hitting the bottle. But hopefully he had now got that dangerous habit in check again. 'Well, you'll just have to be patient with her, and show her as much affection and support as you can. But I know it's difficult when we work such long hours and hardly ever see our families.'

'Yes, sir,' Dorling agreed readily in his blunt Yorkshire accent. He opened his file and began spreading the papers on the desk in front of him. 'Now, with regard to the murder inquiry...I have been back to the building where Judy Wong lived, and interviewed everyone I could find in the tenement. But I haven't learned anything new about her from her neighbours, since she had only been here in Hong Kong since March and, being a northerner from Hopei Province, didn't speak Cantonese at all, which obviously limited her contacts with local people. As for Dora Kam, I have talked to people in the building where she used to live – the block where the witness who found the body, Miss Yui Pui Wah, also lives. But we discovered nothing of any note there, perhaps for the same reasons, since Dora Kam was from Shanghai and therefore a virtual foreigner to the other people in her building. I'm afraid we haven't been able to discover yet where Dora had been living for the last month after she moved out of her first lodging. I'm sure it must be somewhere in Wanchai, but we've had no response to the posters that we have put out around Wanchai and the surrounding areas.'

'That's disappointing, but not unexpected,' Jericho said. 'I still think it likely, though, that the killer is someone that these women met while working in the bar at the Tin Hau Hotel. So that's where we should still concentrate our enquiries.'

'Of course, sir. That does seem the most sensible course,' Dorling agreed. 'We know that Judy Wong worked at the Tin Hau Hotel between April and June, while Dora Kam worked there for a couple of months from May to July. Therefore, since their periods of employment overlapped a little in May and June, they must have known each other, and perhaps had many of the same clients during that time.'

'It seems logical,' Jericho agreed mildly.

Dorling nodded with an affirmative grunt. 'Yesterday, together with Constables Sung and Ho, I spent most of the day in the bar at the Tin Hau and interviewed every girl who works there, plus the hotel staff and bar manager. I asked them all if they had any particular recollections of Judy and Dora's Western clients and whether any of them might have been violent men in their opinion...'

Jericho wondered idly if Dorling had spoken to Cherry Kwok. 'Did any of them come up with anything useful about Judy and Dora?'

'No, not at all. Judy and Dora were Northerners, as you know, and the other girls apparently found them a little stuck up and unfriendly.' Dorling looked at his notes. 'Particularly an ugly little Canton girl called Minnie Tam who seemed quite pleased that these two girls had got their comeuppance.'

'Charming,' Jericho said sarcastically.

'There was however one girl who said that she was quite friendly with Dora,' Dorling went on.

'Oh, who was that?' Jericho asked, expecting it to be Cherry Kwok.

But he proved to be wrong, for Dorling came up with a surprising alternative name instead. 'This was a tall girl called Betty Lau. She looks a real scrubber – wears tight skirts and has an enormous arse that she clearly likes to show off to the men in the bar. But it seems her mother was from Shanghai so she could converse quite easily with Dora. Betty might look a tart compared to the others, but in my opinion she is probably the nicest girl in that place; she was certainly the only one of the bargirls there who had a good word for either Judy or Dora, and the only one who shed any tears for them when I talked to her. But even Betty didn't know where Dora had gone to work after leaving the Tin Hau in July. She thinks it must have been to a much smarter place, though – maybe as a dance hostess in one of the ritzy nightclubs in Central where they could pick up rich men. Dora did boast to her that she was going to make a lot more money where she was going...'

'Then you'll have to make a tour of all the Chinese nightclubs in town and see if their management knows anything of these two women,' Jericho stated flatly. 'For there has to be a possibility that Judy and Dora had left the Tin Hau to work in the same bar or nightclub. Judy might have gone there first in June, then told Dora about how much money she was making, so Dora might then have decided to follow her example a few weeks later. Both Dora Kam and Judy Wong were good-looking young women of Northern Chinese stock - tall and white-skinned and well-spoken – so they are exactly the sort of girls that these fancy Chinese nightclubs like to employ as dance hostesses.'

'In which case, our man might not be a Western seaman at all, for *they* certainly don't frequent expensive Chinese nightclubs,' Dorling commented moodily.

'No, that's true. But then the type of wealthy men who patronize these nightclubs are not usually the homicidal kind either. So, even if these women had moved to work among wealthier clients, it still seems more likely to me that their killer was someone from their past at the Tin Hau, someone who had been a client of both women, and who perhaps went in pursuit of them after they had left the bar...'

Dorling nodded, his mood apparently reviving a little. 'That certainly makes sense if Judy and Dora were friends or close acquaintances. Betty wasn't sure about that, though she says that she remembers seeing Judy and Dora talking together in the bar on a few occasions.'

'That's very good work you've accomplished so far, George.' After paying him this judicious compliment, Jericho decided that now was a suitable time to break it to Dorling that he had visited the bar himself in civvies on Tuesday night, and that he had made some enquiries of his own there. Yet he was wary that Dorling might be justifiably annoyed that his chief had gone behind his back – it did seem like an expression of low confidence in his own team, Jericho had to admit.

Yet Dorling took it surprisingly well when Jericho told him. 'That was probably a good idea, sir, pretending to be a customer. For a lot of these girls clearly don't trust the police, and might just have decided to keep their mouths shut even if they knew something that might help us.'

'Was a girl called Cherry Kwok one of those you interviewed yesterday?' Jericho asked. 'I spoke to her at some length on Tuesday night.'

Dorling consulted his file again. 'Yes, sir. Another Northerner like the two murdered women. But she denied even knowing Judy or Dora. She said that they must have left before she arrived to work in the bar.'

Jericho frowned. 'Well that's certainly not true. She told me she started at the bar in May, that she left briefly last month, and returned to the Tin Hau in August. So Cherry *must* have known Judy and Dora since they were both working in the bar in May and June at the same time as her.'

'Then perhaps you need to talk to this woman again, sir. Maybe she knows more than she's letting on.'

'It certainly seems possible,' Jericho agreed pensively. 'So I think I'll go back to the bar in civvies this evening to have another quiet word with her. Best to strike while the iron is hot...'

Dorling cleared his throat. 'I have also started looking at the case from another direction too, by making a list of overseas seamen who have been in trouble in Hong Kong over the last five years for violent or lewd conduct.'

'Must be thousands of them,' Jericho said ironically.

Dorling smiled. 'Perhaps so. But I limited my attentions to the *real* bad boys, the absolute hard cases, if you like. And I have come up with only six names which fit this bill, the kind of men who might be violent enough to strangle a woman. I'm hoping to discover that at least one or two of the bad boys on this list might have been in Hong Kong during this period from May until now, and might therefore have ventured into the bar at the Tin Hau Hotel. So I have telegraphed inquiries to the two dozen shipping companies who employ Western crews in these waters, to find out whether any of these six dangerous individuals are presently employed on any of their ships ...'

'And?' Jericho asked expectantly.

'Unfortunately there's nothing come back so far that's of any help, sir. The companies who have responded promptly say they have no records of these men. I certainly haven't found any evidence yet that any of these six hard cases have been back in Hong Kong this summer. But I will keep looking...'

Jericho was quietly pleased with Dorling's systematic approach to the investigation, so complimented him again. Yet the warmth of his commendation was as much for the fact that Dorling had apparently taken his advice over his drinking habit, as for the progress he had made with the investigation.

Dorling flushed with pleasure at this unusual level of praise from his superior. 'Thank you very much, sir. Is that all? Can I get back to work now?'

'Yes, of course.' Jericho watched as Dorling stood up, then had another thought. 'George, have you given any thought to the possibility that there might be some connection between the murder of these two women and that of the informer Ricky Sun?'

Dorling froze for a moment. 'No, sir, not at all. Why would you think there could be a connection? Ricky Sun was shot in the back of the head. That's what triads like the Kao Ki-kan usually do with people they consider traitors, so it seems an obvious case of a gangland revenge killing. On the other hand, the two women were strangled in what looks like a clear crime of passion. I have never seen a triad killing like that...in fact they very rarely murder women at all, do they...?'

Jericho was surprised by the Dorling's sudden defensiveness. 'All that is true, of course, George. But these killings did all take place in the same street, Lockhart Road, within a few weeks of each other. And if I remember rightly, Ricky Sun also came from Shanghai originally, just like the second victim, Dora Kam.'

Dorling turned to face Jericho again. 'I didn't think of that, sir. But those are just minor similarities when considered against the very different manner of these killings.'

'Just remind me again how and when Ricky Sun was killed?' Jericho persisted.

Dorling looked flustered for a moment. 'Err...he was killed late on a Saturday night, June the twelfth, in a narrow alleyway between Lockhart Road and Jaffe Road. Two shots to the back of his head in a very clinical fashion. Whoever did it made the poor bastard kneel down on the ground first...it bore all the hallmarks of a classic triad execution.'

'Yet he had been warned that Lucky Lam and the Kao Ki-kan might be on to him, hadn't he? So it's odd that he would have gone willingly into an alleyway like that, late at night. He was also carrying a Colt thirty-eight revolver in a shoulder holster under his coat, but he had the coat buttoned down, so clearly didn't realize that he was in any danger.'

'Yes, that's the way it seems, sir. But perhaps he was just getting complacent. Most of these fellows start to believe they can get away with anything, and end up paying a high price for their arrogance. I *am* sure of one thing, sir: that the names of Judy Wong and Dora Kam certainly never came up during the investigation into the murder of Ricky Sun. I would have remembered those names for certain if I had heard them before.'

Jericho sighed. 'Well you're probably right, George. I'm just clutching at straws, hoping to find a connection between these two cases...'

*

After Dorling had gone back downstairs to his own office, Superintendent Charlie Hebdon knocked on Jericho's open door just as his antique English Station clock chimed for four o'clock. 'Can I have a word, Paul?'

'Yes, of course.' Jericho wondered what was coming, for Hebdon sounded in unusually respectful mood.

Hebdon took over the seat lately vacated by George Dorling, and Jericho speculated that he might be in for another tongue lashing from his superior over the lack of progress on the case of the murdered women. But it turned out to be something else entirely – something rather closer to home.

Hebdon cleared his throat awkwardly. 'I'm afraid that I've instructed Kevin Ball to close down his investigation into the death of your wife, Paul. I think Kevin is very disappointed that he's never been able to trace the driver of the car that hit your wife that night. His theory about what happened is that the driver was most probably a young and wealthy Chinese man who might have been drinking. He was clearly driving quite fast down Kennedy Road. Yet from the evidence of the skid-marks on the road, the driver certainly stopped after he hit her, which lessens his culpability a little. Therefore Ball thinks that Susan must have been in a distracted state that evening, and perhaps walked out into the road in front of this speeding car without looking...'

Jericho knew of course that Hebdon and Ball believed that Susan had been having an affair of some sort, and had been meeting a man somewhere in the Eastern Mid-levels for a liaison that night, even though they had never come out and stated it explicitly. Jericho made no comment in response, though he was equally sure that Susan would never have betrayed him willingly.

Hebdon was still speaking. '...So it was certainly an accident.'

Jericho gritted his teeth. 'Yet the bastard then drove off again and left Susan dying on the road.'

'Yes, that was a truly evil thing to do,' Hebdon agreed uneasily. 'Yet Susan would still have died, even if the man had reported the accident immediately. Ball is convinced that the man who called the police a few minutes later was the driver of the vehicle, but that he disguised his voice using broken English so it would not be recognized. Ball thinks it likely that the man actually spoke perfect English, and is probably a member of one of Hong Kong's wealthy Chinese families. He believes that's how they managed to conceal the accident so successfully; a wealthy Chinese family would certainly have the connections to cover up for one of their own, and the resources to be able to get the vehicle repaired in secret somewhere and back on the road within a few days, or even hours. So there is little realistic chance of finding the driver of this hit-and-run vehicle now unless new witnesses come forward to give evidence.' Hebdon sucked on his brown teeth distractedly. 'But this is not likely after seven months. As a favour to you, we have kept this investigation live for much longer than would normally be the case. But I'm afraid that consideration to one of our own has to end, now that we have many more pressing cases to occupy our time, including the murder of these two young women, and the killing of Ricky Sun.'

Jericho said nothing, so Hebdon carried on, with a slight note of peevishness in his voice now at Jericho's sullen lack of response. 'I'm sure you agree with me that Kevin Ball has done everything humanly possible to find this man and see him prosecuted. I know that Inspector Ball personally checked with every repair garage in Hong Kong in an effort to find the car and the driver – even on Kowloon side. That's the measure of the man's dedication. He could perhaps have spent more time trying to find out whom Susan had been visiting that evening in Mid-levels, yet Ball doubts that would have helped with finding the driver of the car.' Hebdon shifted his gaze guiltily away from Jericho's strained face. 'Both Kevin and I thought it would be better to let those sleeping dogs lie, as a special courtesy to you, Paul...'

Jericho still said nothing, so Hebdon climbed swiftly to his feet. 'Of course, if any new witnesses do come forward, then the case will be reactivated at once. I trust that this is okay with you, Paul...it's the most we can do in the circumstances.' Hebdon adopted a more conciliatory tone. 'Perhaps it's for the best that the case is closed. It will at least give you a chance to put this tragedy finally behind you, Paul, and to get on with your life again...'

*

Four hours later, Paul Jericho was still thinking over what Hebdon had said, even though he was by now seated again in the bar in the Tin Hau Hotel with a cold beer in his hand...

The bar was a little quieter on this Thursday evening than it had been two nights earlier. But then the three destroyers of the US Asiatic Fleet had finally left harbour yesterday after their three weeks stay for a minor refit, so there was now a sudden shortage of American suitors for the bargirls of the Tin Hau Hotel.

Yet even so, three quarters of the tables were still occupied, though now mostly by foreign merchant seamen, with just a sprinkling of the lower ranks of the Royal Navy. The Royal Navy had a significant number of sailors based permanently in Hong Kong at the Admiralty Dockyard, or serving on the floating headquarters of *HMS Tamar*. And there were always some ships of the China Station in port too – sometimes a couple of the elderly light cruisers and destroyers that made up the bulk of the Far East Fleet, but more often "China gunboats", those shallow-draught vessels which were used to patrol the coast of China and up navigable Chinese rivers. Ships of the Royal Navy on this station usually had a distinctive livery of white hull and superstructure and dark funnels, and the men who served on the China Station were equally different from those who served in home waters, Jericho knew from personal experience. Many of these sailors had been in the Far East for years and were old China hands who loved the privileges and the easy life they had out here, far away from the icy grey waters of the Channel and the grimy ports of the North Sea.

Jericho sat by himself again at a table in the very corner of the room, and sipped his San Miguel beer. He had come here partly in the hope of having a further word with the evasive Cherry Kwok, but also simply because he needed a cold drink after a long, hot and tiring day. And despite his best endeavours, he was still upset by Hebdon's decision to close down the investigation into Susan's death. Not that he thought that Hebdon was being unreasonable, or that he was critical of Inspector Ball's efforts to find the driver in question; yet he truly doubted that he would be able to put this matter behind him until he had discovered the truth. Now it seemed that the truth might never be known...

He had come again in civvies tonight since he still had no wish to be identified as an off-duty policeman; he always kept a change of clothes at the station so that he could change after work without needing to go all the way back to his flat in Blue Pool Road in Happy Valley.

Despite the fact that he was the only customer here on his own, he was still not being actively solicited by any of the unoccupied girls. Perhaps his sour mood was obvious even to these bored girls, who had no wish to waste their time on an ill-tempered older man when so many younger and more cheerful sailors were still available.

The Chinese manager of the place – his hair still slicked back and his gold tooth on prominent display – circulated among the noisy sailors with the practised manner of his trade. His eye fell briefly on Jericho, alone at his table, and Jericho thought he might be about to say something. But the man moved on without a word.

The atmosphere of the bar was becoming distinctly uncomfortable with all the accumulating cigarette smoke, which the faint pink wall lamps could barely penetrate, so that the room seemed like it had been enveloped in a sickly London fog. The fancy coin-operated American gramophone was again being worked overtime tonight, but the American tunes of Tuesday night had now been superseded by songs more amenable to British tastes: *Has Anybody Seen Our Ship?* by Noël Coward and Gertrude Lawrence, *Let's Have a Tiddley at The Milk Bar*, sung by Nellie Wallace, and *When I'm Cleaning Windows*, by George Formby. For some reason, George Formby seemed to go down better with the younger British sailors than the cheery Noël Coward song about the ship, which Jericho found a little strange, for it seemed a readymade song for these navy boys.

The cast of bargirls all seemed mostly the same as on Tuesday night, with only a few missing on duty upstairs, and a few replacement faces below whom Jericho had not seen before. The hard-faced Canton girl called Minnie was here – the one who had shown no sympathy at all for her dead colleagues, Judy and Dora. And Betty Lau with her black split skirt and her enormous high heels was very much in evidence too; Jericho remembered that she had surprisingly been the only girl in this place who had been friendly with Judy and Dora.

Jericho had seen no sign of Cherry Kwok so far this evening, but it was still only 8:30 and Cherry, as he remembered from Tuesday, seemed to start work later than most of the other girls. He was just considering whether he should give up his vague notion to speak to her again and head off home for some well-deserved rest, when she appeared suddenly at his side and sat down at his table without even asking. She was wearing a cheap blue cotton dress but still managed to look quite elegant.

Jericho looked at her in surprise. 'Cherry! Hello again. Would you like a drink?'

He bought her another drink of cold tea that cost him five more dollars; this girl was proving an expensive witness...

She sipped her tea and regarded him quizzically. 'Why you come here again? I don't think you want girl.' She kept her voice low as if not wanting anyone else to overhear.

Jericho kept his voice down to a whisper as well. 'I just wanted a drink and some nice company,' he said. 'Is that so bad?'

Her eyes were hostile. 'Not bad...but not true either.' She snorted softly with derision. 'You told me you ship's captain...'

'No, *you* said that, Cherry, not me.'

She clicked her tongue with distaste. 'But you not say I wrong.'

He tried a smile. 'Perhaps I didn't want to disappoint you.'

She studied him with an unwavering eye. 'Too late for that. I very disappoint now.' Cherry ran her finger around the wet rim of her glass. 'I think you policeman.'

Jericho didn't say anything in response. There didn't seem any reason to deny it now; this girl was clearly very smart on the uptake.

'So why come again?' She repeated her demand with vigour. 'Policemen here yesterday, ask many questions about dead girls, Mee-ling and Yu-lan. You must know everything.'

'You told me that you didn't know Judy or Dora,' Jericho pointed out gently.

Cherry was unrepentant. 'I know who they are. But I not friends with them.'

'Why not? I could understand you not being friends with Dora perhaps, who is from Shanghai. But Judy – or Yu-lan as you call her - came from Hopei Province, which is next to your home province of Chahar...'

'Yes, I talk sometime with Judy. But I not like her. She too greedy. She borrow money from me, never pay back...' Cherry drummed her fingers on the table top, playing a discordant tune. 'If I answer question, will you go away for good? Leave me alone? You get me bad name here if they know you a policeman.'

Jericho nodded. 'All right, agreed. Did Judy or Dora ever tell you anything about their clients?'

'Not Dora. I never speak to Dora much. But Yu-lan - Judy – she tell me some things. She not like foreign seamens. Too rough, she say, too dirty. Bad smell...never wash.' Cherry bent down suddenly to retrieve something from the floor.

Jericho saw that it was a gold ankle chain with a clasp in the shape of a dolphin.

Cherry saw him looking at it. 'My mother gave me this. Clasp is broken a little. I must get repair. Keeps falling off my ankle...'

Jericho nodded. 'Did Judy have any regular customers apart from sailors?'

'Maybe. I not know.' Cherry hesitated. 'But I see Dora one time, in June maybe, in Hennessey Road with a Chinese man. He has expensive suit and gets out of big car. Looks like rich Shanghai man, not like coolie. They look like good friends.'

Jericho was suddenly very interested. 'What did this man look like? Was he young? Old? Fat? Thin?'

'I only saw him one time, far away. Not old; quite young. Not fat, quite thin.' Cherry studied him for a moment with a critical eye. 'Younger than you. More handsome.'

Jericho shrugged ruefully. 'That's not saying much.' He had another thought. 'What about the car? What colour was it? What make?'

'Big Yankee car, I think. Dark maybe.'

Jericho guessed that Cherry probably knew as much about cars as she knew about the life of Mahatma Ghandi, so he wasn't likely to discover much more from her in that direction. 'Judy left the bar in June, didn't she? I presume she went somewhere else to work? Do you know where she went? Was it perhaps to a Chinese nightclub with richer customers?'

'She not say,' Cherry said primly. 'But I think you right...'

*

After a few more minutes of quiet questioning, Jericho surreptitiously passed Cherry another ten dollars for her time, then let her go, to her obvious relief. He thought that he had got as much out of Cherry Kwok as he was going to, certainly tonight anyway. He still thought he would have to call her into the station eventually, though, and take a formal statement from her, for she did seem to be the most useful witness in this place, with the possible exception of Betty Lau.

Cherry had been away from the Tin Hau bar for a couple of weeks herself, and Jericho had pressed her about where she had gone to work, thinking it might even be the same place where Judy and Dora had gone. But Cherry denied this quickly; according to her, she had simply taken a few days off because she was ill with a bad case of summer flu.

It was well after ten o'clock by now, and the mood of the bar was becoming rowdier, so Jericho was finally grateful to escape from the smoke and the noise. In the hotel lobby outside, he stood for a moment sucking in breaths of cleaner air, before realizing that someone had followed him out of the bar. But it wasn't one of the bar girls, or even one of the sailor customers; it was the bar manager, Freddie Ling...

The man spoke up confidently in good English with a pronounced American accent. Jericho was no expert on American accents, yet this one sounded like it could be Californian.

'Are you an American, sir?' Ling asked smoothly. His confident manner belied the worn old dinner jacket that he was wearing, which was even threadbare around the shoulders.

'English,' Jericho admitted.

'Never mind, sir. England's a great country too. My name's Freddie Ling; I manage this bar. I used to live in San Francisco,' he said boastfully.

So Cherry had been right about him, Jericho thought: this was encouraging proof of her own reliability as a witness anyway.

Freddie Ling beckoned Jericho towards a quiet corner of the hotel lobby where there was a brass spittoon and a couple of rattan chairs under a wilting potted palm. Jericho went willingly, curious to know what this might be about. He had a feeling that Ling had not recognized him as a policeman, so it seemed he wasn't perhaps as smart as the bargirl Cherry Kwok. Ling sat down in one of the chairs and pushed the other forward for Jericho. 'I couldn't help noticing that you have visited the bar a couple of times, sir, but haven't apparently found any of the girls here to your taste. May I ask why a gentleman like you is visiting a place like this?' Ling cleared his throat with a delicate cough. 'I suppose I should not be denigrating the virtues of my own bar, but it is not designed for the likes of you, sir. I can see clearly from your suit and your manners that you are an English gentleman – a businessman or something in the government, I would guess. And if you will excuse me telling you this, there are more select private places for a gentleman like you to go if you are looking for a girl. Outside this bar, I run a little sideline business of my own where I can arrange a choice of only the highest quality escorts for discerning gentlemen clients. I can arrange everything without embarrassment. A selection of the most beautiful girls can be brought individually to your home, or to any other private address of your choosing. You can talk informally to these young ladies on these initial visits to see if any of them appeals to you. If so, that one girl could stay longer, or she could arrange to come for a further visit. Be assured that all these escort ladies are only of the most beautiful and desirable kind...with the whitest skin and the sweetest smiles and the most obliging natures...'

'These girls are all Chinese, I presume?' Jericho said neutrally, though inside he was congratulating himself that he might have hit on a useful lead by complete chance.

Ling hesitated for a moment. 'Mostly...although we also have a few very beautiful Eurasians on our books. We have some who are half-English or half-French, and even one who is half-Russian...'

Jericho wondered now whether Judy Wong or Dora Kam might have left the Tin Hau bar to work directly for Freddie Ling under such an arrangement. Perhaps their killer might not be a lowly sailor after all, but perhaps a different kind of man entirely? *Perhaps even an expat businessman or someone in the government with a taste for beautiful Chinese girls?* That was a troubling thought...

But when Jericho asked Freddie Ling whether he ever recruited any of his girls from the bar that he managed, Ling was most vociferous in his denials. 'No, sir. Absolutely not. Those girls in there may be good enough for a sailor's short time – a bit of rough pleasure - but not for the likes of a gentleman like you, sir.' Ling reached in his pocket and pulled out a business card. 'If I can be of any help to you, sir, please feel free to call this number and just tell us what you want. Either I or my secretary or my partner will answer...'

Jericho took the card while Freddie Ling stood up and excused himself with a smile and a modest glint of gold, before returning to the bar.

Jericho studied the card, which was written in both Chinese and English. There was a company name embossed in gold – the Blue Heaven Agency – and below it was Freddie Ling's name in both English and Chinese, although Jericho couldn't read the last characters of his Chinese name. The card was discreetly anonymous, without any address at all, and certainly gave no clue that the business of this agency was pimping young women.

Jericho decided that he would have to speak to Mr Freddie Ling again very soon, for something about the man had rung warning bells in his head...

*

Jericho emerged from the Tin Hau Hotel onto the Wanchai waterfront road, and began walking eastwards along his usual route home. Then he heard someone calling his name softly behind him. '*Inspector Jericho*...'

He turned and saw to his surprise that it was the beautiful witness, Miss Yiu. He realized with slight chagrin that she must have seen him leaving the Tin Hau Hotel in his civilian clothes, and wondered if she might conclude that he'd been there for his own pleasure and not for police business.

He didn't attempt to explain his reason for being in the Tin Hau Hotel, though, but contented himself with a brief smile of welcome. 'Good evening, Miss Yiu.'

She was dressed casually in a cotton blouse and a loose fitting purple skirt, yet she still managed to look willowy and elegant even in that simple garb. She stood out among all the stunted and bent Chinese coolie women on the waterfront road like a silver beacon.

'What are you doing here at this time of night?' he asked her. It was only eleven o'clock or so, but it still seemed late for a schoolteacher to be walking the streets of Wanchai alone.

'Oh, I was working late at home marking test papers, and I needed some fresh air and exercise before I turn in.' She turned and looked at the quayside, where the darkened water was still awash with the competing swells of ferries and sampans, and the humid night air filled with the chatter of Hoklo and Tanka women.

'Me too,' he agreed amiably. 'I don't mean the part about marking test papers, but I do always need some fresh air after a long day cooped up inside.' He patted his bulging stomach ruefully. 'And I definitely need more exercise, Miss Yiu...'

She laughed at that. 'There's no need to keep calling me Miss Yiu. I am known to my friends here in Hong Kong as "Maggie".'

'*Maggie*...? That's not a very Russian name. It makes you sound Scottish, like my mother...'

She smiled at that remark too. 'I hope I don't remind you of your mother in any other way,' she joked. 'My Russian birth name is Margarita Maximovna Ivanova; it was the name I used when living in the International Settlement in Shanghai. My father's name is Maxim Ivanov, you see. He lived in Shanghai before the Great War, and married my mother there, which is how I came to be born in the International Settlement. When war with Germany broke out in nineteen-fourteen, he returned alone to Russia to fight. But then the revolution erupted and destroyed the old order; my father was a White Russian and a supporter of the old regime so had to flee Russia in the early twenties and return to Shanghai. I had hardly seen him since I was a baby, so it was a struggle to get to know him again. But we managed to survive as a family until last year when my mother sadly passed away. So I made the decision then to leave Shanghai to find work. I was twenty-four by then, old enough to make my own way in the world...'

It sounded to Jericho as if she had had some sort of falling out with her father after her mother's death.

Maggie Yiu was still explaining her interesting past. 'Since I left Shanghai, I use my mother's family name, which is Yiu, and the given names she bequeathed me – Pui Wah. It certainly makes my life easier in Hong Kong to have a Chinese name rather than a Russian one, which would only arouse suspicion here. But I also use the name "Maggie" here as my English name, which is close to my Russian given name of Margarita.'

'Yet I think I should keep calling you Miss Yiu,' Jericho said regretfully. 'At least while you are still a witness in one of my cases.'

She accepted that with a rueful smile. 'All right, if you must. But once the case is over, then I hope you will call me Maggie. If we ever meet again, that is,' she added enigmatically.

That remark almost sounded like a flirtatious invitation to Jericho, yet he was too out of practice with women to take her up on it and respond in kind. The babble of noise from the quayside increased as a ferry boat landed and a mass of sinewy coolies and women in black pyjamas and conical straw hats emerged onto the stone jetty. Most of the women still wore their hair in a pigtail or queue, the hairstyle that had been forced on the Chinese by their alien Manchu rulers during previous centuries. Old habits died hard with Chinese women, it seemed, although most of their menfolk at least seemed to have abandoned the queue in favour of a cropped Western hairstyle.

'Shall we walk together a little?' he suggested. 'This is my normal way home. I live in Blue Pool Road in Happy Valley.'

She sighed. 'Ah, I wish that I did. I know that road; it's very beautiful.' Her eyes twinkled with good humour. 'Certainly more beautiful than Lockhart Road anyway.'

Jericho and Maggie Yiu began walking together along the waterfront road. Jericho was fascinated as ever by the little Chinese shops and rickety food stalls along the way, with their strange produce and smells. Even at this late hour, shoppers were still haggling over boiled chicken's feet, lotus roots, squares of bean curd, golden mangoes or flattened amber ducks.

Jericho turned to Maggie Yiu and couldn't help noticing that her eyes were long black ellipses, with the eyebrows so perfectly arched that they looked drawn. Under the light of a streetlamp, her cheekbones seemed broader than he'd noticed before, with some hint of Mongolia in them. 'Is your father still alive and well, Miss Yiu?'

She nodded. 'As far as I know. But things are very bad now in the International Settlement in Shanghai, and the foreigners there are effectively trapped by the worsening political situation in the rest of China.'

Jericho was thoughtful. 'The foreign community in Shanghai must be very worried about the Japanese aggression in the North. I wouldn't be surprised if the Japanese air force even launches attacks on Shanghai and other Chinese cities soon; there seems no end to their viciousness. I was always brought up to believe that the Japanese were a most peaceful and obliging race, but they seem to have descended into a new era of barbarism in these last few years.'

Maggie Yiu looked uncomfortable. 'Yet I believe it was the West that caused this problem in the first place, though, by forcing the Japanese to abandon their old feudal ways and become part of the modern world. Japan had been very happy living in isolation from the world for many centuries, but their country was torn apart in the last century by the arrival of Westerners and their mighty new technology. Unfortunately the Japanese have proved themselves to be only too willing and able to learn from the Western powers – particularly with regards to military prowess – and are now using their new-found power to impose themselves on the weaker nations of East Asia.'

'Yes, it seems so,' Jericho agreed.

The talk of war seemed to have upset Maggie Yiu's previously amiable mood, and she now turned to Jericho with a slight frown. 'I have to take this next turning back to Lockhart Road, so I will bid you goodnight, Inspector Jericho.'

Jericho was taken by surprise by the sudden change in her mood.

'Before you go, Miss Yiu, have you had any further thoughts about Dora Kam? Has anything else occurred to you that you never told us on Tuesday?'

Maggie shook her head forcefully. 'No, I haven't had any fresh thoughts, Inspector. Nothing else about Dora has come to mind. So I fear that I am not going to be of any further help to you at all in catching her murderer...'

CHAPTER 6

Friday, 13th August 1937

At 6:30 on the following evening, Paul Jericho was again having a drink of cold San Miguel beer after another hot and relatively unproductive day on duty at Wanchai Police Station. The venue for tonight's evening drink was however certainly a more elegant location than the bar of the Tin Hau Hotel in Wanchai. Tonight Jericho was enjoying the faded splendour of Bessie's Bar in the basement of the Hong Kong Hotel, in the very heart of Central District in Pedder Street.

The Hong Kong Hotel was a great local institution and had been the premier hotel on this island since the last century. Its impressive Victorian facade of stone Corinthian columns and arched and balustered balconies was not to everyone's taste these days, and it had lost much business lately to the impressive and fashionable new Peninsula Hotel on Kowloon side, and to the grandly situated hotel at Repulse Bay with its Lido and its afternoon tea dances. The entire North Wing of the Hong Kong Hotel had also been destroyed by fire on New Year's Day 1926 and replaced by an office building, so the diminished hotel was now reduced more or less to the size of the original building built in 1868, with its entrances onto Pedder Street and Queens Road Central.

Even though its great days were now behind it, Jericho still liked this hotel, and Bessie's Bar remained his favourite venue for meeting old friends. He raised his glass now to his companion, Ronald Grantham. 'Here's to Johnny...'

Grantham raised his own whisky and soda in return. 'Yes, Paul. To Johnny...the best brother a man ever had.'

Ronnie Grantham too was almost like a brother to Paul Jericho, for Jericho had grown up in the same house. Ronnie's father, George Grantham, a kindly Surrey solicitor and devout Quaker, had certainly been a surrogate father to Jericho after the death of his own colonial policeman father in Burma. Paul Jericho had first got to know the Grantham family when he had formed a close friendship with a fellow boarder at school, Johnny Grantham, and Johnny's family had then more or less adopted him unofficially after he was sadly orphaned. So the Grantham home in Guildford – a sprawling untidy Victorian monstrosity of a house, but also an undeniably happy one – had become the nearest thing Paul Jericho had ever had to a real home. Jericho had always remained closest to Johnny Grantham, of course, but he had also got on well with his older brother Ronnie and his three sisters, Ethel, May and Lily. The Grantham family were known for their devotion to charity work, as well for their Christian spirit generally. They were also among the handsomest families in the county of Surrey; all the family members were tall and fair with startling blue eyes. It was said by their many admirers that the younger Granthams "all had eyes as blue as the sea off the Isle of Capri", and that certainly included Ronnie too...

Ronnie excelled at sports so Jericho had always looked up to him in that respect too: Ronnie had won a blue in both rowing and rugby at Cambridge, while he had also been one of the best young rock climbers in England. It was only the fact that Ronnie had already gone out to Hong Kong to join the government service that had persuaded Paul Jericho to take the plunge and apply to join the Hong Kong Police when he was twenty-one.

Jericho reflected that it was exactly a year ago to the day since Johnny had died, killed in a train crash outside Waterloo Station in London. So it was no coincidence that Jericho had chosen to meet up with Ronnie Grantham tonight; this meeting was in the nature of a sentimental salute to the sadly departed Johnny. It was still hard for Paul Jericho to believe that Johnny was gone, even though they had seen very little of each other over the last fifteen years. After school and Cambridge, Johnny had gone on to make a glittering career for himself as a top barrister – a Kings Counsel, and one of the top criminal lawyers in England. Yet it had all ended in tragedy on a rainy August night when a signal had failed just outside Waterloo Station. The collision between the passenger train and the goods locomotive had only been a relatively minor one, but Johnny Grantham had been in the front carriage of the commuter train which had taken the brunt of the impact.

Johnny Grantham's death had been the start of a devastating personal year for Paul Jericho, of course, for only five months later he'd suffered the even worse loss of his wife Susan. Ronnie and his wife Faye had been a great help to Jericho during those first few terrible weeks of his loss in January, and he wasn't sure that he would have got through them without that emotional support...

At the age of thirty-eight Ronnie Grantham still looked so much like his brother that Jericho had to remind himself sometimes that this was not Johnny. Both brothers had always looked like overgrown choirboys, with their flaxen hair and pink complexions that never seemed to age. Jericho was uncomfortably aware that he probably looked ten years older than Ronnie Grantham now.

'How is Faye?' Jericho asked. He had seen very little of Ronnie's wife of late, though he liked her enormously, and thought her a glorious looking woman. Certainly his own wife Susan had been one of the few Western women in Hong Kong who could even compare with Faye Grantham for looks.

Ronnie shrugged. 'She's fine. Looks wonderful as always. We went to a party at Government House on Monday night, and she was the belle of the ball, as usual. Though it wasn't really a ball...more an official reception to try and lift morale among the business community.'

Jericho simply nodded. He knew that Ronnie's marriage was in reality a troubled one. It had been a surprise to everyone when a shy and socially inept young man like Ronnie had managed to win himself such a wife, for Faye was a young heiress from South Africa who had turned men's heads from the moment of her arrival in the colony. Yet somehow Ronnie had won out against all the fierce competition from the wealthy bachelors and business leaders of Hong Kong, probably because of his fresh boyish looks and his gentlemanly manners. Jericho had been his best man when Ronnie and Faye had marched together down the aisle of St John's Cathedral three years ago; everyone had said that they must be the handsomest couple in Hong Kong. Yet that fairy tale occasion hadn't led to a happy ending; even Paul Jericho knew enough to see the obvious tensions in their marriage. Faye had once confessed to Susan that she found her husband to be a little on the dull and conventional side, and it was obvious to most people that the married Faye was still happy to spread her wings and live life to the full, often leaving her staid husband languishing behind. There were even nasty rumours going the rounds that she might have been unfaithful to him, although Jericho hoped that particular piece of tittle-tattle wasn't true...

Paul Jericho had some genuine sympathy with Ronnie in this regard, for he also understood the strain of making a marriage in Hong Kong work, and especially sympathized with the problems of keeping a beautiful wife happy, who was clearly desired by a lot of ambitious and wealthy young men with few scruples. Susan too, like Faye Grantham, had been the object of many young Hong Kong bachelors' fantasies, and probably of many married men's too. Yet despite Susan's occasional propensity to flirt with handsome men, Jericho had never really doubted her, not even when confronted with the mystery of what she had been doing in Kennedy Road on the last night of her life...

Ronnie looked across the room as a small Filipino band began to tune up for their first number. A pretty Filipina girl in a long black silk dress stood a little nervously at the microphone before launching into a rendition of *Smoke Gets in Your Eyes*. Ronnie smiled across the table at Jericho. 'That girl's not bad...better than Irene Dunne anyway.'

Jericho reflected sadly that Irene Dunne had been Susan's favourite actress, and Susan had thought her wonderful in the Astaire-Rogers film *Roberta*. And the song did seem to suit the atmosphere of this room: Bessie's Bar was almost a model of late Victorian English style, with its high moulded-plaster ceiling in duck-egg blue, its fluted Corinthian columns and soft lighting, its leather armchairs and lush Areca palms in giant porcelain tubs. Giant electric fans creaked slowly overhead, relieving the stuffiness and stirring the potted palms into life.

Like his brother Johnny, Ronnie Grantham was also a lawyer by training, though lacking the personality and the skill at the bar to match his brother's stellar career as a top barrister. Ronnie had always recognized his own limitations as a lawyer so had wisely elected for a steady career instead with the colonial government in Hong Kong. Despite his lack of drive compared to his more forceful brother, Ronnie had nevertheless risen to the rank of deputy to the Attorney General of Hong Kong, which was a significant achievement for someone like him. Ronnie might even rise to the top job in time, or so he hoped.

Paul Jericho had never actually met Ronnie's boss, Julian Colby, the present Attorney General – Colby had been away on home leave at the time of Ronnie's wedding, so their paths had not even crossed then. But Ronnie had told Jericho a great deal about Colby's character in passing so Jericho did feel as if he knew the man quite intimately. Colby was only eight years or so older than Ronnie, which was a pity for Ronnie's sake, since he might have to wait another twenty years for that opportunity to replace him. Whether Faye would be happy to stay on in Hong Kong for that length of time was something that Jericho doubted however; he suspected from talking privately to her that she would prefer to return to South Africa in due course to raise a family. He worried that this basic dichotomy in Ronnie and Faye's ambitions might eventually bring all the other strains in their marriage to the fore, and might even lead to divorce in the end. Jericho had a suspicion that Ronnie's yearning to become Attorney General of Hong Kong might even trump his love for Faye, and that he might even prefer to lose her in the end, rather than give up his cherished professional dream...

Ronnie Grantham took another sip of his whisky as the gentle voice of the Filipina singer filled the room with *The Very Thought of You*. 'You look tired, Paul. I hope you're not overdoing things again.'

'Well, we've had a couple of nasty murders on my patch in Wanchai, so I am under considerable pressure to make some arrests.'

Ronnie raised a curious eyebrow. 'Oh, yes. I read that two young women have been murdered there. But I thought you spent most of your time these days on administrative work. I didn't realize that a senior officer like you still got involved in the nitty-gritty of investigative work.'

Jericho acknowledged that. 'Yes, it's true that I do far less real police work than I used to. But I am getting personally involved with this case, because we're concerned about the mood of local people if we don't catch the culprit quickly. We need to avoid any more rioting for the present; the colony is a political tinderbox at the moment, and it will only need one little spark like this to set it off.'

'Ah, so you think it's a Westerner who murdered these women?'

Jericho nodded. 'Yes, I do. Both of these women worked in a pickup bar on the Wanchai waterfront, so the obvious conclusion is that they were killed by one of their more violent customers – a Western sailor probably.'

'It sounds like you think there might be a less obvious solution too,' Ronnie suggested shrewdly.

'Yes, indeed. For these two women had recently gone somewhere else to work – perhaps to one of these fancy dance halls or restaurants in Central or in Western District. In which case, they might have encountered some much wealthier men – perhaps Chinese or even rich Europeans.'

Ronnie frowned. 'Why would a well-to-do Chinese man, or an expat for that matter, murder a couple of Wanchai bar girls? That doesn't make sense at all.'

'No, nor to me. But I can't rule out the possibility yet. Something - or someone - certainly links these two young women together. It may be the obvious fact that they worked in the same bar in Wanchai and met the same customer there. Or the connection might be somewhere else entirely, something much less obvious. If I can find that connection, then I will find the man responsible.' Jericho hesitated. 'I almost hope that the guilty party is just a violent seaman off one of the visiting ships in harbour. It will be a much nastier blow for community cohesion if the killer of these Chinese women turns out to be some privileged expat from up in Mid-levels somewhere.'

Ronnie smiled uneasily. 'Either way, I wouldn't like to be that man with you after him. Because I know you, Paul...*you're a devil for the chase when you're on somebody's tail*...' Then he laughed self-consciously. 'I'm afraid I'm not going to be able to stay long tonight, Paul. There's a bit of a security flap going on at Government House, and our intelligence chief Ralph Ogden has called all the senior staff back for a briefing at eight o'clock. It's probably just another of Ogden's silly panics – the man seems to think that the Japs will invade Hong Kong at any moment. But I suppose I will have to go and listen to what he says...'

*

At 7pm, Edith Starling sat at her own desk in the suite of rooms in the annexe building at the rear of Government House that served as the government communications centre. Her own room was a tiny windowless cubicle packed with shelves of paper files and storage boxes. Her method of filing was unconventional to say the least, and no one else could ever have found a particular document on these dusty shelves. Yet Edith had perfect recall of her system, and could go to any report or intercepted signal with unerring accuracy.

The last three days had been hellish ones for Edith as she had tried to find some new way to decipher a fresh influx of coded signals between the Japanese War Ministry and their Kwantung Army headquarters in Northern China. She had spent fifteen hours a day locked away here in her office as she engaged in her titanic struggle to wrest some meaning from these signals. But the Japanese were now super-enciphering every message, so there was little chance of being able to decode them with her present technique. The only feasible way would be if she could find a "crib" of some sort – that is, a clue which would help determine the plain text of some of the simpler messages. These could then be used as a key to get into the more complex messages. But after three days of trying, Edith had not been able to find any useful cribs; it seemed the Japanese were being ultra-cautious at present as if they couldn't risk the British getting any whiff of what military activities they were planning next against the Chinese.

She and Ralph Ogden had discussed the obvious conclusion from this: that the Japanese really did have an informer somewhere at a high level in the British establishment who had given them the nod that their own signals were vulnerable and that their coding method needed enhancing for reasons of security. Yet Edith still hoped desperately that the leak wasn't somewhere here in Government House, despite what the British embassy in Tokyo had suggested.

Edith heard footsteps in the corridor outside her room, and then the voices of two men. The two men were speaking in little more than a whisper so had to be discussing something sensitive. One of the voices sounded like Ralph Ogden's, but she didn't recognize the other. Edith couldn't restrain her curiosity any further, so got up from her swivel chair and poked her head out into the corridor.

Edith saw immediately that she had been right, for Ogden was indeed one of the men hunched in quiet conversation over the water cooler outside his own office. Edith also belatedly recognized the other man with Ogden too: this was the Commissioner of Police, Gregory Matlock, the head of the entire police force in Hong Kong. Although the SIS had little dealings with the regular criminal police force, they did cooperate with the Special Branch of the Hong Kong Police, who were given such routine tasks as monitoring known political dissidents and activists in Hong Kong, but who were also called upon from time to time to assist with keeping a watch on known spies and informants, and making arrests of suspects when needed.

Ogden looked up and saw Edith at the door of her room. 'Ah, Edith. I think you've met Commissioner Matlock before, haven't you?'

Edith joined them at the water cooler. 'Yes, Ralph, I have.'

Matlock looked a little surprised that Edith should address the stately Ralph Ogden by his Christian name, but then he, in common with the senior civil servants at Government House, was unaware of Edith's true role in this communications centre. Matlock also believed her to be a mere secretary, though he was friendly enough in his bluff superior masculine way.

'Miss Starling...how are you? *Well*, I hope...?' Matlock acknowledged her with a friendly smile. For such a senior policeman, Matlock had been a surprise to her. For one thing he was very young for such a role – in his early forties at most – and for another, he seemed a very cultured and well-educated man. Edith imagined that was why he and Ogden seemed to get on so well together. Matlock certainly made a contrast with another senior policeman whom Edith encountered occasionally - Chief Superintendent of Police Charlie Hebdon. Hebdon was much more what Edith had expected of a colonial policeman: solid, dour and as hard as nails. Hebdon's Rochdale accent was certainly an assault on the ears, and his rough reddened face always seemed to Edith to be on the point of exploding with some inner fury.

Matlock was by comparison a wealthy southerner; his BBC announcer accent and his urbane manners suggested an affluent background in the Home Counties somewhere. Edith had speculated that Hebdon probably found it very distressing that his superior should be so much younger and better spoken than himself. No doubt Hebdon dismissed his boss as a lightweight – a posh boy of the establishment - yet Edith had a shrewd suspicion that Matlock was much tougher and more perceptive than he looked.

Edith started to back away from the two men. 'It seems you have something private to discuss so I don't want to interrupt you two gentlemen.'

Matlock smiled at her again. 'No, not at all, Miss Starling.' He glanced meaningfully at Ogden. 'I think we were just about finished, weren't we, Ralph?'

Ogden nodded. 'Yes, I believe we were, Greg.'

Matlock took his leave with another charming smile aimed in Edith's direction.

Ogden watched Matlock striding away down the corridor with a muted smile of his own. 'It seems you've made a conquest there, Edith.'

'Yet according to Dorothy Parker, *"men seldom make passes at girls who wear glasses*",' Edith said primly, adjusting her own specs with exaggerated effect as she did so.

'Well, you've just proved that particular *bon mot* wrong,' Ogden laughed.

Edith felt like quoting another line of Dorothy Parker to her chief, something just as pertinent: "*Scratch a lover, and find a foe...*" But in the end Edith thought better of saying it out loud, for it was perhaps a little too close to her own dangerous situation.

Ogden however was not similarly constrained by any tact. 'You could do much worse than Greg Matlock, you know, young Edith. He's very well thought of. And still quite young despite being a widower. He lost his pretty young wife to cholera last year, you know.'

Edith shrugged uneasily. 'I didn't know.' She wondered again if Ogden knew about her and Michael Yip – he was an astute old bugger, after all – and was again warning her off such a dangerous liaison. She had to admit to herself that Commissioner Matlock was certainly a much safer target for her to aim at, yet, despite his obvious charm, the truth was that the man left her cold.

Ogden took out a cotton handkerchief from his pocket and mopped his balding head, which was glistening with sweat in the humid heat of the corridor. He beckoned her inside his own office where he shut the door behind them firmly, then sat down at his desk.

'What was Matlock here to tell you, Ralph?' Edith asked as she sat down opposite him.

Ogden held up a hand. 'Don't worry. It was nothing to do with our security problem, if that's what you think. Only you and I so far know about this disturbing leak of ours.' He relaxed back in his comfortable chair, looking more like an ageing Cambridge professor of classics than ever. 'No...Matlock came to tell me that that the murderer of these two prostitutes in Wanchai may be a Western man. According to Superintendent Charlie Hebdon, who is in charge of the case, it may even be a well-to-do expatriate who is responsible, rather than a common sailor. That's what his team of detectives tell him.'

'Why did Matlock come to tell you this? It's none of our business, is it?'

Ogden ran a finger along his sagging jaw line. 'Matlock likes to keep me informed just in case any of his cases might impinge on some of our own intelligence work. Though I doubt that these murders can have anything to do with this network of Japanese agents operating in Hong Kong, which is my main concern...'

As she listened to him, Edith studied Ogden's face with some fresh concern. He was looking quite ill this evening, as if all the pressure of recent events was taking a hard physical toll on him. His sallow complexion had always looked unhealthy, but tonight his face didn't look merely unhealthy, but gaunt and cadaverous. He certainly looked worryingly older than his fifty-three years...

But she decided to say nothing personal on the subject of his health; there was no point in rubbing salt into his wound. Ogden must know well enough by himself that he was not a well man. 'Have you come to any final conclusions yet about this leak of information?' she asked him warily.

'Yes, perhaps I *have* got to the truth...though I scarcely want to believe it.' Ogden seemed visibly shaken for a moment by his own bleak statement, and had to collect his suddenly disordered thoughts. 'That's partly why I've called everyone to this briefing at eight o'clock.'

'Have you invited ABC to this meeting?' Edith wanted to know. Her SIS colleagues - Adam, Broadbent and Casaubon – did not usually mix with the ordinary colonial officials of Government House, but kept a very low profile for security reasons. Edith and Ralph were the only SIS staff who had any regular contact with the ordinary civil servants at Government House, and Edith was only allowed that slight dispensation through the pretence of her being a mere secretary.

Ogden frowned. 'No, I don't think it's necessary for Adam, Broadbent and Casaubon to be there; this briefing is intended more for the general staff at Government House. I want to give everyone a warning about tightening up on security. There are far too many important papers being left lying around for anyone to see. We have got into some very lax habits in Government House, and we need to change those habits quickly.'

'So you *do* think this security leak is coming from someone inside Government House?'

Ogden sighed heavily. 'Yes, Edith, I'm afraid I do.'

Edith gasped. 'Then who do you think it is?'

Ogden looked solemn. 'I can't divulge that even to you at this stage, Edith, not without proper proof. Just be aware that I have set a little trap for our likely man. I have released a tempting snippet of information about the China Fleet solely to this individual – details of a new piece of sounding equipment that the navy is testing. This information is not correct by the way, but should it come to the ears of the Japanese War Ministry in this precise form, then I will know for sure that I am right. I am waiting to hear from our Tokyo embassy whether our informant inside the War Ministry, the *Hyōbu-shō,* has heard anything of this carefully salted secret.'

'Do Adam, Broadbent and Casaubon know about this trap you've set?' Edith asked.

Ogden seemed curiously reluctant to answer that question, so Edith had to wonder why. *Did Ralph suspect that the leak might be coming from one of his own senior SIS men?* That scarcely seemed possible...

Ogden finally spoke up. 'No, they don't know about this. Only you and I know, Edith.'

'What will you do if you find out that you're right?' Edith pressed him.

'We'll have to decide that when the time comes. But probably it would be too risky not to take the man into custody immediately before he does even more damage. Yet I'm not looking forward to it.' Ogden grimaced. 'I hate this damned spying business, you know. I was much happier when I was on the Somme twenty years ago as a mere army captain. That was vicious and bloody all-out war, without much honour attached to it, yet it was still preferable to this miserable game of deceit and counter-deceit that we engage in here...'

*

At a quarter to eight, Edith made her way along the covered walkway that led from the annexe building into the rear entrance of the main part of Government House, then down a corridor to the main entrance hall at the front of the building. She went along to the door of the main drawing room, where she had been told that tonight's security briefing was to be held. But the room was entirely empty, so she stood at the doorway in confusion for a moment, wondering whether she had got the time or the venue wrong. Or perhaps both...

Then, with a feeling of disbelief, she caught a glimpse of a shoe sticking out from behind the leg of the elegant sofa facing the fireplace. The sofa was a Louis XVI revival piece, upholstered in heavy embossed pink fabric, so that the black leather shoe projecting underneath it was hard to miss.

Edith ran over to the sofa and saw that it was Ralph Ogden lying face down on the Persian carpet; he must have been sitting on the sofa preparing himself for the meeting, when he'd collapsed suddenly onto the floor. She took his left arm and felt for a pulse, but there was none, not even a flicker. Trying to control her growing panic, she turned his bulky body over with an effort onto his back. Then she took out her compact mirror from her bag and put it underneath his nose, hoping to see a sign of breath.

But in her heart she already that knew it was too late for Ralph Ogden...

*

Julian Colby was the first person to appear at the door of the drawing room. He recoiled with shock when he saw a white-faced Edith holding Ogden's hand. 'My God! What's happened, Miss Starling?'

'Heart attack, I think,' Edith said numbly. 'Could you make an emergency call for a doctor, Mr Colby? I think it's probably too late to save him, but we should still call a doctor.'

Colby ran a hand over his bristly skull. 'Of course. I'll do it at once,' he said, before departing hurriedly to use the telephone in the administration office.

Edith continued to hold Ralph's hand, with a tear now trickling down her cheek. Yet even in that distraught state, she still couldn't help noticing that there were some slight marks of bruising on Ralph's windpipe. In her fevered imagination, they almost looked to her like the impressed marks of stubby fingers, except that the pattern of circular blue-black bruises was broken at one point by an odd gap.

For a moment a chill suspicion entered her mind, but she quickly dismissed it. Ralph must have made these marks of bruising himself, clutching at his throat with his own fingers as he collapsed. Ralph himself had told her many times that he had a bad heart, after all, and she knew from personal knowledge that he had suffered a severe attack of angina only weeks before, which had put him in hospital for several days.

The handsome young face of Ian Luff appeared next at the door of the drawing room, and Edith had to go through the same explanation with him. Luff looked as shocked as Colby had been, but seemed more in control of himself, and certainly a more useful man in an emergency.

'I have some knowledge of first aid,' he told Edith, 'despite being an economist by training. Do you want to stand back so I can have a look at him?'

Edith apologized profusely and climbed quickly to her feet. 'Of course, Ian. I should have remembered that you are one of the designated first aiders in the building.'

Then she watched with surprise while Luff began applying external compressions to Ogden's chest - fierce and rapid blows with his fists, trying to get his heart pumping again. Edith had never seen anyone do anything like that before – it seemed incredibly violent to her, enough force to crack a rib - but she assumed that Ian Luff must be more up to date with the latest techniques of resuscitation than she was herself.

She became aware that more people had begun arriving for the meeting, including Bob Harmsworth and Ronnie Grantham, who formed a small shocked audience with her as they watched Ian Luff's frantic efforts to revive the stricken Ralph Ogden.

Colby eventually returned too and announced bleakly that an ambulance was on its way, and would be here within five minutes. But Ian Luff finally desisted with his efforts and looked up with a weary sigh of frustration. 'I don't think there's any need for them to hurry now, Julian,' he announced bleakly...

CHAPTER 7

Saturday, 14th August 1937

At ten o'clock on another steamy and enervating Hong Kong morning, Sebastian Ride was at his desk on the top floor of the Saunders Building in Queens Road Central. It was a Saturday, but then he normally worked every Saturday morning as a matter of course. He was dressed impeccably as always in a fine lightweight tropical suit, and knew that he looked extremely well for his forty-one years – tanned, fit and still youthful. The mirror on the wall opposite confirmed that; Ride was not a particularly vain man, yet he was usually satisfied with the way he looked. But inside he felt somewhat different from that confident good-looking man in the glass – increasingly gnawed at by self-doubts and beset with worries.

His major concern at present was for Gloria, of course. He had now hired a full time Chinese nurse – a middle-aged and severe-looking woman called Doris Chow – to look after Gloria's health, and to keep her away from drink. The no-nonsense Miss Chow had been recommended to Sebastian by a compliant doctor friend who understood the problem with Gloria and what must be done to wean her off her dependency. Ride couldn't look much further than that with Gloria at the moment, although it seemed highly unlikely that their marriage could survive in the long term even if he managed to sort out Gloria's problem with drink. That problem was after all only a symptom of a much deeper malaise that existed between them.

Ride had however made up his mind to end his relationship with Faye Grantham. Faye was a wonderful woman, yet the possible dire repercussions of their affair being made public simply outweighed the benefits of continuing his liaison with her, considerable though they were. If he could have regained his freedom quickly by divorcing Gloria without too much distress on both sides, then he might have tried to persuade Faye to leave her husband and throw her lot in with him. Yet that was clearly impossible for the foreseeable future, when Gloria's sanity seemed to be hanging by only a thread, therefore he had decided that, with regard to Faye, it was better to simply cut and run...

A noise from the street below – the honking horn of a motor car and a squeal of brakes - brought his attention back to the present, and made him stretch his neck to look out of the window into Queens Road Central. A taxi – a big American Plymouth – had nudged the wheel of a rickshaw and turned the little painted wooden vehicle over, sending its occupant, a young Chinese man in a cream sharkskin suit, flying across the cobbles. In the usual way of Hong Kong street accidents, a crowd of locals had assembled on the scene as if by magic, and the street was instantly turned into an Oriental theatre of mayhem and confusion. Ride could see the incident was a trivial one, though, and would soon be sorted out after much shouting and shoving, so he quickly closed the window to shut out the jabbering voices from below.

He turned to find Frances Leung, neatly attired as ever in her formal woman's pinstripe suit, regarding him quizzically as she placed a cup of green tea on the desk for him. Frances didn't even bother to ask about what had happened in the street below, for she was an expert at remaining detached from the trivia of life.

Ride thanked her for the tea. Then he looked at the sheaf of papers she had also brought with her. 'So, what's the latest news about the steel rolling mill in Hopei province? I hope you're going to tell me that Chiang Kia-shek has mounted a massive counterattack against the Japanese Kwantung Army and forced them out of Hopei province?' he asked sarcastically.

Frances seemed unsure whether he was joking or not, and looked uneasy for a moment. 'I'm afraid not. The steel plant is already in Japanese hands, so I fear there will be no quick resolution of this problem.'

'Nor are we likely to see any compensation from the Japanese government for them seizing a major industrial asset from our company,' Ride said bitterly.

The unruffled Frances tried to be positive as always. 'Yet we might be able to recover some of the four million Hong Kong dollars from our London insurers. I have just been looking at the wording of our policy in cases of *force majeure*, and I believe we have a very good case to claim at least seventy-five percent of the money.' A look of quiet pride transformed her face for a moment. 'I drafted the precise wording myself to allow for such a possibility as this, since it seemed possible to me that the location of the plant would perhaps be vulnerable to hostile Japanese incursions.'

'That will be wonderful if it's true,' Ride said gratefully. 'What would I do without you, Frances?'

Frances remained apparently unmoved by this praise but Ride thought he could detect a faint sign of pleasure in her placid expression. She turned and walked over to the shelves that occupied one entire wall of the office, and stood on tiptoes to reach a document on the highest shelf. As her skirt rose a few inches above her knee, Ride couldn't help noticing that her thighs were surprisingly shapely and well-developed.

She returned with the file that she had been looking for. 'This is the report I've prepared on this social housing program for the homeless in Hong Kong. I meant to give it to you last night, but you had gone home by the time I finished it, so I left it on the top shelf.'

Ride hadn't gone home until eleven last night, so knew that Frances must have been working on her report until the early hours. Yet she looked as fresh and perfectly turned out as ever. 'So tell me, is it true what James told me? That the government is really planning to spend nearly thirty million dollars of its reserves on this scheme to house Hong Kong's homeless refugees and new arrivals?'

Frances was blinded for a moment by a shaft of sunlight issuing through the office window so Ride leaned back in his chair and hastily pulled down the French blind behind him to shade her face. It gave him the opportunity to study again the strong sculpted lines of her face, which were very striking when combined with her shining black hair and her golden skin. In some lights she did look remarkably European – almost like a Spaniard or a Greek...

Frances gave him a nod of thanks for his consideration. 'It is most certainly true, Mr Ride. Since you told me about it three days ago, I have made strenuous enquiries with all my own contacts in Government House and elsewhere to confirm this.' Frances looked a little downcast. 'I must apologize for not knowing about this much earlier, but it seems that Mr Woo has access to a much better source in the government than I do. Everything he told you seems to be correct: the plans for this housing are well advanced, and four potential sites have been identified for up to twenty-five thousand dwellings on each, including our former quarry in Shaukeiwan, and these three other major sites that we recently purchased on Kowloon side - in Sham Shui Po, Yau Ma Tei and Lai Chi Kok...'

'Do you have any idea who this inside man of Mr Woo's is?' Ride interrupted peevishly. 'I might have a lot more confidence in this scheme if I knew who the hell this man was.'

'Won't Mr Woo tell you?' Frances asked in surprise, before her face fell. 'No, I suppose not.' She hesitated for a moment and looked as if she was about to reveal some deep dark secret. 'I trust that you understand why Mr Woo has been promoting this scheme so assiduously, Mr Ride...and in complete secrecy from you. He is trying to prove to his father – and perhaps also to our investors – that he is a more capable man at the helm than you. I am sure that Mr Woo wants you out of this company completely so that he can be undisputed chairman of Saunders-Woo.'

Ride grimaced. 'Yes, of course I know. But he'll need more than this building scheme to persuade his father and our shareholders to ditch me. I might now have the black mark of that steel mill in Hopei against me, Frances, yet my record of financial successes over the last five years is unmatched in this city...' Ride saw that a look of doubt had flickered briefly across Frances's face. 'What is it, Frances? Is James up to something else that you haven't told me about?'

Frances eased herself down onto the seat opposite him, which surprised Ride immensely, for she was always unfailingly proper in her behaviour in the office and rarely sat down in his presence without being invited. But now she looked almost furtive as she leaned across the desk and lowered her voice to a whisper. 'I think he may well be up to something to try and discredit you, Mr Ride.'

Ride was becoming quite concerned by her unusual manner, which suggested something alarming. 'Why? What have you found out?'

'You remember those two vessels of ours, the *SS Corazon* and the *SS Maribeth?*

Ride nodded. 'Yes, of course. The *Corazon* has been making this regular run since March from Singapore to the port of Dalian in Northern China, while the *Maribeth* has apparently been delivering goods since May from Manila to the port of Tsingtao in the east of Shandong Province...'

Frances looked grave. 'Well, I telegraphed our shipping offices in Manila and Singapore to request original copies of the manifests for these voyages. And it seems the documents I showed you before were all complete forgeries...'

'You mean the ships weren't carrying medical supplies and general provisions?'

Frances bit her bottom lip until it turned white. 'No, they weren't. Both ships had been converted in Singapore last year from general cargo vessels into tankers.'

Ride gasped. 'You mean they were shipping *oil* to the Japanese?'

'Actually marine grade gasoline...which is possibly even worse,' Frances added lamely.

Ride shook his head in disgust. 'So Saunders-Woo has probably been supplying the Japanese Navy in the Yellow Sea with the fuel to deliver military supplies to their army invading China...'

Frances sat back in her chair. 'It seems so...yet I'm afraid it gets worse.'

'How could it possibly get worse?' Ride muttered in exasperation. He knew that they would be in serious trouble as a company if their Chinese investors discovered what had been going on. Ride calmed himself with an effort. 'We need to find out who authorized the conversion of these two vessels to tankers, and then permitted the sale of this gasoline. And if it turns out to be James, I will hang him out to dry, even if he is the son of my oldest friend...'

'It wasn't Mr Woo,' Frances declared. 'At least it's not his signature on the letter that authorized these shipments of gasoline anyway.'

'Then whose it it?' Ride demanded hotly.

Frances took a long breath. 'I'm afraid that it's *your* signature, Mr Ride...'

*

'They are forgeries, Frances,' Ride maintained stubbornly. His mind was still racing as he tried to think how this could have happened.

'Of course they are,' she agreed coolly. 'I have no doubt of that; you would never have sanctioned the sale of gasoline to the Japanese, even though you were in Singapore and Manila in March on business when this letter was apparently signed by you. But I think this forged letter could only have been manufactured with Mr Woo's connivance; he must have paid someone in our Singapore and Manila offices to arrange it. Your signature is not difficult to forge; I had to do it once myself, if you remember, when you had forgotten to sign that building contract in Macau before going on holiday, and our client was screaming for a signed copy to be posted to them.'

'Yes, I remember,' Ride said soberly. He smiled half-heartedly. 'I suppose I should have tried to develop a more mature and less childish signature by now.'

'Your writing is very beautiful, Mr Ride – a perfect copperplate hand,' Frances mumbled awkwardly.

Ride grunted with derision. 'But apparently very easy to copy.' He climbed rapidly to his feet as he came to a decision.

Frances too had leapt to her feet, and stood there expectantly. 'What are you going to do?' she asked nervously. 'Have it out with him now?'

Ride nodded. 'I am. He's here in the building today, isn't he? I heard his voice earlier coming from his office.'

'Yes, I saw him in there a few minutes ago.' Frances hesitated. 'He might be gone by now, though. He only comes in on Saturdays to look at any urgent mail.'

Ride didn't say another word but marched out of his office and along the Edwardian wood-panelled corridor to James Woo's office, which was on the far corner of the building from his own office. But James wasn't there, and the only indication of his recent presence was a cup of half-drunk green tea which was still steaming gently on his antique mahogany pedestal desk.

Ride went to the corner window, which had a panoramic view along both Queens Road West and down Pedder Street to the harbour. He spotted James in Pedder Street almost immediately; he was just getting into a bright red rickshaw outside the entrance of the Hong Kong Hotel. The rickshaw coolie set off at a brisk trot, turning right into Queens Road and heading west into the Chinese part of town.

Sebastian Ride wasn't prepared to leave this matter until Monday morning, so quickly retraced his steps into the corridor, then ran for the main staircase.

Frances looked at him in astonishment as he passed her. 'Where are you going, Mr Ride?'

Ride stopped in his tracks and made a vague gesture towards the nearest window. 'I'm going to follow James and have this out with him right now...'

Frances suddenly took his hand and squeezed it, something she had never done before in all the years that she had worked for him. 'Be careful, Mr Ride. Don't do anything rash...'

*

Mrs Adela Marr had lived in the same grand house on Caine Road since she was a child. She had the *grande dame* looks to match her wonderful Victorian colonial mansion, and was still a handsome and determined-looking woman even at the age of seventy-five. She also had a wonderful memory so Paul Jericho was getting an unexpected history lesson on this hot August morning.

'You know, Chief Inspector Jericho, I grew up here as a girl in the 'sixties of the last century, so I met nearly all the great men who founded Hong Kong. My father was very well connected here - he was Chief Medical Officer to the government - so most of these great men came to our house at one time or another. The Taipan of the Noble House itself – William Keswick - certainly came here many times and sat in this very room; he was a great-nephew of William Jardine who founded Jardine and Matheson, and who had fought an endless business war against his great rival taipans of Dent and Company. The Keswick family still run Jardine-Matheson to this day...

'Then there was Robert Ho-tung, who joined Jardine and Matheson as a lowly young shipping clerk sixty years ago and became the comprador of the company in time, and the wealthiest man in Hong Kong. I remember as a young girl that I thought him very handsome for a Eurasian. He eventually married into the firm to seal his position there. However his first wife, Margaret Maclean – the half-Chinese daughter of one of the Scottish directors of the company - was barren so he simply took a second, Lady Clara, who bore him ten children.' She laughed at that. 'Robert is still going strong of course at his grand house on the Peak, and now has a knighthood to show for his efforts...he is now a very great man indeed...'

Jericho tried to get Mrs Marr back to the real point of his visit, but she was in full flow now. '...There was also Paul Chater, a rather aggressive Armenian, who came to Hong Kong in 'sixty-four at the age of eighteen and had made a fortune as an exchange and bullion broker within ten years.

I didn't like the look of Chater much; he looked a bit of a rogue. But the Scotsman Douglas Lapraik was a kind man: he had come to Hong Kong in the 'forties as a mere watchmaker's assistant, but by the time I met him as a little girl, he owned docks, his own shipping company - the Douglas Steamship Company, and a Gothic baronial mansion overlooking the sea at Pok Fu Lam...'

Mrs Marr looked out of the window of her house on Caine Road and sighed. 'All the old Hong Kong is nearly gone now, of course. I remember when I could see the Praya from this very window, before all these ugly modern buildings were built below to block my view. As a girl I could see Matheson's Point from here, with its original slipway and workshops, and the rake-masted opium clippers, junks and sampans moored along the harbour wall...'

Jericho had learned enough about Mrs Adela Marr's further personal history to know that she had been widowed at forty without any children, so had then thrown all her energies into the daunting task of bringing some sort of education to Chinese girls. At the age of forty-five she had helped found the first girl's school in Hong Kong, so was very widely respected by both the British and the Chinese communities.

Jericho had found himself visiting Mrs Marr on this Saturday morning more or less by accident. He had been to Central Police Headquarters at eight o'clock this morning to speak to Inspector Kevin Ball about the Ricky Sun investigation, and had run into Commissioner of Police Gregory Matlock as he was leaving Ball's office.

Matlock had told him of a sad and unexpected death that had taken place at Government House last night, and Jericho had been taken aback to learn that the dead man was Ralph Ogden, the very man whom Jericho had been discussing with Ronnie Grantham last night in Bessie's Bar. But the death seemed an entirely natural one so Matlock wasn't too concerned about investigating it.

Matlock had been concerned, though, about a personal inquiry addressed to him by letter from the well-known Mrs Adela Marr, who claimed that there seemed to be some sinister goings-on in the large old house next to hers up in Caine Road. Caine Road was one of the oldest and most prestigious addresses in the lower Mid-levels, since it was situated near Government House and the Botanical Gardens. Jericho knew Mrs Marr of course as the founder of the school where Susan had worked - St Stephen's College – so had offered to go and speak with this lady in person and see what was troubling her.

He had taken the opportunity for some exercise to walk up to Mid-levels from Central despite the intense humid heat that soon left his police uniform shirt dripping with sweat. The effort was worth it, though, for the views that he saw on the way. The bustling Praya could still be glimpsed from Caine Road despite all the new buildings: rows of moored steamers, ferries, junks and sampans bobbing at anchor in the turquoise swell. In the other direction, the soaring granite Peak was a striking and ever constant presence, rising up against the intense tropical blue of the morning sky. The arrival of each steamship in Hong Kong harbour was no longer sounded with the firing of a gun and the hoisting of the Union flag as in the old days of the first taipans of Hong Kong, but the famous Noonday Gun was still fired every day as a reminder of those wild pioneering days of the first British merchant adventurers who had settled here...

Now, seated in the main drawing room of Mrs Adela Marr's elegant old mansion, Jericho sipped a cup of green tea and tried to discover what was troubling her so much that she should write a letter to the Commissioner of Police. 'You mentioned in your letter something sinister going on in the next house?' he prompted her.

Mrs Marr collected her thoughts. 'Well, perhaps "sinister" might be overstating the case. Nevertheless something disturbing is certainly going on there.' She stood up. 'Perhaps we should go outside in the garden and have a peek over the wall at this house, Inspector?'

Jericho readily agreed to that, and followed the old lady as she wandered through the house to the conservatory at the rear. The house had been preserved almost exactly as Mrs Marr's father had built it eighty years ago – like an informal museum dedicated lovingly to Victorian style. Soon they were in the garden where palm trees and exotic shrubs vied for space with colourful tropical climbers and dripping ferns. Jericho could see the roof of Government House from here, and below that, the beautiful pale cream stone façade of St John's Cathedral.

Peering over the garden wall, Jericho saw that the house next door was a similarly magnificent old colonial mansion, with ivy-covered walls and balconied windows with beautiful wrought-iron balustrading. The house had a certain look of Portugal about its architecture, like many old and decaying mansions in Macau, and did seem like some transplanted Gothic-styled Bishop's Palace that belonged more in Lisbon or Granada than here in the Far East. The roof looked more Chinese, though, with its porcelain tiles and its stylized dragon profile, which he knew was supposed to halt the approach of any malevolent spirits.

Mrs Marr pointed over the wall. 'No one is living permanently in the house any more, though a group of Chinese servants comes every day to clean and air the rooms.'

Jericho sighed as he began to think that he had wasted his time coming here. 'Then it doesn't sound as if anything too terrible could be going on there. Do you know who owns the house?'

Mrs Marr nodded. 'It used to be owned by Mr Woo Man Lo, though I'm not sure if he still owns it. As far as I know, the members of the Woo

Family now live in a new mansion up in Po Shan Road...' – she glanced up at the Peak far above – '...and in another grand mansion at Repulse Bay that resembles an Italian Renaissance palace.'

'Then I suppose you must mean *the* Woo Man Lo, the owner of Saunders-Woo.' Jericho knew that Saunders-Woo was still one of the wealthiest trading companies in the colony, with assets almost as large as Jardine-Matheson or the Hong Kong Bank. Jericho had also met both Mr Woo Man Lo and his son James after he had gone in person to investigate the report of a burglary at their family house in Po Shan Road last summer. The case had been a simple one: one of the houseboys had gone bad and had let a gang of his accomplices in one night to ransack the place. But Jericho had soon caught the gang and recovered the stolen family treasures, and earned both the gratitude of the Woo family and even the personal praise of Commissioner Matlock for his quick response.

Mrs Marr smiled. 'I *do* mean that Mr Woo Man Lo, of course.' Jericho noticed in the brilliant green light in the garden that Mrs Marr's face seemed ten years younger than inside, with her silver hair as thick and lustrous as a gull's feathers, and her eyes a startling shade of blue that seemed completely undimmed by time.

Mrs Adela Marr continued in her penetrating head-teacher English voice; she might have lived in Hong Kong her whole life but her accent seemed nevertheless to have been manufactured somewhere in Surrey or Berkshire. 'Yet I haven't seen any "For Sale" signs so one must assume that the Woo family still owns it. But I wonder if Mr Woo Man Lo knows what's going on here in his beautiful old house.'

'What *is* going on here, in your opinion?' Jericho interrupted.

Mrs Marr lifted her determined jaw. 'I would say that unsavoury and disreputable parties are being held here.' She hesitated. 'Not every night of course, but perhaps once or twice a month. My sleep has been disturbed regularly by the noise going on late into the night: raucous and unseemly laughter, loud jazz music and even the squeals and cries of vulgar young women. I haven't been able to catch sight of these people arriving or leaving, but they sound a wild crowd. I cannot believe that Mr Woo Man Lo knows what disreputable things are going on in his fine old house, for he is a devout Catholic after all.'

Yet Jericho remembered from his investigation of the burglary at their mansion last year that James Woo was nothing like his sober father, and had a reputation as a playboy and a womanizer. So he had little doubt of the likely origin of these wild parties; it was probable that James Woo liked to entertain his wilder friends safely away from the critical eyes of his conservative father. But he didn't say any of this theory directly to Mrs Marr, who might be shocked at such salacious behaviour in the Woo family. All he did say was: 'Then I promise to look into this, Mrs Marr, and see what I can do to ensure that your sleep is not disturbed in future.'

Mrs Marr inclined her head with regal forbearance. 'Then I would be most obliged, Chief Inspector Jericho.' She led him back to the rear of her own house where an elderly amah, almost as old as Mrs Marr herself, waited patiently for her mistress, then helped her mount the steps back into the conservatory.

Once inside the house again, Mrs Marr said with surprising directness: 'How are you bearing up, Inspector? May I say again how sorry I was for your sad loss? Susan was a wonderful young woman, and reminded me very much of myself at her age. She was absolutely committed to her girls, you know, and was passionate in her sympathies for the Chinese generally. Such sympathy didn't always win her friends with her own community, of course. We do still have some very narrow-minded British people here in Hong Kong, even now, so in some ways things are still much the same here as they were sixty years ago. When I was a girl we had a governor here - Sir John Pope Hennessy – who had some genuine affection for the Chinese and did his best to help them. The Chinese called him their "Number One Friend". He was a fiery Irishman, of course, which might explain his sympathies a little. But do you know what happened when he finally left his post as governor: why, not a single British or American merchant came to the quayside to see him and his wife Kitty off when they departed. I can still remember that shameful day like it was yesterday...*only the Chinese came to see him off*...'

*

Afterwards a thoughtful Paul Jericho wandered along Caine Road to where it merged into Upper Albert Road. The grounds of Government House stood resplendent on the lower side of this elegant street, while the leafy enclave of the Zoological and Botanical Gardens stood on the higher side.

It was nearly noon by now, so Jericho decided to take his luncheon in the gardens since he didn't often get the chance to come here any more. He had often used to come here with Susan in happier days. He had found himself deeply touched by the tribute that the formidable Mrs Marr had paid to Susan, so now felt a sudden need to remember his wife in a setting that she had loved. The eastern part of the gardens, known as the Old Garden, had a children's playground, aviaries, a greenhouse and a fountain terrace garden that Susan had loved in particular. Jericho had just walked past the imposing Memorial Arch, when he saw someone he recognized walking on the path straight towards him: a senior man from the government whom he had met once before through the offices of his good friend Ronnie Grantham. He recognized the man in particular from his gleaming head of silver hair, which was so full and perfect for a man in his fifties that it seemed almost like a wig.

Jericho greeted the new arrival. 'Mr Harmsworth. How are you, sir?'

Bob Harmsworth seemed to struggle to remember him for a moment, so Jericho prompted him. Perhaps it was the police uniform that was confusing him, for Jericho had met Mr Harmsworth at a government function when he had been off duty. 'Paul Jericho.' He offered his hand. 'Ronnie Grantham introduced us some time ago, if you remember.'

'Ah, yes. *Chief Inspector* Jericho.' Harmsworth made an attempt at a smile as he shook Jericho's hand, although he didn't seem pleased at this chance encounter. He was a widower as far as Jericho could remember from their first meeting, and also Colonial Treasurer of Hong Kong, therefore obviously an important man with lots on his mind. Ronnie Grantham had told Jericho that the handsome and well-connected Harmsworth was very wealthy after all his years of service in the East, and owned a wonderful apartment in Kotewall Road high up in the Mid-levels, as well as a grand bungalow out at Shek-O where he could enjoy the scenery and the quiet of the south side of the island.

Jericho suddenly remembered the unexpected death at Government House last night, and realized belatedly that Harmsworth must know the dead man, and might even have been close to him. 'I heard of the death of a colleague of yours at Government House last night - Ralph Ogden.'

Harmsworth seemed startled for a moment that Jericho should know about this. 'Are the police intending to investigate the death, Inspector?' he asked curiously.

Jericho hurriedly corrected him. 'No, I don't think it's a matter for the police. From what I heard, Mr Ogden clearly died of a heart attack.'

Harmsworth seemed relieved. 'Yes, he did. I'm very cut up about it. Ralph and I served together in the war, you know. We were captains together in the Eighth Battalion of the Norfolk Regiment. So we fought side-by-side on the first day of the Battle of the Somme twenty years ago.'

'Then I'm very sorry for your loss,' Jericho commiserated, at which Harmsworth gruffly excused himself and proceeded on his way.

Jericho was just musing on the odd awkwardness of this encounter, when he caught sight of someone else he recognized. A woman had just stepped out onto the path twenty yards ahead of him, and stood for a moment under the shade of a fan palm. Jericho was almost sure that this was the beautiful Maggie Yiu yet again. It seemed like an odd coincidence that he should bump into her here of all places. But before he could call out to her and say hello, she disappeared again as if by magic.

Jericho walked slowly to the spot where he had seen her and looked along a connecting path that disappeared up the hill among the feathery green of the Orchid trees. But there was no sign now of the exotic Miss Yiu so Jericho began to half-wonder if he might just have imagined this encounter.

But no...it had definitely been her.

And what's more, Jericho was convinced that she must have seen him in return, therefore he could only conclude that Miss Yiu had chosen to disappear deliberately. For some reason, Miss Yiu clearly now wanted to avoid him like the plague, which was an interesting fact in itself, when she had been so friendly and cooperative before...

*

Sebastian Ride had engaged a rickshaw of his own outside the Hong Kong Hotel, and his rickshaw coolie was now determinedly following James Woo's rickshaw as it headed west along Queens Road into Western District. The rickshaw man, a lean stringy man of forty years, had looked completely bemused when Ride had hissed to him in fluent Cantonese that he wanted him to follow the bright red rickshaw disappearing into the distance. But the man had soon set off at a fierce pace when Ride promised him ten dollars if he didn't lose sight of that rickshaw ahead: ten dollars was nearly a month's wages for a rickshaw coolie.

Unlike Des Voeux Road, Queens Road didn't fortunately have tram lines down the middle of it to impede the other traffic, but it did have more motor traffic to compensate so that the rickshaw coolie had to weave a dangerous path past all these competing obstructions of pedestrians and vehicles. They were soon in the bustling Chinese section of town, where the elegant colonial style of building soon gave way to a hugger-mugger of Chinese shops and businesses. This might be the modern 1930s yet much of what Ride could see from the back of the rickshaw was reminiscent of an older Imperial China: timeless street scenes, fetid courtyards and dim Oriental interiors. The more prosperous Chinese people on the pavements might have given up wearing embroidered silk gowns in favour of Western suits and hats, but the coolies in their conical straw hats carrying heavy panniers on sagging bamboo poles could have stepped straight out of an old Chinese print...

They passed the solid brick square of Western Market, where James Woo's rickshaw turned left abruptly into a network of crowded, noisy and unsanitary alleyways. Ride's own coolie didn't need any further bidding but followed at once in the same direction. The bright red rickshaw ahead of them eventually took a steep alley that led higher still up the hill to the Tai Ping Shan district – in English, the "Hill of the Great Peace". Ride's coolie followed on at a trot, and - impressively for a man of forty - seemed hardly out of breath even pulling his loaded rickshaw up a one-in-four gradient. Eventually, with sunlit vistas of the harbour opening up behind them, Ride saw that the red rickshaw had stopped in front of a substantial apartment building of six storeys set on a green hillside, with a cobbled entrance courtyard on one side. A flight of granite steps climbed the old stone retaining wall at the back of the courtyard to give access to the rear of the building at first floor level, and was arched over by the dense foliage of fig trees festooned with flowering creepers. In the sunlit courtyard, a boy in Chinese cap and gown was playing with a miniature paper kite, while a group of old men showed off their caged singing birds, feeding them delicately from porcelain water bowls. A line of wrinkled old amahs sat in the sliver of shade near the main entrance, brooding over long-stemmed clay pipes and refreshing themselves from time to time with a flutter of their painted fans.

Every apartment in the building had its own balconies and miniature gardens of pot plants and climbers, so that it seemed like a vertical tower of green set against the glittering blue of the sky and the brilliance of the overhead sun. The building seemed special enough from the outside, but Ride could see that the entrance foyer was even more decorative, with a marble-floor and a carved blackwood interior furnished with silken curtains. There seemed to be only four large apartments on each floor, so this building was clearly a choice residence for wealthy Chinese who were barred from living higher up the Peak in the mainly European enclaves of Mid-levels.

Ride saw that James had paid off his rickshaw coolie, so he did the same, receiving a beaming gap-toothed smile of gratitude and a kowtow almost to the ground from his own coolie in return for the promised ten dollars. Ride pulled the brim of his Panama hat down over his eyes, and kept the rest of his face covered with his arm as he crossed the courtyard for he had no wish to be seen by the people congregated here. He entered the foyer of the building, and saw James get into an old-fashioned birdcage lift; fortunately there was no hall porter at the desk to ask him what he was doing here. Ride watched the indicator of the lift as it moved upwards towards the top floor. Behind the lift cage was an open hardwood staircase that zigzagged from floor to floor to provide access to the same floors. Ride didn't hesitate further but took the stairs at a run instead of waiting for the return of the lift. The lift was slow and creaking, and it stopped at virtually every floor on the way, so that a breathless Sebastian Ride found he had got to the top floor only a few seconds behind James in the lift. He saw James marching along the top corridor to the last door on the floor, and then insert a key in the lock.

In a second Ride had approached silently behind him, and as James entered the apartment, Ride followed him forcefully through the doorway before James had a chance to slam the door in his face.

Ride was gratified to see that he had surprised James Woo for once.

'What are you d...doing here, Sebastian?' James stammered uncertainly. '*How*...how did you find this place?'

'*Easy*...I followed you,' Ride said laconically, as he went further into the apartment without permission and glanced brazenly in each of the rooms to make sure that they were alone. 'Very nice...is this your own private little refuge, James?'

'Yes, it is,' James agreed. He sighed heavily. 'Since you have forced your way in here, Sebastian, I suppose we will have to talk. Shall we go out onto the balcony, though; it's cooler out there.'

Ride followed him through the lavishly furnished Chinese living room and out onto the spacious balcony. Surprisingly the balcony *was* cooler for it faced the lower green hillsides of the Peak and was shaded by a striped canvas awning that flapped slightly in the cooling sea breeze. The view was spectacular as was the dizzying drop of a hundred feet onto the stone retaining wall at the rear of the apartment block.

James stared at Ride coldly, his normal composure now completely restored. 'I'm sure you are going to tell me why you have followed me here from the office, Sebastian. But could you make it quick, for I have some guests arriving in a few minutes.'

Ride wondered cynically whether these guests would be some of James's more disreputable friends, and whether they would be indulging their tastes for the fashionable drug cocaine in the discreet privacy of his flat. Or was James really only expecting *one* visitor, one of his many lovers? That seemed more likely somehow, seeing that it was only just gone noon, therefore a little early for a wild party. Given his suspicions about James's sexuality, Ride wondered whether this presumed lover might even be a man rather than a woman...

'I came to ask you what the hell you think you are doing,' Ride said abrasively.

James frowned. 'What do you mean? You'll have to be a little more specific, Sebastian, if you want an answer.'

'I want to know why you are selling marine gasoline to the Japanese,' Ride said balefully. 'And don't try and deny it. This sleazy deal has got your fingerprints all over it.'

James seemed tempted for a moment to argue, but then finally shrugged. 'It's good business. Do you know how much the Japanese are prepared to pay for marine gasoline? *Three times* the market price...'

Ride was taken aback by the brazenness of that answer. 'Don't you care that this fuel is being used by the Japanese Navy against your motherland of China?'

James smiled at his naivety. 'Not particularly. I never let a little thing like patriotism get in the way of a good business deal.'

'And what happens if our own Chinese investors discover what we have been doing?'

James responded with a sinister chuckle. 'It's not a matter of "if" they discover it, Sebastian, only a matter of "when".'

Ride gasped. 'So this deal wasn't really about making money, was it? It was about setting me up to take the blame for it.'

James inclined his head in sly acknowledgment. 'Indeed so. And even a man as astute as you will not be able to dig yourself out of this hole, Sebastian, especially as it comes hot on the heels of that disastrous project in Hopei Province - the steel rolling mill - that you thought would be such a profitable investment.'

Ride tried to contain his fury. 'It might have been, if your reckless decision to sell marine fuel to the Japanese hadn't encouraged them to invade Hopei Province.'

James was dismissive. 'Now, now, Sebastian. I didn't expect you to be such a sore loser.'

'I'll tell your father the truth,' Ride said desperately.

James shook his head. 'I'm afraid he won't believe you. My father has not got long left in this world, and will not turn his back on me. He will prefer to believe me rather than you, because blood is always stronger than mere friendship at the end of the day.'

'Your sister Grace will believe me,' Ride stated coldly.

'Possibly...she is a little infatuated with you after all,' James agreed mildly. 'But she will have no power to do anything about it. Especially when I bring in this huge new deal with the government to build all this social housing. That will make Saunders-Woo the heroes of the hour, building homes to house Hong Kong's poor and thereby maintaining political stability in these troubled times. I might even get a knighthood out of it eventually like Sir Robert Ho-tung, or at least a sainthood...'

'If I know you, these housing blocks will be built on a shoestring and will be barely habitable,' Ride said.

'Perhaps so,' James smiled. 'Yet they'll still be far better than the shanties on the hillsides and the cardboard boxes on the streets that these people live in at present. And it will certainly be very profitable for our company...though I should say *my* company since I doubt most sincerely that you will be part of Saunders-Woo by that time...'

Ride could restrain his fury no further, but leapt at James and rammed his fist in his face. In a second he had forced a dazed James back to the parapet wall of the balcony, and had his head in a hold like a vice. 'I could settle this right now, James,' he threatened.

Ride could see the sudden terror in James's eyes. 'You won't do it,' James gasped, blood dripping from his nose.

Ride forced James back even further over the parapet until his whole upper body was hanging over the sheer drop. 'I've only got to let go and you're a dead man, James.'

James clearly believed that Ride was going to push him over the edge, and he whimpered with fear. 'Don't do it, Sebastian, please! They'll hang you for it, you know. Plenty of people must have seen you come into this building.'

Ride glowered back at him. 'No, they didn't; I had my face well covered. And even if they could identify me, they wouldn't dare testify against a white man. And who's to say it won't look like an accident anyway?' Ride had had no real intention of killing James Woo when he came up here, but his blood was up now, and for the first time he began to seriously consider ridding himself of this devil for good...

James was near choking with Ride's powerful arms wrapped around his head and neck. But that hold was all that was stopping him from falling to his death on the jagged stone retaining wall far below. 'If you kill me, you'll never learn the truth about the death of your mistress,' James whispered hoarsely.

Ride gripped his head tighter until James's eyes started to pop. 'What do you mean?'

'I mean that policeman's wife you were seeing...*Susan Jericho*.'

'What do you know about her?' Ride demanded, shocked that James even knew Susan's name.

'I was...there...that night it happened. I was at a friend's house in Bowen Road...almost next door to the apartment block where you met this woman. I know you use that company flat in Bowen Road for your assignations...'

Ride squeezed James's head even more. 'What do you know about what happened, you bastard?'

James was gasping, trying to catch his breath. 'I saw it all. I was standing on the balcony of the flat in Bowen Road and I could see almost the whole of Kennedy Road below. I saw Susan Jericho leave the company apartment, then walk down the stepped path that leads from Bowen Road down to Macdonnell Road, and then finally to Kennedy Road. I had met her before at some function at Saint Stephen's College so I knew what she looked like. I guessed she must have been with you that night so I was curious to see where she was going. My friend keeps a pair of binoculars on his balcony, so I was able to get a close-up view of her walking down to Kennedy Road. Then I lost sight of her for a moment in the binoculars as she disappeared under the cover of some overhanging trees, but it sounded like someone attacked her on the pavement...I heard her scream in alarm...'

Ride finally released his hold on James and allowed the man to get his breath back. 'Go on,' he ordered balefully.

James straightened up and felt his bruised neck with a groan of pain. '...The next thing I saw was Susan Jericho running out into the road in a panic. That's when the car hit her. The driver was coming down Kennedy Road too fast, and he couldn't stop in time. The car hit Susan head-on and she was thrown high into the air by the force of the impact. The car skidded to a halt and the driver got out of the car and ran back to have a look at Susan's body. But the driver soon jumped back in his car again, then drove straight off. I ran down into the street, and then down the same path to

Kennedy Road to see if the woman was still alive. But she was dead already by the time that I got there...'

'Were you the person who called the police that night? I heard that someone had called the police from a phone box in Macdonnell Road...' Ride had gone home to Conduit Road that night by the direct route along Bowen Road itself so had known nothing of what had happened to Susan in Kennedy Road below after she had left him. He had only learned the shocking truth a day or so later when he had read about it in the *South China Morning Post*...

James hesitated. 'No, I didn't. The woman was already dead as far as I could see, and I didn't want to have to explain to the police what I was doing there at the scene, especially when the woman was my own partner's mistress. That would have been very embarrassing for the company's good name.'

Ride snorted angrily. 'Oh, you're suddenly worried about the company's good name, are you, James? What about the other person who was there? The person who attacked Susan?'

'Whoever it was had already long fled the scene, and that's what I did too.' James was unrepentant. 'There was nothing I could do to help the woman...'

'And what about the car that hit Susan? Did you see who was driving it?' Ride demanded hoarsely.

James nodded. 'No, my view through the binoculars wasn't good enough to see the driver's face. But the car was an unusual make and colour, so I'm sure I could probably identify the owner of that car if I really wanted to. But I'm damned if I'm going to tell you what I know, you maniac!' Ride could see that James was getting his courage back, and he soon proved it. 'Now get out of my flat before I call the fucking police!' he ordered Ride with all his accustomed arrogance.

Ride stepped forward threateningly again, though in truth his anger was now mostly spent, and the movement he made was a reflex action only. But James Woo misread the look on Ride's face and fell back in alarm against the stone parapet. Suddenly the whole length of the blockwork parapet behind him began to crumble and disintegrate, and a panicked James lost his balance completely as he wavered on the edge of the now exposed balcony. Ride now flung out a despairing hand trying to save his business partner, but he was too late to stop James toppling backwards over the edge.

Quivering with shock, he saw James falling with flailing arms and legs, before he smashed into the stonework far below with a hideous dying scream...

CHAPTER 8

Saturday, 14th August 1937

'Did anyone see you there, Mr Ride? Frances asked anxiously.

It was only an hour since James Woo had fallen to his death, and Sebastian Ride was now back at his desk in the Saunders Building. He had returned here in a daze, and had been about to phone the police immediately and report what had happened. But Frances had stopped him and demanded to know everything that had occurred.

'I don't think anyone in the building saw me. I had my face covered when I went in, and I left by the fire escape and came back here on foot via Hollywood Road.' Ride took another gulp of the Scotch whisky that Frances had brought him, and tried to hold his shaking hand still. 'I don't know why I didn't just ring the police from James's apartment, but I wasn't thinking clearly. I suppose I was in a state of shock and simply wanted to get out of there. There was no point in going down to look at the body; James was nearly decapitated when his head hit the coping of that stone retaining wall.'

Frances took that information with surprising calm; in fact she seemed to him to be almost unnaturally calm since he had returned to the office. It was only he who was shaking like a leaf. Clearly she was one of those people who were at their best in emergencies.

He had confessed everything to Frances, of course, exactly as it had transpired, even the revelation that James Woo had claimed to know the identity of the person who had killed Susan Jericho. Although Ride had never openly discussed his love affairs with Frances, yet he was sure that she knew most of what went on in his private life. The name of Susan Jericho was certainly no surprise to her, Ride could see. Frances truly was more like family to him now – a dependable older sister – to whom he could confide even the worst things without worrying too much about her reaction.

She had been shocked to hear the story of the death of Susan Jericho, though. 'Do you think that's what really happened in Kennedy Road that night, Mr Ride?'

Ride ran a trembling hand through his damp hair. 'I don't know if I believed everything he said. But I think it must have happened something like that, for the details were quite convincing. Yet the fact that he was there on the spot so conveniently makes it very suspicious. I think there's a good chance that it was *he* who was actually driving the car that hit Susan; that would make more sense, and would explain why he wouldn't identify the driver and the car. He was determined to try and discredit me somehow, so this would explain why he might have followed me and Susan to the apartment in Bowen Road. Then he could have parked his car below in Kennedy Road while he waited for Susan and me to reappear. But it was a very cold night so perhaps he simply decided that it wasn't worthwhile waiting around for hours in his car. But in fact, Susan was only with me for a few minutes before leaving on foot via Kennedy Road. So it seems likely that James must have hit her accidentally in Kennedy Road as he was driving away. It's not surprising that he wouldn't stop around afterwards in those circumstances...' Ride gasped as another terrible thought occurred to him. 'I can't believe that he would have run Susan down deliberately: even James couldn't be that evil. And there was no reason for him to kill her deliberately anyway...'

Frances looked a little startled for the first time by his story, but then relaxed her face. 'Yes, it could have been like that – an accident. But it was still an accident that was caused by this man plotting against you. In which case you are well rid of Mr Woo, who was doing nothing but trying to undermine and destroy you...'

'Yet I killed him,' Ride said bleakly. 'The son of my oldest friend. I'm not sure I can live with that, Frances. So I must go to the police and give myself up...'

Frances snorted angrily. 'You will *not* do that, Mr Ride! Not after everything you've done for this company. Saunders-Woo still needs you at the helm; it will quickly die without your inspired leadership. In any case, what happened today was clearly an accident, not murder. That parapet on the balcony must have been unsafe even before you went up there. Perhaps your earlier struggle with Mr Woo helped dislodge some of the concrete blocks a little, but the parapet should never have failed if it had been properly built. Therefore blame the builder for this, not yourself. You actually tried to save the man, after all...'

Ride had to concede that much was true.

'Then you would be very foolish calling the police, when it will help nobody at all,' Frances said firmly. When she checked with him again that no one had apparently seen him enter or leave the apartment building where it had happened, Frances was almost triumphant. 'You see! There's no need to punish yourself any further for this accident, Mr Ride. It *was* an accident, pure and simple, and it is better that you deny ever being there. If anyone asks, I am willing to say that you were here in the office with me the whole morning, except for a few minutes when you stepped out for some fresh air outside. That's just in case the porter at the entrance foyer remembers you going out.'

Ride had a sudden thought. 'Ah, but you forget the rickshaw coolie who took me to Tai Ping Shan. I gave him a ten dollar tip for getting me there; that man won't forget me in a hurry.'

Frances was still cool and unruffled as she considered this. 'Don't worry about the rickshaw coolie, Mr Ride. Leave that problem to me. I know this man, for I recognized the rickshaw that you hired. I will pay him off and ensure that he keeps silent...'

*

Paul Jericho was just entering the main public hall in Wanchai Police Station after his enjoyable excursion up to Caine Road and then to the Botanical Gardens, when he was accosted by an animated George Dorling. It was just after two in the afternoon, so Jericho wondered what was up. Hot and steamy Saturday afternoons were usually very quiet ones for the police, for even the most hardened of Hong Kong criminals found the sticky August heat irksome.

Jericho was glad to see that Dorling was beginning to look more like his old self again, neatly shaved and with clear eyes. He looked reassuringly like a man who might have turned a corner in his life and cured his recent demons.

Dorling spoke up sharply. 'I'm glad you're back, sir. Everybody's been wondering where you are. We've just received a report of a body...'

Jericho had a sinking feeling in the pit of his stomach. 'Not another bar girl, I hope?'

'No, sir, a man. He seems to have fallen to his death from the balcony of a block of flats in Tai Ping Shan.'

Jericho frowned. 'Then why are they calling *us* to investigate? That should be in Western District's patch, shouldn't it?'

Dorling smiled ruefully. 'There are no senior officers available in Western District today – they are all off on some sort of group excursion to Lantau Island.'

Jericho shrugged. 'Very nice for them. But I suppose we'll have to take this one, then.'

Dorling nodded. 'Yes, sir. I took the liberty of ordering your car and driver to come around to the front entrance...'

*

'I wouldn't mind living here myself,' George Dorling said enviously as he looked up at this luxurious block of flats in Tai Ping Shan. 'A lot nicer than Ashley Road in Kowloon. I think even Tess would be happy living here.'

'Yet living here didn't do this poor devil much good,' Jericho pointed out as he looked at the body spread-eagled on top of the retaining wall. He had recognized the victim at once, of course, as James Woo, and was a little disturbed by the coincidence of his visit to the home of Mrs Adela Marr in Caine Road a few hours earlier. For if he had been right in his supposition about the person responsible for these rowdy parties in the Portuguese house next door to Mrs Marr, then her problems with being woken up at night by the noise were most probably solved now, though not in a way that Jericho would ever have foreseen.

The youthful Dr Eric Formby now spoke up, after completing his detailed inspection of the body. 'He broke his neck when his head smacked against the coping of the retaining wall. A clear break between the second and third cervical vertebrae. At least it would have been over quickly for the poor devil; he wouldn't have felt much.'

Jericho was beginning to wonder just how many places James Woo had lived in: for apart from the Woo family homes - the new mansion in Po Shan Road and the even grander mansion at Repulse Bay – it seemed he was also still using the former Woo family home in Caine Road for parties, as well as having this further luxury bolthole apartment in Tai Ping Shan.

Jericho had already been upstairs with Senior Constable Thomas Sung and his regular driver Constable Gary Ho to inspect the balcony from which Woo had apparently fallen. Ho was twenty-five years old, but like many Cantonese men still looked like a smooth-cheeked boy. Constable Ho had recently asked to be transferred from full-time driver duties to regular police work and Jericho had agreed because he was such a promising young officer – another Thomas Sung in the making. But for the present, until Jericho could be assigned a new driver, Constable Ho had found himself having to perform both functions. He was doing this so well, though, that this arrangement might well end up being a permanent one; Jericho had found it very useful to have a driver who was also an accomplished crime scene investigator.

As far as Jericho had seen from his inspection of the scene, the construction of the parapet wall of the balcony seemed to have been the cause of the accident. Parapets like that one were usually built with hollow masonry blocks filled with concrete and reinforced with steel bars anchored into the concrete slab of the balcony. But Jericho had observed that there was no reinforcement in this parapet at all, so the stability of the wall had depended purely on the weight of the blocks and the adhesion of the mortar joints. And the mortar looked like it had deteriorated gradually into little more than a friable weak powder, so it was probably only a matter of time before the parapet failed under even the most modest force. Since the conclusions seemed straightforward, Jericho had left Constables Sung and Ho to search the flat for any other evidence, while he went back to the retaining wall at ground level and the investigation of the body...

The boyish-looking Constable Sung eventually returned from his detailed search of the flat, and Jericho saw that his handsome Cantonese face was grim. 'I found this in the apartment, sir.' He held up a large bottle filled with white powder. 'I'm sure it's cocaine. If Mr Woo had taken some of this stuff, then it might explain how he could have fallen. He must have been leaning heavily against the weakened parapet wall, or perhaps stumbled against it, and in his drugged state couldn't save himself when it started to collapse.'

Formby spoke up again. 'You can see that there's a lot of debris from the broken parapet around the body. But none on *top* of the body so the debris definitely landed here before the body did. So I'd go along with the accident theory.' He frowned. 'He does have some bruising around his lower throat and neck, but that could easily have happened when he landed face down.'

Jericho stepped back a little into the shade of a grand old Bengal Fig tree whose roots grew out of the stone retaining wall like a mass of giant writhing serpents. He spoke to Sung. 'Well, Thomas, we can't tell lies about what we found in the apartment, but we need to be discreet about this. This man was the son of one of the wealthiest men in Hong Kong, so we don't want to deliberately embarrass the Woo family when they will soon be suffering grievous pain from their loss.'

Sung looked uncomfortable. 'Then I could get rid of this stuff, sir, if you want.'

Jericho shook his head. 'No, we will have to keep it as evidence.' He turned warningly to all his colleagues. 'But I want no mention of cocaine to get to the newspapers. *Is that absolutely clear...?*'

CHAPTER 9

Saturday, 14th August 1937

The south side of Hong Kong Island was a complete contrast to the urban and heavily populated north side. Edith Starling had been startled by the difference when she had first arrived in Hong Kong two years ago and been taken by Ralph Ogden for a leisurely drive along the coast road that encircled the island. Until this coast road had been built just after the Great War, and a further connecting road subsequently built over the mountains at Wong Nei Chung Gap in the mid 1920s, it had been impossible to even get to the southern beaches except by boat. These days it was possible to get there by car in one hour from Central District, but even so the south side of the island remained remarkably remote from the mass of people in Hong Kong and was largely the preserve of a privileged wealthy elite.

Edith had seen on her first drive that there were no large settlements built on the delectable bays and inlets of the south coast, nothing except for a few small villages backed by steep forested mountains – Aberdeen, Stanley, Shek-o – and only one place of any note, which was Repulse Bay, which had become an established location for wealthy Chinese to build their luxurious second or third mansions. At the same time Repulse Bay had also developed into a popular place with expatriates as a bathing beach. There were now over a hundred licensed matsheds on Repulse Bay beach – these were large bamboo structures with roofs and walls of rush matting and palm fronds that were used as beach houses. All the big firms in Hong Kong had their own matsheds for use by their European staff, and Repulse Bay was by far the most popular of the bathing beaches, especially since the opening of the Lido at the Repulse Bay Hotel where tea dances were held on the terrace, and the idea was to waltz, tango, foxtrot or rhumba in between lavish helpings of tea and cream cakes, while watching the occasional flying boat land on the water...

Yet none of these bathing beaches on the south coast were open to Chinese, of course. The majority of the Chinese had neither the time nor the money to get out to the beaches, and it was unheard of for Chinese girls to be seen in public in bathing costumes anyway. Yet even if they had, they would have received a cool reception if they had tried to bathe on a beach that was effectively reserved for Europeans.

Edith avoided Repulse Bay as a matter of course anyway, but most certainly today when she had Michael Yip with her. A European woman bathing together with a Chinese man on Repulse Bay beach would most definitely have attracted attention for all the wrong reasons if she had attempted it. So for this afternoon's swimming rendezvous with her lover, Edith had selected the same quiet cove on Tai Tam Bay that they had visited before, a cove which was only two miles east of Repulse Bay, on the other side of the Stanley peninsula, but which was a completely different sort of place, a peaceful cove accessed only by a narrow sandy track. This pretty little cove had none of the facilities of Repulse Bay, of course, but was also far enough from the road to Stanley to be usually deserted even on a Saturday afternoon.

And so, at three o'clock on this hot afternoon, Edith lay on the sand on this deserted beach in the shade of a cuasarina tree with Michael by her side. Her little black Austin Seven was parked a few yards behind them in a grove of red sandalwood and incense trees; she just hoped her little car would be able to get back up the steep sandy track that led back to the main Stanley Road. Last time it had been a bit of a struggle when the rear wheels of the Austin had become bogged down in the soft sand, so Michael had had to get out and push...

There were no matsheds here on this empty little cove, so Edith had been forced to change coyly behind the shelter of a Red Pine tree. Being naked in front of her lover in her bedroom was one thing, but Edith was still far too inhibited as yet to undress brazenly in front of him on a public beach. When she did appear from behind the shelter of the tree, she was still feeling a little nervous, for she wasn't sure how Michael would react to her new swimsuit.

After his insulting remarks about the old black flannel bathing suit she had worn last time - suitable only for a *grandmother,* he had said - she had made the effort this week to go down to Lane Crawford department store in Central and buy herself a new and more stylish one. Yet she was worried that she might have gone too far, for this bright red bathing suit was decidedly risqué and made her feel as if she was practically naked anyway. The neckline plunged at the back three quarters of the way to her bottom, and it had no sleeves at all, while the sides were cut away in a very revealing way. It was also made of the new material rayon, which hugged the body like a second skin and revealed nearly everything else that wasn't already on show. The shoulder straps could also be lowered so as not to leave any tanning lines, though Edith had not been bold enough to go that far.

But she needn't have worried about Michael's reaction, for it could not have been much better. As she sauntered casually from cover and sank down onto the sand beside him, his jaw practically dropped for a second and then he issued a low whistle of delight. 'Wow! I hope that your three grandchildren – little Ignatius, Reginald and Algernon, isn't it? - know what a red hot grandma they have...'

Edith couldn't help blushing with pleasure at this response like a fourteen-year-old at her first dance. But she cleverly concealed her embarrassment by taking off her glasses, then leaping up from the sand again: 'Race you out to that rock!' And without waiting to see if he was following, she splashed immediately into the gentle surf and began swimming a very masculine crawl stroke towards a distant rocky islet with all her might.

Yet she soon found that she hadn't needed to expend quite so much effort, for she beat Michael to the islet by a huge margin. She stretched herself out luxuriantly on the kelp-covered rock and watched complacently as Michael struggled the last few yards to join her. He dragged himself out onto the dripping rock and collapsed in an exaggerated way beside her. 'I didn't realize you were in training for the English Olympic swimming team, Edith,' he complained with a wry smile. He looked at the water, a little nervously. 'Aren't there sharks in these waters, Edith?'

'Probably,' she admitted.

He frowned. 'Aren't you worried about that? Even you can't out-swim a shark, Edith.'

She laughed complacently. 'But then I don't have to, do I? All I have to do is out-swim *you*, Michael.'

He laughed too at her joke, although a little uneasily. 'I see that you have a cruel streak, Miss Starling...'

She laughed again at the expression on his face, but then kissed him tenderly to prove that she was only making fun of him. In fact, if a shark really did ever come for them, she knew that she would probably sacrifice her own life for this beautiful man...

They stretched out on the rock in companionable silence and looked back at the little cove, and the green hills of the Stanley peninsula behind it. Further back beyond that, the mountainous backbone of Hong Kong Island rose steeply into the azure sky, cloaked in a thick green forest of fig trees and evergreen oaks, so that this place seemed from here like some remote uninhabited Pacific island. A few moist tendrils of clouds still clung tenaciously to the upper reaches of the mountains and added their own sense of mystery. In the other direction, looking out from this little rocky islet into the main part of Tai Tam Bay, the amethyst water was almost mirror smooth in the afternoon sun. Only the lightest of cat's-paws disturbed the blue brilliance of the water and left an occasional ripple to spread reluctantly across its glassy surface.

Edith was surreptitiously admiring Michael's lithe brown body as she lay beside him on the wet rock, and it seemed Michael was doing the same for her, for he said innocently, 'That swimsuit of yours reveals your full callipygian perfection, Edith.' He laughed at her reaction. 'You look shocked, Edith. Is it because I know an English word like "callipygian", or is it because I used it about you?'

Edith laughed a little uncertainly in return. 'Both, I think. Is this your retaliation for my joke about the shark? For I believe it means a woman with a big bottom, doesn't it...?'

Michael demurred. 'Oh, not necessarily big, Edith, but certainly exquisitely shaped. That is one attribute where Western women beat Chinese women hands down – you have much more prominent and shapely buttocks.'

Edith coughed dryly. 'I hope that the shape of my bottom isn't the *only* thing you see in me, Michael, is it?'

He leaned across and kissed her tenderly on the lips. 'No, of course not. You're a wonderful person in every way.'

Far out to sea, Edith saw a school of bottlenose dolphins break the liquid blue surface. 'This is such a beautiful place. I wish I could stay here with you forever,' she said with a sudden rush of girlish sentiment.

Michael took her hand and patted it consolingly. 'I know you've had a bad week, so a few hours away from Government House must be a great relief for you.'

Edith had told him on the drive from Happy Valley about the death of Ralph Ogden yesterday evening. She was still struggling to cope with that disturbing event, for she didn't know where her decoding work would go from here without Ralph Ogden's detailed guidance and support. She barely knew her other SIS colleagues in the communications section at Government House apart from Adam, Broadbent and Casaubon, and she had no idea at present who would take over Ogden's demanding role as chief of the section. Probably no one in the short term; Ogden's successor would almost certainly have to come out from England – they wouldn't want to trust such a major responsibility to any of the lightweights who worked in the back room at Government House. Adam and Broadbent were certainly far too young and inexperienced to take over Ralph's role, while Casaubon, although very experienced, was no natural leader. The Japanese were still super-enciphering all their messages from Tokyo to their Kwantung Army so Edith was still locked out completely from being able to read any of them. Something urgent needed to be done, but without Ralph to guide her, she had no idea what...

And then there was the worrying possibility of a traitor within Government House itself; Ralph had seemed completely convinced of that...

She remembered again what he said to her last night – in fact almost the *last* thing he had ever said to her – that he had set a trap for this presumed traitor. And then, within an hour, he was dead. Edith still didn't like the unfortunate timing of Ralph's death, since he had died before exposing this traitor. In fact the secret of the traitor's identity had apparently died with Ralph altogether, since she had no idea of the name that Ralph had in mind, and nor did anyone else presumably. So Ralph's death had been far too convenient an event for this lucky traitor, a fact which Edith did not like at all...

Could this traitor have killed Ralph? The bruises on Ralph's throat meant it had to be a possibility at least, particularly if the man had learned somehow that he was under suspicion...

Edith had tried to tell herself not to imagine such a melodramatic turn of events. She reminded herself again that Ralph had looked truly terrible last night, and long overdue for a reoccurrence of his heart problems. Yet still Edith couldn't let go of this sinister possibility that Ralph had been murdered...

She turned to Michael. 'Yes, it's been a bad week. I was very close to Ralph; he was almost like a father figure to me.'

Michael patted her hand. 'Then I can understand your distress. Mr Ogden did always strike me as a very decent man. For a colonial anyway...' he added with a faint smile.

'How is that you actually knew Ralph?' Edith asked him with deliberate casualness.

Michael shrugged his shoulders. 'I didn't really know him. I had only met him two or three times at various government functions, and I still don't know precisely what his role at Government House was. It was you who told me that he was your boss, I think.'

'Did I?' Edith was completely confident that she had never mentioned Ralph Ogden's name to Michael before this week. That was why she had been so surprised in the grounds of Government House on Monday night to discover that Michael already knew Ralph. She felt a sudden return of her new doubts about Michael as she remembered Ralph's warning to her about him: that he might have engineered their first meeting in the Theatre Royal in the City Hall, and that he was not a man to be trusted. For what he had just said seemed wrong somehow: it seemed far likelier that a well-informed legal man like Michael would know *exactly* what role Ralph Ogden played in Hong Kong – that he was Britain's spymaster in the Far East. And if he knew that much, then he might even know that Edith was no simple secretary but the chief intelligence decoder in Hong Kong.

'Shall we have another race back to the beach?' she asked, rapidly changing the subject.

Michael sighed. 'I see there is a masochistic streak in you, Miss Starling. But all right...just give me ten yards start.' With that he flung himself into the water and started to thresh wildly towards the beach.

Edith didn't try to seriously race him this time, though, and maintained an easy breast stroke back to the shore, her mind mostly elsewhere. She had been reflecting since last night whether she should speak to Susan's husband about her suspicions concerning Ralph Ogden's death...

Edith hadn't known Susan Jericho long – only a little over a year – but something spontaneous had occurred between them from their first social meeting and had made them the best of friends for that short time until Susan's tragic death in January. Perhaps it was because they were both female mathematicians by education – an oddity in a man's world. Yet there had been more to it than that; Susan had been like the older, wiser sister that Edith had never had.

Edith didn't know her husband Paul at all well, but Susan had always claimed that he was the best natural detective in the Hong Kong Police force. So if Edith was going to take her suspicions to anyone, then it would be to Paul Jericho. He would be discreet about this if she asked him to be, and he would certainly keep any knowledge of her suspicions from his superiors until he had made some investigations of his own. Edith definitely didn't want to go directly to the uncouth Superintendent Hebdon, or even the urbane Commissioner of Police Matlock with her suspicions; those two would certainly make her suspicions public at once, and that would cause major problems with her SIS employers if it was discovered that she had been discussing possible intelligence issues with some ordinary Hong Kong policemen.

Yet, if Susan had been right about her husband, Paul Jericho might be the one person in Hong Kong who would be able to tell her whether Ralph had been murdered or not...

Even though she was only swimming at about half her maximum speed, she had still nearly caught Michael by the time they got to the beach. But she was happy to let him have his little moment of triumph for he seemed full of youthful exuberance as he celebrated his "win". In fact she was quite entranced again by his boyish charm and his handsome face. He rushed at her and lifted her up in his muscular arms, then raced back with her to their shelter under the cuasarina tree. Lying side-by-side on the sand again, he began to play teasingly with the shoulder strap of her bathing costume. 'You do look wonderful in this swimsuit, Edith, yet I think you would look even more beautiful without it.'

Edith felt her body stirring under his gentle touch. She smacked his roving hands away, but then slowly lowered the shoulder straps herself...

*

Edith had fallen asleep after making love - her long tiring week, and her more enjoyable exertions today, finally catching up with her. She woke slowly and stretched luxuriantly on the warm white sand. Her eyes looked up at the blue sky, and then at the old stone wall behind the beach, which was covered in a riot of red bottlebrush and yellow oleander. She wasn't yet wearing her glasses again so her view of the world was pleasantly out of focus as if she was tipsy with drink.

She lay still and let her unfocused eyes do the roving around this peaceful scene. Her gaze came to rest next on a breathtaking view of sun-dazzled ocean, of little green islets and jungle-covered hills on the far side of Tai Tam Bay. A crested bulbul sang a pretty song in the feathery branches of the cuasarina tree above her head. Everything was bathed in the brilliant glowing light of the East. The scene reminded her of bathing holidays in Japan as a girl, for the southernmost island of Japan that she'd visited regularly with her diplomat father - Okinawa – was very like this.

Michael was no longer dozing by her side, but she didn't worry about where he had got to. She knew he wouldn't be far away, and that knowledge was a great comfort to her on this perfect afternoon. When he made love to her, all her lingering doubts about him were vanquished in a moment, and she believed in him body and soul. Despite what he had said to her on Wednesday, part of her did dream in those rapturous moments of lovemaking of a permanent future with Michael, though she could scarcely conceive how such a thing might happen.

Then she heard a slight noise behind her – the sound of someone gently opening a car door - and she moved her neck a little to see. She saw that it was Michael, now fully dressed again, who was opening the boot of her little Austin and taking out her briefcase from inside. Her heart jumped for a moment as she saw him open the briefcase and then begin to go methodically through the contents.

She felt a sudden sickness burn in her stomach, a pain like severe heartburn. She wanted to leap to her feet and scream at him accusingly: Please don't tell me that this is all a lie, Michael...

Please don't tell me that you are betraying me...

Yet in the end she did nothing but continue to lie there on the warm sand, pretending to be still asleep, though her mind was now in turmoil...

CHAPTER 10

Saturday, 14th August 1937

The short twilight of the tropics was fading quickly to velvet black as Paul Jericho stood on the front terrace of a grand and sprawling three-storey mansion at the very end of Conduit Road. Apart from the Peak, this road - the highest in the Mid-levels - was the most prestigious residential street in Hong Kong, and with views of the harbour far below that were possibly even better than those from the Peak. Even the wealthiest of Chinese were effectively banned from the Peak, with one or two notable exceptions like the famous comprador Sir Robert Ho-tung, and that restriction also generally applied in practice to Conduit Road too, which was still almost entirely the preserve of distinguished expatriates.

The Woo family were another one of the exceptions to this unofficial rule, since they had managed to get permission to build their lavish new mansion in nearby Po Shan Road. Not only that, they had built a miniature castle of such staggering extravagance and bad taste that its kitsch turrets and towers and faux battlements had put all their expatriate neighbours' houses completely in the shade, and had therefore probably put many English noses out of joint in these highest reaches of the Mid-levels. Jericho had just been to this Woo family home – the same place where he had investigated a burglary last year – to break the terrible news of the death of the scion of the family, James Woo.

He had gone on his own this time, with just his usual police driver, Constable Gary Ho, at the wheel, because it didn't seem appropriate to send a large delegation of policemen on such a delicate task. Constable Ho had seemed impressed by the architectural kitsch of the place, but Jericho thought it one of the ugliest and most tasteless houses he had seen in Hong Kong. Jericho had asked to see Mr Woo Man Lo himself, but that privilege had been denied to him since Mr Woo was seriously ill in bed - perhaps even close to death, it seemed, from the already tearful expressions on the faces of the Woo family's faithful houseboys and amahs. James Woo had several younger half-brothers, but none of them were adults yet, being the sons of Woo Man Lo's much younger second wife. In the end Jericho had been forced to speak to the eldest daughter of the house, Grace, who was James's full sister, and only a year or two younger than him.

Jericho had not met Grace Woo before, for she had been in Europe last summer when he had come to investigate the burglary in this house. She was as handsome as her brother, but seemed a much more wholesome and pleasant personality on first meeting. She had taken the news of her brother's death with apparent stoic calm, although Jericho had suspected that the calm act was a mere front and that she was devastated with grief inside. Jericho had assured her that her brother's death looked like simply an unfortunate accident, which seemed to give her some slight reassurance. Before he left, Grace had asked Jericho with great formality if he would be so kind as to go to the nearby Ride mansion in Conduit Road and tell James's business partner, Sebastian Ride, the tragic news too. 'Sebastian will need to know...' she had added wistfully...

So Jericho had gone in his police car to Sebastian Ride's house in Conduit Road where he now stood on the private terrace at the front, waiting for Mr Ride to be fetched by his houseboy. The house was not as large as the Woo mansion yet it was still a substantial residence. Jericho had never met Sebastian Ride before but knew of him, of course. He had heard that Sebastian Ride came from quite humble beginnings in England, so he had obviously done very well for himself to live in a mansion like this on Conduit Road. The front terrace of the house was a work of art in itself, with granite steps and marble planters filled with strelitzia and canna lilies, and with a large fountain as a centrepiece, splashing water into a lily pond. Jericho glanced at the dazzling lights of Central District far below, and to the thinner scattering of riding lights on the steamers and junks moored in the harbour. From this high up, the harbour looked as if it was the domain of a thousand fireflies...

Jericho turned sharply as he heard a footfall behind him. But it was not Sebastian Ride who had appeared but a woman of forty or so, with untidy red hair and puffy bloodshot eyes. She stood there on the terrace, her head wobbling slightly back and forwards. 'Can I help you...err...' She seemed to notice his police uniform for the first time and fell into an awkward silence.

'Chief Inspector Jericho. I'm here to see Mr Ride,' he announced. He assumed this woman must be his wife.

Jericho could see that his name had meant something to this woman, for she seemed quite taken aback for a moment. Of course his name had been reported a lot in the newspapers in January following Susan's tragic death, so the woman might have remembered his name from those reports. Yet her reaction to his name seemed more pronounced than could be explained in this way. He wondered if this woman might perhaps have been a friend or acquaintance of Susan's, but it seemed unlikely. She did not seem the sort of person that Susan would ever have been close to, and Jericho himself had certainly never heard Susan mention that she knew the wife of Sebastian Ride.

The woman recovered quickly, though. 'I'm Mr Ride's wife,' she confirmed harshly. 'What do you want to see him about?'

Jericho hesitated. 'I think I'd better wait for Mr Ride. The matter is a private one...some bad news, I'm afraid.'

Mrs Ride looked affronted by this reply as if it was a personal insult, and seemed prepared to argue with him about it. But Jericho was saved from an embarrassing altercation with this moody woman by the arrival of her husband. Jericho recognized the man from having seen his photograph in the newspapers from time to time: in the flesh Ride seemed younger and handsomer than in those black-and-white images.

Sebastian Ride offered his hand to Jericho. 'Yes, Chief Inspector. What can I do for you? My houseboy said that you need an urgent word.' Ride seemed to notice his wife's presence for the first time and sighed audibly. 'I don't think you need to be part of this, Gloria. So would you please excuse us?'

Yet Mrs Ride wasn't about to be excused. 'No, I bloody well won't, Sebastian,' she said succinctly, waving an admonitory finger rudely in her husband's handsome face.

Ride sighed and gave in as gracefully as he could. Jericho could see from his weary acceptance that he was used to his wife behaving like this.

Jericho decided to get this awkwardness over with as quickly as possible. 'I'm afraid I have some bad news for you, Mr Ride. Your business partner James Woo has been killed early this afternoon in an accident in an apartment block in Tai Ping Shan...I've just been to inform the Woo family about this sad event, and Miss Grace Woo asked if I could come here and inform you of the tragedy too...'

A shaken Sebastian Ride sat down in a cane chair and ran a hand through his thick dark hair. 'My God! Is it true?'

Even Mrs Ride seemed to be shocked by the news. 'Poor James!' she said, subsiding onto a stone seat.

'How exactly did it happen?' Ride asked.

Jericho was a little reluctant to be too definitive in his judgement. 'Well, that will be a matter for an inquest to determine in due course. But Mr Woo seems to have been leaning against the parapet wall on his balcony, which unfortunately gave way, so that he fell to his death...'

'Did he die quickly?' Ride's voice was hoarse with emotion.

Jericho nodded. 'Instantly, I would say. I'm sure he didn't suffer too much, if that's what's worrying you.'

Mrs Ride stood up with difficulty. 'It seems I must retire after all, Inspector Jericho,' she said, swaying slightly as if she was on a ship at sea. 'My guardian angel is calling...'

Jericho saw that a Chinese nurse had appeared on the terrace with a worried look etched on her sallow middle-aged face.

'Ah, Doris.' Ride greeted the new arrival with apparent relief. 'Will you see to Mrs Ride, please? I think she needs a lie down. We've just had some very bad news...'

After the nurse had led a now subdued Mrs Ride away, Sebastian Ride turned to Jericho again. 'Sorry about that...Is there anything else about James's death that you could tell me? I know he was a troubled man of late. Five years ago his father sent him to the US to study business management at Yale College in Connecticut. This was a precursor to him taking over a much more senior role in the Saunders-Woo company, and effectively replacing his father on the board. But personally I think it was a mistake, for his time in America seemed to have ruined his character irrevocably. Before that he had been a hard working and devoted Chinese son. But when he returned to us, he had turned into an arrogant Westernized playboy with some very dubious habits, and also some very wild friends. I hope that James's death was nothing to do with any of these wilder habits of his, and that it was just a tragic accident that could have happened to anyone...?'

Jericho hadn't been going to mention the cocaine found in James Woo's apartment, yet this did seem like a perfect opportunity. 'Do you happen to know if Mr Woo took stimulants of any sort?'

Ride pulled a wry face. 'I think that's one way of describing them. I know he liked to indulge in cocaine, which seems to be a decadent habit he picked up in America.'

Jericho nodded. 'Then that seems to confirm it. We found a sizeable stock of cocaine in the apartment in Tai Ping Shan. Do you know what he was using that apartment for? Did he live there normally, or did he divide his time between there and the family homes in Po Shan Road and Repulse Bay?'

Ride shook his head. 'I didn't even know about this place he had in Tai Ping Shan, Chief Inspector. I thought he still lived with his family most of the time, although I know that he used the old family house on Caine Road sometimes for parties and the like. I don't think he was allowed to invite his wilder friends to Po Shan Road or Repulse Bay, especially now his father is seriously ill.'

That seemed to confirm Jericho's guess about the source of the noisy parties in the Portuguese house in Caine Road, so perhaps Mrs Adela Marr's sleep really would no longer be disturbed now. Yet it seemed that

James Woo kept the apartment in Tai Ping Shan for somewhat different reasons from the house in Caine Road – it now occurred to Jericho that perhaps Woo met women there...?

'Your partner wasn't married, was he?' Jericho asked.

Ride smiled ruefully. 'No, James still liked to play the field, even though he was thirty-two, and his family were clearly pressing him to find a suitable bride and continue the family line. As I say, James had picked up some *very* bad habits in America...and some very dubious sexual tastes...'

Jericho wondered what that cryptic remark meant. Was Ride suggesting that his business partner was homosexual or perhaps bisexual? Either way, Jericho didn't particularly want to go down that road, which seemed to have nothing to do with the man's death.

Jericho put a different question instead. 'How was your working relationship with him? You say he had some wild habits these days. But did those wild habits extend to his working life?'

Ride took a long time to answer that question as if weighing up alternative answers. 'No, on the whole, he was still conscientious when it came to his work for Saunders-Woo. It was his family's firm after all; I am a mere newcomer to the company by comparison with the Woo family.' He hesitated. 'I had even begun to see some signs of improvement in his personal life of late, so I was hopeful that he was past the worst, and that he would settle down to a responsible life as head of Saunders-Woo eventually.' His eyes fell. 'So his death now is a bitter blow for us...'

'When did you last see him?' Jericho was curious.

Ride had to think for a moment. 'It must have been this morning. He was certainly in the office this morning, though I don't think I actually spoke to him. He usually comes in on a Saturday to check urgent mail. I'm normally in the office all day on Saturday unless I have appointments elsewhere. It's the best day to catch up with my business correspondence.'

'So you didn't actually see him leave?'

Ride shrugged. 'No, we don't keep tags on each other's whereabouts as closely as that.'

'And you had never been to this apartment in Tai Ping Shan?' Jericho asked.

'No, I told you I didn't even know about it.' Ride seemed suddenly evasive for the first time, and Jericho wondered why that should be. 'Why do you ask?'

'I just wondered if Saunders-Woo might have built this apartment block in Tai Ping Shan.'

Ride shook his head. 'I'm sure we didn't. Otherwise I would have known about it, wouldn't I?' His eyes narrowed. 'I'm not sure what point you are making, Inspector Jericho...'

'Only that the builders may have some questions to answer in due course,' Jericho said carefully. 'I'm no structural engineer, but I would say from a quick examination of the parapet on the balcony that it was unsafe. In which case, an inquest may determine that the builders have some important questions to answer. The builders might even have to face a charge of manslaughter in time if the parapet is shown to have been built incorrectly...'

*

Paul Jericho had been working continuously since seven o'clock this morning, apart from that brief walk in the Botanical Gardens at lunchtime. Yet as he returned with his police driver to Wanchai Police Station at nine o'clock on this Saturday evening after his visit to see Sebastian Ride, he was still reluctant to go home immediately to his empty apartment in Blue Pool Road.

Instead he bade farewell for the night to his driver, Constable Ho, in the rear car park, and then walked along the waterfront road to the Tin Hau Hotel where he went inside the entrance lobby and entered the now familiar bar through its swing door. It was his third visit in a week, so he wondered worriedly if he was perhaps developing some strange addiction for this sleazy place. This time he hadn't bothered to change, though, and was still in his chief inspector's police uniform. Something told him that it was past the time for subterfuge, and that he should now be asking some direct questions in this place. In particular he wanted to talk to Cherry Kwok again about the wealthy-looking Chinese man that she had seen in Hennessy Road with the murdered girl from Shanghai, Dora Kam. Jericho had a feeling that this mystery man – the well-dressed young man with the big Yankee car - might hold the key to unravelling some of Dora's secrets at least. But first he would have to try and identify this man before he could find him...

And the other reason why Paul Jericho had decided to come here tonight was that he wanted to have another talk with the bar manager, Freddie Ling. For he was now beginning to have serious doubts about the veracity of what Freddie had said to him - about never recruiting any of his girls from the bar for his own private escort agency. Despite Freddie's denials on this subject, Jericho now suspected that the bar manager would most certainly have chosen to recruit girls from the bar if they were good-looking enough. *After all, what could be easier?* And Dora Kam and Judy Wong had both certainly been good-looking enough to attract wealthy Western men...

The bar was packed to the gills tonight, so Jericho was unable to get a seat. But he was happy to stand near the entrance door and cast his eye over the scene. The tables were all occupied by seamen of one sort or another, mainly merchant seamen tonight. Many of them were impressively tall and blond - Swedes and Finns from their accents - and they were certainly a physical contrast with the representatives of the lower ranks of the Royal Navy, who were mere runts by comparison and who squabbled with each other constantly in the harsh accents of Wapping or Gravesend.

The atmosphere of the bar was as smoky as ever, and the place still stank of beer and sweat. The fancy coin-operated American gramophone was still churning out music – a new cheerful song called *The Lambeth Walk*, and the Old Groaner Bing Crosby crooning *Pennies from Heaven* yet again - though nobody really seemed to be listening to it above the hubbub of conversation...

The cast of bargirls all seemed much the same as on the previous nights, although Jericho could see no sign of his primary person of interest, Cherry Kwok. The hard-faced Canton girl called Minnie seemed to have three giant Swedes all to herself this evening, Jericho noticed, but was managing to keep them entertained somehow with a flow of cheeky and suggestive observations on life.

Betty Lau wandered in front of Jericho in her black split skirt and her enormous high heels, and seemed about to waggle her behind in his direction until she noticed his uniform. She gulped uncertainly and moved on quickly, but Jericho pulled her back by the arm. 'Where is Cherry Kwok tonight?'

Betty looked blank for a moment. 'Oh, you mean Kwok Yaw-lim? She not working tonight...' With that Betty tottered away on her high heels, until a leery middle-aged British matelot wrapped his arm around her satin-covered backside and pulled her down onto his knee.

But if Cherry Kwok was absent, Jericho's other target - the bar manager Freddie Ling -was very much in evidence, and circulating around the tables encouraging all the sailor customers to have another beer, or fondling the breasts of the girls and recommending them to the rowdy sailors for their beauty and their stamina.

Jericho could see that Freddie had not noticed him standing at the back of the room, so was able to examine the man in some detail, taking in again with distaste his gold teeth and his slicked-back hair and his obsequious manner. Jericho noticed that he had however bought himself a new dinner jacket to wear in the bar, so perhaps things were looking up for him professionally. Freddie did seem inordinately proud of his new sartorial elegance, for he fingered the lapels of his new dinner jacket at regular intervals while examining his image complacently in the mirror behind the bar.

But then some sixth sense told Freddie that he was under close observation, and he suddenly looked up, catching Jericho's eye with a guilty start. Freddie took in Jericho's police uniform first, but then realized that he knew the wearer of that uniform from somewhere. Then – from the sudden change of his expression - the truth obviously came to Freddie Ling in a flash, as he remembered that he had spoken to this policeman two days previously and had possibly said some very indiscreet things.

Freddie moved on to the next table as if nothing had happened, but then slyly retreated by stages to the other end of the room by the gramophone, where he slipped quietly through the rear staff door. Jericho realized that he might be about to lose his man for the evening unless he acted quickly. In a second, he had stepped through the main swing door into the hotel lobby, then by instinct followed a dismal brown corridor at the back of the hotel desk that he thought would lead him in the right direction. The corridor stank of old piss and was lit only by a line of naked bulbs dangling from the ceiling, so clearly wasn't a public part of the hotel. Turning a corner in this evil-smelling corridor, he walked straight into the path of a nervous Freddie Ling, who practically jumped when he saw this uniformed policeman reappear unexpectedly in front of him.

'We need to talk again, Freddie,' Jericho said amiably, moving a few paces towards the nearest electric bulb in the ceiling. He flashed his warrant card in front of the man's hostile face.

Freddie responded with a sullen frown. 'What about...' – he peered again at the warrant card that Jericho was still holding up to the bare electric light - '...Chief...Inspector...of ...Police...*Jericho*...?' Freddie made each carefully articulated word sound like an insult.

Jericho didn't dissemble further. 'About Judy Wong and Dora Kam. The two Northern girls who used to work here in the bar, and who are now both dead...*both strangled.*' Jericho let his voice fall to a threatening whisper. 'You told me that you would never recruit any of the girls from this bar for your own escort agency – the Blue Heaven Agency. But that's not true, is it? Judy and Dora had both left the bar here in June and July to go and work elsewhere. But they hadn't gone to work in any fancy dance hall or nightclub in Central as their friends thought; I think they had gone to work for you...'

Freddie Ling looked around him worriedly. 'I don't know anything about those dead girls.'

'But they were working for your agency, weren't they?' Jericho pressed him.

Freddie sighed deeply. 'Yes, OK, they were. But I still don't know what happened to them. I know nothing about the addresses where the girls go, or about the men they meet. My partner in the agency deals with finding suitable clients and apartments, while my part is limited to providing a supply of beautiful girls...'

'Yet you tried to get *me* as a client,' Jericho reminded him.

Freddie grimaced, showing his gold teeth. 'Yeah, and see where that got me...harassed by the police...'

Jericho could sense that, despite his show of bravado, Freddie was a seriously frightened man.

'Why are you so scared, Freddie?'

'Well, it's not because of you and your useless boys in khaki, *Inspector Jericho*,' Freddie spat out contemptuously.

Jericho had a sudden insight as to the real cause of Freddie's nervousness. 'Have you been upsetting Lucky Lam and the Kao Ki-kan?' Jericho knew that the tentacles of this triad extended everywhere in Wanchai; there probably wasn't a Chinese business in this district that wasn't paying squeeze to the Kao Ki-kan, and that would certainly include the Tin Hau Hotel and its lucrative bar cum brothel.

Freddie moved away from the harsh light of the bare electric bulb, which seemed to be disturbing him. He did seem like a man better suited to living life in the shadows, Jericho thought, like a cockroach. Freddie finally spoke up, a catch of tension in his voice. 'I don't know what you mean. I don't know anybody called Lucky Lam.'

No, nor did anybody else, Jericho thought wryly, for Lucky Lam was a shadowy, and half-mythical, figure among the local residents of Wanchai, a man who didn't apparently like to appear in public, or even to be photographed. Lam had never been arrested or even questioned about any crime, which was the measure of his success as a crime boss. Jericho had certainly never met him, and didn't even know what he looked like exactly, though he had heard rumours that he was a surprisingly young man to have reached the top of the organization. Yet everyone knew who ran organized crime in Wanchai through a string of subsidiary organizations, bossed by a select group of Lucky Lam's able and ruthless lieutenants. Jericho had encountered some of these subsidiary mobsters in the course of his investigations, but even they had never been charged with anything. The most that the Hong Kong Police could do was to chip away occasionally and ineffectively at the nastier edges of the organization – at the knifemen and the gunmen and the dope peddlers – but never truly to get anywhere near the beating heart of this ugly beast.

Jericho knew fine well that Lucky Lam's invincibility from the law was not simply to do with his good joss, of course; he was sure that Lam had bought influence in some very high places, and that half the police force was probably taking money from the triad in one form or another. So Freddie Ling was certainly right to be worried if he had transgressed on their territory in some way. Perhaps, Jericho guessed, they didn't like Freddie striking out on his own and creating a profitable escort agency without paying them their proper cut...

Jericho didn't bother pursuing the matter of Lucky Lam and the Kao Ki-kan further with Freddie, because he knew he would be wasting his time to do so. Instead he chose another direction for his questions that he thought might yield more fruit. 'Who is your partner, Freddie? I need to talk to him and find out what clients Judy and Dora had been seeing. And I also need to find out where Judy and Dora met these clients...' Jericho was still more of the opinion that the man who had strangled Judy and Dora was more likely to be someone they had met here in the Tin Hau Hotel, yet he still couldn't rule out the possibility that their killer might instead be one of the wealthier clients they had met elsewhere.

Freddie shook his head in disgust. *'Tell you my partner's name?* He'll kill me himself if I do that! And I wouldn't blame him for it...'

'Then I'll have to take you into custody and sweat the name out of you,' Jericho promised balefully, prodding the man in the chest with his forefinger and pushing him back against the dirty brown plaster wall. 'This is a murder enquiry, Freddie, so you'd better start taking this matter seriously. I only want information from your partner that pertains to Judy and Dora. I'm not interested in the rest of your sordid operation. Judy and Dora could have been seeing the same man, or at least visiting the same apartment where their killer could have met them.'

Freddie weighed that statement up for a good ten seconds before giving way with a great show of reluctance. 'All right. His name is Marco da Silva. He's a half-breed from Macao.' He licked his lips nervously. 'Not a nice man, which is why I don't want to cross him.'

Jericho stepped back a little. 'Where does this man Da Silva live? How can I contact him?'

Freddie shrugged nervously. 'I don't know where he lives...' He saw the look of disbelief on Jericho's face and added quickly: 'No, I mean it. He was living in Western District somewhere, but he's making so much money now that he told me that he has moved into a new apartment up in the Mid-levels somewhere...'

Jericho assumed from this that Freddie was very much the junior partner in this arrangement.

Freddie saw Jericho's continuing look of disbelief. 'He might have said Bonham Road but I can't be sure. I've never been to his house, not even the old place in Western; when we do meet, which isn't often, it's here in Wanchai. That phone number on the business card for the Blue Heaven Agency – that's a room in a building in Pedder Street opposite the Hong Kong Hotel where we keep a small office. But da Silva doesn't go there often; we have a girl who answers the phone and takes messages – Suzy - but she knows nothing about the details of the clients...' Freddie suddenly glanced behind him as if horror struck. 'Oh, my God! They'll kill me for this...*I'm talking to a cop...*'

Jericho turned to look behind him, alarmed at Freddie's expression. A muscular Chinese man in a dark double-breasted suit stood silhouetted by a faint light at the other end of the corridor, watching them silently. The silence of the man was the most disturbing thing about him; he seemed like some vengeful spirit, hardly human.

Then Jericho returned his attention to Freddie only to find that Ling had vanished. Not only that, the silent threatening figure in the corridor behind him had disappeared like a wraith as well...

Jericho swore to himself, then ran down the corridor towards the far end. There had to be a door at the end somewhere because that was the only way Freddie could have disappeared so magically. He found the door without difficulty, even though it was hidden behind a heavy brocade curtain. The door looked like a service exit and led directly outside into a dim alleyway piled high with nameless rubbish and rotting midden heaps. The blank rear walls of old tenement blocks backed onto the alley from each side, forming a narrow artificial canyon which looked much like the alley where Dora Kam's body had been found, though perhaps a little wider. This one didn't look to be a cul-de-sac, though, for it seemed to go on for some way, and probably ended up by joining the north side of Lockhart Road.

Then Jericho heard the ominous sound of a struggle somewhere in the gloom ahead of him, followed by a high-pitched scream of pain that chilled his blood. He took out his service revolver, thankful that he hadn't changed out of uniform before coming here tonight. He moved forward carefully, until he found what he had been dreading: a man's body lying on its back with a bloody knife wound in the chest. There seemed to be blood everywhere; the whole front of the man's dinner jacket – that new jacket that he had seemed so proud of - was so thick with blood and gore that he could have just stepped out of a slaughterhouse...

A quick examination of the man's face confirmed that the victim was indeed Freddie Ling. Of his assailant there was no sign, so the killer must have made a complete getaway somehow. Jericho was almost convinced that Freddie's assailant had to have been the same muscular Chinese man he had just seen inside the Tin Hau Hotel. Perhaps the man had known a quicker way to get out of the hotel and catch Freddie before he could escape...

Jericho swore again with frustration, sure that Freddie Ling must be dead with such a savage wound in his chest.

But then Freddie groaned slightly...

CHAPTER 11

Sunday, 15th August 1937

Paul Jericho, dressed in his best Sunday suit, emerged with the rest of the congregation from the main west door of St John's Cathedral after morning communion and felt the solid humid heat of a Hong Kong summer morning take full possession of him again. He greeted a few familiar faces among his fellow worshipers, but did not stay long to socialize at the entrance. In five more minutes, he had excused himself from the throng and left at a leisurely pace, taking the north path through the cathedral grounds that led back to Garden Road. But halfway along the path he turned back for a moment to admire the square tower of the cathedral, which was glowing a buttery-yellow colour in the fierce tropic sun. The cream-coloured walls of the chancel too made an enticing contrast with the blue sky and with all the tall green palms and fig trees growing in wild profusion around the building.

Jericho was not a particularly religious man, yet he enjoyed the rituals and the companionship of Christian worship, which had been of particular comfort to him after the death of his wife in January. Many people came here to the cathedral, of course, simply to be seen in the company of the great and good of Hong Kong, for the Governor and his staff always attended Sunday worship in the cathedral. Until a few years ago, cathedral pews had been available for rent, and there had been great social competition among Hong Kong's elite to get a pew as close to the altar and the Governor's pew as possible. But those days were now thankfully gone, and even the punkahs, which had formerly been operated by coolies to provide some relief from the overpowering heat inside, had now been replaced by egalitarian electric fans.

But Paul Jericho was one expatriate who did not come here to the cathedral to curry favour with his superiors or with anyone else; this was the place where Susan's funeral had taken place seven months before, so was an important reference point for him to remember her. Jericho had been surprised and touched at the genuine outpouring of grief there had been for Susan at her funeral; he hadn't really understood before her death how well respected she had been for her teaching and her charity work – and even loved by many, it seemed, from many ordinary Chinese up to the then Deputy Governor himself, Norman Lockhart Smith, who had insisted on attending the service personally.

Jericho walked on towards Garden Road where he had parked his battered old Austin, when he heard a voice calling discreetly behind him. He turned and saw a young woman with red-brown hair and glasses hurrying after him.

He stopped in the shade of an Orchid tree and waited for the woman, whom he now recognized as a good friend of his wife's. 'Ah, Miss Starling. How are you?' he said awkwardly, doffing his Panama hat. He didn't know Edith Starling well but knew she was some sort of secretary in Government House. 'I'm afraid I didn't see you inside, or I would have said hello earlier. I don't think you're a regular at Sunday service, are you?'

Edith Starling looked a little embarrassed. 'No, that's true. But my excuse to God is that, like him, I am usually working on a Sunday.' She hesitated. 'And there's no need to call me "Miss Starling", you know; it makes me feel a hundred and fifty years old. I thought you had progressed to calling me "Edith" the last time we met,' she chided him gently. 'Even if you don't, I am still going to be brazen and call you "Paul". *So there...*'

Jericho had to smile at this girl's engaging personality. He didn't think that he'd seen Edith Starling for two months or more, so they were hardly friends in any conventional sense. In fact he doubted that he had met her more than a dozen times in his entire life; she had been Susan's friend, not his. Jericho didn't know how and why Susan had become such good friends with Edith Starling, but the two of them had become as thick as thieves during the last year of Susan's life. Jericho had been pleased at the time that Susan had found such a good friend to spend her free evenings with, for his long working hours as a policeman had meant that he had spent far too little time with Susan himself. It was certainly something he regretted in retrospect, since he would never be able to make up for that lost time with Susan now.

Jericho hadn't chosen to deliberately avoid Edith since Susan's death, but nor had he gone looking to maintain regular contact with her either. With Susan gone, there had seemed no good reason to keep up their slight acquaintanceship. Lingering at the back of Jericho's mind was the possibility that Edith might know what Susan had been doing up in Kennedy Road on the night she died. But he had never been able to bring himself to ask her directly about it; there were some things that perhaps it was better not to know. This way, being left in ignorance of what had happened, he could still cling to the comforting belief that his wife had not betrayed him with another man. And perhaps that was the real reason why he had chosen to let his acquaintanceship with Edith gradually lapse.

Edith pointed the way ahead. 'Shall we walk together a little?' she suggested.

'My car is parked near the bottom of Garden Road outside the Murray Barracks,' Jericho said. Then he remembered where she lived. 'But you live in Wyndham Street, which is the other way from here.'

Edith shook her head. 'Doesn't matter. I need the exercise and a little walk down Garden Road and then back through Central will suit me very well.'

Jericho wasn't sure that he believed her entirely. In fact he was quietly convinced that she had engineered this meeting deliberately for some reason, which might explain why she had attended Sunday service for once in her best floral dress and hat. Jericho doubted somehow that Edith had romantic designs on him, so there had to be some other reason for this meeting. But perhaps it was still some minor and innocuous thing...

They walked out of the grounds of the cathedral into Garden Road proper and began to walk down the hill towards the Murray Barracks and the parade ground. Glancing at her walking by his side, Jericho realized for the first time that Edith was quite an attractive girl. Not beautiful like Susan, of course, but very pretty even in specs, and with a fine girlish figure.

Edith began to talk about the cathedral organ, which Jericho was sure was not the real reason for her being here. 'It sounds dreadful again, doesn't it? The pipes must have been cracked by the tropical heat again, no doubt. I heard from the verger that they spent *fourteen thousand dollars* on repairing the organ only ten years ago, and now it sounds as bad as ever...'

'That's a huge amount of money,' Jericho agreed neutrally. 'I see you've been getting the sun, Edith.' He wondered if that was why she now seemed much prettier to him than he remembered. Her skin was glowing with a nice soft apricot bloom, which complemented her striking eyes and her chestnut-brown hair.

She seemed a little flustered by his remark, and by his long calculated look. 'Oh yes. I managed to get away to the beach yesterday and do some swimming.'

'Oh, really? Which beach?'

'I don't know the name of it. A little quiet cove on Tai Tam Bay that's always empty.' Edith hesitated. 'It was Susan who told me about it.'

Jericho nodded. 'Ah, yes, I know the place. Susan and I used to love swimming there.'

Edith's eyes fell. 'You must miss her greatly, Paul. I know that I do.'

This felt like a perfect opportunity for Jericho to finally ask her that difficult question, despite all his previous determined resolution not to. 'I've never asked you this before, Edith. But do you know what Susan was doing up in Kennedy Road on the night she died? It's just that she had no friends there that I know of, and no one has ever come forward to say that she was with them that night.'

Edith looked pensive. 'Does it really matter now, Paul? In any case, I don't know where she'd been that night...'

Jericho wasn't entirely convinced by that answer, but decided to let it go. If Susan had been seeing a man that night, then - as Edith said - it hardly mattered now.

'You look tired, Paul,' Edith went on quickly. 'Are you very busy with your police work?'

'I am.' Jericho hadn't got back to bed until the early hours after the stabbing of Freddie Ling. The man had been operated on at the Tung Wah Hospital but was still unconscious and in a critical condition. Jericho knew that he had made a complete hash of things last night by his impromptu visit to the Tin Hau Hotel; he should simply have pulled Freddie Ling in for questioning at the station and interrogated him under a formal caution. Even worse, Ling's assailant had got clean away, and Jericho didn't have a clue what the man looked like apart from his general body shape. And even that was based on the assumption that the muscular man whom Jericho had seen in the service corridor inside the hotel had actually done the deed; for Jericho had not seen the stabbing with his own eyes so would have great trouble proving it. The surgeons at the Tung Wah had also told him that Ling only had a fifty-fifty chance of survival, so Charlie Hebdon was less than happy with Jericho's part in this debacle. Ling had been the best lead they had to find the murderer of Judy Wong and Dora Kam, and Hebdon was annoyed that his own most senior inspector, Paul Jericho, had thrown that lead away by his pure incompetence...

'I heard of the sad death at Government House on Friday night,' Jericho continued, deftly changing the subject from his own problems. 'Did you know Mr Ogden yourself?' he asked solicitously.

Edith looked sombre. 'Yes, I did. Actually I worked for him directly. He was my boss...and a very nice man.'

Jericho knew from Ronnie Grantham that Ogden had been a senior intelligence chief. So, if Edith worked directly for him, then perhaps she was a bit more than just a regular secretary at Government House. Susan had told Jericho that Edith had studied maths at Oxford and was an even more gifted mathematician than she was herself, which was high praise indeed from someone like Susan. So there were clearly hidden depths to Miss Edith Starling, Jericho decided.

Edith was still speaking. 'It seems to have been a heart attack; Ralph did certainly have a bad heart. Yet I was still surprised that he died without making a sound or calling for help...' Edith looked as if she was about to say something more about Ogden, but then lapsed into an awkward silence.

Jericho wondered if this was the real reason why she had waylaid him today. 'Do you have any doubts that Ogden's death was due to purely natural causes?'

Edith seemed a little disconcerted that he should say such a thing. 'No, I can't really say that. I just didn't like the ill timing of it, that's all.'

'Isn't that usually the way with unexpected death?' Jericho said tritely. 'The ill timing of it...'

'I suppose so,' Edith replied moodily.

They had reached the Murray Barracks by now, and Jericho pointed out his old Austin on the other side of the street, parked under a spreading banyan tree. 'I could give you a lift if you want, back to Wyndham Street,' he suggested. 'If you don't mind slumming it anyway; I know you drive a very nice blue American tourer.'

'Not any more I don't; I sold the Studebaker last winter after I smashed it up a bit. I have a little black Austin now just like yours.' But when he pressed her again to take a lift, she still wouldn't hear of it. 'No, really, I prefer to walk from here.' She looked at his rusted old Austin with a resigned smile. 'Your car is in even worse condition than my own Austin Seven.' She sighed, realizing. 'Of course, that's Susan's old car, isn't it?'

'Yes, it's the one she used to drive to school and back. That's why I can't get rid of it,' Jericho admitted ruefully. 'I wish she'd used it on the night she died, but it was in the garage for repair.'

'Yes, I remember...' Edith turned away, her face reflecting her sad thoughts.

But Jericho called her back. 'Perhaps we should meet for a drink sometime, Edith,' he suggested.

'Yes, that would be nice,' she agreed absently as she waved goodbye.

Yet Jericho could see that her thoughts were somewhere else entirely...

*

Edith walked away along Queen's Road Central, past the imposing rear entrance of the massive Hong Kong and Shanghai Bank building. She cursed herself for not being stronger and telling Paul Jericho that she suspected Ralph Ogden might have been murdered – possibly by a traitor inside Government House. That was the main reason why she had come to church this morning, after all – certainly not to take communion.

But she had been constrained in the end from speaking openly by the gross impropriety of such an action. If she told Paul Jericho this much, then she would have to tell him everything – about her work for the SIS decoding Japanese military communications, and about Ralph's position as head of the SIS in East Asia. Otherwise her story would make no sense at all. Yet revealing all this to an outsider would be betraying every security principle she had been taught to hold dear by the Secret Intelligence Service.

She was less in doubt about not telling him the truth about Susan's relationship with Sebastian Ride. She knew for a fact that Susan had been in some love nest with Ride near Kennedy Road on the night of her death. Edith still didn't know for sure if Susan had actually slept with Ride – Susan had never admitted whether she had gone that far - but she had certainly been fascinated by him and flattered by the man's attentions. The ironic thing was that Susan had told Edith that she was intending to break off her relationship with Ride that night. Perhaps she had, or perhaps she hadn't in the end, for Edith had seen enough of Sebastian Ride's handsome face last Monday to know that he might be a difficult man to give up.

Yet Edith had known for sure that Susan had loved her husband deeply; just the way that she talked about him had told her that much. Paul Jericho was a very decent man, and Edith could see what Susan had seen in him. He wasn't handsome or showy or witty, but he was steady and affectionate and reliable. Susan had called him her "rock". Well, Edith was not about to make his grief worse by ever telling him about Sebastian Ride...

In any case, she had her own problems to deal with, which were even more pressing than this old tragedy. She was worried to death now by Michael's behaviour yesterday – blatantly searching through her private briefcase. It wasn't the action of an innocent man - that much was clear. Yet who could she go to about Michael? Who could she trust that much? *The answer was nobody, of course*...and certainly not Paul Jericho.

Edith knew that she daren't admit her fears about Michael to anyone else in Government House. She needed to find out the truth about Michael all by herself...

CHAPTER 12

Wednesday, 18th August 1937

Edith Starling did her best to hold back her tears as the coffin was finally lowered into the rich black earth of Happy Valley cemetery. She couldn't help remembering that Ralph Ogden had only been fifty-three; it was no age at all to die. She recalled him telling her only last week, with poignant timing, that he dreamed of giving up the dirty world of intelligence soon and returning to the groves of academia at Cambridge where he could teach the classics again. At heart that was what Ralph had longed to be again: a classics scholar of repute and a trusted mentor to his students. But his ailing heart had let him down; at least Edith *hoped* that was the reason, and that Ralph hadn't been helped on his journey across the Styx, perhaps by one of the very people gathered around this atmospheric graveside...

    Edith glanced around at the view, and thought that Ralph would probably have appreciated this resting place at least, for there were few more beautiful graveyards than this to spend eternity. The cemetery was located on a steep hillside above Happy Valley, with lots of high stone retaining walls smothered in ivy and creepers, and stands of imposing forest trees that formed an intricate green canopy over this miniature tropical paradise. Black kites circled high overhead on the up draughts, while the Peak rose in the distance above the green ridges and steep-sided valleys of the island. All the upper reaches of the island were covered in this dense green forest of bamboo and Chinese banyan and laurel that rippled in the hot morning breezes blowing along the flanks of the mountain.

    Edith had not attended a funeral at Happy Valley since Susan Jericho had been buried here on a cool grey day in January. Susan's grave was only a short distance away from Ralph's, and Edith could see that her white marble headstone was covered as usual with a fresh bouquet of flowers, no doubt from her still grieving husband Paul. Edith could read the inscription on the headstone clearly even from twenty yards away: *Susan Jericho, Born in Hong Kong May 14th 1903, Died January 19th 1937, Beloved Wife of Paul Jericho...*

Edith had been surprised at the modest turnout for Ralph's funeral – far less than the several hundreds who had attended Susan Jericho's laying to rest - for there were no more than twenty mourners here today, and the service itself had been held in the small cemetery chapel rather than in St John's Cathedral as had been the case for Susan. It was a Wednesday morning of course, which had perhaps discouraged a few from attending. But perhaps Ralph would have preferred to leave the world in this unassuming way; he was not a man for great ceremony after all, and despite his long service to the Empire in a difficult and demanding job, he had always retained a healthy scepticism about the colonial institutions of government, and of the unhealthy sense of racial superiority that the Empire had brought to many rather ordinary Britons. Ralph had indeed thought that much to do with the Empire was pure humbug, so perhaps would have been quite satisfied with this modest farewell.

Yet the Acting Governor, Norman Lockhart Smith, was here with his deputy George Carothers to add the full cachet of the establishment to proceedings, so the funeral was still a very respectful tribute to Ralph's memory. There were no SIS people here, though, apart from Edith herself, dressed in mourning black silk. And she was only here in her pretend capacity as Ralph's secretary. The SIS agents in the government communications centre never mixed openly with the colonial civil servants, and led a somewhat shadowy and unacknowledged existence in the annexe building of Government House. None of the people gathered here at the graveside were officially aware of the fact that Edith was also an SIS agent, although she suspected that the more astute amongst them probably had some inkling of the truth.

Most of those who had known Ralph well at Government House were also in attendance. It was natural that Ralph's old army friend Bob Harmsworth should be here, of course, but Edith had been surprised to see his deputy in the Treasury, Ian Luff, also in attendance. Even more of a surprise was that the Attorney General Julian Colby had made an appearance, together with his wife Eileen. Edith reflected that Ralph had loathed the sight of both Colby and his wife, and that feeling seemed to have been mutual as far as Edith knew, so it was odd that they should appear at his graveside and with such a show of apparent grief. Colby's bald head and skull-like features were not flattered by the black suit and trilby that he was wearing – to Edith his features had something of the look of the preserved mummy of Rameses the Great - while Eileen Colby was decked out preposterously as if this was a royal funeral at Westminster Abbey. Edith could feel the woman's eyes dwell on her critically from time to time; it felt like being probed by the scalpel of an expert surgeon. At least her bitter and waspish tongue was being held in check for once, though.

Ronnie Grantham was standing on the opposite side of the grave to Edith, together with his wife Faye. Ronnie smiled sympathetically at Edith as he noticed her quivering lip. His blond hair was shining in the warm humid sunshine filtering down through the trees, and his soft pink cheeks still made him look to her like a lost schoolboy. She thought that he looked even handsomer than usual, although perhaps it was the presence of the sunken-cheeked and sallow-faced Colby standing so close to him that made him appear so. Colby certainly made an unfortunate physical comparison with Ronnie's fresh-faced demeanour.

Faye was in sombre mood alongside her husband, yet Edith had been almost transfixed today by this woman's luminous beauty. Standing there by the graveside in the dappled green light, Faye seemed like some glorious apparition from the heroic age of Greece. Helen of Troy and Diana and Aphrodite all rolled into one...

Sebastian Ride was certainly thinking similar thoughts to hers, Edith could see. She had not been expecting Sebastian Ride to be here at the funeral, for she doubted if Ride had even known Ralph except as a minor acquaintance. And one would think that Mr Ride must have more pressing things on his mind at present, for Edith had read in the newspapers of the death of his business partner, James Woo, in a tragic accident at the weekend. That was surely a death that had far more significance for Sebastian Ride than the death of Ralph Ogden.

So why was he here at Ralph's funeral?

Yet she remembered now that Ralph had certainly known Ride well enough to realize that he was having an affair with Faye Grantham. And from the subtle looks that Ride was presently exchanging with Faye, Edith could see that this affair was still clearly going strong. Despite their best efforts to hide it, Edith could feel the smouldering intensity passing invisibly between the two of them. Edith suspected that everyone here must sense it unless they were completely lacking in all perception; only hapless, innocent Ronnie Grantham seemed entirely unaware of this secret burning passion between his wife and the handsome Mr Ride.

It occurred to Edith that the party at Government House last week had been an ill-omened one, for *two* of the attendees of that soiree were now unexpectedly dead. That bleak thought did make her wonder for a moment about the laws of probability...

The priest – a senior deacon from the cathedral – made the final benedictions over the grave, and everyone began to move away from the graveside in small subdued groups. There was an awful finality about death, Edith thought, as she stumbled away over the mossy earth. Once a human being had left the world of the living to rot slowly in the earth, they instantly became part of that vast innumerable legion of the dead, part of human history, and no longer a part of the present. Eventually - and perhaps even quite soon - they would be forgotten entirely by the living as if they had never existed. This was the fate of even the greatest of human beings, after all, never mind the common man. Some pertinent lines of Thomas Gray came back to her with a sudden rush: *The paths of glory lead but to the grave...*

And in keeping with Gray's *Elegy in a Country Churchyard*, there would certainly be no more human warmth for Ralph Ogden to enjoy, no more hugs, no more smiles, no more friendship...only the cold embrace of wet clay and slithering worms...

She became aware that someone was walking beside her, and turned to find that it was the ever friendly and amiable Ian Luff.

He smiled sympathetically at her as she stopped in the shade of a giant Bengal fig tree. She could feel a tear still trickling down her cheek, but she refused to wipe it away, wearing it instead like a badge of pride.

Luff's voice was gentle for once, not mocking. 'A sad day. I could see that you were very fond of Ralph, Edith, so his death must be a huge shock to you.'

She acknowledged that with a nod. 'Yes, I liked him very much.'

'Yes, me too,' Luff agreed without any particular emphasis. He looked around at the rampant greenery in the cemetery and at the mountains rising above them. 'This is a truly wonderful place, isn't it? Better even than my beloved Peak District.'

'Is that where you're from, Ian?'

'Yes, Hartington in Derbyshire.' Luff smiled modestly. 'My father was only the local dentist, but, as his only child, he was determined that I should be something better. So he sent me to Eton, and then to Oxford, though I was hardly natural public school material.'

Edith wondered at this unusual frankness on Ian's part. 'Yes, I think you told me before that you read economics at Balliol College.'

'Yet I still let my old man down. I didn't get the first that he expected.' Luff appraised her with a penetrating smile. 'I bet that *you* got a first at Somerville, though, Edith, didn't you?'

Edith smiled back. 'I'm afraid I'm far too modest to say.' She did wonder how he knew that she had been to Somerville College, for she was sure she had never mentioned it to him herself. But perhaps Ralph had told him...

Luff laughed at her reply, and Edith was quite taken for a moment by his warm smile and his engaging features. Ian Luff was probably the only expatriate bachelor that she had met in Hong Kong whom she found attractive; he was slight of build, with intense brown eyes and a golden flush to his skin. In this flattering morning light under the leaves of the fig tree, his neat boyish features gave him the look of a matinee idol from the movies.

'I'm afraid that I'm steaming up,' Edith apologized, aware that her glasses had become fogged in the humid shade. She took them off and wiped them with a handkerchief.

'I'd like to think that I might be the reason for that,' Luff joked. 'But I suspect not.'

She looked at him in surprise. That remark almost sounded to her like blatant flirtation. Edith had always been sure that she didn't interest Ian Luff in the slightest in that way, but now she wasn't quite so sure.

'I see that I have discomposed you a little with that remark, Edith,' Luff went on. 'Yet you must be fully aware that you are an attractive woman...'

'Am I really?' she asked dryly, not sure where this was leading.

'And a very interesting woman too,' Luff continued smoothly. 'For I have heard that since Ogden's death last Friday, your male colleagues in that ultra-secret group who hide away in the annexe building in Government House all now defer to you, dear Edith. Which made me wonder why all these worldly and experienced spies should choose to defer to a mere female secretary.' He laughed at the expression on her face. 'Worry not, Edith. Your secret is safe with me. Yet I must admit that this interesting life of yours makes you so much more attractive to me; perhaps I'm attracted by women with a powerful aura...'

Edith smiled wryly. 'I think you're letting your imagination run away with you, Ian. I really am just the dull secretary I appear to be...' Yet in fact it was quite true that Adam, Broadbent and Casaubon had deferred naturally to her for all important decisions since Ralph's death, even though nothing official had been said on the subject. It did seem as if she had just assumed Ralph's role by some magical and unspecified civil service process...

'Then perhaps this dull secretary would like to have dinner with me this evening. I live up in Bowen Road in the Eastern Mid-levels. But I can easily drive down to Central and pick you up there. I've never tried the restaurant at the Repulse Bay Hotel – wouldn't you like to join me there this evening?'

Edith thought that her social life was clearly picking up; first, Paul Jericho had asked her out for a drink, and now Ian Luff wanted to take her to dinner. But she had far too many things on her mind to be thinking about such casual diversions as these. 'I'm not sure that would be a good idea, Ian.'

His face fell and he looked almost crestfallen. Edith guessed that few women had ever turned Ian Luff down, and that he simply wasn't used to refusal.

He finally smiled, though, with characteristic good humour. 'All right. But I beg leave to ask you again in due course. Perhaps I might grow on you with time, Edith...like creeping ivy.'

'Yes, perhaps you will,' Edith agreed with a smile, as she finally took her leave of him and headed off up the steep flight of stone steps that led towards the Stubbs Road entrance, and her parked Austin.

*

Stubbs Road was a steep and winding road that ran along one side of the cemetery before then climbing even higher as it ascended towards the Wong Nei Chung Gap and eventually over the mountains to the south side of the island. Edith had parked her car on Stubbs Road near the upper gate of the cemetery because she loved the view from here of the whole of Happy Valley and Wanchai laid out before her. The climb back to the upper gate was a tiring one in the heat, though, and in these uncomfortable high-heeled shoes. Yet the old flight of stairs was a beautiful thing to contemplate in itself, arched over by densely foliaged trees and with its stone balustrade festooned with flowering creepers. When she reached the upper gate, Edith saw a pretty Hakka girl standing in a pool of sunlight under the trees outside, coiling and ornamenting her sleek black hair before entering the cemetery, as if wanting to look her best for all these dead English people lying in this green patch of Chinese earth.

Edith smiled at the girl who responded shyly in kind. Yet as Edith finally reached her car, which she had left in a small lay-by near the gate, she had a sudden revelation. She'd been thinking again during the funeral ceremony about Ralph's suspicion that there was a traitor inside Government House leaking information to the Japanese. And now those casual thoughts suddenly crystallized into something more definite. She remembered that Ralph had released a tempting snippet of information about the China Fleet to this individual that he suspected – details of a new piece of sounding equipment that the Royal Navy was supposedly testing. He had set this trap a full week ago, so if this person was really a traitor, then the information should certainly have got back to the ears of the Japanese War Ministry by now, and also to the attention of Britain's own informant inside that ministry, the *Hyōbu-sho*. Yet the fact was that Edith had heard nothing back in the last five days from the Tokyo embassy on this subject. There'd certainly been no message from the informant in the War Ministry about any new piece of sounding equipment that the Royal Navy was apparently testing.

Edith felt a sudden flood of relief. *Ralph had been wrong*; the person he suspected inside Government House had *not* passed on this carefully salted secret...

Which meant that there might never have been a traitor inside Government House at all. The only evidence for this after all had been the information provided by the informant inside the Japanese War Ministry.

Suddenly Edith felt the fog disappear from her mind...*the leaks must have come from this informant in the* Hyōbu-sho *himself*. This man had then sensibly muddied the waters by claiming that there was a traitor in Government House in Hong Kong.

Why had she not seen this before? It seemed obvious now; the man in the *Hyōbu-sho* was either a double agent, or else the Japanese had realized the truth about him and had forced the man to start releasing misleading information to the British...

Edith decided that she must get back to Government House urgently and tell Adam, Broadbent and Casaubon what was going on. Yet she was still curious to know who Ralph had suspected in Government House. Ralph was not a man to be easily fooled so there must have been *some* definite grounds for suspicion about this person, otherwise Ralph would certainly not have bothered devising this elaborate ruse to try and prove it. Therefore it was probably better that she *didn't* speak to ABC just yet until she was absolutely sure...

A voice suddenly startled her. 'You look remarkably bright and cheery, Edith, for such a sad day...'

Bob Harmsworth was just opening the door of a splendid new two-door Fiat 1500 convertible that was parked in the lay-by behind her own little Austin Seven. He smiled quizzically at her, his silver hair gleaming in the sun. That hair would do credit to a platinum blonde like Jean Harlow, Edith thought with slight envy.

She recovered quickly from her flustered state. 'Well, it's a beautiful day, Bob. And perhaps we shouldn't feel too sad for Ralph. I'm sure that he would rather be remembered with a smile than a tear.'

'Yes, indeed,' Harmsworth agreed readily. 'I see that you and Ralph had obviously become very close.'

'Yes, absolutely.'

Harmsworth looked like he expected her to say more on that subject, but she decided to disappoint him and keep her thoughts to herself. Instead, she chose to admire his Fiat, which seemed a much safer subject. 'That's a beautiful car you have,' she complimented him. 'It looks expensive.'

'Yes, that it most certainly is,' Harmsworth said with a rueful shrug. 'But at my age I deserve a few innocent pleasures, don't I? And a beautiful Italian car is certainly one of those, now that I am too old for the ladies. Isn't the aerodynamic styling wonderful – all those smooth slinky curves...just like a modern woman, in fact.' Harmsworth eyed her with a twinkle. 'This model was only introduced two years ago at the Milan Motor Show. It has an overhead valve straight-six engine, a four-speed transmission, and a top speed of over seventy. I think I'm in love for the first time since my wife died.'

Edith laughed with him but could see that Harmsworth was genuinely proud of his new toy.

Edith had heard from Ralph that his friend Harmsworth was very well off after all his years of service in Hong Kong, and had a splendid apartment in Kotewall Road high up in the Mid-levels. Ralph had also used to visit Harmsworth occasionally at weekends at his beachfront bungalow near Shek-O where they could reminisce about their memories of fighting together in France. Yet Ralph had also told Edith that, despite his wealth, Bob Harmsworth was a very lonely man since the death of his wife. He had a couple of grown-up daughters in London, but he never saw them these days, apparently...

Harmsworth was about to get into his car, but then apparently changed his mind. He walked back over to Edith and showed her the palm of his right hand. She saw for the first time, with a feeling of slight shock, that his first and second fingers were missing their tips. 'I will never forget Ralph Ogden's friendship and loyalty, not while I carry these shorn off fingers.'

Edith was surprised she had never noticed his truncated fingers before. 'How did you get that injury? Was it on the Somme?'

Harmsworth nodded. 'It was. But not in the heroic way you probably expect. You see I did it to myself...'

Edith was genuinely shocked now. 'Really?'

Harmsworth smiled grimly. 'Yes, really. Though I'm not proud to admit it. Ralph and I were both captains with the Eighth Battalion of the Norfolk Regiment that took part in the attack near Montauban on the first day of the Battle of the Somme, the first of July. We managed to take six enemy trenches before we were relieved on the third day of the battle after suffering nearly four hundred casualties. Then we were ordered back in to take part in the attack on Delville Wood on the nineteenth of July. But I was completely done by then – a wreck. Two years in France had already turned my hair white, though I was only in my early thirties. And I couldn't keep my hands from shaking; I was like an old man with Parkinson's disease. So I took my service pistol and shot away two of my own fingers the night before we were due to go over the top again...fortunately even my shaking hands couldn't miss from six inches...'

'That must have been horrendous,' Edith said lamely.

'It could have been much worse; our commanding officer suspected the truth and wanted me charged with cowardice and dereliction of duty. I could have been put before a firing squad and shot for what I did.'

'Why weren't you?' Edith asked in a subdued voice.

Harmsworth glanced down into the green cemetery. 'It was because of that man we just laid to rest down there. Ralph risked everything and told a lie on my behalf. He gave evidence to our major that I had been hit by a German sniper trying pot luck. This major really respected Ralph so accepted his story, unlikely though it was from the physical evidence of the wound. So I got away with it; ended up with a soft billet on the staff at brigade headquarters twenty miles behind the line. Ralph on the other hand had to go over the top the next day and for many months afterwards. He should have died; only miraculous luck brought him through the rest of the war more or less unscathed.' A tear finally came to Harmsworth's eye and his voice became a low sob of pain. 'He was the finest man I ever knew.' He raised his damaged hand again. 'Unlike Ralph, I doubt very much that I would have been lucky enough to survive another eighteen months of trench warfare. So I'm sure that these missing fingers are the only reason why I'm still here...'

*

Sebastian Ride lay back in bed with Faye in his arms. 'Do you think that your husband knows that we came straight up here after the funeral?' It was three in the afternoon, and they were lying together, their bodies intimately entwined, in the master bedroom of the company flat in Bowen Road.

Faye clearly didn't care what her husband thought. 'I doubt it. I'm sure Ronnie is already back at his desk in Government House and jumping to attention every time Julian Colby snaps his fingers.'

Ride wondered what Faye would say if he told her the truth: that he had brought her up here this afternoon to finish his affair with her. But his willpower was simply not up to the task of evicting this glorious and sensuous woman from his life: no sooner had they walked over the threshold of the apartment than he had started to undress her, piece by intimate piece.

Sebastian looked at her naked body in wonder, admiring her suppleness and her grace. There was something leopard-like in the languorous way she moved. Even with her hair tousled from making love, and with the makeup wiped from her cheeks by their violent exertions, she was still the most beautiful thing he had ever seen. 'I don't know how I managed to get through that funeral today,' he said.

She stirred her bare rump. 'Why? I thought it was a very moving service.'

'No, I didn't mean that.' He sighed. 'It was the sight of you. I was simply mesmerized by your beauty as you stood beside that graveside. I couldn't take my eyes off you. I don't know how I stopped myself from leaping across the grave, and picking you up in my arms...'

Faye laughed. 'Really? In front of my husband? Would that have been wise?'

Ride laughed too. 'And in front of the Acting Governor too, remember. That would have definitely caused a stir. It might even have woken up poor Ralph Ogden from his grave.'

Faye snuggled up to him again and ran her fingers down between the hard muscles of his chest. 'What are we going to do, Sebastian?'

He was surprised at her sudden change of mood; it was as if the sun had vanished behind a black cloud. 'What do you mean? Are you saying that you might leave Ronnie for me?'

Faye kissed his right breast. 'Of course I might. More to the point, though, would you ever leave Gloria?'

Ride took her hand. 'I think that's almost inevitable now, no matter what you and I decide to do. But I would want to get her well again first before I did finally leave her. I owe her that much.'

Faye took a deep breath of exasperation at this, while Ride watched her beautiful slender rib cage rise and fall. 'Have you ever thought of leaving Hong Kong and taking your business skills elsewhere, Sebastian?'

He was surprised to hear such a suggestion because Hong Kong had been his whole life for so long. 'Like where?'

'Like my homeland, South Africa. I want to go back there eventually and settle. And I think you would do very well there. The opportunities are endless there; you would love Natal in particular, which is virgin territory just waiting for a businessman like you to take it into the twentieth century.'

'It would mean starting again almost from scratch,' he protested mildly.

'Hardly. You would still be a very wealthy man if you sold your stake in Saunders-Woo. You own thirty percent of the company outright, which must make you one of the richest men in Hong Kong.'

'And your father literally owns a gold mine in Johannesburg, doesn't he?' Ride countered.

She smiled. 'He does. In fact I own half a goldmine too, all by myself. So we would never need to worry about money. In fact we could spend our time arguing about which of us has the most money...'

'Everyone worries about money. And the more you have, the more worrying it becomes,' Ride said cynically.

Faye tut-tutted. 'You know fine well what I mean, Sebastian. We could live like royalty if we wished. But more to the point, in South Africa we would have a chance to start with a clean slate, away from the reminders and recriminations of all our old mistakes,' Faye whispered. 'I know it would be hard for you to leave Gloria despite what you say. The woman is in a tragic state. But you didn't do it to her...'

'Many people will say that I did,' Ride interrupted harshly.

'Then let them say it. That's why we need to leave and start elsewhere. I have always despised the sort of people who allow themselves to suffer messy and unpleasant divorces, but you may have to accept some pain if you leave Gloria. I think Ronnie would be more understanding, though, if I simply told him that our marriage had run its course and that we should both move on. He knows I would give him a generous settlement...'

'You almost make it sound like Ronnie married you for your money. Is that true?'

Faye laid her head on his bare chest. 'In a way he did. I think he was pleased to win the prestige of having a wealthy wife. That was more important to him than the money itself. Actually Ronnie has very little interest in material things. He is motivated by other things than money; status is what truly matters to him. He is absolutely determined to become Attorney General of Hong Kong in time; it has become his complete obsession. He would do nothing that might rock the boat in that respect, so I'm fairly sure he would accept a divorce without making a great song and dance about it.'

Ride kissed her tenderly on the lips. 'Then I'll give it some serious thought.'

Faye got up from the bed and checked her face in a wall mirror with a sigh. 'Look at what you've done to me! I have to go now, Sebastian. I had better be home in Robinson Road by the time Ronnie gets back.'

Ride got up and embraced her, but then let her go without further protest. He watched her dress hurriedly, and marvelled at how ordinary that process looked compared to the erotic delight of undressing the same woman. She made some quick repairs to her face, then left in a flurry, blowing him a kiss from the doorway.

Ride went and had a shower, and then began to dress too, whistling happily to himself. He found it remarkable how quickly he was getting over the death of James Woo. Four days ago it had seemed like the greatest tragedy of his life, but the horror of that moment had paled now to no more than an uneasy memory.

Frances had been absolutely right in advising him against going to the police and admitting the truth of what had happened. There was absolutely no point in being noble and telling the truth in this case; it would only ruin his life and his business for no good purpose. If he had admitted to the police that he had been there in the apartment when it happened, then no one would have believed it to be an accident. Of course the accident probably would never have happened at all if he had not followed James to his secret apartment – at least not on that particular day. So his actions had certainly led indirectly to James's death. Yet the fact was that the parapet on the balcony had given way under James's weight when Ride had not even been touching him. In fact he, Sebastian Ride, had even tried to save the man at the risk to his own life...

So why should he take the blame for what had happened?

That policeman, Paul Jericho, had the right of it. It was the *builder* of that death trap apartment who should take the blame for James's death, not him...

Ride looked around the apartment as he prepared to leave. James's death had caused a lot of extra work for him, so he needed to get back to the office and go through all the urgent matters with Frances. Yet as he moved around this top floor apartment, he couldn't help remembering another tragedy that he'd been involved in – one that had happened near here: the death of Susan Jericho.

It had been disconcerting that it should be Susan's husband, of all people, who had come to Conduit Road to tell him about the death of James Woo. If James had told him at least part of the truth about what had happened to Susan that night, then it seemed to Ride that the three of them - he and James Woo and Paul Jericho - were all connected oddly by that tragedy...

Ride had met Susan Jericho for the first time at a speech day at St Stephen's College last September. Saunders-Woo had paid for a new science lab for the school, so he had been guest of honour at the school prize-giving.

After that first night, he had pursued her relentlessly like a wolf chasing a helpless hind. Something about her – her gamin-like beauty and her unmatchable charm - had woken up an unlikely passion in Sebastian Ride's world-weary mind. She wasn't as glamorous as Faye Grantham, yet she had soon seemed to him the most desirable woman he had ever met. She had resisted all his attempts to charm her at first, though, as he contrived to meet her "by accident" in various places. Eventually she had given in to his attentions enough to have a drink with him, then a quiet dinner ending with a brotherly kiss on the cheek. By this time he'd fallen in love with her to a quite extraordinary degree for someone like him. He'd never known a woman who had affected him quite like this.

They hadn't even slept together, yet he already knew that he wanted her for his wife. He had been prepared to divorce Gloria without a second thought then. He had even told Susan in the end that he wanted to marry her, and that did seem to finally shock her into a reaction as she realized the trap she had fallen into.

Then the tragedy of that last night, January 19th...

She had agreed to come to this very flat in Bowen Road late that night. Because she had arranged to come at such a late hour, he had been confident that he had won, that she was going to finally surrender to him and spend the night.

But she hadn't. Instead she had come only to tell him that their relationship must end completely there and then. She couldn't betray her husband; nothing would ever tempt her to do that.

Then she was gone, within ten minutes at most. He'd soon left the apartment too, in a quiet daze, as heartbroken as an adolescent boy. He'd walked away from the rear of the apartment block using a cinder path that led higher up to Bowen Road where he usually parked his car when he was here. So he had heard and seen nothing of what had happened on Kennedy Road below: Susan dying in agony after being struck by a hit-and-run driver...

Ride's thoughts returned yet again to James Woo's version of what had happened that night. Yet it still made more sense to him that James had been lying, and that it was actually *he* who had been driving the car that hit Susan. Ride wasn't even so sure any more that James had not done it deliberately: perhaps he had killed Susan Jericho with deliberate intent as an act of pure hatred against his own business partner...

Therefore, if nothing else, the accident that had killed James Woo on Saturday had been justice of a sort for the terrible thing that he had done to Susan Jericho...

CHAPTER 13

Thursday, 19th August 1937

At ten o'clock in the morning, a bleary-eyed George Dorling stood at the window of Chief Inspector Jericho's office in Wanchai Police Station as he waited for his chief to arrive. Jericho was presently at the other end of the corridor having a probably testy meeting with his own chief, Charlie Hebdon, over the lack of progress on the Wanchai murders. This new possible link of this case to the Kao Ki-kan triad was unsettling for Dorling; he had done his very best to ensure that the investigation into the deaths of Judy Wong and Dora Kam should go in *any* direction other than that of the Kao Ki-kan.

The last week had been a nightmare for him as he had tried to pretend to Jericho that he was back to being the old George Dorling – cheerful, dependable, honest. Although he had made a point of keeping off the booze this week, and of always being neatly shaved and wearing a clean uniform every day, yet he always felt as if Jericho would see through the pretence and have it out with him. Paul Jericho was the best natural detective that Dorling had ever come across; a man whose instincts always seemed to hone in on the guilty like an arrow...

At least there had been some good news for Dorling yesterday: the bar manager from the Tin Hau, Freddie Ling, had not recovered from his injuries and had died in the Tung Wah Hospital without regaining consciousness. That did at least close off any enquiries that might lead directly back to the Kao Ki-kan from Freddie Ling. And there had been no progress at all in finding the man's partner, Marco da Silva. Dorling and Thomas Sung had located the room in the office building in Pedder Street out of which the Blue Heaven Agency operated; that had been easy enough. But the room had been stripped bare of any helpful information and was devoid of any witnesses: there was no secretary called Suzy in attendance, and certainly no Eurasian gentleman called Marco da Silva...

Dorling looked right across the harbour to the Kowloon wharf where the P & O liner, the *SS Rajputana,* had just lately berthed. This was the very liner that he and Tess had taken when they had come out to Hong Kong three years ago. He remembered the optimism and joy of that voyage: the delight of his pretty little Nippy waitress as she had found herself on her way to Hong Kong on board such a beautiful liner. That voyage on the *Rajputana* had seemed like a Hollywood movie to Tess; he could remember her glowing happiness as the ship had finally berthed in Kowloon after her six-week voyage.

He wondered now how it could all have gone so wrong in the mere three years since then. Yet he knew the answer, of course...*greed;* he'd seen all his colleagues on the make, minting it in with squeeze, and he'd decided that he wanted some of that easy money for himself...

He borrowed the field glasses on Jericho's desk and turned them towards the *SS Rajputana* to get a better look. Through the glasses he could see quite clearly in the brilliant tropical light that she was disembarking her passengers already. This latest voyage of the *SS Rajputana* had been a grimmer affair than her usual airy voyages to and from Europe; the ship had been hired from P & O by the Hong Kong Government to evacuate the first group of British women and children refugees from Shanghai. George had heard that there were over a thousand arriving today, and more would be due soon. The situation in China was deteriorating rapidly, and the Japanese were now waging a full scale devastating war on the Chinese mainland, even though war had not been officially declared by them. Many people expected that the Japanese air force might soon start bombing major cities like Shanghai. Japanese newspapers were still however referring to the carnage in China as a mere "incident". It did make Dorling wonder what the Japs would consider to be all-out war, if what was going on in China at present was to them no more than an "incident"...

Many of the British refugees had friends and family in Hong Kong, of course, so would be taken in by them. Those refugees without such an easy option, though – up to five hundred of them – were to be housed in a temporary hostel that had been created in the grandstand of the Hong Kong Jockey Club in Happy Valley, with catering provided by the department store Lane Crawford, no less. Yet these were troubling times for Hong Kong, for many worried that it would only be a matter of time before the war in China would spill over into Hong Kong too.

Dorling replaced the field glasses on Jericho's desk, then ran a weary hand through his thick bristly ginger hair. His head ached constantly these days as if it was about to burst with all the pressure building inside him. He was still terrified of the truth coming out, for that would be the end of him. Part of this truth was the fact that he had known Dora Kam: he had met her one night in the bar of the Tin Hau Hotel at the end of May, and had spent an hour with her upstairs in one of the rooms. He had been drunk that night, or else he would never have done it, even though she was a beautiful girl, far better than the usual run of Wanchai bargirls. He could have made the excuse to himself that Tess had just lost her baby then and he was feeling desolated with the pain of that loss, but the real reason was that he had been drunk and had lost his normal inhibitions about paying for sex. In the normal course of events, his little fall from grace wouldn't have mattered a damn; no one would ever have found out about it, least of all Tess. He certainly had no plans to go back and see Dora a second time.

Yet he did see her a second time in even more troubling circumstances: on June 12th, a Saturday night, the night that the informer Ricky Sun had been murdered...

For several months before this, George has been gambling all his squeeze money in illegal gambling dens. At first he had won at dice and at roulette, and it seemed like the good times would never end. He was making so much money that he even began to imagine that he could consider moving back to England with Tess and living on the investments he could buy with all his crooked earnings. Yet his luck began to change in May, and he found himself losing heavily. Soon he found all his squeeze money gone, yet he couldn't give up the gambling which was by now a complete addiction to him. So he began to gamble with money borrowed from a Chinese moneylender in Lockhart Road. In the end he found himself in debt to the tune of fifty thousand Hong Kong dollars, or over two thousand pounds. It was then that he discovered that the moneylender business was owned by the Kao Ki-kan, and that he therefore owed the money to the ruthless triad society who ran organized crime in Wanchai through a string of subsidiary organizations.

He knew then that he was in big trouble, for he had no hope of ever paying back this amount of money. In desperation he did think of fleeing the colony for the safety of England, but something told him that he would not be safe from the Kao Ki-kan even there. The Kao Ki-kan were entirely amoral as far as he could see; their basic aims were only about making money and exercising power. They weren't even patriotic in any real sense, and Dorling had heard rumours that they were quite happy to sell British military defence secrets to Japanese agents in Hong Kong, even though this would hardly be of any benefit to their Chinese homeland.

One night, coming out of the station, he'd been bundled into a car by two men and taken blindfolded to a secret address somewhere in Western District. Dorling suspected the apartment was in Tai Ping Shan but didn't know for sure since he saw nothing of the journey. When they took off his blindfold he found himself in a cluttered Chinese living room, alone with one Chinese man. The man didn't introduce himself, but Dorling was convinced that this was Lucky Lam himself. This individual was dressed in

Western style; he looked like any young Chinese businessman from Central, not the leader of a violent organization like the Kao Ki-kan.

Dorling had been expecting that they would demand their pound of flesh, and that it would have to be something big to compensate for the amount of money he owed them. When Lam told him what they wanted, Dorling was nearly physically sick. They wanted the name of the informer who was passing their secrets to the police. '*Just give us the name, and then we will call it quits...*'

It had seemed like the only way out, so Dorling had given them Ricky Sun's name. He had a shrewd suspicion, though, that they already knew who the informer was, and were merely testing him. So this test was just a likely precursor to what they really wanted, which was total control over him. And that was the way it had proved to be; he was now completely in the power of the Kao Ki-kan. The debt had never been wiped out; it was clearly going to be a permanent debt that would last indefinitely and keep him in their clutches forever.

When they had asked Dorling to lure Ricky Sun into an alleyway in Wanchai on that Saturday night, June 12th, he'd had no choice but to comply. Ricky Sun had not suspected a thing; in his way he had been remarkably naive in his trust of expatriate policemen. After three armed gang members had appeared from hiding in the alleyway and surrounded Ricky Sun, George had refused to wait around and watch the execution of a now terrified man. Yet walking away hurriedly into Lockhart Road with his head down, he had literally bumped into almost the last person he wanted to see there...*Dora Kam*...

He could see that she had recognized him, and therefore could be a witness against him. So, a day later, he had given her name to the Kao Ki-kan triad and asked them to make sure that she didn't come forward as a witness. He had thought that a simple threat from the triad would be enough to stop her coming forward. But when her body had been found last week, he had been sure that the Kao Ki-kan must have done it to make sure of her silence. It wasn't the normal way that the Kao Ki-kan would murder a woman – strangulation was not normally their style – but perhaps they had been clever in this case, and simply copied the style of the earlier killing of the other bargirl, Judy Wong. As far as Dorling knew, Judy Wong had nothing to do with the Kao Ki-kan, and must have been murdered by some drunken violent seaman, exactly as Paul Jericho had thought originally. Or possibly she had been killed by one of the wealthier clients she had met while working for the Blue Heaven escort agency, as Jericho was now coming around to believe.

It seemed certain to Dorling that the Kao Ki-kan had murdered the bar manager Freddie Ling too, though he knew nothing about the reasons for it, or the circumstances. But it was likely that Ling and his partner Da Silva had either muscled in on triad territory by opening up this pimping agency without permission, or else Ling too had welched on a debt to them, just like himself...'

Dorling turned around suddenly as he heard Jericho bustle through the door behind him. Jericho's face was grim. 'I'm afraid we can't have our meeting after all, George. We've just received a report of another body. Just around the corner...*in another tenement in Lockhart Road*...'

*

George Dorling looked at the body on the bed. 'I know this girl from somewhere, sir.'

Jericho nodded expressionlessly. 'So do I. It's the girl I spoke to in the Tin Hau bar twice last week...*Cherry Kwok*. She's been strangled, just like the others...' Jericho swore out loud. 'I'm losing my touch, George. I knew in my heart that this girl was the key to this whole case, and I simply allowed myself to forget it after being distracted by that wretched business with Freddie Ling...'

The police surgeon, Dr Formby, was late on the scene as usual so Dorling bent down to look at the body himself. 'I'd say from the look of the body that she's been dead since last night, sir.' Cherry Kwok was still fully clothed, and wearing the same cheap cotton dress that Jericho had seen her wearing a week ago in the Tin Hau bar. Yet her eyes were protruding in ugly fashion now and her mouth gaped open in a silent scream so that she barely seemed like the same pretty girl that Jericho remembered.

'The killer probably followed her home from the bar,' Jericho realized. 'He must have been waiting outside the bar for her.'

'Couldn't he have gone in and picked her up inside, then left with her?' Dorling asked, as he straightened up.

Jericho shook his head. 'The girls aren't allowed to do that. They have to take their pickups upstairs for short times; that's the only reason the hotel allows them to ply their trade in the bar instead of on the street. They would be banned from the bar if they started making private arrangements and taking men back directly to their own rooms.'

Dorling looked again at the dead girl on the bed. 'I wouldn't have minded picking up this one myself. I'll say this for our killer; he only goes for the best-looking women...'

Jericho was surprised at Dorling's cynical reaction to finding a third young woman murdered; he seemed almost relieved about something.

'What is it, George? What are you thinking?' Jericho asked, wondering if Dorling had perhaps seen something obvious that he had missed. He glanced around this miserable little room, which seemed piled high with the accumulated junk of decades – piles of newspapers, stacks of old clothes, broken china. The heat in the room was so intense that it felt to Jericho as if all these piles of junk might just suddenly burst into flames spontaneously. Yet Cherry had only been in Hong Kong for a few months so most of this junk couldn't be hers anyway; she'd clearly just inherited most of this stuff from the previous occupants and hadn't bothered to clear it out.

Dorling took his time to answer, but did finally offer an opinion. 'I'm probably thinking the same thing as you, sir. This girl Cherry had also left the Tin Hau bar lately to work elsewhere. The chances are high therefore that she had also gone to work for Freddie Ling's escort agency. So it becomes much likelier that the killer is someone these girls met while working with the Blue Heaven escort agency, rather than a sailor from the Tin Hau bar. Otherwise it seems like an odd coincidence that the three girls who were murdered had all recently left the Tin Hau for pastures new. The good thing is that the murders might be nothing to do with the triads...'

'What about the murder of Freddie Ling?' Jericho demanded.

'Ah, that might well be the work of the Kao Ki-kan. We might never get a conviction there, since you didn't get a good look at the man whom you think might have done it. Yet Freddie Ling's death probably has nothing to do directly with the death of these girls. I think these three girls have some direct connection with a particular man, who has turned against them for some reason. He could well be a Westerner, as you've thought from the start. Perhaps this man enjoyed the experience of killing Judy so much, that he now wants to relive the experience at regular intervals.'

'I hope to God that you're wrong, George,' Jericho said moodily. A fresh thought occurred to him. 'There was a difference with Cherry, though. She had returned to the Tin Hau bar to work, unlike Judy and Dora, who never made it back. Which might mean that Cherry was actually working in a different place to Judy and Dora. Or else she was working for the Blue Heaven Agency, but didn't like what she had to do for the customers...'

'Perhaps Cherry felt safer in the Tin Hau bar?' Dorling suggested.

'Yes, maybe,' Jericho agreed. 'That might confirm what you said: that she had no fear of any of the sailors in the Tin Hau bar, but might have left the Blue Heaven Agency to get away from the attentions of some particular threatening individual whom she had met while working there. I wish to God that she'd come clean with me; it might have saved her life if she had. But it seems, like most Chinese, that she didn't trust the police.' He sighed heavily. 'With Freddie Ling dead, and the other man Da Silva gone, it's going to be very hard now to find out what particular clients these girls might have met through the escort agency. Freddie Ling suggested that his girls would be delivered to different private houses and apartments all over Hong Kong, where they could meet potential clients who could then take their pick...'

'Sounds like a real cattle market,' Dorling said with more sympathy.

'Yes, it does that,' Jericho said tiredly. He was still feeling sick at heart that this girl too was dead. Despite what he'd said, he couldn't get over the feeling that he had let this last girl down personally. He noticed suddenly that her gold ankle chain - the one with a clasp in the shape of a dolphin - was gone and wondered whether the killer had taken it.

When he mentioned it to George, Dorling looked doubtful. 'Doesn't seem likely, sir. This was certainly no robbery. Perhaps the thing has just fallen off somewhere?'

Jericho remembered that Cherry's anklet had a broken clasp, so it seemed quite likely that she had lost it somewhere else. In fact she could have lost it anywhere during the last few days so its disappearance might have nothing to do with the circumstances of her murder at all. Jericho looked around the room again, at the damp grey plaster walls and the stained ceiling and the worn floorboards. Cooking smells drifted up the staircase from the even meaner rooms below. 'Yet I'm not so sure we can absolve the Kao Ki-kan completely from these killings, George, for we keep tripping over connections to the triads in this case, don't we?'

Dorling seemed disturbed by the idea. 'Why would you say that, sir?'

Jericho hesitated for a moment, not entirely sure himself. 'These three girls didn't really like each other, as far as I know. Cherry certainly didn't like Judy, even though they were both from the Northern provinces and spoke more or less the same dialect of Chinese. And Cherry and Judy had nothing in common with Dora who was from Shanghai...' Then he remembered something else that might be significant. 'Cherry told me that she had seen Dora once in June in Hennessey Road with a Chinese man. He was wearing an expensive suit and he got out of big car, a big Yankee car according to Cherry. The man looked like a rich Shanghai businessman, not like a coolie. He and Dora looked like they were good friends. The man was quite young, quite thin and handsome. Who does that sound like to you?'

Dorling held up his hands helplessly. 'I've no idea, sir.'

Jericho was surprised that George didn't see it. 'Well I have. Particularly the part about the big Yankee car. I know somebody who fits that description exactly and who also drove a big Cadillac...'

Dorling still looked confused. 'Who do you mean, sir?'

Jericho gave him a dismissive look. 'I mean *Ricky Sun*...'

*

After Dr Formby had arrived and begun to make a detailed examination of the body, Jericho excused himself and went down to the street. The temperature outside felt almost balmy after the boiling heat inside the murder room, and Jericho was desperately in need of some air. It was just gone noon now and the usual curious crowd of local Chinese spectators had assembled in Lockhart Road to view proceedings.

Jericho scanned the silent moody crowd and saw that Maggie Yiu was standing amongst them, a head and shoulders even above all the men.

He walked over to her. 'Good afternoon, Miss Yiu. We meet again,' he said with a smile. He beckoned her away from the crowd to a quieter corner further along the street, as he wanted to ask her whether she had had fresh thoughts about the second victim, Dora Kam – the victim she had known. He saw that he had stopped inadvertently in front of a Chinese funeral paper shop, a place where elaborate paper models were sold as presents for the dead in the afterlife. By the simple expedient of burning the models, the gift was transferred to the departed person: bridges to facilitate their crossing into the next world, bundles of million-dollar notes to keep them in comfort, junks, houses, even whole apartment buildings for the entrepreneurs of the netherworld. The interior of the shop was dim even on this hot August day and, inside, a skeletal old man in shorts and a singlet worked away industriously making more models with paper and glue. Jericho felt a sudden urge to make some offering of his own for the dead girl across the street – perhaps a paper mansion so that she might find the wealth and happiness in her afterlife that she had failed to find in this life...

Miss Yiu had clearly noted his sombre mood, and was equally cheerless in response. 'No, nothing more about Dora has occurred to me.' Her face fell even further. 'Perhaps I have brought bad joss to this street. I always seem to turn up like the proverbial bad penny whenever there's more disturbing news, don't I.' She glanced at the tenement across the street. 'Is this what I think it is?'

He nodded. 'I'm afraid it is. Victim number three. Another young woman who worked in the bar at the Tin Hau hotel.'

'Are you any closer to catching this devil?' she asked with an impatient turn of her head. Even in his present dismal mood, Paul Jericho couldn't help marvelling anew at this woman's extraordinary beauty, which was such a perfect combination of East and West. In the brilliant noonday sunshine, with the sun almost standing vertically above her head like a spotlight, her mass of shining raven hair gleamed like black silk.

He wasn't sure how to answer her question, though. 'We *are* making progress, but it's a difficult and tortuous investigation, I'm afraid,' he said cautiously. He had a sudden thought, after her own remark about bringing bad joss to this street. 'Why *are* you here today, Miss Yiu, may I ask?'

She looked confused for a moment, then said dryly, 'I live here, Inspector, only a hundred yards down the street.'

Jericho smiled faintly. 'No, I mean: why aren't you in school?'

'Ah, if you had children, you would know that without being told, Inspector.' She smiled faintly. 'St Stephen's Girls College is closed now for the summer holidays, as all Hong Kong schools are. So I am a lady of leisure at the moment.'

Jericho tried not to look sheepish at his own lack of awareness 'Ah, I see. I should have realized, of course, despite not having any children of my own. I did catch sight of you in the Botanical Gardens last weekend. Is that one of your regular excursions during the summer holidays?'

She seemed a little put out by this, as if she suspected him of spying on her. 'No, not really. But I *was* there on Saturday, I think. I'm afraid I didn't see you, though, Inspector.'

'No, I don't think you did,' he said, although he was quietly convinced that she *had* seen him and had chosen deliberately to avoid him. It now occurred to him that she had probably been meeting a man on Saturday, for the Botanical Gardens was a popular place for young trysting couples. If she *had* been meeting a man, then Paul Jericho felt a sudden envy of this fortunate individual, whoever he was...

Jericho suddenly realized that George Dorling was calling him from the entrance to the tenement across the street. 'Will you excuse me, Miss Yiu? It seems my sergeant needs me.'

Dorling still had his eyes trained on the other side of the street as Jericho joined him. 'Isn't that woman you were talking to the witness we questioned before, sir? She always seems to be hanging around here in Lockhart Road when there's a murder, doesn't she?'

Jericho gave George a stony look of disapproval in return. 'She's hardly "hanging around", George; she does live in this street, after all.'

Dorling didn't seem convinced. 'If you say so, sir...' he said doubtfully. Then his voice changed to a more excited tone. 'I've got a witness, sir, who might have seen something last night. Or at least I think I have, since she's pretty hard to follow. She's a Shanghai woman apparently, and none of our men can understand everything she's saying. But she definitely lives on the floor below Cherry Kwok, and she does claim to have seen something last night.'

'From Shanghai, do you say? Are you sure? Just wait a moment then, will you, George?' In a second, Jericho had returned across the street and asked Maggie Yiu if she would join him and help question a witness.

Miss Yiu seemed a little reluctant at first, but then assented with a resigned shrug.

Dorling ushered the witness out of the tenement to where Jericho and Maggie Yiu were now waiting. The witness was a white-haired old lady, but she clearly hadn't been in Hong Kong long, for Jericho soon discovered she only spoke a few halting words of Cantonese.

Jericho asked Miss Yiu to speak to the woman in her own Shanghai dialect, which she did. The old woman looked relieved to have finally found someone who could understand her. Her ancient wrinkled cheeks broke into a semblance of a smile, and she soon launched into a breathless torrent of explanation.

Jericho hadn't understood more than a word or two of her Shanghai dialect. 'What does she say?' he asked Maggie Yiu as the woman finally ran out of breath.

Miss Yiu took a deep breath of her own. 'She says that she saw a man leave the room on the top floor last night. Maybe eleven o'clock, or a little later.' She glanced at the old woman who was now silent and brooding. 'She was putting out her garbage in the alley, and had just returned to her own room, when she saw this man coming down the stairs from the top floor. She didn't know anything bad had happened upstairs; she just assumed that the young woman had been entertaining a man. It was dark, and she couldn't see anything of the man's face or hair as he came down the stairs; he had a hat pulled down low over his eyes. But then he stepped into the pool of light from an oil lamp in her room, and she saw his eyes clearly for just a moment.' Miss Yiu hesitated. 'Blue eyes...she says they were definitely *blue eyes...*'

*

At eight o'clock that evening, Paul Jericho sat in the main smoking room of the Hong Kong Club, enjoying a drink with his friend Ronnie Grantham. Jericho was not a member of this club, which was reserved for only the grandees of the Hong Kong establishment. But he was an occasional visitor courtesy of his friendship with Ronnie, who was of course a long standing member because of his high rank in the government service.

The club was housed in a distinguished colonial building in Royal Square. When it was built in the last century, the club building had looked out directly over the harbour with regal importance and style. But with the extensive reclamation schemes of the twenties, the building was now set back a whole block from the new Praya, Connaught Road. Yet despite losing its privileged position on the waterfront, it was nevertheless still the place for ambitious expats to be seen. Being admitted as a member of this club was the ultimate cachet for civil servants and businessmen in Hong Kong, but not many policemen managed to achieve that honoured status apart from a few very senior men like Superintendent Hebdon and Commissioner Matlock. The roll call of present and former members of this club read like a Who's Who of Hong Kong business leaders - or at least of the European ones anyway. This was still one door that the Chinese and other races in Hong Kong had not yet managed to crash, no matter how rich and well connected they were.

The smoking room was almost a carbon copy of similar rooms that might be found in a gentleman's club in Pall Mall or St James's, the main difference being the giant electric ceiling fans that turned slowly above their heads to create a breeze.

Ronnie had just been reading the evening newspaper, but now he put it aside with a frown. 'I hear there has been another murder in Wanchai. You must be getting worried, Paul, that we have a maniac on the loose.'

Jericho glanced up as a man moved past his armchair and murmured a greeting. He hadn't seen who it was, but now turned his head and realized that it was Inspector Kevin Ball. He wondered if Ball had somehow managed to wangle his way into membership of this club; it had to be a possibility with the shameless lickspittle ways that Ball used to cultivate all the right sort of people as friends, particularly Charlie Hebdon, who was a long-time member here. Jericho's only consolation over the dismal progress being made on the Wanchai bargirl murders was that Ball seemed to be making just as little progress with the Ricky Sun investigation.

He turned back to Ronnie. 'Oh, I'm not sure that this man is a maniac. I have a feeling he has a definite agenda, a definite plan.'

'But you still think he's a Westerner?'

Jericho shrugged. 'There seems little doubt of it now. We have a witness who saw the man leave the room of the latest victim last night...'

'Really?' Ronnie looked interested. 'That's good news, then.'

Jericho pulled a wry face. 'It's hardly that. All the witness saw was a pair of blue eyes, nothing else. Half the Westerners in Hong Kong must have blue eyes so it scarcely narrows down my search. I've got blue eyes myself, and so have you. But it does at least suggest that I am on the right lines: that these three women all met a Western man in the course of their work, who has turned violent. The motive doesn't seem to be primarily a sexual one, for the women had not been sexually assaulted in any way. Perhaps he had come to see these women as a threat to his reputation; or perhaps they had learned something incriminating against him which he couldn't afford to have come out. That's what I'm beginning to sense: that there is some order behind these murders rather than just random acts of violence. I get the feeling that this man might even hate what he is doing; that he's doing something which is against his basic nature. I just hope that he stops now, and that there isn't a fourth or a fifth woman who needs to be silenced...'

Ronnie raised his whisky and soda and took a long thoughtful sip. In the subdued lighting of the smoking room, he looked to Jericho even younger than usual, hardly more than a fresh-faced college student. He was still so much like his dead brother Johnny that Paul Jericho felt something like an ache at this constant reminder of his dead friend. 'I'm sure you'll get this man in the end, Paul,' Ronnie said. 'As I told you before, I don't think you're the type of person to ever give up a chase like this. You'll keep going to the bitter end until you catch this devil.'

Jericho rather liked the compliment, but wasn't as convinced of his own infallibility as Ronnie seemed to be. He changed the subject deftly because the last thing he wanted to talk about tonight was his police work. 'It was an odd thing about that man Ogden's death, wasn't it? We had just been talking about him in Bessie's Bar last Friday. Hadn't he called you back that night for some sort of security briefing in Government House?'

Ronnie nodded. 'Yes, he had. But he died suddenly that very evening before he could deliver his talk. I felt very bad afterwards about mocking him and his security concerns, for I know he was a good man at heart, a real old-fashioned English gent. We buried him yesterday in Happy Valley, you know. Very sad business...' He took a long breath. 'Yet the remarkable thing about this whole business is that a little slip of a girl, Edith Starling, seems to have taken over Ralph's role as head of the intelligence section.'

'I know Edith quite well, Ronnie,' Jericho interjected warningly, not wanting Ronnie to say anything about her he shouldn't.

'Do you?' Ronnie clearly had a sudden realization from Jericho's warning tone. 'Ah yes, she was a friend of Susan's, wasn't she? I'd quite forgotten that.'

Jericho turned his head as he heard a burst of raucous laughter erupt at a nearby table, and saw a group of three men getting to their feet in readiness to leave. He recognized one of the men as Bob Harmsworth, the urbane and silver-haired Colonial Treasurer, whom he had bumped into in the Botanical Gardens last Saturday.

The three men walked past their table as they left, and stopped to have a word with Ronnie Grantham, who stood up to greet them.

Jericho climbed to his feet too, so Ronnie introduced him to the other two men. 'Do you know Julian Colby, Paul? He's the Attorney General, and more importantly my boss, so please tell him what a wonderful chap I am,' he said lightly.

Jericho was interested to meet Julian Colby finally, and to see if the man really was the way that Ronnie had described him. He smiled and shook Colby's hand, and they exchanged routine pleasantries. Jericho found that Ronnie's view of the man was just about right: Colby was an unsettling man in the flesh, with a face like a skull and the burning blue eyes of a religious fanatic like Savonarola. His five o'clock shadow was so deep and penetrating that it threatened to spread from his jaw line to take over his whole face.

The other man with him, Ian Luff, was a much pleasanter-looking individual with a passing resemblance to the Duke of Windsor. It seemed that he was one of Harmsworth's right hand men, a sociable young man with an easy and accomplished manner. 'How do you do, Inspector Jericho? I've heard your name from Ronnie, of course, so it's a pleasure to finally meet you in the flesh.'

Jericho had a feeling that he had seen this man somewhere before, but couldn't place exactly when and where. But perhaps it was just the man's vague resemblance to the Duke of Windsor that was confusing him.

Harmsworth too seemed in a much better mood than at their last meeting in the Botanical Gardens, and was positively jovial as he greeted Jericho with apparent enthusiasm. But perhaps he was simply getting over the shock of his friend Ralph Ogden's death by now, Jericho thought.

These three senior colleagues of Ronnie didn't stay long talking and soon excused themselves. Jericho sat down again with Ronnie and watched them leave the room. Next to the Governor and the Colonial Secretary, he supposed that these three men were probably among the most powerful officials in the Hong Kong Government.

Ronnie turned his handsome blond head to follow the direction of Jericho's eyes. 'So which one of those men impressed you the most, Paul? Which of them do you think has the most natural authority and potential for leadership?'

Something about the tone of the question suggested to Jericho that Ronnie already had a clear opinion on this matter himself. 'I wouldn't like to say on such a casual acquaintanceship,' he demurred.

Ronnie smiled disarmingly. 'Well, I know them well enough. And I would say the natural leader amongst them is young Ian Luff. In my opinion, that's a man who clearly knows what he wants in life... *and how to get it...*'

Jericho looked at his friend with surprise, for there was an unmistakable edge of bitterness in Ronnie's voice as he pronounced that last telling phrase. Yet Ronnie Grantham was not usually the bitter sort so it seemed clear that this young colleague of his, Ian Luff, had done something seriously wrong to offend him...

CHAPTER 14

Friday, 20th August 1937

Ralph Ogden had lived on the top floor apartment of a pleasant four-storey block of flats in Macdonnell Road. This road was high up in the Eastern Mid-levels, half way between Kennedy Road lower down the hill, and Bowen Road above. Edith Starling had never been to this apartment when Ralph was alive, but today she had spent almost the entire day here as she sifted through all his belongings for some clue as to whom he had suspected in Government House of passing on secrets to the Japanese.

Edith still felt guilty about prying into Ralph's private life in this way, but she had found nothing in his office in Government House to help her, so coming here and making a thorough search of his home had seemed like the only sensible action to take. After Ralph's funeral on Wednesday, Edith had almost managed to convince herself that he must have been wrong in suspecting a traitor in Government House. She had even gone so far as to send letters on her own authority by diplomatic courier to SIS headquarters in London, and to the British Embassy in Tokyo, in which she had expressed her suspicions about the trustworthiness of the SIS informant inside the Japanese Ministry of War in Tokyo, the *Hyōbu-sho,* and had asked them to be cautious in their dealings with this man.

But on Wednesday night, after she had returned home, she had begun to think a little more clearly and question her own conclusions. For the one undeniable thing about Ralph Ogden was that he had been supremely smart; if he had suspected someone of being a traitor, the odds were very high that he had been right. After all, Edith had only based her conclusion that he had got it wrong on the fact that there had been no comeback on the deliberate trap he had set for the presumed guilty person. That was still the case, in fact: there'd still been no confirming message from the informant in the War Ministry in Tokyo about any new piece of sounding equipment that the Royal Navy was apparently testing. This could of course simply mean that there was no traitor in Government House at all, and that the informant in the War Ministry had simply made this story up.

But what if the informer in Tokyo was being straight with them, and there was *actually a traitor in Hong Kong?* If that was so, *was* there any other explanation why Ralph's trap had failed to catch its intended target? Ralph could of course have leaked his fake secret to the wrong person entirely, but Edith dismissed that possibility for the present. The other possibility was that Ralph had leaked his secret to the *right* person – the real traitor – but that that person had seen through the ruse and not risen to the bait. In fact Ralph's trap might have had exactly the opposite effect to that intended; it might simply have alerted the traitor to the fact that Ralph was on to him and needed to be eliminated as soon as possible...

Faced with this worrying conclusion, Edith had spent the whole of Thursday searching Ralph's office. She had often seen him scribbling notes in meetings into a little private notebook that he always carried with him. But she'd found no sign of any notebook in his office, nor anything else that gave her any clues as to whom Ralph had suspected. She had however found the spare key to his home in Macdonnell Road. She also learned in passing from Bob Harmsworth that Ralph's houseboy and amah were no longer in residence there; Harmsworth had taken the trouble to go to Macdonnell Road this week and pay off these two long-serving servants with a generous gratuity that should tide them over until they could find new employers. 'It seemed like the least I could do for Ralph,' Harmsworth had said. 'He was very fond of his servants who'd both been with him for years...'

So Edith had decided to take the whole of Friday off from Government House and to drive up to Macdonnell Road in her little Austin and search Ralph's flat from top to bottom. She hadn't told anyone what she was going to do; not even Bob Harmsworth (who would most certainly have not approved of such a disrespectful action), nor even her most senior SIS colleagues ABC. Adam and Broadbent were away in China for a few days anyway on an SIS mission to meet the Nationalist Chinese leaders in Nanking, and wouldn't be back until next week, while Elliot Casaubon was still deferring to her for all important local intelligence decisions. Casaubon was more than ten years her senior, and vastly more experienced, yet he seemed quite unable to make any decisions unless she endorsed them too. Edith knew that she should be flattered by this, but was instead becoming increasingly frustrated with the man...

Now, in late afternoon on Friday, with the sun getting low in the western sky, Edith was close to admitting defeat in her search of Ralph's home. She had searched everywhere where he might have kept some secret papers or notebooks – the living room, the bedrooms, the kitchen, even the bathroom – but she had found nothing. As a classic scholar, Ralph had a vast collection of books in his spare room, and Edith had religiously gone through every one. He seemed to have a particular affinity for the works of Horace and Virgil and Marcus Aurelius, but none of these books contained anything but dense scholastic prose.

Hot and fatigued after this long day of searching, she went and sat on a rattan chair on the balcony, which had a fine view of the harbour. Immediately below her was Kennedy Road, and then the steep green slopes fell away further still to the white villas and apartments of the lower Mid-levels and then finally to the grander, taller colonial architecture of Central District. All around her, other elegant white apartment blocks poked their fine roofs above the trees and the greenery that clothed the hillsides. Then it suddenly occurred to Edith that the very spot in Kennedy Road where poor Susan Jericho had died in January was almost directly below her field of view...

That thought jolted her a little. If Ralph had been sitting on his balcony that night, he would have seen the whole dreadful thing. In fact many people might have seen it, for all the wealthy apartment blocks on this green hillside had balconies facing towards the harbour. Yet she remembered that January 19th had been a bitterly cold night by Hong Kong standards, therefore not many people would have been out on their balconies on that wintry night, and at such a late hour...

The line of the Peak Tram crossed over a nearby bridge on Macdonnell Road, and Edith could see a packed tram passing over it on its way up to the Peak, illuminated strikingly by the brilliant red light of sunset. She reflected that Ralph must have sat in this same chair many times and regarded this same view of the blue harbour and the distant line of mountains on the Kowloon side. It was obviously a good place to reflect on things at the end of a long working day; she could just imagine Ralph sitting here and scribbling things in his little notebook – reminders to jog his memory the following day, and to crystallise his thoughts. If she looked below to the west, she could even see the roof of Government House, with its lush gardens of azaleas and fan palms and orchid trees bathed in glowing sunlight. If she turned her head to the east on the other hand, she could plainly see the squat shape of the Japanese consulate building, which was only two hundred yards east of here, and also located on Macdonnell Road.

Edith wondered at that: *had Ralph taken this flat deliberately so that he would be near to the beating heart of his enemy?* Or was it simply a pure coincidence that he lived only a stone's throw from the Japanese consulate? For everyone knew that this particular Japanese consulate was being used to coordinate the activities of the hundreds of Japanese agents and informers in Hong Kong. Yet they were mostly allowed to get away with it, for both the British government and the Hong Kong Governor were extremely nervous of provoking the Japanese too much, so preferred to let them get on with what they viewed as harmless plotting. Nobody in Whitehall really believed that the Japanese would ever be stupid enough to attack British interests in the Far East directly, though some suspected they might do so indirectly through agent provocateurs.

Edith herself was not so convinced about the harmlessness of Japanese intentions, though. From her long history of reading their war ministry signals to their Kwantung Army, Edith had gained a disturbing insight into the Japanese military mind. If the Kwantung Army invaded the South of China, she doubted that people with such rigid minds as these Japanese generals would obligingly stop their troops and their bombers when they got to the border with British Hong Kong...

Edith suddenly sat up in her rattan armchair as she noticed something on the balcony that struck her as odd. Ralph had told her many times that he had a great love of flowers, and had found that watering his balcony plants was one of the most restful and soothing pleasures in his life. Therefore, as she had expected, Ralph had a fine selection of ceramic Chinese flower pots on his balcony, filled with African marigolds, petunias, geraniums, and freesias, which were all beginning to wilt a little after not being watered for a few days - in fact probably not since Ralph's death a week ago. Yet one pot of white lilies was still perfect. She leant over and stroked the petals of the lilies, then realized the truth: these weren't real flowers at all but clever copies made of silk. Even from two feet away they looked like the real thing, so were a triumph of the artificial flower-maker's art.

For a moment Edith was quite diverted by these beautiful silk flowers. But the improvement in her mood didn't last long: she sighed with frustration as she decided that it was time to give up her pointless search and leave the apartment. But as she climbed to her feet, something made her look again at the pot of fake lilies, for Ralph had also told her once that he loathed artificial flowers: '*...I can't see the bloody point of those wretched things, can you, Edith...?*'

She tugged impatiently at the silk flowers, which lifted easily with their hidden wooden base to reveal a small bamboo box secreted inside the main body of the pot. Yet the box was still large enough to contain something interesting: a series of small notebooks filled with copious notes and names...

Edith muttered a small but very unladylike whoop of triumph as she realized that she had found Ralph's secret notebooks. Perhaps this was the only place that he could keep anything safe from the prying eyes of his servants, for he clearly undertook the job of watering these pots himself. She realized that she herself would never have noticed anything special about this pot, but for the fact that the other living plants were presently wilting from drought. And this balcony was certainly a convenient place for him to scribble down his private thoughts at the end of the day, as she'd already realized.

She began to flick through them feverishly. She could see that these notebooks went back several years, so concentrated her attention on what was obviously the latest, for it was only half full. The notebooks were clearly a set of "to do" lists to jog Ralph's somewhat uncertain memory, but also full of seemingly random doodles and scribbles. The pages weren't dated, yet Edith could see from the last completed page that it must be very recent, for the references were all about current issues. Since this seemed to be his current notebook, she wondered why he hadn't had it with him at Government House on the day he died. But perhaps he'd simply forgotten to bring it to work that day, which was fortunate for her.

Her excitement grew when she saw that Ralph had written the question: *Can we trust this informer in the Japanese War Ministry?* He had underlined this three times in red, which proved its importance to him.

Below that he had written: *My source with the Kao Ki-kan tells me that they have members working for the British military who are passing information about our border defences to the Japanese consulate in Macdonnell Road. They are using a woman as their main courier...I need to have this woman watched...she is probably being paid by this bogus company, the King Chung Company, based in Shameen, Canton province...*

Edith knew who the Kao Ki-kan were, of course. But she was surprised to read this because Ralph had never mentioned such a possibility to her: that one of the major triad societies in Hong Kong was apparently colluding with the Japanese.

But none of this told her who the traitor in Government House might be. She quickly collected all the notebooks together again and placed them in her handbag, then took a final look around the flat before closing the front door quietly behind her. She could see that she was going to have a long night ahead of her, for she needed to read all these notebooks through from start to finish.

But then before leaving to return to her car parked below, she had a second thought and reopened the front door of Ralph's apartment. Then she went back to the patio and found Ralph's own watering can, then gave all his real pot plants a thorough soaking. It seemed like the least she could do in the circumstances...for some reason she did not want Ralph's plants to die from neglect any time soon...

*

Edith had just parked her Austin in busy Pedder Street near the Hong Kong Hotel, when, from the driver's seat, she spotted Michael Yip getting off a westbound tram at the nearby tram stop in Des Voeux Road...

She hadn't spoken to Michael since their excursion to Tai Tam Bay last Saturday, although they had arranged provisionally that he would come to her home in Wyndham Street tomorrow evening to spend the night. She still hadn't resolved to herself what to do about Michael. Half of her wanted to break with him completely after she had seen him blatantly going through the contents of her private briefcase. If her SIS bosses ever discovered that she'd allowed her Chinese lover to read through classified documents, she would be for the high jump, and deservedly so.

Yet the other half of her couldn't bear the thought of giving him up, and wanted still to believe in him. But, to have any hopes of clearing the air between them, she knew that she would have to confront him with the evidence of what he'd done, and see what sort of explanation he might come up with. Either that, or receive some sort of excuse or apology for his behaviour, at least...

But, conscious that she would be spending this Friday evening going through Ralph Ogden's notebooks at home, Edith was in no mood to talk to Michael at present. Yet she couldn't help her eyes following him as he walked along Des Voeux Road in the rapidly fading dusk, past the noisy line of rickshaw coolies assembled outside the Hong Kong Hotel, then crossed Pedder Street towards the very parking bays where she had just stopped. For a moment she thought that Michael must have recognized her car and was going to greet her. Yet he walked straight past her car without any sign of recognition, so obviously hadn't seen her at all. He did seem in a highly preoccupied state, Edith thought as she turned her head to follow his progress. He came to the entrance of a modern four-storey office building on the corner of Pedder Street and Queens Road, and entered the lobby almost furtively as if he was doing something distasteful.

Perhaps it was because of Michael's furtive manner that Edith decided she had to know what he was up to. This wasn't his own office building, she did know that much. Michael's law practice operated out of a rundown building on Hennessey Road in Wanchai, which is where she guessed that he'd probably just come from, since the tram he had been on had certainly come from that direction. Whatever the reason, Edith found herself getting smartly out of her Austin and following Michael into the office building.

The building lobby was plain but spotlessly clean: a mosaic tile floor and polished limestone walls. There was a reception desk in one corner, but nobody was about. There was a modern American elevator opposite the desk but Edith saw that Michael must have taken the stairs since the lift seemed stuck at present on the top floor. Edith took the stairs too, and could hear Michael's heels clicking on the stone treads above her head. He left the stairwell at the first floor and Edith did the same. She hung back in the stairwell for a second, though, giving him time to reach his destination. A quick peek around the corner showed her that Michael was just entering an office door at the far end of the first floor corridor. Within a few seconds, Edith was outside the same door. An engraved nameplate on the door announced that these were the premises of something called the "Blue Heaven Agency".

Edith could hear a low hum of conversation coming from inside. She glanced back down the corridor, which was lined with brass spittoons that gleamed like oil lamps even in the subdued electric lighting. No one was about in the corridor so she risked a look through the keyhole. She could see far enough inside to realize that there was a small windowless outer office on the other side of the door, with a water cooler and a receptionist's desk, with another door behind it leading presumably to the main office. There was certainly nobody in the ante-room otherwise the voices would have been much louder. Taking a deep breath, Edith tried the doorknob, which turned easily to her touch. Inside, she closed the door behind her, though not fully, conscious that she might need to make a quick getaway if she was discovered. The thought of being discovered here was more embarrassing to her than anything else; she couldn't imagine what she would say to justify herself if Michael should suddenly step out of the inner office and find her skulking here.

But she wasn't going to turn back now for she could hear the voices with more clarity – still muffled, of course, by the heavy hardwood door, but clear enough to understand their full meaning. Michael was talking to the other unseen man in English, almost as if he wanted her to eavesdrop...

'...so....*Senhor* Da Silva. Why have you asked me to come here?' Michael's voice sounded cold and mocking in tone.

'I need help, Michael.' The other man was clearly more desperate from his voice.

'Why should I help a nasty individual like you, Marco?'

'Because I've been very useful to you, haven't I? I have given you lots of important information...'

Michael's voice became a hiss of displeasure. 'You haven't *given* me anything, Marco. You've been well paid for your services.'

'Yet I don't think you would want my death on your conscience, Michael.' The man's despair was turning to abject fear. 'Lucky Lam is after me. He has already killed my main partner.'

Listening in the outer office, Edith gave a sudden start at this, for she knew the name of Lucky Lam from somewhere. Ralph had mentioned this name to her once. Then it suddenly came to her... *Lucky Lam was the leader of the Kao Ki-kan triad society...*

'Why would he be after you?' Michael's voice demanded.

'He might have found out that I have been giving...sorry...*selling*...information to you.'

Michael coughed cynically. 'More likely it's because this little pimping agency of yours has been trespassing on their territory and costing them money.'

'That could also be true,' the other man admitted. 'But you know that I have been one of your best informers in Hong Kong. And I can be again, if I can only disappear for a few weeks until this fuss dies down.'

'So slither back to Macau, then,' Michael said coldly. 'You'll be able to disappear among all the other Portuguese half-breeds there...'

'Hah! It would be even easier to murder me in Macau than here,' the man muttered. 'But I have another friend who will let me stay at his house on the small fishing island of Cheung Chau. I should be safe there even from Lucky Lam. But I need money to tide me over.'

'Can't your other helpful friend give you that money?'

'He says he can't afford it, not even a couple of hundred dollars.' The man's voice took on a wheedling tone. 'I thought we were friends, Michael.'

'You and I were *never* friends, Marco,' Michael said quietly. There was a long pause before Michael spoke again. 'But here's your money. Two hundred on account for future services. I hope it keeps you alive...'

Edith suddenly realized with shock that Michael was about to leave, and that she had only a few seconds to get out of here before she was discovered. In a moment, she was back through the outer door and racing to the security of the stairwell. Once she was out of sight in the stairwell, she glanced around the corner and saw that Michael was following her down the corridor, an angry frown set on his usually amiable face. Edith quickly ran up to the next landing out of sight, then waited for Michael to enter the stairwell and take the stairs back down to the lobby.

She waited a full five minutes before she dared to venture down to the lobby herself. She had just got back to the lobby when she saw another man enter the main door from Pedder Street. With a gasp of surprise she saw that it was *Ian Luff*...

She stepped back quickly out of sight again, and was relieved when Luff marched over to the elevator, which had just arrived back at that level. Luff spoke to the lift operator, a smartly dressed Chinese youth in a black and green livery uniform. 'First Floor, please.'

As soon as the lift door closed, Edith marched briskly across the lobby and out into the simmering warmth of a Hong Kong summer night. But she scarcely gave any notice to the heat. Her thoughts were instead preoccupied with what Ian Luff of all people might be doing in this building.

Yet the odds seemed very high that he was also on his way to meet this Senhor Da Silva of the Blue Heaven Agency...

*

Paul Jericho was working late on Friday evening in his office at Wanchai Police Station. Jericho had let George Dorling go home early tonight for the poor devil seemed all in after being on duty continuously since yesterday morning when the body of Cherry Kwok had been discovered.

He certainly didn't want George to suffer any relapse of his stress and to turn to drink again for relief. Jericho had told him to take the night off and to take Tess to the pictures: he had recommended a new film opening at the Star Cinema - *The Petrified Forest,* a gangster film with the English actor Leslie Howard and a promising young actress called Bette Davis. Jericho recalled seeing her a year ago in a film of a Somerset Maugham story, *Of Human Bondage,* where she had played a mean and vindictive young harlot with real conviction. He remembered Susan telling him afterwards that young Bette Davis would go far in the acting game...

George had smiled uneasily. 'I think I see enough real gangsters at work, sir, so I might just give it a miss and have dinner at home with the missus tonight.'

Jericho had nodded in return. 'You're probably wise, George...probably wise...'

Now, at nine o'clock, he looked up as Constables Sung and Ho appeared at his door. Constable Ho had now given up completely all his old duties as Jericho's regular driver, in favour of full time investigation work. A new officer had been nominated to take over as Jericho's driver, but this Constable Chang wouldn't be available for another month or so until his driver training was completed. So Jericho was now driving his own car on police duty, though he was breaking regulations by doing so since his little Austin was neither robust enough nor fast enough for police duty, and was a positive embarrassment when compared to the sturdy Morris Fourteen squad cars of the regular police fleet.

Sung murmured an apology for disturbing him.

'No matter, Thomas. What have you found?' From the expectant look on Sung's face, Jericho guessed that he and Ho had found something interesting. He had sent them to the Tin Hau Hotel this afternoon to try and discover if Cherry Kwok had had any clients on the last day of her life – Wednesday.

As the elder statesman of the pair, Thomas Sung did all the talking, while Gary Ho stood at his elbow, brimming with barely suppressed enthusiasm. 'I got this information from Betty Lau, the girl with the show-off walk...'

'I know which one you mean,' Jericho said dryly.

A brief smile flickered across Sung's face. 'Cherry Kwok did get one customer on Wednesday, according to Betty. Which was quite good, because the bar was very quiet that night, no more than half full. Betty said she didn't see the man well, but he looked like an ordinary seaman, maybe a first mate or engineer off a merchant ship. Quite old, she thought. But a lot of the girls like older men, Betty said, because they have better manners than the young ones, and are a bit gentler with them, as well as more generous. Betty didn't see the colour of this man's eyes, but she doesn't remember him as being blue-eyed.'

Jericho stroked his chin thoughtfully. He had cut his chin shaving this morning, and the cut still smarted. 'That doesn't sound like the man that the old woman saw coming out of Cherry Kwok's room, does it?'

Sung shook his head, while Ho did the same in unison. 'No, sir. I think your theory is right: that the man who murdered Cherry was waiting outside and followed her when she finished work for the night. That was about ten thirty, according to the observant Betty...'

'Betty sounds like she would make a good detective herself if we ever choose to let women join the force,' Jericho said.

'Her waggling bottom would be a bit of a distraction to the men, though, sir,' Sung answered, injecting some dry humour of his own into the conversation.

Jericho could see that Sung was building up to making some big announcement. He waited expectantly.

'We searched the room upstairs that Cherry and her sailor client had used on Wednesday, and we found this under the bed...' Sung reached into his pocket and retrieved what looked like a business card.

Jericho examined the card and couldn't help issuing a low whistle of surprise. For the name on the business card was Ian Luff, and his title was given as Secretary to the Colonial Treasurer...

*

Back at home at her flat in Wyndham Street, Edith had spent the last two hours reading through the most recent of Ralph Ogden's notebooks. She sat on the sofa in her living room, under the bright glare of her reading lamp, and pored over the densely written pages. The entries were a mess, random jottings and lists, odd dates and cryptic comments which meant very little even to her.

She did like one comment that Ralph had written, though: *Miss Starling continues to amaze me. Edith is a wonderfully gifted young woman. And a handsome girl too; she often makes me wish that I was twenty five years younger. I do therefore feel some guilt at having to keep her so much in the dark...*

Edith felt grateful for this unsolicited praise from her dead colleague, but some exasperation too at the knowledge that he had been holding so much back from her. She had certainly not found anything yet in the notebook to give her any solid clue as to the identity of Ralph's suspected traitor at Government House.

But her own thoughts quickly turned to Ian Luff. Seeing him tonight in that building in Pedder Street had been a profound shock to her; she had always thought Luff to be the most dependable and trustworthy man in Government House, but now he seemed completely tainted by what she had seen tonight. She didn't doubt that Luff knew this suspect individual Marco da Silva too, who clearly in turn had some connections with the Kao

Ki-kan triad society. It was bad enough that Michael should know such a suspicious character as this Marco da Silva. *But Ian Luff too?* It didn't bear thinking about...

Could Ian Luff even be the mystery traitor inside Government House? She would have laughed at such a suggestion before tonight, but now she was sure of nothing at all. She remembered suddenly that it had been Ian Luff who had tried to save Ralph's life in the drawing room at Government House. But she realized that she was no expert in the resuscitation of victims of heart attacks, so what he had done might just have been a clever subterfuge. He might even have made Ralph's condition worse with his apparent attempt at resuscitation, for all she knew. He could even have been the man who throttled Ralph in the first place and precipitated Ralph's heart attack...

Edith was idly flicking over the pages of the notebook when she happened to see a sentence that caught her eye. In fact the words nearly froze her blood too, for they were almost the last things she wanted to read in her present bewildered state: *I have deep suspicions about the conduct of this Chinese lawyer, Michael Yip. He is certainly playing a dangerous game of some sort. He seems to have his own network of informers here in Hong Kong, and is probably selling on secrets to third parties. But which third parties is he dealing with? His sympathies are supposedly left wing and his official work is mainly concerned with supporting local trade unions and workers. But what if that is simply a front? He could be passing secrets won from his left wing Chinese friends to the Japanese...*

These thoughts were so close to Edith's own worries about Michael that she could hardly believe that Ralph had written these words several weeks ago. No wonder that he had warned her from entering into any friendship with Michael when she and Ralph had encountered him in the gardens of Government House. But Ralph was not to know that Edith had already fallen under this man's spell by that time.

The encounter in that office building this evening also seemed to suggest there might be some connection between Michael and Ian Luff, if only through this intermediary, Marco da Silva.

Edith sat back on the sofa and put her head despairingly in her arms. *What was she going to do now...?*

CHAPTER 15

Saturday, 21th August 1937

On Saturday morning, Sebastian Ride walked in the lush gardens at the back of the Woo family mansion in Po Shan Road. Before going to the office as usual, he had driven here in his blue Bugatti sports car at the special request of Grace Woo, who wanted to discuss plans with him for James's funeral next week. Ride already knew that the funeral was going to be a grand affair as befitting the family's wealth and status, with the finest mahogany coffin with solid gold handles, and a funeral procession two hundred yards long. Professional mourners and pall-bearers would be employed to set the right dignified tone, and there would be at least five bands playing Chinese flutes and other instruments. A fleet of white Cadillacs would carry the family and the most important guests including the Acting Governor Norman Lockhart Smith. All the cars would be covered in white chrysanthemum blooms; no one would wear red colours for this was the symbol of happiness to the Chinese and as out of place at a funeral as a music hall comedian.

Dressed in his best white linen suit, Ride had just been inside the mock castle to pay his respects again to the aged bedridden patriarch of the family, Woo Man Lo. His old friend was only sixty-six – no age at all for a Chinese – but his progressive heart disease had turned him into a pale shadow of the man that Ride had known for the last twenty years. Ride had tried to cheer up the old man with the knowledge that he still had three other fine young sons – the much younger half-brothers of James – therefore the family line was certainly secure. Yet Ride had always known that James had been Man Lo's favourite – his first born son, after all – and nothing was going to console him for his loss. In the end, Ride had simply held the old man's shaking hand for a few minutes, then excused himself. From the sound of Mr Woo's rasping breathing, and his deathly pale colour, Ride did wonder with sadness how long the old man would last now. There was likely to be another funeral in the Woo family very soon, and Ride had to wonder who would then take over the management of the family interests in the company until one of the sons was in a position to do so. The eldest of the remaining sons was presently only sixteen so it would be some time before he or any of the others would be ready for a major role in the company...

Now, walking in the garden, he was enjoying the view of the harbour far below as he thought about his own future, and how he could make the most of the opportunities that had been created by the death of James Woo. And if the father soon followed his son to the grave, then this certainly opened up even more possibilities for Sebastian Ride himself...

Ride came to his favourite place in this garden: a magical little rock pool fed by a natural spring from the mountain above, with moss-covered boulders and scree behind, and everything shaded by tree ferns and tall camellias. Po Shan Road was higher up the flanks of the Peak than even Conduit Road, so the view above the garden was unimpeded by any other visible buildings, and revealed only steep forests clinging dizzily to the rocky slopes, through which a hot August wind blew in fitful bursts.

Ride heard someone delicately clearing their throat behind him, and turned to see Grace Woo standing in the dappled light under an Orchid tree. With the tree above her in full pink bloom, she made a very appealing picture in her long white silk dress, though the overall effect was marred to some extent by the hideous mock battlements and grey stone crenellations of the mansion which rose behind her. The house truly was an architectural monstrosity, Ride thought, which proved the old adage that even vast wealth could not necessarily purchase good taste.

Grace, however, more than lived up to the worth of her name, for she was a beautiful and graceful young woman. He knew of course that she hero-worshipped him a little, and had done so ever since she was a girl of fifteen or so. She was twenty-eight now, and had shown no inclination in the intervening years to marry any of the eligible young men whom her family had suggested for her. Ride had often wondered whether Grace's infatuation with him was so strong and long lasting that she had set her heart on him as a husband, and was simply waiting for him to divorce Gloria and become free. Ride was not a particularly conceited man, but he knew when a woman had fallen for him heart and soul. It made him realize again just what a disaster his marriage had been: not only for him, but for Gloria too. In trying to be loyal to her, he had only made things ten times worse. If he had divorced Gloria two or three years ago, she would have found a new husband easily enough by now with the huge settlement he would have given her, and would probably be far happier than the broken and despairing woman she was now...

And without Gloria to hold him back, Ride realized that he would have a choice of two extraordinary women for his future bride. He could either sell up in Hong Kong and move with Faye to a bright golden future in South Africa, or else he could marry Grace and stay in Hong Kong as undisputed lord and master of Saunders-Woo. These were both enticing prospects...but just dreams while he was still chained to a deadweight like Gloria...

'Thank you for coming, Sebastian,' Grace said, stepping forward, and linking her arm intimately with his. 'Shall we take a turn around the garden while we talk?' she suggested. So they began to wander along a sinuous forest path that led up behind the secret pool.

'Did you hear that there has been a minor outbreak of cholera in town?' she asked. 'Yet for a change it is only you Europeans who are suffering, for the victims are all Westerners apparently. The newspapers say that they had all eaten lately at the Cafe Wiseman in Lane Crawford, so it seems they caught the infection there of all places...'

'Serve them right, then – that's the worst food in town,' Ride joked. The Café Wiseman in the Lane Crawford department store was a favourite meeting place for the English to take tiffin. But Ride had never liked the kind of fearsome memsahibs who patronized the place.

Grace tried not to laugh, but let out a low giggle of delight. 'Oh, you devil.' Yet she soon became serious again. 'How did you find my father's condition? I fear that he is not long for this world.'

He squeezed her hand consolingly. 'Oh, it may not be as bad as that, Grace. He is a very strong-willed man, and I wouldn't be surprised if he recovers his full health again in time.'

'Perhaps he might have in normal circumstances. But James's death has dealt him a cruel additional blow so I doubt he will ever recover now.' Grace looked like she might give in to tears for a moment, but then with a visible effort recovered her usual poise. She glanced back at the house and its castle-like battlements. 'I think this ugly house has been the cause of my father's decline, and perhaps of James's death too. Father did not choose to consult a *feng shui* man when he built this house, you see, and now we are paying the penalty for it...'

Ride was surprised to hear the practical and westernized Grace talk in this way, for *feng shui* had always seemed like hokum to him – a theory of geomancy in which the location of a new house or a piece of furniture had to be sited in a certain specific direction and place so as not to adversely affect the Ch'i or spiritual breath of universe. He even remembered Grace mocking this old Chinese tradition too. But no longer, it seemed...

*

An hour later, Ride was back in the office in the Saunders Building in Queens Road Central. The Oriental clatter and babble of the street below seemed even louder and more intrusive than usual, but it could simply have been the unsettled mood he was in after his long talk with Grace Woo about her brother's funeral. He wondered what Grace would say if she knew the truth: that he had been there with James in that apartment when he had fallen from the balcony. It was exactly a week ago, almost to the hour, and Ride was being haunted by fresh feelings of guilt after going through the details of the man's funeral with his ever loyal sister.

Yet the fact was that he seemed to have got away with it...

No witnesses had come forward with any evidence to implicate him, especially from the group of Chinese boys and old women who had been hanging about outside the building in Tai Ping Shan that day. It seemed that the Gods were favouring him yet again with that familiar "Sebastian Ride" luck that had seen him through so many business ups and downs over the years. And Frances had been as good as her word in dealing with the rickshaw driver who had taken him last week to James's apartment building. Frances had paid the man off so handsomely that this lucky coolie had elected to return to his home town in Canton province and open up a food stall there. So there was now little prospect of anything coming back to bite Sebastian Ride about the death of James Woo. Frances had been entirely right about this, as she was about everything else...

The woman in question now appeared at the connecting door to her own office and marched into his room. She entered his office these days with a newfound assurance, he had noticed, but he could hardly begrudge her that minor liberty when she was such an essential part of his life now. Frances sat down opposite him. She was as perfectly turned out as ever in her woman's dark-striped business suit and her black silk hose. She quickly brought him up to date on the matter of the new steel rolling mill in Hopei province, which had lately been overrun by the Japanese Kwantung Army. 'The Japanese definitely have possession of it, and may even be trying to restart steel production. However, as I told you before, I have been in touch with our insurers in London. As I predicted, since I drafted the clause about cases of *force majeure*, we are entitled to claim back three-quarters of the four million Hong Kong dollars that we invested. I'm afraid that the other one million dollars is lost, though...'

Ride laughed. 'Even so, I think I might just kiss you, Frances.'

She blushed with pleasure. 'It's even better than that, Mr Ride. Even if we eventually regain possession of the asset in the event of a Japanese withdrawal, we won't have to pay the claim amount back, provided we don't get the plant back within two years of the claim being paid.'

Ride was still chuckling. 'That's amazing...how did you manage to get such a clause approved, Frances?' He noted again the strong sculpted lines of her face and her raven black hair and smooth golden skin, and wondered again why he had never been much attracted to her. But he was seeing her in a completely new light now, which made her attractions much more obvious to him...

'Oh, I think these insurance underwriters in London are not as smart as people give them credit for,' she said complacently.

She moved on to her next subject: the secret sale of marine gasoline to the Japanese Navy. 'I believe that we are now in the clear, Mr Ride. I have destroyed all the direct paperwork for these oil shipments or buried the information into files where they will never be discovered again by any auditor. So, now that Mr Woo is no longer here to betray this secret to our Chinese investors, I think the chances of this business ever resurfacing are very small indeed. In fact...' – here Frances reduced her voice to a whisper – '...these sales have made far more money for us than the losses on the steel rolling mill, so we should commend Mr Woo in retrospect for his business acumen if not his trustworthiness.'

Ride could see what she was thinking. 'You're not suggesting that we keep these sales of marine gasoline going, are you?'

Frances rolled her eyes. 'They *are* very profitable. And if we don't sell the Japanese this fuel, someone else will, so it won't change anything in China. And if we were careful, we could make sure that the sales could never be traced back to Saunders-Woo.'

Ride was quite entranced for a moment by the look on Frances's face. Plotting a lucrative deal like this seemed to bring out the natural beauty in her face...

'I don't think so, Frances,' Ride said unconvincingly. 'But I'll give it some thought anyway.'

Frances didn't look discouraged as she continued. '...About this other matter: the massive building program for social housing in Shaukeiwan and in three areas of Kowloon...'

'Yes, what have you discovered?'

'That it might well go ahead. Mr Woo was quite correct in saying that the Acting Governor and his Colonial Secretary want very much to do it. James Woo was also correct in telling you that the individuals in the government who might be able to stop this scheme going ahead are the Attorney General Colby and his assistant Grantham, who are both very close to Lockhart Smith and can possibly change his mind on such matters if they wish. Then there is the Colonial Treasurer Robert Harmsworth, who will obviously have a big say about spending most of the colony's tax reserves on this project. The government intelligence chief, Ralph Ogden, was also believed to be against the scheme, but he has died unexpectedly so is no longer a potential problem...'

'I know, Frances,' Ride said dryly. 'I was at his funeral three days ago...' He looked up sharply in sudden surprise as an unexpected visitor showed her face at his door.

'What are you doing here, Gloria?' he asked in amazement. He doubted if his wife had ever been in his office before, not in all the years that they had been married.

Gloria smiled back, making an effort. Ride could see that she had taken a great deal of trouble over her appearance today, wearing one of best designer dresses in pink satin trimmed with lace, and with her makeup and red hair perfect. Not only that, she appeared entirely sober. Ride was aware that the nurse he had brought in to supervise her, the severe Miss Doris Chow, was doing a sterling job of getting Gloria back on the straight and narrow, but he was surprised at the obvious improvement in Gloria's appearance already. She seemed suddenly much more like the bubbly girl he had married ten years ago. Yet it was still dangerous for Gloria to be wandering around Central District on her own so soon, when there were so many tempting expatriate waterholes in the area, particularly Bessie's Bar in the Hong Kong Hotel, just across the way. He was sure that Doris Chow would not have allowed this visit without his express approval, so it seemed that Gloria might have slipped out of the house on the sly...

'I thought we might have lunch together, Sebastian,' Gloria suggested brightly. 'Knowing how hard you work, even on Saturdays, I'm sure you would like an hour off for tiffin.'

Ride saw that Frances too was clearly taken aback by Gloria's unexpected arrival. Frances had met Gloria several times at company social events so knew her to speak to, at least.

Ride was just wondering what to say in response to Gloria when another person appeared at the door behind her, a young European with fair hair and a handsome smile. 'Mr Ride...?'

Ride inspected the man casually. He thought he recognized him from somewhere – perhaps the party in Government House last Monday week. The man was youthful and clean cut, yet carried the subtle stamp of authority. 'Yes, sir, what can I do for you?'

'I apologize for intruding like this, Mr Ride, since I don't think we have ever been formally introduced before. My name is Ian Luff,' the man announced. 'I need to see you urgently on a matter of business. I'm sorry that I don't have an appointment, but the matter can't wait.'

Ride had a vague feeling that this man might be a member of Harmsworth's team at the Hong Kong treasury, so quickly invited him in. He also seemed to recall now that the man had been at Ralph Ogden's funeral on Wednesday, standing next to Bob Harmsworth, which seemed to confirm that possibility. So, in the circumstances, Ride went over to Gloria and pulled her gently aside. 'I can't go with you at the moment, Gloria,' he whispered, glancing back at Ian Luff, '...because this could be important. Why don't you go shopping for a few minutes in Lane Crawford or somewhere, and then we can meet in the Hong Kong Hotel at one o'clock?

How does that sound?'

Gloria smiled back at him warmly without any hint of pretence. 'Fine, darling...' She turned to the others. 'Goodbye Mr Luff...I think we've met before, haven't we?' Her gaze transferred to Frances. And you, Miss...err...'

Ride was aware that Gloria knew Frances's name perfectly well, of course, and was merely putting her in her place with this display of pretended ignorance.

'*Leung*, Mrs Ride. *Frances Leung*,' Frances said pointedly. 'We have met several times, if you remember.' Frances didn't add that she had worked for her husband for over ten years, but the meaning of that acid look was plain enough to Sebastian Ride.

Gloria took her farewells, while a disgruntled Frances returned to her own room. 'I will just pop out too, Mr Ride, for some *dim sum*, if that's all right?' she said at the door of her own room.

'Of course, Frances,' Ride agreed, as he watched her go back to her own office, collect her handbag, then set out into the corridor beyond.

Ian Luff surprisingly closed the connecting door to Frances's own room after Frances had left. And then – even more surprisingly - he closed the outer door to the corridor too.

Ride was about to protest at the man's presumption when Luff did an astonishing thing: he put a warning finger to his own lips as if they were old friends and confidantes. 'Better that this discussion stays between these four walls, Mr Ride. For I came here to tell you that I know all about it.'

Ride shook his head in bewilderment. 'All about what?'

Luff sighed as if profoundly disappointed. *'I know that you killed your business partner James Woo...'*

*

Ride felt his face turning to stone. 'I don't know what you're talking about, Mr Luff.'

'Oh, come now, don't be tiresome, Mr Ride. You can't argue with the facts.' Luff gave an exasperated smile. 'I can understand your shock at this conversation, for you must have thought you had got away with murder with remarkable ease...'

'I didn't murder anyone,' Ride stated harshly.

The man smiled again, a smile as cold as sunlight glittering on a frozen sea. Ian Luff looked innocuous enough – a fashionably dressed man in his early thirties who looked like he could be a fashion model in his spare time – but Sebastian Ride could sense that there was a formidable personality behind that bland exterior.

'You need to stop this nonsense, Mr Ride,' the man continued. 'You cannot convince me of your innocence, for the simple reason that *I was there* in James's apartment in Tai Ping Shan last Saturday and heard the whole exchange between you and him...'

Ride's mind was racing. 'If you really were there, then you must know that I am innocent, and that it was entirely an accident.' He had another thought. 'And you *couldn't* have been there: I searched the whole place when I first got there to make sure James and I were alone.'

Luff sniffed coldly. 'Yet you didn't search very hard, Mr Ride, for I simply stood out of sight behind the bedroom door when you poked your head in there.'

Ride wondered now if Luff was one of James's secret male lovers; it had to be an unpleasant possibility. 'It was still an accident. If you were listening to us, then you must know the truth.'

Luff grimaced. 'An accident? Really? I heard you say to him: "*I've only got to let go and you're a dead man, James...*"'

Ride knew for certain now, with a chill feeling of despair, that the man must really have been hiding in the apartment. 'Yes, but that was earlier. It's true I lost my temper and threatened James. But I had no real intention of harming him.'

Luff puffed out his boyish cheeks and ran a hand through his thick fair hair. 'I tell you what I heard, Mr Ride: my friend whimpering with fear because you had him hanging over the edge of that balcony. He even screamed: "*Don't do it, Sebastian, please! They'll hang you for it...*"'

Ride glowered resentfully at the man. 'Yet you didn't come to James's aid, did you, Mr Luff? Why not, if you thought his life was really in danger?' Ride stood up abruptly and saw Luff flinch a little in surprise. That told him the real reason why Luff had not interfered last week in the argument: he was a small delicately built man, and perhaps a physical coward too, who had not been prepared to risk his own life to save his friend. That knowledge gave Ride some slight hope that he might be able to deal with this man.

'You only *overheard* this exchange between myself and James, didn't you?' Ride stood towering over the man and tried to intimidate him subtly with his physical superiority. 'You didn't actually see what happened at all, did you?'

Luff swallowed uneasily. 'No, I didn't. That's true.'

'Then you didn't actually see James fall. I swear on my mother's grave that I didn't touch him then. He simply stumbled back against the parapet, which just fell apart like a loose pile of bricks under his weight. I even tried to save him by catching his flailing arm as he went over, but I missed.'

Luff pondered that. 'Well, what you say might even be true,' he agreed reluctantly. 'I have no wish to call you a liar to your face. But the fact is that if I go to the police with my account of what happened, there will certainly be a police investigation. You would almost certainly have to face charges in court – if not of murder, then at least of manslaughter. So, regardless of your actual guilt or not, the fact is this would finish you forever in Hong

Kong. Even if you didn't go to gaol, your career as a businessman would be over.'

'Are you really sure that *you* want to go the police with this, Mr Luff?' Ride said, sitting down again and adopting a more conciliatory tone. 'For it might bring the nature of your own relationship with James out into the open...' he warned balefully.

Luff became defensive. 'I wouldn't speculate on the nature of my relationship with James, if I were you. You're hardly the right man to give anyone lessons in morality...' A cunning look came into his eyes. 'By the way, this argument with James that got you so wound up – about the death of this woman Susan Jericho: James told you the truth about that. He was with me at my own apartment in Bowen Road on January the nineteenth, and he saw the whole incident from my balcony, using my binoculars...'

'Did you see it happen too?' Ride's voice was suddenly hoarse.

'No, I was in my own kitchen cleaning up, which is on the other side of the apartment. But James told me exactly what he had seen when he returned. He had left my building and run down towards Kennedy Road to try and help the woman. Incidentally...' – Luff pulled a wry face – '...if you must pursue other men's wives, I would suggest politely that you avoid the wives of senior policemen in future...'

'Do you know the make of the car that hit Susan?' Ride demanded. 'Did James tell you that much?'

Luff nodded. 'He did. He loved unusual cars so he had recognized this one. I think he even had a shrewd idea who might have been driving it, though he didn't tell me that much...' He hesitated. '...And I might even pass this information about the car on to you some day, Sebastian, if it suits me. I *can* call you "Sebastian", can't I? For we are going to be working together very closely in the future...'

Ride had a feeling this really was the truth about Susan Jericho's death, and that his theory that James himself had been driving the car that killed Susan that night must be wrong.

Then Ride had another sudden realization. '*You* were James's insider in Government House, weren't you? The one who helped him set up this deal for this huge new development of social housing in Shaukeiwan and Kowloon?'

Luff acknowledged that with a quiet look of pride. 'I was...and I can now be *your* insider in Government House, Sebastian.'

'How much do you want?' Ride demanded bitterly.

'It's not a matter of "how much",' Luff stated baldly. 'What I want is to be brought into a senior position in Saunders-Woo in time. Perhaps as your executive assistant at the start, and then eventually a seat on the board...'

Ride gasped in derision. '*A seat on the board?*'

'Exactly...' Luff smiled. 'Don't look so shocked, Sebastian. I will not be a mere passenger for life, but instead a real asset to the company. It was I after all who came up with the idea of the social housing scheme, and I who sold it so assiduously to my government colleagues. James could never have thought up such a subtle scheme; his business imagination was regretfully very limited. It is I who has the ear of the Acting Governor and the Colonial Secretary in this matter. And I have made sure that I have considerable influence over my chief Harmsworth in the Treasury, and also over Colby and Grantham in the Attorney General's department. Bob Harmsworth is fortunately very partial to taking discreet bribes, so in the worst situation we may have to buy his cooperation with some suitable payment. Yet he also has a dark secret of his own that I should be able to exploit, therefore he may cost us nothing in the end. As for Colby, he has been keeping a Chinese mistress in an apartment in Kowloon for several years, so he should be easily persuaded to toe the line in return for our silence on the subject of his risqué love life. Grantham was the biggest problem because he didn't seem to have any skeletons in his closet at all...a real boy scout...'

'What will you do about him, then?' Ride demanded harshly. Despite his predicament, Ride could not completely conceal his admiration for the planning behind this devious scheme.

Luff was clearly pleased with Ride's reaction. 'It's all in hand now. I have enough of a hold now on Grantham to keep him in line. But nevertheless I will need to stay in my job in government until the project is signed off and underway. But in a year or two, after construction begins, I will choose to retire regretfully from the colonial service and take up a post in the hurly-burly world of commerce with one of the leading hongs...'

'You've got it all thought out, I see,' Ride said icily. 'I suppose it was you who persuaded James to start selling marine gasoline to the Japanese, and to try and blame that deal on me.'

Luff still looked imperturbable. 'I did. But that was when I was in partnership with James. You were a potential hindrance to that arrangement so it seemed advisable to get rid of you from Saunders-Woo. But now that James is sadly gone, I need a new man inside Saunders-Woo to hitch my wagon to, and you are it. So you can relax about me concocting any more plots against you, Sebastian; from now on, all my plotting will be in the interests of you and Saunders-Woo. After all, I want the company to be in a healthy state when I officially join the fold...'

Ride fought back a silent scream that was building inside him. He knew that this man would be with him forever now, like a lead weight around his neck...

*

At one-thirty, Frances was just stepping out of the elevator after returning from her lunch when she caught sight of Gloria Ride at the other end of the wood-panelled corridor, standing outside the closed door to her husband's office and looking a little uncertain, as if unsure whether to knock or not. Frances moved cautiously towards Gloria, and was half-tempted to speak to her. As far as Frances had understood Mr Ride to say, Gloria should have been having tiffin with him in the Hong Kong Hotel by now, not hanging about here outside his office. But perhaps Mr Ride had gone over time with his unscheduled meeting with his visitor Mr Luff, so Gloria had simply grown bored with waiting for him and had returned to the building to see where he was.

Yet something now clearly made Gloria Ride change her mind about knocking at her husband's door, for she suddenly turned and almost ran for the stairwell at the far end of the corridor. Fortunately she did not seem to have observed Frances watching her with such undisguised curiosity from the other end of the corridor.

The door to Sebastian's office then opened abruptly and Mr Ride's fair-haired visitor appeared in the corridor. Frances had no idea what this Mr Luff's business with Mr Ride had been. But, whatever it was, it had clearly been of some interest to his wife...

CHAPTER 16

Sunday, 22th August 1937

Edith Starling walked out of the main door of St John's Cathedral, and saw that Paul Jericho was waiting for her outside, with the clear intention of speaking to her.

She emerged from the shade of the square tower of the cathedral, and felt the full blast of summer heat on her face. The power of the tropic sun seemed even more intense than usual for some reason, and she could almost feel it burning her skin like an open flame. Perhaps she simply noticed the heat more today because her mind was in turmoil after the disturbing events of this last week.

Paul Jericho, dressed in his Sunday best again, stepped out from the protective shade of a fan palm and raised his white Panama hat to greet her. 'Second time in two weeks. You're becoming quite a regular again here at Sunday service, Miss Starling...' He saw her look of mild reproof and added quickly, '...*Edith, I mean.*'

She made a weak attempt at a smile. 'That's better.' She glanced back at the chancel: the cream-coloured walls of the cathedral looked very striking against the intense blue of the sky, and with the soaring green beauty of the Peak rising behind it. 'I came here deliberately again because I was hoping to run into you,' she admitted quietly.

She thought that Paul Jericho looked even more tired today than he had last week, so had obviously had a demanding week just like her. His hair was very thick and wiry, and badly in need of a trim, she saw, and he was a little overweight and out of condition. He had aged quite noticeably in the seven months since Susan's death, and clearly wasn't taking good care of himself now that he was on his own. He had lines in his face too that made him look rather older than his real age - Edith had been surprised when Susan had told her last winter that Paul was only thirty-six, for even then he had looked over forty. But she liked Paul Jericho's face nevertheless; there was something reassuring about that square jaw and those intense blue eyes that told you that here was a man who would never let you down.

'Are you still troubled about Mr Ogden's death?' Jericho asked her, before she had the chance to broach the subject herself. 'Last week I sensed that you had some genuine concerns about his death, but were a bit reluctant to say so. So...am I right? Do you have some real doubts that his death was due to natural causes?'

She wavered for a moment, not sure if she should tell him the truth even now. But then, almost by themselves, the words flowed out of her in a sudden rush. 'Yes, I do have some doubts, Paul, if I'm honest.' She took a deep breath. 'I think there is a strong possibility that somebody might have killed Ralph. If somebody *did* do it, then they must have been desperate to silence him, for they took a huge risk killing a man in the public drawing room at Government House. Somebody could have walked in on the killer at any moment. Yet Ralph did have a heart condition and was in poor health, so it wouldn't have been difficult for someone muscular to throttle him or suffocate him quickly with a cloth forced over his nose and mouth. The doctor who signed the death certificate barely looked at the body; he didn't even look at the bruises on Ralph's windpipe which could easily have been caused by the pressure of somebody's fingers...'

Paul Jericho muttered with annoyance under his breath. 'Well, it's a bit late now to tell me this, Edith, with the man already buried. I'd have to have a very good reason to ask for an exhumation order. I can't simply say that Miss Edith Starling now has some suspicions about her boss's death, so I need to dig up the body and check it for signs of foul play...'

She looked at him in alarm. 'No, I don't want you to start digging Ralph's body up, Paul. This is an intelligence matter, and my colleagues would crucify me if I brought in the regular police about this.'

Paul Jericho watched, distracted for a moment, as a sulphur-yellow butterfly fluttered between them and then landed like a feather on the giant red flower of a hibiscus bush. 'Can you not tell me any details about this at all, Edith?'

Edith gulped unhappily. 'No, I can't. Not yet anyway, Paul.'

Jericho turned his head to look up at the Peak, squinting his eyes in the brilliant tropical light. 'The heat is getting worse, isn't it? But it might break soon, for I have heard from a friend at the Observatory that there might be a typhoon brewing in the Pacific east of the Philippines. If there is a typhoon in the offing, then it will usually find its way here eventually.'

'Then I hope it won't be a big one,' Edith said. She knew that these fearsome tropical storms could cause immense damage and huge loss of life along the southern coast of China; it was the last thing she wanted to hear when her whole world was falling apart. She had almost convinced herself by now that the traitor inside Government House was the innocent-looking and charming Ian Luff. This was bad enough by itself, but she was also equally convinced that Michael Yip was probably working with Luff through their mutual contact, the sleazy-sounding individual Marco da Silva. So everything Michael had told her was a lie; he had clearly picked her up deliberately two months ago and taken her as his lover in order to use her and bleed her for information. In fact she now remembered telling Ian Luff beforehand that she had been intending to go on her own to that amateur production of *Private Lives* by the Bowen Players at the Theatre Royal in June. He must have tipped off Michael immediately, who had then waylaid her casually in the bar at the interval. Luff must even have understood enough about her sexual tastes to realize that she was attracted more to Chinese men than Europeans – it was galling to be so transparent to these scheming devils...

Last night she had cooked dinner for Michael in her apartment as planned - she worried that it might look suspicious if she suddenly put him off and cancelled their assignation for no good reason. She had tried to be exactly the same with him as usual, using the same light-hearted banter and the same affectionate gestures that he seemed to like. Then - after their candlelit dinner and warmed with a little wine – she had let him carry her to her bedroom and undress her slowly. She had made love to him just as frantically and feverishly as ever, and had lain afterwards in the warm glow of his arms, feeling the slow rhythmic beating of his heart. Yet, inside, her own heart had been burning with hurt and indignation that this man was betraying her...

But she daren't tell any of this to Paul Jericho. He was a highly competent policeman, but he was used to dealing with the regular criminal classes, not sophisticated spies and agents. Somehow she was going to have to find the evidence against Luff and Michael by herself, and then take it to her superiors. She had stolen a slight march on them because they didn't yet know that she was on to them. She prided herself that nothing she had done or said last night had given her away in the slightest; it had been a performance worthy of Sarah Bernhardt. That might just give her enough of an edge to catch them unawares, even though she knew that she was no field agent but rather a backroom boffin. And a rather naive and helpless boffin at that, she thought ruefully...

But there *was* something she could ask Paul Jericho; this was the reason she had come to Sunday morning service again in the hope of seeing him.

'So, if you won't tell me anything, there's not a lot I can do to help you, Edith,' Jericho warned her bleakly.

'There *is* one thing: do you know anything about a man called Marco da Silva? A Eurasian of some sort – perhaps half-Portuguese from Macau?'

Edith saw instantly from Paul Jericho's reaction that he *did* know something about this man. Yet he seemed reluctant to answer her, until she finally pleaded with him. 'Please...it's important. Tell me what you know.'

'All right. I shouldn't be telling you this, Edith, so please don't pass this on to anybody else. Marco da Silva ran an escort agency from a building in Pedder Street in partnership with a man called Freddie Ling, who also worked as manager of the bar in the Tin Hau Hotel. They were selling the services of good looking Chinese women to wealthy men – probably mostly Westerners. We think this escort agency employed all of the three women who have been recently murdered in Wanchai. So we are looking urgently for Da Silva, although there's nothing to indicate at the moment that he might be directly connected with the murders himself.' Paul Jericho paused expectantly. 'So what's your interest in this man?'

She shrugged uneasily. 'I told you: I can't tell you, Paul. It's an intelligence matter.'

Paul was clearly annoyed. 'That hardly seems fair when I've just told you what I know.'

She took his hand and squeezed it apologetically. 'I'm sorry. But fair or not, that's the way it will have to be.'

'Will you at least tell me if you have met this man Da Silva?' Jericho persisted.

'No, I've never met him,' she answered truthfully. 'And if you know where his office is, why don't you just pick the man up there?'

Jericho shrugged resentfully. 'The office is closed down. And I doubt if Da Silva will ever go back there because he probably knows by now that we want to talk with him.'

Edith was going to correct him in that assumption, since Da Silva had certainly been back in his office on Friday night. But she thought better of saying so since it would only provoke more questions she didn't want to answer.

With that she quickly took her leave, but he called her back. 'Just answer me one more thing, Edith. What do you know about a man called Ian Luff? I believe he works in Government House, and that he has some sort of role with the Treasury...'

Edith tried to maintain a poker face, but it was difficult, given a leading question like that. She certainly hadn't expected Paul Jericho to bring up *that* man's name... 'I know Ian, of course,' she said mildly. 'He seems a pleasant young man, but...err... I don't know him well. Why do you ask about him?'

'We found his business card inside a room at the Tin Hau Hotel,' Paul said laconically. 'A room that had been used by one of the murdered girls on the night she was killed.'

'You think Ian has some involvement with the murders?' Edith asked in surprise. 'I would have thought that very unlikely.'

Paul grunted. 'Yes, me too. Murderers are not often obliging enough to leave their business cards at the scene of their crime. If they were, we'd hardly need a police force at all; the courts could just pick them up directly and cut out the middleman. So the whole thing seems far too convenient to be true.'

'Have you spoken to Ian about it?' Edith asked, pretending to be concerned for a colleague's reputation. Yet her mind was churning at the possibility that Luff might not only be a traitor but a mass murderer too. *Could the murder of these women in Wanchai have something to do with what was happening at Government House?*

'No, not yet,' Paul admitted. 'I need to be careful before I go about making accusations against such a high ranking government official as Ian Luff. Or even bringing him in for questioning, come to think of it.'

Edith finally turned to leave but he quickly called her back a second time. 'Are you *sure* that you're all right, Edith?'

Edith was touched by the clear look of concern on Paul Jericho's face. 'Yes, Paul. Don't worry about me. I'll be fine.' She laughed self-consciously. 'But if you hear that I too have met with an unfortunate and untimely accident, then please feel free to investigate it.'

Jericho looked even more concerned. 'Are you being serious, Edith?'

'Perhaps not entirely,' she said, touching his arm reassuringly...

*

The brief twilight of another hot August day was just fading into sombre black as Frances Leung drove her Chrysler saloon car up the steep concrete drive of Sebastian Ride's home in Conduit Road, and parked it in the spare bay at the top. She had been here to his house once or twice before, but was still surprised at the luxuriousness of this vast white three-storied art deco mansion and its spectacular elevated setting on this, the highest road in Mid-levels.

A houseboy soon answered her knock and let her in to the study on the first floor. The room had a large and spectacular curved plate glass window overlooking the lower Mid-levels below and the sprinkled lights of the harbour beyond, and was furnished in the latest Modernist style: stacking chairs in moulded and laminated plywood, an American art deco desk with a green lacquered finish and geometric patterns in gold leaf. Everywhere was the gleam of modern angular French silverware and Italian ceramics decorated with the fashionable Egyptian lotus motif.

Sebastian soon came downstairs and found her. 'Frances, what are you doing here? It's Sunday evening...don't you ever take any time off?' he chided her gently.

She could see that he was deeply troubled despite his light reply.

She held up the papers she had brought with her. 'You left the office so hurriedly yesterday that you forgot to sign this new contract for the joint venture with that American company in the Philippines...'

Sebastian sighed. 'Ah yes. For the development of the new palm oil plantations in the North of Luzon. It completely slipped my mind. Yet it could have waited until tomorrow, couldn't it?'

Frances took a step towards him. 'Perhaps. But I wasn't sure that you would be in the office first thing.' She bit her lip anxiously. 'I was worried about you, Mr Ride. You seemed almost distraught when you left the office yesterday afternoon. I thought perhaps that there was some fresh problem between you and Mrs Ride...' she added awkwardly.

His eyes flickered. 'No, the problem is not with Gloria. Not this time. She is upstairs, having a long bath.'

Frances ventured a delicate question. 'Did you and your wife meet for lunch yesterday as planned? You were a bit longer with your visitor than I expected.'

His voice took on a bitter note. 'Yes, indeed. He did take up much more of my time than I expected. So I never did get to see Gloria yesterday for lunch. She had already left the Hong Kong Hotel and gone home in a huff, before I could even get there. That's what she told me when I did finally get home last night anyway...I'm afraid that I spent the whole afternoon in Bessie's Bar drowning my sorrows.'

Frances didn't want to add to his problems, but thought she had to tell him the truth about his coarse drunken sot of a wife. 'Your wife didn't go straight home from the Hong Kong Hotel yesterday. When I came back at one-thirty from lunch, I saw her hanging around outside your office door. I got the impression she might have been listening in on your conversation...'

Sebastian went white. 'Oh God, I hope not!'

She tried to reassure him. 'I think she was only there for a short time so probably couldn't have heard too much of what was said.' She hesitated. 'Why is it such a problem if she heard any of your discussion? What did that man Luff actually want?'

Sebastian laughed harshly. 'Want? Why, everything, of course. The moon...the stars...*the whole damned universe...*' His laugh faded into a bleak shrug of despair. 'He wants a seat on the board of Saunders-Woo. He wants to run my life and make me jump to his orders. In fact he wants to own me, body and soul, for the rest of my days.'

Frances moved closer still and put a consoling hand on his shoulder. 'What has he got on you?'

'Everything! Luff is one of James's queer boyfriends. He was there in the apartment in Tai Ping Shan when James fell off the balcony. So he knows everything – not just about that, but about all our business dealings too. He knows all about the sale of gasoline to the Japanese, and about this social housing project here in Hong Kong. In fact he seems to have been the brains behind it all.'

Frances nodded knowingly. 'Ah yes, I didn't think James Woo was smart enough to have come up with all these plans by himself.' She had a sudden realization. 'Luff must have been James's inside man in Government House. That all makes perfect sense now.'

Sebastian took her hand. 'So it seems, Frances, that all your good work to save me has been in vain. I think I will have to go to the police now and admit everything about what happened in Tai Ping Shan. There is no way that I can do what this man Luff wants.'

She squeezed his hand anxiously in return. 'You can't admit the truth, Sebastian...!' She had never called him by his first name before, but in his distraught state he seemed not to notice. 'No one will believe your story now. Your life would be over. The Woo family would break with you permanently and make sure that you were convicted of murder. But I believe in you, Sebastian, and I promise that I will get you out of this.' She hesitated for a moment, but then leaned forward and kissed him hard on the mouth.

This time he did notice that he had reached a new level of intimacy with his long-serving secretary, for he responded suddenly in kind, kissing her back with equal passion and then running her hands over her breasts with mounting fever. But then he stopped suddenly as reality took hold of him again. 'How can you save me, Frances? No one can save me now.'

Frances sighed inwardly: *men were such fools, weren't they*. They really had no idea of the true feelings of the women that they worked with. Sebastian had no comprehension at all of the truth: that she, Frances Leung, had been in love with him for almost the entire ten years that she had worked for him. That she was so devoted to him that she would do anything to save him.

Anything...

Finally she said calmly, 'We need to rid ourselves of this man, Sebastian.'

Sebastian looked bewildered. 'Rid ourselves? *How?* He won't take a simple bribe like that rickshaw coolie, you know.'

Frances turned around to gaze out through the window at the myriad lights of Hong Kong below. 'No, you are right there. *So we will have to kill him...*'

CHAPTER 17

Monday, 23rd August 1937

Dawn was just breaking on Monday morning as Paul Jericho stood with George Dorling on Blake Pier in the heart of the Central District. A police launch was manoeuvring alongside the kelp-encrusted pier pilings, while two Chinese constables on board tried ineffectually to pull an object clear from the water underneath the pier with boathooks. The water beyond the wooden pier was mirror-smooth in the pre-dawn light, touched with green shadows and patches of mother-of-pearl iridescence. Over to the east, the sun was just breaking cover above the mountainous backbone of the Chinese mainland, the tip of its red disc glowing with the promise of another scorching August day to come...

'Not much sign of this promised typhoon yet,' Jericho observed for want of something to say.

'No, sir. It's still as hot as hell.' Dorling clearly was in a dour mood, Jericho could see, and also unshaven and unwashed because he had been called from his bed this morning by the report of a body in the water under Blake Pier. This pier was the place where government officials and VIPs made official landfall into Hong Kong, with brass bands and regimentals on display, so no one wanted a rotting corpse to be left there in the water for long to make an embarrassing spectacle at this privileged location...

Jericho turned his head to look up at the Peak, which carried a few trailing miasmas of white mist in the dawn light. Among all the white colonial buildings that climbed the lower flanks of the mountain, the tower of St John's Cathedral stood out in the emerging dawn because of its glowing primrose colour.

He thought back again with concern to his talk there with Edith Starling yesterday. *Could she be right that her boss Ralph Ogden had been murdered?* One thing was clear to him now from his discussions with her, though: Edith was certainly no ordinary secretary in Government House, as even his wife Susan had believed, but clearly a key member of the Secret Intelligence Service. Jericho knew of the existence of these shadowy people of course, who tended to hide their true purpose in Hong Kong behind vague and innocuous-sounding colonial service titles. But Edith was the first example of these interesting folk that he had ever got to know personally. She was clearly in deep trouble of some sort, and needing help badly. And he wanted desperately to help her in return – particularly as she had been such a good friend of Susan's – yet he didn't know what he could do if Edith herself continued to be as secretive as this, and to resist his offers of help. He certainly couldn't go ahead and get an exhumation order for Ogden's body without Edith's approval.

And what was her interest in this pimping gentleman, Marco da Silva? That was the most puzzling thing of all – how this man Da Silva might be connected, if at all, to the death of a senior British spy chief...

Jericho had a nasty feeling that Edith's life might even be in danger from her enemies, and it would be a bitter blow to him if she too died in mysterious circumstances because of his failure to act. Yet he was at a loss to know what to do for the best...

Jericho looked up as he heard a shout from the police launch. The two strapping constables had finally managed to pull the body clear of the pier pilings and to lift it on board. He motioned George to follow him down the length of the pier, then jumped across the gap onto the gunwale of the police launch. Dorling followed him, but slipped as he landed on the launch, so that Jericho had to help him aboard with a steadying hand. 'Careful, George. I can't afford to lose you...'

They made their way forward to the bows where the body had been laid out on its back by the two heavily breathing constables.

Dorling took a long look at the body. 'A young male. Eurasian, maybe of Portuguese descent from his looks. Are you thinking what I'm thinking, sir?'

Jericho nodded. He didn't want to jump to any assumptions, but he did not really doubt that they had finally found Marco da Silva...

One of the two constables looked up at Jericho. He was the elder of the two and looked like he had seen a good few bodies in his time. 'Shot in the back of the head, sir, three times with a large bore pistol.'

'That's one more than Ricky Sun,' Jericho said dryly. 'They obviously wanted to make completely sure this time...'

*

Six hours later, in early afternoon, Paul Jericho sat in his office in Wanchai Police Station playing idly with the business card of Ian Luff that had been found in the Tin Hau Hotel. He manipulated it through the fingers of his right hand like a playing card, watching how the sunlight filtering through the window shades picked out its gold lettering and its impressive Hong Kong government logo.

Although he had told Edith Starling that he was very dubious about finding such a convenient and damning piece of evidence as this, yet he still wanted to know how and why this card had found its way into the room of a seedy hotel cum brothel on the Wanchai waterfront. It was probably pure coincidence that this card had been found in that particular room, and its presence there was probably nothing to do with the murders of the three women at all. But it would be interesting to know if Ian Luff was actually the sort of man who might patronize the ladies of the Tin Hau Hotel. Although the regular patrons of the bar mostly came from the ranks of ordinary seamen or the lower ranks of the military, yet Jericho was well aware that some of the wealthier types of young male expatriate did like to frequent low class bars in Wanchai on occasion — a chance to see how the masses lived, and perhaps to slum it with an earthier type of woman than they were used to.

Jericho heard a knock at his door and saw George Dorling standing there. George was still bleary-eyed but had at least found the time to have a shave since this morning. His thick ginger hair was still slicked down with water as if he had just come from the communal showers downstairs.

'Come in, George, and sit down,' Jericho said.

Dorling had the preliminary report on the body found this morning at Blake Pier. Jericho had decided not to release any information to the newspapers yet about the discovery of this new body; something told him that it was better to keep this particular murder from the public for the present. At the very least it would keep Lucky Lam and the Kao Ki-kan guessing...

Dorling cleared his throat before speaking. 'It's definitely Marco da Silva, sir. I went and asked Betty Lau from the Tin Hau Bar if she knew Da Silva. It seemed possible since Da Silva was working closely with the bar manager, Freddie Ling. She confirmed she had seen the man in the bar sometimes, and agreed to come to the police morgue and identify the body...she even seemed quite happy to do it...'

'Shall we go ahead and make Betty an honorary policeman then?' Jericho suggested with a wry shrug. 'She seems much better at this game than you and I, George.'

Dorling grunted vaguely, but clearly didn't much care for that sour comment.

'So, we keep coming back in this investigation to Lucky Lam and the Kao Ki-kan,' Jericho went on, after a long awkward silence.

'Maybe,' George said with a frown.

'Perhaps you've forgotten that Cherry Kwok actually saw Dora Kam with Ricky Sun...'

'With a man who looked a bit *like* Ricky Sun, maybe,' Dorling argued. 'There's no other evidence that Dora knew Ricky Sun apart from this chance sighting. And Cherry is dead too now, so there's no way of verifying it.'

'Yet it's one more indication that the Kao Ki-kan is involved in this business somehow,' Jericho persisted.

'But we don't know of any actual reason why the Kao Ki-kan would kill Freddie Ling and Da Silva. Also the ballistics check shows that the gun used to kill Da Silva was definitely not the same one used on Ricky Sun...'

'You're not suggesting they didn't kill Ricky Sun too, are you, George?' Jericho was puzzled that George seemed quite determined to divert this investigation away from the Kao Ki-kan.

'Well, we know they had a motive for killing Ricky Sun at least,' Dorling said uneasily. 'But suppose Freddie Ling and Da Silva were actually killed by the same person who killed the three women? He might just have decided to make those murders look like a triad killing to muddy the water a little...'

'No, I don't accept that, George. I'm sure Lucky Lam is the one who ordered the deaths of Freddie Ling and Marco da Silva. The only question is whether it is something to do with the deaths of the three women, or for some entirely unrelated reason. I suspect the latter: I think Freddie and Marco were a couple of spivs who were probably transgressing on triad territory and got their just deserts for it. But it does mean that our investigation into the detailed activities of the Blue Heaven Agency will be difficult to follow up, with the principals in the business all inconveniently dead. We might never be able to find out now who were the particular clients of these three murdered women. But I'm absolutely sure now that one of those Western clients murdered them – our blue-eyed man. But I'm not confident we'll ever find this man now with so many leads closed to us...'

Jericho saw that Thomas Sung had appeared at the open door to his office, so he beckoned him in to take the chair next to George Dorling. 'You look like you've got something to say, Thomas.'

Thomas Sung came in diffidently and sat down as asked. 'I have, sir. I've remembered something that might help. A year ago last April, I was part of a team from Central Police Station that raided a massage parlour in Western District. It was a place for homosexuals to gather, and the masseurs were mostly Japanese rent boys...'

'I remember it,' Jericho said. 'Somebody in the security services tipped us off that a lot of the staff were Japanese agents trying to pick up confidential military information from Western homosexual men.'

'That's the place,' Sung agreed.

'Well...?' Jericho prompted him.

'I am sure that this man, Marco da Silva, was among those arrested. But he was released without charge for some reason...'

Jericho was immediately interested. 'Do you think that Da Silva was simply enjoying the pleasures of that place? Or was it more? Could he have been one of the owners or managers of the place too?'

'I don't know, sir. I wasn't involved in questioning him. But I heard later from colleagues that this man had been released. I thought it odd, but it's not my place to question decisions like that. Somebody high up had clearly pulled a few strings for him.'

'Well, that's very intriguing, Thomas. Thank you for the information.' Jericho saw the look on Sung's face. 'Was there something else?'

'There was also a young Englishman in the massage parlour the same night. I think this man was allowed to go without even being arrested. I did wonder about it at the time, and asked the inspector about it...'

'Who was in charge of the raid again?' Jericho asked, although he had a good idea already.

'It was Inspector Ball, sir.'

'What reason did he give for letting the man go?' Jericho wondered aloud.

Thomas Sung smiled. 'He said we couldn't take the King of England into custody. And he was right...the man did look exactly like the King of England...'

'This was last year, so Inspector Ball must have meant King *Edward*, not the new king, George?' Jericho suggested.

Sung nodded. 'Yes, King Edward...now the Duke of somewhere or other since he gave up being king.'

Jericho sat back in his chair, realization dawning. 'So this young Englishman who was released by Inspector Ball without charge looked like *the Duke of Windsor...*'

George Dorling looked at Jericho with puzzlement, not understanding his excitement.

But Jericho was excited because he knew of one person who certainly looked very much like the Duke of Windsor...*the increasingly mysterious Ian Luff...*

So it seemed a strong possibility that Ian Luff actually knew Marco da Silva. Which possibility now put an entirely different complexion on the business card found in a room at the Tin Hau Hotel...

*

Edith Starling had found what she thought was the perfect place to keep a watch on Michael Yip's ground floor apartment in Broadwood Road in Happy Valley. She had left work at Government House early today – before three o'clock - armed with the things she needed to maintain a long surveillance of his living room and bedroom. She had confided her plans with no one at Government House, not even her SIS colleague Elliot

Casaubon.

She had been inside Michael's apartment only once, and that very briefly, after she had dropped Michael off after their first day together out at Tai Tam Bay. She had remembered that the living room at the back looked out over a small paved patio with wooded slopes rising steeply behind covered in mulberries and myrtles and Chinese banyan trees. From that brief visit, she recalled a small hillock of scrub Chinese pine trees that looked right down into the living room. Provided Michael didn't close his curtains at night, she would be able to see from that hillock right into his living room.

She had parked her Austin Seven near the cemetery again since she didn't want to leave her car in Broadwood Road itself where somebody might remember her number plate. She had therefore quite a long walk to get herself into the right position, and had experienced a lot more difficulty than expected in finding a useable path through the woods to this convenient hillock. She had certainly ruined her stockings, which were scratched to pieces after her walk through the dense woods, while her skirt was stained with dirt. If she ever had to do this again, she resolved that she would wear slacks...

But finally, late in the afternoon, she had got herself set up in position on the little wooded hill, with a pair of field glasses and a sophisticated camera at the ready. The camera had a special zoom lens which was able to take close-up pictures of anyone entering that living room or stepping outside onto the patio. She remembered that Michael had said several times that he liked to sit out on his patio at night with a cold drink.

Yet for the first three hours of her vigil, she saw almost nothing. Michael was certainly at home, for she caught glimpses of him occasionally. But he seemed to be on his own and behaving perfectly normally. In fact so normally that she began to question her doubts about him all over again. After all, the only concrete facts she had against him was that he had visited this pimp Marco da Silva, and that he had searched through her briefcase one time. The first of these could mean simply that Da Silva had been providing him with information relating to some of his legal cases, while the second could simply have been due to unfortunate male curiosity. She reminded herself that she had never actually seen Michael with Ian Luff, so they might not know each other at all, and their closely-timed visits to the same man last Friday might be entirely coincidental.

But then Edith saw something that thwarted all her hopes of exonerating Michael. For someone else was now certainly in the living room with Michael and engaged in an intense discussion with him. Edith didn't need her binoculars or her zoom lens camera to see that it was Ian Luff...

So this was the dreaded confirmation she was looking for: *Luff was the traitor in Government House, and Michael was his co-conspirator...*

*

George Dorling had barely arrived home at his flat in Hankow Road in Kowloon this evening, when Tess began to interrogate him, over their frugal dinner of spring rolls and fried chicken.

'You were talking in your sleep again last night, George.' Tess's bruises and stitches from her fall two weeks ago were gone now, yet her eyes were red with constant crying. 'You said her name over and over again...Dora Kam. As plain as my own name it was...*Dora Kam*. Who is this woman? Are you planning to leave me for her?'

George wondered what he could say that would end this constant self-flagellation of his wife's. Yet the truth was much worse than the simple affair that Tess suspected. The truth was that he'd had no special feelings for Dora Kam at all. But he had caused that woman's death as surely as if he had strangled her himself, and the guilt of that was clearly tearing him up inside.

Guilt...*and fear*. For he could feel the net of retribution closing inexorably around him. Something would give him away to Jericho in the end, for that man was like a dog with a bone when he was on a case like this. He would never let go of it, gnawing at it constantly, until he uncovered the truth...

He wondered what Tess would say now if he told her the truth: that he was a dirty policeman on the take from the triads, that he had conspired in the murder of one of his own informants, and that his selfish actions had more or less condemned this woman Dora Kam to death.

But all he said was: 'I don't know any woman called Dora. You must be mishearing me, Tess...'

*

The same evening found Paul Jericho back in the select setting of the Hong Kong Club smoking room. Ronnie Grantham had invited him again for a drink after work, and he had accepted, half in the hope that he might encounter Ian Luff again and have the chance to assess the man objectively in a quiet social situation. He certainly didn't have enough evidence to bring in the man for questioning at the moment – at least not without some angry tirade from Charlie Hebdon as to why he was making a nuisance of himself and bothering senior members of the government.

But Jericho found himself disappointed because Luff was not in the smoking room this evening. Instead Jericho found himself at a table with Ronnie and two of his now familiar colleagues – the hawk-like and unsettling Julian Colby, and the more genial-looking man who held the purse strings of the government, the Colonial Treasurer Bob Harmsworth. Harmsworth's silver hair was more impeccably groomed than ever, so Jericho had wondered again if it might be a wig. Yet it seemed not, for at one point he ran a hand through his thick gleaming thatch of hair with perfect naturalness. Jericho did however notice something about the man that he had not noticed before: that he was missing the tips of two of his fingers on his right hand.

Jericho had been tempted to ask these gentlemen some subtle questions about Ian Luff for it would be interesting to know his colleagues' view of the man. Yet in the end he had decided to keep away from any talk of police work this evening, and had been content to sit back and mostly listen to the undemanding chat of his three companions. He certainly hadn't confided in them that yet another body had been found today, for he was still keeping the discovery of Marco da Silva's body out of the newspapers for the moment...

Harmsworth was in the middle of a risqué anecdote about a rubber planter in Malaya who had apparently kept a whole harem of local Malay women at his beck and call, when he noticed that Jericho's gaze had lingered for a moment on the truncated fingers on his right hand. 'Ah, I see you are wondering how I lost these finger tips. Actually I lost them on the Somme, Inspector Jericho.'

'That was careless of you, Bob,' Colby said with leaden humour. He turned to Jericho. 'Don't be too upset for Mr Harmsworth, though, Inspector. For the minor damage to those fingers probably saved his life in the end by allowing him to take a comfortable staff job well behind the lines...'

'I don't think you served in the war at all, Julian, did you?' Harmsworth replied huffily.

'Not in the front line, perhaps,' Colby agreed stiffly. 'But I certainly did my time in the army.'

'You spent the entire war in Egypt,' Harmsworth laughed. 'Enjoying the fleshpots of Cairo, no doubt.'

Ronnie Grantham decided to intervene to try and defuse this increasingly rancorous conversation. 'I call for peace, gentlemen.' He glanced at Jericho by his side. 'But Julian does have a valid point about Bob's injured hand. It did make him technically unfit for front line service, and was a relatively small price to pay for surviving the war, for it hasn't limited him one little bit since then. He still plays a good game of tennis and trounces me regularly even though he's got fifteen years on me. While the strength in those fingers is something remarkable, despite the damage to them. I have very strong fingers myself, for I used to be a very good rock climber in my youth, where a good grip is essential. Therefore I know real strength when I see it. I do seem to remember a Sherlock Holmes story where Holmes proves his strength by straightening a bent poker with his bare hands...'

'*The Adventure of the Speckled Band*, I think,' Colby interjected.

'Quite so,' Ronnie agreed. 'Now, I always thought this bit of the story was nonsense: that no one could do such a thing. But I swear that I saw my silver-haired friend here straighten out a severely bent poker in the drawing room in Government House with his bare hands, and make it look like child's play.'

Harmsworth looked uneasy. 'I think you should take Ronnie's story with a pinch of salt, Inspector Jericho. I believe I did try to straighten out a bent poker in his presence once, but I certainly made no impression on it whatsoever. So I am no circus strong man, as he seems to suggest.'

Jericho could not help noticing that Harmsworth had not been entertained by this complimentary story as most men would have been. In fact he seemed at great pains to deny it. Yet Jericho would have put money on Ronnie's version of the story being close to the truth, so had to wonder why Harmsworth seemed so reluctant to acknowledge it...

CHAPTER 18

Tuesday, 24th August 1937

Late on Tuesday morning Edith waited deliberately near the main portico entrance of Government House in the hope of seeing Ian Luff. She was feeling quite self-conscious as she waited in the fierce tropical heat, for she had decided to be daring today and wear a trouser suit to work. She had a very specific reason for doing this as she had plans for some illegal activities later today that would certainly be easier to accomplish in trousers. Yet she also had a subsidiary reason for wearing such a revealing outfit today too, for she had a vague hope that she might attract Ian Luff's attention by doing so...

She had soon discovered that these sleek white slacks had certainly attracted everybody else's attention in Government House: Julian Colby and Ronnie Grantham had almost spilled their morning coffee when they had seen her in a corridor earlier, while even the staid Elliot Casaubon had made some silly pretence to come into her room and have a long ogle at her legs. She had recognized with some dismay that the balding and bespectacled Casaubon also seemed to have formed some obvious attachment to her of late. This was likely to make their future working relationship a little strained if the man was going to attempt to flirt with her so blatantly all the time. Given his middle-aged schoolmaster looks, Edith couldn't see herself ever being attracted to this man in return. Edith realized with regret that the only type of men she ever seemed to attract were rather sad middle-aged men like Casaubon and Harmsworth, and possibly even Julian Colby.

Yet it was Ian Luff whose attention she was really seeking today by wearing this provocative outfit. She knew he was in the habit of taking a turn in the gardens at lunchtime, so was planning to join him there if she could. She knew now with near certainty that this man was her enemy, and she was determined to expose him as a traitor and a probable murderer. But to achieve that goal, she first needed to know him better. One of the principal things that had been drummed into her during her training with the SIS was this: get to know your enemy, find out what makes them tick, and then establish their weak points...

And the plan worked with surprising ease, for Ian Luff duly appeared at the main entrance and then even suggested without prompting that Edith should join him in his daily lunchtime circumlocution of the gardens. He even cast an admiring glance over her risqué outfit: 'May I say how charming you look today, Edith. I've always liked women in trousers ever since seeing Marlene Dietrich in *Blonde Venus*...'

Edith smiled coyly at that. 'I doubt that there is any resemblance at all between me and Marlene Dietrich, Ian...'

She left the choice of walking route to Luff, and he chose to follow Edith's own favourite path - a meandering ornamental path through the most heavily wooded part of the garden. It was a little disconcerting to Edith to discover that Ian Luff's taste in walking routes should coincide so closely with her own.

They came to a grove of Bauhinia trees in full magnificent flower, where they stopped to rest in the humid shade. The heat was still intense even under the trees, and Edith could feel a trickle of sweat on her brow, and even down her thighs to the tops of her silk stockings. No European women in Hong Kong ever went around in public with bare exposed legs, even in the height of summer, despite the intense discomfort it caused. Yet the flared trousers she was wearing today barely even revealed her ankles, so she had to wonder why she had still put on her silk hose underneath them as usual. It was disconcerting to realize just what a creature of habit she was.

'I fear that I'm steaming up again,' Edith apologized, as she took off her fogged-up glasses and wiped them with a handkerchief.

Luff didn't respond to that remark with any flirtatious banter this time. Instead he tilted his handsome head up to the blue sky as he saw a magpie robin flutter to rest on the branch above his head. He was still looking very cool and collected even in this intimidating summer heat, his slender figure dressed in an open-necked white shirt and drill trousers, and his handsome head protected by a white Fedora hat. He had a fine dew of perspiration on his golden skin, but that only served to make him look even more wholesome. Yet his small delicate hands – almost as delicate as a woman's – gave her some pause for thought, for they did not look like the hands of a man who could have throttled someone like Ralph Ogden to death...

It was nearly a week since they had spoken at any length: that intimate chat after Ralph's funeral when he had invited her out to dinner at the Repulse Bay Hotel. She rather hoped now that he would repeat the invitation for she would certainly accept this time, given what she'd learned about him since then. A long dinner would give her plenty of opportunity to carry out a subtle assessment of this man's character and intentions.

But annoyingly he did not make any repeat of his invitation. Instead he asked her a more sombre question. 'Do you think war is coming to Hong Kong, Edith?'

She hid her surprise at the question. *'Do you?'*

He nodded thoughtfully. 'Yes, I think so. And if it does, the complacent and comfortable lives that all we Westerners lead in Hong Kong might be suddenly ended in a trice.' He looked up at the green splendour of Victoria Peak and at the thin sprinkling of white bungalows and luxury apartment buildings near the very top in May Road and Conduit Road. 'Do you think that all those taipans and diplomats, living up there in splendid isolation from the lower classes below, know that the very foundations of their lives might soon be ripped asunder?'

They walked on and emerged from the cover of the trees on the north side of Government Hill where the dense jumble of buildings in Central District intruded on their view, particularly the stolid bulk of the new Hong Kong and Shanghai Bank building. Beyond all the white colonnaded buildings of the business quarter, the blue of the harbour was almost blinding in its intensity.

'You think the Japanese might take control of the whole of China, then?' she asked.

He laughed, showing his even white teeth. 'It is I who should be asking *you* that question, Edith. For I become ever more convinced that you are no more a meek little secretary than I am an Indian maharajah. I think you know *exactly* what is going on in China...' He stopped suddenly. 'If anybody in Hong Kong knows what the Japanese are planning to do, I bet that person is you, Edith.'

Edith thought this was an odd conversation to be having. She had intended to interrogate Ian Luff, but instead he was questioning her. It was clear that he understood her true position in the SIS here; he had more or less admitted it several times. But if this man was really passing secrets to the Japanese as she thought, then it was a doubly strange conversation to be having, for he should already have a very good idea of Japanese intentions.

So why was he asking her? Was it simply a bluff to make him seem like the innocent treasury official he purported to be? Of course Luff could still be a traitor and yet be entirely ignorant of what the Japanese were planning to do militarily in South China and Hong Kong. He might well be providing information to the Japanese consulate here, but they wouldn't necessarily be returning the favour...

Edith smiled. 'I really think you have misunderstood me completely, Ian. I almost wish I was this mysterious Mata Hari woman you think me to be. But I'm afraid I have no more knowledge of Japanese invasion plans than you do...' She thought this might even be the truth at present, for the Japanese War Ministry was still super-enciphering all their signals to their Kwantung Army, so she had not managed to decode a single one in the last ten days.

Luff sighed resignedly. 'I thought that you would probably continue to deny it. Of course I can't really blame you for doing so; it's probably more than your life's worth to tell me the truth...'

*

Returning to Wanchai in early afternoon from a visit to Central Police Headquarters – and driving his own Austin now that Constable Ho was so busy with other duties - Paul Jericho had just parked his car in Lockhart Road to pick up some *dim sum* for a late luncheon, when he caught sight of Bob Harmsworth walking briskly along the pavement in front of him. Harmsworth's back was to Jericho, and his gleaming head of silver hair was mostly concealed under a Panama hat, yet Jericho was sure it was him.

What was Harmsworth doing here in this seedy part of Wanchai, he wondered. It seemed an odd destination for an urbane man like him, unless he was being fitted for a new suit at one of the many tailors in Lockhart Road. Yet the tailors here catered more to seamen and the lower orders of expatriates, not to senior civil servants, who mostly patronised the more expensive and select tailors in Central District.

But Jericho soon dismissed Harmsworth from his mind, for his thoughts were elsewhere. He had just had a long if rather fruitless meeting with Inspector Kevin Ball in Central where they had compared notes on their respective investigations. He had been late for the meeting because he had got caught up in the huge funeral procession for the late James Woo, scion of the fabulously wealthy Woo family. Jericho had never seen such an immensely long funeral procession before, for it had stretched right through Central District along Queens Road, and into Western District, causing utter chaos to normal traffic. So he had been in a filthy temper by the time he had finally extricated himself from the jam and parked his Austin in the compound of Central Police Headquarters.

The meeting with Inspector Ball had been a testy one as usual. Ball had his own theories about how their investigations might be linked, which Jericho did not subscribe to at all. Jericho was certainly far from sure about any direct connections between the cases, yet he continued to debate with himself whether the murder of the informer Ricky Sun might impinge in some way on his own investigation into the deaths of the three bargirls. Or – more likely at least - into the murders of the two high class pimps, Freddie Ling and Marco da Silva, which might have some connection in turn with the deaths of the Chinese women who had worked for them...

Now, on returning to Wanchai, he had just realized with annoyance that he had forgotten to ask Ball about the raid on that homosexual massage parlour last year, and whether Marco da Silva had been arrested at the time. Or, even more intriguingly, whether this man Ian Luff had been caught up in the raid too but had somehow managed to avoid arrest? Yet he had avoided telling Ball yet about his suspicions about Ian Luff; that was information best kept to himself for the moment, until he was lot more certain about the man's involvement.

Jericho was half-tempted to go back to Central and ask Ball about the raid on the massage parlour, but he reflected that he could do it just as easily with a telephone call. As he got out of his car, he was still muttering to himself over his forgetfulness.

'Talking to yourself is a very bad sign,' a woman's voice said behind him in an amused tone.

He turned to see Maggie Yiu smiling faintly at him.

Jericho smiled wryly in return. 'Indeed so. I just hope no one else heard me, otherwise I could be off to the funny farm in the morning.' He inspected her face with his usual discreet pleasure; she really was a glorious looking creature even when dressed in simple black Chinese pyjamas like today. He realized suddenly that no woman had lately attracted him quite as much as this beautiful Eurasian girl – certainly not since Susan's death anyway. He felt a sudden overwhelming desire to be bold and to run his hands through her silky black hair.

She looked at him oddly as if some second sight had told her exactly what he was thinking.

He quickly lowered his eyes and excused himself. 'I have to get back to the station, Miss Yiu. The investigation is reaching a critical stage now.'

'Have you not caught this blue-eyed man yet?' she asked worriedly.

'No, not yet.' Jericho suddenly realized that he hadn't yet bothered to check a basic fact about his new suspect Ian Luff: what was the colour of his eyes? *Yet he had a nasty feeling from memory that the man had brown eyes...*

'They say a typhoon might be coming to Hong Kong. Perhaps next week, if the rumours are true,' Maggie Yiu went on in a more concerned voice. 'Have you heard anything about this?'

'It seems it might be true. There is a tropical cyclone system building down south of the Philippines, according to a friend of mine at the Hong Kong Observatory.' Jericho's mood was distracted, still trying to recall if Ian Luff had brown eyes or blue eyes...

Maggie Yiu glanced up the street and seemed suddenly disconcerted about something herself. 'I had better let you go, Inspector. You clearly have more important things to do than passing the time of day with me...' With that, she nodded vaguely at him and was gone.

Jericho wondered if he had offended Maggie Yiu in some way. He realized that he had been entertaining some vague hope that she might be attracted to him a little in return. He wasn't sure what he would do about it, though, even in the unlikely event that she returned some of his warm feelings. But it seemed that his slight hopes were just a pipe dream anyway so this effectively laid the matter to rest...

He decided to forget the idea of taking some luncheon at a nearby food stall, and began to walk towards Fenwick Street and the China Fleet Club, which was the quickest way back from here to the police station on the waterfront. But as he reached the corner with Fenwick Street, he happened to glance south towards the much busier Hennessy Road and spotted a little black Austin Seven exactly like his own, stuck behind a broken down tram on the eastbound track. The eastbound roadway next to the tram tracks was presently narrowed because some coolies were working haphazardly at digging a trench for a new sewer across the carriageway. The little Austin had obviously tried to squeeze past the roadworks by using the tram track, but had got stuck behind this stricken tram.

Jericho saw the woman driver get out of the Austin and have an angry word with the tram driver. He recognized at once from her distinctive glasses that it was Edith Starling and that she was in a blazing temper. She was dressed in a cream trouser suit, which surprised him; hardly any Englishwomen in Hong Kong wore slacks except perhaps on holiday at the beach. He had given her almost no thought since seeing her on Sunday and hearing her startling theory about the death of her boss, Ralph Ogden. But he had a sudden compulsion now to know what she might be doing here in Wanchai dressed like that, and where she might be going. She had been Susan's best friend, after all, so he really didn't want any harm to come to her.

In a moment he had turned and retraced his steps at a run back to his own car. Then, quickly starting the car with the starter handle, he leapt in and took a turning south from Lockhart Road that he knew would lead him to a junction in Hennessy Road a little to the east of where Edith was presently held up. He planned to wait there until Edith had freed herself from her little traffic jam, and then to follow her. He had decided that it about time he kept an eye on Edith Starling to see what she was getting up to...

*

Paul Jericho soon discovered what Edith Starling was getting up to, and didn't know whether to be outraged or amused by it. For it seemed that Edith had taken to a career of breaking and entering...

He had followed her to Happy Valley where he himself lived. But she hadn't parked near the racecourse or on Morrison Hill Road as most people did, but had instead turned up Stubbs Road and parked her little black Austin in a lay-by at the top of the hill behind the cemetery. Jericho had parked near to her car, but out of sight behind a large fig tree. From there

Edith had walked down through the hillside cemetery, emerged into the little network of streets above the racecourse, then crossed over Blue Pool Road where Jericho himself lived. For a moment Jericho had wondered if she might be on her way to visit *him* at home, which would make him feel particularly foolish if it was the case. But he had soon dismissed that notion; she could not possibly expect that he would be home on a Tuesday afternoon.

And so it had proved; she had carried on to the next main street, Broadwood Road, then disappeared into the wooded slopes behind. Her manner was decidedly furtive by now so Jericho had followed her with extreme caution, sure she was up to something either illegal or dangerous. She had followed a path through the woods that she was clearly already familiar with, and had arrived at a small wooded hill that looked down at the rear of the houses and small apartment buildings in Broadwood Road. He saw instantly that her interest was in one ground floor apartment in particular with a small paved patio at the back. Through the dense screen of evergreen trees, Jericho could see right inside the living room of this apartment. He also saw Edith wait to make sure the apartment was empty, then descend through the trees to the back patio, where she soon had the back door open with the aid of a skeleton key or something similar.

Then she had spent an hour inside, clearly searching through the whole apartment from top to bottom. Jericho continued to watch from the shelter of the woods, not sure what to do. As a policeman, of course, he should really have followed her down and arrested her. But something told him this was not some personal business of Edith's but something to do with her work for the Secret Intelligence Service. Therefore the last thing he was going to do was intervene...

In the end, she finished her search at four o'clock and emerged onto the patio again. She locked the door behind her with her key, so obviously did not want the owner of the apartment to know he had suffered a break-in. Yet Jericho could see instantly from the sag of Edith's shoulders that she hadn't found what she was looking for: disappointment was written all over her face.

He could of course have challenged her right now and asked her what the hell she thought she was doing. But he decided to let her go; now was not the time to interrogate her about this. Instead he slipped away into the cover of the trees and watched from his hiding place as Edith passed close by him in her distinctive white trouser suit. He assumed she would be going back directly to her car, and then probably back to Government House, so he thought she should be safe enough now.

Jericho waited five minutes more, then descended down through the woods back to Broadwood Road, where he soon found the entrance to the small three-storey apartment block that had attracted Edith's interest. A quick look inside the lobby showed a set of mail boxes with the names of the residents helpfully stencilled on the front of them. The mail box for the ground floor apartment at the rear of the block, 1B, was labelled with the name *Michael Yip*...

Jericho frowned when he read that name. He certainly knew of *someone* by that name, and wondered if it could be the same man: a left wing Chinese lawyer who delighted in haranguing police officers giving evidence at the trials of trade union officials or workers accused of illegal strikes or affray. Given Edith's interest in him, it seemed quite likely that this *was* the same Michael Yip...

Deep in thought, Jericho retraced his steps back to his car parked in Stubbs Road above the cemetery. Yet he was surprised to discover when he got there that Edith's car was also still parked in the same nearby lay-by, so it seemed she hadn't been going back to her car directly as he had thought.

But he couldn't afford to hang around here any longer waiting for her return when he had so many other pressing things to do back at the station. Therefore, reluctantly, he started his car with the handle, and drove back to Wanchai.

*

Earlier, while searching Michael's apartment, Edith had glimpsed someone in the woods watching her. This was a deeply worrying development, which compounded an already frustrating afternoon: first getting stuck for twenty minutes behind that broken-down tram in Wanchai, and now wasting an hour on a fruitless search of Michael's flat that had revealed nothing useful at all.

Now it seemed that someone was on to her, which was the most worrying thing of all...

Yet she left the apartment exactly the same way that she had arrived, and took the same path back through the woods. Half way along the path, though, she suddenly dived off into the undergrowth and scrambled back down out of the woods by an entirely different route. This new route took her safely across Broadwood Road, then to Blue Pool Road, where Susan Jericho had used to live. From there she followed an alternative path back to the cemetery. She knew this path well, for she had walked here several times with Susan during the pleasantly cool days of the previous autumn. She began to congratulate herself that she must have evaded whoever was shadowing her. By the time she got back to the lay-by under the trees in Stubbs Road, she was feeling confident enough to relax her guard again.

But suddenly she felt a pair of powerful arms grab her from behind, then a cloth was clamped tightly over her nose and mouth. She knew at once from the sickly smell that it was dosed with chloroform, so fought feverishly to release the man's hold on her.

But every breath she took made her weaker, and she soon felt herself slipping away into a deep well of unconsciousness...

CHAPTER 19

Wednesday, 25th August 1937

In the offices of Saunders-Woo in Queens Road Central, Sebastian Ride sat contemplating the view through his window of the gracefully arcaded Victorian buildings on the other side of the street. Beyond those buildings a fresh peach-coloured sky outlined the rugged mountains of the Chinese mainland, while the early morning tropical sun already gave promise of another roasting day to come. The wooden shutters creaked fitfully in the early morning breeze blowing in from the harbour. Ride could sense the feverish pulse of the city stirring outside like a living thing...

He had loved the intoxicating feeling of this city from the first moment that he had stepped ashore here twenty years ago – so different from the grim blackened cobbles and mean brick houses of the northern English city where he had grown up. The place had been a total revelation to him: the heavy enveloping blanket of heat, the brilliant light, the strange colourful flowers and trees, the hum of a different world, full of unexpected life, alien noises and unfamiliar scents. The island of Hong Kong had cast a deep impression on him from that first day he had stepped off the boat here at Blake Pier, and had captured his soul completely. Like many Englishmen drawn to this strange Oriental world, he had found the lure of the East to be an all-embracing and captivating one. Yet now this whole life he had built for himself here was under threat because of one man...

He turned around suddenly as he heard Frances Leung enter his room from her adjoining office, a paper file in her hand. Frances had reverted this week in the office to her usual formal behaviour, and had even returned to calling him "Mr Ride". In particular there had been no hint of that erotic intimacy that she had displayed with such devastating effect when she had visited his home on Sunday evening. Yet though she was dressed as ever in her immaculate woman's pinstripe business suit and had her hair worn up and pinned back in a non-nonsense style, she now made an entirely different impression on him. In these last three days he had fallen under her spell so completely that she now seemed to him like the most desirable woman in the world, far more desirable even than Faye Grantham or Grace Woo. He watched her trim figure with rapt attention as she deposited her file on his desk, then picked up the empty cup of green tea she had brought him earlier and took it over to the tray of used cups by the door. As she bent down to leave the cup on the floor boy's tray, his eyes lingered on the tight fabric of her skirt as it stretched taut over her firm buttocks, and the hem lifted slightly to reveal more of the seams of her black silk stockings.

As she turned and retraced her steps to his desk, he had the feeling that she knew exactly where his eyes had been lingering, and might even have planned it that way. Yet on the surface she was the same unruffled and severely professional Frances as ever. She sat down opposite him, while he closed the shutters behind him to reduce some of the constant raucous buzz and clatter of noise from the street below.

'How did it go yesterday at the house, Mr Ride?' she asked.

Ride had spent most of yesterday attending the funeral of James Woo. Afterwards he had gone back to the Woo mansion in Po Shan Road with the closest friends and acquaintances of the Woo family. It had been a hard day because he had felt a complete hypocrite, especially when consoling Grace in her subdued grief. Yet even in her melancholy mood, Grace had still let him know by her usual subtle womanly means that she welcomed his intimate attentions. Ride had always prided himself on his ability to manage his relationships with women, but he now realized for the first time that it was actually women who controlled him. Perhaps that had always been the case, he was forced to admit to himself...

Ride studied Frances's thoughtful expression. 'So, what have you been able to discover for me about this man Ian Luff?'

Frances opened the file she had brought with her. 'Ah, yes. Mr Ian Luff. Thirty two years old, born in the picturesque Peak District village of Hartington in Derbyshire. His father was the local dentist, but somehow found the money to send his son first to Eton, and then later to Oxford...'

'Maybe the father was a bloodsucking blackmailer like the son,' Ride suggested sourly.

Frances's lips twitched slightly with humour. 'Perhaps...anyway, the son read economics at Balliol College, Oxford, and came out to Hong Kong nearly seven years ago. Has done well for himself in the government service, and is well thought of in the Treasury. His social life is a mystery...'

'I bet...!' Ride interjected savagely.

'...He is unmarried, and probably homosexual, but with no obvious scandals to give him away. Lives in Bowen Road in Eastern Mid-levels, in a small and select apartment block next to the one where we keep a company flat of our own for the use of VIP visitors to Hong Kong...' Frances cleared her throat and looked as if she might be about to make some pointed comment about the company flat in Bowen Road, which she was obviously well aware was used by Ride for all his assignations, and not just the tragic one with Susan Jericho. But in the end she said nothing on that delicate subject and merely continued in the same maddeningly professional voice. 'A handsome man, slight of build. He bears some resemblance to a younger version of the Duke of Windsor – many people have commented on it - and is regarded as one of the rising young men in Government House...'

'Is that all you've got, Frances?' Ride complained. 'I was hoping you might discover some real dirt on this man that we could use in return to keep this sordid little blackmailer and crook quiet.'

Frances flushed slightly, and Ride could see that he had angered her. But she held her temper and continued in the same even tone. 'There is an unconfirmed report that Luff was detained briefly last year in a police raid on a homosexual club and massage parlour in Western District. The masseurs were mostly rent boys who are reputed to be Japanese informers and agents...'

Ride jumped on that immediately. 'That's interesting, isn't it? We already know that it was Luff who concocted this plan to sell marine gasoline to the Japanese Navy. So this means that Ian Luff has *two* distinct connections with the Japanese. Can that be entirely coincidental?' He had another even more interesting thought. 'Could Luff be a Japanese agent too? Working in Government House he must have access to all sorts of interesting information, both political and military. Could he be selling information on British military secrets to the Japanese?'

Frances considered that suggestion with a measured frown. 'Possibly. But even if he is, and even if we managed to find the evidence of it, it would be difficult to make use of such knowledge. For if we betrayed him to his British masters, he would still be free to betray you to the Woo family in return...'

Frances had not repeated the remark she had made to him on Sunday night about killing Luff, so Ride had wondered afterwards if she had simply been joking. He remembered that he had once imagined whimsically asking *her* to commit a murder on his behalf, and had even imagined her agreeing primly to do it without a qualm. Now the roles were reversed and it no longer seemed quite so funny. For he knew in his heart that she had not been joking, and that she was simply waiting for him to come to the same inevitable conclusion too in his own time. In truth there was something disturbingly ruthless and implacable in Frances's character that Ride had never fully realized before, something which suggested that she had been deadly serious in what she had said on Sunday night. Perhaps that was the reason why he had suddenly found her so much more sexually attractive than before...

*

At five o'clock that afternoon Ride met Ian Luff outside the imposing entrance of the new Hong Kong and Shanghai Bank in Des Voeux Road and they began to walk together as if this was a chance encounter between old friends. Of course it was no accident in reality for Ride had sent a message to Government House requesting this meeting. Ride was anxious to explore other possibilities than the dread one suggested by Frances: perhaps Luff might be bought off with something a bit less than what he had suggested, though Ride knew that the price would inevitably be high, whatever it was.

Their walk took them across the tram tracks in Des Voeux Road and initially around the stately perimeter of Royal Square, past the imposing statue of the late Queen Victoria in all her bulky bronze splendour.

Luff was amused by the face of Hong Kong's former Great White Queen, which had been rendered in giant epic bronze by the sculptor Raggio and had a face as black as her widow's weeds. 'I wonder if Queen Victoria's darker-skinned imperial subjects might be confused by this statue, which makes her look rather blacker than most of them.' His smile faded. 'Why did you want to see me, Sebastian? It's probably better that we don't meet too often otherwise someone might notice.'

Ride looked around quickly, making sure no one else was within earshot. But the square, with its perimeter of fine old colonial buildings and its row of parked Austins lined up under the palm trees, was quiet for once. The square led down directly to the Praya and to the azure water of the harbour, which was overflowing as usual with boat and shipping traffic. The view across the harbour seemed presently filled with a wind-blown panoply of coloured sails and overloaded junks and sampans. 'I want to know what your minimum price is,' Ride stated bluntly.

Luff froze for a second. 'I thought we understood each other, Sebastian. My "price", as you put it, is a senior position in Saunders-Woo, perhaps as your assistant at the start. But I would expect you would arrange a seat on the board for me within say five years...' He smiled bleakly. 'I am not a greedy man, or a stupid one. I am prepared to wait and follow the usual business protocols. But as I said, I am not really asking you for a favour. Instead I will be doing one for you, for I will bring huge benefits to the company. I believe that I have already demonstrated how effective I am in my business dealings...'

They walked on to the cricket ground and then to the parade ground by Murray Barracks where a company of very smart English soldiers, all muscular and tanned to an unfamiliar golden-brown sheen, were marching and drilling in khaki splendour. Ride finally spoke up again, his voice rising with frustration. 'But you must see that it's impossible, Mr Luff. We could never work together comfortably. At least I could never be comfortable about having someone like you in my inner circle...'

Luff flushed slightly as if Ride had made some insulting remark about his sexual proclivities.

'I didn't mean that as a slur on you, Mr Luff,' Ride added quickly. 'But in business we have to have complete trust between the leading members of a company otherwise the whole system will quickly break down. You will have effectively forced yourself into the company with the use of threats. So do you really think we could ever work together in a spirit of mutual understanding and trust?'

They came to the bottom of Garden Road where they could see the green mass of the Peak rising above the imposing tower of St John's Cathedral and the scatter of white buildings on the lower slopes. Luff looked up at the mountain with a sigh. 'Isn't this the most wonderful place in the world, Sebastian? A place of beauty, yet also a place where real fortunes can be made...'

'*And lost...*' Ride said warningly.

Luff smiled wryly. 'Indeed so. I was told when I first came here that Hong Kong is like a little piece of England set in the South China Sea. But the truth is much more complex than that. If anything, this is still an exotic Chinese island, with only the merest patina of Englishness on the surface. But I love it, that touch of English homeliness and refinement, but now mixed and subsumed like an exotic cocktail by the enticing fizz of Oriental commerce, intrigue and double-dealing...' He finally clapped his hand on Ride's shoulder. 'Don't you see that someone like me is perfect for this place, Sebastian? I promise that I will do Saunders-Woo proud and turn it into the greatest company in Asia in a few short years.'

'And what about me?' Ride said icily.

'*You?* There will still be plenty of opportunities for you to shine too, Sebastian.'

Ride nodded tamely at this but his inner mood was bleak. Frances was right about this man as usual. He bit his lip with despair as he realized the uncomfortable truth: that he would have to kill this man soon, otherwise everything he had ever worked for would be lost.

But how to kill him? That was the question...

*

As dusk was falling, Paul Jericho stood at the iron entrance gate of Government House while he waited for a security pass to be issued by the Officer of the Watch. He had never been subject to this level of security before, and his police uniform and rank had always been sufficient in the past to gain admittance to Government House without question. But it seemed that someone had decided to beef up security, given the present troubled times that Hong Kong was going through. Perhaps the officer in charge was suspicious because Jericho had come alone in his own Austin rather than in an official police car; the guards had certainly made him leave it outside parked on Upper Albert Road.

He stepped back under the line of Bauhinia trees that were planted along the pavement on Upper Albert Road, and which cast a tracery of evening shadows on the white-painted gate lodges on each side of the tall iron gate. He tried to control his impatience but was relieved when Ronnie Grantham finally showed his face on the other side of the gate and soon smoothed the way with the Officer of the Watch for his entry into the grounds.

Ronnie led him down the driveway to the portico entrance of the main building, whose elegant exterior was flushed with pink from the dying rays of the sun. Jericho could see that something serious was afoot so pressed Ronnie to tell him what it was.

Ronnie barely hesitated. 'Young Edith Starling has disappeared. She left work early yesterday lunchtime, and no one has seen her since...'

Jericho stopped in his tracks as he realized the implication of this: that he himself must be one of the last people to have seen Edith before she had gone missing. He wondered instantly if he might have made a profound error of judgement by abandoning his watch on her yesterday after she had broken into the apartment of the lawyer Michael Yip in Happy Valley. He cursed himself under his breath: he should have stuck with her and not let her out of his sight. She had virtually told him that she thought her life was in danger because of some unknown plot to do with the death of her boss Ralph Ogden, but he had done nothing about it.

Yet he didn't feel ready to admit any of his special knowledge of Edith's situation even to Ronnie. 'Couldn't she just have gone away for a few days without telling anyone?' he asked Ronnie hopefully.

Ronnie looked bleak. 'Not at all. She was due to attend a high level meeting with her SIS colleagues today. As I told you last week, she seems now to be in effective charge of the intelligence team here, though nothing official has been said on the subject. Her colleague Elliot Casaubon was wondering where she might be, and had a word with me in case I might know. He knows that Edith and I are friendly and sometimes meet socially. I'm afraid I took it upon myself then to go to Edith's apartment in Wyndham Street and see if she was perhaps laid up with some illness. But she wasn't there, and her amah and houseboy who came to clean her apartment this morning said that her bed had not been slept in...'

'Then you did the right thing to call me, Ronnie,' Jericho said sincerely. He decided that he would send one of his officers to Stubbs Road in Happy Valley as soon as possible and see if Edith's little black Austin Seven was still parked in the same lay-by where he had seen it yesterday. His instincts now told him sadly that the car *would* still be there, and that someone had either abducted Edith or murdered her within a few minutes of him last seeing her at about four o'clock. He had already checked that the Michael Yip who lived in Broadwood Road was indeed the same troublesome criminal lawyer he had assumed him to be. Therefore the question rose quickly in his mind of what Edith had been doing breaking into that man's apartment and conducting a thorough search of the premises. *So how was Michael Yip involved in this mysterious business of Edith's?* It seemed unlikely that he might have anything to do with the business of the British Secret Service in Government House.

They entered the main entrance hall of the building and Jericho took in the sumptuous furnishings and the classically inspired moulded plaster ceiling, which was as fine as anything by Robert Adam. Ronnie turned to Jericho apologetically. 'I should warn you that Casaubon in particular is hopping mad that I should have taken it upon myself to bring in the regular police about this. But I talked him round, and pointed out that Edith's disappearance might have nothing to do with her security work. Therefore I told him that you were the best person to contact for help to try and find her...particularly as you know her quite well through Susan. Yet you will still need to be very discreet in your enquiries here at Government House for fear of upsetting our SIS chums too much...' Ronnie hesitated. 'I have a feeling that Edith might be having an affair with someone, so this might be more the reason for her disappearance than anything to do with her work here. I hardly like to say this, because I sound like such a nasty snitch. But I saw her a few weeks ago in company with a young and handsome Chinese man, walking on the Peak. The man looked like someone I have met professionally: a rather accomplished young Chinese barrister called Michael Yip....' Ronnie paused expectantly. 'Ah...I can see that name means something to you too. But it would, of course, since you have probably encountered this same man in court where he's well known as a stubborn defender of union officials and activists. He and Edith seemed very close, practically walking arm-in-arm along Lugard Road. I did wonder at the time whether Edith might be indulging in a rather dangerous and unsuitable passion. Of course I could be wrong; they might simply be friends and nothing more...'

Jericho was immediately led to the same obvious conclusion: could Edith really have been having an affair with this man Michael Yip? *Could that be why she had broken into his place?* Was her odd behaviour no more than evidence of a lover's tiff or some breakdown in their clandestine relationship? But if Michael Yip really was her lover, then Edith certainly was living dangerously, in more ways than one...

*

Sebastian Ride did not get home to Conduit Road until after eight o'clock. He had gone for a drink in Bessie's Bar after his difficult meeting with Ian

Luff, and that single drink had extended inevitably to five or six whiskies as he pondered what to do. Though he was still not yet drunk by his standards, he decided to leave his Bugatti in its parking space and took a taxi home instead. The taxi had laboured its way up the steep incline of Garden Road – very few cars could manage that hill like his bright blue Bugatti sports car – so Ride had been left with even more time to think in the back of the taxi as it chugged its way in low gear towards his sprawling three-storey mansion in Conduit Road.

The house was quiet as usual apart from the sounds of music coming from upstairs; their servants all discreetly out of sight in the basement for the evening, including Gloria's severe nurse, the efficient Doris Chow. He loosened his tie and climbed the stairs, trying not to make too much noise on the creaking wooden steps. But he found Gloria surprisingly in the study on the first floor, not in her bedroom on the floor above as he'd expected. And the music was not the sound of Hong Kong's radio station, ZBW, broadcasting a live relay of the dance orchestra from The Gripps, but was instead coming from the gramophone in the study. Ride stood at the door of the study as he heard Gloria singing along to the 78 record - *I Wanna be Loved by You* sung by Helen Kane. Gloria's impersonation of Helen Kane's sexy little girl voice was perfect, and he stood there, entranced by her all over again, as she sang along with the record:

I wanna be loved by you
Just you, and nobody else but you
I wanna be loved by you alone
Boo-boopy doo
I wanna be kissed by you
Just you, and nobody else but you
I wanna be kissed by you alone...

He finally poked his head around the door and saw that she was sitting by the gramophone with a wistful expression on her face. He noted to his surprise that she seemed stone-cold sober, and that she had obviously had her hair done today. Her makeup was perfect too, as if she had been waiting here for him with something important to say...

'You look very nice,' he said warily.

She shrugged resignedly. 'So do you, Sebastian, damn you! But then you always do, don't you, darling? Even when you're a little drunk and dishevelled, like now.'

The record came to an end and the sudden silence seemed deafening.

'You didn't tell me how the funeral went yesterday,' Gloria said conversationally.

Ride had chosen not to take her to the funeral, not sure if her recent encouraging period of sobriety would last through the whole of yesterday. And the last thing he could afford to do was to offend the Woo family by taking along a drunken and belligerent wife to a solemn Chinese funeral gathering.

She seemed in a strange fey mood to him – in fact she had seemed to be in this odd mood ever since coming to his office at the weekend.

Suddenly she sprang to her feet. 'Are you thinking of leaving me for that whore Faye Grantham, Sebastian?' she demanded abruptly. In this mood she seemed much more like the determined little daughter of a colonel in the Indian Army that he remembered from their first meeting ten years ago. She walked over to the large curved plate glass window and stared out at the white apartment blocks below and the sprinkled lights of the harbour beyond.

'Why are you asking me this now, Gloria?' Ride muttered petulantly.

She turned to face him again. 'Because, if you are, I would think twice about it, my sweet. If you try to leave me, I will make sure I destroy you. It might perhaps be a pyrrhic victory for me, for we might all go down in flames together. But perhaps I am past caring about myself any more...'

He was taken aback for a moment by the icy contempt in her voice. 'And how would you do that? No one cares about our marriage, Gloria. Everyone else in this place is having affairs. You would just look foolish if you decide to play the embittered wife.'

'Our neighbours and friends might not care about our marriage, Sebastian. But they will certainly be interested when they discover that you murdered your own business partner...'

Ride tried to hide his shock at her brutal statement. 'That's nonsense! Who's told you such a ridiculous thing?'

Gloria came forward towards him until her face was practically touching his. 'I overheard your whole conversation with that man Ian Luff in your office, Sebastian.'

Ride tried to contain his mounting panic. 'It was malicious nonsense that man was spouting. There's no truth in what he said.'

'Then why didn't you just throw him out of your office, Sebastian?' With that, Gloria's harsh expression softened surprisingly into a smile. 'Poor you! Now for the first time, I am finally returning a little of the misery that you have caused me over the years. And you don't like it one little bit, do you...?' But then, even more surprisingly, she leant forward even further and kissed him slowly on the lips. 'You're a complete bastard, Sebastian, yet the sad truth is that I still want you.' She kissed him again, more violently this time. 'Now I want you to take me upstairs, Sebastian, and make love to me as if your life depends on it. Which perhaps - in the circumstances - it does...'

CHAPTER 20

Thursday, 26th August 1937

By nine o'clock on Thursday morning, Paul Jericho was back in Government House making further enquiries into the disappearance of Edith Starling...

As he'd expected, his officers had found Edith's Austin parked in the same picturesque forested spot in Stubbs Road above the Happy Valley cemetery so it now seemed certain that she had either been abducted or perhaps murdered somewhere in the vicinity of Stubbs Road on Tuesday afternoon. Jericho had not explained to any of his colleagues so far how he had managed to divine the location of Edith's car with such magical precision, but George Dorling had clearly understood that his chief was holding something back about his personal knowledge of events surrounding Edith Starling's disappearance. Edith's car had been picked up by a police flatbed lorry and taken back to the police compound at Central Police Station where it was now being assiduously sifted for any clues. But nothing of any significance had been found so far to help in the search.

But Edith's mysterious disappearance had at least provided Jericho with one unexpected benefit, for he now had the perfect excuse to interrogate all her colleagues at Government House, including this man Ian Luff who was now of considerable interest to Jericho in connection with the Wanchai murders. Not that he would be so foolish as to accuse this man of anything directly, of course, yet he could use the opportunity to ask Luff some searching peripheral questions that were not really related to the matter of Edith Starling's disappearance at all.

Bearing in mind Ronnie Grantham's request to be very discreet, Jericho had chosen to come here to Government House on his own this morning to ask questions because he wanted his visit to be viewed as an informal one only at this stage. He hoped this sense of informality might help to lull

Ian Luff in particular into a sense of false security.

He had found Luff in his own room in the modern administration block at the rear of Government House where the senior officials of the Hong Kong Treasury had a suite of offices. The place had the appearance of an efficient government organization: wood-panelled offices, mahogany furniture, polished parquet flooring, a busy scurry of formally attired officials, the chatter of a battery of typewriters in the secretarial pool. It could have been a suite of offices in Whitehall but for the lush tropical palms waving at the tall windows and the creak of the ceiling fans.

Jericho had met Ian Luff formally for the first time a week ago in the Hong Kong Club, and his impression of him this time was much the same as on that first occasion, despite the unfavourable things he had learned about the man since then. Luff was undeniably a well-spoken and pleasant-looking individual. His resemblance to the Duke of Windsor seemed less marked to Jericho than he had thought at their first meeting, but he definitely had a similar head of perfectly groomed fair hair and a similar jaunty charm to the ex-King of England. The sun shining through the window behind him outlined his handsome head in a halo of gold, while his skin was a healthy pink unmarked by any trace of beard stubble even in this unforgiving tropical light. Jericho still had a vague feeling that he had seen this man somewhere before that meeting in the Hong Kong Club, though he still couldn't place the occasion.

'Have you any idea where Edith might be?' Jericho asked him, after Luff had invited him into his room and offered him a comfortable chair.

Luff was smoking a long American cigarette, and he now blew a perfect smoke ring which shifted and changed shape in the eddies caused by the ceiling fan. 'I'm afraid not, Inspector.'

That gesture of Ian Luff's now suddenly reminded Jericho where he had seen Ian Luff before. It had been in the garden at the Woo mansion in Po Shan Road last year when he had gone there to investigate that now notorious burglary. Jericho had not been introduced to Luff at the time, but the man had definitely been there in that garden, talking privately in a nearby grove of palm trees to James Woo. Luff had been smoking in exactly the same languid way he was smoking now. *So was there some close connection between Ian Luff and the late James Woo?*

Jericho now remembered something else important, and took time to examine the colour of Luff's eyes. He'd had a vague feeling from their earlier meeting that the man's eyes might be brown. Yet given the man's fair colouring it had still seemed entirely possible to Jericho that he might be mistaken and that Luff would turn out to have blue eyes after all. But the truth, on close inspection, was that he certainly didn't. Luff eyes were in fact an intense shade of dark brown, and couldn't possibly be mistaken by anyone for blue. Therefore he simply couldn't be the man seen leaving

Cherry Kwok's room on the night she died, just over a week ago. Not unless the old woman witness from Shanghai was wrong anyway. But Jericho didn't think so: that old woman had carried an air of solid conviction in her words.

Yet there was still the fact of his business card being found in the Tin Hau Hotel to explain. And his probable presence in a homosexual massage parlour at the same time as Marco da Silva...

Luff seemed disconcerted by Jericho's long and detailed inspection of him and cleared his throat uncomfortably. 'In fact I hardly know Edith at all since she works in the Intelligence section, who keep themselves very much to themselves...for obvious reasons, I suppose...'

'I'm speaking to everyone in Government House about Edith, even the Acting Governor,' Jericho assured him. 'So please don't feel threatened by these questions, Mr Luff. It's just routine. Even if you didn't know Edith well, you might have seen or heard something that might give us a clue where she has gone.'

Luff took another long draw of his cigarette. 'Well, that all seems entirely reasonable. But I haven't even spoken to Edith since Ralph Ogden's funeral last week.' He seemed to have a sudden thought. 'Oh, wait! I did see her at lunchtime on Tuesday, walking in the gardens here, and we chatted together for a few minutes.'

'Did she say anything significant? Anything that might indicate where she was going later that day? For she does seem to have vanished that very same afternoon...'

Luff seemed to give that some serious thought, as he finally stubbed out the remains of his cigarette. 'It's a filthy habit...I should really give it up...'

'*But Edith*...do you remember what was said between you on Tuesday lunchtime?' Jericho pressed him.

Luff shook his handsome head vaguely. 'We said nothing really of any importance. Just passed the time of day. I remember she was wearing a rather daring white trouser suit on Tuesday, which suited her figure rather well. She reminded me rather of Marlene Dietrich in *Blonde Venus.*' He smiled. 'I hope that doesn't make me sound like a pervert.'

'So you find Edith attractive, do you, Mr Luff?' Jericho asked innocently.

Luff regarded him coolly in return. 'Indeed I do, Inspector. I rather like shapely women in slacks. I even like the fact that she wears spectacles, which suit her very well. And Edith is a very intelligent young woman too who is clearly doing a highly important job here. I did ask her if she thought that the rumours we are always hearing about a possible Japanese invasion of Hong Kong might have some foundation in fact.'

'And what did she say to that?'

Luff made a vague gesture with his delicate looking hands. 'Oh, she was predictably defensive and refused to be drawn on the subject. Just like a loyal government agent would, of course.' He became sombre. 'Do you think something bad has happened to her?' he asked worriedly.

Jericho shrugged. 'I'm afraid it's entirely possible. I don't think she would have stayed away voluntarily from her work for two days without giving her colleagues fair warning of her intentions.'

Luff looked gloomy. 'Oh dear, that doesn't sound hopeful at all.'

Jericho now took the opportunity to suddenly change his line of questioning. 'Have you ever been in the Tin Hau Hotel, Mr Luff?'

Luff frowned. 'Where is that?'

Jericho was studying the man's reaction carefully. 'It's on the Wanchai waterfront. It's a sailors' pick-up place – a brothel by any other name.'

'Ah yes, I think I know the place you mean now. But I've certainly never been there. Why do you ask? Is this something to do with Edith's disappearance?' Luff seemed genuinely puzzled for the first time.

Jericho decided to muddy the waters a little. 'Perhaps it is. Edith was seen near there early on Tuesday afternoon.'

'Well, I can't help you there, Inspector. She certainly didn't tell me that she was planning to visit that rather seedy area of Wanchai. I would certainly have advised her against going there if she had asked me.'

Jericho decided to press home his attack. 'Perhaps you know that we are investigating the murders of three young Chinese women in Wanchai who all worked in the Tin Hau Hotel as bargirls.'

'Yes, I read the newspapers. Although I didn't know that they worked in that particular hotel.'

'Are you *sure* you've never been there?' Jericho persisted.

Luff was becoming irritated now. 'Yes, I'm positive. And what is this to do with Edith's disappearance? I thought you were here to talk about that, not about your other case in Wanchai.'

Jericho pulled the business card from his pocket. 'It's just that we found this business card of yours in a room in the Tin Hau Hotel that had lately been used by one of the murdered women, Cherry Kwok.'

Jericho had half expected that Ian Luff might become flustered by this question. But he seemed more amused than anything else. 'You think that *I* had something to do with the death of this woman?'

It was Jericho's turn to be disconcerted since this was not the normal reaction of a guilty man. This man was either completely innocent, or else a most accomplished and cool liar. 'No, I didn't say that. But how do you explain how your card got there if you have never been inside the hotel as you claim?'

Luff pulled a wry face. 'I simply have no idea. But I give out hundreds of these cards every year to colleagues and businessmen in Hong Kong, so it's not beyond the bounds of possibility for one of those gentlemen to have visited this hotel and accidentally left my card behind. Boys will be boys after all.'

'Do you know the Woo family at all, Mr Luff?' Jericho abruptly changed the line of questioning yet again. 'I mean the wealthy business family who live up in Po Shan Road.'

Luff displayed a little more reaction this time, but was still completely calm and measured in his response. 'No, I don't know the Woo family. I don't move in those kinds of exalted circles. Why do you ask? Is this also something to do with Edith's disappearance?'

'No, not at all. It's just that I thought I saw you at the Woo house last year. You were talking to James Woo in the garden, as I remember. I happened to be there investigating a burglary at the house.'

Jericho wondered if Luff would deny it outright. For a moment it seemed that he might, but then he changed his mind with reluctance. 'Ah yes,' Luff admitted. 'I *was* there at the Woo mansion one time. And I did know James slightly. He had met me at a government reception here and invited me to see some of the artwork in the family home. I have a great interest in Chinese art and porcelain, particularly the Ming period.' He reflected for a moment. 'It was very sad about James Woo. Such a foolish and unnecessary way to die.'

'Yes indeed,' Jericho agreed readily. 'I don't wish to belabour this business of your business card being found in the Tin Hau Hotel, but it would help me exclude you from any further enquiries if I knew where you were last Wednesday evening, the eighteenth.'

Luff smiled, apparently still fully at ease. 'That's easy, Inspector. I went to Ralph Ogden's funeral in the morning of that day. After losing those hours at the funeral, I needed to catch up on urgent work so I was here working from about two in the afternoon until late that night. My boss Bob Harmsworth can vouch for that because he saw me here regularly through the whole evening. I certainly didn't leave before ten-thirty, and I also signed the book in the guardhouse at the main gate when I left Government House...'

*

Bob Harmsworth was fortuitously the next person on Jericho's list, so he quickly asked Harmsworth to confirm that Luff had been working late at Government House on Wednesday the 18th.

Harmsworth smoothed a hand along his silver hair, which was as white and gleaming as a swan's down in the sunlight streaming through his office window. 'What has young Ian done that he needs an alibi for you people?' he asked in an irritated tone of voice. 'Nice young chap like that...we all think the world of him.'

'I'm sure he is,' Jericho agreed amiably. 'But I do have a good reason for asking the question. Was Luff working here until quite late in the evening on Wednesday, August the eighteenth?'

Harmsworth frowned. 'That was...*let me see*...eight days ago. Ah yes, it was the day of poor Ralph's funeral.' He smiled triumphantly. 'So I *can* confirm that Ian and I were here in the office until late that night. We had to rush out some tax forecasts for the coming year – there is an ambitious plan being mooted to begin a program of building social housing in the colony, and the Governor needs to be sure that we can afford it and that it won't overly strain the colony's finances.'

Jericho nodded, but some part of him remained unconvinced that Luff was a completely innocent man. His instincts told him that the man was guilty of something. Yet his alibi for that Wednesday night, *and* the colour of his eyes, did seem to absolve him of any part in the death of Cherry Kwok at least.

Jericho quickly got back to the subject of Edith Starling's disappearance and whether Harmsworth knew anything about it. He had certainly not raised the possibility with anyone here that Edith's disappearance might have something to do with the death of her boss Ralph Ogden, or the even more controversial possibility mentioned to him by Edith that Ogden might have been murdered. For the moment Jericho preferred to stay well away from mentioning that particular possibility, which would undoubtedly cause a severe reaction here in Government House if he were to suggest it.

But Harmsworth was even less help than Ian Luff in connection with Edith's disappearance. 'I had a day off on Tuesday to be fitted for a new suit in Wanchai, so I didn't see Edith at all that day, I'm afraid.'

Jericho remembered now that he had happened to see Harmsworth himself in Lockhart Road on Tuesday, so he already had personal proof of Harmsworth's story. Not that he could seriously consider that a government man as senior as Bob Harmsworth could be implicated in Edith's disappearance in any way.

'I hope you do find her soon, Inspector. Edith is a very sweet girl, and I would hate anything bad to happen to her. She reminds me very much of my younger daughter back in London, whom I sadly see very little of these days...'

*

An hour later, Jericho sat drinking tea with Ronnie Grantham in the drawing room of the main building at Government House. He had seen almost everybody in the building by now who had some personal acquaintance with Edith, including Edith's principal SIS colleagues Adam, Broadbent and Casaubon...

Jericho had seen Adam and Broadbent together: they claimed they had been away in China for the last week, therefore had known nothing about Edith's disappearance until their return to Hong Kong yesterday. Noah Adam was a thin, pasty-faced young Englishman with the air of an Oxford don; he had seemed genuinely concerned about Edith's fate, but had no ideas to offer as to where she might be. Geoffrey Broadbent was a humourless muscular Scot who obviously had a low opinion of women in general, and thought it probable that Edith had simply gone away somewhere with a boyfriend and had forgotten to tell her superiors. Jericho knew this to be nonsense, of course, but didn't contradict the man.

Jericho had then gone to see their superior, Elliot Casaubon. He turned out to be an even more peevish individual than his younger colleagues, and seemed to be boiling over with some hidden rage. 'Why have you not found Edith yet, Inspector Jericho?' he complained. A vein throbbed in his receding hairline and his cheeks were puce with indignation. 'How hard can it be to find one young Englishwoman in a place like Hong Kong?'

'I'll thank you to keep your temper under control, sir,' Jericho had said icily, and their testy exchanges had only become even more sour after that. Jericho had soon realized why the man was so upset: he had apparently formed some romantic interest in Edith, and blamed himself for not looking out for her better. Jericho had some sympathy with that position, for he too felt that he had let Edith down badly.

It was clear enough, though, from his judicious indirect questioning of these three gentlemen that none of them had any suspicions that Ralph Ogden's death might have been due to foul play, or that there might be a traitor in Government House. Such a thing had clearly never occurred to any of these upright British gentlemen, so they were obviously at a loss to explain what might have happened to Edith...

So Jericho's best lead still seemed to be this man Michael Yip, who might or might not have been Edith's lover, and whose flat Edith had certainly broken into and searched just prior to her disappearance...

Now, talking with his old friend Ronnie Grantham in the drawing room, Jericho tried to relax and empty his mind for the moment. Their tea had just been brought on a silver tray by one of the houseboys, complete with a fine bone china tea service and a decorated Chinese teapot in green enamel. Jericho looked around the sumptuous neoclassical perfection of this room with approval. 'I don't usually get my morning tea delivered like this on a silver tray at Wanchai Police Station,' he said with a smile.

Ronnie smiled back. 'No, I don't suppose you do. Nor does your modern little box of an office compare with the splendours of this room, I suppose.' His eyes lingered for a moment on the elegant sofa facing the fireplace, a Louis XVI revival piece, upholstered in heavy embossed pink satin fabric. 'Yet this room has some sad associations for me because it was on that sofa over there that poor Ralph Ogden had his heart attack and died two weeks ago. Young Ian Luff did a sterling job of trying to save his life, but alas Ralph was too far gone.'

'Yes, you did tell me that Ian Luff was a natural leader among the senior government men here despite his youth. Although I got the impression that you didn't particularly like him either,' Jericho added slyly.

Ronnie looked at his friend in surprise. 'Really? Did I say that I didn't like Ian?'

'Not in so many words. Yet it was certainly the impression you gave me.'

Ronnie looked wary. 'Then I see I'll have to watch what I say to you in future, Paul, since it seems you can read me like an open book.' He paused. 'I suppose it's true, though. Ian Luff does seem like the nicest young man in the world. Yet I sense that the man is putting on an act to some extent, and that the real Ian Luff is nothing like as wholesome and gentlemanly as he appears.'

'Would you say that he's the kind of person who might visit disreputable bars like the one in the Tin Hau Hotel?'

Ronnie shrugged. 'Why are you asking *me* this? That's the bar where these three poor murdered bargirls worked, isn't it?' He frowned. 'You can't surely believe that Luff might be your man, can you?'

Jericho realized he might have said too much and cursed himself under his breath. 'No, not at all. But we did happen to find his business card in a room at the Tin Hau, so I wondered if he might frequent the place.'

Ronnie shook his head. 'I doubt it very much.' He lowered his voice and looked around the room as if fearful of being overheard. 'I've long had a suspicion that Ian Luff's sexual tastes lie in a *different* direction entirely,' he added with particular emphasis. 'But that's not to say that he might not have been in the Tin Hau at some time. The place does have a certain reputation that tends to attract young expatriate men. Young gentlemen sometimes need to sow a few wild oats in the bars of Wanchai just as much as the hoi polloi.' Ronnie looked embarrassed. 'I have even been to the Tin Hau myself once or twice, although not for a long time, since before I was married. Even Bob Harmsworth and Julian Colby used to visit the place on occasion when they were younger, I believe.'

Jericho had some trouble imagining senior government people like Harmsworth and Colby mixing with the earthy females of the Tin Hau Bar. But he let it pass and returned to the subject of Edith Starling. He was beginning to feel a growing sense of guilt that he had not done more to save that girl. 'Edith almost told me a few days ago that she thought her life might be in danger,' he admitted. 'Yet I did nothing to help her.'

'Do you think Edith might really be dead, then?' Ronnie asked with a shocked expression.

'I think she might be,' Jericho said dismally.

'Why…? Who would do such a thing to a sweet girl like Edith?' Ronnie was clearly bewildered.

'Edith didn't make it clear to me *why* she was worried about herself,'

Jericho said. Yet this wasn't completely truthful, of course; Edith had certainly intimated that her worries had to do with the death of Ralph Ogden and the possibility that someone had murdered her boss. Yet Jericho knew from personal knowledge that her disappearance had come about within a few minutes of her breaking into the apartment of Michael Yip, which suggested that it might be to do with something entirely separate from her SIS work.

Jericho decided that it was time that he returned to the station in Wanchai as he seemed to have done all he could here for the moment in investigating what had happened to Edith Starling. But Ronnie had something of his own to say first. 'I'm afraid I've got some bad news about me and Faye,' he said with downcast eyes. 'She wants a divorce.'

Jericho put a consoling hand on Ronnie's shoulder. 'I'm sorry to hear it. Is it absolutely certain, though? Can you not dissuade her?'

Ronnie shrugged. 'I don't think so. I believe I will have to be realistic and accept the inevitable. Of course I've known for the last six months that she was being unfaithful to me. She has now finally admitted it, though she won't tell me the identity of her lover at the moment. I have a shrewd idea, though, that the man in question is the chairman of Saunders-Woo, a gentleman called Sebastian Ride...'

Jericho nodded resignedly when he heard that name, which seemed entirely plausible.

Ronnie was still in full flow, his voice breaking with stifled emotion. '... She says that she would like *me* to take the responsibility for the divorce, and to take a lover, either real or pretended, so that she can divorce me without sullying her own reputation. If I do this, she promises me that she will ensure that I get a very generous financial settlement afterwards. Faye claims she wants to move back to South Africa after the divorce although she hasn't made it clear if her lover is going with her. Mr Ride is also married so it may not be as easy for her to arrange as she thinks.'

Jericho didn't know what to say. He had always liked Faye and appreciated the warm support she had given him after Susan's death. But it seemed she was behaving very badly now. But perhaps she simply couldn't help herself; perhaps her infatuation with this man Ride had just destroyed all her usual moral restraint and her sense of judgement.

'I wish I could stay longer and talk to you about this properly. But I'm afraid that I don't really have the time right now, Ronnie,' Jericho apologized regretfully, climbing slowly to his feet. 'But shall we meet again soon and talk about this? Perhaps I can be of some support to you, as you were to me through my bad time earlier this year.'

Ronnie bit his bottom lip. 'Yes, I'd appreciate that, Paul. Divorce may not be quite as final and irrevocable as death, yet this decision of Faye's still feels like an overwhelming grief to me.' He stood up too. 'Have you spoken to Julian Colby yet about Edith's disappearance, Paul?'

'No, I couldn't find him in his office. And I'm not sure that he would be of much help anyway; he barely knows Edith from what I've heard.'

Ronnie nodded. 'That's true. In any case, I would leave Julian out of your questioning, in the circumstances.'

'In *what* circumstances?' Jericho asked, puzzled.

Ronnie looked guilty. 'Perhaps I shouldn't be telling you this, Paul. But it's better that you know so you don't put your foot in it. I'm afraid that Julian has just been diagnosed with pancreatic cancer. He told me himself only yesterday. It certainly put my marital difficulties with Faye into perspective at least when I heard this terrible news. It's a death sentence for him, poor fellow. He has perhaps three months left at most. He's being frightfully brave about his condition – fatalistic even. But in these testing circumstances, it would be best to exclude him from any questioning about Edith. Julian has graciously named me as his temporary replacement as Attorney General, and there seems every possibility that the appointment will be made permanent in time. Therefore every cloud has a silver lining for somebody, I suppose. Yet I am devastated by what has happened to Julian, so my satisfaction at this unexpected promotion is severely limited...'

CHAPTER 21

Saturday, 28th August 1937

On yet another feverishly hot Saturday morning Paul Jericho and George Dorling sat moodily in the office of Inspector Kevin Ball at Central Police Station. Jericho was very much Ball's senior in both rank and experience, yet the request for him to come here with his sergeant early on a Saturday morning had sounded annoyingly more like a summons than a request. An electric fan on his desk provided a little relief against the humid heat of the office, rifling the edges of the pile of papers in Inspector Ball's heavily overstuffed in-tray. Outside the window of Ball's ground floor office, a squad of young police recruits was being put through their paces on the parade ground, marching in tight khaki formation in the harsh tropical sunlight. The parade ground might be fringed with palms and frangipani trees, and the uniforms might be different, but otherwise it was a faithful carbon copy of any British parade ground in Hendon or Catterick...

Kevin Ball presented an even more youthful figure than even his age of twenty-eight years might suggest. His brown hair was gleaming with hair oil and divided on the left with a parting as straight as a knife blade; he had neat boyish features and prominent teeth that seemed far too large for this thin little mouth, and watery blue eyes that seemed to blink in slow motion.

Paul Jericho wasn't offended by Ball's relative youth so much as by his contemptuous attitude to everyone around him. Jericho could feel George Dorling seething with quietly suppressed anger at his side as they were forced to listen to Ball's rambling and patronizing monologue about why their investigation of the Wanchai bargirl murders was going so badly awry. It felt as if the man was merely belittling their efforts, and not asking for their cooperation as was meant to be the case. Ball came from the West Country somewhere, the son of well-to-do yeoman farmers. Yet there was little of the honest countryman about him; he seemed to Jericho more like a

Whitehall politician or civil servant than a down-to-earth man of the red Devon soil: he was devious, slippery, smooth-tongued...in fact a natural weasel...

Yet Jericho had to admit that they had given Ball an open goal to aim at, for in truth they had made no progress at all this week on the bargirl murders. In fact, in many ways, the investigation seemed to have gone backwards. Jericho had thought he might be getting somewhere with the link with this man Ian Luff, yet that was starting to look unlikely now, particularly given that Luff could not be the man who had been in Cherry Kwok's room on the night she died.

It was now also five days since the discovery of the body of Marco da Silva, and nearly two weeks since the death of Freddie Ling, and it still remained unclear to Jericho whether the murders of these two men were directly linked in some way to the deaths of the three murdered bargirls...

Ball had also obviously heard from Charlie Hebdon about the disappearance of an important female government official from Government House, and soon started making provocative comments about Jericho's handling of that case too.

'Why were you called in on that case, Paul, may I ask?' Ball demanded brazenly. 'It should have come here to this station, if anywhere.'

'I have an old friend in Government House who brought me into the matter directly,' Jericho explained, trying to keep his temper. 'This missing lady works for the Secret Intelligence Service, and they didn't want the regular police brought into this at all. But they allowed me to make some discreet enquiries personally because of the recommendation of my friend...'

'Who is this friend?' Ball asked abrasively.

'Ronnie Grantham, the acting Attorney General,' Jericho said evenly.

That seemed to take the wind out of Ball's sails a little. 'I see,' he said uneasily. Clearly no one had told him before that Paul Jericho had these sorts of high-level connections. 'So where have you got with this "discreet" enquiry of yours?'

Jericho didn't want to answer this barbed question. The truth was that Edith had been missing for more than three days now, and that he still had no real idea what had happened to her, or who was responsible. The one reassuring thing was that no likely female corpse had turned up in the meantime so the chances remained high that this was a case of abduction and not murder. Yet there had also been no ransom demand made, so the reasons why anyone would abduct Edith Starling remained puzzling. Jericho now bitterly regretted that he hadn't kept following Edith on Tuesday; that seemed like a huge error of judgement now. The only ace in his hand was his knowledge of Edith's possible relationship with this Chinese gadfly lawyer Michael Yip, and the fact that Edith had broken into his apartment on the day of her disappearance. Jericho had assigned Thomas Sung in civvies to keep a close watch on Michael Yip's movements for the last two days in the hope that he might lead them to Edith. But so far Yip had behaved perfectly normally and had done nothing even remotely suspicious.

Jericho now put Inspector Ball off with a contemptuous shrug. 'I'm afraid I'm not at liberty to discuss that case, Kevin, given that there are security issues attached to it, for which you do not have the necessary clearance. Commissioner Matlock has told me to keep this case *sub rosa*, and not to discuss it with anyone except an approved list of officers.'

Inspector Ball clearly didn't like that response from his stony expression, although George Dorling most definitely did, because Jericho heard utter him a low and almost inaudible whoop of triumph at seeing his chief wipe the complacent smirk off Ball's face.

Ball quickly retaliated though, and with devastating effect. 'Superintendent Hebdon has ordered that I should take over the investigation of the deaths of Freddie Ling and Marco da Silva. These seem to him to be more closely linked to the murder of Ricky Sun than to the deaths of these three women...'

Jericho had to concede to himself that was probably the case. His own instincts told him that Freddie Ling and Marco da Silva had almost certainly been murdered by Lucky Lam and his Kao Ki-kan triad, as had Ricky Sun. Yet it still rankled with Paul Jericho that this case too was to be taken away from him and his team. But he bit back a sharp reply and merely nodded.

'That's why I asked you to come here today, Paul, together with Sergeant Dorling here. I want to see everything you have got so far on the murders of Ling and Da Silva,' Ball continued.

'Are you making any progress with the murder of Ricky Sun, sir?' George Dorling suddenly interrupted with deliberate hostility.

Ball turned his cold blue eyes on Dorling. 'Not as much progress as I'd like, Sergeant. Of course it is only part of a much larger investigation that I am carrying out in order to try and nail Lucky Lam and his organization for good. Apart from their control of organized crime, I have evidence that the Kao Ki-kan are even selling our military secrets to the Japs, so we need to crack down on them urgently. But I find that I'm hampered in my enquiries at every step. It seems that the Kao Ki-kan knows everything I am planning to do with this investigation before I even get to do it. It's becoming very obvious to me that they must have a policeman on their payroll who is leaking all my plans to them.'

'Only one crooked policeman?' Jericho asked sarcastically.

Ball gave him a severe look in return. 'There may be a lot of the rank and file who might be selling minor information to the triad. But I am talking about an individual who clearly is privy to high-level secret information of the most sensitive kind. Only a high ranking officer would get to see such privileged information about a major enquiry. You may be interested to know that I have been having all my own senior Chinese officers watched and monitored for the last two weeks in an attempt to catch this individual. I didn't like to do it, but Superintendent Hebdon backed me up on this. But thankfully all the officers in question have proved themselves honest men. Therefore I am forced to the conclusion that this leak of information about my enquiry must have come from somebody relatively senior at Wanchai Station...'

Jericho's resentment boiled over suddenly at that accusation. 'Now just a minute...'

Ball put up an imperious hand. 'Now just hear me out, Paul. It would explain a lot, wouldn't it? Not just with the way my investigation into the Kao Ki-kan is blocked at every turn, but also with the way that your investigation into the murders of these three Chinese tarts seems to be going nowhere...'

Jericho didn't like the way that Ball had described those unfortunate women. 'That's an ugly way to describe those three victims, *Inspector*. They were all attractive young women doing something that they probably hated, simply in order to survive. They certainly didn't deserve to die like that, and they should be due the same respect as any other victims of crime.'

Ball looked far from chastened but muttered a begrudging apology anyway. 'Yes, of course they should. I didn't mean to be insensitive about this. But I ask you and Sergeant Dorling here to keep a watch on the activities of your colleagues at Wanchai, especially those who have been working on this case. I know that you two must be above reproach. But can you be sure that one of your Chinese colleagues has not sold out to the Kao Ki-kan? The temptation might simply be too much for them, given the money they could make.'

Jericho had to acknowledge that some of his Chinese officers had to be taking "squeeze" from local businesses and the like. But he still thought it unlikely that any of them would have sold their souls completely to the Kao Ki-kan. 'I will look into it, *Inspector*...'

Ball looked resentful at the suddenly harsh tone of Jericho's voice.

To break the awkward silence that followed, Jericho remembered a question of his own. 'There was something that came up in our investigation of the deaths of Freddie Ling and Marco da Silva. One of my officers, when working out of this station last year, took part in a raid led by you on a homosexual massage parlour in Western District. Somebody in the security services had given us a tip that a lot of the staff were Japanese agents trying to pick up confidential military information from Western homosexual men. According to what my officer remembered, those arrested included this man Marco da Silva.'

Ball nodded warily. 'Yes, I remember the raid...it was April last year. And I think Da Silva was arrested. Queer as a nine bob note, he was. But he was small fry; it was the Jap agents we were really after, not their queer customers. We deported most of these Jap masseurs within a day or so. Da Silva was released without charge.'

'I believe that an English expat was also caught up in the raid but was released without even being cautioned. Who was he?'

Ball grew defensive. 'I got instructions directly from Commissioner Matlock to let the Englishman go. This chap was someone high up in the government service, it seems, and we didn't want to drag his name through the mud unnecessarily. A good chap apparently, who just made an error of judgement and went into this place by accident, or so Matlock said...'

Jericho sniffed coldly. 'What was this man's name?'

Ball hesitated only fractionally. 'Ian Luff. He works in the Colonial Treasury where he's a key man apparently.' He narrowed his eyes. 'Is this man Luff connected to your enquiry into the deaths of these three women?'

Jericho nodded almost imperceptibly. 'His name has come up in connection with the investigation. So it's interesting that he might have had some prior acquaintance with this other man Da Silva, who was clearly selling the services of the three women in question.'

Ball looked contemptuous. 'Why would this man Luff have anything to do with bargirls? He's a pansy.'

'I thought you said that he simply made a mistake going into that massage parlour,' Jericho protested mildly.

Ball gave him a cynical smile. 'Not *that* much of a mistake. The chances are that he is still a queer of some sort. Why would a homosexual kill these women? I doubt that a man like Luff has any interest in women at all, except for them to wash his clothes or make his food.'

Jericho sighed with genuine frustration. *It was a good question...*

*

A few minutes later, in the public lobby of Central Police Station, Jericho saw Constable Gary Ho standing in a quiet corner in company with a young coolie boy. The boy looked like a throwback to an earlier part of the century with his shaved head and his emaciated body and his filthy rags.

Jericho was still in a foul mood after his irritating meeting with Inspector Kevin Ball, but he calmed himself and went over immediately when Constable Ho beckoned him and George Dorling discreetly to join him. Jericho saw that the young peasant boy was restrained with handcuffs but that didn't seem to have inhibited him in any way, for he still had a cocky devil-may-care look about him.

'What are *you* doing here, Constable?' Jericho asked him. 'I thought you were off-duty today.' Jericho was still presently having to drive himself everywhere, and even use his own car on police duty, since he had let

Constable Ho move over to regular police duties. So he was a little annoyed that Ho now seemed to have found the time to be doing extra shifts for Central Station too.

Gary Ho looked apologetic as he spoke to Jericho in rapid staccato Cantonese. 'I was supposed to be off today. But Central were short-staffed again on a Saturday, so I volunteered to do overtime and join their foot patrols in Western District. That's where I caught this boy, trying to pick the pocket of a woman tourist from Germany.'

'That's a lie!' the boy protested in street Cantonese, his hands struggling in the handcuffs. *'Her purse had fallen out of her bag, and I was giving it back to her. I didn't run away, did I?'*

Ho patted the boy's cheek almost affectionately. *'I didn't give you the chance to, did I, little one?'* The boy, on the other hand, looked like he might rip out Constable Ho's heart with his teeth, given half a chance.

Jericho knew that the boy would be quickly brought up before a magistrate and would probably get a sentence of corporal punishment rather than gaol. But the boy looked so pathetically thin that Jericho worried how he would be able to stand up to fifty lashings with a bamboo cane. He looked no more than ten or twelve years old.

'Why did you call me over?' Jericho asked Ho moodily, also in Cantonese, not really wanting to get involved in this minor case of street crime.

Constable Ho looked apologetic. 'I thought you might be interested in his story, sir. His name is Ah Yee, though he could be lying about that. In order to persuade me to let him go, he spun me a little story about something he had seen two weeks ago. He claims to have seen a fight between two men on the balcony of an apartment house on a hillside above Tai Ping Shan; the boy says he saw one of the men fall to his death during the fight...'

'Really?' Jericho *was* definitely interested now. The boy had to be talking about the death of James Woo, which had happened exactly two weeks ago today on the 14th of August. Jericho could hardly believe that a different man might also have fallen to his death from a balcony in the same neighbourhood on the very same day without it being reported. But if the boy was telling the truth, *then someone else had been with James Woo when he died...*

Ho was still summarizing the boy's story. 'He said the other man was a tall foreign devil. But with black hair like a civilized person...' Ho looked down at his feet in embarrassment for a moment as he suddenly remembered that he was actually talking to a "foreign devil".

Jericho wondered if the boy was simply making up this story in return for the chance of being let off. The boy might not be able to read, yet he would surely have heard from his friends about the death of James Woo on that day. Therefore Jericho was far from sure that he could afford to take this story at face value. For one thing, he knew from his own inspection of the scene that the parapet had failed because it had been badly constructed. A murderer would simply have thrown their victim over the top of the parapet, not against the parapet wall in the hope that it might fail. So even if Woo had been engaged in a struggle with a second man, his death still looked mostly accidental to Paul Jericho. Even manslaughter on the part of this supposed second man would be hard to prove, never mind a deliberate intent on his part to murder someone.

George Dorling's Cantonese was very poor, yet he had understood enough of Constable Ho's story to follow the description of the second man on the balcony. 'That description fits his partner, Sebastian Ride, doesn't it? I've seen his picture in the papers often enough.'

Jericho shrugged. 'Maybe it does. But Ride was supposedly in his office in Central when Woo died.'

Dorling grunted. 'Yet it might be worth checking that alibi in more detail, don't you think?'

'Yes, I suppose so,' Jericho agreed half-heartedly. In truth he would have preferred to let sleeping dogs lie rather than resuscitate a case like this that was already closed. He certainly had no inclination to start accusing a man like Sebastian Ride of manslaughter or murder without much better evidence than the wild stories of a young thief...

*

By the time Jericho was finished with Constable Ho and his boy pickpocket, it was already after twelve. A disgruntled George Dorling had also taken his leave by this time to return by tram to Wanchai Police Station. Given the time, Jericho had elected to stay in Central and find a restaurant or even food stall to get some luncheon, for he had another destination in mind this afternoon near his own home in Happy Valley. He had decided to take the bull by the horns and speak to Michael Yip directly about Edith Starling. His feeling was that Yip himself was unlikely to be involved in Edith's murder or abduction, yet he might still be able to shed some light on their relationship that might explain her sudden disappearance, or even why Edith had taken it upon herself to break into his apartment last Tuesday...

Jericho found himself standing at the corner of Queens Road Central and Pedder Street opposite the Saunders Building, as he wondered where to buy his lunch. In the end he decided on a simple meal at a food stall so started walking west along the north side of Queens Road, ignoring all the offers of a ride from the assembled mass of rickshaw coolies. This busy thoroughfare pierced right through the heart of the city like a knife, displaying a dazzling array of Chinese signboards and calligraphy, which became even more numerous and dense as the road ran westwards. This was Hong Kong's main commercial street so was dominated at first by modern stone-clad office buildings. But these modern office buildings soon yielded to the normal hugger-mugger of a Chinese city as the road ran further west into the native area of the city. Here the road was lined with food shops and restaurants, while the kerbside was filled with a seething mass of hawkers and food stalls offering everything from shark's fin soup to prawns and lemon chicken. Jericho had always considered that this busy street encapsulated everything about Hong Kong, with its confused mass of humanity, its rickshaws and coolies, and its arcaded Chinese shops providing every service a human being could ever possibly want, from hair cutting to money lending to the sale of children. Like the colony of Hong Kong as a whole, it was a place of infinite hope, frustrated dreams, and dogged relentless toil.

Jericho had reached a narrow-fronted curio shop on the ground floor of a tired old building that seemed in danger of falling into the street from old age. The pastel colours of its plaster walls had long since faded in the intense Oriental sun to grey, while the wizened old man standing at the doorway seemed like a visitor from the past in his dusty Chinese gown and round cap. Jericho was captivated for a moment by the expression of serenity on this old man's face, his eyes as bright as jet buttons and his cheeks with a luminous pink glow like rosy apples. But then Jericho saw the old man's expression change abruptly as he spotted something unexpected across the street. It was if a shadow had passed over the man's soul. Something about this old man's reaction told Jericho that something dramatic was about to unfold in this busy thoroughfare...

On the other side of the street – the south side - a European woman was standing out of the sun in the shelter of an arcade. Her hair was a striking shade of auburn and her face was heavily made up so that her mouth looked like a slash of red in a white mask. Jericho realized that he knew this woman from somewhere but struggled to recall the connection for a moment. Then it suddenly came to him: *this was the wife of Mr Sebastian Ride...*

This immediately struck him as an odd coincidence when Ride's name had just come up under such interesting circumstances at Central Police Station. The woman looked different now, though, from their first meeting: she had obviously been to the hairdresser recently from her sleek new hairstyle, and the heavy makeup – pale foundation, dark eye shadow and ruby lipstick - had transformed her face into a haughty beauty. She did not seem drunk, as she had obviously been at their first meeting, yet there was something unsettling about the fixed rigidity of her gaze, and the burning look of intensity in her eyes. She seemed to be breathing heavily from the rapid rise and fall of her chest, and Jericho was conscious of some feeling of impending tragedy.

Jericho stood watching her uneasily from across the street as a Bedford lorry – a three ton WT model loaded high with sacks of rice - trundled westwards along Queens Road towards her. The lorry was no more than five yards away from Mrs Ride when she suddenly leapt forward into its path. Jericho heard a squeal of brakes and a terrified scream of alarm from a Chinese woman in the arcade, then ran over to where the lorry had jerked to a halt.

He went around the front of the lorry expecting the worst: to see the woman's corpse mutilated and mangled under the front wheels of the Bedford. But it looked as if Mrs Ride had luckily been thrown aside by only a glancing blow from the truck, for she was lying sprawled on the narrow strip of roadway between the lorry and the concrete pillars of the arcade, and was clearly still very much alive...

She was a little dazed by shock but still fully conscious. She made no protest when he started to examine her, feeling her limbs and her abdomen. He checked her quickly for any major injuries, but found none: no broken bones that he could see, and no obvious evidence of any major traumatic injury. It seemed she had had a miraculous delivery from near certain death. She had grazed her cheek when falling, and also skinned a knee which had in turn ripped her silk stockings. Yet all in all, her survival with such minor injuries was remarkable...

The middle-aged lorry driver – a local Cantonese man - got out of his cab, almost shaking with fright. He seemed in a worse state of shock than Mrs Ride, and Jericho had to pull him aside to calm him down.

'Please calm yourself,' Jericho said in Cantonese. He showed the man his warrant card. 'I am a police inspector. I saw the whole thing so there is no need for you to worry. You are quite blameless.'

'That crazy foreign woman jumped in front of my truck deliberately,' the man complained peevishly, his mood becoming angrier as his initial shock wore off.

'I am sure she just didn't see you,' Jericho said warningly, although privately he agreed with the man. He was as sure as he could be that Mrs Ride had just tried to kill herself. Although perhaps she had changed her mind at the last moment, which might explain her improbable survival...

A crowd of curious bystanders had gathered by now, including the old shopkeeper from across the street. He seemed unmoved by what had happened, smoking a long clay pipe with the same placid expression on his ancient face.

Jericho spoke again to the driver of the lorry. 'Can you help me lift the woman into the shade of the arcade before I go and call an ambulance for her?'

'I don't need any bloody ambulance....!'

Jericho saw to his surprise that Mrs Ride had already got to her feet without help and was now standing in front of the lorry dusting down her clothes and regarding the blood seeping from her knee with dispassionate calm.

A concerned Jericho confronted her quickly. 'You need to be checked by a doctor, Mrs Ride. I can't be sure that you have no serious internal injuries.'

She had looked at him in slight alarm when he addressed her by name. But now she seemed to recognize him for the first time. 'Ah, it's Inspector Jericho, isn't it? It would have to be *you* that would turn up and play the white knight, wouldn't it,' she said in an irritated voice, as if resenting his help.

Jericho wondered what he might have done to offend this woman. Her attitude seemed odd when they had met only once before. But perhaps she was suffering from a bit more residual shock than she appeared to be.

He decided to be firm. 'I'm no white knight, Mrs Ride. But I can assure you of one thing: you are not leaving here except in an ambulance that will take you straight to a hospital to be checked.'

Her lips twitched into something like a smile. 'It seems you care about my wellbeing more than my bloody husband does, Inspector Jericho. So I suppose I will have to come quietly.' With that she rolled her eyes and put her wrists together to receive a mock pair of handcuffs from him...

*

It took two hours for Jericho to sort things out after the incident in Queens Road and see Mrs Gloria Ride safely delivered to the Tung Wah Hospital in Po Yan Street, which was just above Hollywood Road in the lower Mid-levels. It seemed that her injuries were just as minor as Jericho had thought, but the young English intern on duty in the hospital said he would keep her in for a few hours for observation. Jericho had not told anyone in the hospital about his conviction that this woman had just tried to kill herself, although he had told the young doctor that she was in a highly emotional state and needed to be watched carefully. That was as much as Jericho was prepared to commit himself at this stage. He knew he would have to follow this matter up himself in the coming days, but it was complicated by the fact that he might also have to interview her husband again in connection with the death of James Woo. Paul Jericho would however have been much happier just to forget the Ride family altogether, because he seemed to be making a rod for his own back by involving himself in their affairs. He knew that he would win few thanks from his superiors if he ventured to accuse a man like Sebastian Ride of murder or manslaughter...

By the time he was finished at the Tung Wah Hospital, it was mid-afternoon so he gave up any hope of having lunch today and decided to drive back instead to Happy Valley for his planned visit to the home of Mr Michael Yip. He had followed the ambulance earlier from Central District to the Tung Wah hospital in his own car – he had left his Austin this morning in the compound at Central Police Station so it was easily retrieved. So now he drove back to Happy Valley, rehearsing in his mind what he would say to Michael Yip if the man should happen to be at home in his small apartment building in Broadwood Road.

Jericho found that the man was indeed at home in his ground floor apartment, for he answered Jericho's knock almost at once. Yip frowned with surprise, though, when he saw who it was at his front door. Jericho had only ever come across the man in court and thought him a little arrogant and supercilious. And from the hostile look on Michael Yip's face, his view of Chief Inspector Paul Jericho of the Hong Kong Police was obviously similarly jaundiced.

'What do you mean by coming here, Chief Inspector?' Yip said, his handsome face twisted in surprise. 'If this is about some legal matter, you should not be calling at my private home. And I can't think of any reason why you would be paying me a social visit.'

Jericho resisted a sharp reply. 'It's about Edith Starling, Mr Yip. I believe that she is a friend of yours. I don't know if you know it, but she has disappeared...'

Yip sighed heavily, but then stood aside to let Jericho cross the threshold. He led Jericho through to the living room at the back that looked out over a small paved patio with a hillside rising steeply behind covered in a dense forest of fragrant mulberries and myrtle trees. The French windows leading to the patio were open, and Jericho could smell the fragrant scent of the trees as they stirred in the hot humid breeze.

Jericho refused the offer of an armchair; he wanted to get this over with as quickly as possible. He did notice however that Yip's apartment was decorated in surprisingly conventional Western style for a man of such avowed distaste for European things.

'Did you already know that Edith has gone missing, Mr Yip?' he asked neutrally.

Yip stood facing Jericho, his legs slightly apart in a belligerent stance. 'I know that she is not at her apartment because I went to see her on Wednesday. Her houseboy told me that she had disappeared. But he said the police already seem to know about it, so I'm afraid I left it at that. I had no wish to go to the police myself since I would no doubt be asked to explain my private relationship with Edith.'

'And what is your private relationship with Edith, Mr Yip?' Jericho asked. 'Please be assured that whatever you tell me will be treated confidentially. I am not here to pass judgement on anyone; I only want to find Edith again and make sure she is safe. She was a friend of my late wife's, so I consider her a friend too.'

Michael Yip was still resentful. 'Is that how you know about me and Edith? Did she tell you herself?'

Jericho decided to be truthful. 'No, Edith is not close enough to me to tell me such things. Someone else noticed you together, that's all – someone from Government House.'

Michael Yip regarded Jericho coolly for a moment before speaking. 'Then I suppose I must trust you with this personal information. Edith and I were friends...*lovers*. I love Edith, if that's what you're asking. But I don't know where she is.'

Jericho thought that admission sounded like the truth. And Michael Yip was a very good-looking man with his shining black hair and his golden skin and his handsome features, so he could see why Edith might have been seduced by this man's charm despite the invidious position it put her in. 'When did you last see her?'

Yip thought for a second. 'I was with her last Saturday night. I stayed at her apartment overnight. We had arranged to meet again on Wednesday night, which is when I found out that she had disappeared.' Yip seemed genuinely distraught for the first time. 'Do you think she has been abducted? Or even worse?'

'I'm afraid I do,' Jericho confirmed bleakly. 'She had told me herself that she thought her life might be in danger because of something to do with her work at Government House. Yet I wasn't sure how seriously to take her remark, because she made light of it herself.'

'That sounds like Edith unfortunately,' Yip said with a reluctant smile.

Jericho nodded. 'Do you know what Edith actually does at Government House?'

Yip seemed evasive for the first time. 'She's a secretary, I believe. She worked for a man there called Ralph Ogden. But he had a heart attack and died a couple of weeks ago, so I don't know who she works for now.'

'Is that all she is? A mere secretary?' Jericho probed.

Yip shrugged. 'Perhaps she's more than that. I think she works in the decoding team in the Intelligence Section. She's a very clever woman, I do know that much. Perhaps even a mathematical genius.'

'Have you no idea who might have abducted her?' Jericho asked. 'Or why?'

'No, none at all.'

Jericho continued. 'Were things between you and Edith the same as usual? Had you had any kind of falling out that might have prompted her to leave Hong Kong of her own accord?' Jericho already knew that Edith would never have done such a thing without informing her colleagues, but he wanted to know if there could have been an argument between Edith and Michael Yip that might explain why she had felt the need to break into this apartment and search it from top to bottom. That search suggested that Edith had some suspicions about Michael Yip himself, though perhaps it was simply part of a lover's tiff and nothing to do with her work at Government House.

'No, everything was fine between us on that last night we met,' Yip said.

Jericho was not sure if he was telling the truth but was certainly not going to reveal to him that he had seen Edith break into his flat on Tuesday afternoon. That was something best kept to himself for the moment...

*

Two hours later and Paul Jericho found himself back in the drawing room at Government House with Ronnie Grantham. He had promised to return on Saturday and bring Ronnie up to date with any progress in the search for Edith Starling. Depressingly, though, he had very little useful to report to Ronnie, for there had been no real progress at all. Edith's whereabouts were still a complete mystery to him.

Jericho was still mulling over his difficult conversation with Michael Yip, and whether he believed the man's story completely. He was quietly convinced that Yip had not told him the whole story of his relationship with Edith, and he had some vague suspicions that Yip might have deliberately cultivated Edith's affections for some ulterior motive of his own. He didn't know of any reason why a lawyer like Michael Yip should be interested in Edith's government work as a decoder in the intelligence team, but perhaps the man was not exactly what he claimed to be...

'So you still have no idea where Edith is, or if she has been abducted or murdered?' Ronnie said disappointedly, stirring his cup of tea moodily with a silver spoon. Their tea had again been brought on a silver tray by one of the houseboys, complete with the same fine bone china tea service and the same decorated Chinese teapot in green enamel.

'I am sure as I can be that she has been abducted,' Jericho said. The detailed search of Edith's car had produced nothing of any note except for a partial footprint of a man's boot in front of the passenger seat, and a thin residue of gravel particles left by the boot. There seemed a possibility that the man who had abducted Edith might have made this footprint, and that he might have lately been walking in a rock quarry or construction site or some similar place. But there were a huge number of rock quarries and construction sites on Hong Kong Island, and even more on Kowloon side, so this information hardly helped at all, while the footprint itself was not complete enough to be able to identify the type and size of boot. Jericho told Ronnie this since it was the only real bit of information that he had. 'Do you know if Edith might have visited a quarry or somewhere similar in the days before her disappearance?'

Ronnie sipped his tea and frowned. 'It's hardly the sort of place that Edith might go.'

'Has anybody from Government House visited a quarry lately?' Jericho asked.

Ronnie gave a sheepish half-smile. 'Well, I have actually. A group of us went on a fact-finding mission to a disused Saunders-Woo quarry at

Shaukeiwan on Monday. It's been earmarked as one of the main sites for the construction of some social housing to ease the colony's dreadful overcrowding problems.'

Jericho's interest was immediately piqued, particularly by the fact that the quarry was owned by Sebastian Ride's company. It seemed that everything he did at the moment led in the direction of that gentleman. 'Who was on this quarry visit with you?'

'Most of the Executive Council was there including the Acting Governor and Colonial Secretary. Bob Harmsworth and Ian Luff were both there, of course, as representatives of the Treasury who will have to fork up the cash for this monster building scheme. And poor Julian Colby was there too; this was just before he'd got that terrible news from his doctor. I suppose we should have known from his appearance of late that he was seriously ill, though it was still a dreadful shock to me when he told me. The man is being so brave that it makes me feel quite humbled by the experience.'

Jericho shrugged ruefully. 'Well, I can't believe that the Governor or any of his senior staff have abducted Edith, can you?'

Ronnie did not seem even remotely amused by the suggestion. '*Hardly*...'

'Were any of Edith's SIS colleagues on this quarry visit?' Jericho could hardly believe that one of Edith's own SIS colleagues could be responsible either, yet it seemed marginally more likely than it being the Governor.

Ronnie shook his head. 'Well, I only really know Casaubon, and two others: Adam and Broadbent. But none of them were on this quarry visit; this construction scheme has nothing to do with our intelligence team. The building scheme is now approved in principle, by the way, so a team of engineering surveyors will be visiting the quarry sometime next week to begin a full topographical survey.'

Jericho subsided into a frustrated silence, not sure what else there was to say on the subject of Edith's disappearance. But then another thought occurred to him. On passing through the entrance hall of Government House a few minutes earlier, Jericho had seen that there seemed to be some sort of great flap going on today, with a group of high-ranking army and navy officers assembled waiting to see the Acting Governor and his staff. 'What is happening today in Government House, Ronnie? I can see something important is in the offing.'

Ronnie lowered his voice to a whisper. 'Something big *is* brewing in China. Edith's SIS colleagues Adam and Broadbent have just returned from a mission to Nanking and have brought back worrying news from the mainland. The indications are that the Japs may be planning to invade Shanghai very soon and take possession of the city. It's looking ominous for the remaining expats there, so we are investigating ways of evacuating all remaining British citizens from the city as soon as possible.'

Jericho ran a hand through his wiry hair. 'It's even more ominous for the Chinese in Shanghai. No one will be offering them an easy way out of there.'

Ronnie looked downcast. 'Of course that's true. I wasn't trying to suggest that English lives are more important than Chinese lives.'

'Yet that's about the size of it, isn't it?' Jericho said cynically.

Ronnie continued to look uncomfortable but wasn't prepared to say anything more about Shanghai. 'Talking about Chinese lives, how is your investigation going into the murder of these three young women in Wanchai?'

It was Jericho's turn to look uncomfortable. 'I thought I had a suspect, but it seems that I was wrong.' Jericho didn't even want to admit that this suspect had been Ian Luff, since this seemed like a particularly foolish notion now. 'So I am back at square one. I have a dreadful feeling that this man, whoever he is, is going to get away with this, unless he now does something stupid to give himself away.'

Ronnie shook his head wryly. 'I doubt that very much, Paul. I'm sure you will get this man in the end. I know you too well; you never give up on a case like this…' He reached into his pocket for his cigarette case, suddenly anxious for a smoke.

Jericho then heard a tinkling noise and saw a flash of gold on the floor.

Ronnie leant down and quickly scooped the gold object from the carpet, which he returned to his inside pocket, before lifting out his silver cigarette case with more care this time.

'What was that?' Jericho asked idly.

Ronnie looked sheepish. 'It's an antique gold necklace chain that I bought for Faye. But just before I could give it to her last week, she turned around and told me she wanted a divorce. It felt like a kick in the stomach to me to hear those dreadful words coming from those beautiful lips…' He smiled faintly with embarrassment. 'So in the unfortunate circumstances I quickly decided to hold on to the gold chain. I've been carrying it around in my pocket ever since like a fool. In any case, the clasp is broken so I would have had to take it back to the jewellers anyway.' Ronnie sighed. 'I suppose it was a stupid present anyway for a woman who owns a whole goldmine in Johannesburg; I can't think what I was doing.' Ronnie's lip quivered with emotion for a moment. 'Faye has broken my heart, you know. I doubt that I will ever recover from this.'

Jericho squeezed his friend's arm. 'I'm sure you will recover, Ronnie. Everyone does in the end…'

*

In the awful heat inside her makeshift prison, Edith Starling groaned and turned over, trying to seek a comfortable place on the hard concrete floor. She had long since taken off her stockings and her white trouser suit and used it as bedding on the dusty floor. Even though she was only dressed now in her underwear – a muslin shift and cotton brassiere and panties – yet the humid heat inside this room was as oppressive as a blanket over her nose and mouth.

She reckoned she had been imprisoned in this building for four days now. Her wristwatch had been taken of course so she could not be sure of the precise length of time she had been here. She had also lost her specs somewhere, probably when she was attacked from behind. She had not known anything more after her abduction until she had woken up inside this bare windowless room. It seemed like a storeroom of some sort in an industrial facility like a quarry or a disused factory, for the ceiling and the floor were rough concrete slabs, while the walls were plain unplastered blockwork. The door was of solid steel plate like a real prison cell so it seemed that something important had been stored in here. She was sure that the door did not lead directly outside, but only to another set of rooms and corridors, for this storeroom seemed like part of a larger building rather than a standalone structure. Despite the lack of any windows, there were a few small chinks of light between the top of the unevenly laid blockwalls and the ceiling slab which had let her know at least when it was daylight outside, and when it was dark. That small unexpected advantage of being able to track the passage of time had been a great blessing to her, giving her some slight hope that she could survive this.

Of her abductor himself, she had seen nothing at all, and no one had come to speak to her or make any demands of her. After the first twenty four hours of suffering in this infernal oven of a room, without any food or water, she had come to the terrifying conclusion: that the man had simply left her here to die. Perhaps he was squeamish and didn't want to kill her directly, so had decided to let thirst and heat do the dirty job for him.

Her rage against this man who had abducted her had only increased with time, despite her growing weakness. Her mind had been in a turmoil as she had wondered about the man's identity. *Surely it couldn't be Michael, though?* Whatever Michael was up to, she couldn't believe that he would be so callous as to do this to her. Even though he had surely been deceiving her, he couldn't be such a monster as this...

She knew by now that her prison must be somewhere remote. For she had shouted herself hoarse crying out for help on that first terrible day, until she had realized with despair that she was wasting her time. There must be nobody within any hearing distance; she was entirely on her own. Left to die here like a dog in this hot dusty room.

She had found nothing in the room except a large pile of broken timber slats from some old crates. The markings on the wood were in Chinese, and she had trouble making them out without her glasses. But these characters were sufficiently like the Japanese *kanji* for "explosive" that she had realized at once that her first guess was correct. This was clearly a storeroom in some old building complex inside a disused quarry, where they had stored the gelignite or dynamite they used for blasting.

It seemed that her abductor had picked on the perfect place for her to die from thirst and heat exposure. Yet the man had made one huge mistake, for there was a potable water pipe fixed to one wall, and the remains of a tap. The business end of the tap had been removed, of course, otherwise her abductor would hardly have missed it. But the stop on the end of the pipe wasn't perfect and she had found that there was a slow but perceptible drip of water from the end of it. That tiny drip of water had been the difference between life and death for her; she was sure that it was the only thing that had kept her alive for the last four days.

That, and her anger at this man who had abducted her...

She was determined to survive this somehow and get her revenge on this devil. That thought of delivering some retribution to this man was an even more potent reason for her to try and stay alive until someone discovered her.

Surely someone must be looking for her by now...?

CHAPTER 22

Sunday, 29th August 1937

On Sunday morning Sebastian Ride walked in the garden of his own home with Frances Leung by his side. They had come out into the garden deliberately, despite the heavy humid heat, anxious that no one should overhear their conversation. The garden at the rear of the house was not as grand as that of the Woo mansion, yet it was still a glorious riot of tropical flowers and trees: pink trumpet trees, Indian coral trees and Chinaberry, all festooned with climbers and epiphytes and ferns dripping moisture. Yet their discussion was much darker and more sinister than the bright surroundings suggested: even Ride had to admit that he and Frances had crossed a line now, no longer just staid employer and docile secretary, but now co-conspirators in an ugly plot...

Yet there seemed no other solution to his problem. He could feel his life unravelling about him like a frayed sweater. Tug at a loose thread and keep pulling, and very soon nothing would be left of the sweater but a pile of loose woollen twine on the floor. That was the way his life felt to him now, being pulled apart seam by seam...

He had told Frances two days ago that Gloria had overheard much more of his conversation in the office last weekend with Ian Luff than she had thought. In fact Gloria knew everything now about the circumstances of the death of James Woo and seemed determined to use that knowledge to try and keep him on a fresh leash of her own.

Frances had seemed curiously untroubled by this additional problem when he had told her. She had seemed confident that she could out-manoeuvre a woman like Gloria and buy her silence just as easily as she had bought the silence of that fortunate rickshaw coolie. Ride had begun to realize that Frances herself was not a woman ever given to panic and confusion: she was instead logical, thoughtful and precise. And a little bit terrifying too, he now had to admit, despite his admiration for her strong character.

Ride had not told Frances that he was now sleeping with Gloria again after many months of effective separation. But Frances seemed to know anyway; she was highly attuned to his moods and could read him like a book.

'How is Gloria today?' Frances asked solicitously, as if talking about a close friend she was concerned about.

Ride was not fooled by Frances's tone; he knew well enough by now that Frances regarded his wife as a drunken coarse harpy. 'She is in a strange dark mood again after her accident yesterday. On Wednesday night she had seemed almost rejuvenated by her newfound power over me, as if she had shed ten years in a single day. But now she seems back to square one again...'

Frances looked at him sternly. 'But you called her bluff, I hope, as I advised you.'

'I did,' Ride confirmed. 'I told her on Friday that there was no hope that we could make a sensible future together. It was better to accept that we could no longer be happy together, and that it would therefore be preferable for both of us to divorce quickly...'

'How did she take that?' Frances said with the placid air of a financial analyst.

'She seemed very calm and even accepting of the inevitability of it. But then something happened yesterday that convinced me that she is in a dangerously unpredictable mood. It seemed she was hit by a lorry in Queens Road and was very nearly killed. They kept her in hospital until the evening, but luckily all she's got are cuts and abrasions. I really can't believe that it was a simple accident, though; it seems far too coincidental in the circumstances. She must have stepped out in front of that lorry deliberately, intent on taking her own life...'

Frances was unmoved. 'She is simply seeking your attention, that's all, Sebastian. And she seems to have succeeded admirably.' She glanced up through the lush green leaves of a fig tree to check that they were invisible from the house. 'I understand my own sex very well – even an unstable woman like your wife. Gloria will never go to the police and tell them what she thinks she knows about the death of James Woo. Despite her threats, she will not kill the goose that can provide her with so many golden eggs for the rest of her life.'

Ride was uneasy. 'I wish I could be as sure of that.'

She took his hand and squeezed it. 'You *must* be sure, Sebastian. This is no time to lose your nerve. All of your present problems are easily solvable provided we deal with this man Luff. *He* is the only real issue. Rid ourselves of him, and we are home free.'

Ride enjoyed the comforting warmth of her hand. 'You really think that killing him is the only solution?'

Frances looked him in the eyes. 'Yes, it is. And tonight's meeting with him would be the perfect opportunity. You have no known connections to this man at present; no one will ever be able to tie his death back to you because you have absolutely no motive.'

'Provided Gloria never talks,' Ride muttered darkly.

'And I've told you that she won't,' Frances rejoined quickly.

Ride had arranged a further meeting with Luff this evening to supposedly discuss the detailed terms for his continued silence. Of course nothing could ever be written down in a formal legal contract therefore even Luff had admitted that there would have to be a measure of trust between them. But Ride knew that once he entered into this informal arrangement with Luff, then he was stuck with this man for life.

Yet the meeting could not be held until late in the evening; it seemed there was a crisis of some sort at Government House and that Luff had been required to attend meetings with his senior colleagues all day. Luff had not told Ride the reason for this panic in Government House, but Ride was sure it was to do with the deepening crisis in China. The Japanese seemed intent on waging all-out war in China now, so the government had to be making emergency plans for further evacuations of Europeans from Shanghai and other Chinese cities to Hong Kong. Luff had however told Ride that he should be free by ten this evening, and had therefore suggested meeting at an address in Caine Road this evening at 10:30, since it was only a short walk from Government House. Ride knew the house that Luff had suggested: a big old rambling Portuguese-style house owned by the Woo family. Luff had told him that the house was presently empty, but he had a front door key given to him by James Woo so they could meet there in perfect security and talk privately as long as they wished. Luff had no wish to be seen in public with the chairman of Saunders-Woo at this stage; their two brief earlier meetings had been as much risk as he was prepared to take.

Ride had agreed to the plan since it was equally important to him too not to be seen in public with this man any more – *especially now that he planned to kill him...*

Frances was talking in exactly the same voice that she used about business matters. 'Caine Road is very poorly lit and overhung with huge old trees. So there must be plenty of dark places where you can ambush Luff and kill him with very little risk to yourself.'

'Couldn't we just hire someone to do it?' he asked uneasily.

Frances pursed her lip. 'We could. And then one more person would know about this, and be free to blackmail us in time. No...you must do this yourself.' Frances reached into her voluminous handbag and pulled out something hard and metallic. She pressed the gun into his hand.

Ride recognized the type of revolver and wondered how on earth she had managed to obtain such a weapon. It was a Colt Detective Special, a six-shot, carbon steel-framed, two-inch-barrelled double-action revolver, with a modern swing-out frame. Ride knew enough about guns to know that it was the first example of a new class of American firearms known to gun enthusiasts as "snub-nosed revolvers". The name "Detective Special" suggested that it was intended to be a concealed weapon used by plainclothes police detectives.

Frances looked at him examining the weapon. 'Don't worry. It's fully loaded. But you should only need one shot. If you are a good shot with a revolver, aim for his head. If you only wound him in the chest or abdomen, though, make sure to finish him off with a second head shot.' She studied him quizzically. 'You do know how to use a gun, don't you, Sebastian?

Ride was a bit unnerved by her cold and callous description of murder. 'I do. I'm a first class marksman with both pistol and rifle. I served with the Hong Kong Volunteers during the political unrest fermented by communists in the twenties, and during the general strike of 'twenty five. So yes...I do know how to use a handgun.'

Frances stood up on tiptoes and kissed him forcibly. 'Then do it tonight! Be a man. Kill your enemy and make him regret ever thinking he could get the better of you...'

*

Paul Jericho was not supposed to be on duty on this Sunday but he had gone to Wanchai Police Station anyway and gone through some routine office work in a half-hearted fashion. He had slept badly again last night, tormented by all the conflicting issues in his life, but particularly by the presumed fate of poor Edith Starling. He was also deeply concerned about the situation of Mrs Gloria Ride too, and knew he would have to do something about that clearly disturbed woman. He couldn't just leave that issue alone. That lady had tried to kill herself yesterday, and he wanted to know why. For it seemed entirely plausible that she might try it again if he did nothing to prevent it...

The station was deathly quiet, with just a skeleton staff working at the front desk in the lobby. George Dorling was enjoying a well-deserved day off with his wife Tess; he had said he might take her for a drive in the New Territories while the weather was still calm. It did seem likely from reports from the Philippines that this big typhoon that everyone was talking about might finally be on its way and would perhaps make landfall on the South China coast by Thursday or Friday this week.

The murder of the three women in nearby Lockhart Road now seemed to be hanging over Paul Jericho's head like the Sword of Damocles, as ominous as that approaching typhoon. He had a strange feeling of foreboding that the case might truly be the death of him – that the process of finding the perpetrator of this evil crime would also destroy him in the end. He had a new suspect in mind now, but it was a theory that he still refused to believe. Every fibre of his being told him that he must be wrong, for the consequences of this being true were just too awful to contemplate...

It was mid-afternoon by now, and Jericho was suddenly struck with a desperate desire to see Maggie Yiu again. He longed to hear that woman's calm and reassuring voice again, to see the way that the sunlight gleamed on her raven hair, to feel the penetrating gaze from those intense dark eyes.

In five minutes Jericho had signed out of the station and was on his way to her home in nearby Lockhart Road. He had forgotten, though, just what a poor tenement she lived in, with its cracked concrete walls and dilapidated rooftop structure of corrugated iron. He entered the main door between the premises of a restaurant and a tailor, and climbed the evil-smelling concrete staircase. The interior of the building still seethed with humanity, but Jericho ignored the gabble of noise and carried on to the third floor where he knocked gently on her door. Yet he was half-tempted by now to beat a hasty retreat, not sure what on earth he was doing here, or what he would say to her. But she gave him no time either to escape back down the stairs or to prepare a few words of explanation, for she opened the door to him at once.

Her eyes widened in surprise when she saw his familiar green khaki uniform and blue peaked cap. '*You...?*'

He smiled uneasily to cover his embarrassment. 'Yes...*me*...'

She frowned slightly. 'What are you doing here?'

He decided to be honest. 'I just wanted to see you again.'

She took a long breath. 'Are you here as a policeman? Or just as a friend?'

He wasn't even quite sure himself. 'A little of both, I think.'

She regarded him with a quizzical smile. 'All right, then. But I don't think you can ever leave the policeman part of you entirely behind, can you?'

'Probably not,' he admitted ruefully. 'But I'll try anyway.'

She finally opened the door fully and stood aside to let him enter. 'Then please come in. As it happens, I need some company today too.'

He saw that she was dressed casually in a cotton blouse and the same loose fitting purple skirt that he had seen her wear once before, yet she still managed to look fashionable and elegant even in such a simple outfit. She seemed to him more than ever like something quite exquisite and exotic – like a wild orchid growing improbably in the drab concrete heart of a busy city. She was a woman who could lift her surroundings simply with the force of her own unmatched beauty, turn the dreary and mundane into something uplifting, and the ugly into something radiant.

Yet something – that policeman's nose of his again - also told him she was not exactly what she seemed to be. He had this strange feeling that she was the key to a mystery that he didn't even understand as yet. He had always nursed a slight suspicion that she knew more about the killing of the three women than she had let on, though he didn't know why...

Jericho looked around the room, this oasis of civilization in this dismal old tenement building. He took in the faded pastel colours of the plaster walls, the dusty windows shaded by a bright awning of red and gold, the functional bamboo and rattan furniture. Dust motes danced in front of the fine silk painting on the wall, while the Java sparrow in his cage seemed as enraptured by Miss Maggie Yiu as Jericho was himself.

'Please take a seat; you look very tired. Can I get you a drink? I have coffee and English tea, as well as Chinese green tea.'

'Then I'll have a cup of English tea to remind me of home,' he declared facetiously. He watched her as she went over to a small gas ring to boil water for the tea. 'Have you really told me everything you know, Maggie?'

She turned and smiled radiantly. 'Ah, you finally called me "Maggie".'

Jericho felt an exultant glow surge through him at the warmth of that smile. Yet, despite his earlier promise, he still couldn't stop himself being a policeman and asking her another question. 'Are you protecting someone, Maggie? A Westerner perhaps?'

The smile faded abruptly. 'There's only one thing I haven't told you. From my window here, late one night, I did once see a Western man walking with a young woman in the street below. They were just passing under a streetlight, which is why I noticed them. I only saw the woman from a distance but she did look a bit like Dora Kam,' she finally admitted. 'If it *was* her, then it was certainly the last time I saw Dora alive. She had already left this building by then and moved somewhere else to live. I only glimpsed the man for a moment too, but he was definitely a European from his size and the way he was dressed. Most of the businesses in the street were already closed for the night, so the pavement was mostly in complete darkness. I soon lost sight of this couple as they walked away together...' Her voice faltered. 'I think it could even have been the night before Dora was found dead, though I'm not absolutely sure of that now...*the mind can play strange tricks...*'

Jericho took a long breath. 'Do you think it could have been the same blue-eyed man who was seen leaving Cherry Kwok's room on the night she died?'

She bit her lip with embarrassment. 'I suppose it could have been.'

Jericho hid his annoyance as best he could. 'Why didn't you tell me this before, Maggie?'

Maggie looked helpless for a moment. 'I had completely forgotten about it until after my interview at the station. I think I was in a state of shock after finding Dora's body. And I was still being plagued by that rat which was visiting my room during the night; my rat poison clearly hadn't worked so I had to employ a rat catcher in the end to trap it and dispose of it. So I was certainly in a very distracted state that week and not thinking very clearly. By the time I remembered seeing that couple in the street, I thought there was no point in going back to the police station and amending my statement since I wasn't even sure that it had actually been Dora I had seen. And - if I'm frank - I was also scared that I was becoming too involved in this police investigation. In any case, I don't think I could identify the man again from that brief look I had. All I could see of him was that he was tall and well built, and moved like a Westerner. He was wearing a hat – a Panama hat pulled down low over his brow - so I couldn't see his hair or much of his face from up here.' Her face looked white and strained. 'I am so sorry that I didn't tell you this before...'

Jericho reflected silently on that; there seemed to be nothing else to say.

She finally came over to him again and offered him the cup of tea with a contrite expression on her face. 'I hope it tastes like English tea.' She sat down at a small bamboo table opposite him and regarded him with concern. 'I really have told you absolutely everything I know about Dora now. There's nothing more to tell. I hope you believe me...I don't want to lose your good opinion because of this.'

He saw the clear signs of hurt in her face, and tried to reassure her. 'Of course I believe you. And you haven't lost my good opinion...I can assure you of that...'

She smiled at him faintly. 'Then I thank you very kindly for that. For I doubt that you bestow your good opinion on many people...' She suddenly leaned across the table towards him and looked him directly in the eyes. 'I think that you are probably a very lonely man, Inspector Paul Jericho, aren't you? A lost soul in a world that you don't really understand or care for?'

He sipped the tea uneasily. 'You're probably right.'

She gave him another melancholy smile. 'I know I am. For I am a lonely soul too. It's a difficult life for a Eurasian here in Hong Kong. Neither the Chinese nor the European races really accept us. We lie imprisoned between two distinct worlds...neither one thing nor the other...'

He looked into her eyes in return. Then he reached out his hand towards her and ran his fingers gently through her thick glossy hair. 'I'm sorry,' he apologized quickly. 'But I've wanted to do that from the first day that we met.'

She hadn't flinched when he had touched her hair, and now she laid her cheek against the palm of his outstretched hand. Finally she stood up, then came around the table and sat on his lap. 'Do it again then...' With that she put her hands around his neck, then kissed him slowly on the lips...

*

Jericho lay in Maggie's embrace, warmed and elevated by her passionate lovemaking. He had forgotten for the moment about everything, even the fact that he now thought he knew who had killed the three women from the Tin Hau Bar...

'I did wonder if I would ever see you out of that khaki uniform,' Maggie said sleepily.

'I think you've seen me out of police uniform before,' he answered.

'Not like this I haven't,' she added with a smile.

He laughed. 'No, I suppose not.'

'You look ten years younger when you laugh,' she said with a further endearing smile.

Then her smile faded as she became serious again. 'I must tell you something, Paul. You are not my first man, you know...you must have realized that...'

'You don't have to explain,' he murmured softly.

'Yes, I do,' she insisted. 'I had a lover before, in Shanghai. He was a good man, a dear and honest man. But he died...it was one more reason why I left...'

'I'm sorry,' he said lamely.

'Don't be. I am happy again now...' With that she kissed him warmly again. 'I'm sorry that this bed is so narrow, though.' She had a sofa that converted into a bed at night. It was comfortable enough, yet too narrow for two, and certainly for two lovers. He realized with surprise that he might even be the first man who had ever shared this particular bed with her. From the feverishness of her lovemaking, she had obviously been as starved of love and human warmth lately as he himself.

'You told me about your Russian father. Have you had any word from him lately?'

'No, I haven't heard anything from him for months. I worry about him being trapped in Shanghai. It's probably just as well that my Chinese mother died last year; I don't know how she would have survived this new and terrible time in her homeland.'

'Your father must be in the International Settlement, though, isn't he? I don't think the Japanese would be bold enough to attack the foreign community, though they may bomb other parts of Shanghai.'

She rested her cheek on his bare chest. 'That's of little comfort to me, I'm afraid.'

He stroked her hair gently again. 'Is there no hope of evacuating your father to Hong Kong?'

He felt her head jerk involuntarily against him as if she had been given an electric shock. 'None at all. The British will not want him: a White Russian man who was married to a Chinese woman? Nor will Soviet Russia take my father back except to execute him or send him to Siberia. I think he would rather take his chances with the Japanese.'

Jericho could feel her mood changing, like a winter freeze stealing its way across a summer landscape. He decided sensibly to change the subject. 'I like your Russian name. Margarita Ivanova...it sounds like a character from Tolstoy or Chekhov...'

'Perhaps I *am* a character from a gloomy Russian novel. Though since I came to Hong Kong, I feel much more Chinese than I ever felt before. Perhaps it's because I use my mother's family name here, Yiu, and the names she bequeathed me – Pui Wah.'

'Yiu Pui Wah...I like that name too.'

She glanced across at him with a flicker of a smile. 'It seems you like everything about me.'

'It seems that I do,' he conceded with a quiet smile of his own.

'Do you want to listen to the radio?' she asked brightly. 'I now own a radio for the first time in my life. I've been dying to show it off to somebody.'

He smiled again at her infectious girlish warmth. In private she was so different from the cool and sophisticated creature that she played in public. 'Then let me hear it.'

He watched as she got up and walked across the room to turn the Bakelite radio on. She had a body like a gazelle: long slender legs, a shapely waist, small breasts. He felt himself harden again just at the sight of her bending over to tune the wireless, and seeing the muscles tighten in her neat rounded buttocks. She had clearly noticed him admiring her body, but did not seem to mind, merely shrugging philosophically at the lascivious nature of men and accepting it as an unspoken compliment.

She had some trouble tuning her new radio at first. But eventually she found the only station that was reachable in Hong Kong, ZBW. Being a Sunday it was not broadcasting a live relay of the dance orchestra from The Gripps but instead only rather slow and ponderous classical music. Jericho thought he recognized it as Tchaikovsky's last major orchestral symphony, the *Pathétique*, which was certainly his least favourite work of that great Russian composer.

Maggie had also clearly recognized it as Tchaikovsky but, unlike Jericho, listened to it with quiet rapture. But her enjoyment came to an abrupt end when the music finished, and the familiar voice of the principal ZBW announcer began to read an emergency news bulletin.

Jericho saw Maggie's face crumple in disbelief as the announcer broke the devastating news that the Japanese air force had bombed the city of Shanghai yesterday with a major loss of civilian life...

*

Edith Starling had spent the whole of this Sunday in her blistering hot prison trying to enlarge one of the small gaps in the top of the blockwork wall, scraping away at it patiently with her fingernails for hours at a time. It gave her something to do, and helped take her mind off her gnawing hunger. She had used the broken timber slats from the old explosive crates to make a small platform three feet high on which she could stand and just reach the top of the wall with her outstretched fingers. The mortar at the very top of the blockwork was dry and friable, yet in her pathetically weakened condition she could hardly keep her arms raised for more than a few seconds at a time. Yet she carried on doggedly, scraping away at the mortar with bleeding fingernails until the small gap had been enlarged into a slotted hole a couple of inches in length. She was still managing to drink sufficient water to keep her alive from the dripping pipe; she had by now tied a handkerchief to the end of the pipe which became slowly saturated with water every few hours, and from which she could then squeeze drops into her mouth rather than having to suck directly on the flanged end of the pipe.

As the light began to fade on this, her fifth full day of imprisonment, she began to consider what she might be able to push through that small hole that might signal her presence inside.

She tried ripping a piece of cloth from her shift, but the material stubbornly refused to tear in her weakened state, even though it was only a light muslin. She considered using her panties, but that seemed like a step too far, even in this desperate situation. But then she had a sudden rush of blood as she remembered that she had been wearing silk stockings under her trouser suit. She thanked God now that she was such a conventional Englishwoman that she had taken the trouble to put on silk hose as usual on Tuesday morning even when wearing slacks to work. Quickly she searched in the darkening room for her discarded stockings. In the deepening gloom she could find only one of them, but that was enough. She climbed back onto the makeshift platform of broken timber slats and tried to push the silk stocking through the tiny hole.

But the bunched-up silk soon snagged on something, perhaps a metal screw or some sort of fixing in the top of the blockwork, and wouldn't go through no matter how hard she tried to push it with her fingertips. She realized with chagrin that all she'd ended up doing was to block most of the light entering the room.

She sank back down on the hard concrete floor in a deeper despair than she had ever known. But then her heart began to race as she heard a sound on the other side of the door. She called out desperately, screaming at the top of her voice for help. But there was only silence on the other side of the door, so that she knew for certain that it must be her abductor who had returned.

Edith felt her blood turn cold as she realized that the man had simply come back to check if she was dead by now.

She imagined him standing on the other side of the door, holding his breath, still not wanting to give his identity away. She spoke to him through the door. 'I know you're there. What do you want with me?'

Still no answer...

She began to plead. 'Is that you, Michael? I know it's you, Michael. Please let me go!'

But she heard nothing more but the faint sound of receding footsteps on the concrete floor outside as the man backed away from the door and left her callously to her fate...

CHAPTER 23

Sunday, 29th August 1937

In the heavy humid warmth of a moonless Hong Kong night, Sebastian Ride waited in the shade of a Bauhinia tree near the wrought iron entrance gate of Government House. A whole line of these floriferous orchid trees had been planted along the north side of Upper Albert Road, and had grown so profusely that they now blocked much of the light from the electric street lamps on the other side of the street. Ride was twenty yards away from the main gate, and also hidden from the sight of the guards on the gate by the corner of the West Gate Lodge. Yet the tree cover along the pavement on this side of the entrance gate was so dense that, in his dark shirt and trousers, Ride knew he would be near invisible even if he stepped out from behind the protective corner of the lodge into plain sight.

It was nearly eleven o'clock now. Ian Luff had not appeared at the empty Woo mansion on nearby Caine Road as promised at 10:30, so Ride had been forced to go looking for him. Leaving the comforting seclusion of that old Portuguese house and garden was a risky business because he was armed with Frances's Colt Detective .38 Special in a makeshift holster under his shirt. Should he be stopped by the police for suspicious behaviour and searched, that Detective Special would take some explaining on his part. Even for a prestigious captain of Hong Kong commerce like himself, the police might wonder what on earth he was doing hanging around outside Government House armed with a deadly snub-nosed revolver...

Ride was beginning to consider giving up on his mission, for it seemed that Ian Luff might be staying the whole night in Government House. It was very tempting to just forget this insane plan, which seemed even more crazy to him as the night wore on. But just as he was about to slink away into the night, he heard the gate clang open and then a muffled interchange between the officer of the guard and a couple of departing visitors.

The gate clanged shut again, and the two men stepped out into plain view in the pool of streetlight immediately in front of the gate. Ride recognized the men as Ian Luff and his superior in the Treasury, Bob Harmsworth. Even from twenty yards away, he could hear their conversation quite distinctly...

*

'Well, that was a long one,' Luff complained tiredly. 'But I noticed that you managed to sneak away from the main meeting with Lockhart Smith for an hour or so.'

Harmsworth's voice sounded huffy. 'I didn't "sneak away" as you so indelicately put it, Ian. I just felt one of my migraines coming on, so I needed to lie down for an hour in a darkened room without any disturbance.'

Luff was unrepentant. 'I wish I'd thought of the same excuse. I didn't know you suffered from migraines, Bob.'

'Well I do.' Harmsworth was becoming irritated now.

Luff modified his tone to a more respectful one. 'It was very brave of Colby to attend today. Of course he's always had a strong interest in China, and the news of the bombing of Shanghai yesterday has clearly shocked him greatly.'

'It's shocked all of us, Ian, me included.' Harmsworth paused. 'I have never liked Colby much, but this terrible illness of his has revealed his true character. The man is a brave English gentleman.'

'Quite...' Luff soon continued, apparently not that interested in the character of his government colleague Colby. 'It seems likely that Shanghai will fall soon to the Japs. They could have complete control of China within weeks.'

Harmsworth shook his head. 'They don't understand what they have bitten off. There will never be enough Japs in the world to control China. And the more brutality they use, the more entrenched and determined the Chinese will become to defend their homeland. The Japs have done what no one else could do: they have unified the Chinese again into one nation.'

Luff nodded. 'Well, perhaps you're right. You have been out here a long time, Bob, and you understand things in a way that I probably never will.'

Harmsworth seemed sceptical. 'Such flattery is unusual for you, Ian. Fortunately I know that you don't mean a word of it.' He looked up at the sky. 'Still very calm tonight. Yet they say that the typhoon in the Philippines is expected to track north over the South China Sea and hit the south coast of China within the next few days.'

Luff was philosophical. 'It seems that their gods have turned their backs on the Chinese completely, doesn't it? First they send them a Japanese invasion, and now a huge malevolent storm. Let's hope this particular typhoon misses Hong Kong at least.'

'Given our present woeful luck, I wouldn't take a bet on that,' Harmsworth said tartly. 'Where is your car today, Ian?'

'I walked to work today; I needed the exercise since I knew I would miss my usual free Sunday at the beach today.'

Harmsworth pointed east along Upper Albert Road with his hand. 'Well, my car is just there. I can give you a lift back to Bowen Road if you like.'

Luff declined politely. 'No thanks, Bob. That's kind of you but I think I prefer to walk tonight.'

Harmsworth laughed robustly. 'Well rather you than me. That's a steep climb ahead of you at this time of night, even for a fit young chap like yourself. I'll bid you goodnight, then, Ian...'

*

Sebastian Ride had been listening intently to this interesting discussion, but now he realized that Luff intended to keep his appointment at the Woo mansion in nearby Caine Road after all, even though he was more than half an hour late. He realized that his original plan to lie in wait for Luff somewhere near the entrance to the Woo mansion would still work, if he now ran ahead of Luff and got himself into a suitable position to spring a trap on the man. There was a big banyan tree just outside the Woo mansion gate that would provide a perfect place to hide and wait for Luff's approach.

In a second he had backed away further into the shadows and started sprinting west along Upper Albert Road in the direction of Caine Road. He reached the Woo mansion in no more than ninety seconds, so he was sure that he must have beaten Luff comfortably to the spot. He stationed himself behind the trunk of the vast banyan tree and pulled the revolver from under his shirt. His heart was already beating rapidly from his energetic run, but continued to race as he waited in the dark to kill a man. He had killed a rioter with the butt of his rifle during his time with the Hong Kong Volunteers over ten years ago. But he had never killed a man in cold blood – not face-to-face like this...

Then he heard the sound of footsteps on the pavement. The pace of them was quite leisurely as if the man had all the time in the world. For some reason that leisurely approach annoyed Ride even more than anything else about Ian Luff, and he sprang out from behind the tree trunk, ready to confront the man.

But his jaw dropped when he saw that the newcomer was not Ian Luff at all but a young uniformed Chinese constable of the Hong Kong Police on patrol. The young policeman saw the snub-nosed revolver in Ride's hand and immediately fumbled in a panic for the pistol in his own holster. Ride had only a moment to react but knew he had no chance of escaping by simply turning and running. So instead he leapt forward and, using the handle of the Detective Special as a club, smashed it into the young

constable's jaw.
Then he ran...

*

A crowd of police officers were milling about in some confusion when Paul Jericho arrived on the scene in Caine Road. He had just left Maggie Yiu's building at 11:30 when he ran into a patrolling constable in Lockhart Road who recognized him and told him of the report of a gunman near a house in Caine Road, a few hundred yards west of Government House.

On arriving just before midnight, Jericho recognized the house in question of course as the Portuguese-style house which was located immediately next door to that of the retired schoolteacher Adela Marr. He remembered that it was a similarly magnificent old colonial mansion to her house, with ivy-covered walls and balconied windows with beautiful wrought-iron balustrading, a decaying palace of a house that at first inspection seemed to belong more in Lisbon or Granada than here in the Far East. Yet the house did reveal its true location more with its distinctive Chinese roof. The porcelain tiles and the stylized dragon profile of the roof were still resolutely doing their part in defending the old house against the incursion of any malevolent spirits. But not apparently against the actions of some madman with a gun, who had assaulted a young police constable just outside the front gate of the house, then escaped without trace...

Jericho's mind was still half elsewhere, as he continued to reflect on the wonderful day he had spent with Maggie Yiu. He still didn't really know why he had left Maggie's home tonight, for she had certainly wanted him to stay the whole night – in fact had almost begged him to stay. The mood between them had certainly become more sombre after she had heard the terrible news about Shanghai, and Jericho had found himself in the unfamiliar role of comforter and supportive friend. Yet even after they had dressed again and shared a dinner of fried rice together, there was still a deep intimacy between them, the intimacy of lovers who were comfortable in each other's presence now, and free to bare their souls to each other. Yet a restless energy took hold of him as the evening wore on, and he found that he simply couldn't stay with her any longer: his mind had begun to dwell too much on the Wanchai murders again, filling his head with a thousand conflicting emotions. He still could not bring himself to believe what his gut instincts were telling him...

He forced himself to deal with the present problem of catching an unknown gunman. The young policeman, Constable David Wu, had been knocked unconscious for a full minute or so by the man, and had not got a clear look at his assailant. Wu had now been taken to hospital to be checked for concussion, but had left his colleagues with a decent description of the man: quite youthful-looking, black hair, lean and muscular build, wearing a dark shirt and trousers. Wu certainly hadn't seen the man's face clearly yet had got the impression that the man might be European, for his hair had seemed curly rather than straight. Yet Jericho doubted that last part, for he could think of no reason on earth why a young European man would assault a patrolling policeman. Assaults on patrolling police officers were unfortunately becoming more common of late because of the volatile political and social situation in Hong Kong, which seemed to be an encouragement to lawbreaking generally, and to the triad gangs in particular. Yet very few Europeans would ever challenge the police: instead the expatriate community were usually staunch supporters of the men in green khaki for somehow managing to keep the streets of Hong Kong relatively safe even in such troubled times as these...

Jericho could have used the services of George Dorling on this job tonight because this sort of rough-and-tumble police work was meat and drink to him. But George was no doubt tucked up safely in bed after his deserved day off with his wife Tess, driving in the New Territories...

As the senior officer present, Paul Jericho put away any thoughts of his own bed. He immediately took control of the operation and began to hand out orders to his assembled men with quick-fire precision...

In another five minutes, Jericho had sent off patrols to every conceivable point in the Mid-levels area, creating a secure ring of steel around the scene of the attack with orders to stop and question anyone found on the streets. He had ordered all his officers to take no chances with the man if they found him, and to use such force as necessary to restrain him. It was a small comfort that the man had not actually fired his revolver at Constable Wu but had only used it as a club to strike him. This suggested that the murder of a policeman was not the man's primary purpose. It was more likely that the man was simply an armed burglar who had walked into Constable Wu by complete accident...

Jericho himself stayed outside the house in Caine Road while he waited hopefully with a young Chinese constable for one of his patrols to make an arrest. But by two o'clock in the morning, with no reports of any arrest, he realized with annoyance that the burglar must have moved very fast to escape the area and had probably already evaded his ring of police patrols. Therefore, with great reluctance, he decided to abandon the operation, and sent word by his runner to tell all his officers to stand down.

In truth he had spent most of his own two-hour vigil thinking not about this resourceful burglar, but more about the murders in Wanchai. He had gradually realized as the night wore on that he must be mistaken in his new theory, and that the truth was that the women *must have* been victims of the Kao Ki-kan triad after all, just as Ricky Sun had been, and probably Freddie Ling and Marco da Silva too.

It seemed obvious to him now what must have happened. This escort agency of Da Silva's – the Blue Heaven Agency – had to be the key to everything. Ling and Da Silva had probably set up their agency without getting the triad's permission, and without paying them their dues. So Ling and Da Silva had paid the price for that mistake with their lives. Yet these three young women must have annoyed Lucky Lam too in some way. It seemed likely that Dora Kam, the girl from Shanghai, had been a friend, or even lover, of the informer Ricky Sun. So that could explain why she had to die. And perhaps Judy Wong and Cherry Kwok had also betrayed the triad in some way...

This explanation now seemed much more likely than the notion that one of the girls' Western customers had killed them. Jericho had certainly abandoned Ian Luff completely as a suspect now, and dismissed the business card found in the Tin Hau Hotel as nothing significant. As Luff himself had said, anyone could have left that card there. In any case, it would be a very careless murderer who would leave his own business card behind to incriminate himself. Luff's vague connection to Marco da Silva – that they had apparently been in the same homosexual massage parlour on the same night – could mean no more than the fact that both men were homosexual.

Yet there was still the matter of the blue-eyed male visitor to Cherry Kwok's room to consider. Jericho had to wonder now about the evidence of the old woman who had glimpsed this mysterious visitor. *Could she really have been so sure that the man had blue eyes?* Or could the local triad man have perhaps threatened her and forced her to give false evidence to the police? It had to be a possibility; the triads were masters of the veiled threat, after all. Yet even if the woman *had* seen what she claimed, there was still no proof that this man had actually killed Cherry Kwok.

And what of the European man that Maggie had seen with Dora Kam in Lockhart Road? This might or might not be the same man who had visited Cherry Kwok on the night she died. But no one could say for sure. The odds were high that this was two entirely different European men, and that these men were simply clients of these two beautiful Chinese women with no murderous intent towards them at all...

Therefore Jericho had become determined by two o'clock that he was going to return to the matter of the Kao Ki-kan's possible involvement in these murders, even if it meant stepping on the toes of Inspector Kevin Ball and his own investigation...and even if it meant ignoring the objections of his own sergeant, George Dorling, who didn't subscribe to this theory at all.

These reflections lifted a huge invisible weight from Jericho's shoulders, and he was almost in optimistic mood again as his patrols gradually returned to Caine Road where he dismissed them all for the night.

Afterwards, alone in the deep nocturnal stillness of Caine Road, he decided to take a final look at the Portuguese mansion, so opened the heavy iron gate. The garden seemed a ghostly place from here, a tangle of greenery in the starlight, dark and uninviting. But something compelled him to enter in spite of that. He switched on his torch and began following the meandering path that led to the front door of the mansion...

*

Sebastian Ride had not run far after escaping from the patrolling policeman, but had instead doubled back towards the Woo mansion, then climbed over the high stone wall at the front and into the depths of the overgrown garden beyond. On reflection this had seemed like a much better place to try and hide than somewhere on the streets. He was sure that he had not done any serious hurt to that young policeman, and that the man would soon recover and summon other policemen to his aid, therefore he needed somewhere secure to hide quickly.

For several reasons he had not ditched the gun yet, the main one being that he was not sure that it could not be traced back to Frances if it was found. It seemed unlikely, of course, for Frances was far too efficient to have given him a traceable weapon to use. But he had forgotten to ask her and make sure, so decided that it was better to hang on to it for the moment.

Fortunately Ride had visited this house in the past often as a guest of the Woo family so had a good idea of the layout of the garden. He remembered in particular a tall Bengal Fig that Grace had once shown him how to climb. She had used to climb this tree many times as a girl, she said. The first part of the climb was quite difficult, getting up through the tangle of lower branches. But after that it was possible to ascend with relative ease and climb all the way to a natural cup-shaped platform high up in the tree that was completely invisible from the ground. It had been Grace's secret hiding place as a young girl, and Ride was aware that she was honouring him by sharing her girlish secret with him. But now, years later, the thought of climbing this tree was less appealing to him. Ride was aware of what a dangerous position he was in: the head of a huge Hong Kong trading company reduced to hiding in a tree like a common criminal. Even worse was the ridiculousness of his situation; in many ways the indignity of his plight seemed even worse than the danger. *What could he have been thinking of to let Frances persuade him to follow such a crazy plan?*

Yet he knew it was the end for him if he was caught here now, so – reluctantly - he began to climb in the starlight, branch by branch. Once he had reached the hidden natural platform high up in the tree and was concealed from the ground in the pitch blackness, he felt better. No one would find him here – the police were people of limited imagination and intelligence after all - so he should be able to simply wait here until the inevitable hue-and-cry died down. He thought he should be invisible even if he was still trapped here at daybreak, although he hoped desperately that his ordeal would not last that long.

Yet he was shocked when he saw the scale of the police operation that his attack on that young policeman had provoked: there seemed to be a small army of police milling about on Caine Road, and much noise and confusion. Yet surely he was still safe here; the police would never think to start looking for him up a tree. But then a sudden bleak thought shocked him out of his complacency: *what if they used dogs to follow his scent...?*

But fortunately there seemed to be no dogs available, for the only sounds Ride could hear were of human bloodhounds. At least he was comfortable in his little prison in the sky: the night was still and warm, with no sign yet of the supposed approaching typhoon.

He began to doze in the balmy night air but then was suddenly jerked back to full consciousness again when he heard the gate of the mansion open. A couple of figures appeared in the starlit gloom below and began a desultory search with torches through the garden. But he could see their heart was not really in the search, and they soon gave up after fifteen minutes of poking about in the dense ferns and green understory of the garden. Not once did they lift their eyes and look up at the trees, but Ride could hardly blame them for that; his was a most unlikely hiding place for a fugitive from the law...

He began to wonder what had happened to Ian Luff tonight. He couldn't believe that Luff and that young policeman were in league in any way; it must have simply been bad luck that a policeman on routine patrol had spoilt their plan to meet. Yet Luff might have been close enough to see what had happened between him and the young copper, and might have observed that Ride had been brandishing a gun. In which case Luff, being a smart man, would soon put two and two together and realize that *he* had been Ride's intended victim, not the policeman. *So what would Luff do if he now realized that Ride had been intending to shoot him down in the street?*

Luff might go to the police immediately and confess everything, in which case the police would soon be looking for him. But Ride had the feeling that Luff would not do anything so precipitous since it would end all his hopes of a glittering future on the board of Saunders-Woo. And Luff would know that he, Sebastian Ride, would fight back if the case ever came to court, and would drag the name of Ian Luff through the mud too, publicizing especially his homosexual nature. Therefore the chances were that Luff would simply choose to lie low and maintain a discreet profile for a few days, waiting to see how events transpired, and whether his plan might still be resurrected...

Two hours or more had dragged by when Ride began to sense that the police were finally dispersing. He realized exultantly that they must think that they had missed him, and were giving up for the night. Ride had already decided that he would not go directly home from here, even if it seemed clear to do so. He would go instead to Frances's apartment in

Morrison Hill in Causeway Bay, and hide up there until he himself was sure that Ian Luff had not gone to the police and identified him as the young policeman's assailant tonight.

He waited patiently as the noise in the street faded away to an uneasy silence. In the distance a watchdog barked twice, but then lapsed into brooding silence too. Ride decided it was time to move, and began to descend the tree carefully, branch by branch.

But then, when he was only ten or fifteen feet from the ground, he heard the iron gate of the mansion creak open again, and a man entered the garden with an electric torch in his hand. Ride froze on the branch he was standing on, trying to stop it from creaking. His rapid breathing sounded near deafening in the silence of the night, and seemed as obvious to him as the snorting of a steam engine. Ride saw the figure of the man outlined briefly by the light of his own torch and realized that this was Susan's husband again, Inspector Paul Jericho. He seemed fated to come across this man at awkward times; first when Jericho had brought him the official news of James Woo's death; and now he seemed to be the only policeman standing between himself and freedom...

Jericho moved forward slowly until he was standing almost directly under the branch of the fig tree that Ride was standing on. If Jericho looked up now and used his torch, he would see Ride for sure. Then it would be a choice of life of death for Sebastian Ride; he would either have to kill Paul Jericho, or else simply give himself up...

It was then, though, that Ride realized that there was now a *second* man below in the gloom, standing only a few paces behind Paul Jericho. This second man was dressed in an overcoat and fedora hat despite the intense humid heat. Ride's first impulse was to believe that this must be a second policeman, a plainclothes colleague of Jericho's come to help him search the garden. But Ride was soon dispossessed of that notion, for it became clear that Jericho was quite unaware of the man behind him, and that this second man seemed to be stalking Jericho with military guile...

Moving as quickly as a cat, the man suddenly attacked Jericho viciously from behind, hitting him over the head with a club of some sort that felled him instantly. The man then knelt over Jericho's body and wrapped his hands around Jericho's throat, throttling the life out of him with powerful fingers.

Ride then acted out of pure instinct and dropped to the ground, landing with his feet on the back of Jericho's attacker. The man screamed with pain and surprise at this sudden impact from nowhere, but was too winded to put up any fight. With an animal snarl, the man leapt to his feet and ran off into the darkness.

Ride bent down over the prone body of Paul Jericho and was relieved to see that the man was still alive. In fact he seemed to be coming to quite rapidly. This had been a disastrous night for Sebastian Ride overall, but finally he felt some relief that he had done the right thing for once tonight: this man was Susan's husband after all, he reminded himself, and Ride felt that he owed the man something for all the pain and misery he'd caused him.

Yet he didn't wait around to be discovered, but took to his heels immediately...

*

Paul Jericho groaned, and became aware that someone was leaning over him.

'Are you all right, sir?'

Jericho saw through a red mist of pain that the man tending to him was *George Dorling...*

Jericho's voice was hoarse and dry. 'What are you doing here, George? How did you get here? I thought you were off duty in Kowloon.'

Dorling helped him sit up. 'I was, sir. I took Tess for a drive to the village of Tai Po in the New Territories today. But we had a little marital argument when we came home, so I went for a drink in the Peninsula Hotel bar tonight. That's when I heard from a friend about the gunman reported outside a house in Caine Road. So I decided to come over and see if I could help. It was after midnight so all the ferries were finished. But I found a walla-walla to take me over. By the time I got here to Caine Road, though, it looked like it was all over. I couldn't see anybody outside the house at all. But then I heard a scuffle from inside the garden and came to investigate...'

Jericho tried to get to his feet. He looked at Dorling with surprise, for he seemed to be breathing as heavily as himself. George was in civvies too, wearing a long coat and hat. 'You didn't see anyone running away?'

'No, sir. Just you, lying groaning on the ground.' Dorling had a thought. 'Who hit you, sir? Was it the gunman you were chasing?'

'It must have been,' Jericho said woozily. 'He must have been hiding in this garden the whole time. I did wonder if he might still be here near the house, because we found no trace of him on the surrounding streets.' He felt his sore head then put a hand to his bruised throat. 'The bastard hit me from behind, then tried to choke me. I suppose it must have been your arrival that scared him off, so it seems you might have saved my life with your fortunate arrival, George.'

'You didn't actually see the man, then, sir?'

'No, I'm afraid not. I got even less of a look at him than Constable Wu did earlier.'

Even in his dazed state, Jericho could not help noticing that George looked relieved by that announcement, for some odd reason...

CHAPTER 24

Monday, 30th August 1937

Standing at the wall mirror in the bathroom of his apartment in Blue Pool Road, Paul Jericho examined his face ruefully as he shaved. He was having to use his cutthroat razor with much more care than usual because of all the bruises and contusions on his throat. That villain last night had made a proper job of assaulting him, and might even have killed him if George Dorling had not happened along...

Yet Jericho had still refused George's offer to take him to hospital afterwards, and had instead just gone home directly and done nothing more than take an aspirin. This casual attitude to his own health seemed to have paid off, though, for he had slept nearly seven solid hours without a break, before waking at ten o'clock, feeling surprisingly fresh and reinvigorated. Yet he didn't look as good as he felt: the mid-morning sunlight spilling through the frosted glass of his bathroom window revealed all the myriad colours of those bruises on his throat and neck in stark detail: some sickly yellow, some a violent red, and one blue-black multiple bruise that looked like a threatening storm cloud.

Yet outside, the morning sky was untouched by any real storm clouds and the morning felt like the beginning of yet another blistering Hong Kong summer's day, with still no sign as yet of this impending typhoon. Despite having to shave with such care around his bruises, the events of last night were not even uppermost in Jericho's mind any more. He was very good at dismissing old failures from his mind and concentrating on the present. That gunman from last night had got away and no one had a clue who he was. So it was better to simply forget this embarrassing failure for the present and concentrate his attentions instead on the cases that he *could* do something about.

Yet even the Wanchai murders did not feel like his main priority today, because the problem of finding Edith Starling was now reaching a crisis point in his mind. He *had* to find that girl somehow; she had come to him for help and he had let her down. So he had to make good his failure by finding her. It also felt like a debt that he owed to his late wife, Susan. Jericho had not been able to save his own wife's life, but perhaps he could save the life of her best friend.

Yet after six days, the truth was that he was beginning to lose hope that Edith would still be alive by now. If they couldn't find her within the next day or so, then the outlook was certainly grim.

Jericho completed his careful shaving, and then stood looking at his mirror image as a new and unexpected thought came to him. It had suddenly occurred to him that he was now sporting bruises on his throat and windpipe that looked very like those that Edith had described about her late boss, Ralph Ogden. The notion struck Jericho as being bizarre at first: these two attacks could not possibly have been carried out by the same man...

Yet he was quickly forced to reconsider that opinion: after all, this gunman who had attacked Constable Wu had been operating only a few hundred yards from Government House. *So could that man also be the person who had murdered Ralph Ogden?* Assuming Ogden *had* been murdered, of course, which was far from certain, for Edith was the only person to claim such a thing. It seemed more and more likely to Jericho that Edith's disappearance was nothing to do with her relationship with Michael Yip after all, but must instead have something to do with her work for the SIS. Edith had not really explained to him *why* somebody should have murdered Ralph Ogden. But presumably it was also to do with his intelligence work. *So was perhaps there a traitor operating at Government House who had murdered Ogden to keep him quiet?* Is that what Edith had thought? And had the same man then abducted and possibly murdered Edith too to stop her talking?

It seemed all too plausible...

So where *was* Edith? If this traitor had abducted her, where would he have hidden her? And with what purpose? If she was a threat to this man, then surely the man would have simply killed her outright. Jericho had clung on to the only small clue that he had: that her abductor had recently been walking in either a quarry or an open excavated construction site. So he now had teams of policemen searching every feasible location on Hong Kong Island and Kowloon side where a woman might be kept imprisoned, including even the Saunders-Woo quarry at Shaukeiwan.

Yet nothing had been found so far. But then again, no body had turned up either as yet, so Jericho was determined to keep on looking until he discovered Edith Starling's ultimate fate...

*

George Dorling had slept late in his third floor Kowloon apartment after his exertions of the night before, but by ten o'clock on this Monday morning he had shaved and was grabbing a hurried breakfast of bacon and eggs in the kitchen, brought to him by their elderly amah. Ah Tong was beaming as usual, and her placid expression was certainly a contrast with the scowl on Tess's face as she hovered uncertainly in the background while Dorling gobbled down his food as fast as he could.

From the kitchen window Dorling could see Ashley Road and the busy junction with Hankow Road that was occupied by the Star Cinema. *The Petrified Forest* had finished its run already without them having the opportunity to see it, and a billboard was now going up for their latest cinematic offering: a new Ronald Colman film called *Lost Horizon*. It seemed like a more appropriate movie for him and Tess to see because that title seemed to sum up their future prospects remarkably well...

He remembered again with some sense of loss how happy they had once been. When he had first caught sight of Tess in her cute "Nippy" waitress uniform in that Lyons teahouse on the Scarborough seafront, he had been completely smitten. And his infatuation had only become stronger through their whirlwind courtship and marriage, and then that wonderful journey to Hong Kong on board the *SS Rajputana*. The three years that had followed had dampened his feelings a little, as they struggled to make a happy life together in their small poky flat in downtown Kowloon. And this struggle had reached its low point in May with the devastating loss of their baby. After that, Dorling had wanted to make it up to his pretty little Lyons waitress by giving her the best of everything, but that wish had only led him to disaster in the end...

Tess told Ah Tong to go and do some ironing in the utility room while she came and sat beside him at the breakfast table. She brushed a piece of fluff from the collar of his clean khaki green summer uniform. 'You've cut yourself,' she pointed out in her flat Yorkshire voice.

'I know,' he said impatiently, as he sipped some sweet tea to wash down the bacon and eggs. 'And I've really got to go...I'm late on duty.'

'Where did you go last night, George?' she asked moodily.

They had had such a pleasant day yesterday, driving in their little Morris out over the mountains to the New Territories and the tranquil village of Tai Po. The place was so quiet – rice paddies and plodding oxen, a quaint Chinese village, an old monastery with a tolling bell – that it had seemed a million miles from busy Kowloon. For the first time in many months they had been happy again together, and he'd felt some rekindling of those warm feelings he had first had for her back in distant Scarborough. But they had not long returned home in the evening before Tess had started pestering him again with the name of Dora Kam. She really did seem to think that he was considering leaving her for this unknown Chinese woman. Dorling had soon given up and stormed out on her. He had spent most of the evening in the bar of the Peninsula Hotel before hearing about the emergency over on the Island...

'I was working,' he said quickly. 'I went over to Hong Kong side when I heard that there was a report of a gunman on the loose in the Mid-levels.' He hesitated. 'It's just as well I did go; I ended up saving the life of my chief, Inspector Jericho. The gunman got away, though...' he saw the look of doubt in her eyes. 'If you don't believe me, read the morning paper. The story will be in there for sure...'

Tess reached across for their copy of the *South China Morning Post*. 'I haven't seen that particular story. But I have seen a story about three Chinese women murdered in Wanchai. And one of them was called *Dora Kam...*' She almost flinched at the look on her husband's face. 'Would you like to tell me what's going on, George? Why are you calling out the name of a murdered woman in your sleep?' Her face had gone deathly pale. 'What have you done...?'

He leaned forward quickly and almost spat the words in her face. 'You'd better not say a word about this, Tess, or else you'll put my head in a noose. Is that what you really want? *My head in a noose...?*

*

In early evening, with no positive news received from his search teams about the hunt for Edith Starling – not even from their search of Shaukeiwan Quarry, which had been his best hope – Paul Jericho drove himself up to Conduit Road to talk to Mrs Sebastian Ride and see how she was recovering after the incident on Saturday. It seemed like the appropriate thing to do in the circumstances, and it would help him understand if she had really tried to kill herself. But he had timed his visit deliberately for the evening in the hope that her husband might also be at home, so that he could do a little more gentle probing into the circumstances surrounding the death of James Woo. That boy thief, Ah Yee, was still in custody and was still sticking emphatically to his story of what he'd seen in Tai Ping Shan two weeks ago. So Jericho understood that he couldn't simply forget this unfortunate bit of evidence, and would have to investigate it formally...

The vast white three-storied art deco mansion seemed even larger and grander than he remembered from his first visit, and its elevated setting even more spectacular. He had parked at the top of the steep drive next to a blue Bugatti sports car, which he assumed must belong to Sebastian Ride himself. His old battered black Austin Seven was certainly an interesting contrast to that stylish Italian sports car, for it displayed the relative wealth of their owners with pitiful clarity: the rewards for a director of a wealthy trading company, compared with those for a painfully honest expatriate policeman...

This time he was not forced to stay outside on the front terrace by the houseboy, but was invited inside on the orders of the lady of the house, up to a Modernist study on the first floor with a vast and spectacular curved plate glass window that overlooked the lower Mid-levels below. The view of the harbour and Central District far below was dazzling: the harbour seemed alive with the riding lights of steamers and junks and sampans. The evening was calm and sultry with still no evidence of this promised typhoon. Perhaps the typhoon had changed course and would not strike this part of the coast after all; Jericho could only hope so, remembering the devastation caused by last year's biggest storm...

Mrs Ride looked less like the rather elegant woman he'd encountered in Queens Road on Saturday, and much more like the drunken and forlorn creature he had met earlier on his first visit to the house. Her red hair was untidy again, and she seemed to have been drinking. Her face was still heavily made up, though, which covered most of the visible bruises and contusions she had suffered on Saturday.

'How are you feeling, Mrs Ride?' he asked solicitously, as she stood up to greet him in the study.

'I'm fine. I have a nurse to look after me, Doris Chow, although her main talent is her ability to hide all the booze in the house.' She smiled faintly. 'Is this follow-up visit a normal part of the Hong Kong Police service? Do you visit everyone who has had an accident? You must be extremely busy if you do...'

Jericho smiled. 'No, it's not a normal part of my job. But I was concerned about you.'

'Thank you,' she said, rather formally. 'It's nice to know that someone cares.' She looked with frank curiosity at his bruised neck. 'You look like you've been in the wars yourself, Inspector.'

He nodded resignedly. 'I have. I had a tussle with an armed burglar last night.'

'What an eventful life you lead,' she commented, without any trace of her usual irony.

Jericho cleared his throat as he came reluctantly to the point. 'Your accident on Saturday, Mrs Ride...'

She straightened her neck and looked him boldly in the eyes. 'I must apologize for my behaviour on Saturday. I was very rude to you, Inspector Jericho. I should have thanked you for your help.'

'Don't worry about it; you were certainly suffering from some residual shock.' He hesitated. 'But is there anything you want to tell me about the circumstances of the accident, Mrs Ride?'

She made a show of being puzzled, although Jericho was sure that she knew exactly what he meant. 'What sort of things do you mean?'

Jericho looked at her sympathetically. 'I mean: how did you happen to fall in front of that lorry?'

She made a casual gesture with her hand. 'Oh that...? I tripped because of my shoe. The stupid heel broke off. That's all there was to it...'

'Are you sure about that? I didn't notice that you had broken your heel.' In fact Jericho was certain that both her shoes had been intact.

Mrs Ride's voice hardened. 'Yes, I'm sure...'

Jericho could have made much more of this – he could have asked to see the shoe with the broken heel, for example – but he decided to let it pass for the moment. He had already learned enough to confirm his opinion that this woman had thrown herself deliberately in front of that Bedford lorry on Saturday. But it seemed she had thought better of it at the last moment, and had pulled back slightly, which gesture had saved her life in the end. Though whether her gesture had been due to an automatic instinct for survival reasserting itself against her will, or whether to a true change of heart about suicide, he could not be sure. 'Can I see your husband, Mrs Ride?'

'For what reason?' She seemed suddenly alarmed for the first time.

He relaxed his face with deliberate intent. 'It's nothing to do with your accident, if that's what's worrying you.'

She didn't seem completely reassured by that statement. 'I'm afraid you can't. Sebastian didn't come home last night; I don't know where he is. He left the house yesterday afternoon by taxi and said he had to do something important at the office. I assumed he was coming back in the evening since he hadn't taken his beloved Bugatti, but he didn't reappear as expected. Nor did he ring to tell me where he had gone.'

Jericho raised his eyebrows. 'Really? Does he do that often?'

She shrugged meaningfully. 'Often enough. My husband and I lead mostly separate lives these days, you see. His secretary should know where he is, though. She's *very* close to him, and keeps close tabs on him.'

'What's her name?'

'Miss Frances Leung. According to Sebastian, Miss Leung is a very accomplished woman. To me she seems more like some desiccated automaton machine, devoid of any real human feelings. I believe she is the daughter of a renowned Chinese doctor and an eccentric Austrian mother, which probably explains a lot about her character. I doubt Miss Leung is at work at this time, though; that would be too much even for a woman as dedicated to the company as her. But if you wanted to see her urgently, she lives in a flat in Leighton Road near the Eastern Hospital in Morrison Hill. An apartment block called Clementi Court, I believe; she has one of the flats on the top floor, the third.'

'I know that apartment building; it's close to where I live in Happy Valley. Do you think your husband could be there with her now?' Jericho asked delicately.

'*Who knows?* But I suspect not. I think Sebastian is probably with another woman entirely.' Gloria Ride gave him a practised if weary smile. 'He has lots of women in his life, you know. And one particular woman at the moment who seems to take up a lot of his time...'

Jericho wondered if, by this, she meant Faye Grantham. Ronnie Grantham certainly suspected that Faye had been having an affair with Sebastian Ride, and, as the cuckolded husband, he was probably right in this supposition. This affair also sounded like something very serious and committed, since it seemed to have been the critical event that had prompted Faye to ask Ronnie for a divorce. Faye was not the type of woman to ask for a divorce on a mere whim, so her feelings for this man must be intense and passionate. Jericho wondered now if he had discovered the reason for Gloria Ride's suicide attempt: *was her errant husband and his latest affair the reason...?*

*

In her baking hot prison, Edith Starling lay slumped on the concrete floor, half-asleep, and with barely the strength to move now. She reckoned that the day just gone was Monday the 30th of August, so this night had to be her seventh in captivity in this grim little makeshift dungeon. Hunger and weakness were now making her lightheaded so that she could barely stand now without feeling dizzy. In her present state she didn't think that she could last more than another day or so, even with that slow drip of water from the pipe on the wall to provide some relief from her constant thirst.

There was still enough light coming through the small gaps at the top of the wall to know when it was light outside, and when it was dark, like now. This was despite the fact that she had blocked the largest hole with one of her own silk stockings, an exercise in futility which had otherwise achieved nothing at all. The sun had set many hours ago so she thought it must now be the early hours of Tuesday morning. Soon it might start to get light again, though that made very little difference to her in her terrible situation.

No one was coming to save her...no one would find her in time.

She was going to die in this miserable oven of a room, and without even knowing who had done this evil thing to her.

She began to drift back into an uneasy sleep. But then she felt a sudden sharp prick in her arm and woke up in terror. The door of her cell was open and a little dawn light seeped in from outside. A hooded man was standing over her, with a hypodermic needle in his hand. 'I'm sorry, Edith. I thought you would be dead by now. I can't let this misery go on...'

Despite the hood over his face, she recognized the voice at once, and for the first time understood who had abducted her. But it was all too late for Edith Starling as she began to slip away into unconsciousness. She felt a great overwhelming darkness possess her, as if she was being sucked down into a black lake of pitch that had no bottom to it...

CHAPTER 25

Tuesday, 31st August 1937

'So where is Mr Ride?' Jericho asked politely.

His Eurasian secretary, Miss Frances Leung, was sitting at her office desk on the top floor of the Saunders Building in Queens Road Central, and looking thoroughly business-like. She was about forty, Jericho thought, but rather beautiful in a restrained and severe way. She exuded an air of quiet if humourless competence so Jericho was tempted to agree immediately with Gloria Ride's somewhat sour assessment of her as an automaton machine.

Miss Leung glanced out of the window behind her at the blue harbour, which was still basking in the usual fierce morning sunlight. 'There's still no sign of this typhoon, is there? Although I have heard by cable from our office in Manila that the city has taken a real battering, so this storm is real enough. I do hope Mr Ride will be all right...'

Jericho frowned. 'You don't mean that he's gone to Manila on the clipper, do you? If he has, his wife doesn't know anything about it.'

Miss Leung turned her face back to Jericho and gave him a wintry smile. 'There must be a million things that Mrs Ride doesn't know about her husband. But no, I don't mean that he's gone to Manila.'

'Then what *do* you mean, Miss Leung?' Jericho asked wearily. Getting information from this woman was as laborious as pulling teeth.

From her icy expression, Miss Leung clearly did not like his tone of voice. 'I mean that Mr Ride has gone out to one of the outlying islands for a little rest. Sometimes his business and personal problems get the better of him, and he needs to get away for some peace and quiet in a tranquil setting.'

'Which island?'

'Lamma Island, probably. Or it could be Cheung Chau. He didn't make it clear where he was going. The company owns a small beachfront cottage on both islands for the use of its directors. James Woo tended to use the one on Cheung Chau, while Mr Ride prefers the one on Lamma Island. But Mr Ride could be using the one on Cheung Chau now that Mr Woo is sadly deceased...'

Jericho sniffed suspiciously. 'Then you don't know exactly where your boss has gone either?' Lamma Island was a large but sparsely populated island to the southwest of Hong Kong Island. Cheung Chau - in Chinese, literally "Long Island" - was a smaller island shaped like a dumbbell further west of Lamma.

Miss Leung still didn't like his abrasive tone. 'I've told you. Mr Ride likes both places, but particularly Lamma Island. So that is where he is likely to be. There's no telephone or any other form of communication there, so I can't contact him directly, no matter which island he is on. The little house he uses on Lamma Island is near the eastern village of Rainbow Bay, but he likes to go hiking in the south part of the island where there are hardly any people, and to look out for the sea turtles that breed at Sham Wan...' Miss Leung finally gave him a smile of sorts. 'No, I don't understand the attraction of turtles either, except as ingredients for soup.'

Jericho had come here at nine o'clock in the morning because he had wanted to talk urgently with Sebastian Ride about his wife Gloria. The woman had seemed in a dangerously unstable state when he had talked with her yesterday evening so Jericho had wanted to warn Ride in case he didn't already understand the seriousness of his wife's situation. From the fact that he had gone off on his own for a few days' rest, it seemed that Ride did *not* *u*nderstand the situation. Or perhaps he simply didn't care...

The one thing that Jericho knew for sure was that Ride had not gone off to his island haunt in company with Faye Grantham; he had called Ronnie last night to talk about his likely divorce, and Ronnie had let him know that Faye was still living in their lavish apartment in Robinson Road, though they were now sleeping in different bedrooms. It seemed, though, that Ronnie was about to move out to a hotel, like the gentleman he was, until he could sort out more permanent accommodation for himself. From the dismal tone of Ronnie' voice, Jericho could hear that there seemed to be no way back for Ronnie and Faye, which was a great personal pity to him too.

Jericho also still wanted to talk with Ride discreetly about the death of James Woo, and the fact that they now had this witness, the boy thief Ah Yee, who claimed to have seen Woo involved in a fight with a Western man just before he had fallen to his death. Given Ah Yee's description of the second man, there had to be a slight possibility that it had been Sebastian Ride. Jericho was doing his best to put this business quickly to rest, but knew that he would have to check Ride's whereabouts for that Saturday morning in more detail. Hopefully the evidence would still stand this closer inspection and remove him from any suspicion. Jericho was fully aware just what a storm of protest would result if he tried to implicate Sebastian Ride in the events of James Woo's death without absolutely irrefutable evidence. The evidence of a young thief was scarcely enough, especially given that Ah Yee probably wasn't even the boy's real name...

Jericho returned his attention to the rigidly loyal Miss Frances Leung. 'Aren't you worried about your boss? Why would he go out to one of the outlying islands when there is a typhoon on its way? The storm is supposed to be here by Thursday from what I've heard, and it will certainly stop all the ferries between the islands.'

Miss Leung looked unimpressed by his argument. 'I'm confident that Mr Ride will ensure that he is back here before the typhoon lands on us. What is it that you want to speak to him about, anyway? It seems rather urgent from your manner.'

Given Miss Leung's rather barbed comment about Mrs Ride earlier, Jericho was not about to tell her his suspicions about Gloria Ride's likely suicidal inclinations. Nor did he really want to raise the matter of James Woo's death with her, since that would merely warn Ride that something was in the offing about it.

'I'm afraid I'm not at liberty to discuss it, Miss Leung. I have to speak to Mr Ride personally...'

'Then please call again tomorrow. I'm sure Mr Ride will be back by then,' Miss Leung said firmly, and then effectively dismissing him by getting back to her perusal of the company mail.

*

After Chief Inspector Jericho had departed, a worried Frances quickly abandoned her reading of the mail, and turned instead towards the window again, deep in thought. She had not been expecting the police to call here so soon, and for a moment had nearly panicked at the thought that Sebastian might have been identified by the police as the fleeing gunman on Sunday night. Sebastian had come to her top floor flat in Clementi Court in Leighton Road in the early hours of Monday morning after the disastrous events in Caine Road, and she had been hiding him there ever since. Fortunately she had no live-in servants so it had been a simple matter to give her visiting Amah and laundry boy a few days off.

Yet she had quickly realized that she would have to find a better place for Sebastian to hide until they could be sure that Ian Luff wasn't planning to go the police. Frances doubted if Luff would do such a thing, even if he had understood from the events in Caine Road that Sebastian had been intending to shoot him. But it was better to be safe than sorry, while they waited to see what happened next. Hopefully Luff didn't even know that much, though - only that the planned meeting at the Woo mansion in Caine Road had gone disastrously wrong because of a patrolling policeman.

Luff seemed to have disappeared too since Sunday night: he had either gone into hiding himself, or else was simply lying low while he decided what to do next. The one ace in their hand was Ian Luff's homosexuality: that would make him very reluctant to go to the police and accuse Sebastian, either of involvement in the death of James Woo, or in the attack on that policeman on Sunday night. Luff must know that he could lose everything if he chose to make a direct accusation to the police against somebody as important as Sebastian, for their counter accusations about Luff's private life would be equally vicious.

Frances was reassured from the informal nature of Inspector Jericho's visit today that none of these critical possibilities had happened yet: Sebastian had clearly *not* been identified as the gunman on Sunday night, while Ian Luff must also have maintained his silence for the moment. Otherwise there would have been whole squads of policemen descending on this office today, rather than just one tired-looking middle-aged police inspector.

She wondered what Jericho had really wanted: *could it be something to do with the supposed attempted suicide by Gloria Ride last Saturday?* That seemed the likeliest reason for Jericho's visit and for his tentative manner. She was pleased that she had come up with that inspired story about Sebastian visiting one of the outlying islands: Jericho would not be able to check that easily, especially not when there was a typhoon on the way. She thought he had believed her story anyway, so would probably simply wait for Sebastian to return from his supposed jaunt to the islands.

Yet there was another troubling possibility: *could a new witness have come forward to the death of James Woo?* Yet Frances was confident they could fight off the claims of any Chinese witness who dared to come forward. Either buy them off, or warn them off. She was sure of one thing: that rickshaw coolie who had taken Sebastian to Tai Ping Shan that day certainly wasn't going to come back from where he was...

Frances thought back with more satisfaction to the last two nights, and having Sebastian sharing her bed for the first time. He was a wonderful and considerate lover, as she'd always known he would be, bringing her to a level of physical pleasure that she had rarely known. And she had surprised him too in return, she knew; for she understood the secrets of how to pleasure a man when she wished. Sebastian had clearly enjoyed that unexpected side to her. But then most men wanted their women to be like that, didn't they? A beautiful virginal queen in public, and a playful erotic whore in private...

Yet, despite his skill as a lover, there was a disturbing weakness in Sebastian's own character that she had never noticed before, a tendency for regret and self-recrimination. For the moment, and despite the sacrifice of her own pleasure after so many years of waiting for his recognition of her as a woman, she had told Sebastian that he must find a better hiding place until all the fuss died down. So she had taken him in her car to the company flat in Bowen Road at first light this morning; very few people outside the company knew of the existence of that apartment. With Sebastian safely out of the way, Frances could then concentrate on resolving this problem.

But one thing remained clear to her: they still had to eliminate Ian Luff permanently...*there was no other way*...

*

After his unsatisfactory meeting with Ride's secretary, Paul Jericho decided in a fit of desperation that he would go and have a look at the disused quarry site in Shaukeiwan in person. Even though a police team had already searched the place unsuccessfully for any sign of Edith Starling, yet he found that he couldn't let the matter lie. He had even talked to the two young constables who had searched there, who both swore they had searched the whole quarry, and also the disused buildings. But Jericho still wondered if they might have missed something, for they had only been there fifteen minutes in total according to their daily report log.

If, as seemed possible, Edith's abductor really was someone from Government House who worked with her closely, then the quarry at Shaukeiwan still had to be the likeliest place that this person would have taken Edith, either to imprison her, or - more likely perhaps - to murder her. A large number of people from Government House had visited this quarry only the day before Edith's abduction, so one of those people could be the guilty party. It would explain the presence of the gravel left by the man's boot-print below the passenger seat of Edith's little black Austin...

The fate of Edith Starling was still like an open sore in Paul Jericho's mind and he was determined to have one last try at finding her before he finally gave up. She'd been missing a whole week now so most people had already given up any hope of finding her alive. Yet Paul Jericho knew enough about Edith's character – her intelligence, her resourcefulness, her feisty spirit – to believe that she might somehow have survived against all the odds.

It was an extremely long shot to try the quarry again when it had already been searched. But there was nothing else that he could think of to do so, after leaving Saunders House, he went to his own car parked in Pedder Street, jerked the engine into life with the starter handle, and followed Des Voeux Road leading west...

In fifteen minutes he had reached Shaukeiwan. The traffic seemed lighter than usual for some reason, while the weather was still sultry and calm. He was a hundred yards past the outlying buildings of Shaukeiwan, when he saw the Saunders-Woo Quarry just ahead on his right. He turned in through the unmanned entrance gate and parked his Austin on an area of waste ground near the former quarry offices. The offices were a substantial building in their own right: an elevated steel-framed building clad in corrugated iron and glazed panels, with an open ground floor below for parking site vehicles. The quarry was much larger than he had expected, but Jericho could still see why it wouldn't take too long to search it for a body, for it consisted of a great open expanse of rubble backed by a perimeter of man-made cliffs behind. The rubble was generally too small in size to conceal a body, so even a quick inspection of the main quarry area convinced him that Edith's body could not have been left here. The disused office building seemed like the only possibility since there were no other building structures between the quarry and the sea apart from an overhead iron gantry bridge that crossed over the coastal road and connected the plant to an old timber jetty for the loading of rock onto ships and barges.

So Jericho climbed the external steel stairs up to the office floor and spent the next hour going through the office building in meticulous detail. The interior had been stripped of most of its furnishings so the search was easier than for a building full of cupboards and storage units and equipment. Yet after an exhausting sixty minutes spent in the hot dusty interior of the building, Jericho finally gave up, sure that Edith could not be here.

Outside, it was noon by this time, and the sun, standing almost vertically in the burnished sky, was beating down fiercely on the quarry, making it seem like a hot and particularly hellish corner of the Sahara Desert. Jericho took off his police cap for a moment and ran a disappointed hand roughly through his hair, which was damp with sweat. He mopped his wet brow with a soiled handkerchief before replacing his cap and continuing with his search.

Jericho wandered further into the quarry and noticed that there was a manmade canyon of sorts leading off from the main quarry area. This little canyon was quite invisible from the quarry offices, so he had to wonder if the two police constables who had searched the quarry yesterday had even noticed this narrow defile. Jericho did not have any great expectations from this little gap in the wall of cliffs but followed it anyway. Within twenty yards, the defile turned sharply through ninety degrees and led to another small complex of buildings. Jericho found this encouraging, for the two constables who had searched here had certainly never mentioned anything about a second set of buildings. The largest of these buildings was a substantial single-storied building sixty feet long, with blockwork walls and a flat concrete roof. It looked like a military bunker, and was surrounded by an earth bund, so he deduced that this must be a store for dangerous materials – explosives or inflammable chemicals. The main door was unlocked and he forced its rusting hinges open, stepping into an interior even dustier and hotter than the quarry offices. There was a small cubicle of an office near the entrance, then the rest of the space was divided up into concrete pens. Jericho checked all of the pens as he went along the central corridor. One of the pens still contained some heavy rock-breaking tools – drills and sledgehammers and picks. Finally, at the end of the corridor, he came to a full height interior wall with a substantial steel-plated door set in the middle of it, which was apparently locked. His excitement was increasing now for this unknown room beyond seemed like a very suitable place to keep someone prisoner...

He went and fetched a sledgehammer, and returned to try and batter the door down. But it was made from tempered steel plate half an inch thick, so he made little impression on it after five minutes of effort. This was more than he could say for himself, though, for his hands were blistered by now, and his uniform lathered with sweat. He decided reluctantly to give up; this door didn't look like it had been opened any time recently. And there was no sound coming from the other side of it to suggest that a woman might be imprisoned there. If Edith was in there and still alive, she would have certainly responded to that attempt to batter down the door to her prison.

He walked back to the main door of the building and was about to leave the area by the same little defile in the rocks that had brought him here, when something made him turn back and walk around the perimeter of the building, between the blank block walls and the surrounding earth bund. He reached the rear of the building, a blank featureless wall which he thought must be the back wall of that room he had just been trying to break into.

At first he saw nothing of interest, but then noticed a sliver of white material poking out through a small gap between the top of the blockwork and the roof slab. His heart began to race as he recognized the material as silk – *part of a lady's stocking...*

In a second he had raced back inside the building to the tool room where he searched for something more suitable to open that door at the end. He found a sturdy metal spike with a flattened end that he thought might work as a jemmy to force the door open. He took this heavy piece of metal with him, jammed the sharper end into the small gap next to the lock, then hit the end with the sledgehammer. The lock soon yielded to this vicious treatment and he was able to force the damaged door open.

He saw at once, with a surge of satisfaction, that he had found the right place...

Yet his self-congratulation was short-lived for he could see that Edith was lying on the floor dressed only in her underwear, and that her pale drawn face had the look of death about it. He cursed himself for not coming here sooner to check this place personally; he should have had the wits to come to come here on Saturday, immediately after Ronnie had told him about the official government visit to this place.

He bent down to examine her body, his mind in turmoil. He checked for any sign of a pulse in her wrist, and for any sign of breathing, but could detect nothing. She was still warm, but then the room was like an oven, and probably warmer than normal human body temperature anyway. Outside, he could hear the wind picking up for the first time and rattling some loose gutter on the roof, heralding the approach of this new and fearsome typhoon. But it was a typhoon that poor Edith Starling was never destined to see.

But then, in a thin beam of sunlight from outside, he saw a pulse beat faintly in her eyelid...

CHAPTER 26

Wednesday, 1st September 1937

Paul Jericho stood in a corridor on the top floor of St Paul's Hospital in Morrison Hill, looking out at the view of nearby Happy Valley and its backdrop of green forested mountains. He lived only a few minutes' walk from the hospital so had come here at first light this morning to see how Edith was faring. She was still alive at least, although that wasn't saying much: the outlook for her seemed bleak indeed since she had apparently been given a huge dose of morphine by somebody...

Jericho had brought a comatose Edith here in his own car yesterday afternoon directly from the quarry, and she had been in emergency care here ever since. Yet despite that care, she had fallen into an even deeper coma, one so deep that the doctors doubted she would ever wake from it. Jericho had gone on to Wanchai Police Station after that and torn a vicious strip off the two young constables who had made the earlier search of the quarry at Shaukeiwan; by their negligence they had probably been the cause of Edith's likely death. The two constables had been to the quarry on Monday, when Edith might have still been in a recoverable physical condition. But sometime between the original police search and Jericho's visit at noon yesterday, her abductor had clearly returned and pumped her full of morphine.

But why had he done that? It seemed that the man had been squeamish about killing her directly, or else wanted to leave as few clues behind as possible, for it looked as if he had simply imprisoned Edith in that room for the best part of a week, presumably hoping that heat and thirst would kill her. But he'd had to change that plan for some reason: perhaps he had heard that the police had been searching there, so had decided he couldn't simply afford to wait for Edith to die. Or else the man knew that a team of engineering surveyors was due to visit the quarry this week to begin a full topographical survey, as part of the plan to use the old quarry as a site for social housing. That latter reason seemed more likely somehow, but made it even clearer that Edith's abductor had to be somebody at Government House who was aware of that planned visit by the survey team.

Jericho didn't know why he had brought Edith to this particular hospital, except that it was close to his home in Happy Valley, and he therefore knew it well. But it was probably an inspired choice anyway, for he was sure that Edith would get the best possible care here, and have the greatest chance of survival. The hospital was known among local people as the "French Hospital", perhaps because it had grown out of the caring activities undertaken by the Sisters of the Roman Catholic Christian order St. Paul de Chartres for the poor and underprivileged of Wanchai and Happy Valley. So its origins went right back to the mid-nineteenth century after this Christian order had first established itself here in the then new British crown colony of Hong Kong...

Jericho looked up suddenly from his painful introspection and saw Eric Formby walking towards him, dressed in a white coat and looking much more like a real doctor than usual.

'What are *you* doing here?' Jericho asked him curiously, for it was still only seven in the morning.

Formby also looked even more like Robert Donat than usual, and even sounded just like that mellifluous actor today. Jericho suddenly felt improbably as if he was in a scene from *The Thirty-Nine Steps*. 'I do two free evening clinics a week here at St Paul's Hospital,' Formby said with a show of reluctance, 'and I help out the resident surgeon during the day when I have the time. Seems like the least I can do, and gives me the chance to do some proper doctoring, rather than just playing with corpses.'

'That probably explains why you never arrive on time at a crime scene.' Jericho's voice was cool, but secretly he was impressed that Formby should be doing such a thing without any public acknowledgement.

Formby laughed. 'It probably does.' His smile faded quickly, though. 'I've just been to see the young woman you brought in yesterday. I have some experience of dealing with overdoses of opiates, you see, so her attending doctor asked me to look at her.'

'What are her chances?'

Formby looked suddenly downcast. 'I have to say they are very poor. To be honest, I don't know how she's still alive. I think she must have been given a dose of more than two hundred milligrams. The textbooks say that an amount of morphine like that should kill a horse never mind a woman. But perhaps her imprisonment and starvation had slowed down her metabolism to such an extent that her body was slow to absorb all of the morphine into her organs and brain...'

'I would have thought that starvation and thirst would make her body even less able to cope with a dose of morphine, not more,' Jericho said.

Formby shrugged. 'Yes, perhaps I would have said the same thing before, yet Miss Edith Starling seems to be defying all conventional medical wisdom at the moment...'

*

Jericho was leaving the building a few minutes later when he encountered Michael Yip in the entrance lobby of the hospital.

Michael Yip's handsome face looked troubled. 'I heard that you have found Edith, Inspector Jericho. How is she? Can I see her?'

Jericho was still not sure how much to trust this man. Although it seemed unlikely, this man could still be the person who had abducted Edith and imprisoned her. Perhaps Yip knew of the existence of the disused quarry at Shaukeiwan for other reasons than its possible designated use for social housing. Or he might even be aware of that anyway, for Jericho knew that Yip was a very well-connected man in Hong Kong who even got regular invites to Government House official functions. Although he was no friend of the colonial government, the authorities here had nevertheless tried to maintain a reasonable working relationship with him, perhaps in an effort to make some positive use of his considerable influence among the Hong Kong masses.

'I'm afraid I can't allow you to see her,' Jericho apologized politely. 'She's under police guard for her safety. In any case, she is in a deep coma, so would not be aware of your presence even if you were allowed in.'

Yip swallowed uncomfortably, clearly emotional. Or he might just be a very accomplished actor, Jericho decided uncharitably.

'I see,' Yip said dismally. 'Then I won't waste any more of your time, Inspector...'

*

Afterwards Paul Jericho did not drive on to Wanchai Police Station as he had originally planned, but carried on along Hennessy Road and then Queensway before turning his Austin up the steep incline of Garden Road leading up to the Mid-levels. It was a route that his wife Susan had taken every day in this same car during term time. He could still feel her presence is this battered old Austin somehow, could imagine her sitting at his side in the narrow seat, with that playful smile on her lips. Getting through the days without her was still a real challenge to him, but his police work, and the busy schedule it entailed, had still been the best means he had of escaping from the quiet melancholy of his life.

Or at least until recently anyway, for he now seemed to have a new woman in his life...

He realized with some dismay that he had been most remiss in not going back to see Maggie since Sunday, but hoped that she would understand how busy he was. The last thing he wanted now was to lose

Maggie Yiu from his life, for she was the one hope of bringing some sweetness and normality back to his jaded existence...

Jericho had decided that Sebastian Ride must certainly have returned from his visit to the outlying islands by now, so was determined to confront him with the evidence of the new witness Ah Yee concerning the death of James Woo, and to see what the man's reaction might be to it.

Yet his more pressing reason for his early morning visit to Conduit Road was to warn Ride about the suicidal intentions of his wife; even if Ride was intending to leave her eventually for a younger woman, the man still owed a duty of care to Gloria. In his own stubborn way, Paul Jericho had become determined to save Gloria Ride from herself. He had failed to save the life of his own wife Susan, and now it looked like he had failed to save the life of her best friend Edith Starling too. So Gloria Ride had become doubly important to him now, a way of fighting back against these past failures...

He took the now familiar route to the sprawling three-storey mansion at the end of Conduit Road, then turned up the steep concrete drive and parked the little Austin in the spare bay at the top. The blue Bugatti sports car was still there in the next bay, as on Monday.

After knocking at the front door, Jericho took the time to turn his head and admire the front terrace and the view beyond. Beyond the marble planters filled with strelitzia and canna lilies, and the lily pond with its towering fountain, the harbour far below was abuzz with steamers and junks. Even this early in the day, Jericho could even hear a hum of activity from the busy streets of Central District below, the sound of industrious people making money, and other, perhaps less industrious, people spending it. He saw, though, that the sky above the harbour was finally clouding over and the wind beginning to gather strength. Despite the gusting wind, though, it seemed hotter than ever, even this high up on the side of the Peak.

There was a distinct feeling of foreboding in the air as the island waited for this approaching typhoon. The latest forecast was that the storm might be of record severity, and that its epicentre might pass within only a few miles of Hong Kong. So, all over the colony, people were preparing for the worst, battening down their possessions and boarding up their property as best they could, for no one really knew what to expect from this approaching monster...

Jericho's knock at the front door was finally answered by an elderly houseboy. But the man merely looked blank when Jericho asked to see Mr Ride. 'Master not here,' he said doubtfully.

A severe-looking Chinese woman appeared behind the houseboy, and Jericho recognized her as Gloria Ride's live-in nurse, Doris Chow. 'Can I speak to your mistress?' he asked her. 'I know it's early...' – it was still not yet eight o'clock in the morning – 'but it is urgent.'

The woman looked worried. 'You policeman, right?'

'Yes,' he confirmed. 'What's the matter?'

Doris Chow bit her lip anxiously. 'Missie has locked door to her rooms. I can't get in. She been there more than one hour. I very worried. Should I break door down? Master not here.'

Jericho didn't delay any further but marched into the house. 'Show me where the locked door is.'

Doris Chow turned and ran up the stairs with Jericho in her wake. She passed the first floor and took the next flight of stairs at a run too, despite her age. On the top floor, Jericho followed her along a passageway, all marble and gilt furnishings, to a decorative white-and-gold door at the end. 'This Missie's private rooms.' She knocked on the door, then jerked at the handle. 'Locked from inside. Can't open.'

Jericho told Doris and the other servants who had followed them to stand aside while he dealt with the door. He took a run at it with his shoulder, and the door, despite its heavy teak frame, splintered at the lock and opened.

Jericho ran inside and saw that the door gave entry to a private suite of rooms: bedroom, dressing room and bathroom. The bathroom door was closed, but he opened it anyway, after only the briefest of knocks.

He stopped in his tracks at what he found behind the door: the white face of Gloria Ride lying naked in a bath of scarlet. One of her wrists was hanging over the edge of the art deco bathtub, dripping blood onto the terrazzo tiles. Yet he could see from the movement of her eyes that she was still conscious...*just*...

Jericho turned to Doris Chow. 'Call for an ambulance...!' Doris had not moved, her jaw hanging in shock at the sight of her mistress bleeding to death in her bath.

'*Now*...!' Jericho ordered her...

*

Six hours later, in the Tung Wah hospital this time, Jericho sat at Gloria Ride's bedside and studied her sleeping face. He had the wry thought that he seemed to be developing some natural affinity for Hong Kong's hospitals, and also for trying to save the lives of women in deep distress. Perhaps he *was* turning into some sort of white knight after all, as Gloria Ride herself had claimed...

He felt some undoubted satisfaction this time, for his prompt action had certainly saved *this* woman's life. He had soon discovered up in the house in Conduit Road that Doris Chow knew no more about dealing with real medical emergencies than Mickey Mouse, and that she was no more than a glorified guard whose sole duty was to keep Gloria away from the booze. But Jericho himself knew enough about tying makeshift tourniquets to stop most of the blood flow from Gloria's wrists and to limit her further blood loss. Yet she had still lost a dreadful amount of blood already, so it had been a close-fought race in the hospital to save her life. She had fortunately only cut the radial artery in one wrist, and the cuts had not been deep enough to reach the ulnar artery in either wrist, otherwise the outcome would certainly have been fatal, despite Jericho's frantic ministrations at the house, and the surgeon's later skill in the hospital in repairing the damaged radial artery.

The elderly Scottish surgeon who had treated her and repaired her wrist injuries, Mr Park, had told Jericho that she might wake up sooner rather than later, for she had been given several pints of transfused blood to replace that lost, and was now making a good recovery. So Jericho had therefore returned to the hospital from Wanchai Police Station in late afternoon and elected to wait in her private room for a while in the hope that he might be able to talk with her. From his seat by Gloria's bedside, Jericho could see the Mid-levels and the Peak through the hospital window, the green flanks of which were now stirring and shaking in the rising wind. Angry looking clouds were racing across the sky, which now seemed like some churning cauldron of liquid being heated over an open fire.

The surgeon's words proved prophetic for Gloria's eyes suddenly flickered open within a few minutes of Jericho's return. She gazed at him uncomprehendingly for a moment, before the full memory of what had happened suddenly returned to her.

She let out a stifled sob of grief. 'How did I get here?'

Jericho kept his voice neutral and matter-of-fact. 'I happened to call at your house early this morning to check on your situation. Your servants were worried because you had locked the door to your private bedroom. So I'm afraid I broke the door down and brought you here to the Tung Wah Hospital again.'

Gloria examined the bandages on her wrists with an embarrassed sigh. 'I am becoming a regular customer here. I should get a season ticket,' she added, with a note of bitter humour in her voice. 'Why do you keep trying to save my life?'

Jericho kept his face expressionless. 'And why do you keep trying to end it when you have so much to live for? You're still a young and attractive woman. What could be so bad that it would drive you to take your own life?'

Gloria was silent, merely staring at him with haunted eyes.

'Is it your husband's behaviour that has driven you to this? The affairs that you told me about...? Why don't you just divorce him? There are plenty of other fish in the sea for a woman like you, Mrs Ride.'

She looked at him with surprise.

'I lost my own wife in a road accident earlier this year, and the grief of that nearly destroyed me,' Jericho admitted. 'So the thought of a woman killing herself for no good reason at all is a difficult one for me to accept.'

Gloria seemed suddenly distraught. 'But I love my husband just as much as you obviously loved your wife. So if he left me, it would cause me just as much grief as you've suffered. Perhaps even more, because at least your wife didn't choose to leave you; it was just an accident of fate that separated you, not a betrayal by the one person whom you love most in the world.'

Her emotions sounded raw and genuine, yet Jericho suddenly wondered if her husband's infidelity was the only reason for her seeming despair. 'Do you know anything about the death of James Woo, Mrs Ride? I think your husband lied about that; I think he was there with James Woo on that balcony when he died...'

Gloria shrunk back in horror. 'No, that isn't true!'

Yet Jericho was suddenly convinced that it *was* true, and that Gloria Ride was well aware of the fact. She was still clearly loyal to her husband, despite everything he had done to her. 'Do you really not know where your husband is? His secretary says he's probably staying out at a company beach cottage on Lamma Island.'

'Well that just proves that Miss Leung doesn't know everything after all. Sebastian likes Lamma Island, but would certainly not go out there with a typhoon approaching Hong Kong. He wouldn't be that foolish.' Her voice rose in pain. 'I think something bad might have happened to him. You have to try and find him, Inspector. I think he might need saving just as much as me...'

Jericho thought the simple truth might be that Sebastian Ride had already left his wife for another woman without even telling her. Yet he didn't say such a brutal thing, for fear of causing Gloria Ride even more heartache. But if Ride *had* gone off with some other woman, then it certainly wasn't Faye Grantham, for she was still at home in the Grantham apartment in Robinson Road.

Therefore perhaps Gloria Ride was right to worry about her husband after all...

CHAPTER 27

Thursday, 2nd September 1937

At nine o'clock in the morning, Paul Jericho stood in Miss Frances Leung's office on the top floor of the Saunders Building in Queens Road Central. He had not been to bed last night but had worked through the night on checking that the Wanchai district and its busy waterfront were battened down and prepared for the approaching storm as well as they could be...

The night had already been a wild and fearsome one, whipping the harbour into waves ten or twelve feet high, and already tearing some ships from their moorings. But much worse was expected today: the Hong Kong Observatory was claiming that wind gust speeds approaching *two hundred miles an hour* might even occur; Jericho had never heard of such a devastating wind speed before. The hurricane signal had been hoisted a few hours previously, and the centre of the typhoon was expected to pass only about ten miles to the south-southwest of Hong Kong Island sometime this afternoon or evening. Now, in early morning, the wind was beginning to moan eerily like a banshee, and the sky was black and ominous. The barometric pressure had been falling like a stone since midnight. If it kept falling like this, then Jericho knew that they really were in for something truly frightening today...

He had half-expected that Miss Leung would not be at work today, for the office buildings of Central District were eerily empty this morning, with most people sensibly staying at home as the government had suggested. Yet Miss Frances Leung was clearly made of sterner stuff than most and did not seem overwhelmed by the mayhem going on outside her office window, although the glass had been boarded up as a precaution therefore she was spared at least from seeing the foaming water of the harbour and the groaning vessels straining at their moorings. She was still looking thoroughly business-like in her smart woman's suit, although she had her hair worn down today which made her look younger than he remembered from two days ago. She was going to have to tie that hair up again, though, when she ventured outside, Jericho thought, for the force of the wind was already enough to lift heavy iron litter bins in the air and send them flying down the street like oversized cannonballs.

'Have you still received no word from Mr Ride, Miss Leung?' he asked, getting swiftly to the point after only a brief greeting. 'You told me he would be back from Lamma Island by now.'

Miss Leung seemed unperturbed. 'Perhaps he misjudged things after all, and didn't get away before the ferries stopped,' she said placidly.

'You don't seem very worried about him, Miss Leung. But I'm afraid I still need to speak to him urgently.'

'Why?' Miss Leung raised her perfectly shaped eyebrows. 'You've still not explained what is so urgent about this.'

Jericho hesitated, not sure if he should tell her. 'His wife tried to kill herself yesterday. In fact it's probably her second attempt to do so in four days.'

'Ah, I see.' Miss Leung's iron composure remained, despite the note of apparent sympathy in her voice. 'Well, I can understand now why you want to speak to Mr Ride so urgently. I assume, from the fact that you used the word "tried", that Mrs Ride is still alive and well?'

Jericho made a wry face. 'Not exactly well. But she is still alive, certainly. In fact, despite her sad situation, she seems more worried about her husband than she does about herself.'

'As any good wife should,' Miss Leung said flatly. 'But why would she think that Mr Ride is in any danger?'

'That I don't know, Miss Leung. But I intend to find out,' Jericho stated bluntly. He looked at her sitting demurely at her desk. 'And I would suggest, Miss Leung, that you go home right now. It isn't really safe to travel now, but it will be even more dangerous by this afternoon. You must remember the biggest typhoon of last year – on August the seventeenth. That one was bad enough. But this one today will be a hundred times worse in terms of the damage it will cause.'

Miss Leung was unmoved. 'So I have heard. That's why I intend to stay here in the office until the storm passes.'

'You might be here all night then, and perhaps most of tomorrow too, before the hurricane signal comes down,' he warned her.

She shuffled some papers and placed them in her out tray. 'Then so be it. I will at least get a lot of work done...'

*

After Inspector Jericho had left, Frances got up from her chair and lit herself a cigarette...

It was a great pity about Gloria Ride's survival; her death by suicide would have solved a lot of their problems in one fell swoop. Yet Frances told herself that all their problems were still entirely manageable provided they could deal with Ian Luff. Given Sebastian's bungling attempt to kill the man, she had decided that she would have to look at other means of getting rid of the man after all, since Sebastian seemed so unreliable in this respect.

But where was Sebastian now...?

The truth was that she really didn't have a clue where Sebastian had got to, for she had been to the company flat in Bowen Road early this morning and found him gone. So it seemed he must have found a new refuge of his own devising somewhere. She was worried now what Sebastian might be planning to do next. It occurred to her, given his uncertain mood after that debacle in Caine Road on Sunday, that he might even give himself up to the police and confess everything.

But another part of her was hoping to see some evidence of the old steel in his character. He still had the Colt Detective Special, of course, so perhaps he was still intending to go after Ian Luff with it, and to do the job properly this time.

She could only hope so...

*

At ten o'clock, Jericho walked into the public lobby of Wanchai Police Station where he was quickly approached by an oddly apprehensive-looking Constable Gary Ho...

It made Jericho remember with irritation that he still had no personal driver yet to replace Constable Ho, and would probably have to continue driving himself for a few weeks more. Yet today his little Austin had been more than just an embarrassment; in a typhoon like this it was a death trap. Even the short drive from Central District back to Wanchai had been a nightmare, and Jericho had been in constant terror that his little Austin was going to be flipped into the air by the force of the wind. Yet he had finally made it back in one piece to Wanchai after slowing the car to a dead crawl in second gear.

Along the Wanchai quayside, all the usual array of ferries and harbour vessels had been moved back into deeper anchorages with the massed ranks of ocean-going vessels, partly to protect the vessels themselves, but also to protect the jetty walls and pilings from damage. Salt spray was being lifted high into the air by the tremendous force of the wind and waves, and drenching the fine new facade of the police station even up to the top floor. The sea was roaring and hissing in a white fury, while the wind created an eerie cacophony of noise of its own.

Once inside the main ground floor corridor of the station, Constable Ho explained himself in a whisper. 'Sir, I have apprehended a member of the Kao Ki-kan triad who I believe might be a very useful witness. There was a street fight last night in Lockhart Road between rival triad members. Two men were stabbed and are in hospital, while two others escaped. But I managed to arrest one, a man called Huang Lee.'

'Well done, Constable,' Jericho commended him with genuine satisfaction. 'Has the man been formally questioned and charged yet?'

'No, sir, not yet.' Ho still seemed peculiarly uneasy.

'I don't have time to do it today myself,' Jericho apologized. 'Can you ask Sergeant Dorling to carry out the interrogation?'

'Sergeant Dorling is out on typhoon duty, like most of the station.' Ho hesitated. 'In any case, this man Huang Lee wants to speak only to you, sir. I mean *alone*...'

'That's against regulations, Constable, as you well know,' Jericho chided him, surprised that a man like Gary Ho should suggest a thing. The only policemen who carried out private interviews were invariably looking for some sort of payola in return for releasing their suspects.

Ho stood his ground. 'I know it's against regulations, sir. But I would still suggest that you talk to this man alone, even if only for five minutes. He says he will only talk to you, because he knows you are the only honest English policeman in this station...'

Jericho was intrigued enough by now to agree to this, provided he could get it over with quickly. In another minute he was inside Interview Room Number Two, sitting across the table from the arrested man Huang Lee. Jericho remembered this was the same room where he had interviewed Maggie Yiu over three weeks ago. That seemed like a long time ago now, yet he was distressingly aware that they had made little real progress in catching the murderer of the three women in the intervening period. Other matters seemed to have conspired to take his attention away from that case.

Today's interviewee Huang Lee certainly bore no resemblance to the beautiful Maggie in any way. Instead he was a scarred and ugly rogue of thirty or thirty-five, who looked extremely dangerous...

*

Jericho's private conversation took rather more than five minutes – more like fifteen – yet it was still over remarkably quickly. When he stepped outside Interview Room Number Two into the corridor again, Constable Ho was standing waiting for him, breathless with anticipation.

'Did he tell you anything interesting, sir?' Ho asked tentatively.

'*Interesting?* Yes, you could say that.' Jericho was still in a state of shock, for Huang Lee had offered to give him the name of a senior policeman on the payroll of the Kao Ki-kan in return for a free passage out of Hong Kong. He had claimed that this corrupt policeman had identified Ricky Sun as a police informer, and had then led Sun deliberately into the trap where he had subsequently been murdered. Yet even without the name of this corrupt policeman, Huang Lee's description of the man's activities, and the circumstances of how the triad had recruited him, pointed Jericho to only one person...*George Dorling...*

Jericho decided he must keep this information to himself until he could decide whether it might be true or not. Yet something told him that it was true since Huang Lee had provided one more convincing detail: that the corrupt foreign devil policeman met his triad contacts regularly in a back room *at the Tin Hau Hotel...*

That detail seemed to confirm the authenticity of this information. It did also explain so much about the lack of progress of the investigation into the murders of the three bargirls. It even seemed to confirm Jericho's most recent theory that the Kao Ki-kan might have murdered these three girls after all, for reasons of their own. But it also suggested that George Dorling had been doing his best afterwards to send the police investigation off into an entirely different direction. Jericho suddenly remembered all the time and energy that Dorling had invested into searching for a number of Western seamen with a history of violence, though there was not the slightest fact linking any of these men to the murdered women. And there was also Dorling's apparent reluctance to believe that the murders of Freddie Ling and Marco da Silva were linked directly to those of the women, even though Ling and Da Silva had certainly employed the three women as escorts.

The truly galling thing was that cocky and patronising Inspector Kevin Ball might be proved entirely right in suspecting a corrupt officer at Wanchai Police Station, while he - gullible and deluded Paul Jericho - had ignored all the evidence of it and continued to believe in the probity of his team.

But could George have done something even worse than betraying Ricky Sun? Could he have been involved in the murder of some of those women directly? For it now occurred to Jericho with deepening dismay that George Dorling had one particular physical attribute that was very worrying: *he possessed a pair of very intense blue eyes...*

A deeply troubled Paul Jericho pulled Ho aside. 'Keep the man in custody, and we'll take an official statement from him once the typhoon has passed and things are back to normal. Don't mention my private meeting with this man to anyone, Constable – is that clear?'

Constable Ho gulped. 'Yes, sir...'

*

Jericho had barely finished with Gary Ho when Superintendent Charlie Hebdon appeared in the corridor with all the restraint of a Pamplona bull and led him into a quiet corner. 'I need you back up in Government House in half an hour to explain to all the senior bods up there what is going on. You found that missing young lady two days ago – and you deserve full credit for that, Paul – but now they are getting extremely nervous up at Government House about this. So you have to make an appearance and give them some sort of explanation.'

'*Explanation?* I don't have any bloody explanation. Edith Starling is in a coma still and can't tell us who abducted her, or why.' Even this far inside the building, Jericho could still hear the screeching and howling of the wind outside. 'And why now? I could kill myself trying to drive up to Government House in this storm.'

'Nonsense , man. You won't be killed by a bit of wind. And I've promised them you'll be there, so just do it...'

Jericho would still have liked to refuse but could see that Hebdon wasn't going to yield. But the one thing he certainly wasn't going to do was to use his own lightweight Austin again today, which was suicidal in this weather. He marched to the front desk where Thomas Sung was standing in for the regular desk sergeant who was, like almost everybody else in the station, out on the streets dealing with emergencies created by the typhoon.

'I'm afraid all the squad cars are out on duty, sir, and I have no drivers free anyway,' Sung said apologetically. But then his eyes brightened as he had a thought. 'But there is a Morris Fourteen still available. It's got a smashed headlight, which is why it's not been taken out. But it's serviceable enough in daylight, if you drive it yourself, sir.'

'I'll take it,' Jericho confirmed laconically. Within five minutes he was driving the Morris up the incline of Garden Road towards Government House. The leaves of the tall palms and tropical figs along the roadside were being shredded into a green soup by the force of the wind, and the rain was falling in a deluge that resembled the bottom of Niagara Falls. Jericho could not believe the frightening power of this storm, which seemed capable of toppling buildings and mountains, never mind trees. Even a car as heavy as the Morris was bucked about by the fierce wind like a toy. Yet, chugging along in second gear through the cascades of water washing across the road, he made it finally in one piece to Upper Albert Road, and was admitted just before eleven o'clock through the main entrance gate of Government House with much less fuss than on his previous visits.

The first person he met inside the Entrance Hall of the building was Ronnie Grantham.

'How are you, Ronnie?' Jericho asked, shaking off his soaking cap, and taking off the raincoat that he had worn to protect his uniform.

Ronnie looked deeply troubled. 'This is quite a storm, isn't it?' he said. 'Certainly the biggest one that I can remember. We had no electricity in the Hong Kong Hotel this morning...'

'Is that where you've moved to?' Jericho asked uneasily. 'You could come and stay with me, you know.'

Ronnie patted him affectionately on the shoulder. 'Wouldn't dream of imposing on you, old man. In any case, it's a lot more convenient being just a short walk from Government House.' Ronnie nodded towards the door of the drawing room. 'I'm afraid they're arranging the Spanish Inquisition for you in there. Even the Governor might show his face, because of the security concerns surrounding Edith's disappearance...while Casaubon, Adam and Broadbent are certainly in there, champing at the bit. You seem to have really upset Casaubon by not coming to see him personally after you found Edith and telling him what had happened.'

'I never agreed to such a thing; I do have lots of other things on my plate, you know,' Jericho said peevishly. Then he had a thought. 'You told me that none of these SIS people had ever been to the quarry at Shaukeiwan, isn't that so?'

Ronnie looked embarrassed. 'I did tell you that. But it seems I was wrong. The SIS and the Military have their own interest in that quarry, apparently. They've identified it as one of the key positions they would need to fortify with artillery if and when they ever need to defend the island from an attack coming from Kowloon. It seems the Military are looking seriously at such scenarios, for the Japanese are beginning to sweep down the length of China, and might even land on our doorstep eventually. So Casaubon and his team certainly know all about that quarry...'

This was a complication that Jericho didn't need, for he had been desperately trying to narrow down in his mind the number of people who had worked closely with Edith, and who also had intimate knowledge of the quarry and its buildings.

Ronnie hesitated. 'There is one other thing: Ian Luff seems to have disappeared now too. Nobody has seen him since he left work late on Sunday night...'

*

Despite Ronnie's warning, Jericho was still taken aback when he entered the drawing room and saw that the entire Executive Council was lined up sitting in a couple of rows of folding chairs to hear what he had to say. He was even more taken aback when he saw that Julian Colby was present and sitting next to Ronnie Grantham in a prominent position. Despite his stepping down as Attorney General, it seemed Colby couldn't relinquish things completely so had come along to this meeting, even in the middle of a typhoon. He looked terrible, though, as if the cancer inside him was already tearing his body apart...

Then the Acting Governor and Colonial Secretary also appeared and took the two vacant seats in the middle of the front row, which had obviously been left for them, so Jericho found he had the attention of almost everybody that mattered in the Hong Kong Government. He noticed for the first time that Commissioner of Police Gregory Matlock was sitting at one end of the front row looking absurdly young and neat for a man of forty-two, with his hair smartly brushed like that of an overgrown choirboy. Even more off-putting was the presence of Edith's three main SIS colleagues in the second row, Casaubon, Adam and Broadbent. Casaubon in particular was staring at Jericho in a barely suppressed rage as if he suspected him of abducting Edith himself.

Jericho stood awkwardly in front of this little assembly, feeling like a nervous young schoolmaster addressing his first school assembly. 'Good morning, gentlemen,' he began hesitantly, a sudden frog in his throat. He cleared his throat with an effort, then went on quickly and told them in a few short sentences the factual details of how he had found Edith, and the condition she was in. But he made no mention of any prior knowledge he had of Edith or the fact that she had told him that she suspected that her chief Ralph Ogden had been murdered. Nor did he make any mention of any connection of the case with Michael Yip; that too was something better left unsaid until he had more of a clue what was going on with that smart young Chinese lawyer.

Jericho paused expectantly as he ended his little discourse. Outside, the wind was howling, while rain lashed in a fury against the main window. He had to raise his voice to be heard above the violence of the storm, which seemed to be shaking the very foundations of the building to pieces. 'So, does anyone have any questions?'

Casaubon stood up with alacrity like a jack-in-the-box, his balding head shining with sweat and his Adam's apple prominent in his long bony neck. 'Why did you happen to concentrate your search at the quarry in Shaikeiwan?'

Jericho glanced at Matlock who nodded faintly in return to signify that he could answer. 'We found a partial footprint in Edith's abandoned car, and a residue of dust and fine crushed rock, which indicated the wearer of the boot might have recently been to a rock quarry...'

'Yes, but why that particular quarry?' Casaubon demanded brusquely.

Jericho didn't want to tell the truth: that he suspected that Edith's abductor came from Government House, and that this man must have been part of that recent visit to the quarry in Shaikeiwan. Instead he said tersely : 'It's the nearest quarry to the place where Edith's car was found.'

Casaubon sat down again but still looked far from satisfied.

Bob Harmsworth then climbed slowly to his feet in the front row; he seemed to have aged noticeably since the last time Jericho had seen him. 'I want to commend you, Chief Inspector Jericho, for finding Edith. It was sterling piece of police work, even though her condition unfortunately looks beyond recovery. But can you tell us this: do you think that my deputy Ian Luff might have been abducted too? And possibly by the same people?'

Jericho glanced again at Commissioner Matlock. 'I wasn't aware that Mr Luff had gone missing, until I came here today. So I wouldn't like to speculate what might have happened to him...'

Casaubon stood up again. 'The police were informed about Mr Luff. He did not come to work on Monday so it was thought he might simply have taken a day off after working all day on Sunday. But when he didn't appear on Tuesday, Mr Harmsworth went to his flat in Bowen Road and found he was not there and had left no word with his houseboy where he was going. So Mr Harmsworth came to me and we agreed that the police would be informed.' Casaubon glared across the room. 'So why do you seem unaware of this, Inspector Jericho?'

Commissioner Matlock quickly got to his feet too and gave Harmsworth and Casaubon one of his practised charming smiles. 'The case was given to Inspector Ball at Central Police Station, not to Chief Inspector Jericho...'

Yet Matlock still made it sound as if this was Jericho's fault somehow, which irritated him considerably.

The Acting Governor, Norman Lockhart Smith, now raised his hand to show he had a question, but didn't deign to stand. 'Chief Inspector Jericho...is there a possibility that Miss Starling was abducted by Japanese agents? And possibly Mr Luff too?' He glanced behind at Elliot Casaubon. 'I see frequent reports from our security people about the scale of Japanese espionage activities in Hong Kong, so could they be moving from mere plotting against us to actual malicious activities? Are we all here in potential danger of abduction or murder from this secret army of Japanese agents?'

Commissioner Matlock spoke up quickly. 'I doubt that Chief Inspector Jericho can answer that question with any certainty, which is outside his normal remit. Our intelligence friends are far better qualified to answer questions like that themselves...'

The meeting became heated after that, and eventually broke up in some disorder. Matlock left the room with the Acting Governor and his aides, and did no more than nod sourly in Jericho's direction as he passed. In a few more minutes Jericho found himself one of the last in the room, with only Harmsworth, Colby and Ronnie Grantham staying behind.

Jericho walked over to the three of them, since they obviously had some private questions of their own.

Ronnie spoke up first. 'So what's the latest news of Edith's condition, Paul? Is she truly beyond hope?'

Jericho had spoken to Eric Formby on the phone late last night, who had told him there was no change in Edith's condition.' 'She's not beyond *all* hope. Patients have come out of comas like this one spontaneously, though no one knows the how and why of it. But her doctors don't put her chances of recovery very highly; perhaps one in ten.'

Colby smiled grimly. 'Then much better than my own chances, anyway, which are about one in a million.' He looked at Jericho shrewdly. 'I see Ronnie must have told you about my condition, Inspector, for you registered no surprise at that last remark.'

Jericho nodded. 'I have heard the sad news, Mr Colby. I can only hope that you prove your doctors entirely wrong.'

'Thank you, Inspector Jericho.' Suddenly Colby relaxed his face and looked much younger for a fleeting moment as he returned to the subject of Edith Starling. 'I liked Edith very much, you know, Inspector, although I was never bold enough to tell her such a thing. I think that is the one thing I am going to miss the most about my life: that I shall no longer be able to enjoy the beauty and grace of the female sex.' He looked up, his face haggard and tired again. 'I hope sincerely that Edith does recover. A very clever girl, and a good-looking one too. I didn't really notice how good-looking, though, until she came to that reception in the ballroom three weeks ago in a very fetching black gown. And I must say that she looked very desirable the last time I saw her, for she was wearing *trousers*. First time I've ever seen a woman wear trousers to work. I've always had a secret yearning for young women bold enough to wear trousers...'

Harmsworth smiled along with Colby. 'Yes, I thought that she looked quite wonderful in trousers too. Made me wish I was twenty years younger...'

Ronnie Grantham had disappeared for a second but he now reappeared with a bottle of Scotch and four glasses. 'It looks like we'll be trapped here all day until the typhoon finally moves on. So shall we have a drink to Edith's recovery?' He looked at Colby awkwardly. 'And to your recovery too, of course, Julian...'

'That will take more than a dram of Glenfiddich, I'm afraid, Ronnie,' Colby said sadly.

Jericho joined in with the toast, but then put down his glass regretfully. 'I can't stay, I'm afraid. I must get back to the station in Wanchai and help with emergency calls.'

Colby, Harmsworth and Ronnie Grantham then raised their glasses to Jericho. 'Take care, then, Inspector,' Colby said with a parting tired smile. 'For the weather out there looks wild indeed...'

CHAPTER 28

Thursday, 2nd September 1937

By two o'clock in the afternoon, Paul Jericho found himself back in Shaukeiwan yet again...

The station desk in Wanchai had received a report of a body found washed ashore in Shaukeiwan near the disused quarry and Jericho had soon spoken to Thomas Sung on the desk about it. There were no squad cars left in the station at all, and every officer was out on emergency duty, including George Dorling, apart from a skeleton staff holding the fort at the station. Jericho had gone outside onto the Praya and thought that the wind force was waning a little, so the worst of the typhoon might hopefully be over. It persuaded him that he should take the Morris with the smashed headlight again and try to get to Shaukeiwan.

Thomas Sung had frowned when he returned to the front desk and suggested it. 'On your own, sir? That's far too dangerous.'

Jericho had looked around the empty lobby with a weary smile. 'I don't see anyone else who wants to go...' He'd had a sudden odd premonition that the body might turn out to be that of the missing Ian Luff, though he had no actual evidence for thinking so, for the message received had mentioned neither the sex nor the race of the victim. Yet just the notion that it might be Ian Luff had spurred him into risking his neck and overruling Thomas Sung's sensible advice...

The journey to Shaukeiwan had been a hundred times worse than his brief trip up to Government House earlier. Jericho had genuinely thought he might die as he drove along Hennessy Road to Causeway Bay and then on to North Point and beyond. The typhoon had ripped this whole community apart leaving the flooded roads littered with debris and partly collapsed buildings. It looked like a war zone, though perhaps not really as bad as the city of Shanghai after the Japanese bombers had finished with it on the previous Saturday. Jericho had seen photographs in the newspapers of the destruction of Shanghai which were truly shocking, and an affront to humanity. The destruction in Hong Kong did not seem as truly bad to him because it was at least only a product of the blind unfeeling power of nature over man, and was not due to the malevolent actions of humans themselves.

Yet somehow Jericho found his way through the devastation, and completed the five mile journey to Shaukeiwan in just over one hour. He passed the wrecked high street of the township with its squalid tenements, dismal workshops and crumbling warehouses, then drove on at a crawl in the roaring wind and lashing rain to the Saunders-Woo Quarry. There was an overhead iron gantry bridge that crossed over the road from the quarry to an old timber jetty on the shore, and he could see a small group of local people – half-a-dozen at most - gathered on the jetty despite the savage weather.

He found a safe place to park his Morris away from the salt spray that was being thrown high in the air by the storm; this was on the flat top of a bare green hillock located fifty feet above the foaming sea, reached by a steep track that led up from the main coast road. Then he walked back down the steep track to the main road, fighting to stay on his feet the whole time, and out onto the timber jetty to see what this group of local fishermen had found.

Yet, on arriving at the end of the jetty, Jericho saw at once from the embarrassed faces of these Cantonese fishermen that they had found nothing of any note, and certainly not a human body. Jericho swore to himself when he realized he had risked his neck coming here for no good reason at all: the "body" - as he soon discovered - was nothing more than the remains of a finless porpoise covered in kelp and dirt...

Jericho was about to give the head fisherman a piece of his mind when he saw the man's face suddenly change expression. The fisherman's normally dark skin seemed to turn to milky-white with shock, and Jericho turned his head out to sea to ascertain what had alarmed the man.

'*Oh, my God...!*'

Jericho thought for a moment that one of the fishermen had surprisingly spoken up in English. But then he realized that the words had come from his own shocked mouth...

For he had now understood the terrible truth: that the savagery of the typhoon so far today had been no more than a precursor to the main event. But that main event was unfolding now in all its terrible grandeur...

Jericho had never seen a sky like this one; it seemed like the omen of some great biblical devastation – the end of the world. The horizon to the south was a blackish purple, above which rolled great masses of cloud of a deep fiery red like the interior of a furnace. The clouds were racing across this tormented sky, with vivid streaks of lightning and peals of thunder like cannon shells. The sea had turned to a greenish white maelstrom, which was now lifting into the air like a monster rising from the deep...

'Run for your lives! Get to high ground!' Jericho screamed in Cantonese to the shocked fishermen, before turning back along the jetty towards the distant quarry. He could feel this giant wall of water rising up behind him and pursuing him like a giant sea serpent, but he dared not stop to look back. Instead he kept running for his life – faster than he had ever run before – on to the landward end of the jetty, across the coast road, through the open gate into the quarry, then in the direction of the former offices which he remembered were an elevated steel framed building with an open ground floor below for vehicles. He had just reached the bottom of the steel stairs leading up to the main floor of the offices when the wall of water finally caught up with him and hurled him against the rusting steelwork like a piece of flotsam.

The breath was knocked out of him completely by the force of the water, but he managed to grab onto the stair railing and pull himself up to the top landing of the stairs which was still just above the rampaging surface of the water. Then he turned his head and looked back in astonishment at the destruction that the freak wave had caused. The wave must have been thirty feet high for it had turned the timber jetty into matchwood and washed the iron gantry bridge away completely, surging far into the quarry which was now a great foaming lake six feet deep. Jericho could see no sign of the fishermen but hoped they had reached some other safe place of refuge from the rushing water. By chance he seemed to have made a good choice of refuge for himself, for the steel frame of the office building seemed to be holding up well against the swirling force of the water. A breathless Jericho finally opened the main door to the offices and went inside to get out of the screaming wind and the rain. He had just stepped over the threshold and closed the door behind him with difficulty when he felt something cold and hard and metallic jammed hard into his left temple.

Jericho turned his head carefully, his heart pumping like the thump of a steam engine. Sebastian Ride was holding a snubnosed revolver against his head. 'How did you find me so quickly, Inspector Jericho?' he asked balefully...

*

They went and sat down in one of the offices that still had an old scarred site table and a couple of cheap wooden chairs. Sebastian Ride sat with his back to the small porthole-like window, while Jericho sat facing him, wondering what the hell was going on. Ride had at least placed the revolver on the table, but it was still within easy reach of his hand therefore still felt like an ominous threat. Yet Jericho was not quite sure how much danger he was in: the truth was that Sebastian Ride was in such a volatile and unpredictable state that he seemed as likely to use the gun on himself as on Jericho...

'What are you doing here, Mr Ride?' Jericho asked him after they had sat down.

Ride raised his head to listen to the terrifying sound of the wind, and to the groans and creaking of the steel roof as it tried to resist these colossal natural forces. It did feel as if the roof was about to be ripped off this building at any moment by these vast suction pressures, and that they would be sucked out into that raging tempest with it. But Ride did not seem even mildly nervous at the prospect of imminent death...

'What are you doing here, Mr Ride?' Jericho repeated. 'Don't you know that your wife tried to kill herself and needs you at home?'

Ride looked uneasy. 'Yes, of course I know. She stepped out in front of a lorry at the weekend, but thankfully changed her mind about it and pulled back at the last minute. At least I'm pretty sure that's what happened...'

'No, I don't mean that,' Jericho interrupted impatiently. 'I mean that she tried again...*yesterday*. She slit her wrists while taking a morning bath...'

'*What...?*' Ride was genuinely shocked by this revelation, Jericho could see. 'Is she all right? You're not trying to tell me that Gloria is dead, I hope...'

'No, she's not dead...' *Not that it's any thanks to you, though,* Jericho wanted to add bitterly. Yet given the feverish look on Ride's face, Jericho decided not to provoke him unnecessarily. 'I happened to call at your house early yesterday morning and I was able to get her to hospital before she lost too much blood.'

Ride took a long breath. 'Then I suppose I owe you a debt of gratitude, Inspector Jericho.'

Jericho raised his eyebrows quizzically. 'Really? Is that your genuine feeling? Yet you don't give me the impression of a man who really cares what happens to his wife.'

'What would you know about my marriage, Inspector?' Ride asked sourly.

'I know that Mrs Ride still loves you, but that you don't seem to love her in return. I think that's the main reason for her unhappiness.'

Ride brooded over that for a moment. 'That may be part of it. But it's not the whole story; something else is tormenting Gloria, something I don't understand.'

Jericho changed the subject. 'How long have you been here? Your secretary, Miss Leung, said that you were staying at a company cottage on Lamma Island.'

Ride looked confused for a second but recovered. 'That's because that's what I told her.'

'But you haven't been to Lamma Island?'

'No, I was staying at a company flat in Bowen Road until yesterday. Then I walked down into Central yesterday evening, not really knowing what to do for the best.'

Outside, the terrifying noise of the storm continued unabated; it did truly sound like the end of the world. 'But why did you come *here* of all places?' Jericho wanted to know.

Ride shrugged. 'I just got on a tram – sitting on the top deck - and it brought me to Shaukeiwan, so it seemed like fate that I should end up here. It seemed as good as any other place. I needed a quiet place to think...and this quarry belongs to Saunders-Woo after all.' He paused. 'So what brought *you* here, Inspector? It seems it wasn't in pursuit of me, as I mistakenly thought.'

'I was here two days ago. A woman called Edith Starling who works in the intelligence team at Government House had been abducted, and I found her here, imprisoned in the old explosives store...'

Ride was clearly puzzled. 'Really? How odd! But I don't know anything about this woman; I've never heard that name as far as I can remember.'

It sounded like the truth to Jericho. So it seemed it was just a coincidence that had brought Sebastian Ride here too. 'I was investigating a report today of a dead body at Shaukeiwan – a mistaken one as it turned out – when that huge rogue wave came crashing in. So I ran into the quarry only to save my life. I certainly had no idea you would be here...'

'You said you went to my house yesterday? Why? Was there any particular reason for your visit?' Ride asked.

'I had *two* reasons,' Jericho said. 'Firstly I was worried about your wife because I had happened to witness her first attempt to kill herself at the weekend. She had denied throwing herself in front of that lorry deliberately, yet I wasn't convinced so I came to your house a couple of times to check up on her. That's when I became aware that you had apparently gone missing somewhere. The other reason I went to your house was to talk to you about the death of your late partner James Woo...'

Ride looked up sharply. 'Oh yes...? *Why?* I thought that was over. You'd examined the balcony where it happened, and you told me yourself that you thought it was an accident caused by shoddy construction of the parapet on his balcony.'

'And I still believe that. But it seems there might have been someone else with James Woo on that balcony when he died. We have a new witness who saw this man with Mr Woo. The description of the man fits *you* perfectly...' Jericho decided to press the matter now despite the risk. 'You were there on that balcony with James Woo when he died, weren't you?'

Ride struggled with his expression for a moment before letting out a long sigh of frustration. 'Yes, I was there. And it feels so good to finally admit it. But I didn't kill my partner, Inspector Jericho. I didn't even cause his death...at least I don't think so. I had followed him from the office to his secret little apartment and confronted him. We had an argument about business matters, and it got a little out of hand. But we both calmed down eventually. It was then that James leaned back against that parapet, and the whole thing just gave way under his weight. I tried to save him – I flung out a hand to try and catch him as he fell. But I missed him, and then he was gone...'

'Why didn't you just call the police immediately and tell us what had really happened?' Jericho asked. He had to raise his voice now to almost a shout to be heard above the fearsome fury of the storm.

'Because I thought I might be accused unfairly of murder, Inspector. I knew how suspicious it would look if I admitted that I had been there with James when he died. There had been a lot of business tension between us of late – many public rows and arguments – so I decided it was wiser to leave the scene and go back to the office. I'm not proud of myself for doing that, but it was too late to help James by that point.'

'Where your secretary would no doubt cover for you if you asked her,' Jericho suggested moodily.

'Yes, perhaps she would have,' Ride admitted. 'But in the end I didn't need to ask her to lie for me because no one made any serious investigation of my whereabouts that day.'

Jericho pondered that. 'So why have you effectively been in hiding for the last three days? Was it because of your wife's problems? Or was it to do with the death of James Woo?'

Ride was choosing his words carefully now as he answered, Jericho could see. 'It was the latter. Someone else was already in the apartment that day when James died, and saw everything, though of course I didn't know he was there at the time. He was one of James's homosexual lovers, a man called Ian Luff...'

'I know Mr Ian Luff,' Ride interrupted grimly.

'But I bet you don't know what type of man he really is: a blackmailer, a cheat, a devious manipulator of human beings.'

Above their heads, the wind was still roaring like a furnace, and all that was keeping them from oblivion seemed to be that thin steel shell of corrugated iron. But Jericho tried to ignore it, even though every second felt like it might be their last. 'So he began to blackmail you about this?'

'Yes. He didn't see what actually happened on the balcony but he had overheard enough of our conversation to get the gist of it. He knows it would finish me with the Woo family if the truth were to come out, even though he also knows fine well that I did not murder James, but was only a witness to his accidental death. But that would be enough to end my business career in Hong Kong...' Ride took the snubnosed revolver in his hand for a moment and squeezed the handle angrily as if he had Ian Luff in his sights.

Jericho could see that the chamber of the gun was loaded and that the hammer was resting on a loaded chamber, therefore could easily go off by accident. Some single-action revolvers had a half-cock notch on the hammer for safety against accidental discharge, but Jericho could not be sure that this Colt had such a thing. Even if it did, this feature did not usually make the weapon drop-proof so Jericho was more than a little uneasy at the cavalier way that Ride was handling the Colt. Jericho's own service revolver was still safely tucked away in his holster because he had not expected to need it today.

'The man is a devil,' Ride went on. 'He has been working secretly on some of his key government colleagues to try and win a massive housing project for Saunders-Woo...'

'And you object to that?' Jericho asked sarcastically.

'I object to the way that he is doing it. I know that he and James were looking for ways to pressurize three key members of the Executive Council: Bob Harmsworth, Julian Colby and Ronald Grantham...'

'What did he have on them?' Jericho demanded quickly.

'I don't know for sure. But Harmsworth apparently takes bribes, while Colby has long kept a Chinese mistress in Kowloon. And Luff seemed confident he had Grantham in his power too, so he must have something on him as well...'

Jericho was glad that Ride seemed to know nothing of his own close relationship with Ronnie Grantham, otherwise he doubted that he would have been so forthcoming.

'...I am sure that it was Luff's influence over James that caused this business rift between James and me in the first place. Therefore he is much more than just a blackmailer; he is the author of all my misfortunes.'

Suddenly Jericho had a moment of inspiration. 'It was *you* who attacked one of our patrolling constables in Caine Road on Sunday night, wasn't it?'

Jericho saw instantly from the look on Ride's face that he had guessed correctly.

Ride became defensive. 'How is that man? Not badly hurt, I hope?'

'No, fortunately Constable Wu seems to have a very hard head.'

Ride looked relieved. 'I was waiting to meet Ian Luff that night. He has a front door key for that old Woo mansion in Caine Road, and we were going to meet there late at night to hammer out a deal for what he wanted in return for his silence.'

'But why the gun?' Jericho asked heavily. 'Were you planning to kill him, is that it? Where did you get a gun like that anyway? I haven't seen too many snubnosed revolvers like that here. It's a thirty eight Colt Detective Special, isn't it?' Jericho made to pick it up, but a suspicious Ride got there first with his hand and gripped it again threateningly.

'It *is* a Detective Special...but I have contacts who can get me anything.' For the first time Ride sounded a little boastful. 'As for killing Luff, I would have liked to. But I don't think I'm quite wicked enough to shoot a man down in cold blood, not even someone like Ian Luff.'

Jericho flinched for a moment as heard a sound like metal tearing, a sound even louder than the general cacophony of the wind and the hammering of the rain on the steel roof. But the roof held for the moment, and he relaxed slightly again.

'I think Luff might even be selling secrets to the Japanese,' Ride suggested unexpectedly.

'What makes you think that?' Jericho kept his voice neutral.

'Because I know for a fact that Luff and James had concocted a plan to sell marine gasoline to the Japanese Navy, which they are very short of. I doubt whether the invasion of China by the Japs would have gone ahead without that fuel that James sold them secretly. And they did it using Saunders-Woo ships without my knowledge. Also I know that Luff was once caught in a homosexual massage parlour in Central that is a known haunt of Japanese agents.' He saw Jericho's expression and hurriedly explained himself. 'After the man made his intentions clear as a blackmailer, I did some background research on him.'

'Do you know that Luff has disappeared from sight too?' Jericho had a sudden bleak thought. 'You haven't killed him after all, have you?'

'No, I certainly haven't,' Ride denied vehemently. 'I swear I didn't even know that he was missing. I'm sure he's just lying low waiting for the dust of Sunday night to settle.'

Jericho had another thought, a more vexatious one this time. 'Was it *you* who attacked me in the grounds of the Woo mansion on Sunday night?' He opened his collar to show Ride the residual bruises on his neck.

Ride laughed bitterly. 'That's gratitude for you! It was *I who saved you*. And it was actually the early hours of Monday morning, to be precise. I don't know if you know it, but someone was stalking you personally that night after all your colleagues had left, a man in an overcoat and fedora hat.'

'Did you see his face or his hair?'

'No, it was dark, and he was well-covered. But he looked a strong fit man, maybe an ex-soldier or even a policeman. Maybe one of your colleagues has got it in for you, Inspector,' Ride suggested dryly. 'The man would certainly have throttled you to death if I hadn't dropped down from the tree where I was hiding. I landed on the man's back, and he fled in a panic...'

'You were *up a tree?*' Jericho said in amazement.

Ride grunted derisively. 'I was. And I saved your life. But perhaps I owed you that much...'

Jericho was hardly listening, though; instead he was wondering if it could have been George Dorling who had attacked him that night. After being chased off by Ride, he could easily have returned a few minutes later after recovering from his own fright and pretended to be rescuing him. George had been wearing a hat and a coat that night, *despite the awful heat...*

The other possibility was that it had been Ian Luff who had been stalking him. Luff had certainly been in the area that night, and could have hung around waiting for the police to disappear. Yet surely Ride would have recognized him if that was the case. And Jericho couldn't think of any reason why Luff should have been targeting him in particular anyway...

Yet his suspicions about Dorling and Luff were curtailed abruptly when he saw Ride take his Detective Special and calmly point the barrel at his own right temple.

'Don't do that, Mr Ride,' Jericho warned. 'Nothing is worth that.'

'Oh, really?' Ride continued to point the short barrel of the gun against his own head. 'I am looking at the end of my business career in Hong Kong, at a possible murder or manslaughter charge in the case of James Woo, at an assault charge on a policeman, and perhaps conspiracy to murder Ian Luff. And I have a wife whom I've driven to try and kill herself. What exactly do I have to live for now, Inspector Jericho?'

Jericho thought quickly. 'You can forget the charge of assault on that policeman; we would never be able to make that charge stick without a signed confession, which I doubt you would give us in the circumstances. And I promise I won't pursue the matter anyway; let's just call it a favour in return for the one you did me. And the same goes with your relations with Ian Luff; nobody can be prosecuted for thinking idly about murdering someone, provided you went no further than that...'

'And what about the death of James Woo? I won't be able to wriggle out of that one quite so easily, will I?'

'There will certainly not be a murder charge against you for the death of James Woo; and you would be unlikely to be convicted even of manslaughter if you tell the truth. The state of the parapet on that balcony still points overwhelmingly to an unfortunate accident, so your defence lawyers wouldn't have much difficulty in getting you off even if the case came to court. I suppose it's true that it would be impossible for you to continue working with the Woo family afterwards, but you're still a young man. You can start again somewhere else; maybe you and your wife could be happy again in another country...'

'That's kind of you to try and talk me out of this, Jericho.' Ride lowered the gun a fraction. 'But let's see if your generosity of spirit is still sufficient to the task when you find out the truth about me. And the truth about your wife Susan...'

Jericho felt his blood run cold. 'What do you know about Susan?'

Ride hesitated, perhaps unnerved by the look on Jericho's face.' She was with me at the same company flat in Bowen Road on the night she died, January the nineteenth. I had met your wife a few months previously at a speech day at her school and I'm afraid I pursued her relentlessly after that. To be honest, I became completely besotted with Susan and wanted her to leave you and marry me. But the truth is she never had more than the mildest interest in me, and the most we ever had was a drink together and one shared dinner after work. If it makes you feel any better, Susan never slept with me. She only came to the flat that last night to give me a final warning to leave her alone. Otherwise she intended to tell you about my pestering of her. She was only there for ten minutes, then she left to walk back down to Kennedy Road. She didn't want me to even give her a lift back to Happy Valley...I think she was planning to walk home though it was already eleven o'clock...'

Jericho was breathing hard. 'And then what?'

'I honestly didn't know what had happened later that night until I read in the newspapers that Susan had been tragically killed by a hit-and-run driver in Kennedy Road. I should have come forward and admitted that I had seen Susan that night, but I didn't. There didn't seem any point; the poor girl was dead and there was nothing I could do about it afterwards. But on the day that I went to James Woo's secret apartment three weeks ago, he admitted that he had been in a nearby flat in Bowen Road that night in January – actually Ian Luff's place - and had seen what happened to Susan through a pair of binoculars. That was the main cause of my argument with James and why it turned so nasty. He said that some unknown person had tried to attack Susan on the pavement and she had run out into the road, perhaps trying to wave down a passing car for help. But the driver of the oncoming vehicle apparently didn't see her until too late and ploughed right into her. The car skidded to a halt, the driver got out briefly to check Susan's body, then drove off again.'

'Did Woo see the driver? Could he identify him?'

Ride shook his head doubtfully. 'He said not. Nor did he see the person who had attacked Susan earlier and caused the accident. But James claimed he knew the make of car which hit Susan because it was a distinctive one, therefore could probably identify the driver if he really wanted to. James died within a minute or so of telling me this. But he had also told Ian Luff earlier what he'd seen. I have an idea that Luff knows both the make of car *and* the name of the driver by now. As a natural blackmailer who deals in deadly secrets, he wouldn't let such a golden opportunity as that go to waste. So find Luff and you might be able to discover finally who was driving the car that ran Susan down...' Ride fell silent for a moment. 'I'm truly sorry about Susan. She was a wonderful woman, and I caused her death by my own stupid selfishness.' He raised the gun to his temple again.

'So, you see, I deserve this end, do I not, Jericho?'

Jericho saw Ride begin to squeeze the trigger and reached desperately across the table trying to knock the gun out of his hand. But he failed in his vain attempt as Ride evaded his clumsy hands...

Ride stood up, the revolver still in his hand, and forced the barrel hard against his temple again, his face contorted with a look of self-loathing.

The sound of the shot was deafening in that room, even with the continual roar of the wind outside...

CHAPTER 29

Thursday, 2nd September 1937

At six o'clock in the evening, Paul Jericho sat down by the bedside of Gloria Ride in the Tung Wah Hospital, and wondered how he was going to tell her what had happened...

Gloria was looking better, Jericho was glad to see, but her face was tense as she waited expectantly for him to speak. 'What is it, Inspector? Has something terrible happened? It's Sebastian, isn't it...?'

Jericho took a long breath. 'He's all right, Mrs Ride. I have found him, and he's fine...'

In the end Sebastian Ride had shown that he didn't really want to die any more than his wife did, for he had not been able to shoot himself, and had instead thrown the gun on the floor in frustrated disgust where it had gone off by accident. Fortunately this stray shot had missed both of them, though coming perilously close to hitting Jericho in the head.

Jericho had given Ride no further opportunity to kill himself and had swiftly pocketed the Colt revolver. Jericho hadn't emptied the gun but he had made sure that the hammer was now resting on the emptied chamber, therefore could not go off by accident again. Then they had simply waited for the worst of the typhoon to abate so that they could leave and make their way back to Wanchai. As if by mutual consent, they had found themselves talking about anything but their present situation: Jericho had told Ride about growing up in Burma and his time in public school in Surrey, and how the Armistice had come along just in time to save him from being conscripted into the army, while Ride had talked about his surprisingly humble origins in his home town of Manchester, and about his father who had been a lowly colliery engine driver in the North of England. Ride had also told him about his years at sea in a tramp steamer as a humble young seaman - a fortunate career choice as it turned out, for it had kept him away from England during the War and ensured that he hadn't ended up as trench fodder like so many of his childhood friends. His career in the Merchant Navy had been even more fortuitous in the end, though, for his ancient tramp steamer had brought him to Hong Kong eventually, and to a life that he could only have dreamed of before...

By four o'clock, there was a noticeable diminution in the power of the wind, though the rain seemed heavier than ever, a tropical downpour that had turned formerly dry land into foaming torrents and cataracts.

But Jericho was determined to get back to the station before dusk fell, so he and Ride went in search of his Morris police car. The seawater had receded from the quarry by now, but had left it looking like a part of the seashore, full of deep rock pools. His decision to park his car on a hillock fifty feet above the sea had proved to be a prescient one, for it was almost the only manmade thing in this area that had survived that terrible freak wave. The jetty and the gantry bridge were completely gone, just wreckage being tossed about in the still violent sea. And there was no sign of the fishermen either, so Jericho had to wonder if he was the only survivor of that ill-fated group who had met on the end of the jetty earlier today.

Unexpectedly, the journey back to town had proved to be easier than the fraught outward journey. The wind was no longer blowing with the same terrifying violence, which certainly helped their laboured progress in the Morris, while teams of firemen and British squaddies had already started clearing the main tram tracks of building debris so that Jericho found it easier to negotiate a way through all the residual carnage on the streets. Jericho had decided not to arrest Ride for the moment, but to let him return to his own home in Conduit Road. In any case he was not sure what Ride could be charged with at present, except some very minor offences like illegal possession of a firearm. Ride no longer seemed in suicidal mood to him, and perhaps Jericho's optimistic view of his situation had cheered him up and shown him that he wasn't in quite as hopeless a position as he'd thought. In fact Jericho suspected that his analysis of Ride's situation might prove to be entirely accurate in the end, and that Ride would not end up being charged with anything at all. He knew he should report Ride's attempted suicide, of course, yet doubted that he would in the circumstances...

Jericho knew that he should have hated this man for what he had done to Susan, for he had certainly caused her death indirectly by his selfish and unfeeling pursuit of her. Therefore he should have been glad to see this wretched man take his own life. Yet instead Jericho felt some satisfaction at having saved the man from himself, and at being magnanimous to him in his hour of need. And Jericho had got something in return today for his generosity of spirit: the proof that Susan had *not* betrayed him. Jericho knew he could never get Susan back again, yet the fact that she had still been faithful to him was a consolation prize of sorts and warmed his sweet memory of her even more.

And he had also learned a lot of interesting information about Ian Luff, who seemed on this evidence a far nastier and more scheming individual than Sebastian Ride could ever be. Jericho wondered if Ian Luff could really be aiding the Japanese. *Could he even be the traitor embedded inside Government House, the man who had murdered Ralph Ogden and then abducted Edith Starling and left her in a morphine-induced coma?* It seemed unlikely on the whole, but then none of the senior people at Government House seemed like likely traitors and murderers...

'I've taken your husband back to Conduit Road,' he told Gloria Ride. 'He is exhausted after being caught out in the typhoon so will rest tonight. But he'll telephone you later here if he can, and will certainly come here tomorrow to see you.' Jericho hesitated before going on. 'Your husband did admit to me that he was with James Woo on that balcony in Tai Ping Shan when he died. But he still denies being responsible for James's death. And I believe him; I am still sure it was no more than an unfortunate accident. But your husband lied about being there because he thought it would mean the end of his relationship with the Woo family. Before going home this afternoon, he insisted on me taking him first to the Woo family home in Po Shan Road so that he could apologize to Grace Woo and her brothers in person for his deceit, and try and clear the air.'

Yet Jericho had seen from Ride's dejected expression when he returned from his brief meeting with Grace Woo that she had obviously not reacted well to his confession. So even though Sebastian Ride might escape having to face criminal charges for what had happened on that balcony in Tai Ping Shan, yet the repercussions for his business relationship with the Woo family were obviously going to be serious indeed.

Gloria Ride did not seem interested in what the Woo family thought of her husband, though. Her mind was entirely elsewhere, and she seemed to be struggling with some deep inner conflict of her own.

Jericho had a sudden insight that her depression and her recent suicidal tendencies might not just be a consequence of her stormy relationship with her husband, but might actually have something to do with the death of his own wife too...

'Did you know that your husband had some sort of a relationship with my wife, Susan Jericho?' he asked her with almost brutal surprise. 'And that Susan had visited your husband in a flat in Bowen Road on the night she died?' He studied her face and noted her quivering lip and her tearful eyes. 'I think you know all about this, don't you? I think you were *there* in Kennedy Road that night in January, weren't you?'

Gloria went white with shock. Then she put her face in her hands and wept bitterly. 'I didn't mean it to happen. I knew that Sebastian was obsessed with your wife after meeting her at some school prize-giving evening. He began pestering her with calls and flowers. I listened in on some of his conversations with her. She always seemed to be politely giving him the brush-off so I wasn't too concerned at first. Yet she was a very good-looking young woman, and I began to fear that Sebastian would eventually succeed in his seduction – he usually did, of course. But this one seemed different from his usual affairs: he seemed genuinely in love this time, and even intent on marrying Susan in time. I heard him ask Susan to marry him on the phone several times, and even though she laughed at him in return and told him she was already married, yet I grew uneasy. I began to follow your wife every day after she left work, and I was reassured again, for she seemed to have little contact with Sebastian apart from those few phone calls. She still seemed devoted to her husband...*to you, I mean*,' she added awkwardly. 'But then I listened in on one more call, and I heard Susan agree to come to the flat in Bowen Road where Sebastian usually met his women...'

'Then what?'

'Late on that cold windy night – it was already after ten, I think - Susan took the last bus from outside her school to Kennedy Road, where she got out and walked up the hill, first to Macdonnell Road, then to Bowen Road. I had followed the bus and parked my car in Kennedy Road. Then I followed her on foot up the hill. But she was only in the company apartment for about ten minutes or so before she reappeared and began walking back down the hill to Kennedy Road again. I thought this was my best chance, so I ran after her. I only wanted to talk to her and plead with her to reject Sebastian's advances. But she saw me running after her. Perhaps I looked a little crazy or something to her, for Susan panicked at the sight of me and ran straight out into Kennedy Road, waving her arms as if trying to stop a passing car for help. But then a big car suddenly appeared out of nowhere and hit her, throwing her poor body high in the air...no one could have survived that terrible impact which threw her body twenty or thirty yards further down the road...' Gloria put her face in her hands and sobbed at the memory.

Jericho too was distraught at hearing the terrible details of Susan's death, and could hardly bear to hear any more. Yet something forced him to keep listening to this woman's confessional tale...

Gloria collected herself with difficulty. '...It almost looked to me as if the car had run her down deliberately; it seemed to be accelerating before it hit her, even though she had run out into Kennedy Road near a streetlight and wasn't that difficult to see. The car then stopped; the driver got out and walked back towards Susan's body. It was difficult to see what was going on by now because Susan's body had been thrown by the collision a long way from the streetlight, and it was very dark where her body had come to rest.

But I am sure that the driver simply looked down at Susan's body quite clinically and made no attempt to help her, before he returned calmly to his car and drove off...'

'It *was* definitely a man, then?'

Gloria looked startled for a moment. 'Oh yes, I am sure it was a man in a dark suit and hat. He was quite tall, but that's all I could see. It was too dark to see his face...'

'Are you sure about all this?' Jericho asked, his mind reeling.

'Yes, I'm sure,' Gloria said with a further sob.

Jericho didn't know what to say. Yet he still couldn't believe that anyone would have driven into Susan deliberately, not even some rich young Chinese man who'd been drinking, as Kevin Ball suspected. *Nobody could be that evil...*

He could see that Gloria Ride was in a deeply distressed state again, so tried to repair some of the damage he'd done with his questioning. 'If that's what really happened, then I can hardly blame you for it. Your husband was more culpable in my wife's death than you.'

'Yet she wouldn't have run out into the road but for me,' Gloria said woodenly. 'But at least I did run back up the hill by another path to Macdonnell Road where I knew there was a public telephone box. I called the police emergency number from there. I put on the voice of a Chinese man because I didn't want to give away my true identity; I can imitate my own houseboy's voice quite well...'

'And then?'

'Then I walked back down to Kennedy Road and stood guard over Susan's body until I heard the sound of approaching sirens. But I couldn't face the thought of being questioned by the police about my part in this terrible thing, so I ran to my own car and left in the other direction.'

Jericho realized that Gloria must have missed seeing the arrival of James Woo on the scene because she had gone to phone for an ambulance. And by the time she had returned, James Woo had already judiciously quit the scene. So it all fitted. He knew everything now except the identity of the driver of the speeding vehicle...

Gloria stared at him with haunted eyes. 'Can you ever forgive me?'

'I've told you already that I can hardly blame you for it.' That night did seem like some convoluted Greek tragedy to him, where everyone was partly to blame, and no one was completely innocent, not even himself. If he'd been a more attentive husband and more attuned to Susan's moods, then she would probably never have gone as far as ever having dinner with Sebastian Ride in the first place. And he might never have lost her...

'You can't tell me anything more about the driver of the car?' he asked with sudden desperation.

Gloria shook her head, the tears still dripping down her cheeks. 'No, I told you - I wasn't close enough. The spot where Susan had been thrown by the collision was a long way from the streetlight where I was standing – thirty yards or more. And that was the closest the driver ever came to me.'

'Did you recognize the make of car at least?'

Gloria seemed uncertain. 'I'm not sure of the make. But I did see the car much more clearly than the driver, of course, as it flashed close by me. It was certainly a big American saloon car. Dark, maybe dark blue or black. I think it could have been a Studebaker President, though I'm no expert on cars. My father had a Studebaker in India, and this car looked a lot like the one Daddy used to drive...'

That mention of a Studebaker President struck a chord with Paul Jericho for some reason, for it occurred to him that he *knew* someone who had driven a car like that. But in his desperately tired state he simply couldn't think of who it was at the moment.

He put his hand on Gloria's thin white arm. 'Try and get some sleep, Mrs Ride. And try not to dwell too much on what happened to Susan. It seems you have been carrying the guilt of that night around with you for a long time, so you have been punished more than enough already for your small part in what happened...'

*

Jericho got back to Wanchai and the waterfront road a few minutes before seven o'clock. The intensity of the typhoon had faded rapidly now, though the gusting wind and the drenching rain were still keeping people off the mostly deserted rubble-strewn streets. He was driving past the Tin Hau Hotel when he caught sight of a man entering through the main front door. Jericho only got a glimpse of the man in the lighted entrance of the hotel, but was sure that it was George Dorling...

Jericho had hardly seen Dorling since their eventful encounter in that garden in Caine Road in the early hours of Monday morning. Jericho's personal mission to find Edith Starling, and his unintentional involvement in the personal drama of Sebastian ride and his wife had kept him away from the station for long spells during the last four days, while Dorling too had been working mainly on street operations this week, before going on typhoon duty today with almost the entire Hong Kong Police force. But something had now brought George back to the Tin Hau Hotel, and Jericho was suddenly consumed with curiosity to find out the reason for it. He still had the words of that evil-looking triad member Huang Lee to consider, and knew he would have to confront George with these accusations soon and not just let this serious matter fester.

Jericho had wanted to put off the occasion to another day when he was better prepared for it, but something told him that he would never have a better chance than now to discover the truth about his own subordinate. In a few seconds, he had pulled his police squad car over to the kerb, and walked back briskly to the hotel entrance. The hotel lobby was deserted, with nobody even at the desk, and the bar, with its familiar swing door entrance like an American western saloon, was closed and in complete darkness. Clearly the compliant girls of the Tin Hau bar were taking some well-deserved rest and recreation of their own during the typhoon, and were sensibly locked up at home with their families and boyfriends this evening.

Jericho heard some footsteps on the stairs so assumed George must have gone that way. He got to the first floor corridor just in time to see a room door opening and closing near the far end. The rooms on this floor seemed mostly empty from the lack of any noise, but then nobody took a room in this hotel for more than a few hours at a time. And with the bar closed and the girls gone, there was no reason why any sailor would be here today.

Jericho stayed at the top of the main stairs for a moment while he pondered what to do. But he had no time to think for very long, for he suddenly felt two powerful hands pinion his arms from behind, then a sack was thrown over his head plunging him into darkness. Before he could struggle further, somebody hit him with some sort of club and his head exploded in pain...

*

When he came to a few minutes later, Jericho found himself inside one of the hotel bedrooms, lying on the double bed with his right hand handcuffed to the heavy bed frame. They were probably his own handcuffs, he thought dismally, angry at himself for getting caught in this stupid way. He looked down at his holster and saw that his service revolver was predictably gone...

There were three other men in the threadbare room, all Chinese and dressed in Western clothes. One was the clear leader and figure of authority in this group despite his slim and youthful figure. Jericho had a feeling that one of the other men was the same muscular barrel-chested man he had seen in this very hotel just before Freddie Ling had been knifed three weeks ago. Jericho had an even stronger feeling that the slim and fashionably dressed leader of this group was none other than Lucky Lam himself...

The third Chinese man was older, a stringy mean-looking individual with the hooded eyes and bitter face of a natural killer. There was no sign of George Dorling, but Jericho didn't have any doubts that he was close by, perhaps in the adjoining bedroom, which was connected to this one by an inner door. Perhaps Lam wasn't sure that Jericho had actually seen Dorling enter this place earlier, and was therefore hoping that the identity of his tame crooked policeman might still be safe. But Jericho realized now with a deepening anger that everything Huang Lee had said today must be right: George Dorling was dirty, and in this filthy business up to his neck...

Jericho guessed what was going on: Dorling must have been called to an urgent meeting in this empty hotel with his triad paymasters, only for Jericho to blunder in and spoil their plans for a cosy private meeting. He could even surmise the reason for this impromptu meeting: one of Lucky Lam's key men - Huang Lee - was in police custody after all, and Lam no doubt wanted him either freed or silenced before he could say anything too incriminating. It seemed from this that Huang Lee must be a much more senior figure in the organization than Jericho had suspected from the man's coarse looks and somewhat brutish manners.

Jericho sat up on the bed and felt his sore head with his free left hand; he had a bump the size of a hen's egg on the back of his skull, which was throbbing with pain. Yet he was fortunate that the injury wasn't worse; he probably had his head of thick wiry hair to thank for the fact that his skull had not been fractured by that vicious blow.

The man whom Jericho assumed to be Lucky Lam stepped forward and sat down on a chair near the bed on which Jericho was sitting. He regarded Jericho with some clear curiosity, like a visitor to a zoo staring through the bars at some exotic and unknown animal. 'Are you here on your own, Mr Policeman?' he asked in perfect American English.

Jericho laughed harshly. 'Of course not. Only a complete fool would walk into a place like this on their own.'

'Yet here you are, so I can only draw one sensible conclusion – you are either remarkably stupid and naive, or else remarkably bold. And please do not try to call out for help: you would be wasting your time, for the only people presently in the building are my associates. We own this hotel, you see...' The man stared at Jericho again. 'I think you know who I am, Inspector Jericho...'

'I do. You are Lam Hok-ling, otherwise known as "Lucky" Lam. Leader of the Kao Ki-kan triad society. ' Jericho sniffed coldly. 'And I see you know who I am.' He looked at the barrel-chested thug behind Lam. 'I believe I am acquainted with this other "gentleman" already.'

'Ah, you mean Mr Teng Chee Hwa. Yes, he's an impressive specimen, isn't he? Not likely to be forgotten easily.' Lam then pointed to the older man, the one with a killer's eyes. 'And this is Mr Cheung...'

The fact that Lam had identified his associates so readily by name was a chilling warning to Paul Jericho; Lam was only doing so because he didn't expect Jericho to ever walk out of this room alive...

Teng spoke up in Cantonese to his boss. *'He's not afraid of us...'* His guttural voice sounded almost disappointed.

Lam nodded and responded to his subordinate in Cantonese too. *'No, he's not, is he?'*

'I wasn't even sure that you really existed,' Jericho continued in English, pretending not to understand this exchange between Lam and his associate. 'For no one seems to know even what you look like. You have an almost legendary status here in Hong Kong.' Yet the rumours he'd heard about Lam had proved to be true: Lucky Lam was indeed a surprisingly young man to have reached the top of such a vicious and demanding organization. He looked to Jericho more like a young and prosperous businessman than a crime boss.

'I could almost say the same about you, Inspector Jericho. For you have almost achieved legendary status in Hong Kong too. You are well known for being...'

'*Stupid and naive...?*'

Lam laughed. 'Possibly that too. But I was going to say that you are well known for being scrupulously honest. That makes you well nigh unique among the Hong Kong Police force.'

Jericho decided to take the offensive at this point because, in moving his position on the bed slightly, he had just felt something heavy and metallic in the left pocket of his khaki trousers that gave him some slight hope of survival. He hardly dared to believe what that object might be, though, for it seemed impossible... 'I know you had Ricky Sun and Freddie Ling killed. And I assume you had Marco da Silva murdered too?'

'It was nothing personal with Freddie and Marco, just business. I couldn't tolerate my underlings setting up on their own and making me look a fool. If I'd let them get away with it, then everybody would try it. We are an organization that rules by fear. Take that element of fear away from us, and we become just a disorganized rabble whom nobody would respect.'

'Did you kill the three women who worked in this hotel?'

Lam shrugged his shoulders innocently. 'Which three women do you mean?'

Jericho wasn't fooled by Lam's show of innocence; he certainly knew exactly which three women he meant. 'I mean Wong Yu-lan, Kam Mei-ling and Kwok Yaw-lim. Otherwise known as Judy Wong, Dora Kam and Cherry Kwok. Dora was a friend or lover of Ricky Sun, wasn't she? And all three women worked for Freddie Ling and Da Silva, didn't they?'

Lam nodded. 'So I believe. But I certainly never ordered the death of these women. Kam Mei-ling may have been Ricky Sun's lover but she did not hold his death against me, not when she learned that Ricky was a police informer and therefore deserved what was coming to him. Mei-ling was actually working for me as a very useful courier so her death was a personal annoyance to me.'

'Are you really selling British military secrets to the Japanese?' Jericho demanded suddenly, remembering what Kevin Ball had told him. 'Is that what Dora was doing for you? Carrying messages to the Japanese consulate in Macdonnell Road?'

Lam smiled complacently. 'It's a very lucrative business, Inspector Jericho. The Japanese pay huge sums of money for even the most piddling pieces of information about British defences in Hong Kong.'

'Doesn't it bother you that you are helping your country's enemies?'

Lam snorted in derision. 'The British are no great friends of China either, Inspector, so why should I care about protecting their military secrets? But Dora never dealt directly with the Japanese; she only passed her information to an intermediary, a woman agent whom the Japanese apparently trust.' He thought for a moment, before finally admitting, 'The truth is that I don't know who killed these three women. And I might even choose to punish this individual myself if I ever find out who was responsible.'

Jericho was convinced for some reason that Lam was being quite genuine in this case. But the thought filled him with a deep depression, for he now knew with almost complete certainty who had actually strangled those three young women...

'What do we do now, then?' Jericho asked. He could see that all three of these men were armed from the bulge of their jackets. They were obviously planning to murder him, but the Tin Hau Hotel was only a hundred yards along the waterfront from Wanchai Police Station. So they wouldn't want to shoot him and make any obvious commotion in this building that might prevent their escape. Even though they might suspect that the nearby police station was short-staffed at present because of the continuing typhoon emergency, they had to know that there could still be up to a dozen armed officers in there who would be here in a flash at the sound of gunfire. So however they planned to kill him, it would have to be done quietly...

It seemed they fully understood the quandary they were in, because a thoughtful Lucky Lam soon stood up and beckoned his two associates to follow him through the connecting door to the adjacent room. They closed it firmly behind them but Jericho could still hear a hum of quickfire Cantonese through the thin wood panelling. They were obviously discussing his fate, so were probably aware after all that he spoke good Cantonese despite his earlier attempt to pretend otherwise. Of course they would know this from George Dorling...

In five minutes, the door reopened slowly. But it wasn't Lucky Lam who entered the room, but George Dorling himself...

*

'I never wanted any of this to happen, sir,' Dorling said, masking his shame with a show of blunt defiance.

'How did they reel you in, George?' Jericho asked calmly, to give himself time to think. His left hand began to feel in the pocket of his khaki trousers again where his fingers soon found the handle of the Colt Detective Special...

He could hardly believe his good fortune but it seemed - unbelievably - that he still had Sebastian Ride's revolver in his pocket...

It had been there ever since he had taken it off Ride this afternoon. And Lam and his two associates had completely missed it when searching him earlier. Yet he could hardly blame them for missing it: they'd taken his own service revolver from his leather holster, of course, and simply assumed that was all the weaponry he would have. For no one would normally expect a Hong Kong Police inspector to be also carrying a concealed snubnosed American revolver on his person...

Dorling winced. 'Gambling, that's how. I got a taste for dice and roulette, and made a lot of money from them at first...'

'They would have let you win, George. That's the way they work.'

'I suppose so. But I wasn't smart enough to see it. I soon found myself losing heavily, and ended up in debt to the tune of fifty thousand. It was then that I discovered that I owed the money, not to some little fat backstreet moneylender, but to the Kao Ki-kan itself. I thought of escaping back to England, but I doubted that I would be safe even there. And Tess had just lost her baby so I couldn't simply make a run for it. In the end I agreed to their price: to give them the name of the police informer...'

'You did more than that, though, didn't you?' Jericho accused him. 'I think you led Ricky Sun into that alley where he was murdered.'

Dorling didn't answer so Jericho continued. 'How does Dora Kam come into your dealings with the Kao Ki-kan?'

Dorling paced the room a little. 'I had a one-night fling with her in May, so I already knew her. Then on the night when I led Ricky Sun into that ambush, she saw me leaving the alley. I told the triad about it, so, when she was murdered a few weeks later, I assumed they must have done it to keep her quiet. But they always claimed they'd never touched her. I certainly didn't kill her. And I had never met Judy Wong at all, while I only met Cherry Kwok when I came here to interview all the girls in the bar. So I still don't know who killed those three women. I did try and lead the enquiry away from any connection with the Kao Ki-kan for obvious reasons, yet it seems I was right about that all along. The killer must be this blue-eyed man who was seen leaving Cherry Kwok's room on that last night...'

Jericho was barely listening to Dorling's rambling self-justification, though, for he was wondering instead what chance he had of surviving by using the revolver in his pocket. The odds didn't look good. He would have to fire the gun left-handed for one thing, and he would have to fire twice to get the first shot off, for the hammer was presently resting on an empty chamber. So...he had five shots in the cylinder. *How quickly could he get those shots off?* Not quickly enough, and not accurately enough with his left hand, to kill four men before they could retaliate in kind.

It was a daunting thought: that his only possible way of surviving this was to kill or disable all four men. If one or more was left alive when he'd finished shooting, then he would be left helpless, with an empty gun in his left hand, and his right still handcuffed to a heavy bed frame and unable to move.

Yet even if he could only take one or two of these men with him, he was going to do it...

Suddenly Jericho became aware of a different note in Dorling's voice.

'...They don't want to kill you, sir. They sent me in here to make you an offer. They'll put you on their payroll too and make you a wealthy man. I know your late wife left you a good amount of money, but you'll make ten times that if you cooperate with these people. You'll be able to retire in a few years with more money than you ever dreamed of. You could buy a house in the Surrey countryside and live like a king...' Dorling's voice tailed away as he saw the look on Jericho's face. 'But I can see I'm wasting my time. I told them as much. You're not a man to sell out – too stubborn...too stupid...to know what's good for you...'

*

Lam and his associates returned within one minute. Lam was grimly philosophical. 'I can see the answer was no. That's too bad, Inspector Jericho; you do seem like a man who's simply too obstinate to see what's best for him.'

Lam turned to Dorling with a grimace. 'This mess is all your doing, Sergeant. So I expect you to resolve it.'

George blanched. 'What do you mean?'

Lam sighed, and took out a vicious-looking knife from his pocket. 'I mean: I expect you to go over there and cut Jericho's throat with this. My men will even hold him down for you. And when that's done, I want you to go back to your station this evening and make sure that Huang Lee meets an unfortunate accident in his cell before morning. Is that all absolutely clear?'

Dorling made a low growling noise of resentment, but he took the knife from Lam's hand anyway.

The other two Chinese men, Teng and Cheung, then each grabbed one of Jericho's arms before he had a chance to reach for the revolver in his pocket. Jericho struggled helplessly on the bed as Dorling came towards him. The muscular Teng had Jericho's left arm in such a vice-like grip that he had no chance of reaching the Colt any more.

Yet something told Jericho that George Dorling would not simply cut his throat on command like this; there was still too much decency in the man for that. Yet Jericho could also see the clear torment in George's face as he approached the bed so still couldn't be entirely sure of the outcome...

Yet he was primed for action, ready to reach for that revolver in his trouser pocket if he should get the slightest chance...

Events then exploded in a confused sequence of brutal violence...

Dorling brandished the knife in Jericho's face, but instead of slitting

Jericho's throat with it as ordered, plunged it deep into Teng's throat, who staggered backwards with blood frothing from a severed artery...

Jericho finally had his left hand free, and pulled out the Colt snubnosed revolver into plain sight...

Dorling launched himself at the other man Cheung, who evaded his knife thrust like a snake...Cheung then pulled out his own knife and stuck it deep into Dorling's ribs...

Lucky Lam reached for an automatic from underneath his coat and aimed it at Dorling, but Jericho fired his revolver...*once*...just a dull click...*then twice more*...deafening explosions this time...which hit Lam in the head and the chest, throwing him violently across the room.

Cheung stabbed Dorling again in a frenzy...*three, four, five times*...

Jericho swung his pistol around to a new target and emptied his final three shots into Cheung at point-blank range...

Then all was silent except for the heavy reek of gunpowder and the sickening smell of blood...

CHAPTER 30

Thursday, 2nd September 1937

Four hours later, Paul Jericho finally left Wanchai Police Station and emerged into the damp night air again. The wind was now no more than a blustery annoyance, though the rain continued relentlessly, now falling near vertically from an invisible black sky. At least eighteen inches of rain had fallen in the last twenty four hours, turning Hong Kong into a water world. Reports from outlying police stations suggested that terrible damage had been sustained during the day: whole villages in the New Territories washed away, many ships run aground or sunk, whole hillsides vanished in massive landslides, buildings collapsed, power lines down...

Jericho had showered in the station tonight and changed from his blood-soaked uniform into clean civilian clothes, yet he wondered if he would ever be able to forget the smell of that charnel house of a room in the Tin Hau Hotel. Yet he had not had to suffer the smell long before the sound of that fusillade of shots had brought his colleagues running from the nearby station to his rescue.

Then a long evening of deliberation and barely suppressed emotion had ensued. Jericho had left the bloody scene as quickly as he decently could, claiming that he needed a doctor to look at his head. But really he just wanted to get away from that room and the stink of death, particularly away from the sightless staring eyes of George Dorling.

Charlie Hebdon and Inspector Kevin Ball had soon turned up at the scene, and even Ball was complimentary to Jericho for once, for not many policemen survived encounters like this with triad gunmen. And the icing on the cake for Ball and Hebdon was that Lucky Lam was finally dead, and therefore not quite so "lucky" any more...

Jericho's account to Hebdon and Ball of what had happened was mostly factual, except for one notable change. According to his embellished account, George Dorling was in fact the noblest of men, and had died a hero, following his chief into the hotel at the risk of his own life and saving him from a brutal fate. Well, that last part was no embellishment at all but the actual truth...

Gary Ho had been listening close by as Jericho told his story, and had looked distinctly sceptical at this elevation of George Dorling to the sainthood. Jericho suspected that Gary Ho had long known the truth about George Dorling, or at least some of it. But he was confident that Ho would say nothing now in the circumstances, and would certainly not contradict his chief. There was of course still the issue of the prisoner Huang Lee's evidence to deal with, but Jericho was confident that the man's accusations of corruption at Wanchai Police Station would be regarded as no more than a tissue of lies invented to try and get him a deal, and could be suppressed or ignored without too much difficulty, now that Dorling was dead.

Jericho didn't really know why he should have chosen to exonerate George Dorling's reputation. Perhaps because he had liked him once and still thought him a decent man at heart. And perhaps even more so because Dorling had redeemed himself again with the final act of his life, when he must have known that it would cost him dear.

The life of an expatriate policeman in Hong Kong was a difficult balancing act because of the temptations on offer, especially for a young working class man fresh out from England who'd never had such opportunities before to make himself rich. It was so easy just to go with the flow and take the squeeze like everybody else, and live with the moral compromises. And before you knew it you had sold your soul to the devil...

And there was another more practical reason for Jericho to defend George Dorling's reputation: it meant that his wife Tess would get a full Hong Kong government pension and would be able to return home in a state of reasonable affluence, and with no stain on her family name.

Standing at the main entrance of the station, Jericho took a long breath of clean night air. If nothing else, a typhoon cleansed the humid dirty air of Hong Kong in a way that nothing else could. Eric Formby had kindly come to the station this evening and tended to his injuries. Formby had whistled with astonishment when he saw the old bruises on Jericho's neck as well as the size of the swelling on the back of his head. Formby had also found massive bruising on Jericho's chest which he himself had hardly been aware of: Jericho realized that it must have happened when that giant wave had caught him this afternoon in the quarry and smashed him against the steelwork of the old quarry offices. Formby had brought him one piece of good news from St Paul's Hospital, though: Edith Starling's condition was improving slightly. The colour of her skin was getting markedly better, and her breathing becoming deeper and more normal. So Formby was a little more hopeful about Edith's chances of recovery now. Yet Jericho had told him to keep that information to himself for the moment; her abductor might be tempted to try again and finish the job, if he heard that Edith might recover her senses eventually after all...

As he stood at the entrance of the police station, Jericho was so exhausted after his long and eventful day that he had to think for a moment where his car might be. Then he remembered that he had left his own Austin in Lockhart Road after returning from his visit to the office of Saunders-Woo this morning in search of Sebastian Ride. That meeting with Ride's secretary this morning now seemed a lifetime ago...

Jericho had to walk a long way to get to his car, for he had parked it well away from the busier shops and businesses in Lockhart Road because of the typhoon. In fact his little black Austin was only parked twenty or thirty yards away from the tenement block where Maggie Yiu lived. As Jericho got to his car and retrieved the starting handle from inside in readiness to leave, his eyes strayed inevitably to the darkened building across the road. He could see a gleam of light in her room on the top floor, but otherwise the building seemed deserted.

He walked across the road and examined the building with concern. The interior did seem deadly quiet as if all the occupants had fled. He noticed that a large sinister gap had opened up between this tenement and the restaurant building next door at roof level, while the main load-bearing concrete wall visible at the side of the building was now marked with large diagonal jagged cracks half an inch wide.

A concerned Jericho was just about to go into the building and look around when Maggie herself appeared at the main door, breathless and flushed. She was dressed in a white cotton blouse and a loose black skirt, and her hair was tied up with pins in business-like fashion.

'Paul...!' she said. 'I saw you from upstairs.'

He looked up at the outside of the building and now saw that many of the windows were broken too. 'What happened here?'

'It was during the typhoon today. There was a great rumbling noise, and then the whole building suddenly lurched sideways with a bang. Everybody panicked then, including me, and we all ran out into the street thinking the building was about to collapse. But then the movement stopped, although a lot of the walls are cracked inside, and all the door frames are warped and the doors won't close properly. All of the other residents have refused to go back, but I had nowhere else to go, so after an hour or so waiting in the wind and rain I went back inside and risked it.'

'Then that wasn't very wise of you.' Jericho had seen cases like this before of old Hong Kong tenements with shallow foundations. 'The heavy rain has obviously weakened the clay subsoil and caused the foundations to settle unevenly. So the structure of the building must be seriously compromised now by the settlement, and it could collapse at any moment.

So you'd better come home with me to Happy Valley. Hopefully my apartment block is still in one piece.'

She smiled at him shyly. 'All right. I know what's best for me. But let me just go and fetch something first...'

Jericho tried to stop her but she disappeared into the depths of the building before he could restrain her. He had thought she might have just gone back for her handbag or for her nightdress - or perhaps even for that new Bakelite radio. But instead she returned in five minutes carrying only her birdcage with her little Java sparrow hopping cheerfully inside. 'I can't leave Ling-Ling behind, can I?'

It seemed she thought more of her Java Sparrow than she did of her expensive Bakelite radio, which endeared her to Jericho even more...

*

Maggie stood with Paul Jericho on the balcony of his apartment in Happy Valley and looked out at the darkened hillside beyond. The wind was dying fast, yet still strong enough to ruffle her hair and cause the soft fabric of her skirt to billow about her legs. They could hear the sounds of the forest stirring on those wooded slopes above, an eerie supernatural sound.

Maggie turned her ear to the hillside. 'That noise sounds more like the sorrowful moans of English ghosts in a churchyard than Chinese ones. Or what I imagine English ghosts sound like anyway, for I have never been to England, or to any part of Europe. That sound seems just like the ghosts of Heathcliff and Cathy haunting the moors in *Wuthering Heights*...'

Jericho smiled at her flight of fancy. 'I see that you must have been teaching your girls Emily Bronte this year...or else it must be your own favourite book...' It suddenly occurred to him that *Wuthering Heights* had been Susan's favourite book too, so it seemed that she and Maggie might have something in common after all, a thought which pleased him. '...Well, Happy Valley Cemetery is full of the remains of English settlers and their families who died here far from home. And some of them might have been from Yorkshire, like Heathcliff and Cathy. So perhaps a few unhappy English spirits do haunt this place...'

Jericho had been relieved to find on returning home that his apartment block still had electricity and running water, so seemed to have survived the typhoon remarkably well.

But Maggie seemed ill at ease in this grand apartment. 'Isn't this an embarrassment for you – bringing a Eurasian woman home to your apartment? Won't your neighbours talk? You could lose your job if you were known to be consorting with a Eurasian or Chinese woman, couldn't you?'

'In theory perhaps, though lots of government people and police do it on the sly. But there are plenty of jobs for Englishmen in the private business sector in Hong Kong where they don't give a damn about a man's private life. I am not so wedded to this job that I can't imagine doing anything else...'

'Oh, really?' Maggie seemed unconvinced. 'You seem entirely wedded to the job to me; I can't ever imagine you being anything else but a policeman.'

Jericho let that remark pass because it was difficult to argue with. 'Don't worry about being here. There are only six apartments in this block – two on each floor. And my neighbours would never say anything. In any case, my immediate neighbours on this floor – a nice young couple called John and Rosie Lawrence – have gone home on leave for three months, so their apartment is presently empty. They left me the key so that I could water their houseplants...' Jericho had a sudden guilty thought. '...Which I haven't done for over a week now, so I'd better do it today before all their beautiful foliage plants die...'

'This really is a beautiful apartment,' Maggie said enviously. 'Is this where you lived when your wife was still alive?'

'Yes. We bought it when we got married five years ago. Susan paid for most of it; her late father was a wealthy English businessman who left her quite well off, while her mother was well known in Hong Kong for her charity work. Susan was actually born and brought up in Hong Kong as an only child, so she loved this place dearly and always had a deep rapport with local people. I have found it tough living in this apartment on my own, though; I miss her presence here more than anywhere else...'

'Then I do feel a little like an intruder,' Maggie suggested awkwardly.

He took her hand quickly. 'It's true that you're the first woman I've invited back here since Susan's death. But no, you are no intruder. This apartment doesn't seem so empty and sad to me any more now that you're here.'

She squeezed his hand. 'Thank you. That may be the nicest thing anyone has ever said to me.' She moved forward and leaned her head against his chest. 'You look exhausted, Paul. I suppose you must have had a terrible day.'

He smiled ruefully. 'Yes, you could say that.' He showed her the old bruises around his neck, and then let her feel the size of the bump on the back of his head.

She flinched in astonishment when she saw the bruises. 'I heard that there was a shooting this evening in the Tin Hau Hotel,' she ventured.

'Yes. Three triad members were shot dead, but I also lost one of my officers...Sergeant Dorling.' Jericho hadn't really wanted to talk about this but it seemed he would have to. 'You met him a couple of times, if you remember.'

Maggie looked up at him. 'Ah yes, the young Englishman with red hair. That's very sad. Was he married?'

'He was.'

'Then it's doubly sad. Was this shooting anything to do with the deaths of Dora and those two other women who worked in the Tin Hau hotel?'

'Yes, I believe it was,' he confirmed vaguely.

'So have you finally got your man?' Maggie asked warily.

'No, not yet.' Jericho could have added that he now thought he knew the man's identity with near certainty, but something made him desist from saying more at this point.

Then Maggie jumped with fright and fell into his arms as she heard a great roaring noise coming from the darkened hillside behind the apartment. The terrifying noise went on for nearly a minute; it sounded as if an express train was moving down the hillside towards them, flattening everything in its path.

Jericho too could feel his heart pounding with shock at this ominous noise, and subconsciously braced himself for some terrible cataclysm. Yet the noise finally faded away into the night, and the apartment still seemed fortunately to be in one piece. Even the lights were still on.

Maggie released herself from his arms and stared out into the night. Nothing was clearly visible from the balcony apart from the dim outlines of trees and scrub at the bottom of the forested hillside, and a vague indication of the darkened hillside rising steeply behind. 'What was that terrible noise? It sounded like the end of the world. But I can't see anything out there...'

Jericho stood beside her and peered out into the gloom too. 'It sounded as if there has been a major landslip on the hillside above. The trees normally do a good job of stabilizing these slopes with their roots, but if the soil becomes saturated with flood water and gets washed away, then a whole section of forest and topsoil can start to slip down the hill and turn into a landslide.' His eyes scanned the darkened hillside again, but he could make out nothing in this near perfect blackness. 'One thing is clear, though; the landslide has obviously missed this building. And there's nothing we can sensibly do about it until first light. Hopefully the landslip hasn't reached as far as any of the houses higher up Blue Pool Road. There is only one other small apartment block on this road apart from this one, and that's further down towards the racecourse. So that building should be all right too, since we seem to be in one piece.'

Maggie sighed with relief. 'That's good. I was beginning to think that by leaving my building and coming here, I had simply jumped from the frying pot into the fire...'

'It's from the frying *pan* into the fire...not the frying pot...' he corrected her with a smile.

She smiled back. 'Are you making fun of my English? I hope not,' she added with mock severity. 'I am supposed to be an English teacher, you know.'

He moved towards her and put his hands around her waist. 'It seems I have a taste for schoolteachers – young and beautiful female ones anyway...'

'And it seems that schoolteachers have a taste for you too - *female ones anyway...*' With that she released the pins in her hair and let her long black tresses fall to her shoulders.

*

Jericho was lying in bed with Maggie sleeping by his side when he heard a discreet knock on the main door of the apartment. He carefully lifted Maggie's arm which was lying draped across his chest and eased himself out of bed, trying not to wake her. He could see from the dim greyness at the window that it was not yet properly daylight, as he put on a dressing gown.

He opened the main door cautiously and was astonished to see a bleary-eyed Ronnie Grantham standing there.

'Sorry about calling so early, Paul,' he apologized. 'But I was concerned about you. I bumped into Greg Matlock in the Hong Kong Hotel last night and he told me that you had got up to some alarming adventures yesterday after leaving us in Government House. I wasn't sure I got the half of it, but I did hear about some shootout at the Tin Hau Hotel so I wanted to see if you were all right...'

Jericho stood aside to let him into the living room. 'As you can see, I'm fine, Ronnie.'

Ronnie grimaced as he noticed the bruises on Jericho's neck and the stiff way that he was moving. 'You don't look exactly fine...' Suddenly the door to the main bedroom opened slightly and Ronnie caught a glimpse of Maggie's black hair as she peered around the corner.

An embarrassed Ronnie began to apologize profusely. 'I can see that I've come at a most inopportune time, Paul, so I will let you get back to bed...err...to sleep, I mean. But I'm glad that you still appear to be in one piece after your heroics yesterday.'

Jericho ushered Ronnie back to the front door. 'Thanks for calling, Ronnie. And for your understanding. I really am feeling much better now, despite the way I look.'

Ronnie smiled as he stepped over the threshold. 'I certainly hope so. I wouldn't want to feel as bad as you presently look,' he joked with a parting nod.

Jericho returned to the living room in a disturbed mood. Maggie now opened the bedroom door wider and joined him in the living room, wearing one of his old dressing gowns.

Jericho could her face was deeply troubled. 'What is going on, Paul?' she asked. 'I don't understand what is happening. That man who was just here...'

'Yes...?' he said warily. 'What about him?'

Maggie seemed shocked. 'I think that's the man that I saw once with

Dora Kam in Lockhart Road.'

Jericho nodded sadly. 'Yes, I know it is...'

CHAPTER 31

Friday, 3rd September 1937

As it was nearly dawn, Jericho didn't go back to bed but had a shave and a shower instead, then dressed for work in his spare summer uniform. He reflected that the uniform he'd worn yesterday was still at the station and heavily stained with the blood that had been spilt during yesterday's violent events. Some of that blood must even be George Dorling's, Jericho realized sadly...

It would take some hard work by the wallahs in the service laundry to get that uniform clean again, and it would take even more hard work on Jericho's own part to put the tragic events of yesterday behind him completely. Yet given the scale of that tragedy, perhaps he never would be able to, not fully...

After he had finished dressing, and while Maggie was in the shower, he went out on the balcony to finally investigate what had caused that frightening and unearthly noise last night. The sun was just rising above the eastern hills and bathing the island in a fresh roseate light. The hot morning rays lit up the flanks of the green mountains above Happy Valley, and revealed the hillside immediately above the apartment with startling clarity. Jericho saw at once that he had been absolutely right in his supposition about the cause of that fearful noise last night, yet the extent of the landslip was much more severe than even that horrendous sound had suggested. A great slice of the forested hillside had slid away from a rocky outcrop and collapsed into the forest below, flattening everything in its path. The rocky outcrop itself was still standing, but it was now stripped bare of the topsoil and forest cover that had previously covered most of its height and was now shown to be an exposed vertical rock face sixty or seventy feet high. A torrent of water was still surging down the hillside above this outcrop of rock, before becoming divided by the granite cliff into two separate waterfalls, which then spilled down into the mud and destruction below. Fortunately this tidal wave of destruction had taken a relatively beneficial direction, for the worst of it lay between Jericho's apartment building and the next house higher up the hill on Blue Pool Road. This area of Blue Pool Road was still quite rural with only a scattering of colonial bungalows at the higher end, which soon thinned to nothing at all as the road climbed higher to join Stubbs Road, before ascending even higher over the mountains at Wong Nei Chung Gap.

When he returned to the bedroom, Jericho knocked on the adjoining bathroom door. 'Shall I make you some tea, Maggie?' But he got no answer, so knocked more loudly. When she still didn't answer, he opened the door discreetly to find the bathroom empty. He was confused now because the dressing gown she had borrowed was lying on the bed, while her own clothes – the white cotton blouse and black skirt - were certainly gone. Then he looked around the rest of the apartment, calling out her name: the small dining room, the second bedroom and the utility room used by his visiting amah and houseboy. But there was no sign of Maggie Yiu...

He went to the front door and realized she must have stepped out for a moment. Perhaps she wanted a little walk along Blue Pool Road in the relative cool of early morning, for it was a delightfully quiet street to enjoy after the crush and constant noise of Wanchai. The other possibility was that she had decided to leave early in order to avoid any encounters with any of his neighbours and to save him from any potential embarrassment.

But surely not without saying goodbye..? That wasn't like Maggie at all. In any case her own building in Lockhart Road was not safe to occupy therefore he couldn't imagine she would go back there without a word of explanation to him. Of course she had been deeply troubled to discover that Jericho seemed to be a close friend and confidante of the very man she had once seen with Dora Kam. Jericho had not explained any of that to her, not sure where he would begin...

He went back into the living room and saw with a feeling of relief that she had left her caged bird Ling-Ling behind at least, which reassured him that she was intending to come back here at some point.

When he heard another quiet knock at the front door of the apartment, Jericho opened it at once. 'Maggie...'

But it wasn't Maggie; it was Ronnie Grantham back again...

'I saw your beautiful lady friend hastily exiting the building, so I decided to come back,' Ronnie said matter-of-factly. 'Is she anybody I know? I must say that you know how to attract beautiful women, Paul. First Susan, now this exquisite girl.'

Jericho limited himself to saying: 'No, she's nobody you know, Ronnie.'

They went and sat on the balcony as if nothing was amiss. Yet the underlying tension between them now was unmistakable. 'Shall I bring some tea, Ronnie?' Jericho asked his old friend quietly.

'No, that's all right. I don't need any tea.' Ronnie glanced at the terrible destruction on the hillside above them. 'My God! Look at that! You've been very lucky, Paul. That mudslide could have come this way and enveloped this whole building. In which case you and your lady friend might have been killed...' Ronnie saw the bleak look on Jericho's face and his own face fell. '*You know everything, don't you...?*

Jericho nodded sadly. 'I think I do...*unfortunately.*'

Ronnie sighed heavily. 'What was it that gave me away?'

'It was that damned gold chain that you dropped when I saw you last Saturday in Government House.'

Ronnie nodded in understanding. 'Yes, I thought you showed far too much interest in that little gold chain, though I didn't understand why.'

Jericho was sombre. 'Well, it wasn't because of any brilliant deductions on my part, or even good solid police work. It was because of the simple fact that I had seen a gold chain like that once before, being worn by a bargirl called Cherry Kwok. But of course you were not to know that I had talked to Cherry Kwok before she died...'

'Why would you think the one I had was the same chain? You only saw it for a second...'

'Actually I *didn't* think it was the same chain at first. But I was curious that you would buy such a simple gold chain for a woman like Faye, for she normally wears much grander jewellery than that. But the oddest thing was that you called it a *necklace* chain. Even from that brief look I had, I could see that it was too small to fit around a woman's neck, even a woman with as slim a neck as Faye. It was obviously an ankle chain. Which meant you couldn't have *bought* that chain from a shop, for no one would have sold it to you as a necklace. Therefore you weren't telling the truth about it: you must have acquired it some other way...'

Ronnie seemed genuinely surprised by that and clearly didn't know what to say in response.

'So I didn't know what to make of your story at first, but gradually the suspicion dawned on me that it might be the same gold ankle chain I had seen Cherry Kwok wearing. That one too had a broken clasp, like yours. Yet if I were to believe such a thing, then I would also have to suspect that *you* – Ronnie Grantham, one of my oldest friends - had killed Cherry Kwok. So I was desperate to find some reason why this couldn't be true, and to prove to myself that your gold chain could not possibly be the same one that Cherry had been wearing. And my policeman's brain finally came up with a solution: for I could see no reason at all why Cherry's murderer would have been so stupid as to have taken the gold chain deliberately from her ankle and kept it on his person as incriminating evidence of what he'd done. And - a further point in your favour - you didn't even know that the chain you had was an ankle chain, therefore you *couldn't have possibly seen Cherry wearing that particular chain...*' Jericho grimaced at the memory of how he had finally absolved Ronnie from his suspicions. 'Therefore...QED...you must have got your chain from someone other than Cherry Kwok. I remember the moment when I thought of it; it was in the early hours of Monday morning when I was up in Caine Road leading a police search in the middle of the night. I was so happy when I thought of it, for it meant you were innocent after all...and that the real murderers of those three young women had to be members of the Kao Ki-kan triad society.'

'And why can't that still be true, then?' Ronnie said quietly.

'Well, for one thing, I spoke to the leader of the Kao Ki-kan last night and he denied doing it.'

Ronnie grunted cynically. 'Well, he would, wouldn't he?'

'Perhaps...but I believed him anyway because he had no reason to lie. He was planning to slit my throat within the next few minutes, and people with such deadly intentions on their mind are often surprisingly frank and honest at such times,' Jericho said with bitter sarcasm.

'Yet you are still right. Only a crazy man would kill a young woman and then keep the evidence of his crime on his person,' Ronnie murmured almost to himself.

Jericho nodded. 'That's true. But it occurred to me that *you might not have known* that you had carried that gold chain away from the murder scene with you...'

'How is that even possible?'

Jericho looked at Ronnie's clothes. Even in the worst heat of summer, he always invariably wore a suit, even if a lightweight one suitable for a tropical climate. And the trousers of his suits always had neat turn-ups at the bottom...

Ronnie saw the direction of his eyes and shrugged resignedly. 'You are a great detective to even think of such a thing.'

Jericho didn't say anything more. But he knew he was right: that gold ankle chain with the damaged clasp must have fallen off Cherry Kwok's ankle when Ronnie had been strangling her, and had slipped into the turn-up of one of his trouser legs without him noticing. Ronnie had obviously not even noticed before that Cherry had been wearing an ankle chain. So it seemed that Ronnie had not discovered the existence of the gold chain at all until he happened to wear the same pair of trousers again ten days later and found the chain by accident inside the turn-up. Then he must have quickly realized the truth and hidden the chain in his inside pocket so he could dispose of it safely later. It was just Ronnie's ill luck again that it was the same Saturday that Jericho had met him in Government House, and that Ronnie had accidentally pulled the gold chain out into full view while reaching for his cigarette case...

Jericho wasn't normally the fanciful kind, but it did seem almost as if Cherry Kwok had managed to lead him to her killer from beyond the grave...that little gold chain had been like the Mark of Cain...

'Is that gold chain the only piece of evidence against me?' Ronnie asked mildly. 'For it *is* gone now, safely buried somewhere at the bottom of the harbour.'

'Unfortunately I now know the truth, so I can hardly just forget this,' Jericho said. 'In any case, there *is* more evidence. A witness saw you leaving Cherry Kwok's room on the night she died and will probably be able to identify you.' Jericho looked at Ronnie's eyes which, like all the Grantham family, were a striking shade of blue. With a feeling of intense pain, he suddenly remembered how their friends in Surrey had described those distinctive eyes: "*...as blue as the sea off the Isle of Capri...*"

Jericho had to fight to keep his voice under control. '...And everything else fits. You did show a great deal of interest in this case of mine - unusually for you - and I obligingly told you everything I was thinking. You must have been pleased at the start that I suspected a common seaman of some sort, but you must have begun to worry when I started to suspect that the murderer might be a client of this escort agency run by a man called Marco da Silva, the Blue Heaven Agency. You *were* one of Da Silva's clients, weren't you, Ronnie?'

Ronnie said nothing so Jericho remonstrated with him with real pain in his voice for the first time. 'I understand everything but why you did such a terrible thing. *In the name of God, why...?*'

*

Ronnie had gone very pale. 'I will try and explain what happened. It doesn't relieve me from this terrible guilt, or exculpate me in any way, yet it might help you understand how somebody like me could have ended up in this dark place.' He paused heavily. 'I was no saint before this happened. Yet my sins, such as they were, were minor things in the great scheme of life. I have never been petty or vicious or evil-tempered, and have always been loyal to my friends. Yet one moment of weakness has ruined everything.' He looked at Jericho. 'Did you know that I had lived here in Hong Kong for sixteen years, thirteen of them as a bachelor, and I had never been near a Chinese woman? I played the game strictly to the rules of this place. I courted a selection of nice English girls, all of whom grew rather bored with me in the end. Yet when I met Faye and found that she liked me equally in return, it seemed I was to get the proper reward for my patience. Yet my marriage has turned out to be a disaster; it's not easy finding myself married to a beautiful woman who has, for a variety of reasons, become steadily more contemptuous of me with time. So I became restless for the company of some compliant local girl who would let me make love to her without complications, and who would treat me with some respect for a change...'

The balcony was growing very hot as the sun rose higher, and Ronnie pushed his rattan chair further back into the shade. 'One night in Bessie's Bar, I ran into a Eurasian man...'

'Da Silva...' Jericho interrupted grimly.

'Yes. He was quite charming in his way, and I didn't suspect his real purpose at first. But eventually he told me about a house in Caine Road that catered discreetly to the sexual pleasures of ex-pats...'

'I suppose that is the former Woo mansion – the one known as the Portuguese House?'

'Yes, that's the place, although I didn't know it belonged to the Woo family at the time. Anyway, Da Silva told me that his agency ran a discreet service from this house, and for a very reasonable price. And – God help me! – I agreed. So Da Silva arranged an evening for me in late June. I got to the house first that evening. Then three Chinese women arrived, all very beautiful and in fine silk cheongsams. I was allowed to talk to them individually, then choose any or all of them...'

'That would have been Cherry, Dora and Judy.'

Ronnie nodded. 'Yes, of course. I found I couldn't choose between them, so I allowed them all to stay. I had never been with a Chinese woman before, and now I had three of them at my beck and call. They were a revelation, beautiful and pliable and submissive, in a way that Western women can never be. Perhaps I've always been a little repressed in sexual matters, but those girls soon ended all my old inhibitions. Yet I never intended to do such a thing again; I was intent on trying to save my marriage by becoming more the sort of man whom Faye had thought she was marrying...' His brow darkened. 'Yet a week later I got a note from one of the Chinese women who had been at the house in Caine Road...Judy Wong. She now showed herself in her true light...'

'What did she want?' Jericho asked, though he knew the answer already.

Ronnie laughed bitterly. 'Money, of course. I arranged to meet her in Wanchai, and she made her demands. I paid up the first time without complaint...and even the second time, though it was only a few days after her first demand. But the third time she asked me for a simply ridiculous amount of money, so I finally refused. She said the other girls wanted a share of the money too for their silence...'

'I doubt that was true,' Jericho said. 'Those three women weren't close, and didn't like each other, so it's unlikely they entered this plot together. It's more likely that it was just Judy on her own...Cherry Kwok would never have gone back to sleeping with sailors in the Tin Hau Hotel if she had been sharing in this windfall.'

'Yet I was forced to believe Judy. She threatened to go to the newspapers and ruin my name with claims of bestial behaviour and drug taking. She began to taunt me, calling me filthy names, and I suppose I just lost my temper. I had never even struck a woman before, and yet I found myself a moment later with that woman hanging dead in my arms like a limp rag doll. I don't even remember strangling her in retrospect, but I must have done it...' He held out his hands in front of him and regarded his strong fingers with a long sigh. 'And once the die was cast, I had no choice but to find the two other girls and eliminate them too.'

'Then those were fully premeditated acts. You can't claim a moment of madness about killing Dora and Cherry,' Jericho said sombrely.

Ronnie hung his head in shame. 'No, I suppose not. But I couldn't let those women destroy me. This wasn't about Faye any more. I already knew by this time that she was having an affair with Sebastian Ride, and that she would probably leave me for him. So I was resigned to that. But the evidence of those three women would have ended any hope of me becoming Attorney General. Now, because of Colby's illness, that dream was almost within my grasp, only for it to be snatched away again. Bad timing indeed...it seems to be the story of my life...'

'Why didn't you just come to me when Judy Wong began to blackmail you? I would have warned her off for you,' Jericho complained.

Ronnie shrugged. 'I wish I had. But it's too late now; I can't turn back the clock.' He ran a weary hand through his thick flaxen hair, the gesture so like his brother Johnny that Jericho was stricken with real doubt for a moment. *Should he simply try and forget what he'd discovered, and let the Kao Ki-kan take the blame for the deaths of those three women?* For this case against Ronnie, if it came to trial, would destroy Ronnie's father, George, and George Grantham was almost like a father to Paul Jericho too. It was almost a relief that Ronnie's mother, Violet, was long dead, so that she at least would be spared from knowing about her son's disgrace, and about Jericho's part in exposing it.

Ronnie began talking rapidly again, as if he wanted to cleanse his soul with this confession. 'Even with the three women dead, I still had a problem, for Da Silva might have put two and two together and realized that the three women who had been murdered were not only all on his agency's books, but had all been with me at the house in Caine Road. But Da Silva then got himself conveniently murdered so I thought I was home free.' He snorted bitterly. 'But I wasn't of course. For I now found I had another blackmailer to deal with. An even worse one than Judy Wong...*Ian Luff*...'

Jericho didn't say anything; he had been waiting for Ian Luff's name to appear in this terrible saga.

'I soon discovered that the whole thing with the three women was Ian Luff's doing. He was a friend of Da Silva – he's probably sleeping with the man – and it was Luff who gave my name to Da Silva to approach...'

'So that's why you deliberately left Luff's business card in the Tin Hau

Hotel?' Jericho realized.

'It seemed like the least I could do – to try and frame him in return.' Ronnie smiled grimly. 'Luff was also a great friend of the late James Woo of Saunders-Woo and wanted to put some pressure on me on behalf of Woo's company to endorse those government plans to build social housing on several sites, including that quarry in Shaukeiwan. That's why they used the house in Caine Road – it belongs to the Woo family, and Ian Luff was able to get the use of it for his honey trap. He and Da Silva probably caught many more victims than just me there, including some no doubt very important people in Hong Kong. But Luff got much more on me than just some ugly sexual affair with Chinese prostitutes; he knows somehow that I murdered those three women so has me totally in his power now. Now there's one man that I could cheerfully kill without any compunction whatsoever...!'

'A lot of people would like to kill that man,' Jericho said, 'for he seems to be blackmailing half of Hong Kong.' Then an uneasy thought occurred to him. 'You haven't killed Luff too, have you? Is that why he's suddenly disappeared?'

Ronnie grimaced violently. 'No such luck. The man has simply gone into hiding until the situation calms down. That man is the devil incarnate, spreading his tentacles everywhere to ensnare them. I am pretty sure that he is also blackmailing Colby and Harmsworth. I don't know what Luff has found out about Harmsworth – probably a hint of some old corruption scandal; rumours have long persisted that Harmsworth can be bought. Luff was probably blackmailing Colby about his Chinese mistress in Kowloon, which is really only a secret from his wife Eileen. Poor Colby will not be worrying too much about that now, with a death sentence hanging over his head, but he might still want to keep his affair private from his wife. I think Luff may also be blackmailing that young Chinese lawyer Michael Yip about his hopeless affair with Edith Starling...'

*

'So what do we do now?' Ronnie asked. 'Are you going to take me in and charge me?' He was calm now after being allowed to explain himself, and seemed to have accepted his fate without complaint.

Jericho made a gesture of helplessness. 'What else can I do, Ronnie?' Yet he was still stricken with real nagging doubt about what to do for the best. The thought of what this would do to Ronnie's father, George, was still the most troubling thing in his mind. *How could Jericho ever look George Grantham in the face again if he was responsible for bringing his son to court and seeing him hanged?* For Ronnie would certainly hang for his crimes based on the facts of the case...

Jericho became aware that Ronnie was no longer looking at him, but at something on the hillside behind that had obviously attracted his interest.

'Look at that!' Ronnie said, suddenly galvanized into action.

Jericho turned his head and saw what Ronnie was pointing at – a small group of figures clinging to what remained of the slope below that tall granite outcrop. There seemed no hope for these people because they had no way of escape: below them the ground fell away into the deep red mud of the landslide, while a foaming cataract of water on each side prevented them moving sideways across the hillside to stable ground. Jericho went and fetched his binoculars and focused quickly on the group; they turned out to an old Chinese couple with two small children of seven or eight. He guessed that they must be refugees from the mainland who had been squatting illegally on the hillside. Through the field glasses he could see that even the thin ledge of soil on which they were standing was crumbling and would soon slip away to join the devastation below.

The only way out for these people seemed to be the granite cliff above, which was stable at least. But Jericho's binoculars showed him that the cliff was a near vertical face of rock that seemed as smooth as a billiard ball from here.

'I'll run down to the telephone box in the street and call for help,' Jericho said, still looking through the glasses.

Ronnie touched his arm. 'Those people will be dead long before help arrives. That slope below is still unstable and looks ready to slip again at any moment.' He pointed at the exposed rock cliff. 'Can you get me to the top of that cliff? I can climb down from there and carry them up on my back. The children certainly...'

Jericho hesitated because the climb looked suicidal from here.

'Let me do it,' Ronnie begged. 'Can't you see – it gives me some small chance of atonement?'

'But look at that cliff face! It looks impossible to climb even *with* the right equipment. And we don't even have proper boots for climbing.'

Ronnie gripped his arm. 'Doesn't matter. I'll manage. Don't forget...I used to be one of the best young rock climbers in England...'

*

Jericho and Susan had often climbed together on these steep wooded slopes during the cool dry days of autumn and winter, and they had often ended up having a picnic at some scenic and vertiginous spot on the hillside where the views below of Happy Valley and the harbour beyond were quite stunning. And one of their favourite picnic spots had been very near that granite outcrop which nature had now turned into a fearsome vertical cliff face.

So Jericho, almost against his own judgement, had given in to Ronnie's persuasion and led him onto the hillside behind the apartment. Twenty minutes of hard uphill walking and scrambling up sodden slopes, then clambering along a fallen tree trunk to cross a cascade of flood water, had brought them to a point at the top of this granite cliff. From the summit of the rock face, the climb down looked a hundred times more difficult than it had seemed through his binoculars. But he could see that Ronnie was still determined to give it a go – perhaps he really saw it as a means of redemption for himself - and so Jericho had allowed him to try, even though Ronnie was only wearing a spare pair of Jericho's police boots.

Then Jericho watched from his safe position above while Ronnie did the miraculous, climbing down the cliff with relative ease, and finding safe handholds and footholds where none seemed to exist. The strength in his fingers was truly astonishing to Jericho; Ronnie seemed to be able to support his own body weight with just two fingers of one hand, which seemed an almost superhuman feat.

Those same fingers that had choked the life out of Judy Wong and Dora Kam and Cherry Kwok were now being put to much better use in saving life, which unexpected notion gave Paul Jericho some considerable pause for thought as he watched this bravura performance…

Within fifteen minutes of arriving, Ronnie had brought the two small ragged children up to safety, and then the old woman who turned out to be the children's grandmother. Now Ronnie was about to return down the cliff face for the old man, who was now lying half-collapsed below from fatigue.

Jericho could see that the two foaming cataracts on each side of the granite outcrop were not abating in strength at all, but that the flow seemed to be increasing noticeably, even in the last few minutes. Suddenly a fresh deluge of water erupted from nowhere and cascaded down the slope below, washing much of the remaining soil away in a great slide of mud.

The narrow ledge of soil on which the old man was half-lying was washed away in this fresh flood, and he was left clinging by his hands to a tiny ledge of granite.

Ronnie started to lower himself over the edge again, but Jericho pulled him back. 'You can't save that man, Ronnie! Let it go. You've saved three lives. Isn't that enough atonement for you?'

But Ronnie only smiled sadly at him, then evaded Jericho's hands with ease. In a second he was on his way to the bottom of the cliff again, moving even faster than before, now that he knew the best route. Reaching the bottom, he managed to lift the old man onto his back, who wrapped his claw-like hands around Ronnie's broad shoulders.

The old man was a much heavier burden than the children or the old woman had been, and Jericho could see that Ronnie was struggling now as he ascended. Perhaps it was the realization that this ascent would be the last meaningful act of his life that slowed his steps: ahead lay only opprobrium, universal condemnation and a mean and sordid death at the hands of the hangman.

Yet he made it to the top in the end and handed the old man over safely into Jericho's care.

But Ronnie didn't climb to safety himself, but lay spread-eagled at the top of the rock face, supported only by his fingertips.

Jericho could see what was going through Ronnie's mind and stretched out a hand to try and reach him.

But Ronnie wasn't going to be persuaded. 'It's better like this, old man...'

Jericho watched in despair as Ronnie released his tenuous grip on the rock and began to slide way into the mud and devastation far below...

CHAPTER 32

Saturday, 4th September 1937

On Saturday morning, the British Crown Colony of Hong Kong was doing its best to recover from the battering of Thursday's great storm. Some people were already saying that it was one of the greatest storms ever recorded in Hong Kong; it was certainly one of the deadliest. Paul Jericho had seen a preliminary police report that suggested that the death toll could be more than ten thousand souls...

The shipping in Victoria Harbour, the seventh busiest port in the world, had been devastated by the storm too; the typhoon wind had been so strong that instruments at the Hong Kong Observatory, which were capable of registering winds up to 125 miles per hour, had simply broken down. So the maximum gusts had possibly been close to two hundred miles per hour, as predicted. The typhoon had been so powerful that it had caused a thirty-foot tidal wave to sweep through the villages of Tai Po and Shatin in the New Territories, where many of the deaths had occurred as a result. That was an even bigger wave than the one which had nearly killed Paul Jericho at Shaukeiwan.

Yet it seemed it was not his time to die...

For here he was on this bright, hot Saturday morning, sitting in his office in Wanchai Police Station, with Superintendent Charlie Hebdon and Inspector Kevin Ball facing him from the other side of his desk. Jericho was now reduced to wearing his oldest summer uniform given that both of his best green khaki uniforms were in the laundry being steamed clean of blood and dirt.

Jericho was mildly amused to see that Kevin Ball's new-found respect for him was still prevailing for the moment, though that respect was also tinged with some obvious envy too. For Kevin Ball was an inveterate glory chaser, therefore would have given his right arm to have done what Jericho had done on Thursday night: to survive a bloody shootout with the Kao Kikan.

And now, to compound things, Jericho had also helped save the lives of a Chinese family, trapped by a huge landslide...

Superintendent Hebdon was equally respectful for a change. 'You have brought great credit on the Hong Kong Police for what you and Ronnie Grantham did yesterday, Paul,' he said, with an almost reverential air.

'I've told you, sir. It was Ronnie who risked his life, then made the ultimate sacrifice.'

Hebdon nodded. 'That's not the way I see it. I know fine well that you must have played a major part too. But I understand your wish to honour your friend Grantham. He proved himself a true Englishman in the end. I'm glad you were able to recover his body at least, unlike so many of the poor wretches who died at Tai Po and Shatin. This week has been a terrible double tragedy for you: first losing young George Dorling, and now your oldest friend in Hong Kong. As a Christian man, I'm not sure I should be saying this, but I doubt that the saving of four rather ordinary Chinese lives was worth the life of that remarkable young man...'

Jericho was still consumed by sadness for his friend's final end, despite everything. But it was still a better end than being tried and hanged for committing brutal and callous murder, therefore Jericho was even beginning to feel some relief that Ronnie had taken this way out. Jericho was now going to do his best to protect Ronnie's reputation, for his family's sake, as he had already done for George Dorling. He would never have done this if either man had survived, but their sacrificial and glorious deaths had bought his reluctant silence about their crimes...

Inspector Ball now spoke up, his voice still tinged with a note of envy. 'So, Paul...have you now come around to my way of thinking about the murder of the three bargirls? I always thought that it must be the triad who had killed those women too, rather than some Westerner as you thought. All three women worked for Freddie Ling and Marco da Silva, after all, so were probably killed for the same reason as their bosses. They must have crossed Lucky Lam in some way.'

Hebdon looked somewhat doubtful. 'Well, Paul. What do *you* think now? Do you still think it was a Westerner? Or could Kevin be right?'

It pained Jericho to have to say it, but he did it as graciously as he could, choosing his words with great care. 'I don't think there's any need to keep the case open and to continue looking for any other suspects, sir.'

Kevin Ball smirked with pride at his clever insight, though Jericho could not remember him actually saying before that he had thought the Kao Kikan had murdered the three women.

Hebdon seemed content with Jericho's vague validation. 'Fine. We'll wind the case down. I'm sure that the murderers of those three women are already dead. I suspect it was probably Lam's two thugs who did the actual deed – Teng and Cheung – so you have already dealt with those two very satisfactorily, Paul. It was certainly lucky that you had that spare revolver on your person...'

'I told you, sir. I had been speaking to Mr Sebastian Ride earlier in the day, and I found he was in possession of an illegal firearm. So I confiscated it, not wanting him to get into trouble with the law.'

'Very wise too,' Hebdon laughed. 'We can't have businessmen roaming about the city armed to the teeth, even if they are worried about their personal safety in these difficult times.' Hebdon had a sudden thought. 'Do you know that Ride came into Central Station yesterday and gave a corrected statement about the death of his partner James Woo? It seems he was present when Mr Woo fell to his death...'

'Yes, sir. I had already spoken to Mr Ride about it, which no doubt prompted his change of evidence. We found a witness who had seen him there.'

Ball intervened again. 'Do you think Ride actually knocked his partner off, then? It will be a huge scandal if he were to be charged.'

Jericho answered quickly, not sure why he was still being so kind to Sebastian Ride when the man's wretched behaviour had been such a leading cause in Susan's death. 'No, I'm convinced that it really was an accident. The unsafe condition of the parapet was the only reason for James Woo's death; Ride lied about being there only to avoid a bit of spiteful public gossip, nothing more.'

'Well, he'll have to face that gossip now,' Ball sniggered. 'He might even have to face a manslaughter charge.'

'I doubt that very much,' Jericho said firmly.

'Well, we'll see,' Hebdon answered heavily. 'But Commissioner Matlock is a good friend of Ride's so I would be surprised if there was any charge laid against the man.' He looked Jericho in the eyes. 'By the way, I spoke to Dorling's widow yesterday. A very nice Yorkshire lass. She used to be a "Nippy" waitress in a Lyons teahouse on the Scarborough seafront, she told me. I could see that she is broken up about George, but she is a strong young woman and will survive this. Of course I expect that she will go back home soon and try to recover her spirits there. I am going to make damned sure that she gets the best government pension we can get for her. And I intend to have a collection for her among the force so that she will have a tidy nest egg to take back to England with her...'

Charlie Hebdon seemed quite emotional for a change, Jericho thought. But he soon became business-like again as he asked Jericho about Edith Starling. 'Have you had any further thoughts about that young woman's abduction? I didn't have time to commend you properly before on finding her, but it was a piece of capital work.'

Jericho smiled wearily. 'I've been busy with too many other things to give it much thought, sir. I sent a team out to Shaukeiwan to make a thorough search of the place where Edith was being held, but they found nothing significant to tell us who her abductor might be.' He turned to Ball. 'I believe that you are looking into the disappearance of this second person from Government House – Ian Luff. Have you come up with anything yet?'

Ball looked uneasy. 'I don't think he's been abducted or anything like that. I think it more likely that he simply went away for a few days somewhere – Macau or one of the outlying islands – and has not been able to make it back yet because of the disruption of the typhoon.'

'Well, you could be right,' Jericho agreed thoughtfully. He hadn't told Ball of his suspicions about Luff – that the man was a blackmailer, and perhaps worse. He could hardly confess what he had heard about Luff, first from Sebastian Ride, and then from Ronnie, without revealing the much greater secrets he was concealing.

Apart from everything else that Jericho was holding back from Ball and Hebdon, he also hadn't told them about what he had learned from Sebastian Ride and his wife concerning Susan's death. And nor did he intend to until the right moment. He had decided instead that he was going to go after the driver of the car himself. If Gloria Ride was right about this, then the car was a big American saloon car, dark blue or black in colour, and might have been a Studebaker President. That was a rather unusual make of car in Hong Kong, therefore it didn't seem as if it would be an enormously difficult task to track it down, given that there were only about two thousand registered cars on the roads of the colony.

Ball and Hebdon got to their feet and packed their notebooks back into their briefcases in readiness to return to Central Station. But Jericho called Ball back with a deliberately casual question. 'Kevin, do you still have that list of all the cars that you checked in connection with my wife's death in January?'

Ball indicated the briefcase he was carrying with a wry nod. 'Not with me, I'm afraid.' Why do you ask?'

'Could you send me a copy of it?'

Ball frowned, and glanced at Hebdon, who was looking similarly disturbed. 'I thought I'd sent you a copy before?'

'No, you promised you would. But you never did,' Jericho stated firmly.

Ball cleared his throat a little nervously. 'Then I apologize. I will have a copy made and sent over to you today. But it will tell you nothing you don't already know, Paul. That list contains all the vehicles I could discover that had sustained some damage to their front bumpers or bonnets, and then been subsequently repaired in a licensed garage between January 19th and the end of May. I whittled the list down to only twenty-odd cars in the end, but their owners were all able to prove that they had been nowhere near Kennedy Road on the night of January the nineteenth when the accident happened. That's what convinced me that the driver must be some rich Chinese who had managed to get his car repaired secretly in a private garage somewhere.'

'Do you remember if there was a Studebaker on the list, perhaps a Studebaker President, dark blue or black in colour?'

Ball glanced again at Hebdon for support. 'No, I am absolutely confident there was no Studebaker President on the list of any colour. Several Austin and Morris saloons, a couple of Chryslers and Fiats, and even one Cadillac saloon owned by a rich Chinese, but definitely no Studebaker...'

'What colour was the Cadillac?' Jericho asked.

'It *was* a dark blue colour, if I remember correctly...' Ball admitted. 'What is this all about, Paul? Have you got some new evidence to share about the case? Has some new witness come forward and identified the type of car?'

'No, not really,' Jericho said evasively. 'It's just a rumour that I heard from one of my own informants.' He gave Ball a long stare. 'So who did the Cadillac belong to?'

'Well, it's a bit of a coincidence, since we were just talking about the Woo family,' Ball said.

'You mean the Cadillac was owned by James Woo?' Jericho asked urgently.

'No, this blue Cadillac is owned by his sister...*Grace Woo*...'

*

At midday Jericho left the station to stretch his legs, despite the heavy humid blanket of heat that had returned to envelop the streets of Wanchai again. The streets were filled with coolies and trades people again, trying to clean up after the typhoon and make patch repairs to broken windows and doors. But Jericho hardly noticed all this intense Oriental chatter and bustle going on around him, for his mind was still reeling with the shock of what Kevin Ball had told him...

Could it be true that Grace Woo had been driving the car that killed Susan? He recalled that Gloria Ride had been convinced that the driver of the car was a man. *But what if she was mistaken?* What if it had been a woman dressed in a man's suit and hat, for example? Gloria Ride had certainly not got a close look at the driver therefore might have simply got it wrong...

James Woo had supposedly seen the whole thing from the balcony of Ian Luff's flat in Bowen Road, and had claimed that he had recognized the make of car but not the identity of the driver. *But what if he was lying?* What if he had recognized the car perfectly well as his sister's blue Cadillac? That would certainly explain his reluctance to tell Sebastian Ride everything.

Yet it seemed a huge coincidence that both James and his sister should be there that night unless Grace Woo had some individual motive of her own for her presence there in Kennedy Road. *Could she be sweet on Sebastian Ride too and have seen Susan as a potential rival to be removed?* Could she perhaps have followed Susan to her rendezvous with Sebastian Ride, just as Gloria Ride had done?

It was possible, of course...

Gloria Ride had said that the car made no attempt to brake prior to the collision and seemed to have hit Susan almost deliberately. Yet Jericho had met Grace Woo and she did not seem like the sort of evil person who would do a thing like that...

Kevin Ball had also checked the whereabouts of Grace Woo on that January night, as he had for the twenty or so other drivers on his list who had lately damaged the front bumpers of their cars. Grace had affirmed that she had done this damage to her Cadillac when she had recently grazed a street lamp in Conduit Road, while she had also claimed to be at home with her family on the night of January 19th. Well, James Woo had certainly not been home that evening, so Jericho had to wonder just how well Kevin Ball had checked Grace's alibi...

Jericho looked up suddenly as he realized that his perambulations through Wanchai had brought him to Maggie Yiu's tenement block again. Yet perhaps it was no accident that had brought him here. He had not seen her since she had disappeared from his apartment yesterday morning without a word, and he was beginning to fear that he had offended her in some way. Either that, or else she had been frightened and disturbed at Jericho's apparent amiable relationship with the man who might have murdered poor Dora Kam...

Jericho was desperate to see her again and to explain what had happened – or as much as he could explain to her without it jeopardizing Ronnie Grantham's reputation. He could hardly believe that Maggie would have come back to her old room to stay, though – Jericho had made sure yesterday that the building was marked with clear warning signs in Chinese and English that the building was unsafe and should not be entered under any circumstances.

Jericho did however poke his own head inside the front door and listen for a second to hear if anyone had returned to the tenement. Yet the building was as lifeless as the grave, so he gave up after five minutes and retraced his steps back to the station, where he had a million pressing things to do...

*

At nine that evening, Jericho finally left Wanchai Police Station after being on duty for fourteen hours solid, apart from his brief excursion at midday. This long working day had at least helped him catch up with his paperwork and other administrative tasks, which was the one part of this job that he really detested. One of his tasks today had been to recommend someone for promotion to replace George Dorling. He knew Hebdon would expect him to propose one of the young expatriate officers in the station, of which there were several who were showing great promise. But Jericho was determined to try and promote Thomas Sung this time after all his years of honest and dedicated service. So, regardless of the consequences, Jericho had drafted a memo to Hebdon putting Sung's name forward for promotion. He knew that Hebdon would be unlikely to accept his recommendation, of course, but it still felt like the right thing to do. It would at least be one small positive to take from the sad death of George Dorling, if Thomas Sung finally made it to sergeant...

Even at nine o'clock in the evening, the humid heat on the waterfront road felt like the interior of a Turkish bath, and Jericho could feel the beads of sweat rise instantly on his face in response. He had again left his Austin in Lockhart Road this morning because of the present congestion of vehicles in the station yard, so started walking.

Now that he was finally done with his mundane administrative tasks today, Jericho's thoughts began to return to more interesting matters, in particular the matter of the egregious Mr Ian Luff. He wondered again what had happened to this disreputable individual. Kevin Ball could of course be right, and Luff might have simply decamped from Hong Kong for a few days rest, and been trapped on one of the outlying islands until the typhoon was over. But the fact that he had not returned was ominous: it might mean that one of his enemies had finally caught up with him.

Jericho knew for certain that Luff had been blackmailing both Sebastian Ride and Ronnie Grantham, and he was almost equally certain that Luff was blackmailing Julian Colby and Bob Harmsworth, and perhaps Michael Yip too. So God only knew how many other people this charming viper might be blackmailing. Luff also seemed to be the corrupting agent who had caused the rift between James Woo and his conservative Chinese family, so the Woo family too would have very strong reasons for hating this man if they knew the truth.

Jericho remembered that he had suspected Luff at one time of some involvement in the murders of the three women in Wanchai. That suspicion seemed rather foolish in retrospect. Yet he recalled the accusations that Sebastian Ride had made about Luff: that he was not only a cynical blackmailer and an exploiter of human folly, but might also be selling secrets to the Japanese. *Could Luff be the man who had abducted Edith Starling and left her to die?* Could he have murdered Ralph Ogden too? He had certainly had that opportunity...

If Luff did reappear in Hong Kong and was charged with any offences, then it would of course have one unpleasant consequence: for he apparently knew that Ronnie Grantham had murdered the three women in Wanchai, and he might even make that knowledge public if he was ever brought to trial for his own crimes. Of course Luff might have no direct evidence of Ronnie's guilt, yet just the accusation against Ronnie would undo all of Jericho's own work in trying to save Ronnie's reputation. Jericho felt suddenly uneasy that he was now becoming complicit in Ronnie's terrible crimes by his willingness to protect his dead friend from scandal, even to the extent of suppressing evidence...

Jericho finally reached his car, and glanced down the street to Maggie Yiu's tenement building, which was all in darkness and devoid of even a single gleam of light. He wondered if Maggie had found herself somewhere new to live and if he would ever see her again. Perhaps she wanted no more to do with him after she had seen him consorting in such a friendly manner with Dora Kam's murderer? *Perhaps she even distrusted him now and didn't feel safe in his company...?*

Jericho felt his mood plummet to one of despair at the thought. His mind suddenly went back to that awful moment when Ronnie had released his finger hold on the rock and had spiralled down that cliff face to disappear into the mud and debris below...

He wondered now if he would ever have suspected Ronnie if it had not been for the business of that gold ankle chain. The truth was...*probably not...*

So it seemed that Ronnie had been found out only because he had happened to wear a pair of trousers with turn-ups at the bottom; it seemed a bitter irony now that Ronnie's impeccable fashion sense, even when committing a murder, had been his downfall.

The thought seemed to trigger another memory in Jericho's mind, though, something else to do with trousers...

What was it...?

Then he remembered... Edith Starling had been wearing trousers on the day that she had been abducted. Jericho had seen her himself by chance that day in Wanchai and had followed her when she had broken into Michael Yip's flat. So he realized belatedly that the fact that she had been wearing trousers that day probably had something to do with her intention to break into his flat and search the place.

But it wasn't that which was nagging at Jericho's memory. It was something else -something to do with the remarks that various people had made about the way Edith looked in a trouser suit. Julian Colby had said something about her looking very desirable in trousers because he'd always had a secret passion for young women bold enough to wear them...

And then Bob Harmsworth had agreed with Colby and said something similar: *I thought that she looked quite wonderful in trousers too...*

But there was a difference. Colby had actually been present in Government House that Tuesday so could certainly have seen Edith in her trouser suit. *But Harmsworth had not been there;* he'd had a day off to get measured for a suit of his own right here in Lockhart Road. Jericho had even seen him here...

So how could Harmsworth have seen that trouser suit? Edith had never worn such a thing at work before. In fact there was only one way Harmsworth could have seen Edith's outfit that day; he must have followed Edith to Happy Valley too and then abducted her...

Harmsworth was the man...

He was the traitor who was selling secrets to the Japanese, and who had then killed his old friend Ogden when Ogden had begun to suspect him. Then he had abducted Edith when she had gone in search of this traitor too...

It all fitted: Jericho remembered the strength in the man's fingers, stronger even that Ronnie Grantham's, able to straighten a bent poker as a parlour trick. Certainly enough strength to strangle his old friend Ogden to death. And certainly enough to throttle a blundering policeman from behind: Jericho had no doubts now who had attacked him in the garden of the Woo mansion in Caine Road.

Harmsworth had also been to the quarry at Shaukeiwan with his government colleagues on the day before Edith's abduction, so would still have had quarry dust and grit on the soles of his shoes. So he had probably not really been to a tailor's for a new suit that day in Wanchai; he had come to Lockhart Road for another purpose that day.

Near Maggie's home...

Jericho suddenly remembered that, three weeks ago, Harmsworth had also been up in the Botanical Gardens at the same time as Maggie too; Jericho had seem them both there himself. That seemed like too much of a coincidence now when he remembered what Lucky Lam had said about Dora Kam: that she had only passed her secret information to an intermediary...*a woman agent whom the Japanese apparently trust...*

Harmsworth and Maggie...

Jericho felt a wave of despair wash over him: *Maggie was working with Harmsworth to sell secrets to the Japanese...*

A dejected Jericho glanced up at the top window of Maggie's tenement building and now saw a gleam of electric light from inside.

The power was still on in the building apparently. But more importantly than that, *Maggie was home again...*

CHAPTER 33

Saturday, 4th September 1937

The rundown restaurant and the dismal tailor's shop that flanked the tenement on each side were both closed and dark. But the door of the tenement itself was partly open which seemed to confirm that somebody had entered here since Jericho's last visit at noon. He began to climb the stained concrete staircase using his torch to see by, remembering as he went the first time that he had entered this building with Maggie. It seemed impossible to him that it was less than four weeks ago, for she had forged a place in his heart since then with her beauty and her grace. Yet now she was revealed to be yet another deceiver...

Though the building was now deserted, it still stank like an earth privy. Yet he recalled that Maggie had not seemed at all embarrassed that first time by the degrading poverty of her surroundings, but had looked instead like some glorious angel ascending through the fiery pits of Hell, untouched by all the squalor around her. The interior of the building no longer seethed with humanity, and the former gabble of noise and the ubiquitous clatter of mah-jong tiles were now replaced by a sinister and threatening stillness. And there was another difference about this building now: the internal walls were heavily cracked and the floors were uneven and sloping visibly. Jericho could hear that the whole structure was creaking and groaning like a living thing, and seemed ready to collapse at any moment.

He came to the second floor, and to the room where Dora Kam had lived briefly. He opened the door with an effort and flashed his torch inside, and saw that the room was as he remembered it from his previous search: partitioned into bed spaces with sacking. The room seemed entirely empty now, though, so he prepared to move on. But then he saw something stir in the darkness.

Yet it wasn't a desperate coolie as he'd expected, but a young Chinese girl of seventeen or eighteen. In the light of his torch, Jericho saw that she was a very pretty girl, white-skinned and tall. She reminded Jericho unexpectedly of Cherry Kwok except for the fact that she was dressed in peasant clothes.

No doubt she was yet another new arrival from China, and one who preferred to take the risk of sleeping here in this condemned building rather than being out on the streets. Soon she would be forced by economic circumstances to work in one of Wanchai's notorious palaces of joy - Chinese hotels like the Luk Kwok, or bars like Nagasaki Joe's or The Black Dog – and would no doubt soon find herself selling her young and slender body to the lowest type of Western seamen.

The girl screwed up her eyes in the glare from his torch.

He spoke to her in Cantonese. 'I'm a policeman. Leave here at once. The building is not safe and could collapse at any moment.'

But she didn't seem to understand so he tried some of his limited Mandarin on her.

This time she seemed to get the gist of what he was saying. *'All right...'* The girl might have only been in Hong Kong for a short time, but she'd learned one useful English phrase at least.

Jericho carried on up to the third floor and Maggie's room. The door was ajar, and he could see that there was a light on inside so he switched off his torch to save the battery. He knocked on the door, then pushed it fully open.

The main ceiling light was on, revealing the interior of the room: the faded pastel colours of the plaster walls, the windows shaded by a bright awning of red and gold, the bamboo and rattan furniture, the lacquer work cabinet and the fine silk painting on the wall. Her new Bakelite radio was still in pride of place by the window.

Jericho couldn't see Maggie from the doorway so stepped inside to look around. Then he turned his head and saw her sitting on the sofa that doubled as a bed. But she wasn't free to move; her hands and feet were bound together with rope, and her mouth was gagged tightly with a handkerchief...

'Come in, Chief Inspector Jericho,' a voice said behind him. 'We've been waiting for you. I was sure you would come eventually to find your lady love if I left a light burning in the window...'

Harmsworth came into Jericho's view and waved a Webley revolver in his face. 'I think I'll relieve you of that weapon in your holster, Inspector.' This was a different Harmsworth from any that Jericho had seen before: the handsome face and the silver hair were the same but the manner was subtly else – efficient, ruthless and deadly. He was using his left hand to hold the revolver – the one with all the fingers intact – so his damaged right hand obviously had some limitations when using a firearm.

Jericho stood his ground and wondered if he might be able to disarm Harmsworth if he rushed him. But the man looked formidable with that weapon in his hand so it seemed a suicidal plan.

Then Jericho felt the concrete floor suddenly lurch a little under his feet, followed by a low rumble of vibration as if the building had been struck by a slight earthquake.

Harmsworth eyed the ceiling curiously, from which a thin rain of concrete dust had begun to fall. But he didn't seem truly concerned about the perilous state of this old tenement. 'Give me your gun now, and use only the first finger and thumb of your left hand to lift it by the barrel,' he ordered. 'If not, I shall be forced to shoot Miss Yiu immediately.'

Jericho doubted that the man was bluffing, so reluctantly did as he was told.

Harmsworth pocketed Jericho's service revolver with his damaged right hand with deft skill. 'You don't seem surprised to find me here?'

'No, I'm not. I have been rather slow on the uptake, but you did eventually give yourself away. The only thing that surprises me is that you've trussed up your confederate Miss Yiu over there.' Jericho went over to her. 'She looks very uncomfortable. Can I at least take that gag from her mouth now?'

'Ever the gentleman, I see.' But despite the cynical remark, Harmsworth allowed Jericho to remove Maggie's gag without further comment.

Harmsworth studied Jericho with frank curiosity. 'I knew I was in trouble when I realized that you and Miss Yiu had become lovers. I came here late on Sunday night after working most of the day, because I needed to see Miss Yiu urgently. But then I saw you leaving her building very discreetly so then I knew the worst. I followed you back up to Government House, thinking you might already know everything and were about to denounce me. But it seemed you had only gone to Mid-levels on other police business. Yet I hung around in Caine Road in the hope of silencing you permanently. But it seems you think of everything for you had someone guarding your back...'

Jericho said nothing to that: clearly Harmsworth had not recognized that his guardian had been Sebastian Ride...

Maggie now broke into a rush of words. 'Paul, it's not the way it looks. I had to help them...'

'Why did you have to help them?' Jericho asked stonily.

'I found out last year that my father has been working secretly for the Japanese for the last ten years; he was their top informant in Shanghai. But I had nothing to do with his activities; I only found out that he was betraying his Chinese friends by accident. I am just a schoolteacher, exactly like I said. But my father's Japanese paymasters heard that I was moving to Hong Kong to work, so they forced me to agree to act as a courier for their agents here. That's all I did: I picked up messages from this man here, or from various triad agents, and delivered them to the Japanese consulate in Macdonnell Road. Dora was one of the triad agents who brought me information to pass on, but I couldn't tell you that when you were trying to find her murderer. But I know nothing about any killings or abductions. You've got to believe me. They don't even pay me for doing this...'

'Why not?' Jericho asked, still heavily subdued. 'Surely treachery like this is worth something.'

Her eyes were pleading with him to understand. 'They have my father as an effective hostage. If I didn't do as they asked, they said that they would give my father's name to the Chinese Nationalists as a Japanese agent. He is of limited use to them now, since they will soon be in possession of Shanghai anyway. So I am sure they mean it. And my father will die a terrible death if his neighbours ever discover the truth about him.'

Harmsworth spoke up behind them. 'For what it's worth, Inspector Jericho, she is telling the truth. She has been a very reluctant courier. Therefore I have never been quite sure of her loyalties, or how much I could really trust her.'

Jericho turned to face him. 'And what of you, Mr Harmsworth? How did a respectable English gentleman like you - a soldier who fought with valour in France, a long-time government servant - end up as a traitor to his own country, selling our secrets to the Japanese for filthy lucre...'

Harmsworth smiled sadly. 'Oh, there's nothing filthy about money, Inspector Jericho. I am not a greedy man, yet I have grown used to a certain level of comfort in my life. But I was in danger of losing everything I had worked for because of a few bad investments – my wonderful apartment in Kotewall Road, and my weekend bungalow out at Shek-O. I couldn't bear the thought of losing those things in my old age, so I had to find a new source of income quickly. That's all there is to it... I can't say anything more in my defence.'

'But to kill one of your oldest friends? How could you do such a thing?'

'Yes, that was the hardest thing to do. Ralph and I fought together with the Norfolk Regiment in the attack near Montauban on the first day of the Battle of the Somme.' He held up his right hand to show his damaged fingers. 'And he even saved my life after I did this to my hand. I did this injury to myself, you see, to try and get away from the Front. Ralph covered for me...I would have been shot for cowardice and dereliction of duty if he hadn't backed me up on my story.'

'And yet you still killed him,' Jericho said accusingly.

'I couldn't do anything else. It was either him or me. Ralph always understood me better than any other human being, and I could never get away with lying to him for long. He could always see right through me, as he had on the Somme when I had deliberately shot away two of my own fingers in order to get a transfer away from the Front. So I knew he was on to me; he even told me a tempting snippet of information about the China Fleet – details of a new piece of sounding equipment that the Royal Navy was supposedly testing. But I could read Ralph just as well in return, so I knew he had rumbled me and that this was simply a trap designed to expose me. I also knew Ralph would have kept such suspicions to himself until they were definitely proved, so I had a small chance of survival. But it meant I had to act quickly; I couldn't leave him alive to tell anyone else his suspicions...'

'Yet lots of people seem to know the truth about you now – myself and Miss Yiu for a start. Was Edith on to you too? Is that why you abducted her?' Jericho paused expectantly as the building seemed to shift slightly under his feet again. He began to wonder if any of them would get of this building alive. Yet Harmsworth seemed remarkably unconcerned, as if he had all the time in the world, so obviously didn't really understand how close this whole building was to complete collapse... 'Why did you not just kill her straightaway? Why did you leave her imprisoned there at the quarry for so long?'

Harmsworth looked sheepish. 'Because I liked her, Inspector. And she was smart too; I was sure she would get to the truth about how Ralph died in the end, and follow the trail to me. Yet I found I couldn't just put a bullet through her pretty head. I've never killed a woman, you see. I was quite amazed by her resilience and fortitude, though – dazzled really, despite it causing me such a huge headache. I even slipped away from Government House on Sunday afternoon – I know a secret way out of the grounds that avoids going through the security on the main gate – and I was astounded to find her still alive after five days without food or water. Even two days later, she was *still* alive, so I had to end it then and give her a large dose of morphine, because a team of engineering surveyors was due at the quarry very soon to start a topographical survey. My Japanese friends provided me with the morphine. I think Edith recognized me just before she succumbed to the drug...' His voice became harsh. 'You did her no favours by finding her, you know. Without that, she would have simply slipped away into a pleasant oblivion. Because of you, she may linger for a long time, reduced to a vegetable existence...'

Jericho was relieved that Harmsworth had not heard about the small improvement in Edith's condition, for she might be in real danger if it was discovered that she had a slight chance of recovery.

'So you have a soft heart, it seems,' Jericho sneered. 'Is that why you didn't shoot me immediately when I arrived?'

Harmsworth looked uneasy for the first time as the building shook yet again. 'No, I just needed to make sure that no one else knows about me apart from you and Miss Yiu...'

LOCKHART ROAD

Suddenly Jericho realized with despair that Harmsworth fully intended to kill Maggie too. He wasn't going to take the chance of leaving her alive to talk either.

'Then you've got it wrong,' Jericho said with apparent confidence. 'I've already made my suspicions about you known to several of my team at Wanchai Police Station. So there is nothing to be gained from killing me and Miss Yiu. You would be better just surrendering yourself to me. That might be a small mitigating factor when you come to trial...'

'They would still hang me, though, wouldn't they?' Harmsworth said ironically. 'And I think I'll take my chances on you being as close-mouthed with your colleagues as you are reputed to be...'

'There's still no point in killing us. You've forgotten one thing...'

Harmsworth frowned. 'What is that?'

Jericho played his trump card, which had just become clear to him. 'I mean Ian Luff...'

Harmsworth tried to look unconcerned. 'What about him?'

'He's blackmailing you, isn't he? If he isn't yet, then he very soon will be, for he knows that you've been selling secrets to the Japanese.'

Harmsworth became philosophical. 'Mr Luff will soon discover that he has bitten off more than he can chew this time. My Japanese friends will make him pay a heavy price for his interference; in fact they probably already have...' Harmsworth gave Jericho an almost admiring look. 'You *are* very well informed, aren't you, Inspector? Though it seems to have done you little good. For here we are, and I have a gun in my hand, and you do not...'

Jericho heard a huge explosive bang then, and thought for a moment that Harmsworth had fired his revolver without warning. But then he saw with a feeling of disbelief that the whole fabric of the building was beginning to tear itself apart. A great chasm had opened up in the floor and Harmsworth was nowhere to be seen...

Jericho picked Maggie up from the sofa at once and put her over his shoulder like a fireman; there seemed no time to undo the ropes tying her hands and feet – the building felt as if it was only seconds away from complete collapse...

He ran to the staircase, but instead of going down the stairs, went *up*, towards the flat roof with its homemade shanty structures of old sacking, rotting wood, and corrugated iron. Maggie yelled out in astonishment that he was going up the stairs and not down. But on the roof he saw what he had hoped to see: that the gap to the adjacent building was only five feet or so, and that they should be able to jump across to the relative safety of that more solid looking roof.

He laid Maggie down and began trying feverishly to undo the knots on the ropes that constrained her hands and feet. But Harmsworth had made a good job of them and they were devilishly hard to unravel. Jericho had just managed to get her feet untied, and was working on her hands, when they both realized that there was no more time: *the building was collapsing completely under them...*

'Save yourself!' Maggie screamed, her hands still not free.

Jericho ignored her and pulled her roughly to her feet. 'Jump together...*now*...!'

Then the building collapsed as if a bomb had gone off...

A moment later Jericho found himself lying on the roof of the next building, engulfed by a huge cloud of dust and concrete debris.

When the rain of debris finally began to disperse, he saw that Maggie's tenement was gone - no more than an ugly mountain of broken concrete and timber over which a pall of dust hung like a funeral shroud.

But his heart filled with despair when he looked around the roof of the building he was standing on, and could see no sign of Maggie at all...

CHAPTER 34

Sunday, 5th September 1937

At ten o'clock the following morning, Paul Jericho left Edith Starling's private nursing room in St Paul's Hospital, and rubbed his unshaven chin wearily. He nodded to the two Chinese constables who were on guard duty at Edith's door. 'Make sure that you let no one in, except hospital staff,' he ordered in Cantonese.

Both men jumped smartly to attention. 'Yes, sir...!'

Jericho began to walk down the corridor towards the main staircase, but was only half way along it when Michael Yip suddenly appeared from a side corridor. His handsome Oriental face was drawn with worry. 'Can I talk to you, Inspector Jericho?'

Jericho agreed resignedly. 'If you must...'

They went into a quiet alcove with a window view that looked out towards Happy Valley and the great sweep of verdant hillside and mountain beyond. From here everything looked deceptively normal for there was no visible sign from this privileged window of the damage and havoc created by the recent typhoon.

'How is Edith?' Yip asked gently.

'She's still in a coma. It's been five days now since she was found, so it's not looking good.'

Yip swallowed painfully. 'That's not what I wanted to hear...'

Jericho saw that Yip's expression had become even more melancholy as he digested the unsettling news about Edith, so he added a small note of optimism. 'Yet her doctors say there is some small improvement in her vital signs over the last two days, so they haven't given up all hope that she might recover spontaneously.'

Yip weighed that information up but didn't seem particularly reassured by it. 'I can't help thinking that I might have been partly responsible for what has happened to her.'

Jericho took pity on the man and shook his head firmly. 'No, that's certainly not true. I know who abducted Edith now. And take it from me, it was nothing to with her personal life, or because of her friendship with you.'

Michael Yip seemed a little reassured by that. 'So who was it who imprisoned Edith and then left her in this condition?'

Jericho fought back a painful yawn. 'I can't tell you that, Mr Yip.'

Yip eyed him shrewdly. 'You look as if you have been up all night, Inspector,' he suggested moodily.

'That's because I have been,' Jericho stated flatly. 'A building collapsed in Wanchai, and I was there the whole night helping the rescue team to look for survivors.' He hesitated. 'But there were none.'

Realization dawned on Michael Yip. 'Ah yes, I heard the sad news about this collapsed tenement. But it seems the death toll has been small – only two people, according to what I was told...'

'That seems to be the case,' Jericho affirmed. 'Most of the residents had already left because the building had been declared unsafe.'

'Then why was anyone inside at all?' Yip frowned, before continuing. 'I have even heard that one of the victims is the Colonial Treasurer, Mr Harmsworth? Is that true?'

'It is; I identified the body myself, for I knew the man slightly.'

Yip looked mystified. 'What on earth was he doing in a condemned tenement in Wanchai?' He suppressed a world-weary smile. 'Or shouldn't we ask?'

'No, we probably shouldn't,' Jericho agreed grimly.

'Who was the other victim, though?' Yip asked, obviously still intrigued by this little mystery.

'A young woman who has been identified as a Miss Maggie Yiu, a teacher up at St Stephen's College. She rented the top room in the building.' Jericho didn't add that he had identified that body too.

'Then presumably Mr Harmsworth and this Miss Yiu were "friends"?' Yip suggested tartly.

Jericho could see that Maggie's name meant nothing at all to Michael Yip, which was something at least. 'I wouldn't like to speculate, Mr Yip. And it's probably better if you don't either,' he admonished him gently.

Yip looked suitably chastened and mumbled an apology. 'Of course...I don't mean to denigrate anyone, especially the dead.' But he wasn't quite done yet. 'Is there any chance that you would let me see Edith now? I expect to be leaving Hong Kong soon, and it would mean a lot to me to see her before I go.'

'Where are you going?' Jericho asked sharply. 'I'm not sure I can allow you to leave the colony when you have clearly been up to some dubious activities during your time here...'

'What do you mean... *dubious activities*?'

Jericho pressed home his attack. 'Who do you really work for, Mr Yip? You are reputed to be a communist sympathizer...so is that who you've been working for during your time here? The Chinese communists...?'

Yip looked at him frankly. 'I make no apology for my political allegiances, Inspector. I am certainly a man of the Left...a socialist if you like. But my motherland of China is now facing an existential threat from outside that outweighs any other considerations or political rivalries. Therefore I had accepted a request from the Nationalist government to use my influence here to aid our fight against the Japanese...'

'You've been doing more than that,' Jericho asserted. 'You've certainly been acting as a direct agent for the Nationalist government. Were you trying to find out what the British intend to do concerning this latest Japanese aggression? Did you deliberately cultivate Edith's affections because of her key position in the intelligence team at Government House?'

Yip seemed tempted to deny it for a moment, but then thought better of it. 'I did. But then I found to my discomfiture that I really had fallen in love with Edith. It had never occurred to me that I could fall for an Englishwoman.' Yip made a dismissive gesture. 'Englishwomen had always seemed to me to be peculiarly sexless and unattractive examples of womanhood.'

Jericho ignored this slight on his own race. 'What was your relationship with Ian Luff?'

Yip looked surprised to hear that name. '*Relationship?* Why, none at all. I had met Luff at various government functions, of course, and knew him to be an important official in the Treasury, but that's as far as it went. For my pains, I did know a man called Marco da Silva, though, who I believe was a friend and confidante of Luff's. I did buy information from this man Da Silva from time to time, because he owned a homosexual massage parlour that was frequented by many British homosexuals, including some high up in the military who could be very indiscreet when indulging their secret sexual pleasures. Luff is also homosexual, I believe, and may have encouraged some of his fellow countrymen to go to Da Silva's establishment. But I had nothing personally to do with Luff at all until...'

'Until what?'

'Until he discovered somehow that Edith and I were having an affair. A couple of weeks ago, he brazenly came to my home and demanded hush money. I would have paid him too, just to protect Edith's reputation with her own countrymen. It would have been far worse for Edith if the truth had come out, than for me. Yet I never got to the point of paying Luff anything, for Edith was abducted soon after and I had more urgent things to think about than a miserable blackmailer like Ian Luff. And now he seems to have disappeared from sight, thankfully, so perhaps I never will have to pay him anything at all...'

Jericho nodded grimly. 'Yes, Luff is still missing, so you may be right. The man is a devious individual, to be sure, who clearly enjoys preying on people. Therefore I have some sympathy with you about being in the power of a man like that. I believe there was once a French king in the Middle Ages called Louis – the eleventh, I think - who was known as the "Universal Spider" because of his constant plotting and machinations. But I think this King Louis could have taken a lesson or two from our Mr Ian Luff...'

Michael Yip gave him a sour smile in return. 'If you think that I've had Luff killed, then you're quite wrong, Inspector Jericho. I am not nearly as ruthless and efficient as that...*unfortunately*...'

'So you said you are planning to leave the colony. Where are you intending to go? Back to China?'

'Yes, to Nanking, at least in the short term,' Yip said.

'To get new instructions?' Jericho asked cynically.

'Perhaps,' Yip admitted. 'We know the English are quite happy for the moment to stand back and watch China being torn apart. But the Japanese may soon become emboldened enough to threaten your empire too. So we may well find ourselves unwilling allies in the not too distant future, Inspector Jericho...'

'Yes, that possibility has occurred to me too,' Jericho said soberly. He gave a long sigh of exasperation as he came to a decision. 'I will have a word with my men who are guarding Edith. If you want to go and sit with her for a few minutes and say your farewells, then it's all right with me.'

Michael Yip bowed a little in gratitude. 'Then thank you very much, sir. I really think that she might respond if I can hold her hand for a few minutes and say a few words of endearment to her again.'

Jericho said nothing to that, but he suspected sadly that it would take a lot more than just a few kind words to bring Edith Starling back to the world of the living...

*

Jericho was just entering the entrance hall of Wanchai Police Station an hour later when he noticed George Dorling's wife Tess sitting patiently on one of the wooden benches in the public waiting area...

He would have preferred to just walk on, for he had no idea what he could possibly say to her that would be of any help. But his innate good manners wouldn't allow him to simply walk past and ignore her, so – with great reluctance – he stopped and spoke to her.

'Good morning, Tess. What are you doing here on a Sunday?' he asked kindly. She seemed to be reasonably in control of her emotions, he was glad to see. Her eyes were a little red from constant weeping, yet she had made an effort to look presentable this morning, for she was dressed in one of her smartest summer silk dresses, and her hair was freshly washed and shining.

'Inspector Jericho...good morning...' Tess stopped in mid-sentence, as if struggling to think. 'Oh, I'm here to see Superintendent Hebdon. He has promised to book me a passage back to England at the beginning of October...'

'So soon?'

Tess tried to smile. 'Yes, I think it's for the best. I want to thank you and all your men for the money you have donated to me so far in George's memory. Superintendent Hebdon thinks the fund could end up in the thousands of pounds so I am very grateful to you all.'

Jericho could see that she was still just a girl, and a very pretty one, who would hopefully get over this tragedy quickly and make a new life for herself again back in Scarborough.

He couldn't help wondering, though, if Tess had suspected the truth about George – that he had gone bad. 'I should tell you, in case you don't know, that George gave his life for mine, and died a real hero.'

A tear trickled down Tess's pale cheeks. 'Yes, I never doubted his bravery. But he was a troubled soul, so perhaps it's better like this,' she added emphatically.

Jericho held his breath. *It seemed she had known the truth...*

There was a moment of awkwardness between them while Jericho wondered what to say next.

But Tess solved the awkwardness by standing up and kissing Jericho gently on the cheek. 'Thank you for all you have done, and for saying what you did about him. I know George let you down badly at times, so it's good of you to protect his name when he didn't really deserve it...'

*

Jericho ran into Superintendent Charlie Hebdon himself in a corridor on the top floor of the station a few minutes later.

Hebdon did a double take when he saw Jericho's face. 'Good God, you look terrible, Paul. Why are you even here today? You should be resting at home after what you've been through the last few days...'

'Oh, I will be leaving soon, sir, and taking the rest of the day off. There were just a few things I needed to do urgently...' Jericho paused. 'I saw Tess Dorling a little earlier. Have you spoken to her yet?'

Hebdon nodded. 'I have. She's a pretty little thing, so I was glad to bring a little glow back to her cheeks when I told how much money we've raised for her so far.' He pulled Jericho aside into a corner and lowered his voice. 'So is this body you found in that collapsed tenement last night really Bob Harmsworth?'

Jericho kept his voice low in return. 'There's no doubt of it, sir, even though he was badly smashed up.'

Hebdon shook his head in disbelief. 'That's a sordid and miserable end for a top man like that. The Governor has lost some of his best men in the last few days: first Ronnie Grantham, and now Bob Harmsworth. And I've also heard talk that Julian Colby has not got long to live; he's ailing fast. So these are troubled times up at Government House...' Hebdon lowered his voice even more. 'What do you think Harmsworth was doing in a building like that? Do you think he was there with that woman who was found with him?'

Jericho had to fight to keep his face under control. 'Perhaps...'

'You identified the woman as a Miss Maggie Yiu. Wasn't she that nice-looking young woman who was a useful witness for you in the recent murder case?'

'She was...'

Hebdon frowned. 'That's an odd coincidence, then. But if she was Harmsworth's woman on the side, then I have to admire the man's taste at least, if not his judgement. This woman has cost him dear in the end, though...'

Jericho said nothing to this, his face turned to stone.

Hebdon turned to go, but stopped for a second. 'By the way, Paul, I have accepted your recommendation to promote Constable Thomas Sung to Sergeant to replace George Dorling...'

Jericho was even more amazed when Hebdon went on. 'And I also agree to your proposal to promote Constable Gary Ho to Senior Constable. I think it's about time that we started to promote some of our local lads. I'm surprised it's taken you so long to appreciate them. Some of these Chinese officers have the making of top policemen in time if we can give them the proper training and motivation...'

Jericho walked away in a daze, wondering if he had truly heard right...

*

On the way home to his apartment in Happy Valley, Paul Jericho stopped his little Austin again at St Paul's Hospital and went up to the floor where Edith Starling was being treated.

He nodded to the constables on guard outside her door and went inside. Then he took a chair by her bedside.

He saw that her face had much better colour than before, no longer deathly pale and drawn, but quite healthy looking and pink. She was being fed intravenously, so her cheeks had lost their sunken gauntness and her breathing seemed quite normal. In fact she seemed simply asleep to him rather than in a deep coma, so perhaps Michael Yip's visit this morning had done more good than Jericho had expected.

He took hold of her right hand and began talking to her as if she was fully conscious. He told her everything that had happened to him since he had last talked to her outside St John's Cathedral two weeks ago. He told her about the typhoon and the giant wave that had nearly killed him, about his fraught meeting with Sebastian Ride at Shaukeiwan, about his encounters with Michael Yip, about the sad deaths of George Dorling and Ronnie Grantham. He even told her what he had now discovered about Susan's death. And then he told her finally about Bob Harmsworth – that *he* was the man who had abducted her and then tried to kill her with a huge dose of morphine...

His long rambling monologue seemed to have some cathartic effect on himself at least, if not on Edith, for he felt as if a huge weight had been lifted from his shoulders by the mere act of sharing this knowledge honestly with someone. He found himself drifting away in his chair into a deep, deep sleep, the sleep of utter exhaustion...

But then he was jerked back suddenly into consciousness again when he felt a flicker of movement in her fingers...

*

The sun was just dipping down over the western mountains of the offshore islands as Paul Jericho finally returned to his apartment in Blue Pool Road.

Yet he didn't go into his own apartment, but instead entered the other one on the same floor, the one that belonged to his close friends John and Rosie Lawrence. He went to the spare bedroom and knocked gently on the door. 'Are you awake?' he asked through the door.

He heard her answer distinctly so opened the door slowly. She was still in bed but sitting up with her head against the backboard. She smiled a welcome, despite the bruises on her face and the scratches and lesions on her arms. Her caged bird Ling–Ling had clearly resented his intrusion, though, and hopped about his cage, chirping wildly.

'I thought you'd forgotten me,' she said, still smiling.

He smiled back. 'Never...' He went and sat on the bed beside her. 'Are you feeling a little better?'

'Still a little sore all over, but I'm sure it's nothing serious...' She looked around the room. 'Won't your neighbours mind me using this room? I feel like I am taking a terrible liberty.'

'They won't mind; they're both very nice people,' Jericho assured her.

Jericho thought back to the drama of last night, and how Maggie's life had been saved by a miracle. She had been blown off the roof of her own tenement as it collapsed, and against the wall of the adjacent building where she should by rights have fallen to her death. But she had been saved from that fate when the ropes binding her wrists had caught on a sturdy metal vent pipe sticking out of the wall. Jericho had found her there, hanging perilously from the vent pipe, and had managed to pull her to safety.

So, in an odd way, Harmsworth had been the means of saving her life in the end, for if her hands had not been bound she would have almost certainly plunged to her death...

Once he had discovered that she wasn't badly hurt, Jericho had quickly decided to get her out of there, and had brought her back by car to this apartment. He couldn't put her in his own apartment for his laundry boy usually came on Sunday to collect his dirty washing. Jericho knew that he was taking a huge risk now in helping Maggie – far more risk than he had over the matter of George Dorling and Ronnie Grantham – for he was now actively misleading a police investigation. He would go to gaol if his colleagues ever found out about this; Charlie Hebdon for one would throw the book at him if he were to discover the truth.

Yet a plan had begun to crystallize in Jericho's mind almost immediately - a plan to save Maggie's life if he could. The first part of the plan was to make it appear that Maggie was dead; that seemed like the only way to save her from the vengeance of her Japanese employers. The fact that another woman's body had been found in the wreckage of the tenement had been a major help in this plan, yet Jericho had felt huge shame at having to deliberately misidentify the body as being Maggie. It had to be in reality the body of the young Chinese girl he had seen there last night – the new arrival from China. Yet despite his pity for that poor girl, Jericho had gone through with this deception and had identified her bruised and battered body as that of Maggie Yiu. He doubted that anyone else would ever see the body or seriously question its identity.

So the first part of the plan was complete. The second part would be far more difficult to accomplish, though, for he would have to get Maggie out of Hong Kong somehow and establish a new identity for her somewhere else. If not, and she stayed in Hong Kong - even under a different name - the Japanese would soon realize their mistake, and Maggie's life wouldn't be worth a cent...

Yet even as he'd thought about this possibility, Jericho had known that he simply didn't have the power or the personal connections to make this happen. The only people who might be able to do this, and who would be happy to leave the Hong Kong Police in the dark about Maggie's survival, would be Edith's employers, the Secret Intelligence Service. But they would only oblige if they got something in return for their help. Fortunately Maggie claimed to have in her possession something that the SIS might be willing to trade for: a complete set of Japanese military and naval code books, which her father had secretly given her before she left Shanghai, as leverage for just such an eventuality as this...

Jericho first told Maggie the good news about Edith. 'The woman that Harmsworth abducted and then tried to murder...'

'Yes...? What about her?'

'She's just come out of her coma. She started to wake up while I was there in her room this afternoon. That's why I'm so late...I wanted to see if she would open her eyes...'

'And did she?'

'Yes, she did...and she even seemed to recognize me,' Jericho said warmly. 'I'm very happy because Edith was a good friend of my wife Susan's...'

'That's wonderful,' Maggie said with genuine emotion. 'It still causes me great pain that I was helping that man Harmsworth, even if in only a small way. And also helping the Japanese against my own country...'

'You were doing it to save your father,' Jericho reminded her. 'No one can blame you for that.'

Maggie looked downcast. 'Yet I can certainly blame myself. If I'd known what it would entail, I would have refused and let my father take his chances. When I heard the terrible news that the Japanese had bombed Shanghai, I resolved then that I had to stop this. But I simply didn't know how...'

He took her hand. 'Well, I do know how. At first light this morning, I went to Government House and spoke to a man called Elliot Casaubon. Since Edith's absence, he is the effective leader of the British Intelligence team in Hong Kong. I told him the situation and the offer of a trade: a new identity for you somewhere safe, in return for your code books. He did look most curious that this offer should be coming from a senior policeman. But he has agreed to this trade in principle provided the code books are what you say they are...' He frowned. *'You do still have these code books, don't you?'* he asked a little nervously. For it now occurred to him that she must have lost all her personal possessions last night when her tenement building had collapsed, and surely the code books must have been among them...

But she only smiled with a faint show of complacence. 'Yes, I still have the code books.'

'Good...' Jericho still wasn't entirely convinced, though. 'Then where are they?'

Maggie eased herself out of bed and walked over to her birdcage where she pressed a small lever to reveal that the cage had a false bottom. 'Here they are,' she smiled. 'Ling-Ling has been keeping them safe for me...'

CHAPTER 35

Wednesday, 8th September 1937

Morning sunlight flooded the private hospital Room in the Tung Wah Hospital as Sebastian Ride sat beside his wife's bedside.

'You look much better, Gloria,' he said with genuine surprise. She did seem much more like the bubbly redhead he had first met eleven years ago when she had come out to Hong Kong as part of the "fishing fleet".

'So do you, Sebastian,' she responded. It had been a full week since the policeman Jericho had saved her life and brought her to this hospital, and the stay seemed to have done her the world of good, both physically and mentally. A psychiatrist specialized in the treatment of depression, a Mr Fortescue, had been visiting her every day for counselling sessions, and these seemed to have helped her wellbeing too. This Mr Fortescue seemed confident that Gloria was in a much stronger frame of mind now and was unlikely to repeat the attempt to take her own life provided she continued to receive proper counselling.

Ride spoke up, slightly nervously. 'I've just had some good news from Commissioner Matlock. There's not going to be any fresh inquest into the death of James Woo, and I am not going to be charged with any offence. I think Chief Inspector Jericho's opinion has carried the day: his evidence about the poor condition of the parapet on that balcony has convinced the authorities not to take this any further.'

Gloria looked pensive. 'We both owe that man a great deal, Sebastian. He certainly saved my life. And now he has saved you from a possible manslaughter charge. Yet the man should hate us for what we did to his poor wife...'

Ride looked down at his feet. 'I'm well aware of it.' They had both confessed to each other their parts in the sad death of Susan Jericho, which had been a trying experience for them both. But Ride knew that he owed even more to Paul Jericho than that: he had kept from Gloria the truth of what had happened at Shaukeiwan – that he too had come close to killing himself in despair. And that he had earlier been considering committing murder to save his reputation...

Yet Jericho had pulled him back from the brink, even though he knew that Ride had been so instrumental in causing his wife's death.

Gloria pointed at the newspaper lying on her table. 'I was reading about the death of Ronnie Grantham. Apparently the man proved himself a great hero in the end by saving a coolie family trapped on a hillside during the typhoon. Obviously there was more to that man than met the eye.'

'Yes, he did very well.'

Gloria smiled almost in triumph. 'And – how convenient! – it means that Faye Grantham is now the most beautiful and wealthy widow in Hong Kong. You won't even have to endure being cited as co-respondent in a messy divorce case now. You can just dump me, then run off to South Africa with Faye where you can live together in gilded splendour for the rest of your lives...'

'I'm not going with Faye,' Ride said soberly. 'I have told her it's over between us.'

'Then that's a bit cruel of you, isn't it, coming so soon after she has lost her doting husband?' Gloria eyed her husband with reluctant curiosity. 'Then what are you planning to do, Sebastian? Stay here in Hong Kong?'

'No, that's quite impossible. I don't want to be a constant embarrassment to the Woo family, and to Grace in particular, especially now that her father has just died too. The break between Grace and me is irrevocable so I have agreed to sell all my holdings in the company to her at half their market value. It seems like the least I can do. She will have to bring in a new partner and chief executive from somewhere, but she's not willing to accept my help to do it.'

Gloria seemed genuinely sympathetic. 'That's a pity, because you and Grace always had such a close friendship. So what are you going to do?'

Ride had also been to see Frances and explain to her that he was leaving Hong Kong for good. She had taken it very badly and had even sworn at him in an ugly and crude way, which had shocked him. Yet he had promised her that she was entirely in the clear, and that nothing about that business with Ian Luff would ever come back to bother her. He had also left her a cheque for a hundred thousand Hong Kong dollars, which was a fortune and should set her up for life, even if she was forced out of Saunders-Woo by the new management regime. Yet despite his generosity, she had still looked at him with utter disdain when he left her, like a scorned and rejected lover. *Which she was, of course...*

Ride moved his chair a little closer to her bed. 'I think I need a new start. But not in South Africa. I fancy California more – orange groves and

Spanish missions and dusty blue hills thick with Californian lilac and manzanita. Doesn't that sound enticing?'

'What would you do there?'

'Oh, real estate development probably. But I might like to branch out into movie making...I have an old English friend at Warner Brothers who has offered to help me get into movie production...' Ride couldn't keep the enthusiasm out of his voice. Less than a week ago he had been close to putting a bullet through his own head, and now, thanks to that man Jericho, he felt as if he was riding high again, with his whole life still ahead of him.

Gloria shook her head in mild amusement. 'And what about me? What sort of divorce settlement will you give me?'

He laughed. 'None. For I don't want to divorce you, Gloria. Why can't we start again and get on the Pan Am clipper from Manila to San Francisco together next month? They've just inaugurated the first regular air service across the Pacific, isn't that exciting?' He had realized in the last week that he really did still love this woman, and wanted her to come with him, despite her drinking and her sometimes impossible moods. For she did truly make him feel alive like no other woman...

She gazed at him in complete bafflement. 'But the problem is that I now want to divorce *you*, Sebastian. Don't you understand that now – that I've finally come to my senses?'

Ride was shocked to hear this. 'Why? I promise I'll change and become a much better husband to you once we make a new life together in America.'

'And how long would that resolution last when you started mixing with Hollywood starlets like Carole Lombard and Dorothy Lamour?' Gloria took his hand almost consolingly. 'For both our sakes, we need to end this marriage, Sebastian...'

And Sebastian Ride realized with dismay that she meant it and would never change her mind. This really was the end...

'Then what will you do, Gloria?' he asked painfully. 'Will you be all right?'

Gloria sat up in bed and looked with dispassionate frankness at the scars on her wrists. 'I'll be all right. Mr Fortescue will bring me through this. Then I intend to see if I can return to being the sort of woman I used to be. Perhaps there are still some decent civilized people somewhere out there in the world whom I will be able to call friends, and some decent civilized place that I can call home...'

*

The Noonday Gun was just going off with a ferocious bang in nearby Causeway Bay when Paul Jericho stepped ashore in the blazing heat from the police launch at Wanchai ferry pier. He had just been out to the picturesque fishing island of Cheung Chau, and to a beachfront cottage in the centre of the island...

The body of a Western man had been reported first thing this morning to the small police station on the island, and Jericho and his new sergeant, Thomas Sung, had been summoned by radio to have a look. Jericho had been particularly interested to go when he had discovered that the cottage was owned by the Woo family and was therefore presumably the one that, according to Sebastian Ride's secretary, had been used as a holiday getaway by the late James Woo.

Jericho had not therefore been too surprised when he and Sergeant Sung had got to the cottage and discovered that the murdered man was Ian Luff...

So it seemed that one of his victims had finally caught up with him. If any man had been tempting fate, then it was certainly this man Ian Luff, for he seemed to have woven a web of evil and deceit wherever he went, embroiling so many helpless people in his schemes, and uncovering so many dark secrets. He had certainly corrupted Ronnie Grantham and turned him into a killer, which was something that Jericho could not forgive in particular. The rough justice of Luff's death did at least ensure that he would never come back to expose Ronnie Grantham's own dark secret, for which Jericho had to be grateful...

Yet Jericho had been unable to avoid some pity for the man when he'd seen the gruesome manner of his death. Ian Luff certainly hadn't died quickly; whoever had ordered his death had definitely intended to send a signal to someone, for the man was hanging naked by his neck from a roof beam, while his body showed the marks of sadistic torture – cigarette burns and slash wounds from a sharp knife. From the look on Luff's face, he had died in absolute terror as his killers had finally tied a noose around his head and then hauled his squirming body into the air...

The manner of Luff's death seemed to preclude a simple act of revenge by one of his blackmail victims; Jericho could not seriously entertain the notion that Sebastian Ride or even Michael Yip could have ordered this savage murder. Jericho guessed that Harmsworth had been right about this, and that Luff's death had been ordered by Japanese agents in Hong Kong, though – from the brutal manner of the killing - they may have sub-contracted the actual murder to local criminals.

Yet Jericho thought there was another possibility too: that the Woo family might have paid for this murder. The Woo clan certainly had good reason to hate Ian Luff for the unsettling influence he'd had on the eldest son of the family, the late James Woo. But this theory still seemed less likely on the whole to Jericho than the notion that the Japanese had ordered this murder, for Jericho had heard that the head of the family, Woo Man Lo, had just died, and it seemed improbable that anyone else in the Woo family would have taken it upon themselves at such a sensitive time as this to order such a nasty and bloody killing. Jericho could certainly not believe that Grace Woo was in private some kind of vicious scheming dragon lady who could order a man's death without any qualms.

After learning from Inspector Ball about Grace Woo's damaged blue Cadillac, Jericho had however made some discreet inquiries of his own about Grace and about her whereabouts on the night that his wife Susan was killed. And Grace Woo seemed to be in the clear; Jericho was as sure as he could be that she had been at home that evening at a family party. And he had also discovered no dark rumours about Grace's past life that might suggest she was anything other than what she seemed; everything he had heard about her revealed her to be a quiet, intelligent, studious young woman of good character and quiet decorum...

As Jericho stepped ashore from the launch at Wanchai, he turned to Thomas Sung and spoke in Cantonese. 'Will you draft a report on the murder and then send a copy to Inspector Ball at Central. He was leading the search for Ian Luff, so I presume he will take over the murder investigation too.'

Sung looked relieved; the killing of a white man in such a brutal manner was a case best left to someone else.

Jericho then parted from his new sergeant. 'I'm not going back to the station directly, Thomas,' he said. 'I have to go to St Paul's Hospital first and talk again with Miss Starling.'

Sung nodded dutifully. 'I'm glad that she has recovered so well, sir.' His tone became one of almost reverential awe. 'You saved her life by finding her when you did. I hope she understands that.'

Jericho flinched a little at this level of praise; since his promotion, Thomas Sung was now as devoted to him as a grateful lap dog, and seemed to think it was part of his duty to compliment his chief at regular intervals. 'I think she does...'

*

Jericho had kept a permanent guard on duty outside Edith's room, but he had relaxed the rules a little of late to allow her friends and colleagues to visit her, now that she was sitting up again and able to talk freely.

He had just reached the door to Edith's room and nodded a greeting to the two constables on duty there, when the door opened suddenly and Faye Grantham appeared.

Jericho had not been to see her since Ronnie's death five days ago, and he was conscious that this must seem like odd and callous behaviour on his part. He had been best man at their wedding three years ago, after all, and had also actually been with Ronnie when he died. In truth he had deliberately put off a meeting with her, worried that he might give away some of the terrible truth about Ronnie. But he had also not been sure what level of sympathy to offer her; he knew of course that Faye had been having an affair and was planning to divorce Ronnie, but perhaps the less said about that the better, in these sad circumstances.

Faye looked at Jericho in surprise. '*Why, Paul...*' She seemed unsure what to say next.

Jericho saw that the tragedy had not dimmed her beauty in any way; she looked as stunning as ever. In fact even more beautiful, because a few days of grieving, and perhaps guilt, had given her face an ethereal white-cheeked beauty that was straight out of a Titian masterpiece.

'I'm sorry I haven't been to see you, Faye,' he apologized in a rush.

Her blue eyes misted over, and she had difficulty swallowing for a moment, so Jericho could see that Ronnie's death had really affected her. 'It's all right, Paul. I know you're a busy man...'

'I will come and see you one evening this week, if you wish,' Jericho offered. 'I can at least tell you what happened on that hillside, and how brave Ronnie was at the end.'

Her eyes were brimming with tears now and she brushed them away impatiently. 'I just wish I had been a better wife to him. But it's too late now to make amends.'

Jericho wondered if she might marry her lover Sebastian Ride in time, now that Ronnie was conveniently dead. But of course he couldn't ask her such a thing directly. It was clear at least that she didn't suspect the truth about Ronnie for she suddenly burst into tears, then fled down the corridor sobbing her heart out...

*

Edith was looking so much better that Jericho was thrilled by the improvement in her. She had sent someone to her home to fetch her spare pairs of glasses so that she could see properly again, and even read if she wanted. And she was wearing one of her own nightdresses.

'I feel like a complete fraud,' she complained. 'I have no idea why I'm still in here. Although I do wonder if it might be *your* doing, for it seems to be your Dr Formby who is insisting I stay in hospital for a few days more. Is he taking his instructions from you?'

'Not at all. And he's certainly not *my* Dr Formby. He probably just likes you, and wants to practise his bedside manner on you,' Jericho suggested lightly.

'I like him too, though I wish he would shave off that stupid little Robert Donat moustache that he sports. If he wants a moustache, he should at least grow it into a proper Ronald Colman or a Clark Gable...'

'You sound in good form,' Jericho said with a smile.

'Yes, thanks to you. I've heard from Dr Formby that everyone else had given up looking for me. *Everyone except you...*' She leaned across the bed and touched his arm affectionately. 'I know from Susan that you're not one for sentimental hugs and kisses from strange women.' She patted his arm again.

'But consider this a big hug and a warm thanks from me for saving my life.' Then her face darkened. 'I still can't believe that Bob Harmsworth was the one.'

'Greed does strange things to men,' Jericho observed.

'It certainly does. I recognized Harmsworth's voice, as he stuck that needle into me, and I thought it would be the last thing I would ever hear. But thanks to you, I'm still breathing. It's a pity in a way that Harmsworth has cheated justice by dying in that building collapse, though; I would have preferred to see him hang for what he did. And it would have also given us the chance to interrogate him properly; he must have known a lot of useful information that would have helped me break the new Japanese codes...' She stopped guiltily as she realized she had said too much.

'It's all right; I am fully aware now of what you do, Edith,' Jericho reassured her. But this seemed like the perfect opening to begin telling her the truth about Maggie Yiu...

He told her everything about his relationship with Maggie Yiu, just as it had happened, and how he was now hiding her - a woman who had worked for the Japanese and who was supposed to be dead...

Edith didn't say anything through his surprising story, but did whistle softly in astonishment when he told her what had really happened in that condemned tenement in Lockhart Road. 'And I thought you were as straight and predictable as they come,' she said in wonder. 'Obviously I was wrong...'

But then he went on and told her about the Japanese code books that Maggie had in her possession, and about the deal he had made with Elliot Casaubon on her behalf. This time he saw Edith's eyes light up with real excitement...

'Oh, I hope this is true, and that I'm not just dreaming,' she said exultantly.

'Can I trust Casaubon over this? Will he honour the deal? He has agreed that the SIS will give Maggie a new identity, and that she will fly from Kai Tak airfield to Penang in the next two weeks. He even claims that he can find her a job as a teacher in a school in Georgetown...'

'If these code books are what Miss Yiu claims them to be, then we will certainly honour the deal. For information like this, Miss Yiu could get a room at the Ritz for life, and a personal visit from the King.'

Jericho laughed. 'I think Maggie will be more than happy with a teaching job in Penang. It is a beautiful island, I'm told, the pearl of the Orient.'

Edith was still busy calculating what she could do with these codebooks. 'Oh, yes. I believe it is a wonderful place. Very quiet after Hong Kong, of course...'

'I don't think Maggie will mind some peace and quiet after what she has been through lately,' Jericho said.

'And what are you planning to do, Paul? Are you going with her? Perhaps you could get a transfer to the police in the Malay States? It sounds as if you are in love with her, so you must want to go with her?'

Jericho shook his head. 'That's not part of the deal. In fact, Casaubon has vetoed that explicitly. If I were to think of such a thing, it would jeopardize Maggie's safety and future life. He says that Japanese agents are probably well aware from Harmsworth that Maggie and I were lovers, and that if I move to take a job in Penang, there is a real risk that I would simply lead them to her. And the SIS wouldn't be able to protect us for the rest of our lives.'

Edith sank back against her pillow. 'I'm afraid Casaubon is probably right in this case, though I hate to say it. So to save your lover's life, it seems that you will have to give her up. That seems so unfair when you had already suffered the tragedy of losing Susan earlier this year.'

Jericho found himself saying, with unexpected abruptness: 'You knew about Susan and Sebastian Ride, didn't you, Edith?'

Edith gave a long sigh. 'What have you found out, Paul?'

Jericho told her everything about that terrible night that he had learned from Sebastian Ride and his wife Gloria.

Edith listened intently. 'That all fits with what I knew. Susan did tell me that Ride was actively pursuing her, and that she did find him charming in an oily way. But it seems she did reject him in the end, as I expected her to. Yet you still don't know who was driving the car that hit her?'

'No, that's the one piece of the puzzle I don't possess. But I am pretty sure the car was a big American car, black or dark blue.' Jericho grimaced wryly. 'I thought the car might have been a blue Cadillac belonging to James Woo's sister Grace. But I've discarded that theory now. Gloria Ride thought the car might have been a dark blue Studebaker President, though she admitted that she's no expert on cars...'

Edith was nonplussed. 'But *I* had a car exactly like that. Don't you remember? You must have seen it once or twice. A Studebaker President series FE7 passenger Tourer...'

'Ah yes, I knew I had seen a blue Studebaker somewhere.' Jericho couldn't help smiling faintly, though. 'You think that *your* car might have been the one that killed Susan?' He shook his head in mild derision. 'Do you know what the chances of such a thing are? That would be a strange coincidence indeed...' He thought for a second. 'Did you not still have this car in January anyway when Susan was killed?'

'No, I had an accident with the car in the New Territories in December and took it to a garage in Nathan Road for the front to be repaired. But the owner of the garage then offered me a huge sum of money for it, even in its damaged state, so I accepted his offer.'

'What was the name of this generous garage owner?'

Edith had to think for a moment because her coma had left some odd gaps in her memory. But she finally remembered the name. 'Dominic Tien...that's it. A rich Eurasian who owns a lot of motor dealerships in Hong Kong and Kowloon. He said he thought the car would be a nice gift for someone in his family...'

Jericho pondered that for a moment and wondered if it would be worth talking to this Mr Dominic Tien to find out who now owned the blue Studebaker. But it still seemed a completely implausible coincidence that Edith's old car might be the very one that had mown down Susan that night. It was far more likely that Gloria Ride was simply mistaken, and that the car wasn't even a Studebaker at all...

It seemed time to Jericho for yet another frank admission. 'Err...I also spoke to Michael Yip when you were missing...and then again on Sunday when he came here hoping to see you...'

Edith stirred in surprise. 'You know about me and Michael too? You really are a detective, aren't you? I didn't know he'd been here, though; I must have still been comatose... Will he come again? I'd like to see him.'

'He's gone back to China, to Nanking,' Jericho told her bluntly. 'I think he sees his duty there for the moment, perhaps fighting in the front line against the Japanese, rather than indulging in his comfortable Western life here.' Jericho paused. 'But he might be back at some point to use his political contacts here. The Chinese are desperate for Western help against the Japanese...'

Edith only nodded silently, and Jericho could see clearly from her suddenly stricken expression that Michael Yip had meant as much to her as Maggie did to him. Finally she said, 'Faye Grantham just came to visit me, and told me the sad news about Ronnie – how he died a hero saving a Chinese family. This has been a terrible week for everybody...'

*

Despite all his reservations about the possibility of Edith's old car being the one that had killed his wife, Paul Jericho did take the ferry across to Kowloon side in late afternoon and walk up Nathan Road to the garage owned by Mr Dominic Tien.

The buildings along Nathan Road were displaying a similar level of damage to the buildings on Hong Kong Island as a result of the recent typhoon, but Jericho's destination seemed to have survived the storm remarkably well, with a spotless forecourt, perfect glazing and fresh paintwork on the offices, and a large stainless steel sign that proclaimed the owner's name. From the cars on the forecourt it seemed obvious that the garage did specialize in stylish American cars. Mr Tien turned out to be a handsome Eurasian in his early forties, with a charming manner and a twinkle in his eye. He was the sort of man, Jericho was sure, who could sell you a complete rusted wreck of a car, and yet still make you feel you had got a bargain. Jericho was only glad that he wasn't in the market for a new car himself...

Mr Tien continued to smile charmingly, even when he discovered that Jericho was here on official police business. Jericho asked about the damaged blue Studebaker that Tien had bought in December.

Mr Tien also spoke perfect English. 'Ah yes, I remember it well. It belonged to a young English lady called Miss Starling who'd driven it into a ditch near Fan-ling, and made a bit of a mess of the front. But I have the best panel beaters and spray painters in Hong Kong in my garage, so I knew I could make it look as good as new.'

Jericho was hot and uncomfortable after his long walk from the ferry terminal, and wondering again why he had wasted his time on this long shot. 'Miss Starling told me that you were going to keep the car in the family and give it to one of your relatives as a present?'

Mr Tien smiled. 'I was thinking about it. But in the end I sold the blue Studebaker to a friend in Canton instead. He happened to be here on a visit, saw the car as it was being finished off, and offered me cash on the spot. And it was such a nice profit for me that I couldn't turn it down. Family is one thing, but business is business...am I right, sir?' Tien's near-permanent smile faltered for a moment. 'May I ask why you are so interested in this car, Inspector?'

Jericho took out a handkerchief and wiped his dripping brow and neck. 'The car matches the description of a car that was involved in a fatal accident in Kennedy Road on the evening of Tuesday the nineteenth of January. When did you sell the car to your friend from Canton? Was it after the nineteenth of January? Or before?'

Mr Tien jumped to attention. 'It should be easy enough to check. We must have a copy of the bill of sale...' With the help of a subdued male clerk in the office, Tien soon returned, brandishing a piece of paper and a photograph. 'Here it is, Inspector. I sold the car to Mr Yee of Canton on the sixth of January as you can see from this date stamp. And not only that, Mr Yee sent me a picture later of the car at its new home in Canton, where it is mostly used by his eldest son. This photo shows Mr Yee and his son with the car near their family godown on the waterfront.'

Jericho looked at the bill of sale and at the photo; the car certainly looked like Edith's Studebaker...

He sighed heavily because it seemed like his last lead was gone. Kevin Ball must have been right all the time. The real car that had killed Susan must have belonged to some rich Chinese family who had got it repaired in secret without any paperwork to incriminate them. So he realized that he was wasting his time trying to find the car in the records of any official garage...

It was probably time to give up and let Susan rest in peace...

*

Evening had already fallen over the business area of Central District as Frances Leung sat at her desk. She studied her own reflection in the darkening glass, and was reassured that she was still a handsome woman at the age of forty-two. She was still nursing her grievous disappointment at Sebastian Ride's unforgivable behaviour. She had given him ten years of devoted support, and yet the man had walked out on the company, and on her, in a matter of minutes. The money he had given her was something, at least, but still didn't make up for the hurt.

She had to wonder now what she had ever seen in him. He *was* physically beautiful, it was true, but then many people were beautiful. In truth there was far too much emphasis placed on the way a person looked, when such things were just a lottery anyway, decided by nature and chance. Strength of character was a much more appealing trait to Frances than mere superficial beauty, for it was something that a person could forge for themselves, regardless of the hand that nature had dealt them.

Sebastian had certainly shown himself to be a weak-willed man in the end, despite all the help and advice she had given him. The man had let her down badly in the end. He should have killed that man Luff himself and proved his worth to her. Then he would have been hers for life – in her power completely - as she'd always intended...

And as for the death of James Woo, he could have easily brazened it out and denied ever being there. *Who was there to say otherwise?* A coolie boy, and his own drunken wife as witnesses against him? It would have been laughed out of court. There had certainly been no need for him to pour out his soul to James's sister and almost beg for her forgiveness. Grace had been entirely right to throw him out of the house after that and refuse to have anything further to do with him.

If he'd done what Frances had asked, Sebastian's position in the company would have remained unassailable. He could have divorced his drunken sot of a wife with ease and then married her, Frances Leung, in the end. Some people would have looked down on him for marrying a Eurasian woman, of course. But not for long, for she and Sebastian would have turned Saunders-Woo into the greatest business house in Asia...

Now it seemed he was planning to leave Hong Kong for America to make movies of all things, and might even take his pathetic slut of a wife with him...

She hoped that they both rotted in Hell...

The telephone rang suddenly, the sound a jarring strident note in the quiet of the office after business hours. She took the call and heard her cousin's familiar voice. She and Dominic had grown up together and were truly more like brother and sister than mere cousins on their Austrian mothers' side. She listened intently as he told her about Chief Inspector

Jericho's visit.

She had been expecting that the man might find his way to Dominic eventually. He was known to be a very diligent and accomplished policeman so he was hardly likely to give up easily in the matter of his own wife's death.

But Dominic had covered for her perfectly, saying exactly what she had told him to say. She remembered that Dominic had been most annoyed when she had told him that she had damaged the blue Studebaker that he'd only given to her as a birthday present a week before on January 12th. She'd asked him to repair the car a second time in secret and then to dispose of it safely where it would be difficult to trace. So he had taken his gift back and repaired it a second time, then sold it quickly to a friend in Canton, while she had gone back to using her old Chrysler saloon car. Dominic had even sensibly altered the date on the bill of sale for the Studebaker – changed it from 26th January to 6th January, which was easy enough.

Dominic hadn't known before how she had caused the damage to the car, but he was a close friend and supporter who had always covered for her in the past without asking too many questions. And there was no reason why Jericho would ever find out the truth now unless he learned by some chance that she and Dominic were cousins, and put two and two together. But she was safe enough, for hardly anybody knew about their family connection, which they had sensibly kept very private...

Frances had always planned that Sebastian would marry *her* in the end. She had known that she would be able to get rid of Gloria Ride easily enough: she had even arranged through a compliant houseboy in the Ride household to keep Gloria always provided with enough alcohol to feed her addiction. The woman would certainly have drunk herself to death in due course...

As for Sebastian's other women, Frances knew that most of his affairs were harmless, and that he swiftly tired of his conquests, so were of no real consequence. Faye Grantham certainly fell into that category; he would never marry a woman like her despite her money and her looks.

But Susan Jericho was different somehow; Frances had judged shrewdly that Sebastian might even be tempted to marry her in the end, which would have been a disaster for her own carefully laid plan. Susan Jericho was no empty-headed socialite but a hard-working and intelligent teacher with a strong social conscience. She was so unlike any other woman that Sebastian had pursued that it had set the alarm bells ringing in Frances's mind. So she had begun to think of some way in which to end this affair before it became too serious.

Frances thought back to that night in Kennedy Road...

She had been watching Susan Jericho for a few weeks before that night because she had learned from listening in on their private telephone calls just how much Sebastian had fallen for this young married teacher. From listening in on one particular telephone call the day before, Frances had known that Susan had finally agreed to come to the company flat in Bowen Road after some evening function at her school. The apartment in Bowen Road was where Sebastian always took his women, therefore Frances had feared the worst.

So she had followed Susan Jericho in her new blue Studebaker when she left her school at ten o'clock that night, and then took a late bus to Bowen Road. As usual when driving at night, Frances had dressed in a man's suit with her long hair worn up and concealed under a Fedora hat; male disguise suited her dark purpose on these nights. But on this particular night, Frances had soon spotted Gloria Ride hanging around outside the apartment building in Bowen Road too, so it seemed that both she and Gloria were concerned about this new woman in Sebastian's life.

Frances had soon begun to see the ridiculousness of the situation, and that there was nothing she could do that night with Gloria there, so she had decided to leave quickly, and had driven down the steep road connecting Bowen Drive to Kennedy Road. Then, as chance would have it, she saw Susan Jericho suddenly appear, running into Kennedy Road in an apparent panic, almost directly into her path. Susan Jericho must have only been with Sebastian for a few minutes, which Frances should have found odd, and perhaps reassuring. But she had not given it any thought, for she had already pressed the accelerator on the Studebaker, anxious to take her golden opportunity to rid herself of this problem woman...

She had killed Susan Jericho quite deliberately, driving into her at high speed. She had felt no remorse at all, only a strange exultation as her car ploughed into the woman. She'd even stopped briefly to check the woman was dead, and almost enjoyed the sight of her broken bleeding body lying sprawled on the road. Frances had always been like this from a child: *if anything got in her way, she destroyed it...*

Like the miserable rickshaw coolie who had taken Sebastian to James Woo's apartment in Tai Ping Shan. Frances smiled at the thought that Sebastian had really imagined that she would simply have paid the man off. That would have been a foolish and unnecessary waste. She had instead paid two hired killers a piddling amount to murder the coolie with no questions asked, and to dump his body where it would never be found.

And then there was Ian Luff...

Ian Luff had already made a nuisance of himself when he had started blackmailing Sebastian. But when Frances had learned that James Woo had witnessed the death of Susan Jericho and had apparently passed his knowledge on to his friend Luff, she suddenly had a double reason for wanting to get rid of this man. When Sebastian had failed miserably in the task of killing Ian Luff, Frances had been forced to go back to the same two hired killers. She had always known where Luff was likely to hide – at James Woo's cottage on Cheung Chau – so she had sent the same two killers there yesterday with instructions to make his death slow and painful...

Frances looked up in sudden surprise as she saw another reflection in the darkened glass of her office window. She stood up quickly and turned to face her visitor.

Grace Woo smiled obligingly at Frances, and spoke in Cantonese. 'I thought you would still be here, Frances, so I called hoping to see you. As usual, you seem to be the last person to leave the office. And you were no doubt the first person to arrive here this morning...May I sit?'

Frances could not hide her surprise at such praise for she doubted if Grace Woo had ever spoken more than half a dozen words to her in all her time with Saunders-Woo. 'Of course. Please sit down, Miss Woo. Can I bring you some tea?'

'No, thank you, Frances. I wanted to thank you for the card of sympathy you sent me about the death of my father. Did you write it yourself?'

'I did, of course.' Frances finally sat down too, wondering what was coming. She guessed that Grace already had a new executive director in mind for the company to replace Sebastian, and that there was unlikely to be a place in the new organization for her, since she was viewed by the Woo family as no more than Sebastian's faithful old secretary. Sebastian's fall from grace would inevitably mean the end of her own career here too...

Grace nodded. 'I thought so. The words on the card were chosen with exquisite care and sensibility, I think, while your calligraphy for a non-Chinese is quite astounding.' Grace leaned forward across the desk. 'May I say that I have long been impressed by your diligence and resourcefulness? In fact I have long suspected that much of the credit for the work done by Mr Ride should actually be *yours*...is that not true?'

'Well...' Frances did blush this time, but then she was very adept at blushing to order.

'You know of course that Mr Ride has left the company. He had betrayed my family by lying about the death of my brother, therefore there could no longer be any real trust between us.' Grace sat back again and studied Frances from across the desk. 'Frances, I will get straight to the point. I want *you* to take over the daily management of this office...'

Frances was truly astounded for perhaps the first time in her life. '*Me?* A woman in charge of this office?'

Grace frowned. 'I'm a woman too, Frances, in case you haven't noticed. And for the moment, *I* am the person who has complete control of all the Woo holdings in this company. And I believe you are entirely capable of running this office, and perhaps even eventually running the whole company.'

Frances bowed her head. 'You do me too much honour, Miss Woo.'

Grace smiled. 'Please call me Grace. From now on I think we shall be firm friends and allies in this great adventure…'

EPILOGUE

Sunday 19th September 1937

Early on this hot Sunday morning, Paul Jericho waited with Maggie Yiu in the small brick building that served the civilian passengers using RAF Kai Tak. The airfield had originally been the brainchild of two local imaginative businessmen, Kai Ho Ai and Au Tak, hence the name. But the government had taken it over ten years ago for public use, and it now doubled as both a small RAF base and as a new civilian airfield.

The RAF only had a thin scattering of planes on the grass strip and in the matshed hangars — three Hawker Horsley biplane bombers and a couple of De Havilland Tiger Moth trainers. Most of the aircraft using Kai Tak were seaplanes and flying boats that landed on the nearby water. But the newly inaugurated regular air service by Imperial Airways from Hong Kong to London used a relay of De Havilland Express DH-86A biplanes to go all the way on this epic journey - first to Penang via Saigon in French Indo-China, and then onto Rangoon and various Indian cities before overnight stops in the Middle East and Egypt; then further onto European cities - Athens, Rome and Marseilles - before finally reaching London after a full ten days.

Yet the present state of the airfield, with its uneven bumpy grass strip and its untidy jumble of hangars and sheds, was hardly a worthy match for the epic journeys now being undertaken weekly from here. The runway still crossed the main road from Kowloon to the Saikung peninsula so that traffic still had to be stopped every time a plane took off...

Maggie had worn a disguise of sorts today — dark glasses and a silk headscarf to cover her hair — just in case anyone she knew might see her on the car and ferry journey to the airfield. Jericho was in civvies too because he certainly didn't want to be noticed either with Maggie today. But he had found that he couldn't bear to simply take her to the airfield, and then drop her off to wait by herself for her aircraft to depart. So he had risked the chance that he might run into somebody he knew here among the departing passengers. Yet nobody seemed to be taking any notice of him and Maggie so perhaps the risk had paid off for both of them. Now that they were in the small passenger terminal, she had finally taken off the headscarf and dark glasses to reveal her beautiful glowing face and shining hair again.

Maggie had been forced to remain in complete seclusion for the last fortnight, for it would have spoilt everything if she had been seen alive and well on the streets by someone who knew her. She had felt worst about deceiving her teaching colleagues at St Stephen's College, and about all the grief it must have caused all her girls at school, who were reported to be distraught at the loss of one of their favourite teachers. Yet there was no other way...

Yet Jericho and Maggie had made good use of those two weeks of seclusion: they had spent that time together in his apartment building, living quietly as man and wife, like an idyllic honeymoon couple. Yet unlike a honeymoon, Jericho had always known that this would be all the time he would ever have with her; there would no long happy years of marriage to follow. Knowing that had added a bittersweet note to these otherwise joyous days he had spent with her.

The De Havilland Express was already on the grass making final preparations for leaving on the first stage to Saigon; all the luggage stowed and the last safety checks being made on the aeroplane.

Maggie was looking quite exquisitely beautiful today, Jericho thought, with her golden skin and her raven hair and her wonderful dark eyes. He felt almost numbed by so much beauty, perhaps because he knew it would probably be the last time that he would ever see that perfect face. Casaubon had been as good as his word in return for those priceless code books, and had provided Maggie with everything she might need in her new life in Penang: a wardrobe of elegant new clothes and the luggage to carry them in, a new name and passport, and enough money to tide her over until her school job in Georgetown started in October.

She was excited, Jericho could see. 'I wish I could stay on this plane and fly all the way to London...'

Jericho smiled. 'You would find it very cold and grey in late September. And all the leaves are beginning to fall, and the chimneys will be smoking, and your fine clothes would get covered in soot...'

'Sounds wonderful.' She looked at him with real gratitude. 'I can't believe I'm going.' She took out her new blue passport and admired the gold lettering on the front. 'I never knew it was this easy to become a British citizen,' she said complacently. 'It seems we are fellow citizens of King George now. I like my new name too...*Mrs Margaret Turner*. I am a widow of Malay Chinese extraction, it seems...my husband was an English rubber planter in the state of Johore, who sadly died of cholera, so I have returned to my first love of teaching.' Then her happiness faded as she saw her fellow passengers start to move towards the door. 'It looks like it's already time to leave...I didn't expect it would be this quick...'

He looked at the queue of passengers with quiet despair. 'I think you need to go.'

'Will you come and see me in Penang when you have time?' she asked, almost desperately.

He smiled. 'Just try and keep me away.'

'I wish I could give you a kiss,' she said. 'But all these white people might be shocked.'

'So let's shock them a little,' Jericho said as he kissed her discreetly.

Then he watched with an ache in his heart while Maggie walked out of his life. She called back to him at the departure door: 'Please take good care of Ling-Ling...'

He stayed there in the building, watching her board the aeroplane, then went outside a few minutes later in the hot morning sunshine to watch it take off into the deep blue sky. He watched the plane for a long time until it had faded to a small silver speck in the sky, then he finally turned and retraced his steps to his car.

*

As the sun dipped low towards the blue horizon on this Sunday afternoon, Edith Starling stood on the Praya in Central District watching all the activity around her. She took a deep breath of the sea air; it felt so good to be alive today, perhaps because she knew just how close she had been to death only two weeks ago.

The harbour seemed to have recovered well from the recent typhoon - a storm which she had missed entirely in her comatose state, so she had some difficulty believing that it had been quite as bad as some had claimed. The main channels were filled again with lines of tankers and freighters and other modern shipping, yet there were still many reminders of the old Hong Kong to see and enjoy: rusted old steamers chugged through the clutter of sampans and red-sailed junks, while ferries beat an erratic path of their own through all this disorganized confusion, and ships' horns competed with the raucous shouts of boatmen and waterside traders. Edith listened to that babble of noise and was captivated anew by the spirit of this waterfront with its exotic people and its enticing smells.

Despite what had happened, her affection for Hong Kong and its people was still undimmed. She turned her head and looked at the row of elegant waterfront colonial buildings that ran along the Praya, and at the white buildings rising beyond – at the clock tower and the cathedral, and the domed civic buildings, and at the green hillsides rising up to the Peak. From here Hong Kong truly seemed a lush green paradise, a once bare and rocky Oriental island that had been transformed by elegant buildings and the planting of a million trees into a miniature tropical replica of England.

Yet she knew that this sunny peaceful mood today was deceptive, for there was no doubt in her mind that war would be coming to this place before very long. Edith had been back at her desk in Government House this week and making full use of the Japanese code books that had been provided by Paul Jericho's friend, Miss Yiu. And with the help of these incredible documents, Edith had found she had been able to start reading Japanese military communications again, particularly between the Japanese War Ministry, the *Hyōbu-sho* and the Kwantung Army in China. And what she had read in these signals was truly terrifying: it gave her no doubt that the Japanese intended to subjugate the whole of China in time. But their plans didn't even stop there, for the Japanese High Command seemed determined to sweep down into the whole of South-East Asia eventually, and to force the European colonial powers out of Asia completely. Yet the Japanese plan did not seem intended to replace Western colonialism with any form of benevolent independence for the people of these Asian states, but to subject them instead to an even more ruthless tyranny than any they had known before...

She wondered if the limited British forces in the Far East would really be able to hold off a Japanese army, battle-hardened by the long war in China, if they came marching down south backed by their mighty air force. Conventional wisdom said that they would be no match for the fighting skills of the British Army. Yet Far East outposts like Hong Kong and Singapore were defended by mostly second rate troops and reservists, so perhaps none of these places were truly safe, and certainly not Hong Kong. And what about the sanctuary the SIS had found for Miss Yiu? The island of Penang? How safe a sanctuary was that in reality?

Edith looked up suddenly and saw Paul Jericho in a white linen suit and Panama hat approaching along the waterfront road. He seemed in a very melancholy mood, but then she knew that he had seen Miss Yiu off at Kai Tak airfield this morning, so must be missing her already. Her heart went out to him when she saw the doleful expression on his face, and she did feel like running up to him and giving him a hug. He looked like a man who was presently in great need of a warm hug from somebody. It seemed he had finally found a woman to help him get over the loss of Susan, only to lose her too...

His mood lightened, though, when he saw her waiting for him as planned. 'I'm sorry I'm late,' he said with a smile.

'I thought you had stood me up,' Edith replied, tongue in cheek. She decided not to spoil his day even further by mentioning her own doubts about the long-term safety of the place they had sent Miss Yiu to.

They began to walk together along the Praya, trying to avoid the swirl of people around them. 'By the way, I have been and talked to the garage owner who bought your blue Studebaker last December. But it seems he sold the car to a rich man in Canton even before Susan's death. So you'll be happy to know that it certainly wasn't *your* car that killed her.'

Edith looked sheepish. 'I suppose I am relieved to hear it. It would have been very unsettling to think that my own car might have been the instrument of Susan's death...'

'I don't think I'll ever find out who was driving that car now. The trail is too cold,' Paul admitted to her. 'Perhaps it's for the best. At least I know what happened, and that Susan never betrayed me, which is something.' He looked at her curiously. 'How has it been for you back at work? Are you sure that you're well enough to be back doing full time work?'

She touched his arm. 'I am perfectly well now, Paul, and back to my old self.' It wasn't quite true, of course, but nearly. 'We are making good use of Miss Yiu's code books; you have no idea how valuable these are to us. I still can't quite believe that I have these code books in my own hand.'

'How is the mood at Government House? It must be sombre.'

'It is. Colby is now in hospital after his condition suddenly worsened. And then we had to bury poor Ronnie Grantham, as you well know of course, since you were there...' Edith saw the sudden look of grief on Paul's face and wished she hadn't mentioned Ronnie's name. Paul was still clearly grieving deeply for his friend who had sacrificed his life so bravely during the recent typhoon. Yet she couldn't help wondering if there was something about Ronnie's death that Paul hadn't told her; she had a feeling that he was holding something back about it... 'The Acting Governor is in a state of shock about the loss of so many of his closest colleagues and advisors, and seems quite distraught; it means he has put a halt to a massive program of social housing that he and his team were planning for the homeless of Hong Kong, which is a great pity in my view. So it seems that the quarry at Shaukeiwan, where I nearly died, will not be built on after all...at least not in the foreseeable future...'

She continued quickly. 'We even had to give Ian Luff and Bob Harmsworth respectful funerals too, for nobody in Government House knows the truth about them, apart from SIS people, of course. Actually, in retrospect, it was quite fortunate that Harmsworth died in this accidental way, rather than being tried and hanged for treason, as I initially thought he should be. Given this fortunate circumstance, it is important now that the Japanese continue to believe that Harmsworth and Miss Yiu died in an accidental building collapse, and that he had not been exposed as one of their agents. So I had to stand at their gravesides and pretend that Harmsworth and Luff were both the finest of men...'

Edith could see that Paul was surprised by her last remark and that she had clearly given away too much to him by her inclusion of Ian Luff in her condemnation. For Paul had not told her anything about Ian Luff's career as a serial blackmailer himself, or about the details of his sordid end. But she had her own sources now, and she had soon discovered just what a despicable individual Ian Luff had really been. Luff might not have been a traitor or a murderer, yet it seemed he had been an amoral individual who had caused great suffering with his devious plotting and schemes.

'Have you had any word from Michael Yip since he returned to China?' Paul asked, apparently wanting to change the subject. 'I assume he must be in Nanking by now...'

Edith flinched slightly at the mention of that name. 'No, and I don't expect to.' She left it at that, not wanting to say anything further to Paul on this difficult subject. But in truth she was deeply concerned for Michael's safety, for the Japanese were now besieging the city of Nanking with ferocious zeal and seemed determined to inflict a terrible punishment on the Chinese inhabitants of that city for their stubborn refusal to submit. If Michael really was in Nanking now, then he would soon be trapped in that city too by the encircling Japanese Army. It was still hard for Edith to believe that the Japanese people she had loved and respected so much as a child should now be inflicting such terrible violence on their Chinese neighbours.

Yet Edith was also mourning the loss of Michael as her lover and soul mate. She had been almost shocked to discover that she still had an overwhelming physical desire for him, which her recent ordeal seemed to have done nothing to dampen at all. And now that Michael was gone, and never likely to return, she had been forced to re-examine her life and think of some alternative future for herself. Yet in the short term at least, the simple – and perhaps unpalatable - truth was that she needed a man to share her bed occasionally. But not just any man, of course – she certainly drew the line at Elliot Casaubon, for example. She didn't like that pompous individual at all, and it was always a bad idea to sleep with a colleague anyway. In any case, Casaubon had been politeness and deference itself since her return to work, with no hint of his previous clumsy attempts at flirtation. The young police doctor who'd looked after her in St Paul's Hospital, Eric Formby, was certainly a better option; he had called her a couple of times this week and seemed genuinely interested in her. Yet she had put him off for some reason, though she hardly knew why.

In truth the only man she was physically attracted to at present was standing right beside her. They were both nursing broken hearts of sorts, so it now occurred to her that perhaps they could find some consolation in each other...

They stood together and watched the sun as it began to slip below the mountains to the west. 'I think Susan would have liked it that you and I should become proper friends,' Edith said.

He turned and smiled at her. 'Yes, I think she would.'

The sun finally dropped out of sight, leaving a vivid orange glow smeared across the sky. 'So shall we go and have that drink that you promised me a few weeks ago?' she suggested.

He offered her his arm with another smile. 'Yes, let's be off to join the regular gin drinkers and the other inebriates in Bessie's Bar.'

She smiled back, then looped her arm tightly through his as they began to walk again. The brief twilight was already fading fast as they crossed the Praya into Pedder Street, and night began to descend again on the island of Hong Kong.

THE END

ABOUT THE AUTHOR

Gordon Thomson is a retired civil engineer by profession, a Geordie by birth, and Sunderland supporter (and therefore masochist) by inclination. His professional engineering career took him all over the world - Africa, the Far East, South America, as well as Holland and the UK - and this experience of exotic places and different cultures is what gave him the urge to try writing.

He has a Japanese wife and two grown up sons, one of whom was born in Holland, so he does claim to be a citizen of the world, if a very English one.

Apart from this book, he has also published the Victorian thrillers *Leviathan* and *The Last Bridge,,* and the WWI thriller *Gotha,* as well as the Molly Titchen series set in 17th century Restoration England, which begins with *Winter of the Comet*. Other books include the romantic thriller *Draught of Life,* the 1960s American thriller *Crystal River,* and a 1940s English courtroom drama and whodunit *In Winter's Grip*.

Printed in Great Britain
by Amazon